THE IVY CROWN

Also by Mary Luke

BIOGRAPHY

Catherine, The Queen
A Crown for Elizabeth
Gloriana: The Years of Elizabeth I

FICTION

The Nonsuch Lure

MARY LUKE

The
Ivy Crown

DOUBLEDAY & COMPANY, INC.
Garden City, New York   1984

Library of Congress Cataloging in Publication Data

Luke, Mary.
The ivy crown.

1. Katherine Parr, Queen, consort of Henry VIII,
King of England, 1512–1548–Fiction. 2. Henry VIII,
King of England, 1491–1547–Fiction. I. Title.
PS3562.U46I9 1984 813'.54
ISBN: 0-385-18823-4
Library of Congress Catalog Card Number 82–46014

For
CLINT WADE

AUTHOR'S NOTE

A few words concerning the reasons for writing *The Ivy Crown* might interest the reader. My inspiration was a visit several years ago to Sudeley Castle in Gloucestershire. There I saw Katherine Parr's tomb, the effigy of which bore little resemblance to her known portraits. Later, I learned the original tomb had been desecrated on at least two occasions and the present carved likeness dated only from the Victorian era.

Though I had written extensively on the Tudor period, I realized how little I really knew of Henry VIII's last queen. My knowledge was that of most people: she'd survived her royal husband and been (though the term would have been strange to her) the first Protestant queen of England. Because I was familiar with the stories of Henry's children, I knew that Princess Mary, Princess Elizabeth and Prince Edward had all adored this warm and engaging woman who served—for Elizabeth and Edward at least—as the only mother they'd ever known. I knew that while Katherine had accepted Henry's offer of marriage reluctantly, she'd been a popular queen, with sufficient intelligence and integrity to be made Regent of England during the king's absence from the country. And one of Henry's last deathbed wishes had been for her future welfare. Beyond that, the life of Katherine Parr was a mystery.

I was especially surprised then to learn that she'd been educated in the royal classroom with the king's daughter and nieces; that her mother was one of Katherine of Aragon's ladies-in-waiting and her father a close boyhood friend of young Henry; that her blood was even more illustrious than that of the Tudors who'd stolen the English Crown from the Plantagenets a generation before. In the royal classroom, little Princess Mary, Katherine Parr and Kate Willoughby, the daughter of Katherine of Aragon's dearest Spanish friend, Maria de Salinas, had absorbed the teachings of a gifted tutor brought to England on the advice of Sir Thomas More. A greater gift of those classroom days was the strong emotional bond between Mary, Katherine and Kate; they were a triumvirate for life.

While the closely interwoven relationships of Katherine's childhood were intriguing, I found her adult life even more surprising. While much has been made of Henry's six wives, I was startled to find that Katherine had had four husbands. She was married very young to satisfy her family's desire for wealth, land and a title, as well as to insure her own social and financial security. Certainly Katherine never questioned her fate, for Tudor women depended on their men—father, husband, uncle, brother or cousin—for guidance and protection. Some bore innumerable children, others died at an age we'd consider to be quite young. It was not at all unusual for a man to have three or four wives during his expected life span of fifty to sixty years.

Yet these women did not think their lives hard and often possessed great ambition of their own, an ambition directed toward furthering their families' social and economic standing as well as increasing the influence of the church which ruled their lives. They were a hardy breed, often unscrupulous, not the greatest parents in the world and, at the time of which I write, extremely well educated in comparison with the average woman or man. They were truly the sixteenth-century forerunner of the "liberated woman" to the extent it was then possible.

Katherine Parr and her contemporaries, however, always knew that real power lay in the hands of men. Yet she and her friends, with delicate skill, often attained their own ends by using their brains, avoiding notoriety or anything that would upset the balance of influence on their husbands who were statesmen of note or councillors to the king, sometimes both.

As if all this wasn't sufficiently exciting, the story was there waiting to be brought to life. I knew I could reconstruct scenes from letters or the known result of any particular action or episode. Indeed, in many instances, much of the dialogue is factual. A few examples will illustrate: Jane Grey's happiness during the brief time she lived with Katherine is well known and her description of her home life is in her own words. Lady Jane served as Chief Mourner at Katherine's funeral and it was more than an honorary duty for, without the queen's protection, Jane was ultimately forced to return to the abusive treatment of her parents. It was not difficult, therefore, to "imagine" several instances of such abuse.

Bessie Bellingham, Anne Askew, Robert Aske, though less well known than Lady Jane or Princess Mary, touched Katherine Parr's life as surely as did her husbands and numerous stepchildren. Princess Mary's letter to Thomas Seymour rejecting his suggestion that she urge Katherine to marry him has often been published. It was not difficult to "imagine" the emotional impact this had on Katherine. Similarly, an account of Elizabeth's banishment from her father's presence for over a year is true and her later exile to Cheshunt after the early-morning escapades at Chelsea manor house is historical fact. But it is from her subsequent letters to Katherine that we know the two parted close, loving friends on an occasion when Elizabeth might have been even more severely chastised. It was easy, then, to "imagine" the parting scene.

It is only recently, however, that historians have discovered that Katherine Parr was involved in the downfall of Thomas Cromwell, the king's chief minister, who was beheaded for treasonous activities. Yet Katherine's part in the tragedy was managed so adroitly that her contemporaries undoubtedly never knew it occurred. It was a typical example of how, in one way or another, a group of very bright women influenced and changed the course of their country's history. And these were the same women from whom came the sons and daughters who were to shape Elizabethan England. It was Jane Dudley's son Robert, who later became the great Earl of Leicester, one of the most powerful men about Elizabeth when she was queen.

All these many factors led me to believe that Katherine Parr's story could be as inspiring as any of those of Henry's other queens. In commencing it, I chose the novel form rather than biography to avoid the restrictions and limitations of the latter form with its quoted documentation and citation. And as the story evolved, I realized it was a wise choice for it allowed me the freedom to "imagine" what occurred—always within the framework of what we know actually *did* happen. R. F. Delderfield, the eminent British novelist, once told me that—providing one did not invent characters that hadn't lived, or change or invent situations that hadn't occurred—that an appreciation of history was often better served in this manner. This only the reader can decide. Certainly the same amount of care and concern has gone into this book as went into my Tudor biographies.

And there was, in addition to completing this life of a very compassionate and learned lady, a personal reward for the author. While leafing through a book of Holbein's sketches for a description of young William Parr (one of the few reliably identified by the noted painter), I was impressed by an unfinished sketch of a young woman that I'd first seen at Windsor Castle some years ago. But this time my eye was caught for another reason. For, above the face, was the lettered title, "Lady Borow," a good example of the Tudor people's inclination to spell phonetically. Often, in the documentation of such portraits the sitter's family name is given. But here, other than "Lady Borow," there was only the word "unknown."

But I submit that the portrait now in possession of Queen Elizabeth II is really that of a nubile Katherine Parr when she was briefly, Lady Borough of Cantley Hall, Gainsborough, Lincolnshire, a painting commenced by Holbein but never finished.

MARY LUKE

Ridgefield, Conn.
Winter 1983

PREFACE

Many ceremonies had been celebrated within the chapel of Sudeley Castle in Gloucestershire. Centuries old, the aura of countless weddings, christenings and funerals, as well as generations of devotional worship had limned the stone walls and walk. The ancient windows, venerable monuments and great flagged floor impressed the reverent; the chapel's beauty was transcendent with grace. It welcomed the mystic, the devout and the dreamer to worship.

And so it had remained, longer than any mortal could remember, for its age was measured in ownership, not dates. Sudeley would endure. Had it not been coveted by a king? Had it not housed a queen? Would not its history, beauty and isolation provide a protection that the lack of a moat or high walls might otherwise guarantee?

In the latter half of the eighteenth century, the answer was evident in the ruined and despoiled building where gaunt roofless walls were the target of neighborhood plunder and mischief. Empty and decaying, it provided a temporary if uncomfortable shelter for vagrants and itinerant passersby. For years, the townspeople had helped themselves to building blocks and panels of linenfold or pried great fieldstones loose from fireplaces that had long ago lost their impressive mantels. Chambers that had once echoed to music and laughter now housed rusting farm equipment or sheltered livestock and feed.

In the spring of 1784, Sudeley's chapel was further desecrated as local ruffians, drunken and rowdy, passed the ruins on their way home. Loudly, they weaved among sanctified walls, stumbling over those broken stones too heavy to steal. Spying an imposing piece of alabaster in the north wall, one gestured to his companions and, in moments, with the strength of the inebriated, they'd removed the stone.

Shouting with success, they peered into the dark hole, muttering amongst themselves. One, braver than the others, thrust his hands into the opening and to his companions' encouraging cries, pulled forth a long, heavy, leaden coffin. Viciously, the marauders battered it with large rocks until the cover broke revealing a long inner box of lead. This, too, was quickly mutilated. Then, with triumphant shouts and wild laughter, human hands touched the figure that had lain undisturbed for over two centuries.

Roughly, it was pulled from its resting place, which, being tightly sealed, had kept it from decomposition. Now the drunken figures held it up for view, parodying sweeping bows and obeisances before making obscenely foul gestures in its direction. The body, still as immaculate and uncorrupt as the day it had been laid to rest, was clothed in a russet-colored velvet gown; the color almost matched the red-gold hair and delicately arched brows above the sleeping eyes. As the roisterers held the figure aloft, small sandals of the same velvet swung limply beneath the full skirt. A velvet cap, generously edged with pearls and bands of gold embroidery, was rudely plucked from the hair and, as everyone wished to see the richness of the gems, the corpse itself was flung on a heap of rubbish nearby. Quickly, the pearls and rich golden trim were divided among the motley crew.

As each pocketed their find, the cool morning air and lightening sky—as well as the hard feel of the gems—had a sobering effect. Seemingly, a measure of sanity returned as several signaled farewell to each other. They separated silently, each going in different directions, all ignoring the violated corpse on the rubbish heap.

There it lay overnight and all through the next day as the curious came to view it. At last the vicar of the neighboring town objected. No one decently and reverently buried should suffer disinterment and the rude gaze of the people, he said. Certainly not a queen of England! Though the people muttered (for their contact with royalty was nonexistent and the event brought some titillation into their hard and tedious lives), they complied. By nightfall, the velvet-clad figure was returned to its leaden enclosure and the coffin replaced in the gaping aperture. After which the people left to tell the story in their cottages and hovels, in the manor houses, inns and taverns.

And thus it passed into local legend until a later time.

THE IVY CROWN

Maud

1524

CHAPTER I

My Lord, seeing this matter has been so long in cogitation, I am right sorry on my part it cannot take effect, for in good faith . . . I never had communication for a marriage for her that I would have been so glad should come forward as this. . . .
Maud Parre to Lord Dacre,
From the court at Greenwich,
March 15, 1524

Katherine Parr was almost nine when her mother, Maud, began to think seriously of her daughter's marriage. The thought gave little pleasure for the girl's absence would create a great void in her own life. But concern for Katherine's future, plus the duty owed to the memory of her beloved Thomas—whose loss four years ago had so devastated her—set her to thinking of a suitable choice. Pride in her own heritage, as well as that of the Parrs, demanded nothing less than a peer's son for the sunny, smiling child, so much a replica of herself. If she could secure a proper husband for Katherine within two or three years—and such matters often took that long—then the girl could be married, as she herself had been, at thirteen.

Maud did not discuss the subject with Katherine. The girl would never object or question her mother's choice; there would be time for talk when a suitable list of prospects had been drawn up. And for that Maud meant to rely heavily on Sir William Parr, Thomas's brother, who'd been such a mainstay during her widowhood.

Maud knew she could also ask help of the king and his Spanish wife, Katherine. She'd devotedly served the queen as a lady-in-waiting and even named her eldest daughter for her. At little Katherine's birth, the queen had sent a gleaming circlet of gold, fragile and small, wrapped in a napkin with the initials K.I.P. delicately embroidered in each corner. Later, visiting Maud, the queen had nostalgically traced the initials. "For *Katerina. Infanta Princess. Plus Oultre,*" she told the new mother. "I remember the nuns in the Granada convent spending months embroidering these initials and those four little trumpeters at the corners. My mother, Queen Isabella, had a whole set made for me, as well as this little crown. She told me that since all my older sisters would become queens, there might not be enough thrones to go around! So she gave me the little circlet. Crowns for my sisters, she said, and a circlet for Katerina. . . ." Little Katherine Parr never tired of hearing her mother tell the story.

Maud's dead husband, Thomas Parr, had also grown up with young Henry Tudor. Once, Thomas had told her of how severely the austere old king, Henry VII, had cloistered the young boy, especially after his oldest son, Prince Arthur, had died. For then, Henry was the sole Tudor heir to inherit the throne his father had taken from the Plantagenets. Yet as soon as he was old enough to outwit the old king, the prince had had his first sexual encounters in the back lanes at Windsor Castle—indiscretions tolerated by his father when he learned they'd occurred in Tom Parr's company. All the Parrs were close to the royal family and, in something as important as her daughter's future, Maud knew she could rely on their help.

Thomas had died during one of the outbreaks of "the sweat," that mysterious disease brought to England a generation back by English mercenaries who'd fought in France.

Periodically it engulfed London, carrying off noble and commoner alike in a matter of hours. After an idyllic summer with his family at Kendal Castle, the ancient seat of the Parr family in Westmorland, Thomas had returned to London for an early sitting of Parliament, leaving Maud and the children to follow.

Arriving at Parr House in the Strand on that day which changed her life forever, Maud heard the tolling of the great bell of the Blackfriars Church next door. Weeping servants filled the courtyard, quickly glancing away from her as she rode through the archway. Light-headed with fear, but captive among the wagons and carts carrying their belongings home, Maud watched her steward dismount and question one of the grooms.

"What is it, Appleton?" she called anxiously.

"He is dead, my lady." Dazed, the steward passed a heavy hand over his forehead. "Sir Thomas is dead and is even now being placed in his winding sheet."

Screaming in disbelief, Maud ran into the house, straight into the protecting arms of Sir William, who forbade her to go to the chamber she'd shared with Thomas until it had been cleansed of all disease.

The two smaller children, two-year-old Will and three-year-old Ann, frightened by their mother's shrieks, were quickly taken in hand by their older sister. "Shush!" Katherine whispered, stunned. "Mother is crying for Father. She'll tell you about it later." She urged them toward the nursery where, after leaving them with a sobbing nurse, she ran quickly back to her mother's side.

By then, Maud had quieted. With swollen, listless eyes, she stared out the window at the vast panorama of the Thames. Katherine put her arms about her mother's tiny waist and was comforted when Maud drew her close. Wisely, Sir William left to deal with the servants. Once her shock wore off, he knew his sister-in-law's real despair would commence and she'd need their help.

Sir William was right. Each night, lying in the big bed she'd shared with Thomas, Maud recalled each line in his face, deliberately instilling each feature in memory, lest she ever forget. Her body warmed at remembrance of how Thomas had held her and whispered his love for her, his pride in her beauty. Each night, she prayed to join him in some heaven which, shocked and grieving, she found hard to believe existed. Thomas had opened up such a world for her—little lighthearted Maud Green—who'd never been far from home at Boughton in all her thirteen years. Thomas had given her the world of a woman loved and loving, linked in a spiritual and physical union with a kindred soul. She knew she'd never find his like again.

Friends and relatives helped. Katherine, aware she was the eldest, kept her boisterous smaller brother away from her mother's chamber when despair took over. But she, too, missed her father and when the tears came, it was comforting to have the consolation of her grandmother, Lady Elizabeth Parr, who asked her help in the garden or, as a special treat, brought her a pretty piece of new needlework.

And there were her studies. Each day, Katherine attended the palace schoolroom where the newly arrived Juan Luys Vives tutored six-year-old Princess Mary and other children of the court. Katherine was Mary's best friend and both girls studied and played with five-year-old Kate Willoughby, the daughter of the queen's dearest friend, Maria de Salinas Willoughby, who'd accompanied the fifteen-year-old Katherine of Aragon from Spain a quarter of a century ago.

The children were all awed by their new teacher, a brilliant Spanish scholar from Bruges, whom Sir Thomas More himself had advised the queen to bring to England. Senor Vives had shown visible pride in little Katherine Parr's easy ability to translate Latin into English and then into Greek. Recently he'd given her the Epistles of St. Jerome and St. Augustine for study and had promised that she might read Cicero, Plato and the tragedies of Seneca. Before leaving for his last summer at Kendal, her father had requested that in the fall, the older children be allowed a diversion in reading the *Utopia* of his good friend, Tom More.

Katherine remembered a day when she'd had her father all to herself—a day when he'd taken her on horseback to watch the king and his companions shooting at the butts at Moorfield. She could still recall how snugly she'd fitted into the saddle, her father's body strong against hers, one arm holding her tightly. Henry had just finished his turn as her father hoisted her from the saddle and, holding her by the hand, approached the group. The king, tall as a giant, was mopping his sweating face. Handing the towel to a servant, he'd leaned down and ruffled her hair. "That's a winsome wench you have there, eh, Tom? She's very like her mother." Katherine remembered how happy she'd been because she knew her mother was the prettiest lady at court. Everyone said so. And she could see her father had been very proud.

Her best friend, Princess Mary, sensed Katherine's sadness. "You'll get used to it, Kate," she said. "I never see much of my father. He's always busy with great matters and days go by before he summons me." She pressed her friend's hand. "Never mind. You still have your mother and, when her year of mourning is over, she'll probably wed again."

Katherine felt herself grow hot with anger and she longed to strike Mary, princess or not. "No one can take my father's place!" she cried. Her little companion appeared startled at her friend's vehemence. "Don't you ever again say anything like that! My lady mother will never marry again!"

Silent with embarrassment, the two returned to their books. Katherine knew Mary had meant well and she felt the little princess' silent rebuke. But she didn't know what else to say. The thought of her mother wed to another man had simply never occurred to her.

* * *

For months, Maud Parr's despair enveloped Parr House. Then the queen, aware of the suffering her lady-in-waiting bravely tried to hide, asked her to supervise the royal classroom. Already her two children, Katherine and Ann, were students there. Who could better assist Senor Vives than Lady Parr who read so easily, spoke so well and wrote so beautiful a hand?

"You'll have your hands full, Lady Maud." The queen spoke in a heavy accent after almost a quarter of a century away from Spain. "Senor Vives is a fine master, but he needs help and all the children know and love you."

Maud was reticent for her depression was still deep and constant. Vives was an intellectual, a champion of the "New Learning," that maddeningly puzzling, radical philosophy that questioned and challenged every aspect of religion, education, ethics, morals and politics that had been taken for granted for centuries. Not everyone at court thought as Vives did. The older, more conservative element certainly did not believe that women were as teachable as men and deserved to learn something more challenging than to draw prettily or embroider expertly. Vives thought they needed more than a smattering of philosophy, science, Latin or instruction in Scripture. The queen, mindful that one day her daughter might rule, agreed with the scholar. "It will also be a change for her to learn from a man," she told Maud pensively. "Jesu knows, she sees little of her father."

Maud sensed the queen's sadness. As everyone at court knew, it was not that Henry didn't love his little daughter. He was very proud of Mary's quick mind and her skill with the needle, her love of music, dancing and her ease with languages. It was simply that Mary should have been a boy—his heir. One he might have helped groom for a tournament, the hunt or taken proudly on progress to show to his subjects.

Katherine encouraged Maud to take the post. "You should do it, Mother," she insisted. "The queen has asked and she knows how well suited you are. I'm sure you can manage those awful Brandon children who make Senor Vives so angry. He cannot understand how the king's nieces can be so careless and not wish to study!"

The queen's decision had been a sound one. Later, as Maud strove to accept her loss and rebuild her life around her children, she recognized the responsibility had undoubtedly saved her reason. Three years later, Thomas's mother, Lady Elizabeth, passed away peacefully in her sleep and now it was Maud's duty to be up at dawn to meet with the steward, to discuss the duties of the cooks, scullions, laundresses, fire boys and brewers, as well as the cleric, the resident priest and apothecary who all lived in the rooms, lofts and crannies of old Parr House. Listening to the stablemen and grooms' complaints, settling arguments between boatmen and yardmen or consulting with the nurses and rockers who cared for little Will in the third-floor nursery, Maud realized she needed help. How long would it be before the servants took advantage of the fact that for a good part of each day they were comparatively unsupervised? How long would it be before carelessness or dishonesty resulted in damage or loss to Parr House?

Her solution was to send for Bessie Bellingham. The Bellinghams were an old Northern family from Burneside in Westmorland near Kendal Castle. Their eldest daughter, Bessie, was fifteen and Maud immediately liked the large-framed sensible girl with her rich chestnut hair and speech with its resonant Northern burr. The girl was overjoyed at the thought of London and her parents were grateful. For, although Maud didn't promise, it was understood that if matters worked out the way they usually did, a suitable hand might later be found for the girl. When Bessie arrived, her cheeks glowing with that special tinge of pink all Northerners seemed to possess, Maud made her welcome in a room near the children. In no time at all, she'd won them over, especially ten-year-old Katherine. The servants, too, had sensed the girl's authority. In Maud's absence, Bessie's orders were as meticulously followed as old Lady Elizabeth's had been.

So each day, after prayers in the chapel and a light meal with the children in the old nursery, Maud went to the classroom—three rooms under the eaves in a turret of Westminster Palace—to observe and sometimes chastise the children, discuss the curriculum with their tutor and be certain the servants kept the place reasonably tidy. By the first morning light, she'd direct her sleepy brood into the litter and, on horseback, follow her steward from Parr House in the Strand as he led them through the awakening City to Westminster. By seven o'clock, classes in ancient languages, to be followed by logic, rhetoric and mathematics commenced, and Maud then left for the queen's quarters. At the day's end, after again conferring with Senor Vives, she and her children retraced their steps to Parr House.

Each night, Maud shared the evening meal with Bessie and Katherine, who'd been excused from nursery supper fare when she was nine. She looked forward to discussing her daughter's studies and later told Bessie and Katherine the daily occurrences in the queen's chamber. After they'd dined, when Bessie had left to see to the younger children, Maud helped Katherine with her needlework, never failing to find pleasure in the round face with its perfect rose and gold complexion, the bright hair, its reddish sheen high-lighted by candleglow and the flickering bursts of light from the fireplace.

Katherine's deep sea-green eyes, so like her own, sparkled with a lively in-telligence. Her ease in absorbing Senor Vives's teachings compensated some-what for the boisterous rudeness of Frances and Eleanor Brandon, the saucy wit of little Kate Willoughby and the earnestness of Princess Mary, whose aptitude for languages and music was as startling as her inability to grasp an abstraction or theory.

Once, when Katherine asked what Maud had been taught at her age, her mother replied, "It was not like today, Kate. I was brought up to read easily, write carefully, know my manners and embroider. I learned to cast simple sums, to know that the Continent is east of England and that Norsemen came from countries farther north to plunder. But I knew little of philoso-phy or sciences—or even of religion, other than what the priest said. My father—what a tyrant he was!—felt women needed or deserved little learn-ing except how to run a household and bear children. Anything else set him to shouting and my mother to her bed with a throbbing head! It was easier to do as he said. But here in London, the king's grandmother, Lady Mar-garet, helped change all that."

Katherine barely remembered Lady Margaret Beaufort who'd been her own grandmother, Lady Elizabeth's, closest friend. Lady Margaret, the mother of Henry VII, had seen her son win the Plantagenet crown at Bos-worth Field, only to die from consumption after which her eighteen-year-old grandson ascended the throne. Katherine recalled the tall almost emaciated figure, her ascetic bony features emphasized by the stark, snowy-white head-band and black mantle she wore at all times. Margaret Beaufort's gaunt ap-pearance, combined with a loud assertive voice, often frightened the chil-dren. Katherine clung to her mother's skirt whenever the king's grandmother came into sight. When she told Maud the court children even called her a witch, her mother had thrown back her tiny head and laughed, "If she's a witch, she's a good witch! Don't be afraid of her, Kate. She's a clever lady and a pious soul if ever I've seen one. And, Jesu knows, they are rare at court!" Afterward, Katherine regarded Lady Margaret with less temerity.

Fondly, Maud recalled Margaret Beaufort. "I still miss her, Kate. She was so kind to me when I first came to court. She let me sit at her feet with her ladies and listen to her talk. She had a self-assurance that was rare. She said we—all her ladies—must use our feminine influence to assert our indepen-dence and have more in our heads than the latest fashion or gossip or how to wheedle yet another bauble from our husbands. She insisted everyone should learn to read, for how could they know the truth otherwise? She made her friends Master Linacre and Master Grocyn and dear old Dean Colet of St. Paul's help her. She wanted girls to be able to read as well as boys. She wanted *everyone* to be educated so they might read and combat superstition and tyranny, to understand how the universe functioned and the wonders of our everyday world."

"She would have liked Senor Vives then," Katherine replied, "for he feels the same way."

Maud sighed. "Ah, she would have, Kate. I remember a long time ago she told me she'd helped Mr. Caxton print all those religious and political tracts and how angry your dear father used to be with her! But later I read them all for anyone who didn't was rarely asked back to her presence. And now that she's gone—God rest her soul—the queen wants to carry on her teaching. She says her mother, Queen Isabella, was like-minded and made certain all her daughters were as well educated as her son. The queen wants the same for Mary—and for all of you."

Katherine had heard such stories before—memories of a happier time that made Thomas Parr live again for his mourning wife. She interrupted her mother's reverie, pointing to the hourglass near the fireplace. "We've talked the evening away, Mother." She put aside her needlework. Leaving the fire and candles to the servants, the two went to their chambers. At her door, Katherine bent her knee in a slight curtsey and impulsively brushed her fingers along Maud's cheek in a gesture more caressing than a kiss. Then the door closed behind her.

Touched, Maud prepared for bed. Katherine was such a sensitive, caring child, secretly her favorite. She loved Will and Ann, of course. Will, with his exuberance and charm, his great fondness for sports and his small boy sense of mischief. Ann was as dark as the Parrs and had a seriousness, even at six, that reminded Maud of her father. But Katherine was so like herself; the closeness between them was intensely gratifying. She was proud of her daughter's intelligence and the promise, even so young, of great beauty.

Whoever won her would be a lucky man, indeed. Katherine had a proper dowry, a lineage which included Talbots and Throckmortons on Maud's side and those of the deTaillebois, Tunstalls, Nevilles and Marmions—which went back to before the Conquest—on the Parrs'. Had the king and queen had a son, they might have looked favorably on Katherine Parr. But princes and princesses, Maud knew, were most likely wed away from home, just as Queen Katherine had been, coming from Aragon so long ago in a political union to benefit England and Spain.

With Katherine approaching her tenth birthday, Maud knew she could put the child's marriage off no longer. She wrote her kinswoman, Lady Dacre, and asked her help in finding the girl a suitable husband. Sir William Parr had advised, "She will understand that Thomas would want his daughter to wed with the same good Northern stock from which our own family has sprung." The Dacres were a prominent Northern family and close to the Parrs of Kendal. Lady Dacre knew all the Darcys, Talbots, Cliffords and Husseys and numerous other nobles who headed small fiefdoms containing thousands of acres of land, dozens of castles and manors and retainers by the thousands. She'd know that Katherine Parr's husband must have a distinguished lineage, be a prosperous landowner with sufficient wealth to secure her future and that of their children.

Maud sighed as she completed the letter. She'd have three years in which to search, for, by law, a marriage could not be consummated until a girl was at least twelve and a boy fourteen. Somewhere in the North, a young lad was growing up to become Katherine Parr's husband. The girl would probably not see him before the wedding, just as she'd not seen Thomas. But how lucky she'd been! She prayed she might find the same happiness for her beloved daughter. And that it might last longer than the eight blessed years she'd had with Thomas.

Often, Maud had been urged to wed again. She was only twenty-two when widowed, independently wealthy and one of the acknowledged beauties at court. Yet never once, even as she now sought marriage for her daughter, did it occur to her to do so.

To belong to anyone other than Thomas Parr was unthinkable.

CHAPTER II

Awaiting word from the North, life went on at Parr House, part of an old Norman stronghold, Montfichet Castle, built by a baron who'd come to England with William the Conqueror. Its foundations, now underground, were covered by the Blackfriars Church and monastery next door; the monks' fruit orchards bordered Parr House's gardens. On its farther side, westward toward Whitehall, lay the greensward of drum-shaped Temple Church enclosed in its little park of plane trees. Along the riverbank the nobles' houses with their terraces, gardens and fruit orchards sloped to the Thames, mingling with the palaces of the bishops—Exeter, Salisbury and Durham—names which conjured up princely wealth as well as the church's authority.

It was from this terrace that the children and adults of Parr House often watched the daily extraordinary drama of the river. Everyone—passengers in their wherries or slips, those aboard ferries which took them from bank to bank, even the Lord Mayor in his colorful barge—all savored the sights, sounds and smell of the river as their craft dodged among the snowy swans gliding imperiously among the vessels. Along the riverbank, citizens swam when the tide was in and others, usually children of the poor, hunted eels when it was out.

Everyone used the river. It was safer, cleaner and quicker than the muddy roadways, some little better than paths, beset with petty thieves and deep ruts, a danger to horse, cart and limb alike. Prosperous merchants, hailing their boatmen at the City waterstairs, jostled the nobles and other courtiers who rode the river from the Tower to Whitehall. There, if one was lucky, one might even see the king and queen boarding the royal barge at the Privy Stairs for a short ride downriver.

On rainy days, all the Parr children and Bessie watched—through the rivulets of water splashing against the windows—for the foreign vessels from Muscovy or the Indies, from the Mediterranean or Africa. On fine days, Maud would let Katherine and Will romp with the servants' children in the decaying courtyard of old Baynards Castle. There, Bessie watched as they played stickball, quoits, or blindman's buff, before hurrying home at dusk through the back alleys of Bridewell Palace, then standing for a moment on the new little bridge over the Fleet River to drop stones in the water below.

These excursions were never mentioned to anyone; it was unthinkable

Lady Parr would allow her children to play with the offspring of those who served her. But Maud remembered her own lonely childhood and was determined her children would never be friendless.

One day in early spring, Maud assembled her family on the terrace to await the arrival of the French queen, Mary Tudor, the king's sister. The wife of tall, darkly handsome Charles Brandon, the Duke of Suffolk, one of the king's closest friends, Mary was the mother of the troublesome Brandon girls who so provoked everyone in the classroom. Katherine knew her mother's patience with the eldest, Frances, was about exhausted. The girl was spoiled and arrogant, rarely hesitating to use rank or create mischief, bedeviling servant and tutor alike. Privately, Katherine thought the girls deserved a good beating with a stick. She knew that sometimes parents did beat their children, although she couldn't imagine her mother doing so. And she didn't think the French queen would either, much as her daughters deserved it.

Suffolk House, the great stone mansion across the river at Southwark where the Brandons lived, was just a stone's throw from the end of London Bridge. Even now, the French queen's barge must be on the river. Katherine prayed she was not bringing the girls. As they waited, she asked her mother why Mary Tudor, for whom little Princess Mary had been named, was called "the French queen."

"Because for about six months, when she was just a little older than you, she was queen of France," Maud explained.

"Did she like being a queen?" How would it feel, Katherine wondered, to be queen for six months and then come home and be a mere duchess?

"No, she didn't," Maud replied. If Katherine was old enough to be inquisitive, she was old enough to know what marriage for a princess might mean. "She hated everything about it for by that time she was very much in love with Charles Brandon. He was older than Mary and, though the king was very fond of him, he didn't want his youngest sister to marry Brandon, who'd already had two wives."

As Katherine pondered her mother's words, Maud recalled the day she'd first met fifteen-year-old Mary Tudor. The princess was clearly the darling of the royal family, an elfin girl, round of face with the fair pink and white coloring of all the Tudors. Her red hair, with brilliant golden highlights, defied her governess' comb and remained, under her pretty caps, a bright mop of curls. Fourteen-year-old Maud, now pregnant, had been shy at meeting the king's sister. But Mary's blue eyes had sparkled at the thought of a friend near her own age and soon the two, despite vastly differing personalities, became inseparable.

While Maud looked forward to her studies with Lady Margaret Beaufort, Mary Tudor sought pleasure with the same intensity as she disdained books, saying she had neither the wit nor the desire to learn. Laughingly, she chided Maud for spending so much time listening to her grandmother and reading her dull treatises. Lady Margaret had long ago lost patience with the rebellious Mary who'd shrugged her shoulders and cried, "I shall marry my heart's desire and have many children and wed them to the thrones of Europe!" When Henry later reprimanded her for paying little attention to her tutors, she'd retorted, "Why should I spend my days with my nose in a book? Why bother with all that when someone else can always tell me what I need to know?" When the queen complained she absented herself from the court's religious services too often, she told Maud with tight lips, "I go to Mass weekly, sometimes more. I confess and study the lives of the saints. If the queen wishes to hear Mass three times a day and my brother wants to attend daily vespers, let them! Jesu—do I have to spend more time on my knees and walk the halls with a Bible in my hand so they'll leave me alone?"

Katherine, aware her mother's thoughts were far away, mused. "I think it was very brave of her to go to France, away from her family, especially when she was in love with someone else."

"The king thought Mary would get over her attraction for Charles Brandon, though your father and I were just as certain she wouldn't! When the king said she had to go, we did everything we could to help her. But she would not be quieted. She cried and raged and said her husband-to-be was fifty-two years old, with no teeth and everyone said he smelled bad. She threatened to kill herself if the king made her go to France. But in the end, of course, she went."

"I don't think she could have done anything else, if the king willed it," Katherine replied soberly. "Was she just as unhappy in France?"

"For six months, she bore it all, Kate," Maud replied, "but her marriage was a source of great grief and humiliation to her." That was all Maud intended to say. Never, she thought, would she describe the sexual degradation to which Louis had submitted his young wife. Henry had assured his sister the union would be in name only. How could a man so ill and diseased as the French king—who could barely mount a horse—be expected to consummate a marriage?

But, confronted with the girl the English called "the Tudor Rose" with her startlingly blue eyes, fair complexion, the graceful hands and shapely figure, Louis XII had had other thoughts. Though she successfully put him off for weeks, at last Mary was forced to share his chamber where, as she'd tearfully written Maud, "he has wrestled with me until I am limp. It has hurt his pride and made him angry, but I am still intact. He fondles me so roughly and meanly that often I protest and to punish me, he uses my poor body in ways he says are agreeable to him and makes it easier for him to caress me. He thinks of nothing but his pleasure, but I have refused to respond to other loathesome suggestions. I find it all disgusting . . . but I know he will not, indeed cannot, violate me. At least not physically."

Mary, the French queen, had solved the problem in her own way. If her husband wished to be pleasured, she decided, he should have his wish. Night after night, there were balls, masques and plays. Early the next morning, hunting parties were formed and lackeys lifted an exhausted monarch into the saddle. There was feasting and dancing enough to make the royal physicians complain. But Louis was determined to please his young wife. In six months, he was dead "of the excess" his family said. His queen, in formal mourning, counted the days until she could return to England.

"And when she came home to find her true love, did she marry him right away?" Intent upon her needlework, Katherine felt a little glow of pleasure that her mother was treating her as an adult confidante.

"No, she married Charles Brandon in France. The king sent him to bring Mary home, for he wished to be certain her jewels came with her. He told Charles he'd expected the marriage to last longer and had wasted a large dowry for naught! But once there, Mary made Charles wed her for if she waited until her return, she was certain the king would marry her elsewhere. She was pregnant when she came home."

Katherine thought the story exciting. To give up a throne for love—no matter how old the king was or how badly he smelled—was thrilling. "And they lived happily ever after. . . ." she sighed.

Maud nodded. Katherine needn't know, even as he'd accepted Mary's jewels, how enraged the king had been that his closest friend had dared seduce his sister. Or of how, at their first meeting, the French queen had shouted for all to hear that if there'd been any seducing, *she'd* been the seducer! In a matter of months, Mary had regained her brother's love, if not her jewels, and the only reminder of her dismal time in France was the persistence of her title.

Out of the corner of her eye, Katherine saw the Suffolk barge, distinctive with its ducal markings and the blue and gold fleurs-de-lis, being secured at the Parr House waterstairs. In a moment, the French queen, tall and graceful, stepped onto the pavement, accompanied by a slight child who clung to her hand as they began the ascent up to the terrace. Katherine was happy it was Princess Mary and not one of the Brandon girls. Nearing the top, the little girl caught sight of Maud Parr and waved, running ahead to greet her friends.

"My lady! My lady!" she cried in a voice startlingly deep for one so small. "We're to go to Richmond with my mother, the queen. Richmond, for a whole week, my lady!"

Both Maud and Katherine dropped deep curtseys as Mary reached them. Then, opening her arms, Maud hugged the child as the French queen drew near. Dutifully, Katherine bobbed a curtsey before receiving a kiss on the cheek from the king's sister.

"Richmond is it?" Maud hugged the little girl again. "Well, now, that should please you. You'll have all the friars' orchards to romp in and can sail boats on the river. We'll see if Lady Willoughby won't let Kate come too, shall we, since her father is very ill? It would be good for the child to get out of that place of gloom! And," nodding toward the French queen, she whispered, "we might even persuade your aunt to join us!"

"I can never resist Richmond, Maud dear, you know that," Mary smiled.

Turning to Katherine, she said, "You're growing up too fast, Kate, you make me feel old! Soon all the young lads of the court will be noticing this daughter of yours, Maud. She's much too pretty and smart for them. You'll do better than that, Kate—your mother will see to it!"

Katherine felt a momentary pang of sadness at the thought of leaving her mother and the peaceful security of Parr House. But she said nothing, knowing it was not her place and only hoped she'd be allowed to remain while the two adults visited with each other. She never tired of watching them—surely they were the prettiest ladies in all London? One, her mother, petite and rounded, her silky blond hair and large green eyes, looking for all the world like a beautiful elder sister instead of her mother. And the French queen, taller, with that matchless skin and red-gold hair tamed at last under its green-hued damask cap lavishly trimmed with seed pearls framing the perfect oval of her face. She, too, looked younger than her twenty-five years. Katherine listened shamelessly as her mother spoke to her companion about her daughters' behavior.

"My darling Maud," Mary Tudor laughed aloud, "neither Charles nor I are students, as you know. He finds it difficult to read more than three sentences and I am no scholar! How can you expect our children to be so different?"

"They are intelligent enough, Your Grace," Maud replied steadily, "but they do not apply themselves. They don't think they *have* to. It makes it difficult for the other children."

"Ah, they can be nuisances, I know. Well, I will see what I can do with them." Mary sighed. "Sometimes, I wish they were boys. Boys usually have more wit than girls and do better in the classroom."

Maud did not argue that neither the queen, Senor Vives, nor she herself would agree with such a premise. If there was no improvement in the girls' behavior, Queen Katherine might insist they be tutored at home. Maud devoutly hoped so.

As the servants brought wine and spiced cakes, she suggested Katherine take Mary to the terrace's far end where they might play cards at a small table already set up for their use. Taking two spiced cakes, Katherine sighed; she'd hoped to be allowed to listen to the adults' conversation.

Maud wanted to discuss her daughter's marriage prospects. "She should be affianced soon, Your Grace," she told Mary Tudor. "Her father would have wanted it that way. I don't want her turned loose at court. As you can see, she's going to be comely and there. . . ." Her voice trailed off.

"And there," laughed the French queen, "she will see that virtue does not always have its own reward! There she will find those who look to her good name and money to fill their pockets. Or, should they already have enough, they will wed for her connections and then solace themselves with some other *jeune fille,* such as my dear brother has done with that Boleyn wench . ."

"That will not last, Your Grace. You know that once the king satisfies his fancy with the girl, he will return to the queen."

"I hope you're right," Mary sipped her wine delicately. "This girl seems not to care whether Henry pursues her or not. There is nothing to pique a man's interest more than aloofness—and my good brother is not used to that!"

Maud's heart ached for the queen. She knew how much Katherine of Aragon loved her husband, how disappointed she was that there'd been only one living child—and that a girl—for the man who so desperately needed a son and heir. The queen had borne seven children in nine years, all stillborn, except Mary and one little prince who'd lived a few months. Now, nearing forty, her childbearing years over and prematurely aged, she had to face the challenge of a younger rival for her husband's attentions. There was little sense in complaining; it would only drive the king further from her.

"It is the fate of queens," Katherine once told Maud Parr. "I'll never know the same closeness you and Maria have with your husbands. Remember, queens rarely wed for love. If it happens, we're lucky! We've had good years together, my Henry and I. He is still young and has to answer to no one. I have no regrets. My lord may not need me as he once did, but I am still queen and mother of the heir!" Maud had thought Katherine of Aragon very brave.

The French queen drew the pale green velvet cloak close about her as a breeze blew off the river. "Henry says he will name Mary the Princess of Wales. The queen is very pleased, for it means Mary will have the throne. But my brother is not happy, Maud, at the thought. He says female sovereigns are easy prey for power cliques within the court or else they might wed in a foreign alliance which could prove disastrous for the realm. A fine one he is to talk!" Mary Tudor's bright blue eyes, so like her brother's, sparkled with anger. "The best thing about my brother since my grandmother died has been the advice and help he's had from the queen! He knows this deep down in his heart, of course, but with Mistress Boleyn to keep him dancing attendance, he finds it easy to forget."

Maud Parr had seen Anne Boleyn only a few times in recent years. She remembered her best as the eleven-year-old girl who'd gone off to France as a maid of honor at Mary Tudor's marriage. Anne had remained in France, living at the French court, for eight years. Upon her return, Maud had scarcely recognized the slim black-haired beauty. Anne's straight carriage lent emphasis to a long neck and the oval, well-shaped head from which two deep, lustrous black eyes sparkled. The sleek, raven hair, drawn back in a large cluster of curls, gave her a mature look for her nineteen years.

"She is very proud, this Anne!" The exasperated Mary continued, "Maria de Salinas has threatened to box her ears if she ever again mimics the old Duchess of Norfolk, or anyone else. I would have thought she'd have been taught better manners at the French court than to make fun of her own aunt!" Maud turned her face away so Mary would not see her smile. The old duchess, garrulous and demanding, was no favorite of hers and she'd laughed as long as anyone else at the deadly accuracy of Anne's impersonation.

Continuing to talk about the king's new favorite, Maud realized her daughter and Mary had joined them. Undoubtedly, they'd heard the last of the conversation. The little princess' face was a study in doubt and bewilderment. She'd certainly heard "Boleyn" whispered in the queen's chambers and realized it was the name of a girl who often made her mother weep. Maud knew the child would probably like to ask her elders how such an ordinary girl could hurt a queen? But Mary had been taught that manners were important and she must not act unbecomingly.

As the French queen prepared to leave, Maud knew the little princess was returning home with a heavy heart. As they walked to the terrace edge, she put a comforting arm about Mary's thin shoulders. The child was gnawing nervously at her lip and, at the older woman's touch, turned and clung to her tightly. Maud wondered how much Mary—even her own Kate—really knew. Servants gossipped. Some even relished telling their charges much that would better be left unsaid. Though she'd taught Kate that gossip was harmful, she knew children could be malicious. And in the schoolroom, they were all fair game. There, even rank was no protection.

After her guests had departed and Katherine had gone to find Bessie, Maud went to her chamber. There, on her table, were the names of her daughter's marriage prospects: their age, the extent of their land and tenants, their wealth, county connections and titles, as well as a general assessment of their status at court. Many were old families: the Poles, Abergavennys, Staffords, Percys and Montagues. There also were the newcomers—the Comptons, Dorsets, Boleyns, Greys and Howards—the "new men" the king preferred to have about him. Maud's own preference inclined toward the older, more conservative families. But she knew that in the end, it came down to hard facts: land, money and influence at court. Often, pondering the list, she felt as though she was playing a game and longed for Thomas to be there to fit the puzzle together. At stake was her beloved daughter's future and she wanted security, position, wealth—and love—for Katherine. Thomas had once said it was everyone's birthright to have love. But she had only to look at the court and many of her friends, including the king and queen, to know that love, true and enduring, was perhaps the hardest of all to find.

* * *

Richmond Palace. The very name conjured up peace and tranquillity. Sun-dappled orchards, meadows and lawn gracing a river which the old king had once likened to a silver ribbon. Henry VII had built Richmond; it replaced the ancient palace of Sheen destroyed in a fire in 1499. It rose from the banks of the Thames, three stories high, almost flamboyant in the raw redness of its brick, the tall slim windows emphasizing the cupolas and turrets—fourteen onion-shaped domes—topped by the King's Beasts. When the wind was just right, so the local people said, they often seemed to roar.

Old Henry had meant Richmond to show that royalty no longer needed securely fortified strongholds such as the Tower or Windsor Castle. There were gates and sentries, but no moat or bridge guarded the approach. Instead, the main entrance was from the river, while those arriving with horses and wagons used the great arched gate at the opposite end where Henry's arms were chiseled in bold relief. It faced a large level, well-turfed field or green where jousts and tournaments were held and, once a year, the common people were allowed to use it for their fair.

Inside its thick walls, the palace of Richmond was a mélange of parks and orchards, with shady walks where pavilions were set for chess or other games. Bowling alleys and tennis courts were bordered with flowering beds or rows of neatly trimmed shrubs behind which sculpture had been tastefully placed.

Richmond was an especial favorite of Queen Katherine—not only for its beauty but as a place of refuge when the plague or intense winter cold settled on London. Here she could easily visit her favored Order of the Observant Friars, whose chapel and orchards abutted on the palace's east flank. And here she could relax. In contrast to Greenwich, where complete formality and court protocol was always strictly observed, at Richmond everyone felt on holiday.

Often, the queen, her ladies and their children piled into the royal barge and, with a minstrel to sing the old songs or one of the Fools to tell stories, spent hours on the river, singing, trailing small baubles in the water as they watched the herons and other shore creatures.

Young Katherine Parr loved Richmond. There she and the other children were also allowed to roam, enjoying the same freedom as the peasant—the pleasure of searching for the fallow deer, the wild flowers and small wildlife that teemed in the verdant countryside.

Long ago the children had formed the habit of saving tidbits of nursery fare or food from their place at table in the Great Hall. Once the meal was over, they'd bide their time, ready to flee to what they considered their own enchanted forest. As soon as they were dismissed, they ran past the friars' garden where the brown-robed monks responded to their shouts as they skirted the orchards on the way to the nearby woods. There, with no adults about, they'd huddle down in a glade or clearing, eating their scraps from none too clean hands with all the gusto of a dairymaid or a farmer's lass.

It was on just such a day, warm and hazy with heat from the river, that the children met the gypsy.

Bessie Bellingham and Katherine accompanied by Princess Mary, Kate Willoughby and the visiting Brandon children, had settled in high spirits into their forest sanctuary to eat their hoarded food. The man, wizened and gouty, appeared from nowhere into the clearing, shuffling along the path which led straight to their secret picnic ground. Bessie was the first to see him as he approached. His piercing black eyes looked straight into hers, causing her an involuntary shudder. Yet in spite of his dirty clothing and formidable walking stick, none of the children seemed afraid. Katherine, startled at his bedraggled appearance, was about to speak when a look from Bessie silenced her.

In a low voice, the old man asked for food. Bessie remembered the many gypsies along the banks of the Kent near her Northern home who never traveled without food. But, silently, she handed over some scraps of bread and cheese. Princess Mary, ever mindful of her mother's admonition to be kind to the poor, dutifully offered a grubby fistful of sweetmeats. The old man said nothing, but wolfed away at the food.

"Have you come a long way?" Bessie asked. "If you have nothing, the friars will help you."

"I go to Lunnon," the old man muttered between bites. "I thank you for the food. I was set upon at sundown yesterday."

"You were robbed?" The princess' eyes shone as Katherine edged closer to hear the story. The old man, his stomach rumblings somewhat eased, recounted the episode. He'd been walking along, minding his own business, traveling to Lunnon to join his brothers when, seemingly out of nowhere, half a dozen rogues had set upon him, beating him about the head and then running off with his horse, wagon and trunk. It was a sorry experience, he wheezed, when one could not travel the king's highway without losing all one's possessions.

Bessie saw the princess' lips tighten. Any criticism of her father was likely to provoke a small storm in Mary. Quickly, she suggested everyone gather up their things and shake out their skirts. The old man wiped his fingers on a handful of leaves. For the first time, Bessie noticed bruises along his arms and about his neck. As he turned to go, he said, "You have been kind. I will go to Lunnon more comfortable now. Let me repay you. . . ."

"I thought you didn't have any money!" Little Frances Brandon pursed her lips and, for a moment, looked so much like the king one might have thought her his daughter rather than his niece. "You said you didn't have any money!" she accused.

"I don't have any money, little wench, but I have more up here!" The old man tapped his head. "Gypsies have the gift of sight and we usually tell it for gold, didn't you know that? But I'm sure you have no gold, same as me, so I'll repay you in my own way. Now, my little one, let's see your hand. . . ."

Dutifully, Frances offered a smudged hand, her fat little fingers outstretched so the gypsy might see. The others, laughing, clustered around as he promised great riches, handsome suitors when they grew up, and always good health, good fortune and happy times ahead. At last he turned to Katherine, saying, "And now it's your turn."

Shyly, Katherine offered her hand. For the first time, the man seemed quietly thoughtful, easy words and promises failing him. He muttered a bit to himself, drew her nearer the edge of the clearing where the light was stronger and looked at her palm. "Young miss," he said, looking into her eyes, "you have a good hand." Peering more closely, he said, "Well, young miss, I see castles and a title. A title, young miss! I see wealth and travel and not one man, but many!" Katherine blushed at Bessie's smile and the old man continued, "You'll be much wedded and you'll work also. But with your mind—you'll never work with your hands. You will influence many others with your learning." He released her fingers, bowed slightly and said again, "You'll not work with those hands, my young miss. Those hands are meant to touch crowns and scepters, you'll see. . . ."

"What are scepters?" Princess Mary asked, tugging a basket filled with plants she'd dug for the friars. "Kate will have a scepter? What's a scepter?" But her question went unanswered. The old man bowed again and was soon lost among the trees.

As Bessie led the group back along the orchard path, Katherine lingered behind. The old man's words were seductive and she felt dazed by their spell. Ahead, the others were laughing and talking excitedly of what they'd heard. Yet none had been told anything as impressive as what the old gypsy had told her.

Katherine wondered what her mother would say when she heard the prophecy. Undoubtedly everyone would have a merry time discussing the scene. Katherine felt a momentary resentfulness that they might even laugh at the old gypsy's words. Then, common sense asserting itself, she laughed aloud and ran ahead to join the others.

"Don't, for the love you bear our Saviour, tell the princess what a scepter is, Kate! She'll only say he made a mistake and told the fortune to the wrong person!" Bessie admonished. Katherine nodded and, taking Mary by the hand, told the child of the gala the court ladies were planning for the following evening when the king and Charles Brandon would arrive from London. Maud Parr had said the queen looked so beautiful in her dark royal blue velvet. . . .

Yet along the way, amidst her companions' laughter, the words recurred in her mind. Crowns and scepters, the old gypsy had said. Crowns and scepters. . . .

CHAPTER III

Young women have said that they could not love, nor find it in their heart to marry someone whom they did not know before. . . . But if the maid will only marry a man because she is already used to his love, she is not very different from a mistress. . . . She spends the love (which ought to be kept until after the wedding) before the marriage, and so it is said, "They that marry for love shall spend their lives in sorrow."

—Juan Luys Vives, royal tutor

When Katherine told her family of the gypsy's prophecy, little seven-year-old Ann cried, "I'll be your chief maid of honor!" while the exuberant Will bent a childish head, promising undying loyalty. Joining in the fun, Maud brought out the slim gold circlet the queen had sent at Katherine's birth. The three children eyed it solemnly. Impulsively, Maud lay it atop her daughter's shining hair and, catching the mood, the girl drew herself up regally, holding out her hand for an invisible escort as she paraded slowly about the chamber while her brother and sister followed deferentially.

Maud watched them fondly, forgetting for a moment her disappointment in finding a husband for Katherine. She'd even taken the matter to the queen. Her daughter had been raised with royalty and deserved the best. "There are only forty peers in England, Your Grace, and most of their heirs are already married or betrothed. But I will not have Kate wed beneath her. . . ." It troubled Maud there were so few candidates from which to choose.

The queen, agreeing her namesake and godchild must have only the best, had patted Maud's hand comfortingly and promised to mention the matter to the king.

Henry suggested the fourteen-year-old son and heir of Lord Scrope of Bolton. Lady Dacre wrote she hadn't suggested young Henry Scrope because, despite a sound family background, she suspected the family was virtually penniless, a fact the present lord had probably kept hidden from the king. As soon as negotiations commenced, Maud saw that Lady Dacre's suspicions were correct for, from the beginning, Lord Scrope was well aware the advantage lay with him. He knew the extent of the Parr wealth and the family's close connection to the Crown. Several of his manors abutted on Parr holdings which would be particularly advantageous to the bride's family. What his son lacked in money, he had in land. Marriages to enlarge or secure family estates were hardly uncommon and always the result of shrewd bargaining. And Lord Scrope, a land-poor peer with a great need for cash, was determined his son's marriage would be the means of obtaining it.

In the midst of negotiations, Maud was further disheartened when a court progress to Newcastle and Easthampstead was announced. Torn between duty to the queen and leaving her children for over a month, she especially disliked being away while the bargaining between Lord Scrope and Sir William Parr continued. As Sir William swore softly at Scrope's demands, Maud's cousin, Cuthbert Tunstall, the Bishop of London, whose help she'd also asked, only shook his head. Not only did the old peer want a larger dowry than offered, but over half must be paid before the marriage was even consummated.

"And that could be at least two years away!" Maud cried. "He says also if Katherine should die in childbirth—which Jesu forbid!—no part of her dowry will be returned and, once wed, they must live on our property, not his. Wretched man! Let him wait now for our answer! I want to discuss this with the queen."

The queen and Maria de Salinas, aware their children would have only governesses and servants for companionship while they were away, had arranged for the Parr children and Kate Willoughby, to occupy rooms near Princess Mary at Westminster Palace. In that way, Mary would not be so lonely, and each day Bessie could accompany them to the schoolroom and return them to their quarters in the afternoon. Lady Margaret Bryan, Mary's devoted governess, would supervise their activities and send daily messages to the queen.

"But remember, Kate," Maud advised at their parting, "you're the oldest and must be helpful to Bessie and Senor Vives. I've told Bessie that if Will misbehaves, the threat of the rod is usually enough to quiet him. Mary and Kate will miss their mothers, too, and if there are tears, remind them the king feels it's his duty to meet his people. Everyone here must behave. They must do their duty as the king and queen do theirs."

Maud's words hid her apprehension in leaving her family at a time when Katherine's future might be decided. She knew William Parr would do nothing without consulting her, but being absent from Parr House would cause delay. Yet any delay meant Katherine would be with her longer. Maud still hadn't forgotten the old peer's callous remark about the girl dying in childbirth.

Whenever she thought of her daughter's marriage, she missed Thomas more than ever. He'd have known just how to deal with the miserable Scrope—how to be certain Katherine's future would be as bright and happy as she deserved. Without him, she now realized it might not be as easy as she'd thought.

*   *   *

Katherine's marriage was not the only one under discussion for recently the king had chosen a husband for seven-year-old Princess Mary. The alliance with the French dauphin, settled when the child was two, had foundered as relations between the two nations worsened. Then Queen Katherine insisted Mary be affianced to the twenty-four-year-old Charles V, the Holy Roman Emperor. When the announcement was made, the little princess made every effort to appear pleased. But Katherine knew only the queen's joy in the union between her nephew, the son of her sister, Juana of Castile, kept Mary from tears at the thought of leaving her parents to live in Spain.

Several days after the court left London, the fear was still on the princess' mind. Kate Willoughby had gone to the Barbican house to visit with her ill father and, awaiting her return, Mary and Katherine rode to the king's mews above the great cross at Charing, to meet Robert Cheseman, the royal falconer for a morning of coursing through the woods to Chelsea.

It was a day of clear blue skies and rain-washed air. The two girls were greeted by Mary's pair of matched greyhounds running wildly about the mews' courtyard. Joining them, Cheseman said, "We'll go by way of the abbey and palace, Your Grace, and then on into the woods." As everyone mounted their horses, he said, "Mind the dogs now. Let them have their head, but stay close together!"

At his signal, the animals bounded ahead, ecstatic at the fresh pungent smell of the spongy wet earth. Their sleek bodies responded to the whoops and shouts as everyone tore off through the great wooded area. Then, as the riders' pace slowed, they disappeared amongst the sun-dappled trees while small animals scurried for protection.

Breathless from the swift ride, Katherine and Mary rode in silence until suddenly the princess asked, "Will you like being married to Lord Scrope's son, Kate?"

"It doesn't matter, Mary." Katherine knew she was not truly answering her friend's question. "My lady mother will know best, I'm sure. However, she's very angry with Lord Scrope and says he must change his mind before she'll let me go."

"Well, at least you won't have to leave home," said the princess apprehensively. "When you wed, you'll remain here. But Kate, my mother never saw her parents after she came to England. If I go to Spain, it will be the same and I couldn't bear it!"

"Ah, that's a long time off, Mary, for you'll not wed until you're fourteen or more, the queen says. And you must remember, you'll not be going to a strange land, but to your mother's *homeland*. . . ."

They'd reached the river at last and Cheseman, pointing to the sun, signaled a return along the river. Katherine recalled the last time the queen had talked to them of Spain. "It's nothing like you'll ever see in England, my girls. It's a golden land—especially Granada—where the sun shines all the time. There is no damp and no fog and the land is fragrant with lush gardens of oleander and jasmine. The sky stays blue for days, with great clouds looking for all the world like a sheep's fleece hanging over pastures and fields of figs and limes and almonds." The queen's voice had trembled with nostalgia. "Near our mosque there were great orange groves with cypress trees to cut the heat and provide shade. Each hour a great bell tolled. . . ."

"I still don't want to leave home!" Mary's voice was sharp, interrupting Katherine's reverie. "I want to stay here! I'd wed such a one as Henry Scrope if it meant I didn't have to go away. Although of course, it wouldn't be proper. . . ."

Katherine, mindful of her mother's words to solace Mary, replied, "When it comes time to go, you'll be happy to leave. Remember, your mother was happy to come to England and marry a prince. But you'll be an *empress*, Mary! And the emperor is very noble-looking! Remember what Senor Vives said? That marriages arranged by parents who love us are much better than those made for romantic love?"

Only the previous day, as if aware of questions in his feminine students' mind, Senor Vives had dwelt at length upon the fact that a woman left to her own device and marrying for love was likely to be duped. In an unusual lecture, Vives said such women spent their lives in sorrow, for men were wont to use romantic love as a weapon, trapping foolhardy young girls into liaisons which could lead to perdition. His feminine audience had sat entranced as he described how romantic love led to a wretchedness where girls —often from good families—ended up in brothels, ill with disease, forever destined to spend their lives begging on the streets. How much better, Vives stressed, not to lose one's virginity, to keep one's reputation free from blemish, and not become the subject of idle gossip.

Mary remembered Vives's words. "He said romantic love is such a great danger to us all. What do you think, Kate? How can a love be romantic when you don't even see your husband until your wedding day?"

Katherine had pondered the tutor's words. Young as she was, she knew that at any given moment, the court was always alive with several affairs in various stages of dalliance. Was that romantic love and was it so bad? How could she reconcile her tutor's teaching with the great love—surely a *romantic* love—that had existed between her parents? Maud Parr had so adored her husband she'd refused all offers for her hand. Surely theirs had been a love not only of respect and liking, but passion and delight as well, the very kind their tutor prophesied led to sorrow.

Undoubtedly, Mary was thinking of her own parents' marriage which almost bore out the truth of Vives's words. Katherine of Aragon, the widow of Henry's older brother, Prince Arthur, who'd died at sixteen, had wed young

Henry when he was eighteen and she was twenty-four. It had been a love match. Even today, some fifteen years later, there was still affection and friendship between Henry and his queen. Yet, as the king's attention appeared to wander more often, it had caused much heartbreak and sorrow for the queen.

"I know when our parents choose for us, it will be for our own good," Katherine told Mary soothingly. Privately, she found it all very taxing to think upon.

She was relieved to see the princess looking more cheerful and, following the falconer's lead, they rode toward Westminster, making for the roadway past the ornate new York House that old Cardinal Wolsey had recently completed. Katherine could guess how Mary felt. How would she feel if her mother found her a husband from Italy, France—or even Scotland? Surely, however, everything would turn out all right for Mary if the king and queen —and even the French queen—all approved the Spanish match?

Who would want to send Mary where she'd be unhappy?

* * *

After days of dividing their time between schoolroom, chapel, and their palace chambers, Lady Bryan, cheeks pink with excitement, announced the court would be returning in a day or so and, for their good behavior, she'd planned a special treat.

"Oh, tell, tell!" little Kate Willoughby jumped up and down, tugging at the governess' arm. But Lady Bryan would only say that Senor Vives had excused them from classes and they must be ready in simple dress, at the Westminster waterstairs.

"Then we're going on the river!" Katherine cried. But Lady Bryan merely pursed her lips and would say no more.

Early the next morning, Bessie brought Katherine and Kate Willoughby to the palace where Randall Dodd, one of Princess Mary's stewards and Lady Bryan, with the little princess, waited. Although the royal craft was tied up nearby, they all entered a plain barge and, within moments, the oarsman had them midriver. As they glided downstream, the children cried out in excitement at the familiar sights, which looked so different from the river.

"There's Lady Parr's favorite tree just behind the Blackfriars' bell tower!" Kate Willoughby exclaimed. Along the beaches at Bridewell and Baynards Castle, Katherine saw several of the children she'd often romped with, playing at the water's edge. Lady Bryan and Mary held out pieces of stale bread that the governess had brought for the swans that swam beside them, water dripping from their beaks as they snapped at the tidbits. "Careful, young miss, they'll give you a nip," the old man said. It was then Katherine realized he'd not recognized the princess and that part of Lady Bryan's treat was that they were all incognito.

"Look to the bridge!" the governess pointed to the gaudy shops that lined the long structure. "We're almost there." Her speech was drowned out as the oarsman shouted, "Hold tight, we're going to shoot the bridge. Hang on to the sides very tightly!"

In a moment, the little craft was bobbing like a cork amidst boiling, foaming water as it shot through the bridge's pilings. For a fearful moment, Katherine wondered if it might founder and they'd all be thrown into the river. But, in a moment, the craft had reached quieter water and there, on the left, was the Tower with its great guns lined up on the beach. The oarsman made for the stairs where, after Randall Dodd gave him a coin, they all entered the Lion's Gate.

"Now the choice is yours," Lady Bryan said, "you may go to the Tower and see the beasts. Or we may walk up yonder to Tower Hill and on to Moorfield for the sporting and to Cheapside to see the markets."

It was a heady thought—to walk the City streets the same as any commoner!—and the girls looked to Katherine for guidance. Recalling the day she and her father had seen the king at Moorfield, she suggested they head in that direction. They'd all seen the Tower lions before and the ravens, too.

Waiting at the Tower's entrance for Randall Dodd to rent horses, everyone was pushed and jostled. With no one to cry, "Make way for Princess Mary!" it was another world. On unfamiliar mounts, they rode through the crowded area surrounding the Holy Cross Friars into Fenchurch Street and on to the Corn Hill. At the entrance to the Augustinian Friary, pedlars with dancing bears showed their wares, while beggars in foul, ragged clothing that barely covered filthy bodies, exhibited raw and open sores as they cried for alms. Neither Katherine nor her young companions had ever been so close to the sight, smell and sound of poverty and disease and their eyes were wide with shock and distress.

On into Moorgate, its Norman postern in the shadow of St. Mary of Bethlehem Church, where everyone reverently crossed themselves as they passed. In moments, less than a mile from their start at Tower Hill, they were in open country, with fresh clean air sweeping along the one good road lined with elms. It was heavily wooded on either side with small cottages, an abbey, a church and several farms.

"Make way there, young misses, do move to one side," one farmer growled, as huge wagons filled with fruit, cheese, butter, hens and eggs, lumbered toward the London markets. The three girls pressed close to each other at the roadside, the smell of the cheeses mingling with the animals' sweat. Following them, a group of bakers from Stratford-le-Bow stopped as Randall Dodd bought a penny loaf, hot and dripping with butter, for everyone.

When the sun was highest and the London bells could be heard tolling the midday hour, cloths were set upon the green of an old churchyard and everyone, rank and protocol forgotten, devoured the simple food. Never had cheese, bread and fruit tasted so good. Lady Bryan even allowed the girls half portions of ale mixed with water.

With the sun warm upon her skin, Katherine wanted to run so the breeze might caress her bare body; it felt so different to be in a simple thin cloth dress rather than the heavy velvets and damasks she usually wore. It was almost like being at Kendal except the sun was never so warm in the North and there it would be impossible to just slip away and melt into a crowd. At Kendal, everyone bowed, curtsied or tugged at forelock or cap.

Princess Mary and Kate were also in high spirits. "This has been such good sport, my lady!" Mary hugged Lady Bryan. "And tomorrow, my mother will be home. I can't wait to see her again! And, of course, my father, too!" she added loyally.

Regretfully, they all helped Bessie and Lady Bryan clean up the remains of the meal, feeding leftovers to the horses. Silently, with Randall Dodd leading the way, they returned along the country road until it became more crowded and again the sights and smells of the great City surrounded them. Soon they entered Cheapside, making for the vendors' stalls opposite the splendid row of houses and shops known as Goldsmith's Row. They watched, wide-eyed as apprentices ran errands, dashing past pedlars displaying sacks of fruit or arranging stands of vegetables with great wheels of cheese. As Mary brushed near a stand containing little pyramids of fruit, the vendor cried angrily, "Careful, young miss, look where you're going!" and roughly indicated she move on.

Mary's eyes sparkled. No one had ever told her to "move on" before!

As they waited patiently at a lacemaker's stall while Lady Bryan fingered a scarf, intricately woven as a cobweb, and Bessie purchased some ribbons, Randall Dodd rewarded them by bringing little dishes of oysters and mussels. As if they hadn't eaten less than an hour before, they devoured them with gusto as the old steward haggled for live periwinkles to take to his lodging above the palace kitchen. As they licked sticky fingers, wiping them surreptitiously on wrinkled skirts, a loud commotion could be heard down the long marketplace. "The king—the king is coming—make way for the king!" Almost at once, a mounted herald appeared, blowing one long blast for attention and shouting, "Make way for the king!"

Katherine's heart beat faster. Her mother was home! Mary and Kate Willoughby, shouting happily, started to run into the street, colliding with merchants who muttered angrily at the interruption, even as they pushed their stalls and wagons to one side.

"Kate, come here at once!" Lady Bryan, aghast, called to the girls. Katherine knew she'd not expected the sovereigns' return until the next day or even later. What would Their Majesties say if they saw their daughter and her companions jostling at the roadside with those who now shoved for a place to watch or pushed their merchandise away from the thieving fingers that a crowd always produced? Visibly upset, the governess looked to Randall Dodd who shrugged his shoulders and shouted, "Keep them out of sight!"

"No! I want to see my mother!" Princess Mary's square little chin, so like her father's, jutted out ominously, as tears welled in her eyes. Suddenly she was a princess again. "I won't hide!"

Quietly, Bessie took charge. "Your Grace, we must not cause trouble. I know you all want to see your mothers." She patted Mary's shoulder, leading her away from the road. "Why not just stand back and all have a peek as they go by? Just don't run out where they can see you." Katherine and Kate followed quickly finding places behind the scarlet pillar of a goldsmith's shop. Relieved, Lady Bryan cried, "Now for the love of Jesu, stay quiet. Pull your caps further down and don't wave or call out! I don't think your parents would want to see you here. Oh, this will make trouble for me!" Chastened, the girls did as they were told; they could see Lady Bryan was close to tears.

Katherine put a hand on her arm. "Madame, we'll be like mice." She pushed her two companions almost out of sight behind the pillar. "I promise you we'll all stay very still." She saw Mary purse her lips. Katherine whispered to the little girl, "My Lady Bryan has given us a treat, Mary, and I'm sure the queen would not disapprove. You can tell her later. But we shouldn't make trouble for my lady now." She was relieved to see Mary shake her head in agreement and, turning, push Kate Willoughby farther behind the pillar.

In a moment, the royal entourage came into view and a loud roar erupted from the crowd. Safely out of sight and caps pulled nearly to their eyebrows, the three girls could barely contain their excitement as the king, magnificently clad in a glowing hunter green velvet riding suit, appeared. Astride his favorite stallion, his plumed cap set at a rakish angle, Henry's smile was broad as he nodded his head and raised a gloved hand to acknowledge his subjects' greeting. Sunlight glinted on his red hair and beard, catching the glint of pleasure in blue eyes alight with goodwill at the adulation. He laughed aloud as caps were tossed high, even catching one in his gloved hand and sending it spinning back to its owner. The king's lean figure exuded energy and confidence and he turned often in his saddle to be certain he missed no one, even waving to those who called from upper stories or the roofs of roadside buildings.

Mary, being the smallest, was first behind the pillar and her little feet danced in excitement, even as she remained in place. Eagerly, everyone looked past the king for their mothers. The queen and Maria de Salinas followed, seated in an open litter and opposite them were Lady Maud Parr and the Duchess of Norfolk. Katherine felt tears in her eyes and her throat ached. She hadn't realized how much she'd missed her mother. And how proud she felt watching beautiful Lady Parr sitting quietly gracious as the queen responded to the people's acclaim by bowing her head from side to side and raising her hand in greeting. Behind the litter came the rest of the court, each wearing their badge of honor or carrying their rod of office. The cheers and shouts continued until the last wagon was out of sight.

Still tingling with excitement, the girls emerged from hiding to mount the horses that Randall Dodd brought forward. In the Parr House courtyard, Katherine and Bessie kissed Lady Bryan goodbye. "Thank you, madame,"

Katherine curtsied to the older woman, "this will be our secret unless the others wish to tell their parents." She didn't mention that her mother had let her play along the riverbank with the neighborhood children. She had no wish to scandalize the good soul who'd given them such a memorable outing.

Quickly, she went to her chamber to change to clean clothing and arrange her hair properly. Katherine knew it would be hours before Maud was back at Parr House. Even now the procession was probably entering Westminster Palace yard and surely there'd be a ceremony of thanksgiving at the old abbey before everyone returned home?

The thought sent Katherine to the small prie-dieu at the end of her room where, clean and expectant, she knelt and gave thanks for her mother's safe return.

As an afterthought, she also prayed an especial blessing for Lady Bryan.

* * *

Katherine thought her mother looked very tired when she returned to Parr House. "There's nothing really wrong with me, Kate," Maud insisted, hugging her children and Bessie. "Just too much traveling, too much riding, too much wondering how you all were at the palace. And too much anger with that wretched Scrope."

Immediately, Maud became embroiled in Katherine's marriage negotiations again. One day, surrounded by papers, her face flushed with anger, she cried, "He will not change his mind. He wants too much money! The Scropes were always a pinchpenny lot and if my own kin, Tom Dacre, can't do better than this, then we must look elsewhere!"

"I hate to see you so upset," Katherine whispered. "You worry too much. Maybe we should change our plans." She sought to cheer her mother, "Remember, if I can't have a crown and a scepter, perchance I'm fated to have nothing!" She was relieved to see the first genuine smile on her mother's face; they both laughed heartily as Katherine straightened an invisible crown on her hair.

In the days that followed, between studies and chapel, after time left over from classroom studies, as she sought her mother in the queen's chamber or while returning to Parr House with Bessie, Katherine prayed someone would be found to marry her. There was no one at court; on that point, Maud Parr was firm. It was the first time Katherine had seen her mother so frustrated and disappointed.

One day, crossing the courtyard toward the queen's apartments, she heard someone singing. It was a trained voice, velvety and smooth, its deep tones confident and sure, taking higher trills with ease. Curious, Katherine crossed the green, entering a long gallery, hoping to see the singer. Such a beautiful voice might surely be used in the court entertainment the queen and her mother often helped plan. The king still liked merriment and games in the evening, though the queen's poor health often kept her from his side.

The long gallery was superbly furnished with handsome tables, benches and beautiful oak panel-back chairs. There were no rushes on the floor; here the wide floorboards gleamed in the pale sunlight that streamed through a long oriel window. It fell upon the singer who, with several companions, sat amidst a pile of cushions on the floor.

As Katherine watched, the girl announced a tune "straight from the king's hand." The melody was true and clear and, as she lingered over the phrasing, her long tapering fingers stroked the mandolin almost sensually. Katherine, awkward and ill at ease in the face of such self-assurance, found it difficult to tear herself away. Mistress Anne Boleyn was not only a talented singer, she was alluringly beautiful, unlike anything Katherine had previously seen at court. Her dark hair, parted in the middle and half-hidden under a deep lavender cap trimmed with pearls, accented the olive skin now flushed with pleasure. Anne's black eyes sparkled with an infectious gaiety and, as she sang, her voice rose joyously. Katherine watched quietly, remembering her mother's dislike of this girl, yet fascinated by her vivid presence.

She couldn't wait to find Bessie and tell her she'd just seen the king's new lady. Then, immediately, she was consumed with guilt. How often had her mother warned against gossip which could often hurt the speaker more than anyone else? How often had the tutor Vives repeatedly told his students that loyalty and learning were more important than words and innuendos? Vives called such malicious tongues "great babblers" who usually came to no good end. Even so, Katherine and Bessie had always cherished the spicy nuggets which came their way and sent them flying to their chamber to discuss the puzzling actions of their elders which seemingly caused so much grief and hurt.

Later, she told her mother of the incident. "Mistress Boleyn is very beautiful and she sings like an angel." Despite her mother's surprise, she kept on. "Mistress Boleyn is much older than I and still unwed. She has a place at court. Perhaps, if there is no suitable match for me, I could become a maid of honor to the queen and later a lady-in-waiting."

"Kate, you're cut out for finer things than Mistress Anne Boleyn will ever have!" Maud's voice was tight. A steely loyalty to the queen and a strong disinclination to gossip warred with a desire to voice her fears to Katherine. As much as her disappointment with the Scrope negotiations, it was Henry's interest in Tom Boleyn's daughter and worry for the queen that contributed to her anxiety and fatigue. "Mistress Boleyn looks only for her own good and considers no one else. When she returned from France, the queen—out of the goodness of her heart!—made her one of her own maids. And now she repays such kindness by staying up late to sing and dance and play at cards with the king. To devise new dances and masques, to rise early and hunt and hawk with him. All the things the queen's age and health do not permit her to do easily!"

"And how does Mistress Boleyn feel about what she does?" Katherine wondered if Princess Mary knew all the things her mother was telling her.

"Who knows how she feels?" Maud replied angrily. "At times she laughs at Henry's attention—and lets it go at that. She doesn't encourage him, as almost any other woman would. I think this is what intrigues him. He's not used to being treated so casually." Her mother sighed. "I think the less said about Mistress Anne, the better, Kate. The king's infatuation may then die a natural death. I pray it is so!"

Katherine hoped so, too. Anything that disquieted the queen made Princess Mary and Maud Parr unhappy also. And Maud had enough to concern herself with in finding her daughter a husband. Katherine hoped someone would soon be found if for no other reason than to give her mother peace of mind.

* * *

In early fall, Lord Willoughby, the husband of Maria de Salinas, died suddenly, sending Maria to bed in shock and a tearful little Kate to stay at Parr House. For days the queen's dearest friend lay at her home in the Barbican, turning a deaf ear to the royal plea that she was missed and her daughter needed her. But Maria, who'd adored her husband, did not respond and, in a few days, the French queen came to take Kate to Westhorpe. The child did not go willingly. On her last day in the classroom, she broke down and cried, "I don't want to leave! I want to stay here with Mary and Kate Parr! I don't like my lady duchess' girls . . . !"

Katherine and Princess Mary didn't blame Kate for not wanting to live with the Brandon girls. Much as they all adored the French queen, her daughters were another matter. Lately, Mary Tudor had spent most of her time at her country home rather than at Suffolk House across the river. Maud had said it was Mary's way of showing her brother, the king, how thoroughly she disapproved of the way he was treating his queen.

Maud at last accepted how much the king's attention to Anne Boleyn had devastated the queen and frightened Princess Mary. The queen had been sent to Greenwich and Mary learned from Lady Bryan she had not gone of her own choice. "She's there because your father has ordered it, Mary." Lady Bryan's face was grim. "I cannot and will not lie to you. She'd rather be here with you, but your father wishes her to stay at Greenwich. When she's here, she doesn't tolerate his excesses easily and it angers him."

When Katherine asked her mother if the story was true, Maud shook her head sadly. "Yes, it grieves me to say, it is." Katherine wondered aloud what the French queen would do when she heard of the king's actions.

"Doubtless she'll have something to say," Maud replied dryly. "I've never known Her Grace to be at a loss for words when she feels strongly about anything!"

Mary, too, now accepted that she was summoned less often to her father's presence. When she did see him, she tearfully told Katherine, "It's almost as if my father is angry with me because he's angry with my mother. . . ."

What with spending time with the queen at Greenwich and then returning hurriedly home only to read Kate Willoughby's letters begging Lady Parr to convince Maria to let her return to London—and all the while watching the Boleyn girl take the queen's place in so many court celebrations—Maud often felt overwhelmed with responsibility. Too many changes were taking place at court and she'd never liked change. The Scrope marriage negotiations were foundering; she was convinced she must look elsewhere. She was still determined that nothing less than a peer's son would do for Katherine. When William Parr told her bluntly, there were none available, Maud's lips tightened. "Then she'll have a peer himself! For the rest of these court layabouts, they can all hang from Tyburn gibbet!" she cried heatedly, causing Sir William to throw up his hands in disgust and, for the first time, leave his sister-in-law's presence without a farewell.

It didn't help when, shortly afterward, Princess Mary came flying to her arms because the king had refused a birthday visit to her mother at Greenwich. Maud was shocked at the order. "He's using the child to hurt the mother!" she cried to Lady Bryan and her companions, indifferent to who might hear the criticism.

It had not helped her disposition or peace of mind that she could hardly explain to the weeping child that personal harassment was affecting others of the court. She suspected the king's new lady was using her influence to settle some old scores, as well as create an exciting new mischief. Anne still kept the king dancing attendance. She accepted Henry's gifts, attention and compliments with solemn gratitude. But her black, almond-shaped eyes remained gay and mocking, even as she flirted outrageously with others of the court, such as her cousin Tom Wyatt.

Once, when Maud Parr openly reprimanded her for being so much in the king's company, Anne answered resentfully. "Is the court to be like a church? That's what it is when the queen is here! What have I done wrong, Lady Parr? The king wishes to ride—I will ride. He wishes to dance—I will dance. He wishes to give me this"—she indicated a slim gold tablet hanging from a belt at her waist—"and what am I to do? Throw it back in his face? If you feel so strongly, tell the king, Lady Parr, do not tell me!" The girl swung on her velvet-shod foot, leaving Maud with her anger and frustration.

When the French queen, bringing Kate Willoughby for a visit to her ailing mother, came to Parr House, she said, "Henry vows Anne is not his mistress. And, strange as it may seem, my dear Maud, I don't think she is either. At least not yet. She's not that easy and is clever enough not to give in to Henry. One day he says she's a witch because she won't bed with him. The next day, he endows her with every saintly quality because she's so virtuous. In many ways, I pity the man, for he's his own worst enemy!" It was the first time, Mary Tudor said, the king had ever encountered one whose moods could change within the hour—or less. Who welcomed him if she felt like it or, cross and withdrawn, begged to be excused, leaving a bewildered and frustrated monarch behind.

It also puzzled Maud and made her more determined than ever to protect the princess and queen as much as she could from the effect of the Boleyn's actions and to find a husband for her daughter before Katherine, too, was caught up in a court of increasingly divided loyalties.

CHAPTER IV

*My Lady Princess came hither on Saturday; surely, sir, of her age,
as goodly a child as ever I have seen . . . she is joyous and dec-
orous in manners.*

—A message from an anonymous spectator to Cardinal Wolsey upon the
arrival of Princess Mary at Ludlow, September 1525

Sir William Parr spent much of his summer at Kendal seeking a
husband for his niece among his Northern neighbors. While his sister-in-law,
Maud, remained in London with the queen, he called upon Edward, Lord
Borough at Cantley Hall, a handsome manor house near Gainsborough sev
enteen miles from Lincoln. Lord Borough owned other fine dwellings at
Newark and Catterick in Yorkshire—legacies from his first wife, a Cobham
of Kent. Borough was wealthy, his family distinguished, with a long record
of service to the Crown. Though he now lived wholly in the North, his connections at court were still strong.

Relatives had told Sir William that Lord Borough was not eager to marry
again. He was sixty-four years old, with two sons and several grandsons to
preserve the title and his daughters had made fine and prosperous marriages.
But Sir William was not deterred. The Boroughs were prominent Northerners in a land where Parr roots were deep and Parr blood was strong. If
he'd have her, Katherine would be among her own kind and her inheritance
would be safe.

Visiting Lord Borough, Sir William found the old gentleman gracious and
reminiscent. "Each summer I miss Thomas all the more, Will. I suppose returning to Kendal makes you feel the same. He was a fine man, with a good
wife and family. It was a great tragedy, sir, to lose him, a great tragedy. He
was too young." Then, more brightly. "But Kendal remains prosperous and,
praise God, he left a son to carry on."

There could not have been a better opening for Sir William. He described
Maud's search for a husband for Katherine and her insistence on a peer's
son. Lord Borough sat, fingertips touching, agreeing earnestly. "There are
fewer than ever, Will. The French wars and the plague have taken too
many of our fine boys. I was very lucky Henry and Thomas remained
unharmed and before they wed, you may be sure I was besieged with con-
tracts for them."

"I'm aware, my lord, your sons are taken and happily so, I hear. But I've not come about Henry and Thomas. I've come to inquire about *your* state since the sad death of your good wife. You had many happy years together, I know. You must miss a wifely presence here." He gestured about the great chamber rimmed with dusty deer's antlers, family banncrets and pennons, one bearing damage inflicted at Flodden Field almost twelve years ago.

The old peer smiled. "Ah, Will, you flatter me. At my age, it's best to content oneself with memories of one's good luck and fortune." He laughed outright. "However, in addition to my sons, the county ladies have not been backward about approaching me! But no, Will, I have my home and hearth and, Jesu be praised, a healthy family to share it with. I'm not eager to undertake a new life at my age." He reached for the small enameled medallion that Sir William handed him.

Lord Borough examined the portrait, which had been painted when Katherine was eleven. He peered closely at the perfectly rounded face with its halo of red-gold hair and the most startling green eyes he'd ever seen. Skillfully, the artist had caught the pinkish cast of the young girl's clear smooth skin and flushed cheeks, the sheen of her delicate neck and bosom above budding breasts covered with deep green velvet. Katherine's nubile beauty and direct gaze appeared to fascinate the older man. Quietly, he held the small medallion between long fingers, walking to the window to examine it in better light.

Returning, he remarked, "She is comely, Will, and if she's anything like her mother, personable and intelligent, with a soft disposition." He looked at the portrait again. "I don't know . . . I don't know. . . ."

Sir William knew better than to press the subject for he knew he'd aroused the old peer's interest. And there would not be that bothersome difficulty about the dowry which had marred the Scrope negotiations. Katherine would be no charge on Edward Borough, although, of course, he'd be expected to provide for her in his will. There was more than enough Borough wealth to go around. The attitude of the old man's children—who must be in their twenties at least—would be important, however. What would they think of their father marrying again?

Disdaining any offer of wine and cakes, Sir William rose to leave. "I have duties at Kendal, my lord, which will keep me there for at least another two weeks. Think upon what I've proposed. She is Tom Parr's daughter. A kind and intelligent girl and, as you say, comely. Her mother fears for her well-being at court. It isn't as you remember it now, my lord. There are too many new families looking to profit from the older ones. And Tom always meant for Kate to wed in the North. I think she would make you very happy."

Leaving the room, Sir William knew instinctively he'd won a husband for his niece. And what a proud union it would be! He could hardly wait to write the good news to Maud.

* * *

Two weeks later, as Katherine returned from the palace schoolroom, she met her mother in the courtyard. "Come to the river room, Kate! There's something we must talk about." Katherine hadn't seen her mother so smiling and happy in weeks.

Puzzled, she handed her books to Bessie, dutifully following Maud. On the worktable where her mother checked her household accounts and attended to her correspondence lay a pile of papers in disarray. On top was an important-looking document from which several seals dangled. The little medallion painted on her birthday was close by.

"Kate, we have wonderful news! Your Uncle Will has seen Lord Borough about your marriage!"

"But I thought the Borough sons were wed, Mother. I remember you and Father attended the weddings and told us how beautiful the brides were!" Then, quietly, "I hope there's been no grief." Death in childbed often followed a festive wedding, with the man inevitably marrying again only to suffer the same tragedy months later. Katherine found the thought depressing and wondered at her mother's lack of sensitivity. It was so unlike her.

"My darling Kate, it isn't one of the Borough boys. It's Lord Borough himself! Uncle Will has seen him and they've talked very seriously about a marriage between you. Will says my lord had no idea of marrying again. But—for the love he bore your father and the security it will give you—he's willing to take you to wife! Kate, how lucky you are! Think—you will be a peer's wife!" Maud waved the document in the air and danced a little jig about the room. "Oh, Kate, this would have pleased your father so! And wait until the queen and Maria and the French queen hear! They will be so happy for you!"

Shaken by the news and knowing instinctively she must conceal it and not spoil her mother's happiness, Katherine picked up the medallion which she now saw was not hers. The face gazing out from the deep gray background was of a handsome and strong-featured gentleman with wine-red hair and beard, kindly eyes the color of chestnuts, above sensitive lips. Katherine was relieved; Lord Borough was not disagreeable to look upon, though obviously years older than she. But that was not important, she knew. He *was* a peer and she would be a peer's wife. Curiosity and apprehension gave way to pride and, catching her mother's gaiety, she laughed aloud, holding out the medallion. "Lord Borough sent this for me, Mother?"

"Yes," Maud put an arm about her daughter's waist. "Kate, I'd be less than honest if I didn't wish he were younger. But he's quite kindly-looking, don't you think? The Parrs have always highly esteemed the Boroughs. His home is very noble and well managed, for I've visited there often. You'll have nothing to fear, my darling Kate. He was a good husband for many years and will provide well for you. He's had a long talk with your uncle and says he's perfectly content to settle the marriage details now. But you're to remain here until you're old enough to go to Gainsborough. And that could mean another year or perchance two!"

Returning the medallion to her mother's eager hands, Katherine was ashamed at her relief. She *should* be pleased with the match which her uncle had so thoughtfully arranged and which made her mother so happy. She'd wed the devil himself if it made Maud Parr less weary and frustrated and give her some of the joy she'd had when her husband was alive.

"Lord Borough was most sensible about the dowry," Maud was saying. "He bears a fine honorable name, Kate, and we are all very fortunate. And now I must talk to your uncle about the ceremony. It will be soon, very soon!"

Katherine repressed a smile. She could see her mother wasn't going to risk losing such a fine catch.

"I want to be the one to tell Bess!" She hugged her mother and, medallion in hand, ran from the room. Bessie was in her chamber, writing her weekly letter to her parents. "Wait 'til you see what I have, Bess!" Katherine lay the medallion on the table, explaining quickly what had happened.

Bessie grinned broadly. "You'll be a proper Northern lady, Kate"—she hugged the girl—"and a grand one, too. My parents are good friends of the Boroughs." She looked at the portrait again. "Yes, it will be good for you, Kate, and I'm even happier for your mother. She's been so worried. And now she's naught to think about than to get you wed! I must tell my mother the news right now. . . ." She returned to her letter writing and Katherine walked slowly back to her own adjoining chamber. Examining the medallion she wondered—suddenly shy—how to tell Mary and Kate that very soon, even though she was apparently going to remain in the classroom, she'd be no longer a maid, but a married lady.

Four days later, simultaneous marriage ceremonies were held at Parr House in London and at Cantley Hall in Gainsborough. Katherine stood alone at the chapel altar. Her family sat in the pews behind her with the French queen, Charles Brandon and their daughters, representing the king and queen, sitting opposite. Little Mary Tudor, as Katherine's chief maid of honor, stood apart from the bride as cousin Cuthbert Tunstall, the Bishop of London, intoned the marriage ceremony. Later, there was much signing of documents, heavy with crested seals and ribbons, after which everyone returned through the courtyard to the terrace where a small feast had been prepared in celebration. Everyone knew that, several hundred miles away, a similar occurrence was taking place. At one o'clock precisely, upon Sir William Parr's instructions, the Blackfriars' bell tolled and he raised a glass. "A long life to Lord and Lady Borough," he cried. Solemnly, everyone repeated the toast. Blushing, Katherine sipped her wine, aware of the tears in her mother's eyes, the joy on the guests' faces and wondered how she should respond. Kate Willoughby saved the day. "My lady"—she curtsied deeply as Princess Mary, laughing, did the same—"a long life to you, Lady

Borough!" Everyone clapped merrily as a proud Maud Parr signaled the servants to fill the wine cups again.

In the following months, Katherine found her marriage made little or no change in her life; in a few weeks it was all but forgotten. Whenever Bessie, Princess Mary or Kate Willoughby pointedly addressed her as "my lady" or "Lady Borough," they all collapsed in mirth. The short respite from the classroom soon ended and she found Vives's curriculum, especially laid out for her since it was her last school year, demanding and arduous. Katherine spent hours translating Latin and Greek, studying Plutarch and, for a change, devouring the Humanistic literature that poured into Parr House from her mother's friends on the Continent. The movement, which Lady Margaret Beaufort had so enthusiastically furthered, had already gained great momentum, embracing not only a "New Learning" in the arts, philosophy and science, but in religion as well. Mary was not as interested in the tracts that Katherine and her mother eagerly read and discussed. She refused to argue with Katherine. "You feel one way, Kate, I feel another. I cannot refute the church and the holy priests. I don't believe the new thinkers in Switzerland and Germany should dispute the ancient church fathers. Who are they to know better than the Holy Father in Rome?"

It was the one area in which Katherine and Mary thought differently and, by silent consent, they avoided the subject. It was better to enjoy one's company unmarred by dissent. In a year or so, Kate knew she'd be sent North to join her husband and Mary would undoubtedly be in Spain, wife of the Holy Roman Emperor. Probably, they'd never see one another again. It was a sobering thought and whenever even hinted at, both girls became saddened and quiet.

*   *   *

Less than two months after her proxy wedding, as Katherine and her mother sat working a long piece of carmine satin, each turning their edge with precise neatness, they were summoned by Randall Dodd to attend Princess Mary at Westminster Palace. Laying the work aside, they followed Mary's old steward to the waterstairs. "What is it, Dodd?" Maud was puzzled. She'd seen the child earlier that morning. "Is the princess ill?"

"They're sending her away, my lady." The old man's mouth worked for a moment and then, with a little shrug, he said, "She's to go to Ludlow."

Maud gasped and appeared stunned. "Jesu, I'd heard at Greenwich he might do this, but I prayed it would be at least another year, that she might remain with her mother until she goes to Spain. Oh, this will sadden the queen!"

"Mother, what is it?" Katherine cried, alarmed. "Tell me, what will make the queen so sad?"

"It means that Mary—who the king has named Princess of Wales—must go to live at Ludlow."

Katherine wanted to tell her mother that Mary was more fearful of being sent to Spain. Yet she knew that anything which took her away from her mother would devastate the little princess. Ludlow was on the Welsh border and notorious for its violence; the natives were considered semibarbaric by the English. Katherine felt sick at the thought of her dearest friend living in such a dangerous place without her parents or anyone close to her. In Spain at least she'd have a husband and protector.

Princess Mary's household was in a long row of chambers in Westminster Palace. Leaving their barge at the waterstairs, Maud and Katherine swept past the sentries guarding the river entrance, hurrying down the long black and white tiled corridors, skirts rustling against the soft velvet of their slippers. They nodded to the officer guarding the princess' chamber. Opening the door, he closed it as soon as they were inside to still the sound of sobbing that came from behind Mary's door.

It was nearly twilight and the candles were still unlit. In the dim light, Katherine saw Lady Bryan at the room's farther end. The princess lay on the bed, her clothing rumpled and twisted, her face swollen with tears. She was hiccuping badly.

"Oh, Mary, my dear child! Please—you'll only make yourself ill!" Maud Parr gathered the little girl in her arms. "Your father means well, you know that! It's a great honor, Mary, a very great honor to be Princess of Wales. It means you'll be queen someday, Jesu willing . . . just as the emperor will be king."

"My mother's the only queen!" Mary cried belligerently, "and she's going to live a long time!" Throwing herself back on the bed, she burst into a paroxysm of sobs. "I don't care whether I'm queen or empress. I just want to stay here with my mother, even if I don't see her much."

Katherine felt her eyes smart. How would she feel if, not yet ten, she was ordered off to some remote castle hundreds of miles from Parr House? How would she like to be sent away from her family—to act as a princess should —to a people who didn't really like or want the English in their country? Wasn't Ludlow where Henry's older brother, Arthur, the queen's first boy-husband, had died of consumption? Old castles weren't always pleasant. She felt she had to say something comforting.

"Mary, when you get there, we'll all come and visit! When I go North, we'll be even closer, Mary, and perchance my lord husband would like to see Wales." She stroked the girl's damp little hand, aware her words sounded empty. "Maybe even the French queen would come too and then we'd all be together just like at Richmond and Greenwich. We'll keep the holidays the same as we've always done, only we'll come to spend them with you."

When Mary made no reply, she appealed to the royal pride. "You'll be very important, you know! *You* are the first Princess of Wales, Mary! Before you, there was only a *Prince* of Wales. Your father has paid you a great honor and you'll have your own court and officers and maybe even your own Fool!" The others nodded their heads encouragingly. Only recently Lady Bryan had requested Henry's council to appoint a Fool for Mary's household, thinking it might cheer the child who missed her mother now that she remained at Greenwich so much of the time.

Katherine's words caused Mary's tears to lessen and Maud, impressed with her daughter's common sense and adult graciousness, was relieved. Katherine had appealed not only to Mary's pride but to her strong sense of parental obedience as well. Once she quieted down, Maud prayed the child would accept her fate with serenity. It would be so much easier for the queen.

"Lady Bryan and I will go to our supper now and leave you two together," she said, "and the steward will bring your meal here." The princess' tears had ceased and she was swinging her small thin legs over the bed's high edge. Maud bent down to kiss her, motioning to Lady Bryan to leave. As they closed the door behind them, Katherine was still talking brightly about Ludlow and Mary was listening with great interest.

Sometimes, Maud realized, it took children to calm children.

*   *   *

Mary's departure was more imminent than anyone had thought. In the following days, she was fitted for new clothing and met with those who would serve in her new household. Her father told her she'd have a proper council, just as he had and, with the advice and assistance of the Bishop of Exeter and Lord John Dudley, she would be titular head of the council that ruled the Welsh. Dr. Wotton was to be her Dean of Chapel and Senor Vives had selected a Mr. John Featherstone to be her tutor. As plans unfolded daily, even Mary appeared impressed.

"It's going to be very different in the classroom without her," Katherine told her mother. "I'm glad this is my last year."

"Then think what it will be like for the queen, Kate. She hasn't seen much of Mary since we returned from progress and now they'll be even farther apart."

Katherine felt sorry for Katherine of Aragon. Suddenly, she remembered the gypsy's prediction. Crowns and scepters, he'd said. She was glad it was only a foolish prophecy for crowns and scepters, as far as she could see, appeared to bring little happiness to those who had them. She was grateful she was only Katherine Parr—*Lady Borough*, she corrected herself—whose family had recently arranged a good marriage for her. Nothing royal, only a family of good blood, sufficient wealth and a respectable amount of land. That's where her happiness would be found. So much for fantasy crowns and scepters!

Within a few days the queen returned to Westminster. Katherine hadn't seen her in months and was surprised at her appearance. Though she still possessed a regally kind and gracious manner, her pallor had heightened and she moved more slowly. "I should exercise more," she told Maud as Katherine stood respectfully by, "but the river's damp seeps into these Spanish bones and causes me great pain."

She held out a hand to raise Katherine from her curtsey. "Kate, you're already taller than I. And I see you still have Bessie with you." Katherine of Aragon smiled as the older girl curtsied again. "I wish Mary had someone her own age as close as you two are to each other." Then, sighing, "But that's not the way with royalty, it seems. One hesitates to become too close. It means one must trust and trusting is a luxury we cannot afford. . . ."

"I think the princess is looking forward to Ludlow, Your Grace," Katherine replied, "even though she was sad at first because she didn't wish to be so far away from you."

"I know," the queen smiled, "your mother tells me you've done little else in the past weeks but tell her how lucky she is to have so large a household in such a beautiful part of England." She laughed throatily, her accent becoming more noticeable. "Once there she'll find it gloomy enough, Jesu knows! But my good friend, the Countess of Salisbury, will go with her and there will be enough young people with children so she'll have companions her own age. But they'll not make up for you dear friends. Even when you're young, like Mary, you can miss what you leave behind."

* * *

During the next few weeks, Mary—conscious of her newly elevated status —struggled to adapt to what was expected of her, putting aside her own feelings, so as not to distress her parents, particularly her mother.

"She has great pride," Maud Parr said fondly, "she's a remarkable child." Only the day before, they'd all had a wonderful day on the strand at Chelsea where Henry had asked the French queen to look at a site he'd chosen to build a small manor house. It would be near London, but with clearer air and convenient to Windsor and Cardinal Wolsey's new palace at Hampton. With his little house at Chelsea, the king could forgo the long trip back to Westminster by barge or up the rough "king's road." The French queen had liked the flat wooded ground which overlooked the river and that evening they'd all stayed at the Chelsea home of the Howards. During the night, Lady Bryan told Maud the next morning, she'd heard Mary cry herself to sleep.

At last it was time to go. Katherine rose the morning of Mary's departure, depressed and saddened. When would she see her best friend again? What could Mary do if she disliked living in that vast castle overlooking the Teme which the queen said was bigger than any castle in England except Windsor and possibly Warwick? "She'll do nothing, Kate, that's not Mary's way," Maud Parr said, "she'll do everything her parents tell her."

An unfamiliar resentment stirred Katherine. Why were things always so mixed up where royalty was concerned? Mary and her parents hadn't really seen much of each other for nearly a year and now she was to be sent away. She felt a surge of sympathy for Mary, anger at the king and frustration for the queen. She wondered aloud why the king couldn't just send all those other people to Ludlow and leave Mary home?

"Because she's his heir, Kate, and the Welsh must see who one day will rule them." Maud also felt sad at Mary's departure, but loyalty to the sovereigns kept her from showing it. "She is Princess of Wales and belongs now to Wales."

Several hours later, everyone gathered in Westminster Palace's courtyard to say farewell. As the main part of the princess' entourage waited at King's Langley, only the more important officers and her new governess, the Countess of Salisbury, would accompany Mary from London to Hertfordshire.

Arriving at the palace, the Parr family found a large throng in the long corridor outside the Presence Chamber where Mary was having a few precious moments alone with her parents. Everyone spoke in hushed tones. "If Mary's with the king and queen now, we won't get a chance to say goodbye," Katherine whispered, an aching lump in her throat. "I thought we might see her a little before she left."

Maud pressed her daughter's hand, her other arm about Kate Willoughby, whose mother, Maria de Salinas, was witnessing the little princess' farewell. She could visualize the scene: Mary, standing very straight, hoping to appear as grown-up as possible, mindful her parents were charging her with great responsibility. The king would probably try to hurry the meeting while the queen would be watching her daughter, struggling to memorize her young features, knowing it would be awhile before they met again.

Suddenly, the blast of a herald's trumpet signaled the opening of the heavy double doors and, slowly, the king and queen entered the corridor. Both were sumptuously dressed—Henry in tawny velvet with an outer robe of deep golden brown trimmed with ermine. The queen was majestic in a robe of pale lavender, trimmed with several rows of lace which had been stiffened and brushed with powdered gold leaf.

But everyone looked to the Princess of Wales, following at a respectful distance. Mary was less than five feet tall, but it seemed to Katherine, she had grown overnight. She, too, was richly garbed in a serge riding costume of her favorite deep green. It was embroidered at the neck and sleeves with golden scrollwork and on her bonnet was the large creamy plume of the Prince of Wales's feathers—the first plume Mary had ever worn. Her gloved hands were clasped in front, much like her mother's. She looked neither right nor left as, her little figure ramrod straight and chin held high, she followed her parents to the palace entrance.

Everyone knelt as the royal trio passed into the courtyard and there, protocol forgotten, they clustered about the princess to say goodbye. Katherine and Maud curtsied and quickly embraced Mary. There was no time for words, for it was obvious the king wanted the procession to be off before mother and daughter became emotional. A litter was brought forward and, outside the gates, Londoners waited with loud cries and cheers for the royal pageant to commence.

As the herald signaled everything was ready, the queen turned and put her arm lightly along her daughter's shoulders. For a moment their eyes met and Katherine saw the raw sadness in the queen's gaze. She felt her own eyes mist over as Katherine of Aragon hugged the little princess and, smiling bravely, pushed her gently toward her father. Henry leaned down, took her by the shoulders, kissed her lightly on both cheeks and whispered something that caused her to smile broadly.

The sad moment passed. Then Mary was in the litter, sitting quiet and poised, as six husky men, clad in Tudor green and white, hoisted the poles onto their shoulders and began their way toward the curving drive that led to the gates. Waving and calling farewell, several others ran alongside. Near the gate, half in the shadow of Westminster Abbey's spires across the road, Katherine and Kate Willoughby caught up with the litter.

"She looks so small," Katherine whispered to her companion. She wanted to call out but knew she'd be unheard in the din. "Be brave, Mary," she said almost to herself, even as the litter passed so close she and Kate could have reached out and touched the child. Again, Katherine felt the aching lump in her throat. Rounding the last curve at the gate, she knew Mary could see them. Frantically, she and Kate waved and blew kisses.

But the Princess of Wales was aware her father's subjects were almost in sight waiting to cheer her on her way. Now she could not afford tears—not even for her dearest friends. So, raising her hand in greeting, she smiled graciously and then looked the other way. In a moment, she was out the gates and those inside heard the huge roar that greeted her appearance.

Swallowing her tears, Katherine clutched Kate's hand. Something dear and familiar in her life had just ended. That part with a king and queen who'd been as close as her family and her friendship with their daughter who was dearer to her than her own sister, Ann.

"Come along," she said, pulling Kate Willoughby out the gate toward the old abbey across the roadway. Already Londoners were following the litter and the long line of horses down the street toward Cardinal Wolsey's York House. The dust stirred up by the cavalcade still lingered in the road as the two girls entered the great abbey where a few monks knelt in prayer for the princess. Kneeling near the tomb of the Confessor, Katherine let the tears spill from her eyes. "Well, Kate," she said between sniffles, "let us say a prayer for Mary. And then one for ourselves. There's only two of us left now, just you and I."

CHAPTER V

Katherine's studies did not cease when she left the schoolroom for good. "Your daughter is a natural scholar, madame," Senor Vives told a proud Maud Parr. "She's as well educated now as any university graduate, yet I pray she continues to learn. She is inquisitive, with a fine memory and an appreciation of what she learns. It would be a pity for her to stop now."

"There's little danger in that, senor," Maud smiled. "Lady Borough can scarcely pass a bookstall in Paternoster Row without purchasing a new work or translation or some new book on the new religious thinking from the Continent." She frowned. "At times, I confess it worries me, for it discourages friendships with those who are not as studious or like-minded."

Maud knew, too, that Katherine's preoccupation with reading and studying, while a natural continuation of schoolroom habits, also helped diminish the loneliness she felt with Princess Mary at Ludlow and Kate Willoughby away now at Westhorpe with the French queen. Within three months, Katherine had lost the companionship of her dearest young friends. All had been so close they'd needed no other and now there was no one to take their place. The queen had thoughtfully offered to make Katherine one of her maids of honor, but Maud found the courage to ask her forbearance and let her daughter remain at Parr House. Katherine of Aragon needed no further explanation. Her own deteriorating status at court left her with little influence to guide or protect such a young beauty as Lady Borough from those "new men" her husband now favored, and whom she regarded as a distasteful result of his attraction for Anne Boleyn.

Katherine was content to remain at home. With a proper steward in attendance, she and Bessie often rode throughout the City or on the river, though her days of romping with the neighborhood children were over. She helped her young brother with his lessons, exclaiming, "Will, if you'd just put your mind to it, you'd find it's not so hard. Think!" Often Maud suppressed a smile as she let her daughter harass her son. Will was no scholar and never would be, but he adored his older sister and tried hard to please. The younger daughter, Ann, had no use for Katherine's help. "Leave me alone," she glared at her older sister, "I'll do it my way!" While Maud grimaced, Katherine shrugged her shoulders and left the little dark-eyed girl to her own devices. When she was Ann's age, she'd always been grateful for help from her father or mother. Half the fun of learning was sharing it with someone else. Couldn't Ann see that?

The winter passed with a quiet Christmas, unusual for the court, with the queen remaining at Greenwich, the king at Westminster and Princess Mary at Ludlow. Henry's affair with Anne Boleyn was now common knowledge. "The king's great matter," as people called it, was openly discussed by Privy Councillor, royal scullion, merchant and citizen alike. Gossip filled the taverns and alehouses of London as well as little county inns. Kings had had mistresses before, everyone said, although it was rumored this one was not his mistress. Anne Boleyn was aiming higher, for the Crown itself. For that, there'd have to be a divorce which, said William Parr, was quite possible.

"On what grounds?" a stunned Maud Parr asked. "The queen has done nothing! It's the king who is . . . misbehaving." She glanced at Katherine who sat, needlework in hand, her head bowed industriously, although Maud knew she hadn't missed a word.

"She hasn't given him the son and heir he wants, Maud. It's as simple as that—or was, until the Boleyn woman appeared on the scene. Now he believes that since the queen was once wed to his older brother, his marriage is damned, though it is no secret the marriage to Prince Arthur was never consummated. Henry can even quote Leviticus' biblical prophecy that when a man marries his brother's wife, such marriages shall be childless."

"Childless? With six dead babies and one living daughter?" Maud cried angrily. "Jesu knows the queen has tried! Have you forgotten her heartbreak when the first little prince lived only a few weeks? Have you forgotten the joy when Mary was born?" Maud's voice shook with indignation. "That's why the king made her Princess of Wales—to be his heir!" She threw aside her needlework in distaste.

"The king wants a male heir. And what Henry doesn't have he usually wants most. If he can't have one by this queen—and we all know she's too old now—then he may try again with another wife. He's asking the Pope to put aside the dispensation given when they were married and hopes the queen will enter a convent. After that, who knows?"

"But Uncle," Katherine dared ask, knowing what misery such a move would bring Mary, "how can one Pope void the dispensation another has already given?"

William Parr smiled faintly. "Your mother can best answer that, I believe. With all the "New Learning" or "New Thinking" or whatever you two call it, you must know one of the religious criticisms is that papal influence—all in the name of Holy Mother Church, of course!—may be purchased with gold, land or anything else valuable! And especially it may accommodate any king, queen, emperor, prince or princess in matrimonial matters where the succession is concerned. Henry may be successful. We'll have to wait and see."

"Pray the matter be over quickly," Maud said quietly, picking up her needlework. "The queen doesn't need anything more to worry about. And if Mary finds out about this, she'll be concerned for both her parents."

* * *

On days when the queen was unwell, remaining in her chamber with only Maria de Salinas for company, Maud stayed at Parr House, grateful for the time to attend to her household accounts, listen to servants' squabbles and instruct the seamstresses who arrived twice yearly to make her children's clothing. On those days, she was grateful for Katherine's quiet presence. It was at such times that she still missed Thomas the most.

While enjoying a brief respite from the queen's chambers, a courier brought a letter from Lord Borough. Maud had previously written that on their way to Kendal later in the year, she'd bring Katherine to Gainsborough. Her daughter was thirteen and it was time for her to take her place at her husband's side. She'd written the letter with a wrench, realizing what a loss it would mean. But it was her obligation to the man who'd married her child and her duty as a mother to send Katherine away from the court where the "wolves without pity," as the French queen called them, singled out the young maids with proud names and substantial fortunes for their dubious attentions.

Lord Borough had other thoughts. "It's a pity to wait another six or seven months, my lady," he wrote, the handwriting strong and clear. "The roads are now passable for travel and I see no reason for further delay. I'm eager to meet my wife and our family wishes to greet her also. I'm sure Sir William would agree Katherine is old enough for marriage and I understand her studies are now complete."

Katherine entered the room as her mother, stunned, finished reading the letter. Silently, she handed it to the girl who quickly scanned its contents. "Oh, Mother, so soon! You said we could go together when we went to Kendal next summer!"

Katherine was angry. The French queen had promised to bring Kate Willoughby for a visit when she was next in London. Why need her pleasant leisurely life at Parr House with her adored mother be interrupted now? She was about to cry out, "I don't want to go!" when her mother replied, "That's what I'd hoped, Kate—to take you to Gainsborough myself on our way to Kendal. We could have visited back and forth all summer and it would have been easier for you, being away from home for the first time. But if Lord Borough wants you now, my darling, there's nothing I can do. You're of age, you're his wife and. . . ." Suddenly, the thought of losing Katherine overwhelmed her and she burst into tears, covering her face as she struggled for control. ". . . And there's no way I can keep you here any longer, Kate!" Wrenching sobs engulfed Maud who turned away to hide her emotion.

Shaken at the sight of her mother's grief, Katherine put an arm about her shoulders. She felt the same breathless numbness as when she'd had a bad fall with her neighborhood playmates or tumbled from a pony while learning to ride. She'd planned, as she knew her mother had, to have the spring and early summer months to put her trousseau together, to pack books and those childish souvenirs so important they were still treasured, which would be her link to home. She'd hoped to see Mary before she went and, most of all, she'd depended on her mother's presence all the way to the very door of Cantley Hall.

But now, Katherine knew she must do what she could to lessen her mother's obvious despair. Giving Maud a little shake, she laughed, "Mother, this is what we've both wanted, don't you remember? I've been wed for months now and of course I want to see my husband!" Guilty at the lie, Katherine picked up the letter. "He seems very eager and it is our duty to do as he wishes." It was becoming more difficult to speak for her throat was aching, just as it had on the day Mary left. Swallowing hard and waving the letter gaily, she cried, "Don't you remember how you felt when your mother sent you to London to meet Father?" Katherine tried to focus on Thomas Parr. The image was comforting; it lessened her fear and disappointment. "Father would want me to go. . . ."

"Yes, he would," Maud managed a smile, "and it's selfish of me to want to keep you here, Kate. Of course, you should be with your husband! Jesu knows, we had trouble enough finding you one!" They were both laughing merrily as Bessie entered the room. "And you'll have to go too, Bess!" Maud waved the letter at the puzzled girl. "Lord Borough has asked that Kate come now. So you'll be able to see your parents more often. Yes, it will be best for everyone."

Tears suddenly filled Katherine's eyes; she dared not trust a reply. Noting her pallor, Bessie said that Will and Ann had just returned from the schoolroom and needed her help in the old nursery room. Grateful for Bessie's understanding, Katherine hugged her mother and fled. If Will and Ann needed her—and she doubted they did—they'd have to wait until she'd had a good cry.

Left alone, Maud reread Lord Borough's letter. With Bess leaving also, it was almost like losing two daughters. Yet there was no way out. Katherine was obviously elated, anticipating a household of her own and Maud knew she mustn't spoil her daughter's happiness for her own selfish reasons.

After replying to the letter, she summoned her barge. She would go to Greenwich and have a long talk with the queen. There she could weep for as long as she wished. Katherine of Aragon, who'd recently sent her own daughter away, would be the first to understand.

* * *

There was little time for dejection in the following weeks as Katherine submitted to endless fittings for the new clothes proper for Lady Borough of Cantley Hall, Gainsborough, Lincolnshire. There were numerous trips to the City shops for gloves and caps, for silver lace, cambric and sheer lawn, for bolts of shining velvets, satins and damasks, yards of tissue cloth of gold and silver and lengths of richly embroidered trim. Maud insisted Katherine select pieces from her grandmother's jewelry as well as her own and together they chose Parr linens, silver and pewter for the boxes, trunks, heavy bags and bundles that servants carefully packed into the wagons and carts that would follow Katherine northward. She secreted small trinkets and bibelots from Parr House into her trunk, burrowing them deeply among her precious books lest someone accuse her of childish sentimentality.

And one memorable day she accompanied her mother to Greenwich to say farewell to the queen. Mary's mother was gracious and gave her a gift—a small lacquered box inlaid in red and black which had been part of her own dowry. "I once had to sell a good deal of my plate when I first came to England, Kate, because I didn't have any money. It was after Prince Arthur died and, since I had no husband, my father, King Ferdinand, refused to pay the rest of my dowry. Ah, it made Henry's father, the old king, very angry and he withdrew all support from my household." Memories of those seven dreary years at Durham House before she'd married young Henry marred the queen's pleasant features. "So I sold the plate but no one wanted this little box—it didn't seem worth much. Yet I've always loved it for it was my mother's. I couldn't give you anything more valuable."

Katherine, touched by the queen's gift, curtsied and kissed her hand. "I will treasure it forever, Your Grace," she whispered, overcome at owning a possession of great Queen Isabella. She clutched the box tightly all the way back to Parr House, wishing Mary were there to share her pleasure.

Two days before leavetaking, Maud obtained an audience with the king. It was impossible that Tom Parr's daughter's departure go unnoticed by the court. Maud suggested Katherine wear the new crimson damask gown with the fashionable farthingale and double sleeves, slashed with shining cloth of gold. But even she was startled when Katherine appeared. Her maid had swept the girl's hair into a shining perfect coil. A tiny cap of the same scarlet lay atop the coil into which small gems had been intricately wired. Katherine's eyes were glowing. Maud felt her own grow moist with pride even as sadness swept over her that this suddenly adult young lady, her own Kate, the sometime tomboy of the back lanes of Baynards Castle, should so soon be missing from her life.

Entering the Presence Chamber at Westminster Palace, they found the king talking with Charles Brandon, the Duke of Suffolk and several of his Privy Councillors. Maud was relieved the Boleyn woman was not present. As the herald announced their arrival, they went directly to Henry and knelt at his feet.

The king greeted them affably. "Ah, Lady Parr!" He nodded to his companions who quickly withdrew to the room's far end. But not before Charles Brandon had winked broadly at the two kneeling women. Katherine had to restrain a smile. The French queen's husband was as jocular as his daughters were difficult. She could understand why his wife adored him.

"You've brought the bride, we're happy to see," Henry exclaimed graciously. Katherine hadn't seen the king since the day of Mary's departure and, on that day, she'd had eyes only for her friend. Heretofore, Henry had been only Mary's father—a man she'd known as long as she could remember —one she'd watched in chapel processions or abroad in the City with his courtiers. On her way to the schoolroom, she'd often glimpsed him walking in the palace yard with the queen or seen him in palace corridors as she'd romped with Mary and the royal nurse while her mother attended the queen.

But now the king's smile was just for her. Henry was only a few years younger than her father would have been, had he lived. Katherine felt the man's personal magnetism, a splendid male presence made more vivid by the shining mauve jacket and doublet, the magnificent rings which adorned his hands. The jewels sewn into his collar were as carefully chosen, Katherine noted, as the rosy plume of his cap. Now with the royal attention and smile seemingly just for her, she forgot all about the queen's unhappiness and Mary's reluctant absence in Wales.

"We will miss you, Kate," Henry pressed her hand gently, his blue eyes sparkling with appreciation of her crimson-clad beauty. "Lincolnshire, is it? That's strong country, but you'll do well there in the North. That's where your stock came from—and there was no one more true than Tom Parr! We miss him to this day. You have our good wishes and affection, Kate. Tell Borough our pleasure in your marriage."

Suddenly, he bent down and kissed Katherine on both cheeks. It was a signal honor and, overcome, she knelt for his blessing. Backing away from His Majesty's presence, she passed the councillors returning to his side. Yet even another wink from a smiling Charles Brandon could not lessen the lingering seductive spell the king had evoked with only a few words and two kisses such as he might have given his own daughter. Now more than ever, she pitied Katherine of Aragon. To have had the love of such a man and lose it would be overwhelming. She understood why Mary revered her father and how much she must miss him so far away in Wales.

But what was more puzzling was how such a man—even a king—could be so kind, just, learned and, above all appealing—and treat his wife so dishonorably and his daughter with such aloof unconcern.

Both she and her mother were silent as they returned to Parr House. Tomorrow would be her last day at home.

*   *   *

Two weeks later, Katherine arrived in Gainsborough. Just before noon, the steward who'd ridden ahead to inform the Boroughs of her arrival, returned to the long cavalcade of riders. Pointing to a far ridge, he exclaimed, "That's it, my lady, Cantley Hall."

Everyone clustered about Katherine, excited at arriving at their destination. "It's a very noble-looking house, Kate," Bess whispered, "and larger than I'd expected." All the way north, Katherine had been grateful for Bessie's close companionship. Together, they'd winced at the rough clothing and the crude dialects of the people they'd passed on the road, at the plain food the stewards brought from taverns and roadside inns on those occasions when they had not lodged at the home of relatives or friends. "Yet I was brought up on just such food and I still speak a bit like these people," Bess commented. "It's all your fault, Lady Borough! You've almost made a proper lady out of me!" She made a face at her companion and the two laughed merrily.

Now they stared at the imposing house in the distance. A solid three-storied brick building with small old-fashioned windows and parapets broad enough for a man to walk on. Crowstepped gables and chimneys of fancy brickwork were obviously new; the brick was deeper red than the weathered rose of the original. To the west a range of buildings, built of the same old brick undoubtedly housed servants, the buttery, bakehouse, brew and firehouse, which must grace any estate as self-supporting as Cantley Hall would be.

The sight of her new home brought Katherine's nervous fears which she'd managed to hide during her journey to the surface. The day was warmer than she'd expected and, dressed in her heavy, best traveling finery, she missed the cool, bracing Lincolnshire air. Behind the doors of that far manor house, her husband waited. As they rode forward, nervousness gradually gave way to curiosity. How would he receive her? What should she say? How should she address her stepchildren? Before leaving London, she'd asked her mother about such situations. Always, Maud had replied, "My darling Kate, of all three of my children, you are the most gracious. You have natural good manners. Just be yourself and act the same as you would at home."

At the great carved doors of Cantley Hall as she watched her horse being led away and heard the clatter of the entourage breaking up as servants wound their way to the back courtyard to begin the unloading, she remembered her mother's words. Inside her expensive fawn gloves, her hands were moist and sweat beaded her lips. Glancing back toward the road they'd just traveled, she realized Cantley Hall was built on the rim of what must once have been a great forest. It sat now like a jewel in an earth-bowl of green, russet, flame and brown, with the distant hills forming a protecting arc. Outside her home was beautiful. Inside must be similarly impressive and there a man with eyes the color of chestnuts waited for her.

Stepping inside, Katherine looked for the man in the medallion. Where was he? She was about to whisper her concern to Bessie when, suddenly, a stooped figure, elderly and frail, came forward. With those streaks lining his thin hair and chin, he'd have been called a "graybeard" at court. Katherine thought it odd her husband should have such an old man as steward or chamberlain.

At last, he was directly in front and, unbelievably, with both hands on her shoulders, was kissing her on each cheek. "Welcome, my dear! I've asked everyone to come forward and greet you. I hope you've had a pleasant journey?" Then, Katherine realized, the frail old gentleman was her husband. The enameled medallion she and Bessie had pored over had to be at least a quarter of a century old.

She wanted to cry out in angry disappointment. Was this why she'd come to Gainsborough? Her mother hadn't said her husband would look so old! Behind him, the Borough family and guests were waiting. Remembering Maud Parr's words, Katherine clasped her trembling hands tightly and replied, "A perfect journey, my lord." Thankfully, her voice was firm. Yet her heart was beating so rapidly, she was certain everyone could hear it. Nearby, although she was as stunned as Katherine, Bessie shook her head approvingly.

Lord Borough introduced his children. The older son, Henry, strongly resembled the man in the medallion. The younger son, Thomas, bowed while his sisters, Elizabeth and Ann, curtsied. Several grandchildren, dressed in replicas of their elders' clothing, bobbed their heads and appeared solemn. The Boroughs were a large, close and united family, Katherine realized. However, as she moved about, accepting a glass of wine, she sensed a certain withdrawal in the older children and was suddenly acutely aware of her youth. Though it was hardly unusual to be married at fourteen, how many brides inherited stepgrandchildren almost their own age?

Lord Borough suggested that Katherine and her companions refresh themselves, and then a relative, Lady Hamel, would guide them about the house. "You must see it through a woman's eyes, my dear," he explained. "My former wife is responsible for most of what you see. She supervised the inside for over thirty years. . . ."

For the next hour, Katherine and Bessie followed Lady Hamel about Cantley Hall. When Bessie remarked it was really more like a small castle, their guide explained, "Parts of it are old, very old indeed. But the courtyard is new, as you can see from the cobbling. And," she gestured out the window, "you can see the old moat was filled in about the same time." At the window, Lady Hamel pointed out the bakehouse and other buildings containing the slaughterhouse and fishhouse. Main barns, near the woodyard, housed the stables, the falconer's quarters and the hawks' mews. In spite of herself, Katherine was impressed. Kendal had similar outbuildings and accommodations for servants and animals, but here there were so many! Unlike Kendal which was lived in mainly in the summer, Cantley Hall was a year-round residence for a large and growing family. And now she was the mistress of it all.

Bessie smiled approvingly when shown her quarters. Already the servants were unpacking her belongings and placing them about the room. Both she and Katherine were appropriately silent in the suite where Lady Borough was certainly expected to share the large canopied bed with her lord and master. For the first time in years, Katherine realized, Bess would not be next door. Again, she felt nervousness returning and had to force herself to listen as Lady Hamel described the portraits in the Long Gallery which the first Lady Borough had arranged in the proper sequence and which had never been changed.

Late in the afternoon, after a brief rest in Bessie's chamber, Katherine sat with her husband at the head table for her first meal at Cantley Hall. It was, he said, the last of three "messes" served daily. "Lady Hamel will explain, my dear. We set up additional tables each day for visitors or for those working on the premises, or for the couriers or messengers who might be passing through and have a right to expect hospitality. But this is the family meal and it is now that we happily welcome you to your new home."

Smiling, Katherine sat in the high-backed chair, very aware of the man at her side. He ate delicately, indicating several of his favorite dishes as they were presented by serving men. His son, on her right, was equally gracious, rising to propose a toast to "Katherine, Lady Borough," at which the whole hall rose as one and drank her health. Several paces away, Katherine noticed Bessie surrounded by strangers. Did she, too, feel sad—almost lonely—in the midst of so many strange people?

With the arrival of minstrels, Katherine was spared the effort to make conversation. As the meal progressed and at its conclusion, Lord Borough's children and several of the older grandchildren danced. Since no one asked her to join them, she sat, straight and silent, watching the festivities.

It was all so different from home. She remembered when she and Bessie and even little Princess Mary had been allowed to observe similar occasions at Parr House or at court. They'd watched as their elders formed the long procession before entering the banqueting hall. In colorfully splendid clothes, elaborate headdresses and flashing jewels, they'd chattered, whispered and laughed, calling out to their friends. Others, heavily rouged and scented, had flirted with their lovers or, executing little turns and· pivots to the music's beat, drew loud applause from their fellow celebrants.

But here at Cantley Hall, everything appeared stately and ordered, everyone quietly gracious. Katherine found it puzzling that, though everyone was certainly as aware of her as she was of them, no one paid her the slightest attention. She'd been welcomed in a formal toast and that apparently was all anyone considered necessary. Although Bessie was now whirling around the floor with one of the Borough grandsons, no one asked her to dance. It was then she realized that if her husband didn't wish to dance—as he obviously didn't—no one would ask her. At the end of a long and tiring day, full of expectation and disappointment, she found the thought depressing.

At last the minstrels put their instruments away and everyone waited for Lord Borough's departure. Rising, Katherine caught Bessie's eye. More than anything, she wanted to flee to her friend's chamber and talk about the memorable day; she knew Bess felt the same. Instead, she took her husband's extended hand and, emulating him, bowed left and right as they went from the room. Bessie, nearest the door, bowed as deeply as the others.

In the room with the great canopied bed, her maid was waiting. Usually there was much chatter between maid and mistress, but tonight both were silent as Katherine undressed. In a short time, she was alone in the large bed, wondering what she should do next. What side of the bed was she supposed to sleep on? Should she have waited until her husband joined her? How was she to address him other than "my lord"? Edward was his first name, she knew, but to address someone so old by his first name seemed deeply disrespectful. Her nervousness returned and she longed more than ever for Bess. She dared not even think of her mother.

The door opened and Lord Borough, in nightcap and robe, entered. A servant helped him off with his robe, bowed and left. Katherine wondered why the man hadn't snuffed out the large bedside candle. Did her husband sleep with a light burning all night? As he joined her in bed, she caught the faint odor of perfume and the scent of a good French soap used by many at court. The familiar fragrance brought back home and her mother—everything that seemed so far away. An aching lump in her throat only made her more tremulous and again, she wondered, what she should do or say. Why didn't her husband console her? Didn't he know she was uncertain and afraid? Was he waiting for her to speak?

All at once, the old man caught her to him. Katherine raised her arms to protest and, startled, felt the rough, scented beard against her face and neck as he kissed her cheek and his hands fondled her body.

"You mustn't be afraid, Katherine, I'll not hurt you," he said gently. "This is not enjoyable for a woman the first time and you are small." As he spoke, his hands groped about her nightrail and suddenly, his beard and lips were all over her face and mouth. Though his words had soothed her fears, Katherine felt stifled and suffocated and she wished at least it was dark. Then she wouldn't have to see this old man, tasseled nightcap bobbing, whose face was suddenly suffused with a red flush, whose eyes held a surprising glint of anticipation. What was he going to do? She twisted her head to avoid his lips and clenched her hands so she would not protest as he removed her nightrail. Yet she wanted to cry out and cover herself. But to whom could she cry? If this was what her husband wanted to do, what could she say?

Finally, she lay as naked as Lord Borough desired. Murmuring to himself, he stroked and caressed her, his soft words of appreciation stilling a growing panic. Even as she lay rigid and silent, he wound the long red-gold hair away from her face, exclaiming in delight at the smooth line from chin and neck. He fondled her small breasts until they hurt. In spite of herself, Katherine felt a limpid warmth growing in her and, thankfully, her panic was subsiding. If it was no worse than this, she could bear it. And perhaps he would stop right there, for he was old. Certainly, she was pleasing him and she felt a little glow of pride as he ran his hands over her hips and down her legs. She saw his face had become darkly red and now, as he fumbled with his night clothing, Katherine thought perhaps he would stop. He'd exposed her body and seen and caressed every part of it. Now, old as he was, he would want to sleep.

Then, inexplicably, he was hovering above her. The little warmth in her body, that pleasant relaxed sensation aroused by his caresses disappeared and, rigid and frightened, Katherine felt his weight upon her. Stifling a scream—which only seemed to excite the man—she turned her face into the pillow to escape the bobbing beard in her mouth and eyes. Suddenly, a jolting, tearing rush of pain sliced between her legs. Biting her lips as she lay quiet, holding back tears of pain and anger, her discomfort continued as he heaved and thrust, muttering to himself. She knew she must not shame herself and her husband by crying.

Soon it was over. After one giant thrust, her husband reared up, his eyes bulging, his mouth open and, as if in great relief, fell limp upon her, almost burying her slight body beneath his own.

Katherine lay still, letting the tears finally fall. She didn't care now if Lord Borough saw them. Never had she felt so humiliated, ashamed or degraded. Her husband was extremely sweaty and she, herself, was bloodied with the result of his exertions. But she knew that to clean herself would be unwise. The sheets would be examined in the morning for proof of her virginity and her husband's virility. Certainly, he'd have little doubt of her condition for, while he'd done nothing deliberately to hurt her, she'd never felt so sore and aching.

Beside her, Lord Borough lay quiet and, brushing away her tears and wiping her face and breasts of the feel of his beard, Katherine wondered if he was asleep. She sat up, pulling her nightrail back over her head, noting the servants would have ample testimony to her maidenly condition in the morning. She wondered if she should wish her husband good-night, but the old man was very still. She pulled the covers over them both, then leaned over and snuffed out the candle. A gentle snore at her side told her her lord and husband slumbered, satiated and at peace.

It was some hours before she herself finally fell asleep.

Lady Borough

1530

CHAPTER VI

Katherine's days soon settled into a pleasant round of county activities. Neighbors—aristocracy, gentry and common citizen alike—were all curious to meet Lord Borough's new wife. Each morning began with Mass in the family chapel where a resident priest conducted services for family and servants. Later Katherine met with the master gardener, brewer, baker or cook —anyone who wanted advice or a decision. Unlike London, where her mother's household was directed by a chamberlain who often consulted Maud Parr, Katherine soon realized a Northern lady was expected to be the source of all knowledge, direction and benefits, one familiar with the needs of family and servants as well as the tenants housed in nearby cottages and farmhouses. Monks of the abbey on the other side of the valley also looked to Cantley Hall for help with the poor, the ill and the homeless. In addition, she had to remember everyone's name and rank, so as not to confuse the one hundred and seventeen lackeys, stableboys, scullions, shepherds, farmhands and laborers who kept her new family in reasonable comfort.

From the first, her husband was patient and kind and never spoke demeaningly to her. "And Jesu knows, he's had reason to do so!" Katherine told Bessie a month after their arrival. "I find it takes all my wits just to remember the servants' names, to know who's to do what, to learn the county customs." Cantley Hall was a world apart from Kendal Castle. At her father's Northern manor, it had always been holiday time; London was their true home. But Gainsborough was now her world and she might see London —if she was lucky—once a year. Rising each day with the early morning light, Katherine often thought of her mother, several hundred miles away, going through the same motions before leaving for her duties at court. She wondered if Maud Parr missed her as much as she was missed.

Her new family—stepsons, their sisters, wives and children—continued aloof and withdrawn. "They're waiting to see what you will do," Bessie explained. "You're mistress of the house now and, mercifully, they don't realize how little you really know about properly running a household!" Laughing lightly, Bessie ducked to avoid the pillow Katherine tossed her way. "I'd advise you, my dear Lady Borough," she smiled, "to let well enough alone and when you don't know, go to Lady Hamel. She seems to know everything."

Her husband's grandchildren reminded Katherine of her brother and sister. She was shocked to find they'd had little formal tutoring, that even their mothers were almost illiterate. Distressed, she'd told Bessie, "They can barely read and they all write most poorly. And when I offered to teach Elizabeth and Ann or my lord's sons' children, they looked at me as if I had two heads with horns!" Katherine didn't offer again. Her husband's word was law. If he hadn't wished his daughters and grandchildren to learn to read and write decently, it was unlikely he'd desire or appreciate her help.

Katherine was fondly tolerant of her husband. Bessie, admitting to being curious about what happened each night when her friend disappeared behind the large carved doors of her bedchamber, had been spared no detail. Every ten days or so, Katherine said, the old man still quietly undressed her, stroked and fondled her for what seemed forever and then repeated that ridiculous huffing performance. Now, instead of turning her face into the pillow to hide her pain, Katherine said she did so to conceal her laughter. "It doesn't hurt anymore, Bess, and I just lie there and let him do whatever he wants. It seems to give him pleasure and it could be worse I suppose. He *is* kind. . . ."

"You make it sound like a pig a-mootin' a sow," Bessie laughed, lapsing into her broad North country dialect. "It would appear I'm not lacking much!" She'd recently returned from a week at Burneside where her father had voiced his disappointment that Lady Parr hadn't found her a husband.

Katherine also worried that Bess, now twenty-six, was still unwed. "I'm almost a spinster maid," the girl admitted without rancor, "but I told my father your mother hadn't forgotten. It was only that she had to provide for you first and she still has another daughter and son to look for. I told him the London gentlemen want large dowries and he reminded me he has three other daughters!"

"Do you mind it, Bess, not being wed?"

"I don't mind it at all, only that other people seem to make so much of it. Even Lady Hamel talks about how my family should look to my future!" Bessie smiled. "But I'm happy enough as I am, Kate. Perhaps I'm not meant to wed. . . ."

Other than impressive furnishings, Katherine had found little evidence of great wealth at Cantley Hall. Lord Borough was a good landlord and provided well for his tenants, workers and others less fortunate. But he was a hard taskmaster for those who served him. His wine must be the best, but Katherine thought he served it sparingly. His food was ample: boiled beef, neat's tongue, baked mutton or rabbit, sometimes a venison pasty. But it was plain and unadorned—so much so that she often dreamt of the rich sauces, exotic viands and sweetmeats she'd so taken for granted in London. Lord Borough's cattle must produce the best yield and his fields the greatest harvest and woe to the unlucky fellow who failed in his duty. If the yearly books didn't measure up to his master's expectation, a tenant might find himself turned out of cottage or farmhouse.

When Katherine found the courage to protest one such incident, Bessie defended Lord Borough. "It's the way of the North, Kate. It's always been so," she explained, "my father is the same. We're self-supporting up here. It's hard for you to realize, but if your husband doesn't provide—and provide well—there'd be serious hardship in the winter and other times, too. Everything depends on one's doing one's work well, for everyone is dependent upon one another. Remember, the North is self-sustaining! There's no London purveyor over on Cheapside to get you anything you want from the Continent!"

Chastened, Katherine threw herself into her household duties. When huge bolts of cloth arrived from London for the servants' new gray and white livery, they'd accepted the cloth, silent and self-effacing, in great contrast to their Parr House counterparts where such an occasion always called for celebration. Katherine missed the humorous little exchanges with those who served her. Again, said Bessie, such was the way of the North. "Wit doesn't put food on the table or clothes on your back," she explained, "and they'll think you light-headed if you try to change them."

Katherine had better luck with the laundresses and dairymaids. Several were nearer her own age and did not live on the estate, coming to Cantley Hall only to help out in times of need. As she knew was expected, Katherine worked along with them, and later, these same young girls helped the Borough women pickle, preserve fruits, vegetables and berries from the estate gardens and orchards. Toward autumn, neat rows of jellies, jams, marmalades, syrups and comfits in the cool manor house cellar provided ample evidence of their efforts. All the Borough women collected herbs and dried blossoms which they made into potpourri to scent wardrobe, cupboards and musty-smelling chambers. Potions, salves, teas and other remedies were meticulously made from recipes contained in the first Lady Borough's ledger.

Katherine and Bessie often laughed over their first morning in the stillroom. Tremulously, Elizabeth Borough had offered to remove her mother's recipe book. Obviously, her new stepmother had her own.

Startled, Katherine thought quickly. Already her stepchildren regarded her as odd; to admit she had no recipes would make her appear even more so.

"The recipes belong to my lady mother and I left them at Parr House," she said confidently. "Remember she was here several times and knew of your mother's skill." She turned quickly so as not to see Bessie's broad grin. "I'll be happy to use whatever you wish, Elizabeth." She knew it would be useless to tell her stepdaughter that while Maud Parr was familiar with a stillroom, she preferred having others work in it so she might spend her time studying and learning, the same as her daughter. Happily, everyone set to making the familiar concoctions.

But Katherine's words brought unforeseen results. Later in the day, the Borough ladies arrived in Katherine's chamber for their first visit. When Katherine ordered the wine and biscuits she usually enjoyed in the late afternoon, they did not disdain the refreshment which, by their looks of surprise, they obviously considered an unusual treat. Within moments, everyone was chattering together easily and Katherine knew from Bessie's pleased expression her time of probation was over.

The manor of Gainsborough ran like a finely wound clock and, in time, Katherine came to share her husband's pride in the beautiful house and land which belonged to him as far as the eye could see. Though she had no recipes of her own, she determined to become knowledgeable in the use of the stillroom remedies and, with the Borough ladies' help, soon she could dispense them with confidence to anyone with a cut, bruise, boil, fever or cough.

By the end of her first year of marriage, as she prepared to celebrate her fifteenth birthday, even Lady Hamel spoke of Katherine's skillful adaptation to her new life. A fire in the bakehouse, rats in the scullery, butter that wouldn't turn, a drunken maltman in the brewhouse, Lady Borough seemed equal to them all.

*   *   *

Letters from home helped. Sir William Parr had taken Katherine's brother and sister to Kendal for the summer because, her mother wrote, Katherine of Aragon had recently returned to court and she didn't want to leave her side. "The king will ask for a divorce, Kate," Maud Parr wrote, "and it now appears the queen's nephew Charles, the Holy Roman Emperor, threatens war if he does. Jesu, Kate, war for a divorce! What will happen to Charles's promise to wed Mary when she is of age? Ah, I pray God will enlighten His Grace. . . ."

The letters helped Katherine through what she and Bessie had come to call their "Borough boring days." Both girls missed the easy camaraderie of London and the court. Katherine still craved the latest philosophical books, the political pamphlets, and the religious and ideological treatises she'd read from childhood, picked from the piles about her mother's rooms. Maud sent the latest books and pamphlets, but it wasn't the same as being at the hub of royal life. With her duties complete and making certain her husband was napping—he never insisted she bed with him except at night—Katherine often sped to Bessie's chamber to talk of life at home.

"Remember the old marketplace and all the crowd near the abbey across the road from the palace where everyone bought eel pies? Remember the beautiful view from our terrace and the way old Wolsey's great house looked with those waterstairs twice the size of the ones at Westminster?" Soon Katherine was tearfully homesick while Bessie only sighed. It wasn't that they meant to be disloyal. It wasn't that Gainsborough was ugly or Cantley Hall uncomfortable or even that they were unhappy. It was all simply different and very dull.

Each month, Katherine hoped to find she was pregnant. "Then I'd have a good excuse not to work in the stillroom!" she told Bess. "I'd just say it made me nauseous! And it would give me something to do, for I'd take care of the

child myself. Think how that would shock everyone! And I trow I'd teach it
to read whether my lord says so or not!"

Childless at the end of her first year of marriage, Katherine gave it no further thought. Her husband still pleasured himself with her frequently, but
aroused no feeling in her. Was that lack of response the reason she could not
conceive? When the Borough women and those of the neighboring gentry
came to work on the large pieces of needlework for the Gainsborough
church altar, they talked about babies and why some miscarried or bore living children. Or even how *not* to have one. Katherine was startled to learn
that sponges tucked into one's innards had often prevented an unwanted
birth while potions, similar to those brewed in her own stillroom, when
mixed together by someone "good with herbs" could often bring a pregnancy
to an end.

Yet behind all the chatter, there was a reluctance to talk of personal matters. Katherine longed to ask, as Bessie had asked her, just what husbands
and wives did in the privacy of their bedrooms and whether the women
liked it. Several times she'd seen bruises on several of her new friends' arms
or necks; if any were on their legs, their long gowns hid the sight. Yet no
one ever questioned the women who bore a haunted frightened look; the
purplish-black markings were completely ignored.

Clearly, Katherine thought, she was lucky. Lord Borough would never deliberately hurt her. Indeed, after that first night, he never had. She was simply an instrument of pleasure and, were he younger and if she'd enjoyed the
act more, she might have become pregnant. But she knew with a certainty
now she never would.

It was consoling to think that her mother—with troubles enough of her
own—would never have to mourn a beloved daughter lost in childbirth.

*   *   *

Cantley Hall was often filled with visiting relatives and friends. The
Askew family of Stallingborough, old friends of the Bellinghams, Bessie's
parents, was one of Katherine's favorites. "Will and I were knighted by the
old king for our services in France years ago, my dear," Lord Borough told
his wife. "He married later than I and now visits us once or twice a year."

Katherine looked forward to the Askews' visits. Not only did they relieve
the tedium of her Gainsborough days, but she especially delighted in the
company of little nine-year-old Anne Askew—a high-spirited, smiling child
with the Northerners' pink cheeks and long flowing red curls no bonnet
could contain. She was so different from her plain-faced mother and
dignified father, only a few years younger than Lord Borough, that Katherine could scarcely believe she belonged to the same family. On her first
visit, Anne became Katherine's shadow, plainly cheered at finding a hostess
only a few years older.

One day, as everyone had disappeared for an afternoon nap, she followed

Katherine into the room she'd made for her own where she might read, study and leave books and papers about without anyone disturbing them.

"These are all yours, my lady?" The little girl was clearly awed. "May I choose some to read?"

It had been a long time since Katherine had seen any enthusiasm for study, indeed had seen anyone other than Bess read. Impressed, she piled the little girl's arms with books, certain of protest. Instead, smiling happily, Anne had clutched her treasure and run off to her own quarters. Each day, she returned a book and chose another, sitting for an hour or so to read through Katherine's pamphlets. When the Askews' visit ended, Anne asked if she might take some books back to her home.

"The child devours everything in sight," her mother explained when Katherine marveled at how easily Anne read. "But she is careful, Lady Borough, and I'll see to it these come back to you in good order."

Within days, the neatly trussed books were returned by an Askew servant with a note in Anne's neat handwriting asking for more reading material. Carefully, Katherine chose some classics: Cicero's *Epistles*, Ovid's *Metamorphoses* and Aesop's *Fables*. She also sent along Senor Vives's own book, *The Education of a Christian Woman*, dedicated to the queen.

When these were returned with an enthusiastic note in which Anne discussed what she'd read, Katherine was stunned. "She couldn't have understood half of what I gave her," she cried to Bessie, "she's only nine!"

"You were reading much the same when you were ten, my fine Lady Borough," Bessie replied, looking through Katherine's collection. "You had a tutor to help, of course. But remember, loneliness is a great teacher. The child has nothing else to occupy her mind. Shall we send her some of your mother's new books?"

When Lady Askew visited Cantley Hall alone one day, Katherine asked if so much study might not be taxing to Anne's young mind. "Her nose is forever in a work," Lady Askew sniffed, "but she enjoys reading and perchance one day she'll be able to teach her own children as well. Her father—he does not read too well himself—is not as content as I that she studies so much. But it is harmless, I tell him! I just hope it won't hurt her chances of a good marriage. Her father says whoever he selects will have to be as well read as Anne or she'll make his life a misery!" she exclaimed, rolling her eyes heavenward.

The day after Lady Askew's departure, everything was swept from Katherine's mind by a letter from her mother. The papal legate, Maud Parr wrote, had finally arrived in London to render a verdict on the king's request for a divorce. Even though the queen had been asked to appear in the Great Hall of the Blackfriars, everyone thought the decision would be in the king's favor. But before anyone had testified, Katherine of Aragon had taken matters into her own hands. "It was unbelievable, Kate!" Maud Parr wrote:

You know how the queen is quite modest and shy. But now, she was a giantess! Everyone was there; Campeggio, the papal legate, and Wolsey, who I think is quite ill from worry over this affair. Rochester, Canterbury, the lawyers and judges—all who were supposed to testify.

But before they had the opportunity, the queen came forward. She was dressed all in black and, ignoring those who tried to stop her, went directly to where the king was sitting, some paces away. She knelt before him and, Kate, it would have brought tears to your eyes to hear her words. She spoke of their early happiness and asked what she'd done to wrong herself in his heart? She told of her exile from court, of the people who now shunned her, and asked what had caused his displeasure?

The king said nothing, but he was pale and his hands trembled. I truthfully think he was angry and frightened and later Charles Brandon told me that was so. The hall was so quiet—no one wished to miss a word. The queen recalled how her parents had arranged her marriage, how happy she'd been even though she'd shared his heartbreak that they'd had no son. She said she was proud of their daughter, Mary, fulfilling her duties so far from home and whom she longed so much to see. . . .

Katherine felt tears in her eyes. Someone—perhaps even Maud Parr—would write this sad news to the Countess of Salisbury at Ludlow. There was no way Mary could not know what was happening between her parents. She continued reading the letter.

The king remained quiet and it seemed he planned to make no reply. So the queen rose from her knees saying, "I commit my cause to God." She walked away from him then, very slowly, even though the crier insisted she return to her seat. She called out, "There is no justice for me here—I will not tarry!" And then she went out the door. The crowd was waiting and oh, Kate, how they cheered her! You know how they've always loved her. The king sat very still, almost stunned, while the hall erupted. After things had quieted down, he spoke for a few moments. He said he wished for a divorce so he might wed again and beget a son for the good of the realm. He vowed he found no fault in the queen except she could not give him an heir. Of course, everyone knows about the Boleyn and I fear it did the king little good. Later on, he was heard to say that another such happening and he'd make a few heads fly. . . .

As she finished the letter, Katherine wept openly. The scene remained in her mind for days. "Crowns and scepters!" she cried to Bessie as they reread the letter. "My mother says this will kill the queen—and that Boleyn will do everything she can to make Mary miserable when she marries the king. Do you suppose a crown ever brought happiness, Bess? I think we're better off here! At least everyone is honest and means no harm!"

It was the last letter Katherine was ever to receive from her mother. On August 20, 1529, Maud, Lady Parr, was found dead in her bed. She'd been unwell for days, Sir William Parr wrote, but had not wished to bother her children, thinking it only a minor indisposition. She was just a few months short of her thirty-fourth birthday.

* * *

At first, Katherine was incredulous, certain there must be some mistake. It was impossible to believe her pretty green-eyed mother was gone. She lay, tearless, in her chamber, staring at the ceiling, trying to comprehend her loss. Outside the door, an uncertain Lord Borough waited, wondering what he might do to ease his wife's pain. With great relief, he saw Bessie Bellingham flying down the corridor, her face pale with anxiety. Shaking her head at his unspoken question, he was relieved when she firmly closed the door behind her.

Silently, Katherine handed her the letter. But Bessie put it aside and took her grieving friend in her arms. At the girl's touch, Katherine's shock gave way to tears.

"If only I'd been there!" she cried, her face contorted with anguish, "perhaps she could have been saved! Oh, Bess, it can't be true—there must be a mistake!" She threw herself back on the bed, great wrenching sobs enveloping her body.

Lying beside Katherine, Bessie wept also. Solace would come later, she knew, but for now the girl must grieve. Later, when a maid timidly ventured into the room bringing the wine and biscuits that a startled Lord Borough learned was his wife's custom each afternoon, Bessie insisted Katherine take some refreshment. As she became more calm, they reread Sir William's letter. London was in the grip of the sweating sickness, he wrote, and for that reason, Maud Parr had been buried immediately beside her husband in the Blackfriars Church. Under no condition was Katherine to return. He'd sent her brother and sister, with several servants, to Lady Maud's parents at Boughton Green. Once the sickness had passed, he'd bring them home and, in the meantime, he'd look after Parr House and her mother's estate. Katherine might return to London when the Borough family came for the sitting of Parliament. However, he frankly doubted that Wolsey would call one as the king's personal affairs were a mess and taking most of the cardinal's time.

Katherine knew her uncle was right, but the stunning shock of her loss lingered. Her husband and his family were sympathetic and, at the funeral Mass in the Borough chapel, their kind understanding helped numb her grief. As the days went on, however, her sadness continued. Never before had she realized how much she'd loved and depended on her mother. She still found it impossible to believe she'd never see Maud Parr again.

Bessie was her greatest comfort. "Mourning is only natural, Kate, and yours is doubly painful because you and your mother were so close. You are so like her—not only your features, but in other ways, too. Soft-appearing on the surface, yet iron and granite underneath. And stubborn about principle. Remember how angry you both were when those who easily shifted loyalties shunned the queen while the Boleyn lorded it over everyone? Remember how you hated it for the queen and Mary?"

Within days, her uncle sent a small box of her mother's trinkets. While the really valuable jewels were held as part of her mother's estate, Sir William hoped these more modest pieces might be a comfort to Katherine. She and Bess pored over the contents, tearfully recalling the occasions they'd seen the baubles on Maud Parr's gown, cloak or bonnet. Katherine was touched when, one by one, the Borough ladies and their children came to exclaim shyly over the pretty pieces. It allowed Katherine to talk of her mother and share her grief. Bess was pleased by their visit. "Northerners don't show sadness easily, Kate. It's a sign of weakness—or so they think. You've won them over or they'd not be wanting to comfort you now."

The Borough family was further involved several days later when a courier clad in Tudor green and white brought a letter from Princess Mary. As the family listened wide-eyed, Katherine read it aloud:

> "Ludlow Castle
> September 1, 1529
>
> My dearest Kate,
>
> Word has just arrived here of Lady Parr's passing. Ah, Kate, it is like losing my own dear mother, the queen, whom I so long to see. I have spent the last hour in tears with Lady Salisbury who was also so fond of her, telling my lady of the many times when your mother took such good care of me. She would always listen to what I had to say, no matter how dull or how selfish! She was so pretty, Kate, and as good a companion as my Lady Bryan was when I was little and as Lady Salisbury is now here in Wales.
>
> I am heartbroken she has gone, Kate, and I grieve for you and all who loved her. I will write more later, but I wanted you to have this quickly, for I know the misery you must feel. God give you comfort in this time of your distress, even as I know He has Lady Parr in His care. . . ."

It was not often that royalty, on such an intimate note, was encountered at Cantley Hall. Through tears of sadness and pride, Katherine smiled as one by one her husband's little grandchildren came forward to solemnly examine the seal of the Princess of Wales that dangled impressively from Mary's letter.

Katherine's sorrow lingered on through the beauty of a Lincolnshire autumn. She counted the days until her return to Parr House where, Parliament or not, Lord Borough had promised she could stay as long as she wished. "Henry usually attends to my London affairs, my dear. As the oldest son, I wanted him to have the experience. But this year, we'll go together and you'll have plenty of time to see your family and old friends." He pressed her hand kindly. "I've been selfish, Katherine, in keeping you here. I never realized you might be so homesick." Sighing, he drew her closer. "I forget how much younger you are for you've brought me so much happiness."

"You are kind, my lord," Katherine whispered. "I've been happy here. But I'd like to see my family again. And visit my mother's grave. . . ."

Shortly afterward, an advance courier rode into Cantley Hall's courtyard to announce the king's sister, Mary, the Duchess of Suffolk, would arrive the next day. While visiting friends in Northamptonshire, she'd heard of Lady Parr's death. Would it be convenient for her to see Lady Borough? With shining eyes, Katherine sped the courier on his return and immediately summoned the head servants to prepare to receive her mother's dearest friend.

The next day, everyone gathered in the hall where Katherine had been welcomed over a year ago and as the tall figure of the French queen was silhouetted in the doorway, all bowed deeply.

"Your Grace, you are indeed kind to come." Katherine swept a deep curtsey. Rising, she introduced her husband and stepchildren as they came forward. A few pleasant words of welcome and then, as if by silent agreement, everyone withdrew leaving Katherine and the duchess alone. Mary Tudor opened her arms and Katherine, respectful restraint gone, threw herself into their embrace, her tears dampening the heavy, gold velvet gown.

"Oh, Kate, my dearest, I've thought of you so often these past few days. I know how you must feel! I can't believe Maud is gone!" The duchess drew a handkerchief from her sleeve, wiping her own tears and Katherine's as well. She urged the girl to a deep window embrasure and, for a moment, they sat silent, each waiting for the other to speak. Outside the velvety green of Cantley Hall's lawns reminded Katherine of Richmond. "It was so wonderful in those days, Your Grace," she said softly, "but it seems long ago now and it lasted such a short time."

Though her eyes were still wet, the French queen smiled. "You're still little more than a child, Kate. But you've done so well here. Your husband and family have become very fond of you. Believe me, word travels fast when it's otherwise! You should know how proud your mother was of you. She always said you had to have the very best! The finest in education—remember, she saw to it that you were educated with royalty!—and your companions were a princess and the child of the queen's closest friend, Maria. Maud had a great deal of faith in your common sense and your willingness to accept responsibility. You are so much like her, my dear Kate," she finished, echoing Bessie's own words.

Later that afternoon, the French queen shared a meal at Lord Borough's table. Katherine strove to keep the conversation lively for her husband and his family were clearly awed at the sight of the king's sister conversing with their fifteen-year-old stepmother as an equal. At the moment of departure, they thoughtfully left the two alone and Katherine mentioned her concern for her brother and sister.

"Your uncle will see to their best interests, Kate. They are both almost finished with the schoolroom and surely will join the court. But I cannot bear to be there myself! Wolsey's days are numbered for my dear brother, the king, will have his divorce, no matter what." The French queen's eyes were troubled. "I don't even see as much of my own husband now as we'd both like, Kate. He finds it difficult to leave Henry—you know how close they've always been. But I'm glad Charles is there for he is a good restraint for the king."

"A restraint, Your Grace?"

"My brother has never learned to use his power wisely, Kate," Mary Tudor sighed. "It's a weakness on his part. Our father kept him too close when he was young. He never had much freedom and was not allowed to make decisions of his own. After the coronation, everything came his way too soon and too easily! As long as the queen was close to him, she tempered and held him back more than anyone realized. But now the Boleyn and her family urge him to all sorts of base behavior and this appeals to Henry. He's finally realizing his power—but in the wrong way! He treats the clergy—because they won't accommodate him with this despicable divorce—as if they were puppets! Now, he says, he will be the head of the church and the Pope will be less than nothing in England, only the Bishop of Rome! He rewards the wrong people for the wrong reasons. With no one to curb him and with the fear he's aroused, everything comes easily to him. It represents a victory to him—and a vindication as well."

Katherine asked after the queen.

"She took courage when the papal legate refused to declare for a divorce and now lives at court." Mary's lips tightened. "But Henry never visits her. She spends her time in her own apartments and lives quietly with her ladies. She was shattered at losing your mother, Kate. And she misses Mary more than ever. She never ceases begging Henry to let the child return for a visit. But he refuses. It's a petty way to repay her for fighting the divorce and refusing to enter a convent." Mary embraced Katherine tightly. "Ah, Kate, stay here in the North. It is not good at court anymore. . . ." Katherine recognized the words as her mother's own.

Later, her husband snoring peacefully at her side, Katherine tried to sleep. But the French queen's words haunted her and, restless, she lit a candle and sped quickly down the corridor. Bessie was still awake and eager to hear what the duchess had had to say. Katherine held nothing back and, as the two talked together, their words recalled court life as it once had been. Long lazy golden days at Richmond, Windsor and Greenwich. A devoted royal couple, delighted with their little daughter. They wondered if they'd ever see Princess Mary and Kate Willoughby again. What would happen to Will and Ann Parr? Would their uncle live at Parr House or must it be sold? In all their reminiscing, the figure of Maud Parr loomed as large in memory as she had in life.

It was the emotional catharsis Katherine needed. The French queen and now Bessie had helped her mother live again for a little while. But now Katherine let go. She must live her own life, using her level head and that sense of responsibility of which her mother had been so proud. Memories of life at court, insidiously bewitching as they were, must be laid to rest. If what the French queen said was true, the old court had changed and not for the best. For now, the North was her home. It was, as the king had said, where her roots lay. The brilliance of court life, the splendid pomp of sovereignty were not for her and if she yearned for grandeur, she must look to the misty valleys and Gainsborough's craggy hills to find it. It was the life her mother had chosen for her and, still anguished and saddened, Katherine found solace in the thought.

                                         * * *

During his next visit, Sir William Askew asked Lord Borough if his daughter Anne might spend the next few months being tutored by Lady Borough. "She's read everything your wife has given her, Edward, and we are not great readers at home." Clearly the man was puzzled about his daughter. "She's greatly attached to Lady Borough and wants to study with her. If you'll have the child, it would be a great kindness, for my wife is at her wit's end what to do with the girl."

Katherine was excited at the prospect of having Anne Askew for she knew she'd enjoy teaching the child. And, in an odd way she couldn't even explain to Bessie, it would be a tribute to her mother, who'd learned so much from old Lady Margaret Beaufort and passed it on to her own daughter.

On the day a beaming Anne arrived, she flew to join Katherine in the chamber set aside for study. There was a joyous reunion with her hostess and Bessie Bellingham and, together, they showed her about the room. All Maud Parr's books, as well as Lady Borough's, were laid out in neat rows upon shelves and tables. Two desks were set up near a good light with papers and writing materials close at hand. Anne could hardly wait to begin work.

Katherine set up a program of grammar, rhetoric, moral philosophy, Latin, physic and science, insisting they study the same time each day. Anne arrived each morning, freshly scrubbed and neat, eyes sparkling, obviously relishing the discipline and challenge. Soon Katherine added Malory, Froissart and the works of the English Humanists, Linacre, Grocyn and Latimer. Within weeks, without realizing it, the royal classroom of Juan Luys Vives came alive again in a back chamber of a Lincolnshire manor house.

"I don't know who's enjoying this more, Anne or me," Katherine told Bess.

Her pupil was a delight to teach and heartbreakingly grateful to be rescued from her prosaic life at Stallingborough. Katherine was amazed at the child's quick ability to learn and soon embarrassingly aware Anne regarded her with an affection bordering on adoration.

"You're so pretty and kind, my lady, and the smartest person I know! I'd like to stay here with you always!" she cried fervently.

Katherine found such child worship difficult. "Anne dear, you have a nice home and parents who are very concerned with your future. That's why they've let you stay for a visit. But you must never depend upon anyone but yourself! What you learn here will remain with you when you return home and you can continue to study there. But I can only give you so much. You'll have your own life to live and must make of it what you will." Somewhere, deep inside, there was a tiny roil of resentment against such veneration, especially from one so young.

Anne brought the same intensity to her religious studies. Her imagination was stimulated by the religious controversies now circulating in England as part of the "New Learning." Though Katherine knew Lord Borough would have disapproved, she had Martin Luther's Ninety-five Theses tucked amongst her papers. The monk, now excommunicated from the church he'd likened to a heathen Babylon, had become something of a champion to the Humanists, his daring in marrying an ex-nun as controversial as his friendship with other freethinkers, such as Melanchthon and Zwingli. Anne was full of admiration for Luther, reading from his works. "I was born to fight with devils and factions. It is my business to remove obstructions, to cut down thorns, to fill up quagmires, and to open and make straight the paths . . . let me speak the truth with too great severity than once act the hypocrite and conceal the truth."

"You see, my lady, he seeks the truth!" Anne cried, her cheeks pink with elation. "Is that why his books are burned in England? Yet even the king cares naught for the Pope and says he will be the head of his own church! Why does he fear what the new thinkers say when it appears he feels the same?"

Katherine had no ready answer. Seemingly, Anne Askew absorbed knowledge as others consumed meat and drink. Often she wondered what Senor Vives would have made of the child. "Don't you find it all confusing?" she asked her protégé. "Perhaps one day you'll join the convent life, Anne?"

The little girl shook her head. "No, my lady. No convent for me! I would die in such a cloistered place!" Then, more puzzled, "I don't see why we have to read Scripture in Greek, Latin and German. Why can't we have those great words in English? How do we know what Jesus Christ or His followers really meant when their words or actions have been translated so often into so many languages? *How do we know it's the truth?*"

Again, Katherine was startled at Anne's precocity. She had once asked the same question which, Maud Parr told her, even old Lady Margaret Beaufort had often discussed.

"I don't know the answer, Anne. I suppose it's because it's always been so. At times, I admit, it's easy to see subtle differences in a translation. Is that what you mean? Do you doubt these learned men know what they are saying?"

"No, my lady," the child answered respectfully, her freckled face under the tangled red hair breaking into a wide smile, "Oh, I do understand what they mean! But sometimes it seems they don't agree with each other in what they say—even in small ways! Is it the translation which makes the difference?" Before Katherine could answer, she hurried on, "I wish to know everything, madame! And it's not easy to study where I live for it's not like in London where you lived and where these books came from, my lady." Her small fingers caressed one of Maud Parr's volumes.

Touched, Katherine replied, "I know, Anne, and I'm so glad I can help. You must rely on Bessie, too. She's much smarter!"

Over her pupil's head, Katherine caught Bessie's eye. She knew her friend was equally stimulated, her curiosity aroused and challenged by the little girl's questing, seeking mind.

Clearly, Bess's expression said, tutors might learn from pupils—especially one as clever and confident as little Anne Askew.

* * *

As Martinmas approached and Katherine eagerly anticipated her promised return to London, she noticed Lord Borough was failing. His breathing became more labored and his mind often wandered. Several times he called her "Alice," the name of his first wife. Though his children were as concerned as she, he insisted upon hunting and riding as usual, attending to his myriad estate duties with tenants, farmers and overseers. Bessie also noticed his decline and both she and Katherine tried not to leave him alone for any length of time.

It was shortly after an early hard frost that had taxed everyone's energies getting animals and foodstuffs under cover that Katherine tiptoed into their chamber. An early darkness had settled over the valley and it was well past the time Lord Borough usually arose from his nap. Katherine found her husband peacefully asleep on the wide bed and hesitated to wake him. He'd ridden hard all morning and might need this extra rest. Approaching the bed, however, she suddenly felt uncertain, knowing instinctively something was wrong. "Bessie! Bessie! Come quickly . . . !"

In a moment, Bess was at her side. "Kate, what is it?" She looked at the slumbering figure on the bed. Katherine's face was white and her hands were shaking.

"I don't know. He looks so . . . different. . . ." Quietly, she spoke to the sleeping man. "My lord." She shook his shoulder gently. At her touch, the old body turned on its back.

"Jesu!" Bessie shrieked, as Katherine stifled a scream. Lord Borough lay with one arm twisted against his chest, as if clutching it in pain. His eyes were wide open and distended and his mouth usually invisible in the scraggy gray and russet beard, grimaced as if uttering a silent, indignant cry. His expression was one of surprise, mingled with pain and an impatience that death had caught him unprepared, with no time for charges to his wife and staff, no sentimental farewell to his family.

In death, Lord Borough appeared no different from the lowliest laborer in his fields. Bessie put an arm about Katherine's shoulders and whispered, "Come away, Kate. There's nothing you can do for him now."

Katherine was numbed at the sight of the forlorn body on the bed. *Was this the way my mother looked when they found her?* She was overwhelmed by nausea at the thought for, genuinely fond of Edward Borough, she was outraged that death had once more invaded her life. People crowded into the room as a servant silently covered the body with a sheet. Again, Bessie tugged at her elbow. "Do come, Kate. Someone has gone for my lord's sons. Come away, now."

Katherine let herself be led back to her study chamber. She still could not believe her husband was dead. He'd been kind to her, generous and patient, and had taught her many things. Once again, death had robbed her of someone to whom she owed much, without even a chance to say goodbye. The thought brought remembrance of her mother and she felt tears start in her eyes.

From her study window, she saw the Borough sons leaping from their horses and racing inside. Henry and Thomas had loved and respected their father; their grief would be genuine. She recalled their kindness when Maud Parr had died and hoped she could remember what others had said that had given her some little peace. Though their sadness would be greater than hers, it was her duty to grieve with them.

Giving the boys some time to be alone with their father, as she returned down the long corridor, the thought arose that she was no longer Lady Borough of Cantley Hall. That title now belonged to Henry's wife. Unbidden —even undesired—came the similar thought that now that her lord and husband had gone, there was nothing to keep her in the North any longer.

* * *

Six weeks later, Katherine left Gainsborough for good. Henry, now Lord Borough, had begged her to stay. "We are all fond of you, Katherine, and the children are upset that you're leaving. You must always consider this your home."

Touched, Katherine shook her head. "I'm anxious to see to my mother's affairs, my lord," she said, "and to see my brother and sister. . . ." Bessie, standing nearby, shook her head approvingly. Only the night before, she'd urged Katherine not to be swayed. "You're too young to be the Dowager-Lady Borough," she said grimly, "and if you accept, you'll be buried here for life. Marriages have to be found for your two stepdaughters before anyone would consider one for you."

Katherine wanted to reply she wasn't eager to marry again. But little Anne Askew, flinging herself on Katherine, had cried, "Oh, my lady, I hate to see you go! I'll miss you so! I'll have to go back home and there's no one there to teach me." Katherine had hugged the child, but Anne would not be consoled. She'd only burrowed her head in her benefactress' lap and wept all the more.

On the day of departure, the child was still sad. Katherine embraced her whispering, "When you're older, maybe even next year, perhaps my lord, your good father, or Lord Borough will bring you to visit me." The girl's face brightened. Katherine smiled and said, "Just give me time to get settled back home, Anne!" She kissed the girl's wet cheeks. "Keep all the books we used in class, my dear. There's a tidy number to see you through the winter. And in the spring, or next summer—if we come to Kendal—perchance, you can visit us there. Send me letters, Anne. . . ." She embraced the little girl again. "I'll not forget you." The child hugged her tightly. Misty-eyed, Katherine hurried to join the escort waiting outside the doors she'd entered so tremulously in what now seemed another lifetime ago.

Her last sight as she and Bessie waved goodbye to the Borough family who'd assembled to see them off was of a forlorn Anne Askew, clutching the new Lady Borough's hand, her face still wet and looking as if her world had just come to an end.

CHAPTER VII

*God knows what I suffer from these people, enough to kill ten men,
much more a shattered woman who has done no harm. I can do
nothing but appeal to God and Your Majesty on whom alone my
remedy depends. For the love of God, procure a final sentence from
His Holiness as soon as possible. . . . The Pope's tardiness makes
many on my side waver, and those who would say the truth, do not.
Speak out yourself, that my friends may not think I am abandoned
by all the world . . . !*

—Katherine of Aragon to Charles, the Holy Roman Emperor, November 6, 1531

Katherine celebrated her sixteenth birthday quietly a week after she
returned to Parr House. Each day of the year that followed made her more
aware of how life in London and at court had changed during her absence
in the North.

On that first day home, there was a joyful reunion with the servants
who'd clustered about her in welcome. Later, everyone tactfully withdrew
and she'd wandered through the familiar rooms so alive with Maud Parr's
presence, she almost expected to see her mother. In each room, a fire burned
brightly reminding Katherine of the remark her mother had made after her
grandmother's death. Old Lady Parr had been chary of such luxuries but
now, Maud vowed, she'd have fires in every room whether in use or not!
Gazing into the chamber her parents had shared with its vast tester bed
hurt; Katherine decided to keep her old room near Bessie.

On the terrace, too cold to sit or stand, she'd hurriedly walked to the garden,
now brown and frozen, the dead leaves of winter skittering in the cutting
winds from the river. The dark earth and icy grayness of the Thames
reflected her mood. "I feel a bit like I'm not altogether here, Bess," she said
quietly when her companion joined her. "I don't belong in Gainsborough
anymore and here it still looks the same, but it's so different! I'm an orphan,
a widow and I feel as rootless as those old dead leaves there near the wall."

"That's only natural, Kate." Bess drew the girl inside from the cold.
"You've had two severe losses in a year and you're very young to be so
alone." Suddenly, the great bell of the Blackfriars Church next door tolled

the hour and, within seconds, other church bells pealed loudly throughout the City. It was a familiar and beloved sound, so much a part of her childhood, that Katherine laughed with genuine joy. "Hear the bells, Bess! They're welcoming us home!"

Later, she'd slipped away alone, entering the Blackfriars Church to seek out the Parr tombs. The lettering on her mother's stone was simple and brightly new. MAUD, LADY PARR, BELOVED WIFE OF SIR THOMAS PARR. BORN BOUGHTON GREEN APRIL 6, 1495, DIED LONDON AUGUST 20, 1529. SHE IS AGAIN WITH HIM.

Tearless, Katherine touched the stone, recoiling at its damp coldness. Yes, her mother was with Him and with that man who'd meant life itself to her. She took some comfort in the thought.

Katherine of Aragon, learning of her return to London, invited her to take her mother's place at court. It was a formality, out of the queen's fondness for Maud Parr. "She doesn't expect you to accept, Kate," Mary Tudor, the French queen, said on a welcoming visit. "The queen has fewer ladies about her now. Most of the others left when Wolsey insisted they spy on her. They said they'd rather leave than shame their queen. Jane Seymour is the youngest and she's twenty-two. You're much too young for the life the queen leads these days. She rarely leaves her quarters and only Maria is with her constantly. She still misses Mary very much."

Within days, Katherine had assumed her mother's duties, supervising the servants, keeping her household accounts, attending to correspondence with her Borough relatives and those others who'd only learned of her double loss. Each morning, along with Bess and the servants, she attended services in the Parr House chapel, often reading aloud from the Psalms, returning to her seat for the Mass conducted by a priest from the Blackfriars next door.

Katherine was shocked in talking with her mother's old friends how public "the king's great matter" had become.

"The king is going to divorce the queen, Kate, there's no doubt of that," her uncle, Sir William Parr told her, his fine eyes betraying his distress. "I don't know how—I don't think *he* knows how—but he will do it. Old Wolsey failed to get him that papal dispensation and has been sent into house exile at Esher. I think Tom More will be the new Lord Chancellor. He's a good man, but he won't like the men he has to work with, especially if they continue to harass the clergy."

Katherine repeated the French queen's observation that opposition always brought out the worst in the king. "What does the king intend to do with the clergy, Uncle?"

"If they continue at odds, he will take away as many of their powers as affect the Pope to show His Holiness he means business." Her uncle sighed, "Ah, whoever would have thought the affair with Tom Boleyn's girl would last almost five years? And ever since that debacle at the Blackfriars, the king has completely ignored the queen. One night at court he even let the Boleyn sit in the queen's place of estate and the French queen and old Norfolk's wife were seated below her. They haven't been back to court since."

As if tiring of the subject, Sir William asked Katherine if she expected to remain at Parr House. It was a large place, rather gloomy for a young girl, he thought. She could spend her summers at Kendal Castle, have a suite of rooms at court if she wished and he'd be happy to lease the house for her.

Katherine was startled. "But of course I mean to keep it, Uncle. This is my home!" Puzzled, she asked, "I can afford its charges?"

Her uncle laughed, "My dear Kate, the charges should not concern you! With your father's inheritance and what Edward Borough provided for you, you'll never have any worries. If you're content here, by all means stay. I doubt that you'll see much of Will and Ann, however."

Ann Parr, now almost fifteen, had been made a legal ward of the king. "That's in case anything should happen to me," her uncle explained. "Then Henry will be responsible for her welfare and her marriage. When your mother died, the queen insisted Ann come to court, asking who else would keep an eye on her? I thought it best, but I think she finds it rather dull. Will is much more happily placed, I'm glad to say, if it all doesn't go to his head."

Shortly after Katherine had gone to Gainsborough, Maud Parr had sought a marriage·for her young son. Nothing less than union with a peer's daughter would do, she insisted, and in Anne Bourchier, the only child and heiress of the Earl of Essex, she'd found what she wanted. As a great many Parr lands joined those of old Essex's, one day Will would inherit not only the title, but holdings respectable enough for a duke. But the marriage had been costly.

"Your mother found great satisfaction in the union, even though I advised her otherwise," her uncle explained. "She said Thomas would have wanted it. Bourchier took a great deal of her money—money that should rightfully have been yours and Ann's. But I could not dissuade her, Kate. Will is too young to live with his wife, of course, but old Bourchier insisted the marital endowment to be paid anyway. I secured the boy an appointment to the household of the king's son. They are of the same age and, as you know, I serve there as chamberlain."

Clapping her hands, Katherine laughed merrily. When her uncle appeared puzzled, she said, "It reminded me of something the French queen once told me. She said my lady mother was determined we be educated with royalty. Now when you tell me Will has been appointed to the household of the king's son—bastard though he may be—I see she also meant us to *live* with royalty! I would imagine this makes Will very content." Though she'd been only six years old, Katherine could still remember the horrified whispering and scandalized look on her mother's face when informed that Henry's young mistress, Bessie Blount, had presented him with a son. The boy, Henry Fitzroy, was now about the same age as her brother.

When her sister and brother arrived at Parr House the following day,

Katherine was astonished. Regarding the handsome pair, she cried, "You're both taller than I!" Ann had grown from a sullen, silent child into a pretty girl, slim and well-groomed, with the darker complexion of her father's mother. Thick winged black brows emphasized her pointed chin and the gray eyes which missed nothing. She was splendidly dressed in a deep blue velvet with a cloak trimmed in miniver; matching gloves and tiny velvet slippers showed her delicate hands and feet to advantage.

"You must come to court, too, Kate, when your mourning is over," she advised her older sister solemnly. "It's not as lively as it might be for the queen is often sickly, but she wants to see you whenever you wish." She glanced about the familiar river room of Parr House. "I don't see how you can bear to be here alone."

"I find it very comforting, Ann." If one had to explain, thought Katherine, better to keep silent.

She found her brother, awkward and clumsy at thirteen, a shade more confident than need be. He, too, was richly dressed in glowing satin the color of canary wine, his doublet heavy with lace and several jewels Katherine recognized as her mother's. He gazed at her mourning dress with obvious disdain and, remarking at one point that the view from Richmond House terrace was so much better than his old home, postured about the room until Katherine felt her patience wearing thin. She was not unhappy when they left, realizing again, how little she had in common with either.

* * *

As her year of mourning ended, Katherine was amused at the suitors who flocked to Parr House. "You'll not be a widow long, Kate," Bessie laughed, as one elegant gentleman left after what was obviously an inspection visit for his young son. "Not with your great house and fortune—not to mention your pretty face! Do you want to wed again, Kate?"

Remembering the hard anticipatory glint she'd seen in my lord's eyes as he gazed at her parents' riches, Katherine shook her head. She still vividly remembered Edward Borough's stroking and fondling, of forever being at another's beck and call with little privacy to study and less freedom to decide how a day might be spent. Of never being able to talk openly or privately as she could talk to Bess.

"No, I'm a respectable widow now, Bess, and widows, you understand, are allowed all sorts of freedom and privileges you unmarried lasses can't have! So I'll stay a widow at least for a while. Why give up my life here? Unless of course, my prince comes riding with that crown and scepter!"

And, as always happened when the gypsy's prophecy was recalled, the two girls fell to laughing with Katherine vowing again, "If I can't have a crown and scepter, I mustn't settle for anything less!"

Along with those who came to Parr House, Katherine met many young men on occasions when her uncle took her to the court functions honoring visiting dignitaries and foreign ambassadors. Many flirted openly, begging that she receive them at Parr House or accept an invitation to a court revel or a picnic in the family barge on the river. Often she saw her sister in the company of Anne Boleyn and her companions; it was obvious Ann preferred the lively chambers of "the king's lady" to the dark incense-laden rooms of the queen.

"She's a foot in each camp, that one," Bessie observed wryly as she and Katherine rode to a ceremonial at Westminster Abbey, passing Ann riding with the royal party for a day of hunting at Eltham. The king raised his hand in greeting and the Boleyn woman nodded as Katherine passed. The sight of Maud Parr's daughter in the entourage of the queen's sworn enemy did not appear as unusual to others as it did to Katherine. It was another example of how things had changed since she'd gone to Gainsborough.

She often wondered how much Princess Mary knew of "the king's great matter." Certainly an effort would be made to keep the situation secret, for the queen would hardly write such distressing news to her daughter. But in one of Mary's replies, she sensed that even at distant Ludlow, the princess had learned the extent of her parents' unhappiness.

> Ludlow Castle
> Ludlow, Salop
> April 6, 1530
>
> My dearest Kate,
>
> I have your letter from the hand of your courier, Ives, and our good servant, Dodd, will bring you this in reply. He brings letters for my good aunt Suffolk and for Kate Willoughby who is still with her while her mother Maria remains with the queen.
>
> My days are much the same, Kate. I continue studying with Master Featherstone and I still play on the virginals. Lady Salisbury says when I return home my parents will be pleased at my progress. When will that happy day ever come?
>
> Without Lady Salisbury's company and that of Susan Clarencieux, my maid of honor, it would be very lonely for me. And worrisome, too. Kate Willoughby writes her mother never leaves the queen and neither goes to court anymore. Lady Salisbury says I must leave everything to God, Whom I do trust in, but it is very hard, being so far away.
>
> Kate, will you see to Dodd's care at Parr House? He doesn't wish to go to court for, at his last lodging, when he asked to see the queen, he found much ill will. . . .

Katherine made a point of seeing old Randall Dodd when she read the letter. The man had aged, his weatherbeaten features testifying to many grueling hours on the road, serving as courier between Ludlow and London.

"The princess is well, Dodd?" Katherine gave him a few coins along with a package of books and her letters for Kate Willoughby and the French queen.

"Aye, as well as one can be in that place that's so dark and with weather the devil himself conjures up to test us," the old man replied grimly. "'Tis no place for my young princess, my lady, and I'd tell the king himself if he asked me," he concluded angrily with the privilege of one who'd known Henry Tudor since boyhood. "Which he won't. The king pays no attention to those of us of the old days now, my lady, he's too bent on the new." He bowed and thanked Katherine for the coins. "I'll be back on my return, my lady, and thank you for my lodging here. 'Tis warmer than my old place at the palace—even if it was over the kitchen!"

Old Randall Dodd had just about reached Westhorpe when Ann Parr visited Katherine with welcome news. Mary Tudor was coming home! "It's because of her marriage, Kate," Ann explained, her cheeks pink with excitement. "Mary's fiancé, Charles of Spain, is very unhappy over the king's treatment of his aunt, the queen. They've had words and Charles's army even sacked Rome and imprisoned the Pope! It has made the king very angry and so he looks for a new marriage to show the emperor how little he and Spain matter in England anymore. The king is considering a marriage with France and soon the French ambassadors will arrive to discuss the terms. Think of it, Kate, Mary will be the queen of France!" Twisting her fingers nervously, Ann said, "I understand the queen took to her bed in disappointment."

Rereading Mary's letter, Katherine's apprehension increased. "It will be hard for the princess," she told Bess. "She doesn't know the emperor has broken the betrothal or her father's new plans. And she had such pride in Spain!"

It angered Katherine that after so long a time away from her parents, Mary was being brought back again only to serve her father's wishes. No matter how she felt, she knew the princess would do her parents' bidding. It would never occur to her to resist as her aunt, the French queen, had once done.

* * *

As preparations for a festive ball to receive the French ambassadors were made, the queen returned from Greenwich to occupy her old quarters in Westminster Palace. Angrily, Anne Boleyn moved into York House which the king had taken from old Cardinal Wolsey when the minister fell into disgrace. "My Lady Anne says there's no place for a queen at Whitehall— that's what she's renamed the place—where she'll live with the king when they wed. She says she prefers the cardinal's gilt to Westminster's grime!" Ann Parr told Katherine with some satisfaction.

"I doubt the queen will notice her absence," Katherine replied tartly, "and if she does, she'll be thankful for it. I hope you're going to accompany Mistress Anne? I think when Mary returns she should find only friends about her." She was rewarded with a slight flush of embarrassment in her sister's cheeks.

Within days, Margaret Pole, the Countess of Salisbury, Mary's governess, arrived at Parr House to see Katherine and express her sympathy at Maud Parr's death. She described the emotional reunion between Mary and her mother. "It set everyone to weeping—even the king had tears in his eyes." Answering Katherine's question, she said that Mary had accepted the emperor's rejection philosophically, agreeing her parents should make whatever match they considered best.

"I think she's more stunned by her father's plans for the ball, Katherine," Lady Salisbury laughed. "Mary has lived a very different life for the past few years. I've worried about how quiet it was for one so young. Now, suddenly, her father can't give her enough! The dressmakers are flocking to her chambers with all sorts of patterns and fabrics, for the king vows she'll have a wardrobe worthy of a queen. When he brought in a coffer of jewels and told her to select anything she wanted, all the poor child could do was burst into tears!"

Katherine understood, although she said nothing. The king would obviously spare no effort or expense to beautify the daughter who would be the future queen of France as well as England. Certainly, that would show the emperor—and his own stubborn queen as well!

* * *

On the night of what had come to be called "the Frenchmen's gala," Katherine, escorted by Sir William Askew on one of his rare London visits, joined others at Westminster Stairs to await conveyance to Hampton Court. The last dying rays of the sun glinted on the red roof of Lambeth Palace across the river and colored the old abbey behind them in a roseate glow. On the river, the horse ferries hurried to land before dark. All about her, celebrants dressed in shining satin, burnished velvets or damask embellished with lace, jewels, gold or silver trim waited for their barges. Plumed caps and embroidered hoods vied with the birds of paradise, the ribbons and flowers—real or jeweled—tucked into intricate coiffures. Katherine was happy her year of mourning was over so she could wear her gown in the newly popular shade of "lady blush"—a pale-pinkish cream velvet. She'd swept her hair underneath a hood of the same material bordered with double rows of pearls and diamonds. Her mother's favorite necklace of deeply glowing emeralds was clasped about her neck. "Without those eyes of yours, you'd never think of emeralds with that gown," Bessie had said as Katherine twirled for her approval. "But they're perfect. They look as lovely on you, Lady Borough, as they did on Lady Parr!" Katherine rewarded her companion with a flourish, a curtsey and a kiss.

Now, waiting with Sir William, she felt her excitement mounting. Not only would she see Mary again but now, after her year of mourning, she could dance the night away! Tonight the petty bickerings and jealous animosities which had split the court since the royal estrangement had seemingly disappeared; everyone was genuinely lighthearted and exhilarated. Tonight, the king and queen would be together and their daughter would be with them. Everyone wanted to share the royal happiness—to make Mary's homecoming a happy event.

Soon, an attendant was holding out his hand to help Katherine into what she recognized as one of the queen's own barges, one she'd often used with her mother. Quickly, Sir William found a place and the barge, filled with music and the excited chatter of guests, pulled away from the waterstairs, joining the others on their way upriver to Hampton Court.

Katherine gazed at the other occupants, recognizing the pale, older girl near the far end as Jane Seymour, one of Queen Katherine's attendants. Her companion, a beauty with luxuriant dark hair, her full figure displayed to great advantage in a low-cut green velvet gown, was a stranger.

As they proceeded upriver, the soft swish of the oars mingling with the laughter and conversation of her companions, Katherine's gaze returned to two men seated near Jane Seymour. The dark-haired beauty seemed preoccupied with one, a strong-featured man of distinctive elegance with a short beard and cream-colored plumed cap atop reddish brown hair. The other, several years younger, was clean-shaven and resembled the older man. His gray velvet doublet was embroidered with a thick silver trim; a cloak of similar material was tossed carelessly over his knee.

As his gaze met Katherine's, he inclined his head and, in a pleasantly musical voice, asked, "You are Lady Borough?" Surprisingly, Katherine felt a blush arising from her bosom as she replied, "I am, sir," and presented Sir William Askew.

"Thomas Seymour, madame," the man acknowledged the introduction, "and my brother, Edward, and his betrothed, Anne Stanhope." The couple broke off their animated conversation long enough to smile in greeting. Edward Seymour, his brother explained, was Master of the Horse in the household of the king's son, Henry Fitzroy. He knew her brother as well as her uncle.

"I met Sir William, madame, when I went to France as a page at the time the king's sister married the French king. He has been very kind to the Seymour family. My sister, Jane, serves the queen who is not well, as you must certainly know. The princess' return has made her very happy!" Thomas Seymour appeared so genuinely solicitous, Katherine was touched. It had been a long time since she'd heard Katherine of Aragon spoken of with such respect and affection.

By the time Hampton Court, ablaze with candles and torchlight, appeared in view, everyone was talking together as if they were old friends. "And now it begins again," Thomas Seymour laughed, "another English princess will wed with France. Pray this one will be more successful than the last!"

Crossing the moat into the enormous courtyard, they reached the Banqueting Hall where Cardinal Wolsey had so often entertained foreign ambassadors and other dignitaries. Hundreds of candles hung on wheels from the great carved hammerbeam ceiling, illuminating the vast hall bedecked with the most valuable tapestries for the occasion.

"We've come a long way, Lady Borough," Thomas whispered with amusement as he gazed about the hall, "at least we don't have fires in the middle with smoke going out a hole in the roof as it did in our grandfathers' day!"

It was almost the last opportunity for speech. At that moment, a brace of heralds, hidden behind a bower of green branches adorned with multicolored flowers shaped to form a Tudor rose, raised their trumpets as the great center door opened. There were the king and queen, together if only for this momentous occasion. Katherine caught her breath in excitement. Henry was magnificent in purple velvet with gold and white slashed sleeves. Proudly, he led Queen Katherine, stately in cloth of gold tissue trimmed with Spanish lace into which tiny jewels had been sewn, into the hall. Her graying hair was almost hidden under a bright golden cap which gleamed with pearls and diamonds. Reaching the dais, she turned to face the now silent throng and her smile was as bright as the gems which adorned her gown.

Another trumpet blast and there, suddenly, was Princess Mary, alone and as regal as her mother in a dress of pure white satin and lace, similarly embroidered with diamonds and pearls. A filigreed net, crossed with silvery bands, held her hair high on her head, giving her an adult look. Mary had never appeared more beautiful and, as she began the long solitary walk through the crowded room, Katherine recalled the day she'd passed through the palace corridor, looking neither right nor left, on her way to Ludlow. Everyone, awestruck and silent, bowed deeply as she passed. For most, it was the first glimpse of the child to whom they'd said goodbye almost five years ago.

As, with slow dignified steps, Mary passed to join her parents, Katherine felt a lump in her throat. The princess was no longer the sad little girl who'd wept at leaving her parents and friends. Now nearly fifteen, she was old enough to wed a king's son and sufficiently attractive to merit what was obviously an astonished approval from a sophisticated court. And, from the radiant look on her face, she was enjoying every moment of it. As she passed, Katherine longed to run and embrace her old friend, but only bent her head and bowed as deeply as the others.

Behind her came the foreign visitors: the Bishop of Tarbes with François, the Vicomte de Turenne and La Viste, president of the Paris *parlement*. Once everyone was assembled with the king and queen, the musicians began to play. Taking Mary by the hand, the king led her to the middle of the floor and, to laughter, shouts and then loud applause, began to dance with his daughter as the queen, beaming with happiness, looked on. Soon others joined in the whirling circle or made their way to the dais to speak to the queen. Katherine, happy to see "the king's lady" was nowhere in sight, whispered to Sir William Askew she was going to talk to the queen.

As she started forward, someone clutched her arm, swinging her about abruptly.

"Lady Borough," Thomas Seymour smiled down at her, his dark brown hair and white teeth gleaming in the luminous candlelight, "our queen will be here for a while. I want to dance with you while I have the chance!"

"Sir," Katherine laughed, aware once more of that warm sensation in her breast, that little spurt of excitement deep within, "chance is nothing to depend upon! Are you often at court?"

"That's what I meant by saying while I have a chance!" As the music's tempo changed, he led her expertly into a sprightly galliard. "No, I am not at court as much as I would like. I am, madame," he bowed in exaggerated fashion, "a glorified messenger for His Majesty over there, leaping as if he were still a boy. Even I, at twenty-three, cannot leap like that! Where does he get the strength?"

Katherine laughed happily, "The king has always danced well. My mother often said there was none better. . . ."

"I met your mother at Greenwich the last year you were in Lincolnshire," Thomas replied. "She was a beautiful woman—one of the most beautiful I've ever seen." He held Katherine off, gazing at her approvingly, "You're very like her, you know."

"So I've been told, my lord."

"My sister, Jane, was very beholden to your mother. Lady Parr made it especially easy for her when she came from our home in Somerset to serve the queen. She is hoping, of course, to be of service to the princess, too, now that she has returned."

Katherine understood. Thomas Seymour was saying, in the obliquely innocent way everyone had adopted in the last few years, where his loyalty lay. She replied as she knew was expected, "I'm certain the princess will be grateful for your sister's concern."

As the music stopped, Katherine was still far away from the queen and Mary. Sir Thomas Cawarden, Master of the Revels, strode to the center of the floor to announce "a diversion by Master Holbein." Everyone must be seated, he said, indicating a few cushions near the wall or, to much laughter, on the hard floor, if necessary. Gratefully, Katherine sank onto a cushion, noting that Signore Spinelli, the Venetian ambassador, had placed himself between her and Thomas Seymour. When her partner suggested they change places, the older man glared indignantly, vigorously shaking his head as Thomas, smiling in his relaxed way, shrugged his shoulders and reluctantly sat a few paces away.

Another trumpet blast and, near the musicians' bower, a long golden curtain parted as eight masked men in gold doublets, their helmets adorned with the Princess of Wales's plumed feathers, strode forward pushing a huge *papier-mâché* "mountain" painted in glowing pastels with small gilt towers and rocks of coral, lapis lazuli and crystal. As the "mountain" turned, indentations in the substance provided seats for eight young ladies, all dressed in cloth of gold, their hair hanging freely about their shoulders. In the middle was Princess Mary. At the sound of trumpets, she rose and stretched out her arms. As the music became louder and more insistent, the court erupted in a roar of approval. When the masked men pushed the painted "mountain" about the room, the visiting Venetian sitting next to Katherine applauded, crying, "She is dazzling to see! She is like an angel!"

In a moment, the men and women stepped out and down from their painted perches and, as the music swung to a different beat, performed several intricate dances which, Katherine knew, were the result of days of practicing. Then Princess Mary joined them and suddenly the music switched to a Spanish *seguidilla*. As the beat became faster and louder, so did the spectators' cries and applause. Katherine felt herself caught up in the almost sensual sound and, quickly glancing toward Thomas Seymour who was thumping the floor with his hand keeping time to the music, saw he was similarly elated. Between them, the Venetian, Spinelli, cried that Mary was an angel, that he'd never seen such jewels, that the musicians must have come from outside this world with their heavenly music and no one in the world was more fortunate than the French dauphin.

Then, quickly, to a loud crash of drums, it was over. Amidst great applause, the king and French ambassador appeared together, joining the princess who kissed her father and embraced the foreign envoy. Spontaneously, Henry reached out and plucked the net from Mary's hair, causing it to tumble in a dark cascade about her shoulders. At that, Spinelli, who was being helped to his feet by Thomas Seymour, cried, "She is a most heavenly sight!" Not to be outdone by his French colleague, he darted forward.

Already, everyone was filing into the courtyard. There tables ladened with dishes of silver, gilt and gold were filled with mounds of food and great beakers of wine and other drink awaited the thirsty. In the throng, Katherine glimpsed Sir Thomas More, the new Lord Chancellor, his great golden chain of office, glistening in the myriad light of hundreds of thick candles. Sir Thomas had been her father's great friend; his hair was more gray than she remembered. She bowed in answer to his pleasant smile. Undoubtedly, he'd recognized her because of her resemblance to her mother.

Moving toward the dais where throngs surrounded the royal couple and their daughter, Katherine was strangely moved at the sight of the now adult princess, the majestic grace of the queen and the king's beaming cordiality. This, she thought, is what the court must have once been like in that time her mother had called "the old days."

Waiting to greet the royal trio, Katherine felt something else as she watched the retreating figure of Thomas Seymour who was joining his brother in the courtyard. Anticipation? Excitement? Intrigue? It was all so unfamiliar a feeling, so unexpected and odd.

But very definitely pleasant.

CHAPTER VIII

Within days after the gala, Katherine hurried to Richmond for a joyous reunion with Princess Mary. The French queen had brought thirteen-year-old Kate Willoughby from Westhorpe to see her mother, Maria de Salinas. She and the queen shared the happy moment when, after curtseys to princess and queen, Katherine and Kate rose to embrace Mary warmly. Happily, the queen greeted them, "You look so much like your dear mother, Kate. There isn't a day that I still don't miss her." Impulsively, she hugged her namesake, asking proudly, "And how do you find our princess?"

"A welcome sight in everyone's eyes, madame," Katherine replied, "and it's wonderful to be back at Richmond." She thought how much her mother would have enjoyed the scene: the queen, sitting down now to embroider a small hanging, with skeins of silk in the vivid Spanish colors she loved about her neck. Mary and Kate whispering together as the French queen and Maria spoke quietly, Maria gesturing broadly, her speech still littered with familiar Spanish phrases. How impressed she must be with the daughter she hadn't seen for so long! Kate, mature for twelve, was now a head taller than Mary. Her thin, almost angular features were animated by a bright intelligence; rust-brown hair rippled in waves to her shoulders, framing a fair English complexion enhanced by her mother's dark Spanish eyes. Kate had tiny wrists, ankles and feet and, even quiescent, seemed on the verge of movement. When she walked, she strode rapidly, yet gracefully and when she spoke, her words tripped over themselves in her eagerness and enthusiasm to be heard.

"And you must see the princess' trousseau, Kate!" she exclaimed. "I had a peek at Greenwich on my way here. Ah, there are gowns of silver tissue and black velvet. One has purple sateen sleeves, another is one of crimson velvet that Mary almost wore to the ball until the queen said white was best. She has nightrails, bonnets and hoods and a cloak trimmed with ermine! There are shoes to match each gown and dozens of Spanish gloves in all colors! I trow the dauphin will be dazzled, for the French will not have seen anything like it!"

"You're right, they have seen nothing like it," the French queen said almost to herself, her eyes shadowed with unpleasant memories. "Mary has an innocence and integrity which will be more shining than her garments, Kate. That's what will make her noticeable—like a clear crystal glass set beside an overly bejeweled goblet!" Sensing the princess' puzzlement, her aunt laughed lightly and said, "But it will be different for you, Mary. Your husband is young, mine was an old man. It will be happier for you!"

Soon the group settled down to gossip of the court. No one mentioned Anne Boleyn or the king. "The most important discussion in my rooms right now is whether Jane Seymour will wed Rob Dormer," the queen smiled, deftly threading her needle. "She is a gentle and sweet girl and should make young Dormer a good wife if his parents will only consent. But I fear they wish to look higher. They are ambitious for their son and think he should do better. Fools!"

Katherine was about to comment when a steward announced visitors from the king. The queen's features, so animated as she spoke of her favored lady-in-waiting, lit up in anticipation. She still loves her husband, Katherine thought, no matter that he treats her so poorly or keeps her apart from the court. She watched as Mary helped her mother rise, asking if she might accompany her to greet their guests. The queen shook her head and left the room.

Mention of Jane Seymour brought her brother Thomas to mind. Katherine had hoped to see him again at court and was disappointed to learn he'd returned to France with the ambassadors to assist in the details of Mary's betrothal contract. She still remembered, with intriguing clarity, each moment of their evening at Hampton Court. The meeting in the queen's barge, the light in his eyes as they'd danced. No one had ever made her feel so beautiful and desirable. Any thought of the handsome courtier still caused a quivering excitement that even her uncle's somewhat mysterious dislike of the Seymours hadn't dampened. Edward and Thomas Seymour, children of Sir John and Lady Margaret Seymour of Wolf Hall in Somerset, so her uncle said, had come to court only to make their fortunes amongst the covey of "new men" with whom the king now surrounded himself.

Sir William made it plain that, despite the royal favor, he considered them—as well as their sister Jane—*arrivistes*. Katherine had wanted to question him further but hesitated to appear too interested in a family he so obviously disdained. She hoped there would be an opportunity to talk alone with Mary and Kate. But could she adequately describe to her two best friends that strange warm sensation that even Thomas Seymour's name provoked?

Her pleasant thoughts were interrupted by a heated conversation from beyond the door. As if to stifle the unpleasant sound, Maria quickly began to talk as Kate Willoughby prattled on how they must all go one day to Chelsea to see the little manor house which the king had built. Katherine joined in, hoping to keep the conversation going, even as the voices outside became louder. Mary's face was pale and she bit her lips nervously, hiding her trembling hands in her long skirt as she rose to pace about the room. At last, all talk dwindled as everyone put pretense aside and listened incredulously to the drama taking place on the other side of the door.

Someone was vehemently telling the queen that once again the king had decided she must renounce her title. If she would comply, her husband would make her a handsome gift of money and estates, the courier said. She would be treated with great reverence and respect, while all honor would be paid to her daughter who would be the heir unless, of course, the king had a son. But Henry Tudor must have his freedom. His marriage was illegal and he would brook no further stubbornness from his wife.

The queen's voice was clear as she replied, "First, tell my good husband and lord, the king, I already have great honor and respect, as does my daughter. Tell him there is not a family in this whole land that does not regard me as their true queen and Princess Mary as the heir. Only those at court with something to gain for themselves tell him otherwise!"

Obviously somewhat abashed, the speaker answered that the king's conscience was troubled. "His Majesty does not think his marriage a true one and cannot live with such an assault on his spirit."

"God grant the king a quiet conscience," the queen replied, "mine is clear! I have right on my side and the love of my people. The Pope issued a dispensation for our marriage and the king knows I came virgin to his bed. His claims are senseless! I will not be forced into a convent or the single life!"

Boldly, someone taunted Katherine of Aragon. She was already living a single life, he said, for the king continued to absent himself from her presence and, as he would soon be Supreme Head of the Church, if she continued to balk him, he might be forced to punish her severely.

"Then tell His Majesty I live a single life only because *he* chooses to remain away from me and my daughter. The princess has seen her father only twice since she returned from Ludlow! Give His Majesty this message —that if he wishes to be Supreme Head of the Church, he may." Katherine's laugh was contemptuous. "He knows as well as I there is only one head of the church and he lives in Rome! I acknowledge my husband to be my lord and master on earth, but in spiritual matters, I will be governed only by the Pope! If my husband is impatient, tell him to send others such as you to Rome and harass His Holiness for a decision. I am as eager for it as the king because I know what that decision will be!"

When there was no reply, Mary paused near the door, as if to go to her mother's aid. Quickly, Maria sped toward her, shaking her head. They listened as the queen continued, "I am passing my time with my maids, for who else shall I rely on except my Holy Father and my nephew, the emperor? But they, alas, are far away. . . ." Her voice trailed off, "You may go now. Tell my husband I am not well and this cruel treatment does not help me. . . ."

The door opened and Mary quickly assisted her mother to her seat. The queen was distraught, fingering the skeins of silken thread about her neck with shaking hands. Sinking to her knees at her mother's side, Mary cried, "Miserable men! How could they torment you so?"

"It was Norfolk," the queen replied in a trembling voice as she picked up her needlework. "Norfolk, the Boleyn's uncle! I don't think he much relished his task, but I think he and I understand one another now. Supreme Head of the Church, indeed! In the name of Jesus—I think my good lord and husband has been bewitched! I marvel there is no one to tell him of his folly!" There were tears in her eyes as she pressed Mary's hand. "But, daughter, this should not change your feelings for your father. He is not himself these days, but he loves you and he will honor you. Always remember, Mary, you were born of love and with legal sanction. Accept nothing less. No matter what happens to me, you are the king's true daughter. And as long as I am alive, I'll not let him forget."

Mary looked wretched and Katherine's heart ached for her. For all her younger years, the princess had had everything—loving parents, freedom of palace, court or country house. Now she must know her days with her mother were numbered. Soon, with that glorious trousseau, she'd be sent to France to marry a boy she'd never seen. Had she wed the emperor, at least she'd have returned to her mother's native country. But France? Stories of the French queen's trial there had circulated about the court for years. Mary must have heard them. How could she look forward to her marriage?

* * *

"It makes me feel guilty," Katherine told Bessie Bellingham the following day as they rode in the park adjoining the king's new mansion of Whitehall. "I have so much and the princess has so little." Ahead, on marshy land which had formerly been a home for leper maidens, the king was building, in honor of St. James, what he called "a house in the fields." Katherine was eager to see what would probably be another home for "the king's lady." Drawing their mounts to a halt, the two girls watched as the builders hurried to complete their work before the inclement winter weather set in. It would be a handsome dwelling, Katherine thought, noting the giant red-brick towers stark against a lowering sky. Already cobbles were being set to form an impressive courtyard and, some distance away, workers were piling brick upon brick for a thick wall. Two magnificent new dwellings for a new queen. One here at St. James's and another a stone's throw away at Whitehall. And all the while the real queen lived apart virtually friendless while soon her daughter would be sent away to marry for England's political convenience. Probably they'd never see one another again.

"It's all so unfair," Katherine said crossly, turning back toward Whitehall. "Well, I wish the king much happiness in his new palace. Once he's there, perhaps he'll think more kindly of his wife and child! This divorce is beginning to affect everyone, Bess. Kate Willoughby has to live with the French queen because her mother wants to share the queen's exile. And my own sister prefers the company of the woman who has caused all this trouble. Even Mary's betrothal is to spite the queen's nephew, the emperor! People are confused about their loyalties. Where will it all end?"

The answer came sooner than even Katherine expected. Two weeks later, the Pope at last affirmed the legality of Henry's marriage to Katherine of Aragon, pronouncing their daughter the legitimate heir. Should the king not put the Boleyn aside and return to his wife, the Holy Father said, he might suffer excommunication.

Within days, the king's answer swept London. The Pope could be damned, he told Eustace Chapuys, the Spanish ambassador. "He can issue ten thousand excommunications and I should not care a straw for them!" Henry shouted. "I shall settle this matter in my own way, senor, and care naught for the opinions of the Bishop of Rome or your master, the Holy Roman Emperor! My daughter will wed with France. If the emperor sends his armies, France and England will be ready!"

Seemingly, however, the French king did not share Henry's optimism. Each day as she rode down the Strand, Katherine noted the crowds outside Durham House where Anne Boleyn lived. There she saw Anne's clean shaven prelate, Dr. Thomas Cranmer in deep conversation with Thomas Cromwell. Cromwell, a protégé of old Cardinal Wolsey, had risen in the royal favor when the old prelate died. He was a stockily built man, usually dressed in a plain black gown and cap which emphasized the heavy-lidded gaze and gave him a scowling, almost predatory, look. By contrast with Cranmer and Cromwell, handsome Stephen Gardiner, the Bishop of Winchester, always wore impressive church garments of shining gold or silver, heavily embroidered in a lavish trim. Each day, accompanied by the French ambassador, he appeared more gorgeously dressed causing his goddaughter, Kate Willoughby, to comment, "He vies with the peacock for splendor, but the bird is the winner because he has more brain!" Kate's witty barbs, unusual for one so young, were rapidly winning her a reputation at court.

Often the London merchants, fearful for their foreign trade should the king upset the delicate balance between France and Spain, joined the solemn-eyed churchmen and councillors as they arrived to discuss "the king's great matter." As the days wore on, the City held its breath. At last it appeared the emperor had won. The marriage between Princess Mary and the dauphin would be canceled. France, seemingly, was not as eager to risk a reprisal from Spain or invite an angry reprimand from Rome for allowing the dauphin to wed the child of a monarch courting excommunication.

Katherine, secretly relieved for Mary, was unprepared for the effect on the court of the French snub. A distraught Ann Parr told her sister bluntly, "The king means to have his divorce, Kate, and the queen is only making it more difficult for herself by being so obstinate." Ann defended Anne Boleyn. "You must remember, she's tolerated this situation for almost five years. Five years of keeping the king at arm's length, even separating herself from the court because at times she was so discouraged they might never wed. Five years of watching another woman, her lover's wife, hold on when she knows she's unwanted and cannot give him the son he must have. Why shouldn't she encourage the king who refuses to live with that woman who won't step gracefully aside? Other queens have had to do so!" Then, angrily, "One day, mark you, if the queen doesn't come to her senses, the king will take extreme measures. Even Mistress Anne will not be able to hold him back. Already he is incensed with such as Gardiner and old Archbishop Warham who mumble he must return to his wife. He will never do so! He'll get rid of the bishops first!"

Listening, Katherine only marveled how easily her sister rationalized an excuse for a situation rapidly becoming intolerable for everyone.

But as Ann Parr had predicted, the French rebuke and papal threat at last loosened Henry Tudor's anger. Cromwell told the king that England was a "two-headed monster, with two rulers—a Pope and a king—and his bishops swore fealty to him only *after* they'd sworn loyalty to the Pope. He challenged Henry to follow the example of the German princes who'd thrown off the papal yoke. With the church brought to heel, the divorce could be accomplished and the realm set in order with a new marriage and a possible male heir.

Cromwell's suggestions horrified the clergy. Threatened with a fine of one hundred thousand pounds if they continued in their Romish loyalty, old John Fisher, the Bishop of Rochester and one of the queen's staunchest supporters, roared at Cromwell, "It is not the good of the church ye seek, but the goods!" Stephen Gardiner, the Bishop of Winchester, and old Stokesley, the Bishop of London, were appalled. For years, they'd actively encouraged the king in his papal-baiting as a means of securing Cardinal Wolsey's downfall, hoping in the meantime the king would tire of Anne Boleyn. Now Henry was using their own tactics to bait the church itself and Mistress Anne, everyone now realized, would be queen whether the clergy or country desired or approved it. The king was smitten, the Pope was in the way and something had to give.

At last, at a Convocation held in the old Chapter House at Westminster Abbey, the terrified churchmen finally acknowledged their sovereign as "Supreme Head of the Church and Clergy of England." When one prelate asked that the words, "as far as the law of Christ allows," be inserted, no one spoke in favor of the tempering phrase.

Later, Katherine was startled and proud to learn from Sir William Parr that their cousin, Cuthbert Tunstall, now the Bishop of Durham, had had the singular courage to rise and ask the clerk to record his personal protest against the king's new title.

* * *

One result of the king's action was soon evident. Within days, Sir Thomas More surrendered the seal of the Lord Chancellor's office, telling Henry he could no longer serve, in good conscience, a country where the church was controlled by the state and not the Pope. It was a measure of the king's regard for his childhood idol that he and the elder statesman parted in friendship. A short time later, the office was given to Sir Thomas Audley.

"He has everyone in line now—Cranmer, Cromwell and Audley." Sir William Parr grimly told his niece. "He even calls them 'my Thomases'! They will all do his bidding and care naught for the effect on the country."

"Dr. Cranmer seems harmless, Uncle. He's preached at the Blackfriars once or twice. He has a pleasant manner." Katherine was certain her uncle disliked the prelate because he served Anne Boleyn.

"Cranmer will always bend with the wind, Kate. But not Cromwell! He's grown big with his own success! Remember, he was the one who urged the king to papal schism. Now he's looking at the church's property. He says he will send commissioners to all the abbeys and monasteries to look for abuses. I am worried for a good deal of our family holdings are adjacent to lands belonging to religious houses."

"Abuses, Uncle?" Katherine was puzzled. "What abuses?"

"There are some, my dear, but not as many as Cromwell intends to find. The religious are only human. There are, I suppose, such frailties as gluttony, cruelty, pride and greed. In some instances, even carnal living, as the pious Master Cromwell likes to call it. But a few should not damn the whole!"

Later, pondering her uncle's words, Katherine wondered if the Vicar-General could really threaten a house of God. She'd grown up in the shadow of the Blackfriars knowing the monks to be kind, understanding and helpful. As a child, she'd fallen asleep to chanting or, waking in the early dawn, had listened to the shuffling of sandaled feet as the brethren walked in procession in the semidarkness to the first Mass of the day. The monastery bells were a part of Parr House life; she could not imagine them silent. And, just a short ride away, was the Charterhouse where devout Carthusian monks lived in isolation, subject to severest disciplines of mind, body and spirit. She remembered the splendid Northern abbeys of Whitby, Rievaulx and Crowland where, on their way to Kendal Castle, the Parr family had often stayed overnight. Everywhere she'd seen only devoted service to God, honest care of the sick and poor, warm hospitality for the traveler and food at the gate for the poor. Why would Cromwell want to make trouble for the religious houses?

The apprehension of the clergy and those families who still favored Queen Katherine and her daughter were put aside at the marriage of the French queen's daughter, Lady Frances Brandon to Henry Grey, the Marquis of Dorset, whose late father had been a close friend of Charles Brandon and the king. A welcome gaiety, engulfed the court as it assembled at the Church of St. Saviour in Southwark for the solemn ceremony, afterward walking the few steps from the church to Suffolk House for the wedding festivities.

Observing that young Grey seemed enamored of his fifteen-year-old bride, Katherine wished him well. Frances Brandon, the source of much mischief during her schoolroom days, had never been a favorite. She was still difficult,

Kate Willoughby said, mistreating servant and horse alike, riding the beast like a man and cursing the other with the tongue of a commoner. "But she doesn't trouble *me* anymore," Kate whispered during the ceremony. "I give as good as I get and she leaves me alone. We understand one another now. But I mislike the girl and can't understand how the French queen could have such a daughter!"

Katherine had hoped to see Mary at the ceremony, but the princess remained at Richmond, apart from her mother whom the king had ordered to The More, an old hunting box of Wolsey's in Hertfordshire. "It's a miserable place and she hates it," Kate told Katherine as they waited in line to enter Suffolk House. "But she went. The king has reduced her allowance and left her only a few of her ladies. My good mother went, of course, and I'm to stay with the French queen at Westhorpe when she leaves after the ceremony." As her companion's lips quivered, Katherine realized how young Maria de Salinas's daughter actually was.

"What's going to happen to us all, Katherine?" the girl cried. "I don't want to stay at Westhorpe for the rest of my life! I want to be with my mother. . . ." Katherine clutched her friend's hand tightly. Though there was not quite five years' difference between them, Kate's vulnerability made Katherine feel old.

At last they were inside beautiful Suffolk House, gay now with court merriment. Usually it was empty because the French queen refused to live near the court and her husband remained almost constantly with the king. There were all the familiar "new people": Cromwell, Cranmer, Gardiner, the Boleyns, with a few sprinklings of the aristocratic old families who'd been her parents' and grandparents' friends. Thomas Cromwell moved easily through the throng, his plain black gown and cap replaced by a long cloak of bronze velvet trimmed with sable, his manner confident and obliging. A graying Charles Brandon enjoying his daughter's triumphant marriage shook the hand of a smiling Sir Thomas More after which, Katherine noted, the ex-Chancellor soon departed. At last they came to the French queen and, after curtseys and embraces, Katherine raised her wine cup to her mother's old friend and said, "May God bless this marriage, Your Grace. They seem a devoted couple."

"They will do well together, Kate. They are much alike. But I don't worry for Frances—she can take care of herself! It is these others that concern me for what they do to my brother." She gestured about the room. "Look at them—those vultures that surround Henry—they sicken me! Cromwell—even Henry calls him 'a knave'—and Cranmer, so slippery and eager to please. And that toady, Stephen Gardiner. Our father would have sent the lot to Tower Hill! Gardiner is a bishop, yet he works against the Pope, fawns all over the Boleyns and thinks because he keeps a woman in his house, every priest does too!"

Suddenly, a coughing spell gripped the woman, causing her delicate body to tremble even after the seizure had passed. Katherine noted the famed complexion which had earned Mary Tudor the endearing title of "the Tudor Rose" had faded to a pallid translucency. Even though she was swathed in furs and the day was mild, the French queen still shivered.

"Soon I will go on pilgrimage to Our Lady of Walsingham, my two Kates, and I ask your prayers for my health. After that I intend to stay at Westhorpe for good." As her husband approached, she smiled affectionately. Katherine noticed Charles Brandon's face was more lined than she remembered. Yet he was but forty-two, the same age as the king. The handsome courtier's fine black eyes, usually smiling and full of banter, appeared fatigued. Beside Brandon stood a radiant Anne Stanhope, recently married to Edward Seymour. Beaming, she curtsied to the French queen who, patting her companions on the shoulder, moved off with her husband to greet other guests. Aware she risked arousing Kate Willoughby's suspicions, Katherine asked after Anne's brother-in-law, Thomas Seymour.

"Ah, he is with his father at Wolf Hall," Anne explained, "the old gentleman is ill, Lady Borough, and one of the sons had to go. Edward, of course, was needed to help with the wedding." Out of Anne's sight, Kate grimaced and rolled her eyes heavenward, making a great effort at restraint. But Anne had no such thought.

"The king has made my husband a Squire of the Body. I'm sure you've heard, Lady Borough. Soon, I'm pleased to say, His Majesty will honor Edward with a viscountcy." The woman preened so flagrantly, Katherine wanted to slap her and then wondered why she was annoyed. Anne was intelligent, certainly beautiful and if she wished to behave with such unnecessary arrogance, she demeaned no one but herself.

But Kate, apparently, had had enough and not trusting to restraint too long, mumbled an excuse and joined the old Duchess of Norfolk who was watching the festivities from the sidelines. The dancing had commenced and, as Jane Seymour, looking somewhat downcast, danced by with her brother, Anne's husband, Katherine asked, "And how fares Mistress Jane's romance with Rob Dormer? The queen has said it would be a good match." And little thanks she'll get for such support, Katherine thought. All the Seymours now seemed eager to serve the king. So much for their vaunted sympathy for the queen!

Anne's handsome features flushed. Too late, Katherine realized she'd touched a sensitive nerve. "Ah, Lady Borough," her companion's eyes narrowed and she attempted a condescending smile, "the Dormers regard themselves too high it appears and have forbidden the match. It has caused my sister-in-law great heartache and her brothers swear they'll not forget this insult to the family honor! What can they be thinking?" Her eyes flashed angrily and Katherine knew Anne thought the comment had been made to humble. She knew she'd irked Madame Seymour and, though not intentional, was glad her question had found its mark.

Suddenly, Anne dropped a deep curtsey. Turning, Katherine saw the king himself, his face wreathed in a wide smile.

"My dear Lady Borough," Henry was jovial as he raised both ladies to their feet. "It has been a long time since we've seen you! Honor us with this dance, my lady!"

Before she could reply—and as she saw her companion bow her head and move away—Henry's strong arms encircled her and she was whirled to the center of the room as others moved back to give His Majesty space for twirling his partner, before lifting her high in the air to the music's quick tempo. When, at last, the minstrels changed to a quieter piece, Katherine glanced up at the man who held her so lightly. Henry was smiling happily, much at ease at the pleasant sight of his young partner. His auburn hair was still thick about his brow and shone in the light of hundreds of candles. The deep blue eyes, so like his sister's, were beaming with joy of the dance.

"You're as light as a feather, Kate, the same as your mother!" The king laughed again and, as the music swelled, circled his hands about her slim waist and lifted her high again, as the spectators applauded and stamped their feet to the clear sensual beat of the viols, lutes and rebecs.

"My mother always said dancing with Your Grace made her feel just like that—like a feather!" Katherine cried as the dance ended.

Henry acknowledged the compliment by signaling the musicians for another tune. As his tall frame moved easily through the intricate steps, Katherine felt the warmth of royal approval and, catching the spirit, deftly matched his every move, accepting each challenge of step and beat which the king could devise. Watching his partner's tiny feet follow his every move, Henry's spontaneous laughter rose above the music, filling the room. A magnetism flowed from his fingers to hers—an elusive pleasure she could no more prevent than she could refuse to follow his lead. She forgot how angry she'd been with this man for the way he'd treated his wife and daughter, for the dissension he'd caused at court and in the church. How could she have looked upon him almost as an enemy? It was pleasant to feel so gay and lighthearted! She gave herself up completely to the delight of the dance, the challenge of her partner and the applause of the spectators who shouted and cheered their approval.

When, at last, the music ended with a great fanfare, the king did not relinquish her at once. "You remind us so much of happier days with your parents, my dear," he said, his arm lightly about her waist. "You're still unpledged, Kate? What is that sober uncle of yours thinking?" As his companion's face flushed, he smiled again, noting her remarkable eyes, so like Lady Maud's, seemed suddenly wary. "Shall we find you a husband, Kate?" he teased. " 'Tis the least we could do, for we held your mother and father in great affection!"

"Sire," Katherine carefully kept her tone as light as the king's, "my good uncle has my future in mind. I am grateful for your concern. . . ." Already, she could see Henry's interest was waning as, over her shoulder he nodded to Anne Boleyn, who'd applauded his dance as loudly as the others. Anne Stanhope was standing nearby and she returned Katherine's glance with one of utter dislike. She's angry, Katherine thought, because she thinks the king should have danced with her. And she wonders if I asked after her sister-in-law to humble her. The intense hatred in the woman's eyes made Katherine shiver. She did not want Anne Stanhope Seymour as an enemy.

Suddenly, the king motioned a sensitive-faced man to his presence. As he knelt, Henry said, "Kate, this is Master Hans Holbein. He has made us many a pretty pageant at court and is now painting our portrait. Later, we will have other work for him. But for now," he turned to the young artist whose features were alight at the royal interest, "we charge you, Master Holbein, to draw this pretty face as well. We present to you, Kate Parr, Lady Borough, whose parents were dear to us. This is a face you should enjoy painting, my good Hans!" He smiled again, bowed to Katherine and, clapping Holbein on the back, moved into the crowd.

Holbein gazed at young Lady Borough and thought himself fortunate. As the king had said, he'd drawn other likenesses, many of which he had not enjoyed. It was his blessing—or his curse—to draw what he saw and often envy, dissipation, cruelty or cunning was too evident for all to see. Anne Boleyn had not cared for her portrait, although the king had been kind about it. But here was a face worthy of a crown itself.

Katherine, still dazed by the king's attention, smiled at the young artist's appreciative scrutiny. As her gaze met his, Holbein caught his breath. Already, he was mentally clothing her in a pastel sea-green damask to match those incredible eyes. Her skin would be a challenge but one to which he felt equal. He knew the portrait would take all his talent, but when it was finished, he knew the lady would be pleased.

And, as important, so would he.

CHAPTER IX

*Tell the queen that we do not want any of her goodbyes and have
no wish to afford her consolation. We do not care whether she asks
after our health or not. She has caused us no end of trouble and obstinately refused the reasonable request of our Privy Council. She
depends, we know, upon the emperor, but she will find God Almighty is more powerful still. Have her send no more messages. Let
her stop it and mind her own business.*
—Henry VIII to Queen Katherine, July 11, 1532, upon leaving her at
Windsor Castle without any final farewell

With the advent of spring and a recurrence of "the sweat," London
was soon deserted by the court. The king and a few close companions went
to Hunsdon in Worcestershire, the sturdy brick manor house, a seat of the
Duke of Norfolk, built during the reign of Henry VI. The duke's niece,
Anne Boleyn, returned to Hever Castle in Kent with her father, now the
Earl of Ormonde. And at Parr House, Sir William advised Katherine to
leave early for Kendal Castle and he would follow; her brother and sister
had fled to friends' homes in the countryside.

"You're the only one of Tom's children with any real love for the place,
Kate," her uncle said, "they'd be bored within a week." Remembering Kate
Willoughby's reluctance, despite her affection for the French queen, to
remain at Westhorpe for a prolonged period, she asked that the girl accompany her.

Within days, a joyful Kate danced into Katherine's chamber. "You saved
me from a dull pilgrimage to Walsingham!" she cried, flinging her arms
about her friend, "but, oh, Kate, the French queen is sick unto the death."
Kate's fine dark eyes, so like her mother's, filled with tears. "Her cough wors-
ens and the duke is wild with worry. He wants to be with his wife, but the
king demands his presence at the council table. And the duke wants to be
there because he says the king is like clay in the hands of Master Cromwell.
The French queen argues with the duke and says he is too biddable—that
he should tell the king he is following a knave."

"And the duke will not?"

"The duke will do nothing, Katherine. He says the king is his brother-in-law and best friend. He'll not oppose him for those who do so are as good as dead. He says he doesn't care to die for something he cannot help."

Remembering Charles Brandon's fatigued appearance at his daughter's nuptials, Katherine thought, for the hundredth time, how the Boleyn and Cromwell's association with the king was, in one way or another, affecting everyone. Even her portrait had been delayed because Anne insisted Holbein first paint her sister-in-law, Lady Rochford. "I can do nothing about it, my lady," the artist had shrugged when Katherine arrived at his Westminster studio. "I'm eager to commence your portrait and trust we can do so when you return to London in the fall."

Once at Kendal, Kate had quickly fallen into the pattern of Northern days, delighted to share with Katherine the demands of field and beast, the responsibility for a small cordon of servants and laborers whose families had served the Parrs for generations. For Kate, virtually homeless since her father's death and her mother's desire to remain with the queen, Kendal Castle was almost a fairyland.

They spent hours outdoors. Passing a field of daffodils and primroses, Kate impulsively gathered the flowers, urging her companion to hold out her skirt so she might take them back to her chamber. With a catch in her throat, Katherine remembered how often she and her mother had stopped to pluck the same bright blossoms. Kendal still bore happy memories of her parents. Their favorite horses were cosseted in the stables and the choice hawks and merlins Tom Parr had flown enjoyed a comfortable old age in the mews. When Kate, waving her arm in a broad sweep to encompass fields and castle, cried, "You're so lucky to have all this!" Katherine nodded. "Not just for its beauty, Kate," she whispered. "It's the place where I also feel closest to my mother and father."

The memories were all happy; Katherine was not saddened by their remembrance. Instead, she threw herself into her duties, delighting in instructing young Kate in making the scented potpourri and herbal remedies in the stillroom, in overseeing the fragrant bakery, buttery and brewhouse. The Parrs were popular with their tenant farmers and freeholders who took great pride in working the castle land. During the summer, Katherine invited her Borough stepchildren and Throckmorton relatives from Coughton Court, while other friends arrived from Szigerh Castle, keeping the chambers and lofts of old Kendal full.

One visiting family, the Askews from Stallingborough, arrived during midsummer bringing their daughter, Anne—the first time Katherine had seen the girl since they'd parted at Gainsborough over two years ago.

"I know I broke a promise and you never came to London," Katherine hugged her guest. "There was so much happening, Anne, and after my lady mother died, I had to learn to take her place! I kept thinking that soon I'd be back at Kendal and would see you then. But I never forgot you!"

Anne Askew had matured since the Gainsborough days. Though nearly twelve, she obviously cared little about her appearance, for her slim, pretty figure was hidden under nondescript clothing, while her curls, tightly plaited, were captive at last under a simple cap. A healthily pink complexion, that heritage of every Northern lass, was deeply tinged with olive, the result of hours in the saddle. High cheekbones accented Anne's golden-brown eyes which were now level with Katherine's own.

"I'm so glad to see you again, my lady," Anne whispered, her voice shaking with excitement. "I've never forgotten how kind you were to let me stay so long at Gainsborough. It's all right I didn't come to London! My lady mother always said you had other more important things on your mind. But now we can work together again, can't we, my lady?" Even as she impulsively hugged her hostess, Katherine felt a slight reprimand. How could Anne so easily make an adult feel like a wayward child?

After her guest had gone to her chamber, Lady Askew said, "Anne may be a bit taller, Lady Borough, but you'll find she hasn't changed. She's still always with her nose in a book, talking about theories and arguments that I cannot untangle and don't wish to hear! Gossip bores her and you can see she cares little about pretty clothing. She dresses herself with whatever comes first to hand! I despair of ever making a proper marriage for her!"

Later, alone with Bessie Bellingham, Katherine asked, "What is it that makes her so different? I love the child, Bess, but I trow there are times she makes me uncomfortable!"

"She's not unlike other Northern girls, Kate. Most have a lonely upbringing here because they live in remote parts of the country. She appears to have little in common with her brothers and sisters and you know her parents only tolerate her—they make no effort to understand her!" Bessie clasped Katherine's hand. "Through your teaching, she had contact with London and the court. You gave her books. How many of Anne's family or friends are as well read as you? Or, God knoweth, can even read at all? You opened up a whole new world for her!"

"I know, Bess, but she is a forward child and what I meant as a simple diversion, she's made into an obsession. I wish she'd think of something else instead of study. It's not natural! And it makes me uneasy. . . ."

In the following days, however, Anne Askew made it clear she meant to continue where she'd left off at Gainsborough. She spent hours in Maud Parr's library, poring over books, pamphlets and tracts on religion and politics, especially those Katherine had brought for her own summer reading. When her hostess suggested she ride with the Borough grandchildren or visit other families in the neighborhood for a day of simple pleasure, Anne only shook her head and waved Katherine away.

"Don't worry, Kate," Bessie consoled Katherine when her young guest was particularly trying. "The seeds were there. You've given her a few tools, that's all. She'll outgrow all this learning once she's wed. . . ."

Katherine wasn't so certain. She knew now, after her last year in London, that the "New Learning" had come to mean different things to different people. For her grandmother, Lady Elizabeth Parr, it had been a mental stimulation, a renewed interest in Greek, art and literature. Old Lady Margaret Beaufort, the terror of her childhood, had thought of a revolution in education, a challenging and rare opportunity for those who might learn. Both women had given their enthusiasm and zest for study to young Maud Green Parr who'd passed it on to her own daughter.

Katherine doubted if Margaret Beaufort, her grandmother or her mother had even considered this renaissance of thought in regard to religion. They'd hoped the springlike winds of learning might blow needed fresh air into the musty realms of science, philosophy and art. But Scripture was Scripture and would remain undefiled. Yet during the past year, Katherine had seen such seeking lead to a questioning of religious principles resulting in less reverence for the established Christian form and ritual. Was it possible such a challenge could diminish respect for religious order and authority?

In spite of herself, Katherine found much of the new religious thought stimulating and intriguing. Her faith was deep; observance of her religious commitment was a daily part of her life. But it confused and even dismayed her that she could be even mildly receptive to what, on the surface, appeared to be a rebellious opposition to established religious form. Yet why, she wondered, was it wrong to question someone else's religious philosophy?

Anne Askew was fond of quoting the Swiss reformer, Zwingli, who'd rejected the Pope and church hierarchy, stating the Bible was the only spiritual authority the common man needed. Scathingly, Zwingli had cited abuses in the papacy and church and called for a spiritual cleansing in religion.

"He would restore the church to the primitive faith and authority of the ancient church fathers," Anne told Katherine earnestly. "You remember, my lady, that Savonarola preached that only Christ should be king in the hearts and minds of people and not the petty opportunists—which many of our churchmen are!—for they use fear to impress the ignorant so they might gain for themselves!"

"Yes, I remember, Anne, and what happened to him?" Katherine replied dryly. "He was burnt at the stake and his ashes thrown into the Arno! You work that clever brain too hard, my dear. There's more to life than arguing and disputing—which you do very easily and expertly. But where is it all going to lead? You should be thinking of pretty clothes and a new way to do your beautiful hair so you wouldn't have to hide it underneath a cap. You should make more friends! Books and study are wonderful but they are cold comfort when you want to talk to someone! And aren't you interested in the marriage your good father will arrange for you someday?"

"I shall never wed," Anne's tone was determined. "I am called to do a work and I shall do it. When I am old enough, I will go to London and I hope you'll let me live with you, Lady Borough. But whether you do or not, I shall see London one day!"

Abashed, Katherine could only answer it must all come with time and Anne's parents' consent.

When news reached Kendal that old Warham, the Archbishop of Canterbury, had died and the king had appointed Anne Boleyn's chaplain, Thomas Cranmer, as his successor, Anne seemed to know more about court affairs than Katherine thought possible. When Sir William Parr said at the evening meal that the king would now have little trouble with his divorce since his mistress' chaplain was its highest official, Anne answered tightly. "And why not? Why should our king—or anyone else?—pay monies and tribute to the Pope? He lives a life of sin like any other man, not as one appointed to be the Vicar of Christ on earth! The church must be cleansed of such hypocrisy, sir, and spend its time and money for the poor and suffering as Jesus did." Turning to Katherine, she asked, "You remember, my lady, what Luther said . . . ?"

Katherine did, indeed, remember what Luther said. She, herself, had given the German ex-monk's writings to little Anne almost three years ago. Then it had all seemed so simple. Idealistically, she herself had responded to Luther's purpose, if not his methods. But now, aware of her uncle's patience in not chastising Anne, she recognized the true consequence of Luther's philosophy. It was all happening in England—setting king against church, church against would-be reformers or protesters, family against family and king against queen. With a princess and a mistress caught in the middle.

* * *

During her summer at Kendal Castle, Katherine felt her family's pressure to wed again. "It's better that you do, Kate," her stepson, Henry Borough, advised, when she sought to make light of his concern. "It's unnatural you should remain a widow. Your cousin Tunstall must find you a husband. Shall I speak to him?"

"My cousin Tunstall has already spoken to me." Katherine hoped her impatience was not evident. Several times during the past year, the bishop had mentioned likely candidates for wedlock and each time, Katherine had found it difficult—as she now found it impossible—to tell her stepson that she relished her orderly life, its freedom for study, for friends and spending her time as she wished. "I'm aware of his concern and yours, Henry. . . ."

William Parr was another who wished to see his niece wed. Considering the vast Borough and Parr lands which were hers by marriage and inheritance, her continued widowhood was intolerable. Such sizable holdings, he intimated, should be used to acquire even more property and income in a marriage that would bring honor to all! Privately, he thought any wealthy, beautiful, green-eyed widow fluttering about London and the court, only invited those gentlemen with impressive names and empty purses who sought out the vulnerable. He knew his niece to be levelheaded and sensible and, thankfully, her interest in young Tom Seymour seemed to have waned. But there were still many unsavory ones at court waiting to take advantage of the naïve.

Katherine was often depressed by the news visitors to Kendal brought

from the court. The queen, now confined at Ampthill had been refused any
visits from her daughter, Mary, who'd been ordered to Woburn Abbey.
Charles Brandon wrote her uncle:

> What my wife heard from the court makes her heartsick. I don't tell
> her half of what I know. She remains at Westhorpe, away from it
> all. There is still much public support for the queen and princess.
> This only makes Henry angrier and more determined to keep them
> apart. My wife would like to see them, but knows it will only make
> it worse for them if she does. We sent Mary books and when my
> steward returned from Woburn, he said whenever she appears in
> public, she is cheered by the people. When the king heard of this,
> he was enraged. So now Mary makes fewer outings.

Remembering the princess' passion for coursing with her greyhounds or
walking the miles of wooded paths outside Westminster's gates, Katherine
could only guess what this had cost her friend. She wasn't surprised by later
news that Mary had long bouts of depression and melancholy and suffered
debilitating headaches as well as great pain with her teeth.

Brandon also said that many influential courtiers had chosen to remain
away from London, hoping not to endanger their lands, wealth, castles and
titles by being forced to choose sides. While they all lamented the queen's
deplorable condition—and were sympathetic to the princess—they sensibly
admitted there was little they could do to change their circumstances. All of
which only further convinced William Parr that his niece should be in a
more settled position.

One day, as she discussed her uncle's attitude with Kate Willoughby,
Katherine was amused at her friend's reaction. "No one pays any attention to
a match for me!" Kate cried with an unusual petulance. "With my lady
mother staying with the queen and the French queen so ill, I'm not liable to
be contracted for and I'm almost fourteen! I suppose the duke will be the one
to seek for me as I am his ward. But I'm certain no one at court will want to
wed with a family so close to the queen! Shall we become spinsters together, Kate, you and I?"

"And Anne, too," Katherine motioned to the Askew girl, quietly studying
in a corner. "Remember, she says she'll never marry!" Anne, absorbed in her
reading, did not reply.

At the close of her Kendal summer, Sir William again discussed Katherine's future. "I promise to think upon your words, uncle, and I shall be
guided by what you do. But next time I would like to wed as my heart tells
me."

"And when your heart tells you, Kate," William Parr smiled, "you must
tell me, too! Edward Seymour writes the Boleyn has been made a marchioness! Her goal, I promise you, is the throne! God knows what we'll find in
London!"

Any mention of the Seymours always brought Thomas Seymour vividly to mind. Katherine wondered at her feelings for she hardly knew the man. Yet he'd impressed her as few had. When visitors from court mentioned that he still spent much time abroad, she pretended little interest. It was all so new and puzzling—this eagerness to find out everything she could about a man she might not see again for months or years.

Yet she listened, wondering if she dared ask why he'd never married.

At last the tingle of cool dry weather, the withering of leaves and the harvest celebration signaled the end of another magical Kendal summer. Lady Askew arrived to take a tearful and reluctant Anne Askew, laden with books and gifts, back to Stallingborough. Later, Katherine and Kate rode among the Parr tenants to say goodbye, taking samples of their jellies and comfits, warm woolen clothing for the winter ahead and, always, a small embroidered gift for each new baby born on castle lands that summer. Once more the wagons were packed, the carts loaded and preparations made for the long journey south. But at the last moment, Sir William Parr announced he must again visit their cousin Tunstall at Durham. In his place, John Neville, Lord Latimer, had kindly offered to escort his niece home. Latimer was a relative of Katherine's Borough stepdaughter-in-law and was returning to his Charterhouse home for the sitting of Parliament.

Katherine was disturbed. She'd told Kate Willoughby—permission or no permission—that she meant to see Princess Mary on her way home. It would be easy, she said, as they enjoyed friends' hospitality, to evade her uncle for a few hours and visit with Mary at Woburn, before anyone became concerned at her absence. But how could she do that with a man she barely knew overseeing her safety?

Katherine also knew her uncle had little real reason to visit Durham and was deliberately pairing her with Lord Latimer. But, as Bess suggested, possibly someone as impressive as Latimer might be helpful. Katherine had always liked John Neville. The tall, sandy-haired man was forty-three and twice a widower. His last wife, by whom he'd had two children, had been dead five years. When Katherine asked why he hadn't married again, William Parr replied that every widow in the North as well as London had set her cap for the attractive Yorkshireman. Latimer was immensely wealthy with lands in Yorkshire, Richmondshire and several manors nearer London. Obviously, her uncle said, there was little need to marry for land or money and he'd chosen to remain single for reasons of his own.

"Look kindly on the man, Kate," he whispered on the day of their departure, "you can't stay unwed forever. John Neville is a gentle and pious man and very well regarded in the North and at court. It would be a fitting match. . . ."

Riding beside him, with Kate and Bessie just behind, Katherine found Lord Latimer easy to be with. He spoke with a familiar and endearingly rich Yorkshire dialect. His love for his home, Snape Hall in Yorkshire, and his other lands and manors was evident.

"But I avoid London like the plague—especially when there *is* a plague!"

he smiled at his young companion. "I'm a Northerner, Lady Borough. I like the old ways and customs. This 'New Learning' or whatever it is called and which everyone at court speaks of has caused more trouble than good! And I like the honesty of our Northern people—their loyalty to each other and their lack of greed. . . ." He sighed. "London is too filthy and the court makes me uncomfortable. My father was the same. He served the old king faithfully, but could scarcely wait to return home. We Northerners are not easily transplanted!"

At last, on the final day of their journey as they neared Woburn Abbey, Katherine confided her desire to see Princess Mary. "You must help me, my lord," she touched her companion's arm. "The princess is an old and dear friend and isn't well. If I don't see her before we get to London, I may not have another opportunity. Will you do so, my lord?"

John Neville looked at the deepest green eyes he'd ever seen and felt the stirring of feelings he'd thought gone forever. Had he been more articulate, he might have called Lady Borough winsome and appealing, even beguiling. But few Northerners were eloquent; blunt honesty usually sufficed. Now he wondered at his own forwardness in wanting to involve himself in something better left alone.

Helpless, he placed a hand on Katherine's and nodded. Though he also knew Princess Mary and the queen as well, it would never have occurred to him to go against the royal command forbidding visitors. But how could he deny this beautiful young lady looking for help and with every expectation that he'd not fail her?

For the next half hour, they made plans. Kate Willoughby was brought into the conspiracy and, as the vast pile of Woburn Abbey appeared on the horizon, Katherine disappeared into Bessie's litter, emerging a short time later, dressed in one of her companion's simpler day garments, a gray wool devoid of adornment or embroidery, with only a long white scarf about the neck. She'd wound a large kerchief about her head and removed her jewels, the good gloves and sensible shoes she always wore on a long journey. The beautiful Lady Borough of the exquisite furred and velvet riding dress had disappeared and in her place was only a simple lass, perhaps a maid to one of the great ladies of the court.

Within moments, a Latimer steward rang the abbey bell at the gate and, almost at once, a monk appeared. Lord Latimer explained a lady traveling south in his company had suddenly become ill. Would one of the good brothers—an apothecary perhaps—help?

The monk nodded kindly and without further ado motioned his visitor through the gate. Kate Willoughby, dressed in Katherine's clothing, lay silently in the litter, her arm across her face so her features were partly hidden. Quickly, the Latimer and Borough stewards dismounted, the grooms taking the horses to the stables, while other monks were summoned to provide light refreshments for the distinguished Lord Latimer. In all the activity, no one noticed as a slim girl, dressed in gray wool, quickly disengaged herself from the others. "God speed you well, Kate," Bessie whispered, as her companion disappeared around the abbey wall.

Katherine knew Woburn well for the Parr family had often stayed there on their way north. One special house was set apart from the monks' quarters for important visitors or royalty. If Mary was at Woburn, there was no other place for her to be. Katherine prayed the princess was still there and all the pretense she and Lord Latimer shared would not be in vain.

She was encouraged by the activity about the house. A few women walked in the garden while others sat with their needlework in the shade. Several dogs ran free and, as one loped toward her, Katherine held her breath, opening her arms to still any barking. The animal licked her hands and face and then ran happily alongside her as she sped toward the arbor at the end of a long pleached alley. Katherine's heart bounded at the sight of Margaret Pole, the Countess of Salisbury, sitting on a bench near the entrance. If the countess was at Woburn, so was Mary Tudor. She came upon the woman lightly, waiting for her to look up from her sewing as the dog sat watching the two with a cocked head.

"Katherine!" The countess' long Plantagenet features were incredulous. She dropped her work to the ground as she rose, embracing the girl tightly. "Jesu, child, you gave me a turn! How did you manage this? Do you come from the court? Is there anything wrong with the queen?" She looked at Katherine's simple gown. "And where did you get that dress?"

Close to tears with relief, Katherine explained, stressing she must not linger long or she'd worry Lord Latimer. And how long could Kate pretend illness?

Immediately, the countess understood. She clasped Katherine's hands crying, "Come at once, child. Oh, Mary will be so happy to see you!"

They found the princess at her desk. "Mary, here is a visitor," the countess spoke softly and then quietly closed the chamber door behind her.

Mary turned, at first not recognizing the visitor with her head so severely bound. Katherine curtsied and then, unable to hold back her laughter, plucked the kerchief from her head. "Mary—'tis I, Kate!" she cried.

"Kate!" Mary flung down her pen and ran to hug her friend tightly. "Oh, Kate, what good fortune brings you to Woburn? Do you know you're the first visitor I've seen in months? How did you get in? You look so well!" She held Katherine off, looking at her intently, "And where did you get that dress?"

Almost breathless from shock at seeing her old friend, Mary's voice shook. But there was more than just excitement at greeting a visitor; the princess' emotions were raw. Tears lingered just behind her eyes and in the tremulous tone of her voice. With trembling hands, she guided Katherine, who quickly explained the situation, to the one remaining chair in the simply furnished room. It was not a room the king or queen—or even her own mother—would have been given on a visit to Woburn.

Mary saw the question in Katherine's eyes. "My room is as simple as your

gown, Kate, but not for the same reason. The good monks have been ordered
to keep me this way, although they mislike what they do and they tell me so.
The king has told the Pope his place is in hell and soon he will wed that
woman. I do believe no one quite knows what to do with me—even the emperor and the French king seem to have deserted my lady mother and me!
And, in the meantime, Woburn is where I am to stay. . . ." At which the
sixteen-year-old princess' control vanished and the tears came freely. Kate
put her arms about Mary's shaking shoulders as the girl described what had
happened.

It was not a pretty tale. Privation. Not real hardship, Mary stressed, blowing her nose. But deprivation of things which meant something to a princess: proper clothing, attendants and sympathetic guardians. "Only my Lady
Salisbury and Susan Clarencieux are true friends, Kate," she said, "the rest
are all spies, reporting to that woman or Master Cromwell." Mary said she
yearned for some semblance of normalcy when she'd not be awakened in the
middle of the night and ordered to a new dwelling. Above all, she wanted
an acknowledgment of her position as the king's legitimate daughter, with
access to her mother who was ill and depressed.

Mary rustled amongst the papers on the desk. "Here is a letter from my
lady mother, Kate. Listen to what she has written:

". . . and an emissary came from the king and said I must render
my jewels to him, that they did not belong to me. I told the king's
messenger I would not give one jewel until the king, himself, wrote
asking for them. The messenger told my chamberlain, Jorge, that
the lady is to be made a marchioness and wants to wear the jewels
at the ceremony. How I fear for your father's soul, Mary, that he
should submit to such an influence and treat his wife and daughter
in such a cruel way!"

Katherine rose and embraced Mary. "Jesu, how much longer must this go
on? This summer at Kendal, a messenger said the king was keeping you
from your mother because he felt if you were together you might plot against
him. And your father was frank to say you had enough support to cause
trouble!"

"I've heard the same rumor, Kate, but you know my mother would never
oppose my father! Nor would I—we plot only for justice! How much longer
can my mother stand such persecution?"

Suddenly the door opened and the countess, with Susan Clarencieux,
called out. "Come quickly, Kate!" Her face was ashen. "I've sent the others
to an early Mass. You must join your escort while they are in the abbey
church. You were not seen coming in—it would not do for you to be seen
going out!"

Wordlessly, Katherine embraced Mary once more and, touching the wide-
eyed Susan and countess affectionately, sped through the doorway. Down
the long corridor she ran toward the nearest entrance and, emerging into the

sunlit courtyard, saw the countess' companions entering the church. John Neville, waiting patiently, was already astride his horse. He looked at her inquiringly and motioned toward the litter nearby, its curtains still drawn.

"Our sick friend is better," he smiled. "The apothecary says Lady Borough has a bit of the ague. Nothing which should worry us and we can proceed now." The words were as much a question as a statement.

Relief flooded Katherine as she watched the old church door close upon the last of Mary's household. Now no enemy would know of her visit. She knew that without John Neville's help, she probably would not have seen the princess. The monks would have been too fearful and asked permission of those sent by the king.

Respect and admiration for her companion mingled with her relief. Others, more fearful of royal retaliation, might not have been so eager to help. Yet John Neville hadn't hesitated. He reached over now as she prepared to join Bessie in the litter and patted her shoulder encouragingly. "We'll talk about it later," he whispered, "we must be on the road now."

Katherine reached up and took his hand, pressing it gently in response. Her heart was still pounding from her flight down the long hall, yet she felt very protected by this tall, kindly Northerner. Suddenly, she was glad John Neville was to be in London, too. He was her friend, as well as the queen's and Princess Mary's. She watched now as he raised his hand, signaling the many wagons and carts behind him to fall in line. He was someone she could depend upon, much as she relied on her uncle or cousin Tunstall.

"Thank you, my lord," Katherine pressed his hand again. "Yes, we will talk later." And then, eager to tell Bessie and Kate of her visit with Mary, she opened the litter curtains and disappeared inside.

CHAPTER X

In London, Katherine learned from her sister, Ann Parr, of the impressive ceremony held at Windsor Castle by which Anne Boleyn became the Marchioness of Pembroke. Though the Duke of Suffolk had been prominent during the festivities, his wife, the French queen, had remained at Westhorpe. Their daughter, Frances Brandon Grey, arrived at the last moment because, said Ann, she was furious Anne Boleyn would now take precedence over her at court ceremonies. Thomas Cromwell, the king's minister, had convinced the king's niece it would be only sensible to appear.

As Ann chattered on about news of the court, Katherine asked if there was any hope the queen and Princess Mary might be allowed to see one another.

"Not until the Spanish woman acknowledges her marriage was illegal, until she agrees to forsake her title and be called the 'Princess-Dowager,'" Anne replied.

"Then they'll be apart until death unites them," Katherine was angry. "You have so little pity, Ann! Don't you know if the queen does as you say, she makes her daughter a bastard? Can't you find it in your heart to understand their position and have some sympathy?"

"I understand they are obstinate, if not stupid." Ann, like her formidable grandmother, Lady Elizabeth Parr, rarely minced words. "It's time they realized they have nothing to gain, only a great deal to lose. The Spanish woman is ill and God in His infinite mercy may be kind and soon put an end to her unhappiness. But my lady Mary has much to learn! I can pity them, yes, but there's nothing I or anyone else can do about it, Kate! You'll do well to remember that before you return to court."

"I have little desire to be there, Ann. And I'm afraid there are many—including your new marchioness—who know where my loyalty is. They'd be just as happy not to receive me."

As Ann made ready to leave, she said, "It's rumored my lady Anne is pregnant, Kate, but you must keep that quiet. Even I'm not supposed to know! Lady Rochford, her sister-in-law, tattled that the marchioness has been acting very queerly lately. You remember how smug that woman is! She must know everything and then can't wait to tell it!" Ann embraced her sister, giving her a little shake. "Now don't be as obstinate as the queen and as stupid as Mary," she whispered, "come back to court. You know how highly the king regards you! When you stay away, people spread rumors and it jeopardizes us all. Don't put yourself in such a position for something you can't help. Believe me, Kate, the king and his lady *will* wed!"

Alone after Ann left, Katherine pondered her sister's words. Secrets, gossip, power plays—all compounded by envy, greed and ambition—how easy it would be to become so involved that one's life and property might be endangered. Everything had changed so much. There were people about the court now with whom she suspected her parents might have been uncomfortable. The king and his lady caused the Duke of Suffolk to remain away from his wife, kept Kate Willoughby from her mother and the princess from the queen. Henry's new title, "Supreme Head of the Church" had caused debate, resentment—even a tart, rancorous humor—throughout the land. And now, possibly, Anne Boleyn was pregnant. If so, Katherine realized there would be little pity for anyone who stood in the way of her marriage.

The more she dwelt on the subject, the more angry and depressed she became, vowing again to remain away from court. But a visit to Chartreuse, Lord Latimer's London home, changed her mind.

Her uncle brought John Neville's invitation to visit his home so that Katherine might advise him on a refurbishing of the Long Gallery, neglected since his wife's death. He also wished her to see new plantings from the Continent for the garden next to the Charterhouse, the old Carthusian monastery next door. Recalling the man's kindness at Woburn, Katherine was pleased to accept.

"Latimer's been widowed for so long, he says his house is in great disrepair for his steward has been lax," William Parr explained as he and Katherine, on matched bays, rode up Ludgate Hill toward Smithfield. "But you and I don't play games, Kate. You know Latimer is looking for an excuse to see you again. I think he's quite surprised at himself—he's been a widower so long. Look kindly on the man, my dear. He's lonely—and you can't remain unwed forever!"

Lord Latimer was at the door of the handsome ivy-covered red brick house. "Welcome to Chartreuse, Lady Borough," he exclaimed warmly, taking her hand in his, a broad smile of welcome on his face. Obviously he'd been awaiting their arrival, not trusting a servant to be on duty.

"A lovely home, my lord," Katherine curtsied as her uncle relinquished their horses to a groom and hurried forth to greet his host.

"When my father died, I discovered 'Chartreuse' was the original name for this land," Lord Latimer explained as he led his guests inside, "but our noble English tongue found that difficult, so it became the 'Charterhouse.'" Katherine paused at the garden entrance where life-size statues of Roman emperors graced the walks set between hedges of privet and whitethorn. A burst of scarlet color from roses climbing a trellised arbor was a blurred rainbow-like prism seen through the pink marble fountain's spray. "This whole area," Latimer continued, "was once a pesthole. Several hundred years ago, it belonged to the Carthusians next door. It was called 'Pardon Churchyard' because criminals and even plague victims were later buried here." As the sound of the monastery's chimes floated over the adjoining wall, he smiled, "But, as you see, it is now a place of peace."

Entering the house, Latimer suggested they have refreshments with other guests before seeing the Long Gallery. Katherine put her hand on his as he escorted her into the main hall where guests, some seated at long tables, were being served by servants clad in the Latimer colors of brown, cream and tawny. Others stood in small groups, drinking wine from silver goblets.

Nodding to several acquaintances, Katherine heard her name. "Lady Borough! What great luck! It is such a pleasure to see you again, my lady!" Thomas Seymour, his strong features alight with welcome, held out his hands. A new short beard and mustache gave him a more mature look than Katherine remembered; their blackness accented his tanned skin and strong white teeth. He exuded confidence and good humor and, though the room was crowded, his smile seemed only for her. Beside him, the stocky figure of the king's sergeant-painter, Hans Holbein, clad in a simple russet gown, seemed out of place.

Again Katherine felt the impact of Thomas Seymour's forceful personality. In his black and white doublet, a cap with its long creamy plume tucked beneath his arm, he dominated the room with a quiet elegance. As Latimer relinquished his hold, Seymour caught her hands in his. "It has been a long time, Lady Borough. I've looked for you at court on the few occasions I've been home and always you seem to be in the North or visiting relatives in the countryside. My sister Jane has brought me here today for Master Holbein is to paint her portrait at my Lady Anne's request."

Katherine sought the poise which always deserted her in Seymour's presence. The man was plainly delighted, relishing the unexpected meeting. As his vibrant, dark-eyed gaze held hers, she was pleased she'd dressed with care, choosing a gown of deep blue velvet, its sleeves slashed in rose-pink damask. Several pieces of her mother's simple jewelry were wound about her neck and Bessie had swept the back of her auburn hair into a shining coil, covered with a delicate net, into which small gems had been sewn.

She felt a deep flush rising to her face. Suddenly, her heart and pulse were racing. She hoped her hands, which Seymour kept clasped in his, were not trembling. Attempting to match his easy spontaneity, her voice wavered. The artist rescued her.

"I'm indeed honored to paint Mistress Seymour and Lord Latimer has been kind to let us use a chamber here for the sitting. When it is finished, my lady, I hope to start your portrait! You remember the king requested it?"

"I haven't forgotten, Master Holbein, and I promise to come soon." Katherine's voice sounded far away and, though Lord Latimer and her uncle were waiting patiently, she was reluctant to leave. "You've been away, Master Seymour?"

"I'm always away, my lady. The king's business is everywhere! Yet I'm not complaining. It is interesting abroad. Our painter friend here—who has also traveled a good deal—can testify to that, eh, Holbein?" As the artist laughed, Seymour pressed Katherine's hands again. "You're very much missed at court, Lady Borough." He bowed once more. "I see I'm keeping you from our good friend Latimer. But I trust to see you soon. . . ." Katherine returned his bow and followed her host and uncle toward a table for refreshments.

Later, as she admired the gallery—its long spaciousness and the two massive stone fireplaces blackened from centuries of use—the image of Thomas Seymour kept recurring. Katherine admitted the pargeted ceiling certainly needed attention; it was flaking and cracked in spots. She agreed, even as Seymour's resonant tones reverberated in her memory, that a thorough cleaning of the old Flemish tapestries might help, as would a good polishing of the impressive silver collection that graced the sideboard. A glazier should see to the dusty spotty windows, and perhaps a touching-up of the gilt on the embossed carvings around the doorways and windows was needed. A general refreshing of the handsome velvet-covered chairs and benches would make a world of difference she suggested and, warming to her talk, advised that Turkey carpets, now much in vogue with those who could afford them, would lend warmth and color at the gallery's northern end.

And all the while the evanescent charm of Thomas Seymour lingered. Her hand still tingled with his touch; she felt warmed at recalling the appreciative light in his eyes. He'd been as happy to see her as she'd been to meet him. No one had ever stirred her as deeply. When Lord Latimer clasped her hand, she felt his eagerness, that was all. And the one thing she recalled about her husband's touch was that it had been kind. What was it about Seymour that made him so different?

As she rode home with her uncle—who was so pleased with the day he'd said nothing about Seymour—Katherine wondered if Thomas was right. Already, Ann Parr had said how foolish she'd be to remain away from court. Over a period of time her absence would be noted. Would it hurt to be polite to the Boleyn? She wasn't queen yet! Why not be pleasant to the king who'd been so fond of her parents he'd asked the most famous artist in London to paint her portrait? Henry meant to be kind. What good did it do to sit alone at Parr House and let what she saw as a great injustice fester within?

Bidding her uncle goodbye at the courtyard of her home, she ran inside to talk to Bessie. Already, her mind was made up. Ann Parr was right. To absent herself from court would serve no purpose nor would it help the queen or Princess Mary. Everyone—her sister, brother and uncle—seemed to be facing up to the royal situation. Why shouldn't she?

* * *

In the following months, John Neville, Lord Latimer, allowed nothing to hinder his courtship of Katherine Parr. "The man is smitten, such as I'd never have believed!" William Parr told his niece with a satisfied chuckle.

"It would be well for him, Kate, if you put him out of his misery, marry him quickly, and go north with him in the spring!"

But Katherine would not commit herself. It had been something of an embarrassment, as she attended festive masques at Whitehall or Greenwich, or joined friends in the royal barge for river fêtes or rode out the courtyard of the new St. James's Palace for an early morning hunt, to realize she'd momentarily forgotten the searing anguish of the queen for whom she'd been named and the heartbreak of a princess who was her closest friend. Then, passing the life-sized King's Beasts—those painted mythological animals that graced the green turf of Whitehall's gardens like giant chess figures—some remembrance of Mary's conversation or the queen's voice would remind her of their misery and, penitent, she'd flee to Parr House.

"Don't feel guilty about enjoying yourself, Kate! You're still very young and, God knoweth, there hasn't been much gaiety in your life," Bessie solaced her companion.

As Ann Parr had predicted, Anne Boleyn was, indeed, pregnant. Proudly so. At court, she'd welcomed Katherine warmly, saying how fond she was of her sister. "We will make a good marriage for her, Lady Borough," she told Katherine, who wondered at the woman's ease in using the royal "we."

It wasn't long before the entire court had the answer. Already it appeared, Anne *was* a queen. Earlier that year, on St. Paul's Day, January 25, 1533, she and the king had been married in a western turret of Whitehall with Dr. Rowland Lee officiating. Only the bride's immediate family, the Duke of Suffolk and Henry Norreys, a close friend of the king, had witnessed the ceremony. Everyone was sworn to secrecy for the papal bulls—by which Thomas Cranmer would be made Archbishop of Canterbury and thus in a position to free Henry from his stubborn Spanish wife—had not arrived in England. By early spring, however, couriers from Rome finally brought the fateful bulls and the archbishop was duly appointed. His first official act was to pronounce Katherine of Aragon's marriage illegal and Henry's union with the Marchioness of Pembroke good and valid.

At Chartreuse, when Katherine spoke of her fear for Princess Mary, Lord Latimer attempted to explain the political and religious implications of the king's divorce and remarriage.

"She'll not have an easy time of it, our princess, for she's as proud as her mother," Lord Latimer said quietly. "And everyone—Cromwell, Cranmer and the new queen—have vowed to break her spirit, to make her accept that she's no longer the king's heir. For Mary, this will be impossible! The Countess of Salisbury told Norfolk—who was here at Chartreuse yesterday after the council meeting—that the girl is in delicate health. She has trouble keeping her food down and is plagued with headaches so strong that at times she's almost blind! I don't think she's seen anyone, my dear, since you saw her at Woburn and that was months ago! Even the king still refuses to see her until she accepts and acknowledges her mother is not the queen."

"Then Mary has seen the last of her father," Katherine whispered tearfully. "She'll never compromise her position or degrade her mother. Oh, my lord, what will happen to her? She's only seventeen and has her whole life before her!"

Latimer put an arm about Katherine's shoulders and she sensed he'd like to embrace her. She felt the comforting warmth of his touch, but that was all. "You're good to understand, my lord," she said, wiping away a tear as she gently disengaged herself. It would hardly be fair to encourage this man whom she'd come to cherish as a friend. She was unhappy enough with the events at court without embroiling herself in a relationship for which she had no heart.

* * *

As the warm summer months passed, all England awaited the birth of the royal child. At court, Anne Boleyn cradled her stomach, remarking upon "the royal imp" who would soon make his parents' life complete. Lady-in-waiting Ann Parr worried that the years of waiting to be queen had exacted their price for, at times, her royal mistress was moody and tense, preferring the company of her sister, Mary Boleyn Carey. When she ordered them away, Ann and several companions often rode to Parr House. Obviously bored with the absence of masques, gambling and the hunt, with no countryside excursions or river fêtes, the girls laughed merrily at Katherine's suggestion that they spend their quiet waiting time reading or studying. She offered them several of her new books from the Continent, suggesting they read the writings of a new scholar, John Calvin, the great friend of Erasmus, Ulrich Zwingli or even the challenging preaching of Martin Luther.

Seeing the blank look on their faces, she changed the subject. Did her sister and friends think of nothing but pleasure? They'd all been taught to read, but did they ever do so?

Katherine spent many a satisfying hour in the Parr House garden with her books and writing tablet, tantalized by the provocative words of those reformers who protested or challenged the basic tenets of her faith. Often, contemplating the great cross of the Blackfriars monastery next door, she crossed herself as the pure golden chimes floated over wall and river, signaling the bells of other City churches to peal also. She was there one midsummer day when, following a great commotion in her courtyard, Lord Latimer strode into the garden accompanied by a young lady. It wasn't until the visitor ran toward her crying, "My lady! My lady!" that she recognized Anne Askew, her eyes bright with happy tears.

"Anne! What a great surprise!" Katherine hugged her, pleased at the sight of the almost statuesque girl in her somber traveling cloak of Kendal green cloth. A matching feathered cap atop her neatly dressed red hair, provided a perfect frame for the flushed and shining face. Anne's skin was still as freckled as ever and the large golden-brown eyes with their light reddish lashes had a look of maturity Katherine had not seen before.

"Oh, my lady, I'm so happy to be here with you at last!" As Lord Latimer beamed, she clung to Katherine, as if still not believing her good fortune.

Later, after an astonished Bessie had taken Anne to her chamber, Latimer explained. "I didn't think you'd mind, Katherine. The girl was so eager to be with you. She said—and her family agreed—that you'd promised to have her visit you in London. She was bereft that you hadn't sent for her before. If her visit is inconvenient, I'll take her to Chartreuse, of course." Accepting the wine his hostess handed him, he remarked, "She's a little firebrand, however. I think her parents were relieved to have her go! She's been 'gospeling' as some call it in the North, in the neighborhood churches and has greatly distressed her family. She's old enough to wed, but her father thinks her behavior has spoiled any chance of a good marriage. That's one reason she wanted to leave. She says she'll never marry!"

Katherine laughed, excited at Anne's appearance and delighted Latimer was home again. "I'm glad she came, John, for I did promise her a long time ago that she could visit London, though I suspect she'll live in the bookstalls at Paternoster Row. We'll have to be certain she doesn't confront the archbishop at Lambeth or the king at Whitehall with her convictions! I tell her she's but a young girl and should listen to her elders who have more authority and knowledge. Yet I know—and so does she—that few of our elders have studied as much as she."

"I can't imagine her listening to anyone—except perhaps you, Katherine," Latimer answered. "Do you know she was so eager to be here with you we stayed on the road a little longer each day and arrived almost half a day earlier than usual? Are you certain you don't mind her being here? I don't think she ever plans to return home. You must know, she worships you, my dear." Latimer cleared his throat as Katherine gazed at him fondly. "She's not the only one—you know that. You won't think upon my suit?"

Katherine pressed his hand. "My lord, you know with what great respect I look upon you. But I'm not ready for another marriage. My family wants me to wed again, but I'm too troubled in other ways to be a good wife. Let me wait a bit longer, John." She was grateful Latimer didn't urge further. It was one of the things she admired most about the gentle Northerner.

A servant arrived to escort him to the door. "Enjoy your guest, my dear. I hope she doesn't wear you out!" As Katherine rose from her curtsey, Latimer put an arm about her and kissed her briefly on the forehead. "Bring her to Chartreuse soon and we'll let Prior Houghton from the monastery next door put a few things to right in her head."

Suddenly, the door burst open and her sister Ann, white-faced and distraught, rushed into the room, a piece of paper clutched in her hand.

"The queen—the queen—she's dead!" Katherine felt an icy faintness enveloping her as Latimer rushed forward to take the message. "It's Mary, the French queen," he said sadly, "she's gone. Well, God rest her soul." All three quietly crossed themselves. "She died in her bed, with Brandon and

Kate Willoughby at her side. The message is from Joan Guildford who was visiting Westhorpe at the time. I'm certain by now the king and everyone else knows." He glanced at his hostess. "Katherine, are you all right?"

Katherine had turned aside, her eyes brimming, as grief clutched at her heart. Suddenly, her mind filled with the many images of Mary, the "Tudor Rose." It was the French queen who'd always listened to childish confidences or fears, had remembered their birthdays and brought thoughtful gifts from her travels. She'd praised their schoolroom efforts, never scolding, admitting freely that learning for itself had little meaning for her. She'd laughed away its lack and become, in the process, more warm and loving than anyone Katherine had ever known, except Maud Parr. Her beauty, in a court where physical attractiveness and fashionable dress were highly prized, had shone with the quick pure gleam of the almost translucent colors she favored. Swathed in furs, smart boots and supple, richly embroidered gloves, the French queen had been the epitome of elegance, beauty, amiability and love.

And now she was gone.

The remembered pain of her mother's death caused great wrenching sobs to tear at Katherine as Latimer led her to a chair. "The queen and princess will be devastated, Ann," she whispered, "have they been told? Did anyone realize how ill she really was?"

"You mean the Princess-Dowager and my lady Mary?" Color had returned to Ann's features and her voice was tight as she confronted her sister. "You know their titles, Kate! I know how you feel, but don't call them that outside this room! Cromwell's been ordered to bring in anyone who challenges Queen Anne's title. Do you want to bring shame upon us all?"

Tears drying on her face, a cold bitter anger replaced Katherine's sorrow. "Well, Cromwell can be damned to eternal hell!" She faced Ann, shouting. "It's that sort of treatment of Queen Katherine and Princess Mary—yes, Ann, *queen and princess*—that has hurried the French queen to an early grave! Go tell Cromwell, Ann—go tell him that your own sister thinks our blessed Queen Anne is a fraud! Go tell anyone—I've had enough!" As Latimer touched her arm, she shook him loose. "I hope the king is content that his behavior has caused so much unhappiness. He's helped his sister to her death! You can tell him that for me, too, Ann! Now leave me to my sorrow —and rush to tell everyone what I've said. Just go—*get out!*"

Over Katherine's head, Latimer's glance urged the girl to leave. Shocked at her sister's outburst, Ann needed no prompting. He held the paper out to her and, as the door slammed behind her, took the sobbing Katherine in his arms to comfort her.

CHAPTER XI

The thirty-seven-year-old Mary Tudor was buried in the abbey church at Bury St. Edmunds near Westhorpe, with the full court in attendance. While his queen remained impassive, Henry wept at the ceremonies, later ordering a great alabaster monument to mark her resting place. In the murky light near the shrine of St. Edmund, Katherine sat with the Brandon family—the very pregnant Frances, the Marchioness of Dorset, her younger sister, Eleanor and a grieving Charles Brandon. Kate Willoughby wept softly, desolate at the loss of the woman who'd been a second mother to her. Her own mother, Maria de Salinas, had remained with the exiled queen.

"She wanted to come, but felt she might not be allowed to return to Her Grace if she did," Kate explained to those who asked after her mother. When Brandon urged her to speak more cautiously and not refer so openly to Katherine as queen, Kate replied tartly, "I speak only for myself, my lord. If everyone spoke their conscience, we might not have this sad situation. The court is full of toadies! Even the lackeys have more courage!"

She invited Katherine to remain at Westhorpe after the funeral. "Someone has to go through the French queen's possessions and make an inventory as required for the king," Kate said. "Neither her husband nor children read that well. You'll do just fine, my dear, and we'll make short work of it."

Katherine agreed, sensing that fourteen-year-old Kate also needed companionship and cheering as much as anything else. For almost two years, she'd provided not only loving companionship for her benefactress, but had helped run Westhorpe as well.

It was the first opportunity to be together since their Kendal summer and, in the weeks that followed, their old closeness deepened. They spoke of the child Anne Boleyn would have and the very real possibility that Queen Katherine would die without ever seeing her daughter again.

"Oh, Kate, you've been well out of it here with the French queen!" Katherine told her friend. "It's been lonely for you, I know, but you haven't had to choose your friends carefully or speak discreetly. That would be difficult for you, my girl. What will you do now? Return to London?"

"I don't know," Kate shrugged her thin shoulders. "My mother cannot have me with her. I'm fourteen and not yet contracted for! Who's to arrange my marriage? I'm the duke's ward, but I've already told him I'll not be foisted off on some sick and ailing old man like you and the French queen were obliged to have! I can go home to the Barbican house but that would mean being at court and fawning all over the Boleyn and her family." Kate drew herself up impressively. "And who shall we find there, my dear Lady Borough? My Lady Frances, now a marchioness and so pompous she might burst from her own wind, especially if she doesn't have that child soon! The Howards? So engrossed in their own importance and so fearful someone might find out how spineless they are, they float about in a sea of indecision! The Russells? Sir John—old 'Swearing Russell' himself—with his vulgar profanity that bespeaks a brain the size of a pea? The Seymours? Especially that haughty Stanhope wench who was only dreadful until the king made her husband a viscount? I shudder to think of her arrogance now! One could drop the whole lot into the Thames and the splash would be little, for their learning would not fill a thimble. I doubt that between them they could compose a decent rhyme or read or pen a simple phrase. They are a passel of fools!"

As she spoke, Kate's features and voice had magically taken on the characteristics and tone of those she ridiculed with such deadly accuracy. Katherine laughed delightedly.

"They are fools, indeed, but we must suffer them, like it or not," she said, wiping her eyes. "You can't stay here, Kate! I'll ask my uncle to speak with the king—or my lord of Suffolk should do so. You deserve to be more settled than you have been in the past."

One early fall night, as they prepared for prayers in Westhorpe's chapel, a note arrived from Charles Brandon informing his ward that two days previously, on September 7, Queen Anne had had her child at Greenwich. He said that proclamations, already drawn up announcing the birth of a prince, had been hastily recalled so two additionals "s's" might be inserted before they were hung or cried at Paul's Cross, the Temple and the parish churches.

"But she is a comely child and while the queen was disappointed it wasn't a boy, she made light of it, reminding everyone she's still young enough to bring forth a prince," wrote the duke. "But the king left the lying-in room very quickly and, later, as we had wine, he dashed the goblet to the floor. He is very upset to have another girl. . . ."

In a postscript, obviously added hastily, Charles Brandon said Mary had been summoned to court as was the custom at the birth of a royal child. She'd arrived in great excitement, hoping for a reconciliation with her father. But, when Henry only suggested she pay honor to the queen and then curtly left, her disappointment was touching to see. "She didn't see her father again, nor did she visit the queen," wrote the duke. "When everyone was visiting in the queen's chamber, Mary and the Countess of Salisbury slipped out and returned to Woburn."

Brandon said the baby was very pretty, with the red hair of the Tudors and her mother's long expressive fingers. "She's to be called Elizabeth," he ended the letter, "after the king's mother."

*   *   *

Returning home two weeks later, Katherine found Parr House in a turmoil. Her uncle had occupied the house during her absence as his own home near the Austin Friars was being reroofed. His fine handsome features, so like her father's, were agitated. At Katherine's concerned questioning, he explained.

" 'Tis that rogue Cromwell, Kate. He's created a fine stir at our Uncle George's Coughton Court and it has all the Throckmortons ill with worry. He's suing over the ownership of land which he says belongs to his manor of Oursley—land which has been Throckmorton land for centuries! He's using his authority with the council and influence with the king in a way to make a highwayman blush!"

In addition, Sir William was upset over the way Cromwell's agents had acted in confiscating the holy house of Sion near London. "They've turned all the nuns—good women all!—into the streets with insulting charges of poor organization and lax supervision. None of this can be proved, of course," Sir William was grim, "but I vow it's only a beginning, Kate. He's testing to see how far he can go."

But the matter which appeared to distress her uncle more than anything else was her guest, Anne Askew.

"You've got to get rid of the girl, Kate, for she's nothing but a troublemaker. Bessie can scarcely control her. She takes her leave when she chooses and walks about London unaccompanied, poking her long nose into places where she's not wanted or welcome. It's a wonder she hasn't been harmed! Last week, she even challenged a priest who was preaching at Paul's Cross! She called out to the good father that his words were but jests and advised him to read Holy Scripture more closely—and preferably in the original Greek! She disputed his each and every point, telling the congregation just where he was wrong. It's a miracle they didn't shout her down, but they didn't. They listened! And that angered the priest so much he had to have her forcibly removed!"

Katherine was appalled. Priests were used to drunken harassment or a beggar's piteous cry, perhaps even a cynical hoot now and then. How startling it must have been for the holy father to hear Anne's clear voice speaking with such intense conviction, challenging his learning and thinking.

"What happened to her?"

"She was brought home, Kate, much to Bessie's distress and told by the sheriff to keep to the house and never disrupt the peace again. Yet the very next day, she was gone! She eluded Bess and went to hear that miserable soul, Elizabeth Barton, who thinks she's a nun and cries out against the king and queen! Anne had mentioned the woman was preaching in the sanctuary at Westminster so Bessie went after her and almost had to beat Anne to get her home. The girl was very overwrought saying she wanted to follow the nun! You remember the woman, Kate? She was creating disturbances even before the French queen died."

Katherine remembered. Seeing Elizabeth Barton preaching in the vicinity of Westminster Abbey, she'd marveled that the woman—a former epileptic servant in old Archbishop Warham's household—had won such a large following. After the archbishop's death, she'd been sent by a priest, Father Bocking, to St. Sepulchre's in Canterbury where she'd become a nun. Now, as the "Holy Maid of Kent," Elizabeth Barton preached to all who would listen, crying with an impressive authority, that she'd seen the Saviour's Mother who'd sent a loving message to Her sinful children on earth. The woman, attributing her heavenly visions and voices to the Holy Ghost, obviously reveled in the attention, the improved material comforts and the inevitable comparison to the Maid of Orleans. The day Katherine heard her, she'd predicted the king would be sent to hell unless he put aside his new queen and returned to his good Spanish wife.

"Surely such a creature won't last, Uncle? The streets are full of unfortunates like the beggars and Abraham-men who pretend illness so people will give them coins. This nun, as she's called, doesn't want money. She wants attention!"

"Well, she's getting it, Kate, and that's dangerous. I've seen Cromwell's agents listening while she speaks and they report her activities to the Council. I think she's being used by some who have little conscience and would have her speak what they themselves would be afraid to say! That's where the Askew girl is so foolish—she can't throw her lot in with someone like that! The king refuses to punish the witless woman, saying it will only make her a martyr. But Anne must be kept at home or she'll make trouble for us all, Kate!"

"I'll see to the girl, Uncle, and I sorely regret the distress she's caused you. I'll tell her she must behave more strictly or go back to her home. I plan to take her home in the spring when I go to Kendal."

"You have a nuisance on your hands, my dear, and you must watch her," William Parr was adamant. "There are eyes and ears at court these days such as I've never seen before, looking for any evidence of disloyalty and even treason. The king is not pleased with his queen who failed to give him a son. The queen is not happy with her stepdaughter because Mary's insistence on her legitimacy imperils—or so she thinks—the future of her own baby, Elizabeth. The wily Cromwell is angered with the church because they won't tell him the extent of their wealth, their income or how they spend their monies. We don't need someone like this foolish Askew wench stirring up trouble by her careless tongue."

Sobered, Katherine pressed her uncle's hand, promising she'd see to Anne. And she'd go to court the very next day. It had been over two months since she'd seen the king and she had yet to offer congratulations on Princess Elizabeth's birth. She mustn't forget, either, to remind Henry what a comfort

Kate Willoughby had been to his sister. Perhaps now—how would she word it?—it was time the king and his ministers did something for the girl.

* * *

On the day she obtained an appointment to see the king, Katherine entered Whitehall through the palace garden, wondering why the area she remembered as thronged and lively should be so deserted. Walking through a long hallway toward the Presence Chamber, she suddenly realized how easily one could be seen through the myriad windows that overlooked the handsome gardens. Its triangles and knots, usually so filled with color, were now dimmed by autumn. Only the King's Beasts, standing upright in their box-bordered plots, were on solitary sentinel duty. Obviously, people chose now to stay in groups rather than chance an encounter with someone in the king's or Cromwell's disfavor. Upon her return to court, Katherine had found the atmosphere—while outwardly gay and festive—subtly changed. Cliques, hardly unusual and each with their favored person or cause to further, seemed more numerous and less restrained. She'd stepped warily, not allying herself with any. Now, near the Presence Chamber, she saw a small gathering, standing together as if for protection. They merely nodded as she passed. They don't know where to place me, she thought, amused. Whose side am I on?

Aware of the whispers as she passed, she soon reached the Presence Chamber where a gentleman-usher called out her name, "Lady Borough!"

Katherine was relieved to see only one occupant in the two chairs of estate at the room's end. She'd dreaded meeting Anne Boleyn. The king, seated in one chair, was talking animatedly with Edward Seymour, the new Viscount Beauchamp. Reaching them, Katherine made a deep curtsey, grateful the king appeared to be in a good mood.

"My dear Kate," graciously Henry raised her, "you bring us good cheer by your presence."

"It is my honor to be here, sire." There was a moment's silence as Katherine wondered how she could talk with another person present. As if reading her thoughts, the king turned to Seymour. "We would see the Lady Borough in private, Edward, so we may hear of our sister's affairs." Gratefully, Katherine watched as the door closed quietly, leaving her alone with Henry Tudor.

"Sit here with us, Kate." He gestured to a nearby chair. "We are in your debt for staying at our sister's house and helping Mistress Willoughby." He pressed her hand, sighing, "Ah, Kate, it is sad to lose a sister. We loved her, you know, but she would fight us. Ah, she would fight. . . ." Henry's eyes filled with tears and he was silent, as if reflecting upon happier times. Katherine knew better than to speak and, in a moment, the king was smiling again. "It is good to see you, my dear. You look well and very handsome. You still wish to remain unwed, Kate? Surely we must have dolts at court, they cannot ensnare a beautiful woman? 'Twas not so when *we* were young!" Still smiling, the king was gazing at her with something more than the impersonal fondness she'd always known.

Katherine felt a flush rising to her cheek. She'd never been alone with the king before, had never sat in his presence unless the court was dining. All at once her brain and voice seemed laggard, for his immense vitality, jovial graciousness and sheer sensual presence blotted out every other thought. She wondered how to respond to his jest. She'd heard rumors of his wenching; there were always light women at court eager to be counted a royal conquest. Now as he watched her keenly, she knew something other than an empty retort was expected.

"Sire, you honor me. If I have beauty, I must thank my parents—your good friends. And I am well, God be thanked. He has blessed me with good health. I remain unwed of my own choice, sire." Hoping the king would not think her family remiss, she explained, "My uncle, however, is anxious to settle me."

"With the good Lord Latimer?"

Surprise must have shown in her face, for Henry laughed, throwing back his head with such gusto his cap fell from the fine auburn hair, now thinning, and a shade lighter than his lush beard. He was still chuckling as he retrieved it from the floor, placing it jauntily on his head, satisfied he'd confused her.

"Tongues wag continually, Kate, but we're happy to have surprised you, if only to see you blush so prettily! Latimer is a good man—you'd be wise to accept him. He has strong roots—as we told you with Borough—in the North. His father served our father long and well and now he serves us nobly. Think upon him, Kate." After a moment's reflection, he said, "But you didn't come here, my dear, to talk of the good Latimer. What can we help you with?"

"Sire, I haven't yet spoken of my delight in hearing of the Princess Elizabeth's birth. I was still at Westhorpe when we heard of the queen's safe delivery. I am sorry not to see Her Grace. . . ."

"The queen is at Hatfield with the child. We've sent her there for the better air, although she is, God be thanked, a healthy child." Henry's tone was short, as if remembering his many dead babies.

Quickly, Katherine told the king of her uncle's concern over the disputed land at Coughton Court. She stressed that ownership had never been questioned until Thomas Cromwell had purchased the adjoining land. As she spoke, a small smile played around the king's lips.

"Ah, he's a knave, that Cromwell, a roguish knave, Kate." Henry slapped his thigh. "He's turning the screw, just as they do on the rack, hoping to intimidate George Throckmorton. Eh, is that it?" As Katherine nodded, he laughed again. "Well, he's met his match, my dear. We'd gamble on your uncle who's long been our friend—and who doesn't even let us win at cards, my dear Kate!—against Cromwell any day. Let the farce play itself out—that's our advice to your cousin. It may teach Cromwell a lesson and if he tries any of his tricks—and he has a bagful—then you may be certain of our help." As if wondering if his sanction of such behavior might appear unseemly to his young guest, he patted Katherine's hand. "You must know, Kate, that men like Cromwell have great value. He can do things we cannot. Dirty work to be sure—and much of it we deplore." The king's voice sank.

Observing the question on Katherine's face, he went on. "Why do we allow him his head? Because he's useful! Cromwell has great ability and skill. But he has little conscience as well as an undeniably healthy urge to line his own pockets as quickly as he can. Yet he's as good an organizer as Wolsey without any of the cardinal's inappropriate attacks of remorse and he has no connection with Rome, except when he served there as a soldier. . . ."

"Sire, my uncle will be grateful for what you say." Katherine was relieved it had all gone so well. Then, remembering her promise, she mentioned Kate Willoughby's future. "She was a great comfort to the duchess and is worthy of Your Majesty's notice. She cannot stay at Westhorpe and her mother. . . ." Katherine stopped, abashed.

"Yes, we know where her mother, the sainted Maria, is. And where she's liable to remain, God pity her." Henry's voice was sardonic. "Kate was as faithful to our sister as her mother is to our former wife. We are aware of those debts, Kate." He rose, signifying the audience was over. "We'll think on Mistress Willoughby's future right soon." He pressed Katherine's hand and she felt the rough beard on her neck as he kissed her lightly on the cheek. "Come again, Lady Borough," he bowed as she curtsied, "you cheer us always, my dear. We'll watch Cromwell and young Mistress Kate." As an attendant came forward to escort her out, he called after her. "And next time you come—come to see your king!" He was still smiling as Katherine left the chamber.

*   *   *

As 1533 drew to a close, Katherine celebrated her twentieth birthday with a gathering at Parr House. Although the snowy weather prohibited the planned fireworks from her terrace, there was dancing, feasting and even a small masque enjoyed by her family and Borough stepchildren. During the evening, Sir William Parr announced another cause for celebration—the betrothal of Ann Parr to William Herbert.

True to her word, Queen Anne had made a good match for the youngest Parr girl. Will Herbert had distinguished himself during the French War, later serving the king as a Squire of the Body. Katherine was happy to see that it appeared a genuine love match, though privately she thought young Herbert, whose father was the illegitimate son of the Earl of Pembroke, somewhat uncouth and nearly illiterate. For the first time in several years, Ann stayed in her old room overnight, so she and Katherine might make plans for the wedding.

The next morning, after prayers and breakfast, the two sisters and Bessie assembled in the river room. Outside, servants swept the heavy accumulation of snow from the terrace. All three had just settled themselves close to a roaring fire, when a servant entered with a letter written on the French queen's long creamy paper with its deep Suffolk insignia. Puzzled, Katherine broke the seal, wondering who might be using the dead Mary Tudor's device. She quickly scanned the contents, ending with a peal of delighted laughter. "My dears," she cried, waving the letter, "good news! Let me read this to you!

> "Westhorpe
> December 6, 1533
>
> My dearest, dearest Katherine,
>
> Charles has told me of your visit to the king when he returned from court. He said you'd reminded His Grace of my care for his late sister, our beloved French queen, and asked him to think upon my future. At the same time, because I was also his ward, Charles had questioned the king about where I should be placed. He was told in reply that the matter would be taken up by the council and, in the king's words—as Charles told them to me—'see what young blood with enough marks in his pocket, a lusty desire in his loins, and fitting lands to support Mistress Willoughby's fancies' might be available."

"I think young Kate takes a good deal upon herself to call the duke so familiarly." Ann Parr's lips pursed and again Katherine thought how much the girl was like their grandmother. She took up the letter again:

> "Charles said the king had mentioned one of the Greys. (Jesu, Kate, that would mark me as Lady Frances's sister-in-law!) The younger Seymour—the one with the great panache, of such courtly fashion and magnificent voice, but somewhat empty in matter, I think—was also suggested. Then there was a Dudley and the younger brother of the good Herbert that Charles tells me your sister will wed. Those were the best. After thinking upon them for some hours, I told Charles I did not wish to consider those or hear of any lesser ones the king might later think upon."

"She'll refuse the king's choice?" Bessie exclaimed, while Ann Parr only shook her head, muttering, "foolish, foolish child. . . ." Hurriedly, Katherine resumed her reading:

> "I slept on the matter by night and thought upon it by day. One thing kept recurring. I could either choose my own fate (and know the exact burden I would face) or I could let the king and his council place me with little thought for that which I regard as important —temperament (I could never abide a fool!), mutual respect and a physical union I would not feel degrading. I am not, dear Kate, as

you know, easily pleased. The four men the king mentioned are so alike as to leave little choice.

So, after debating with myself for several days, I finally arrived at what I think might be the best solution, although I am certain you, my dear and honorable friend, may (when I tell you what is in my mind and heart) believe my senses have departed my poor addled head. After great weighing of the matter (and trusting to God to help in the weaving of my plans), I finally confronted the duke with my answer and told him I wished to marry him."

As her two companions gasped, Katherine laughed again. "She's not speaking in jest either, my girls. Now follow closely!

"Now, dearest Kate, we know that Charles is not given to devious manner in his thinking or action, so he does not look for such ignoble devices in others, except perhaps at court, where—when he has to—he can be as cunning as any other rogue or knave. But in this instance, I think he thought me either foolishly stupid or guilty of some contrivance of which he was ignorant. I sought, of course, to convince him. I pointed out we'd lived under one roof for several years, we knew each other well, that I had loved and honored the French queen and always regarded him with respect and affection.

When his shock wore off, I could tell he was not overly displeased with me or my proposal. He is much older, being the same age as the king, while I will not be fifteen for nearly eight months. But as I told the duke, the youthful spirits and overweening pride of the king's choices might fain put me in an early grave. But with him, I will feel easy, comfortable, knowing. There will be no surprises. The more he thought on it, the more attractive my suit became and I felt I must prove to him that our union would be mutually agreeable. I have always thought the duke pleasing to look upon and it was not difficult for me to make him look at me with new eyes. . . ."

"God's blood, she's seduced His Grace!" Bessie's eyes were O's of astonishment while, for once, Ann Parr appeared speechless. Stifling her laughter, Katherine continued:

"This has been a long manner of saying, Kate dear, that on Tuesday of this week, Charles and I were wed in the same church where we buried the French queen. I felt her presence and know she approves our union. You know how she loved him, yet would never admit his faults. I don't think I shall be as easy of his shortcomings. He swears by our Saviour he'll never leave me alone for a long period of time. He says if I will come to court—as the French queen would not—we can be together for all time. I mean upon mine honor to see he keeps his word.

So, Kate, I am now a wedded woman and I like what I have. The king, when informed, told Charles's messenger to say he thought, 'My Lord of Suffolk is daft, but he has won a good honorable wench who will keep his bed warm and take care of him in his old age.'

We will be returning to court within a short time. Both of us pray to hear from you after you have this letter. I would tell you much more, my dear Kate, but my poor hand—lame with this effort —can write no more. . . ."

Handing the letter to her still silent sister, Katherine murmured, "Notice the signature, Ann." She traced with a slim finger *"Katherine of Suffolk"* across the ivory paper.

"This makes our Kate second only to the Duchess of Norfolk," she explained. "Next to the queen and my Lady Norfolk, Kate will be the reigning lady at court and in all London! Jesu, I would give all next year's wool money from our Kendal sheep to see Frances Grey's face when she hears the news! Lady Frances—a mere marchioness—with a not quite fifteen-year-old stepmother, the Duchess of Suffolk!" Katherine's eyes sparkled with amusement as Bessie clapped her hands gleefully. For the first time, a trace of a smile appeared on Ann Parr's envious face, as all three envisaged the tall, gangling Katherine Willoughby Brandon moving among the courtiers who'd often scorned her, sparing none her cunning wit or blunt impatience.

"She's done well." Katherine folded the letter, placing it in her workbox. "Kate's got her mother's good head and has refused to settle for second best. Oh, how I wish I could be there when Maria hears the news—that her daughter is now my Lord of Suffolk's wife! She'll be surprised, but very pleased, I trow. But oh, my ladies," she placed a hand to her forehead in mock horror, "I wonder if the duke realizes what he has on his hands? Kate has a mind of her own and a tongue as sharp as a blade. Can he handle her? And, I wonder, does he know how lucky he is?"

* * *

As winter closed in on London, the Thames froze to a depth of twenty feet, drawing hundreds of eager spectators to walk upon the solid water from the Tower to Southwark on the opposite shore. Hurriedly, merchants erected tents and booths to hawk souvenirs of the great Frost Fair of 1533, while others built bonfires upon the ice to sell mulled wine, roasted birds and hot eel pies. The novelty of the river being frozen only occurred perhaps once in a lifetime and, everywhere, people promenaded on the ice, calling out their delight in the phenomenon. Upstream, downstream and cross-stream, the populace flowed—much as the river itself—during a holiday occasion wrought by the unusual temperature and the miracle of seeing the mighty Thames stand still.

It was on the Fair's third day—as the weather showed no sign of breaking

—that Katherine, accompanied by Bessie and a steward, went to Suffolk House where Hans Holbein waited to commence her portrait. The new duchess, Kate Brandon, had suggested the artist use a small chamber facing the river where the light was good and the delicate linenfold paneling would make a proper background for Katherine's portrait.

Gingerly, the two girls picked their way down the frozen Blackfriars waterstairs sliding onto the ice. They walked carefully, dodging children and adults on crude skates made of animal bones. Halfway across, they stopped to admire a tent, its pennants flying while the occupant, a juggler, performed seemingly impossible feats with varicolored balls. Nearby, a ragged man put a dancing bear through its paces. When the steward bought hot spicy wine from a vendor, the girls drank it gratefully, their smoky wisps of breath mingling with the steam from the wine cups.

Kate Brandon was waiting for her guest. Katherine swept the youthful duchess a deep curtsey, murmuring, "Your Grace. . . ."

"You foolish girl—I've told you I will not have it! You will not bow to me, Katherine Borough!" Kate flung her arms about her visitor. "I've just heard that Lady Frances almost gave birth prematurely when she heard I'd married her father! She finds it impossible to believe I have precedence over her—I, the homeless nobody whose mother lives with a Spanish woman who still calls herself a queen!"

After a brief visit, Katherine joined Holbein. The duchess' words lingered in her mind as she greeted the artist, relieved when he admired the smooth ivory damask gown, its heavy velvet sleeves of deeper tawny tinged with pale green and laced throughout with finespun gold and silver thread. The delicate sheen of the cloth emphasized Katherine's gleaming hair which lay neatly parted beneath a gossamer cap of sheerest ivory and reminded him of the old-fashioned wimple his grandmother had worn.

Katherine followed the artist's instructions as he found the pose he wanted —a three-quarter face to show the symmetrically perfect line of brow, cheek and chin which gave his sitter such dignity.

"That's fine, Lady Borough, if you could just sit that way. Be comfortable, you must not sit stiffly." Quickly, he began mixing his paints, making broad daubs of color on the canvas.

Katherine watched his sensitive face—the highly colored flat cheeks, the straight, almost classic nose beneath his neatly trimmed brown hair. Already, he was completely immersed in his task. Should she speak while he was painting?

"By all means, my lady," he replied, "talk if you wish. It will put you at ease. What shall we talk about?"

Katherine asked about his life before he'd come to England. Holbein told her of the fine education he and his brother had received from their father, the elder Hans, after which he'd gone to Lucerne and Basle to paint the renowned Desiderius Erasmus. The old scholar had later sent him to France.

"And there I saw His Majesty's collection of the da Vinci paintings and drawings and received my first commission from the Duc Jean de Berry to paint him and his wife. The French king sent me to England where Erasmus insisted I paint Sir Thomas More—who wanted not only himself but his whole family put on canvas! And then he took me to the king. I haven't lacked commissions since, my lady."

"You've painted so many at court," Katherine reflected, "who is your favorite? Who was the best subject for the king's great artist?"

Holbein waved his brush, warming to his task as well as the compliment. "Ah, my lady, my favorite? The king, of course—His Majesty is an impressive subject. And the queen, too, although she wasn't well when she sat for me and I'm afraid it shows in her expression. I cannot paint except what I see! And now, Mistress Seymour's portrait is finished and I shall do her brothers Thomas and the Viscount Beauchamp."

Katherine had not seen Thomas Seymour since their meeting at Lord Latimer's house. Shortly thereafter, he'd gone to France to take the Order of the Garter to the French king. And from there, she'd heard, he would go to Spain to meet with the emperor and smooth over, as best he could, the king's divorce from the Spanish sovereign's aunt.

"I think it will be difficult to keep Master Seymour home long enough for him to sit for you."

"He'll be here more often from now on, my lady." The artist stood away from the canvas, his brow furrowed. "Now that his sister is so favored by the king, I think we'll see more of him. Viscount Beauchamp has grown so much in the king's esteem, surely he'll see to it that his brother gains as much?"

Katherine was startled at the artist's frankness; he discussed the king and his courtiers as though he were their equal. Impelled, as always, by some urgency at Seymour's name, she asked, "And what is the talk at court? I had not realized Mistress Jane was regarded so highly by the king." She held her breath, feeling like a conspirator.

"Oh, yes, that is so." Holbein's voice was quiet. He might as well have been discussing a family problem. "The queen is angry at the king's interest in Mistress Seymour and even angrier at the brothers who continually urge her to seek even more favor. I feel sorry for her—she has made many enemies and the king constantly harangues her for not having given him the son she'd promised."

Again Katherine wondered that Holbein would discuss his sovereign's life so intimately. Undoubtedly, he was in and out of the court and courtiers' homes often, had observed them at ease and overheard their conversations. The man was hardly a servant, but he had a servant's opportunity to listen when others spoke. Whereas a good servant would have remained silent, however, Holbein seemingly had little restraint.

That evening as they dined together at Parr House, Katherine recounted the conversation to her uncle. William Parr did not deny the artist's words.

"He sees a good deal, Kate, for he has easy entry to court. Henry dotes on the man and has commissioned him to design a new gate for Whitehall. He discusses things with Holbein, the same as he does with his Fool, Will Somers. Not that the two souls are one and the same, of course. Holbein has a remarkable talent. But then so has young Will! Who else can call the king 'Hal' to his face and not chance a box on the ears or banishment from his presence? I think the king regards them both as simple souls, who mean no harm, who have little self-interest in court happenings. He trusts them both and so speaks openly in front of them."

"And you think, Uncle, that the Seymours are working against Queen Anne?"

William Parr fingered his knife thoughtfully. "Kate, there's nothing in our experience to say what might happen. You know how different the court is today from the time when your mother and the French queen were there. The king is no fool—we must not underestimate him! He's been through a tremendous experience, unlike anything the old king ever faced. It was difficult for him to put Katherine away and it is not easy now for him to keep Mary in exile. Henry is no monster and he's been very patient with them both. Queen Anne, more's the pity, doesn't seem to have the attraction she once had for him. Remember, he courted her for six years before they wed! She never gave him an easy moment then and she mishandles him now. When she's angry, I trow, she uses words I doubt the old queen ever knew! She complains of Princess Mary, calls the Privy Council spineless toads and gives the man no peace. He has other things to worry about— Spain and France, for instance. Remember, they have centuries of loyalty to Rome and could combine against England anytime. The king doesn't want war! He feels perchance, if war comes, the old queen's supporters might rise. Remember, many of our friends in the North like Dacre and old Lord Darcy are troubled and dissatisfied! They'd rise in the old queen's defense quickly enough, especially if they thought her nephew, the Spanish emperor, would come to her aid—for it would be a defense of the church, too." William Parr sighed. "So who can blame him if he turns to the Seymour when she treats him more kindly and with a respect he lacks in his own chambers?"

"And the Seymour brothers?"

"Ah, now, there's a different situation. Edward, the estimable Viscount Beauchamp, is devoted to the king and is, I deem, an honorable and well-meaning man, despite his unbearable wife. And Thomas? Well, I grant you I cannot say why, but I don't trust the man. Between them, however, they'll do anything to forward their sister and Cromwell will help them. To his credit, he's done away with a great deal of waste within the court from those petty opportunists who think themselves important and exploit their positions. He has contempt for the small thief and a high regard for the clever rogue who plots for a fortune. Naturally, he's made many enemies—like our cousin Throckmorton who refused to bend to his will. He takes great pleasure in degrading those of noble birth as well as those who have little courage and are unwilling to stand up to him." Sir William reflected a moment. "Yes, I think the situation is just about what that fellow Holbein told you."

Yet it was Anne Askew who finally convinced Katherine of the rivalries, the deep undercurrent of discontent and uncertainty at court. After Anne's confrontation with the sheriff, she'd told the girl bluntly, "You're welcome here, my dear, as long as you do not bring dishonor or danger upon the household. You cannot go rushing about London upbraiding priests! You may visit with me or my friends and you may study, but I'll not have you airing your freethinking opinions to anyone who will listen!"

"But many of the things I speak of, *you* also believe, my lady! *You* read the same books! *You* were the first to tell me of the religious truths found in ancient Greek!" Though her words were rebellious, Anne hung her head.

"You're right," Katherine replied, penitent, "but you've taken what I feel are interesting theories, perhaps even strong truths, and used them in a way I would not. Of course I'm interested in discovering the ancient dogmas which concern God and man! I would do away with superstition and seek old truths by putting heart and mind to study. But that doesn't mean I wish to challenge everyone else who thinks differently! You make a fool of those smarter and cleverer than you—the very ones who may gradually change what is wrong with religion! *They* will deal with any wrong-thinking. You can't help by ridicule, for you are but a young girl! If what we think is right —then it will come in time."

Anne had flung her arms about Katherine, wept copious tears and cried she'd never meant to embarrass or endanger anyone. She'd do anything to stay in London and not be sent home where her father was eager to marry her off.

When Katherine mentioned Holbein's comments about Jane Seymour to Bessie, she was surprised at her young guest's reaction. Anne rolled her eyes heavenward. "They'll have their way, you'll see, my lady. Something will happen to Queen Anne. I don't know what, but it will all be part of some-thing bigger, so the king will be as free of the Pope as the followers of Lu-ther are. It is all part of Cromwell's plan. . . ."

"And what is Cromwell's plan, pray?" Bessie asked with an amused look at Katherine.

"Why, to put away those who oppose the king, who pretend with their tongues that he's their churchly sovereign but who really are popish. That's what Master Cromwell, Queen Anne and Archbishop Cranmer are working for. Luther's work in Germany was truly religious, though it had great politi-cal consequences. Cromwell's intent is mainly political, but it will have great religious consequences. Don't you see all this?" Anne appeared irritated. Couldn't anyone understand what was happening right under their noses? "That's why Master Cromwell will pursue those who oppose the king. He will use religion as an excuse. That's why the Nun of Kent has been arrested and kept in the Tower and soon the Countess of Salisbury will be made to leave my Lady Mary."

Katherine was indignant. Once more, it seemed her guest was talking above her head and knowledge. "Anne, how do you know all this? What do you know of my Lady Salisbury?"

"I see, my lady, I must tell you." Anne bent her head for a moment and then looked up defiant. "I went to the Tower to see the nun. I went with no one knowing who I was and I went very quickly. I dressed as a serving girl, bringing fruit from the nuns of Bermondsey." As Katherine bit her lip, Anne cried eagerly, "It was all right, my lady, it was all right! There was no danger. They let me in and I saw the nun for a long time and she told me everything."

Bessie, thunderstruck at Anne's words, advised in quiet exasperation, "Then perhaps, my girl, you'd best tell *us* everything! How does the nun know such things? She's been locked in the Tower for weeks!"

For the next half hour, Anne recounted her visit to the woman so many thought mad. "But she's not, my lady, she's not mad," the girl said breathlessly, "she has her visions and hears her voices. And she's been in contact with many—she won't say who—that come from the court and they've told her things she's put together in her own way. She says there's a conspiracy to get rid of Queen Anne and put forth the Seymour and later to close all the holy houses. Now that the king no longer honors the Pope, those who still do, like Lady Salisbury, must go. And you know how faithful she is to Rome! You know her son lives there and her whole family is very popish! I trow the king might do away with the Lady Mary if she weren't his daughter! No one will touch the old queen for she may die soon anyway. But Mary will be kept close until she swears to her father's sovereignty in the church. Master Cromwell—and anyone else who looks to the future without the Pope—have all vowed that those who oppose him must change their beliefs or be put away. No matter who, my lady, no matter who."

Bending over her needlework, Katherine's thoughts raced through her head. She was frightened, for everything Anne Askew said made sense. Margaret Plantagenet Pole, the Countess of Salisbury, was indeed the mother of Reginald Pole, whom Cromwell called "Brainsick Pole" because he'd written diatribes from Rome against the king for his treatment of Queen Katherine. Pole had called Anne Boleyn a "Jezebel and a sorceress" and Cromwell, the "Vicar of Satan." All the Plantagenets were loyal to the Pope and likely to remain so. Katherine wondered if they knew the danger they were in. Then, irrationally, she wondered how anyone as lustily vigorous as Henry Tudor could be interested in the shy, plain-faced Jane Seymour, so different from her brothers.

Shivering, she put her needlework aside. It was too much to think upon all at once. She suggested everyone go to bed, telling Anne to put out her candle at once and not read the night away. The girl's mouth trembled at the reproach and, guiltily, Katherine put an arm about her shoulders. "It's all right, Anne, I know you meant no harm. Go to sleep now and let us pray there will be no more trouble for those we love."

Anne hugged Katherine. "I'll pray for you, my lady, and I'm sorry if my words have troubled you. What I said tonight will soon be common knowledge at court. It will not harm you, my lady."

Later, lying in bed, Katherine thought of everything that had happened since the French queen's death. The birth of the Boleyn's child, the bitterness of Princess Mary, the elevation of Jane Seymour in the king's affections and now a danger to Lady Salisbury, the church and those who still resented the king's supremacy. What was happening to the court, to those she loved, to the church and to England? She was twenty years old and, for the last four years since her return from Gainsborough, each day had brought new threats to her peace of mind, if not outright fear for the safety or well-being of loved ones.

How much longer could such conditions continue?

CHAPTER XII

My lords, as touching my removal (to Hatfield), I will obey His Grace, as my duty is, or to any other place His Grace may appoint me; but I protest before you, and all others present, that my conscience will in no wise suffer me to take any other than myself for princess or for the king's daughter, born in lawful matrimony; and that I will never wittingly or willingly say or do ought whereby any person might take occasion to think I agree to the contrary . . . should I do otherwise, I should slander the deed of our mother, the holy church and the Pope . . . and dishonor the king, my father, and the queen, my mother, and falsely confess myself a bastard. . . .

—Princess Mary to the Privy Council, 1533

In mid-December, Henry announced the Christmas holidays would be held at Greenwich Palace. There, in an atmosphere of good cheer and celebration, the Lord of Misrule, whom some called the Abbot of Misrule— a direct reflection of the royal regard for church opposition—would reign for the Twelve Days of Christmas.

In the City, citizens bedecked themselves with scarves, ribbons and laces. Tying handkerchiefs about their legs and astride hobbyhorses and dragons, they danced throughout the night in the shadow of the huge bonfires that graced each parish, providing a shield of warmth as well as protection from the cutthroats, prostitutes and petty criminals mingling with the celebrants.

At court, the holiday meant almost constant attendance upon the king and queen as well as preparing for one's role in the festivities. For weeks beforehand, seamstresses, laundresses, wigmakers, jewelers and embroiderers spent long hours creating lavish new dresses, doublets and sleeves for both men and women, while others knitted brightly colored hose. Petticoats, jeweled hoods, underskirts and farthingales, long cloaks trimmed with fur or embroidered with broad bands of gold or silver were meticulously produced for those who could afford them, while the more frugal had their dress refurbished.

Richard Cecil, a Groom of the Wardrobe and Yeoman of the Robes, along with his young son William, home from school in Grantham, went through the Wardrobe, a crumbling building near the courtyard of Baynards Castle, to select costumes for the indoor masques. Young Will often accompanied his father to court, enjoying those occasions during school vacations when he helped find suitable garments for plays and mumming, even assisting old Tom Cawarden with planning the jousts and tournaments so much a part of the holiday season. As the new queen loved playacting and spectacles, Cawarden had commissioned Hans Holbein to create a "Riche Mount"—a play upon Richmond, the old king's title before his accession. The artist worked day and night on his creation, a large rocklike substance on wheels, upon which—when it appeared as if by magic from behind curtains of shimmery gold tissue cloth—the king and seven courtiers would be seated. Eight maidens would be hidden inside, waiting to emerge at the proper moment to dance with the king and his companions. While Holbein was pleased at the commission, he'd regretfully told Katherine that work on her portrait must again wait until the Twelve Days were over.

At Greenwich, Katherine was reunited with the young Duchess of Suffolk, an event made more joyous by the news that she was pregnant.

"Charles says it's all my fault for making him promise to stay with me and not spend so much time at court!" Kate Brandon was glowing. "He went to Richmond with the king only once in three weeks!"

"You'll be a wonderful mother, Kate," Katherine hugged her friend. Love had certainly changed the impatient Mistress Willoughby's brusque manner. "I envy you."

"Then why don't you do something about it?" Kate laughed, waving her hand for emphasis. "Charles says Latimer is so besotted with you it would be an act of mercy if you married him. And many of our court gallants—no matter if their brains or purses permit—would storm Parr House and help you attain this enviable position if they thought they had a chance! Remember, my dear, your mourning period has long since passed!"

"My uncle reminds me constantly and I know I'm getting no younger," Katherine replied. "Oh, Kate, I do want to be settled! But I want to choose for myself the next time. Just as you did! I remember how devoted my parents were—how right they were together. I want that, too!"

"Charles says the lackey and serving wench are luckier than we and usually happier, because they choose for themselves," Kate embraced her friend. "I'm not taking my good luck for granted, my dear," she said soberly, "I know how lucky I am and I'll fight to keep it that way."

Katherine asked for news of Princess Mary. Who would know better than the wife of the king's closest friend?

Kate said that only the previous week the king had ordered Mary to Hatfield. "It was Charles's sad duty to escort her there. He asked the king's leave to get someone else to take her, but Henry insisted. Old Norfolk read her the declaration that from now on she will be called the 'Lady Mary' and must live with her half sister. But, God be thanked, she still has Lady Salis-

bury and Susan Clarencieux, and Charles said old Lady Bryan will soon
leave to serve as nurse to Elizabeth."

"Then Mary will have at least one more friend at Hatfield. I'm sure the
new queen had forgotten she was also once Mary's nurse."

"But oh, Katherine, confinement will be very difficult for her there! To be
forced to live in the household of the baby who's taken her place as heir, the
daughter of the woman who's responsible for the misery her mother suffers.
You know the old queen has been sent to Kimbolton and is allowed no visitors at all?" Kate stamped angrily about the room. "But that's not the worst.
Sometimes I fear for Mary's reason. I think this whole affair has given her
fantasies."

"Fantasies? Mary? The princess has as level a head as anyone I know,"
Katherine was indignant. "Mary is not one to chase rainbows, Kate!"

"Yet she told Lady Salisbury an incredible story," the duchess replied.
"You remember Mary came to court when Princess Elizabeth was born? I
think she heard talk from that nag, Jane Morley, who married George
Boleyn and is now our dear Lady Rochford. Jane hinted—and the Seymour
girl and that Saville wench who came to court two years ago agreed—that
Mistress Anne had played loosely with several gentlemen of the court, especially that ballad player, Mark Smeaton. You know how he's been posturing
about with love for her for years! The Seymour girl said Anne even fancied
Tom Wyatt who pens such pretty rhymes. They said she passed the babe off
as the king's!"

Cold fear settled about Katherine's heart. Mary must be desperate if she'd
told such a tale—even to such a one as trustworthy as the countess. Mary
had always found it difficult to see bad in anyone. Solitude had certainly
loosened her tongue and regarding something that would never be proved.

"Oh, Kate, Mary should be silent! Surely someone will tell the king or
queen! She must be told to say nothing!" Katherine was quiet for a moment,
then whispered, "Do you think it is true?"

"Well, if it is there's no proof, nor likely ever to be. Even you and I know
better than to meddle with such fantasy, Kate. Better to forget I even mentioned it! But do you see how much worse it is for Mary? To lose her title is
one thing. Yet to be forced to relinquish it for a child she fears is not her father's is another matter entirely. If anything should happen to the king—
which Jesu forbid—and he have no son, this child would be queen! It must
make Mary sick with worry and more stubborn than ever not to acknowledge the illegitimacy which has been foisted upon her. Yet she can hardly
explain her feelings to her father, so everyone regards her as obstinate and a
troublemaker!"

Katherine then told the duchess of Holbein's comments on the king's
fancy for Jane Seymour. She was surprised at her friend's reaction.

"That woman!" Kate's eyes were pinpoints of fire. "That whey-faced,
placid smug little prig! She pretends great friendship for Mary—and then
tells her a story which breaks her heart and puts her in great danger if she

repeats it. It could even be a trick to get Mary to accuse the queen or make her father so angry he'll make her life even more difficult. I don't trust her any more than I do her brothers. Charles says they urge her to all sorts of ruses to catch the king's attention and she's been so upset at losing Rob Dormer, she does as they say. She's vowed to make a good marriage to show old Lady Dormer. No good will come of this, mark you!"

In just a matter of days, Kate Brandon's prediction came true.

Anne Boleyn, once again pregnant, had ordered all her maids of honor to assemble in her chamber where each might choose the dress or costume they would wear for the Christmas Eve revel. Everyone from the Duchess of Norfolk to little Joan Guildford, now wed to John Dudley and recently the mother of little Robert Dudley, was present. After making their selections, the ladies formed small groups for games of primero and dice while others worked at needlepoint or embroidery for New Year's gifts. Gesturing toward Jane Seymour in the group near the queen, Kate Brandon whispered to Katherine that her husband wondered what the king saw in her.

"After all, she's hardly a stranger here. She was a maid of honor to the old queen when our lady mothers were in attendance and she's nearly twenty-six, almost as old as Queen Anne! Hardly one to fascinate the king, I should think. Yet Charles says he is quite smitten."

"Perhaps it's because she's so different." Katherine glanced at the demure Jane. "She's so quiet and meek."

"And there's always the lure of the forbidden," Kate grimaced. "The king doesn't see that her nose is too long, her eyes too sly and that, like a serpent, she'll sting when prodded! Believe me, Katherine, she's just as ambitious as her brothers and probably smarter than either one. Which is not saying much, I grant you, for they were born for the battlefield, the tiltyard—and the boudoir. Charles says the younger one, Thomas, will soon be a Gentleman of the Privy Chamber. Which means he won't be hatching another covey of bastards from Calais to Paris!"

Katherine felt herself blushing. Silent, she wondered if Tom Seymour was really the rakehell court gossip insisted he was. It was impossible to reconcile her picture of the man—charming, handsome, solicitous—with the irresponsible, hardened courtier pictured by Kate Brandon. Would the king really tolerate someone so conscienceless with the important business of the court?

Her thoughts were interrupted by the rising tone of the queen's voice. "And I say, Mistress Seymour, that I would see the locket!"

Jane had risen from her cushion, clasping her hand defensively about a chain which hung from her neck.

"It is but a pretty bauble belonging to my good mother, Your Grace," she stammered, "it would not interest you."

"I shall be the judge of that." Anne's dark eyes narrowed. Suddenly, before the girl could move, she reached up and tugged the chain so hard that

Jane, tears springing to her eyes, cried out and rubbed the raw skin of her neck.

Anne opened the locket and gazed at the newly painted miniature of Henry Tudor. For a moment, she stared at it unbelievingly and then, furious, flung it to the floor. In the next instant, her hand swung a wide arc, leaving a deep red imprint on Jane's thin, almost translucent cheek. The girl screamed loudly as Anne berated her for her impudence in owning such a memento, much less wearing it. As everyone looked on in shock and embarrassment, the terrified Jane, without asking leave, fled from the chamber. Quickly, the distraught queen turned and dismissed all the ladies except her aunt, the Duchess of Norfolk.

Within a day or two, Jane Seymour left the court, pleading her mother's illness. When her friends asked the true nature of her relationship with the king, she replied, pale lips pressed tightly together, "The least said, the soonest mended," and was gone.

The following week, as the artist Holbein at last completed his great mountain and loaded it on a cart with cleverly concealed wheels, whispers swept the court that the queen would not be present at the holiday festivities. After the locket incident, she'd confronted her husband and harangued him with her suspicions. At first the king tried to placate her, pointing out the gravity of her condition and the danger of overexcitement. But Anne Boleyn would not be solaced. She gave her husband no peace until finally, patience gone, he shouted that she must learn to close her eyes to such incidents just as her betters had done before her.

Shocked, Anne had turned silently and left. Hours later, amidst tears and terror, she miscarried. As the great "Riche Mount" waited, concealed behind the golden curtains at Greenwich, word swept the court that the king had left for the revels without visiting her.

* * *

Katherine was relieved when the holidays were over. With one queen in exile at Kimbolton Castle, the other ill at Whitehall and an ex-princess incarcerated at Hatfield, the revels had been, as Kate Brandon said, a "mockery and a travesty." Once the New Year's gifts were presented, everyone was free to go and, within the day, the chambers and courtyards of old Greenwich Palace were empty. As they made ready to leave, Katherine and her uncle met Thomas Cromwell emerging from the Presence Chamber. The king's minister bowed and then, surprisingly, asked leave to accompany them back to London, explaining he'd been detained by the king at the last moment and his own entourage had already left.

Katherine was curious about Cromwell. Old Wolsey's protégé, the son of a Putney blacksmith, had been prominent during the holiday merriment, mingling as an equal with those who bowed respectfully and then whispered behind his retreating back. This was the man, she realized, whose actions and influence would help determine Mary Tudor's future. What mischief would he make of her belief that Elizabeth was not the king's child? If what Anne Askew said was true, even the futures of the Countess of Salisbury, Jane Seymour and the Nun of Kent, were shadowed by Cromwell's intent. How, Katherine wondered, had he gained such power so quickly? And what made the king so dependent upon him?

During their journey back to London, Katherine found some of the answers. Thomas Cromwell was in rare good form, deferring to her uncle with courtesy and, though a sardonic humor filled the small and narrow black eyes, he listened respectfully each time she spoke. Not that there was much opportunity. Cromwell appeared determined to vanquish any questionable impression his companions might have of him.

"I come from the trade, my lady, as you know. It is no secret. I wasn't born to wealth and honor such as you. I'm no longer young, being almost half a century old. I've been a soldier with the French in Italy and worked with the rich Frescobaldi bankers in Venice. Ah, there is a way to learn some of life's more worthwhile tricks! I was once a merchant in the Netherlands. To come from the land of the Borgia and Machiavelli and the court of Urbino—from the marketplace at Antwerp where they view we English as sloths in financial matters—to return home and see England struggling with matters our continental cousins put behind them years ago—ah, my lady, it was very enlightening!"

"I pray, sir, I find you confusing. . . ."

"Then let me explain further. In Italy, France or Spain—who is it who holds the countries together? The bankers? The farmers? The educated gentry? Ah, no, my lady, it is the church! The novitiates, the monks, the abbots, the bishops and cardinals—the church, always! It owns property which, if it is lucrative enough, it might lease to the banker, farmer or merchant. It decides who goes to school, what they will learn and how they will learn it. It decides who will be employed and how. It secures the fate of unborn millions by letting them be born only to perpetuate a cycle of illness, poverty, brutality, hunger and violence. And it does nothing—or very little, my lady— to alleviate the suffering. The supremest politicians in France and Italy are not those of the court. They belong to the church. They are more regal than your Francis of France or Charles of Spain. They live in palaces as rich as royalty and their power is absolute. Royalty knows this, of course, and serves the church well. They coexist. . . ."

"Sir, would you have a country where there was no church, with people who did not worship God, but lived as pagans?" Katherine wondered what Anne Askew would make of the conversation.

"Of course not, my lady. I am a Christian. I believe in one God, one Father in Heaven. I believe in Jesus Christ, His True Son. I believe one should live by the tenets of that faith. But I do not believe in a hierarchy owning half the civilized world's land, governing and ordering the lives of people by some senseless ritual they don't understand, which demands they worship at the feet of clay saints and pay their hard-earned money to Rome for the remittance of some minor grievance or transgression that our Saviour would have laughed at! Why, the religious community—be it the Carthusians in the Charterhouse or the nuns at Bermondsey—take more, use more and continue to ask for more—much more than they give! If Jesus Christ could return today, my lady, He would laugh—or perhaps weep—at the sins of pride, greed and corruption committed in His name!"

Her uncle spoke. "You damn all the church, Master Cromwell, with no regard for those who live godly lives, those who do great good such as, let us say, at Butley Priory. We know the fathers at Butley well, for our land adjoins theirs. They serve all. They seek no one's fortune nor do they dominate anyone's lives."

"Ah, yes, Sir William. Butley is, I grant you, an excellent house! So excellent, I think, that the late lamented French queen often stayed there with all her ladies and gentlemen. She'd be there for weeks, hunting in Staverton Park, dining with the canons who were flattered by her attention and, when her husband, the good duke, was building Suffolk House and knew not what to do with seven of his retainers, he sent them to Butley where they were put up at the church's expense for, I believe, nine months! This is the privilege or duty of a holy house? Is it redeemed by the fact that they educate a dozen parish boys and provide a living for about twenty-five monks of doubtful intelligence? Why even at St. Mary's of York, only about fifty boys are being educated! Do you know the revenue of a house like St. Mary's, my good Sir William?"

As the flush on her uncle's cheeks deepened, Katherine recalled the many times the Parr family had stayed at various abbeys on their way north. Boldly, she asked Cromwell, "What is it you would do, Master Cromwell? Close all the houses such as has happened at Sion? The king is willing to do this?"

"It has happened before, my lady, only there was not much made of it. Holy houses have given up land for universities, for hospitals and colleges since the time of the king's grandmother, the esteemed Lady Beaufort. There is nothing new here, my lady, except we—the English king and I, his good servant—are now doing it. Not Rome. Not the Pope. And not for money."

"Not for money, Master Cromwell?" Sir William smiled wryly. "Where did the wealth of Sion go? Where will the monies, the lands, buildings and treasures of the religious houses go if they are closed? Not to Rome, I'm certain!"

Cromwell acknowledged the barb with a light bow. "You are astute, Sir William. Of course, the church's possessions will revert to the Crown. The religious houses which are old, ill-run, decrepit or mismanaged will be closed. But I still say not for money, but rather because they are a symbol of a religious disease which can no longer be tolerated in England. I know they are still closely allied with Rome, that those inmates—in their deepest hearts—believe in the supremacy of the Pope and not the king. So they must go. I will be the one to see to this and the king shall value me more. I know people will not understand, but I cannot allow that to dissuade me. There can no longer be two rulers in England—the Pope and Henry Tudor. The king must be the only sovereign. So I shall be blamed as the great godless destroyer of much of the old faith." He laughed easily, yet a slight perspiration beaded his forehead as he said, almost to himself, "It will not trouble me. I know that, no matter the cause, an evil name, once gotten, will not lightly be put away. . . ."

*   *   *

A week later a distraught Countess of Salisbury appeared at Parr House, telling Katherine she'd been ordered to leave the princess and return to London. Tom Howard, the old Duke of Norfolk, had brought the king's orders that the countess' services to the king's illegitimate daughter were no longer required.

"But what they really wanted, Katherine, was to make me go for the pain it would cause the princess and because, for some twisted reason, I believe her father and that woman think Mary and I plot against them. It is all nonsense, of course." The elderly woman wiped her eyes and Katherine saw her deep fatigue and despair. "It was very difficult to leave her."

"And I can imagine Mary's grief," Katherine whispered. "But she is all right, madame?"

Margaret Pole twisted her handkerchief. "She is bearing the burden, but that's all, and it is making her physically ill with worry. Mary was overcome when her father declared her a bastard. There were several dreadful scenes with Norfolk over whether she'd go to Hatfield or not. She knew that once there she'd be at the mercy of those in Elizabeth's household, most of whom are Queen Anne's relatives. So she refused to go. Old Norfolk had to threaten physical violence if she refused to obey the king's orders."

"He wouldn't dare!" Katherine cried, appalled at the thought of anyone mishandling Mary Tudor.

"Ah, Kate, nothing surprises me anymore!" The countess let her tears flow freely. "Even when I said I'd pay my own charges if I could stay with her, I was refused. I could see Mary was almost numb with shock at the order and all the servants were whispering or crying for they couldn't believe what they were hearing. Now I know how Maria felt when she gave up her home and daughter to go with the old queen! But I knew if we both refused to accept the order, there'd be no pity for Mary. So I took her aside and told her I'd come to court and plead her case with the king and Master Cromwell, that otherwise Norfolk would remove her by force. I told her she must never allow such an affront, that she must go with as much dignity as her mother, the queen, had gone. I told her she must go as a *princess*. . . ."

Tears filled Katherine's eyes as she visualized the scene, the shock and heartbreak and Mary's wounded pride. Suddenly, she remembered Anne

Askew's prediction that the countess would be made to leave the princess. Embracing her guest, she said, "You did all you could, madame. And Mary knows it. Now you must think of yourself. You have a place to stay?"

Lady Salisbury nodded. She would lodge with her sister Gertrude, the wife of Henry Courtenay, the Marquess of Exeter, at Exeter House. They were all grieved and apprehensive at Mary's detention, only too aware that Lady Salisbury's son, Reginald Pole, had hurt their standing at court by his outspoken criticism of the king's new marriage.

"But one cannot change what is in one's heart overnight, Katherine." The old countess seemed anxious to excuse her son. "I cannot believe what the king does these days. It is almost as the old queen used to say—that he is bewitched! And there seems to be no one to say him nay. But oh, I fear Mary is going to try!"

*   *   *

To buttress Mary's illegitimacy and complete Henry Tudor's supremacy in the church, an Act of Succession was passed by the Parliament. Now, by law, every subject of the king—noble, ecclesiastic, merchant, farmer or humble peasant—must swear on oath to maintain the succession. At the same time, the Parliament refused to send further church revenues to Rome and specifically exempted the bishops from papal control. All ecclesiastical matters formerly settled by the Pope, Cromwell said, would now be handled by the King's Court of Chancery. While the structural foundation of the church was completely transformed, creed and ritual remained the same, with the English now swearing loyalty to the monarch instead of the Pope. Refusal to comply with the law would be considered treasonous and the offender liable to suffer the penalty of hanging, drawing and quartering.

Within several weeks, the result of the parliamentary action was evident. On a windy, overcast day, Elizabeth Barton, the Nun of Kent and her companions suffered a traitors' death at Tyburn. Several days before the king's soldiers had also apprehended one of the queen's staunchest supporters, John Fisher, the venerable Bishop of Rochester, and taken him to the Tower to await the king's pleasure.

Shocked at the old prelate's detention, William Parr predicted ominously it was only the beginning. When commissioners came to exact the oath from the Parr family and servants, everyone swore willingly except Bessie who appeared reluctant. Still bewildered that the Pope she'd honored since childhood was no longer her spiritual father, she asked Katherine how the tradition of centuries could be changed overnight?

"Bess, it's not that you must regard the Holy Father as an enemy. He is the spiritual leader of the church as it has come to exist since the time of our Lord." Katherine chose her words carefully. For years, Bess had read literature on the "New Learning"; she was steeped in the Humanistic principles,

Katherine knew. Yet now, faced with forgoing her long loyalty to the Pope, everything she'd read and discussed appeared forgotten.

"Bess, remember, during the long centuries since the time of our Lord there has been a great increase in the power and position of the Pope so that perhaps—if one considers the true nature and original intent of Jesus in sending forth His emissaries to carry on the true religion—the Romish faction has strayed very far from what He truly desired. All our king has done is cast off such alien influence. No longer will our church send monies to the Pope or the one who follows him so he may live in such a grand style, or acquire more treasures. This was hardly Jesus' wish! But when you go to church tomorrow, it will be just as it's always been, only we will pray for our king instead of the Pope. Remember, Bess, for all the fact that the Pope is the anointed representative of our Lord on earth, he and his predecessors have stained their office many times—that's no secret, my girl!—by greed, their abuse of power and their personal living habits! Now the Romish church has grown bloated with its own wealth and ambition and our king hopes to undo such practices. I trow, Bess, in the end, this will be for the best." She was relieved when Bessie whispered her assent to the commissioner's questioning, yet the girl remained troubled and, when their visitors left, she'd slipped away alone to the Blackfriars Church. Katherine knew she went to seek forgiveness.

Though she spoke comfortingly to her household and companion, Katherine was not confident that the country's religious loyalties could be changed so quickly. While most swore the Oath, many refused. Either they could not accept the king's supremacy, or they could not accept the Princess Elizabeth as the heir. On the morning the Nun of Kent suffered, Katherine had dealt with a hysterical Anne Askew who had to be physically restrained from rushing to Tyburn where she threatened to defend the nun and harass her tormentors, even if it meant her own death. In her anger, she'd spared neither the king nor queen and damned the new Archbishop of Canterbury who'd lifted not a finger to save Elizabeth Barton. "And yet old Bishop Fisher thought she was a saint!" Anne had screamed, her freckled face blotchy with tears. "But that spineless toad Cranmer pretends it isn't happening and looks the other way! I curse them all for their evilness—he and that loathsome Vicar-General Cromwell—may they die as pitiful and wasteful a death as that poor woman!"

Shaken with the violence of the scene, it had taken Bess and a steward to help Katherine lock Anne in her chamber. For hours, everyone listened to her screams and threats until, finally, knowing her mentor was gone, there was only silence. Creeping into the room, Katherine took the exhausted girl in her arms.

"Oh, my lady, she didn't deserve to die!" Anne sobbed quietly. "She meant no harm. She only spoke what she thought was true. Why is the truth always feared?"

Smoothing Anne's hair, matted with tears and sweat, Katherine could only shake her head as she lay beside her guest until the girl finally slept.

* * *

In answer to the Act of Succession, Pope Clement issued a brief proclaiming the marriage of Henry Tudor and Katherine of Aragon valid and named their daughter, Princess Mary, the legitimate heir.

"The Pope can wipe his arse with his briefs," said Thomas Cromwell when it was placed before him. "It makes little difference to us now."

But it was making a difference. The Act of Succession claimed many victims who refused to swear the Oath. It set friend against friend and families against each other. Within months, Sir Thomas More, the ex-Chancellor, joined Bishop Fisher in the Tower and Margaret Pole, the Countess of Salisbury was detained. Speechless at the thought of her mother's old friend in prison, Katherine sought Lord Latimer, asking what could be done.

"There's nothing to be done, my dear, nothing at all. As your uncle said, this is only the beginning. Cromwell and the king are finding more loyalty to the Pope and the old queen than they expected. There will be others, you'll see." Only this morning, he said, a delegation had visited the monks at the Charterhouse. "They were not easy on the holy fathers, Katherine, insisting they swear the Oath and shoving them about when they refused. I went to see what the trouble was for Prior Houghton has a voice that carries far! But there was little I could do. The men all refused and the soldiers carted them off like so much cattle."

Katherine pressed John Neville's hand; she could see he was deeply disturbed. Weeks before, he'd sworn the Oath and it had been difficult. "You know my heart is with the old queen and the princess, my dear," he'd told her at the time. "I abhor what the king has done, but it is final. He has married, fathered another child and I pray daily he may yet have a son. If I objected as others have done, I'd be stripped of everything I own, imprisoned—perhaps even executed. I'm not afraid for myself, but is it worth the ruin of my children's lives? What right have I to forfeit their inheritance?" Now, he closed his eyes wearily, "It may not be praiseworthy, my dear Katherine, what I did. I hope you don't think less of me for it. I don't have the sinew and pith of the crusader or the martyr. . . ."

When Lady Salisbury's detention continued, Katherine wrote Kate Brandon awaiting the birth of her child at Westhorpe, asking what she could do. By return courier, Kate replied:

> I dare not write all that I know, dear Katherine, but will return to Suffolk House as soon as this babe is born. Which I pray will be soon, for I am quite unwieldy! I long to see you to find out how you do in this time of great unrest.
>
> Charles says the king is very puzzled about those who oppose him. You know how proud he's been of his people's loyalty and he

cannot stand opposition. I fear Cromwell will try to win favor by persecuting those he thinks are the king's enemies—even Mary who causes him so much trouble. And Tom More, too, even though his reputation for godliness and fairness has won him much esteem. Cromwell cannot tolerate their stubbornness.

Charles says the king is determined to make Mary swear the Oath, for Queen Anne never ceases to taunt him that he cannot govern his own daughter and thus imperils Elizabeth's rights, unless she has a son.

Ah, for one who bragged so much before she was wed, she's taking a long time in producing a boy! Perchance now she knows how the old queen felt with all those dead babies! But I say too much. . . .

I pray for Lady Salisbury. She went to court and told the king to his face his treatment of Mary might put the girl in an early grave. I think the king might have overlooked her criticism—for the friendship she bore his mother and father—but Cromwell would not. Lady S. is old and unwell and confinement will be a hardship. But her greatest danger is from her son whom I pray will remain silent. . . .

Katherine put the letter aside, despondent. The king's action—handled differently and impartially—might have resulted in much good for England. But now, she could see, the price might be exorbitantly high—and cruel. Everything Anne Askew had predicted appeared to be coming true. Now those individual power plays and court intrigues over which she, her mother and Kate Brandon had so often laughed appeared trivial. No longer was it a mere jostling for honor, wealth and authority. Now an insidious, covert poison aimed at one's deepest and cherished religious belief, long upheld by tradition, had seeped into the very fabric of English life and threatened not only reputation and property, but one's very life as well.

*　*　*

Several weeks later, Katherine rode to Suffolk House where a radiant Kate, blooming with health and joy at the birth of a son, laid little Henry Brandon in her arms. "We named him for the king who will be godfather and we want you as godmother," the duchess smiled happily. "My good stepdaughter, the Lady Frances, has nigh suffered a seizure since I have a boy and she has only two girls. Now the title will go to my babe, not hers!" Katherine laughed at her friend's evident satisfaction. Apparently many old schoolroom scores were now being settled and not to Frances Brandon Grey's satisfaction.

Later, riding home with Bessie and a steward, Katherine reflected on the duchess' happiness and the obvious pleasure—for all his years of previous fatherhood—which the arrival of his first son had given Charles Brandon.

While not denying her old friend, Katherine felt a twinge of honest envy. That soft little body in her arms, the sweet smell and mewing sounds from tiny Henry Brandon had provoked a strange and unfamiliar yearning.

At London Bridge, her reverie ended. All about were carts, wagons, cattle and the pedestrians who jostled good-naturedly for precedence onto the bridge. Her steward muttered at the traffic ahead and Katherine settled down to wait. Near the bridge entrance, she crossed herself, avoiding looking up at the rotting heads of criminals that adorned poles at the bridge's South-wark end.

At last the line began to move slowly. Reaching the bridge's opposite end, she heard a tumult near the Lion Tower entrance to the Tower of London. A throng of several hundred people crowded about the exit, further imped-ing traffic as it left the bridge. Katherine suggested her steward ride ahead to seek the cause of the unusual gathering. Within moments, he returned, white-faced and distressed.

"We must leave quickly, my lady. We'll keep straight ahead. Follow me now and don't lose sight of me!" Before Katherine could reply, he'd begun to maneuver through the throng.

Obediently, Katherine spurred her mount and followed. She wanted to question the man and wondered what could have so disturbed him.

As they clattered off the bridge, heading for Byward Street, a great roar went up from the crowd. Suddenly, it began to shift and move as mounted soldiers, emerging from the Lion Tower, ordered onlookers to move back. Katherine's steward held up his hand. "We're too late, my lady. We must stay or we'll be surrounded by the mob. Stay close to me now, please. Oh, I had hoped to spare you this!"

"Spare me what?" Katherine cried, annoyed at the man's protectiveness. Had they pressed on ahead, they'd have soon left the crowd behind. Beside her, she heard a woman cry, "Oh, Jesu save us all . . . !" Following the woman's glance, she saw the team of horses, gray and heavyset, as they pulled something which caused the crowd's roar to turn into a wailing cry of repugnance, a keening sound of grief and sorrow.

As the group of soldiers rode forward, the sound changed to anger as sev-eral onlookers raised their fists and cried out.

"What is it?" Katherine strained to see and, as the soldiers passed so close she could see the sweat on their faces, her throat constricted with disgust and a thrusting hot rage. There, behind the two horses, lying bound together on a rough wooden hurdle, were three monks. One she recognized as Lord Lat-imer's neighbor, Prior John Houghton of the Charterhouse. He lay bound and trussed like a dead animal, his hands crossed on his breast, feet tied to-gether, his body chained with the others to the rough hurdle that would drag them through the City to . . . where?

"In God's name, what are they doing to them?" Katherine could barely speak. Her gorge rose as she pictured the monks' pain as they were dragged over the stones, through the mud of London's streets. She wondered if she was going to be sick right there at the end of London Bridge.

"They've been sentenced to die because they would not swear the king's oath," her steward mumbled. "They will die like criminals, my lady. It is a traitor's death of hanging, drawing and quartering they're headed for, God save them." The man appeared near tears.

As the horses dragged their human cargo toward Eastcheap, Katherine stared at the retreating spectacle, unable to believe what she'd just seen. All about her, people rode silently, their faces horror-stricken and pale; others sobbed loudly. Sickened, she urged the steward to hurry. She wanted the sheltering protection of Parr House. There she and Bess would go to the chapel and pray for the soul of John Houghton and his companions. Perhaps prayer would release the frustrating, almost numbing wrath within her.

Later that evening, lying awake, staring into the darkness, she thought what a sad, tragic place Chartreuse, Lord Latimer's home, would be. Next door, the good brothers would almost certainly be in prayer for their comrades who'd suffered so horribly that day. Katherine prayed they would find peace also.

The next morning, still disturbed, she rode with her steward to Chartreuse to offer what solace she could to Lord Latimer. It was an overcast day and, halfway to her destination, a fine misty rain commenced. Nearing the entrance to the Charterhouse, she heard voices raised in hearty and triumphant song. Hardly proper under the circumstances, she thought. Or, perhaps a miracle had occurred and Houghton and his companions had been pardoned! Perhaps this vigorous inspiring music was a song of thanksgiving?

Hastening toward the church, she suddenly caught sight of a mutilated thing hung high on the arch of the Charterhouse gate. Katherine stood, struck dumb with horror and that surging sickness which again threatened to overcome her. There, atop the venerable stone gate, was the bloody quarter —an arm and a shoulder—of what had been a man. The flesh was bruised and torn, and the rain was softening the caked blood so it dripped to the earth below. Houghton had not been saved. Part of what was left of him was there for all to see, while inside his brethren sang, honoring his memory in the only way they knew how.

Ignoring her steward, who appeared as stricken as she, Katherine slipped from her mount and ran toward Chartreuse, the ghastly sight imprinted on her mind. She found John Neville sitting quietly in the garden, heedless of the gray day or the fountain's melodic splash. The caged birds were all singing lustily to the sound of the music from the monastery. As she ran toward him, the man opened his arms, saying, "Oh, my dear, you've seen—you've seen it! I would have spared you that had I known you were coming. . . ." Even as John held her closely, Katherine still struggled for composure, anything to still that aching sickness in her throat.

Suddenly, the great Charterhouse bell rang out, its rolling resonant tones rising above the monks' singing.

"Some may think they are mourning, John," she whispered, as he urged her into the house, "but you and I know better. They are singing in defiance! The bell tolls because they want everyone to see what has happened."

"There's nothing to be done for that godly man now, Katherine." John was still pale. "Just pray there will be no more sacrifices. They are needless! This is no way for the king to fight the church! He listens to such poor advisers, I fear there will be yet more trouble." As a servant approached, bringing a tray with wine, wafers and fruit, he gave her a warning look. "The fewer words we say, my dear, the better. There are eyes and ears everywhere looking for treason of any sort."

John Neville's words remained with Katherine for days. How different the court had become—even in those few years since she'd returned from Gainsborough! She was not close to the new queen and was uncomfortable with those who'd so easily forgotten Queen Katherine and Mary. She had little in common with her brother and sister. Kate Brandon was her closest friend but, once the christening was over, she'd most likely spend her time at Westhorpe where her son could enjoy the good air while his mother avoided court life.

"Now everyone distrusts one another. They spend as little time at court as they have to, unless there is some immediate gain," she told Bessie. "There are too many factions, all pushing for their own good and I don't seem to belong with any of them. It's a blessing my parents cannot see this."

"Maybe you should live at Kendal," Bessie mused. "With the princess and duchess away, you'll have to depend for companionship on others who might not think as you do. And that will be difficult for you, Kate. You're much too loyal." Her companion smiled, taking the sting from her words.

The next morning, after prayers and breakfast, Katherine took her books and needlework to the garden. The everyday sounds of the river traffic over the wall that separated Parr House from the Blackfriars Church was comforting. She could hear music coming from the old building and, in the garden, the monks' laughter as they turned the cold earth, cleaning up the winter's damage, awaiting the grace of spring, was comforting. It all sounded normal, yet she knew their conversation masked a fear and resentment as present in the streets outside as it was in the monastery. For days, people had cried out or angrily turned away at the loathsome sight of quartered bodies hung about the City. Certainly the Blackfriars brethren must be aware a similar fate awaited them if they refused to acknowledge the king's supremacy? It could make for little real peace in the cloisters.

All day, Katherine walked in the garden or, lost in thought, watched the Thames traffic from the river terrace, noting the children playing at the water's edge, just as she had so many years ago. Slowly, an answer was evolving and with it a certainty she hadn't felt in a long time. Glancing up at old Parr House, still so alive with memories of her parents, she felt tears in her eyes—then again that silent awareness she was taking the right step. On her way back to her chamber, she stopped in the chapel to offer a prayer of thanks.

That evening, when her uncle arrived, Katherine calmly told him that, after much thought and prayer, she'd decided to wed John Neville, Lord Latimer.

"The sooner the better, Uncle. I've no wish to remain here any longer. Perhaps we could even go north at once—that would please me very much." She was sad at the thought of leaving Parr House. And all the strain of the past months—Mary's confinement, Lady Salisbury's detention, Prior Houghton's agonizing death, her own uncomfortable situation at court—was soon evident in unrestrained tears. William Parr spoke soothingly, though he could scarcely hide his joy in her decision.

"It's a wise move you're making, Kate," he embraced his niece. "Oh, John will be so happy! And, mark my words, he'll be good for you! Remember, my dear, he's much admired in the North—you'll be better off there with him. There's not much to hold you here anymore, Kate. If your father were alive today, he'd be the first to say 'go.'"

Drying her eyes, Katherine accepted her uncle's kiss and then went to tell Bessie her decision. Tomorrow, William Parr would see Lord Latimer and, within a short time, she'd be married, probably right in the Parr House chapel. Then there would be the long journey north. She'd urge her uncle, for sentiment's sake, to use Parr House as his residence for it was doubtful if she'd ever return to London permanently. If she did, Chartreuse would be her home. From the time of her marriage, her life would be in the North and she didn't intend to look back.

Then, irrationally, the thought appeared that—as if fate had decreed it—Master Hans Holbein would have to wait once again to complete her portrait.

Lady Latimer
1534

CHAPTER XIII

Katherine's arrival at Snape Hall near Ripon in Yorkshire was very different from her first day at Gainsborough. Her husband was no stranger; now he was there at her side. There were no adult family members inwardly resentful of a young stepmother. Lord Latimer had been a widower for nearly ten years.

Snape also was quite different from either Gainsborough or Kendal Castle. Unlike neighboring hilltop manor houses or fortified castles, Snape stood in a vast wooded park. Three stories high, its gray granite stone, mellowed to a pearly yellow, was mottled with a green patchwork of ivy with stems as thick as a child's wrist. Across the roof line, graven images of knights paraded about the battlements, guarding against invisible marauders.

"That was a fancy of our ancestor who built Snape about a hundred years after the battle at Hastings," John explained. "The tale is that this was the only place in the valley where wood, water and stone were so easily available and he chose it even though it was difficult to defend or guard. Every Neville has left his mark, of course, but it's still very much the same building of four hundred years ago."

While Snape differed physically in almost every way from Gainsborough, Katherine spent her time in much the same fashion, consulting with John's chamberlain and stewards who ran the estate in his absence. Over seventy servants worked in the house while outside a similar number staffed the stables, laundry, dairy and brewery. An especial satisfaction were the Snape gardens, famous throughout the district due to the ministrations of old Torrey, the gardener, the fifth of his family to serve the Nevilles. At the garden's end, an immense dovecote stood sentinel, facing the back courtyard which ended at a stream where carp and trout were often taken for food.

The welfare of the shepherds, grooms, tenant farmers and laborers who lived on Snape lands, as well as the nearby villagers, was Katherine's responsibility. "They all look to us in time of need," John explained, "so you must get to know them. Don't be disappointed if they are wary at first. Our people don't make friends easily. You have to win their loyalty."

Katherine understood. Her summers at Kendal and her years at Gainsborough had given her a knowledgeable and sympathetic awareness of the Northern people whom she knew to be frugal, honest, hardworking and deeply religious. Protective of their way of life, they were suspicious of strangers who might want to change their customs. "You'll have no trouble," Bessie predicted, "they know the Parrs are of Northern stock."

From her first day at Snape, however, Katherine's stepchildren became her special charge. John Neville, a twelve-year-old miniature of his father, and eleven-year-old Margaret, black-haired with enormous violet eyes, had easily won her heart. Deep curtsies and bows had immediately been followed by shy embraces and a whispered "welcome, madame" that Katherine found touching. John told her only young John could remember his mother; they were happy memories and he had not grieved long.

Katherine had insisted the children accompany her as their father showed her about her new home. Through rooms regal with handsome arras and painted cloths on the old stone walls, she admired the gold and silver plate, the sturdy furniture of the North and the tapestries depicting local and religious legends. In one chamber, an ancestor's suit of armor stood majestically, while the antlers of some of the countless deer struck down by his bow hung over the cavernous fireplace. Shyly, the children showed off their favorite hiding places and pointed with laughter to the gargoyle an unknown woodcarver had slipped into a panel composed of angels. With a child by each hand, she'd exclaimed over their favorite view from a deeply embrasured window wide enough for John to seat his daughter upon. Through diamond-paned glass, several of which were set with the Neville coat of arms, Katherine exclaimed at the sight of the vast park where hundreds of sheep kept the short sweet grass of the North tightly cropped. As she walked through her spacious home, servants curtsied or bowed, and outside workmen tugged at greasy caps, welcoming her in the dialect Katherine knew so well.

After a month in her new home, Katherine felt she'd won her place in that tightly knit fabric of Northern life, threaded as it was with intermarriage and the jointly owned lands that had remained in families for centuries. She'd made no startling changes allowing the servants to follow their familiar routines. She knew she'd won their trust as much as her stepchildren's love.

"They are a credit to old Dame Nan," Katherine told their father, knowing the remark would find its way back to the old nurse who'd raised their father as well as his children. Dame Nan had been happy to relinquish her charges frequently for study and games, returning to the servants' hall where she was sure of a toddy and a place near the fire to warm her aging bones.

On such occasions, Katherine would take the children and a groom for a swift ride in the park. Later, after a picnic of good Snape cheese, bread and ale, they'd search for wild flowers which grew damply at the woods' edge. Together, they'd collected smooth rounded stones, vying with each other for the most perfect or unusual. Katherine pointed out the purple heath, the bilberries and white-bolled cotton grass found on the moors over which the curlew and lapwing watched the skylark soar in song. Often, as she walked or ran with John or Margaret, there were throat-catching memories of Maud

Parr, skirts hoisted high, running through the rough bracken of Kendal with her children tumbling at her side. At such times, Katherine realized how much she still missed her mother, dead now for five years. It made her more determined than ever that John and Margaret should have similar memories also, for old Dame Nan had been too old to take them on such excursions.

When Margaret was twelve, she helped her plan a new wardrobe, suggesting colors and materials that would complement the little girl's vivid coloring. Pleased with the attention and the delightful vision she presented to her father, Margaret rewarded her stepmother with a loyalty bordering on adoration. Katherine also won her stepson's undying gratitude for tactfully suggesting to his father that he spend more time on the music lessons and art studies which he loved and at which he excelled, rather than waste time and energy on the ceaseless hunting, fencing and other sports which he tolerated more for his father's satisfaction than his own. And, during their first Christmas at Snape when John played the virginals, accompanying himself in a clear soft tenor that brought tears to Katherine's eyes, her husband had groped silently for her hand, pressing it gratefully.

Within months of her arrival, when ill health caused the children's tutor to return to London, Katherine had taken over their studies, unpacking once again the textbooks she'd used in the palace schoolroom and later at Gainsborough when she'd taught little Anne Askew.

Katherine never thought of Anne without a twinge of guilt. "I'll never feel right about that girl," she told Bessie. "I took her to London, I gave her the books, I encouraged her to read and seek for herself. It made her different, Bess, you must see that! So different I wonder if she'll ever find a life that will make her content."

"Kate, there's no reason for you to take the girl's behavior so to heart. You didn't make her different. She was born that way! She used what you taught her as a means to prove to herself—and others also—that she *was* different." Bessie shook her head, pursing her lips. "If it hadn't been you, it would have been someone else. Anything to satisfy that craziness of hers!"

Katherine was silent, remembering the day Anne learned her mentor would wed Lord Latimer. "You'll return to the North, my lady?" She'd looked at Katherine, aghast. "What will happen to me?"

"You'll go home, Anne, of course," Katherine had replied, trying to keep her voice even. She still remembered the girl's outburst when the Nun of Kent had been executed.

"With you, my lady?"

"No, Anne, it's time you went home." Ashamed of her cowardice, Katherine had forced herself to look the girl in the eye. "You're nearly fourteen, my dear, and your parents, I know, will want to look to your future." She'd paused, waiting for the torrent to burst, but Anne had remained silent. When Katherine tried to embrace her and stress how they might visit each other, Anne—her face white with shock—had merely stared at her hostess with unbelieving eyes before running from the room. She'd locked herself in her chamber and Katherine had wisely left her alone. On rejoining the household a day later—and all through Katherine's nuptials and feasting afterward—she'd been docile and quiet. She'd accompanied the Latimers on their journey and they'd left her, outwardly compliant and reserved, at her father's Lincolnshire manor. Katherine had been ashamed at her feeling of relief as the door of her home closed behind Anne.

Within the next few months, word had filtered over the hills, carried by churchmen traveling to or from Fountains Abbey, Jervaulx, Bolton or Whitby, or by pedlars selling their wares at Snape Hall's gate, that the Askews had not had an easy time at Anne's return. The eldest daughter, Martha, had been contracted to wed Thomas Kyme, a wealthy Lincolnshire squire. Soon after Anne's return, the girl developed a consumptive cough and, at the onset of Katherine's first winter at Snape, had suddenly died. The shocked family had quickly rallied and, not wanting to lose a prosperous son-in-law, had suggested Anne as a replacement.

Eyeing the tall, redheaded, freckle-faced girl, Kyme had seen only a calm exterior and a shapely body garbed in clothes selected by her mother to enhance her bright coloring. Anne Askew appeared healthy and capable of childbearing. If the girl's eyes were remote, concealing a boiling hostility, Thomas Kyme—stolid and unimaginative—did not see it. They were married a month later and Anne's father was heard to utter a great sigh of relief as the two set off for the Kyme home.

When she heard of the marriage, Katherine had sent Anne a letter and a delicate ivory cross on a thin gold chain. But there had been no reply. Several months later, Lady Askew wrote that Anne had given birth to a daughter.

"You see, all your worry was for naught!" Bessie cried a year later when Lady Askew wrote that Anne had just borne a son as redheaded as his mother. "All the girl needed was a strong hand and some young ones to take up her time."

Katherine nodded, but somehow the picture of a subdued Anne Askew did not ring true. It was difficult to imagine the girl relinquishing her studies in favor of caring for her children; it was equally impossible to imagine her as a loving and obedient wife.

After her second year of marriage, Katherine was well aware how fortunate she herself was. She was genuinely fond of her husband and, by an arrangement worked out by her uncle prior to her marriage, she was even wealthier than before, with lands, manors and Chartreuse given to her outright.

"Parr House is now your uncle's, Katherine, and it's only right I deed the place to you," John had said. "My children will spend their lives in the North, but should anything happen to me, you might want to return home." The income from her estates was hers to do with as she pleased; she need not wait to be a widow to claim it. She was proud of her home, one of the loveliest in the North, with competent, self-effacing servants, clad in the Latimer colors of tawny, brown and cream, seeing to her every wish and comfort. She had friends from Kendal and her Borough stepchildren for long visits and John and Margaret, growing taller each day, loved her as if she were their own mother.

Katherine enjoyed a free hand in running her home, but on the subject of his children's education, John had been firm.

"I want them taught as I was taught, my dear," he'd told her firmly. "I know you received another kind of education. I respect your thinking and want you to read and believe as you choose. But for my children—I would have them taught as others here in the North are taught. You may read your foreign books and you may believe Luther has reason to vilify the Pope and church, but I will not have such books put in my children's hands. Your thinking will not be popular in the North, my dear, though I know it is fashionable at court. But it demeans the belief of my father and his father before him. Another decade of this "New Learning" or "New Thinking," or whatever you call it and we may be questioning the existence of God Himself!"

John suggested his children study languages, but insisted it be Latin or French, not the Greek so fashionable at court. "Keep their studies simple, please, and let them learn what they will use during their life. Music and art for the boy if that's what he wants—he already rides and hunts passably well. Drawing, dancing, some simple mathematics and history for the girl. But for philosophy, dissertation, for rhetoric or science—they will have little use for those in the life they will lead when I am gone."

Katherine agreed, not too disappointed, for the memory of Anne Askew still lingered. It was more important that John loved his children and had no wish to place them out in another home considered more prestigious, where they might learn more pretentious social graces and later be bartered in marriages that would bring more wealth, honor and land to the Neville family.

Though London seemed far away, often she and Bessie were engulfed with nostalgia. Katherine missed the stimulation of court life—the tournaments, processions, masques and revels. She missed the king and his court. She missed the old queen and, most of all, Princess Mary and Kate Brandon. As she recalled the splendor of a band of knights, standards hoisted high, silhouetted against a dying sun as they raced across a Greenwich hilltop to be home and stabled before twilight, Katherine's homesickness was almost unbearable.

Letters from home helped. Her brother and sister were still in attendance upon the king and queen and popular at court, her uncle wrote, though Will Parr—now living with his young wife—was not making her very happy. The old queen still lived at Kimbolton Castle with only Maria de Salinas for company. Lady Mary, stubborn and still refusing to swear to her father's supremacy or accept her loss of title, had been forced to remain, bitter and hostile, in little Elizabeth's household. No one had seen her in months.

Letters from Kate Brandon were cheerier. Within a year of her first child's birth, she'd borne another boy named Charles for his father. "Now I have two Charleses and two Henrys to deal with—a husband, a king and two babies! It is exciting, Kate, and I love them all dearly. But oh, I do miss our long talks and our time together. But I'm certain you are happy and so I am content."

After reading them, Katherine always folded the letters and tucked them into her letter box for those moments when recollection of home overwhelmed her. Yet each day made her more thankful she'd chosen John Neville and her life in the North. Her relationship with her husband had held no surprises. On their wedding night, John had said almost apologetically, "I know how women feel about this, Katherine. I will not hurt you, my dear, and you must tell me if I tax your strength too often." As with old Lord Borough, there'd been no lit candles nor had she been naked when their union was consummated. Instead, after embracing her during which she felt his hands linger on her breasts, he'd gently lifted her nightrail and, in a few moments lay back, satisfied. Katherine wondered, puzzled, if she was now pregnant. She'd felt nothing. Why didn't women feel the same lust as men?

Later, when one of her new friends hinted of married intimacy, another smiled scornfully, saying, "Bed-loving was only for the begetting of children. There was no pleasure in it." Another called it a good sample of original sin —the pain of childbirth was the wife's penalty.

"And pray, what is the husband's penalty?" Katherine asked, while her friends looked surprised that one should be expected.

The following months had been repetitious of that first night. Although Lord Latimer was nearly forty-two, he could still embrace and mount his wife at least twice a week. Each time, Katherine held him lovingly, her spirit as quiet as her body as he used it. Each time she felt nothing, wondering again if this lack of feeling accounted for her failure to conceive. Other women had babies every ten or eleven months—why couldn't she? It puzzled her even as she submitted to her husband's desire. Yet she could not speak of it. It was easier to lie quietly in the clean nightrail John would lift only as far as necessary, than to embarrass him with questions he might think unwomanly. Satisfied and content with his own children, he never mentioned the possibility of having another. Nor did he seem aware that Katherine might long for a child of her own.

*   *   *

After two years in the North, John told Katherine, they must return to London for a sitting of the Parliament. Previously, he'd made many excuses to Cromwell for absences, explaining his estates needed putting in order in view of his recent marriage.

Katherine was not eager to go.

"It will take me weeks to find out who the new favorites at court are and what we can talk easily about," she told John, startled at her own lack of enthusiasm. She still missed her old home and friends but now she'd have to live at Chartreuse, acquaint herself with new servants while attempting to pick up the thread of her old life. After which, a few months later, she'd be whisked off to the North again.

In the past, when John had been absent for a few days hunting or stayed in York overnight on estate business, Katherine had relished her privacy and solitude. There was always a shipment of new books from the Continent waiting to be unpacked and savored and, during their father's absence, she and Bessie could indulge the children in long walks in the hills or extravagant excursions into Ripon on market day. She'd won the affection of her neighbors—the proud Darcys, Talbots and Montagues—and never longed for companionship. After months among her Borough stepchildren or friends visiting from Kendal, the thought of the court—still divided in its loyalty to the new or old queen—was stifling and frightening.

Kate Brandon had written that the Act of Succession had claimed many victims for refusing to swear the Oath of Supremacy. Prior Houghton and his brethren had been only the beginning; others continued to suffer martyrdom for their consciences' sake. It was all she could do, the duchess wrote, to pass through the City where gruesome sights assaulted one's senses everywhere. Bishop Fisher, Thomas More and the Countess of Salisbury still languished in the Tower. There was even a rumor that if the Lady Mary did not soon oblige her father with her submission, she might be imprisoned also.

Yet, in the end, Katherine knew she had little real reason to remain in the North while John stayed in London for so many weeks. She'd only disappoint him and the children seemed eager for a change. Even Bessie was curious about living at Chartreuse; she'd known no other home in London but Parr House.

So, toward midsummer the Latimer caravan of wagons, carts, servants and family lumbered southward. Katherine wondered what she'd find in London. She'd see Kate, but not Mary. The former princess still lived in little Elizabeth's household and, in a battle of wills with the king and Cromwell, still stubbornly refused to admit she was illegitimate and that her mother had lived in sin with her husband for twenty-five years. Katherine wondered what old Lady Margaret Beaufort would have made of the sad situation. Undoubtedly, she'd have been appalled and angered at the imprisonment of old Fisher whom, on her deathbed, she'd named to be young Henry's spiritual and political adviser. And what, thought Katherine, in the name of sweet Jesus, would she have done had she known her grandson would force his subjects to accept him in the place of the Pope?

Within days of her arrival at Chartreuse, however, it was as if she'd never been away. During a visit to Parr House which her uncle had maintained splendidly, she chose several of her favorite pieces for her new home. Parr flagons, pewter goblets and silver gilt cups were soon stored in handsome cupboards bearing the Neville coat of arms. A red marble table—always at her mother's bedside—was placed alongside the great oaken bed Katherine shared with her husband. She filled chests with her own precious books and made room in cupboards for her stepchildren's games. She chose a comfortable chamber overlooking the Charterhouse gardens where they might study and work with their dancing master and music teacher. With a practiced eye, she'd sorted out their reading materials, sending Bessie to the stationer's shop in Paternoster Row for more paper, paints, chalk and hornbooks.

Still, she put off returning to court. Chartreuse was enchanting as long as she avoided looking at the adjoining Charterhouse gate. She was still haunted by the mutilated thing which had hung there almost three years ago.

An early joy had been an affectionately tearful reunion with Kate Brandon. The Duchess of Suffolk brought her two boys—three-year-old Henry, very like his jovially handsome father, and little Charles. Tall and imposing, her hair bound into a tight coif nearly hidden by a heavy pointed hood delicately embroidered with seed pearls, Kate Brandon appeared much older than her seventeen years. She was handsomely dressed in a rich blue velvet riding costume, adorned with several pieces of jewelry Katherine recognized as belonging to the French queen.

"It smarts my Lady Frances that I wear her mother's jewels," Kate laughed with some satisfaction, "but I tell her they go with the title, not the person!"

Katherine laughed delightedly. Elegance aside, she thought, her Kate hadn't changed. She was still irreverent, still contemptuous of a lesser mortal's frailties. Later, admiring the two handsome Brandon children, she wondered aloud at her own failure to conceive.

"I've been married almost a total of six years, with two husbands and yet every month I'm disappointed. . . ." Then, guiltily, "I love my stepchildren of course—all of them! They are a great comfort. But I wonder if I'm barren, Kate?"

"Nonsense, you've had two old men for husbands," Kate spoke assuredly, "and older men don't spend their seed as fruitfully as younger ones."

Katherine almost replied that Charles Brandon was as old as Lord Latimer, but the duchess had quickly changed the subject.

"What you need is a change of scene from those Yorkshire hills with their cold wind to London's filthy streets and its icy damp! Come back to court, Kate! You don't have to be a lady-in-waiting like your mother. The queen would never ask you—she's well satisfied with your sister. You can't stay buried here at Chartreuse or at Snape. The court isn't as you remember it or as you'd like it to be. But it has its rewards—if only to watch the artificers and intriguers, the power plays where whenever one wins, another loses. It can be exciting if you leave your conscience at home, close your eyes to things you can do nothing about and remember to let others prattle while you guard your tongue."

"That's easy for you, Kate. You're the Duchess of Suffolk and everyone bows to you! Your husband bears an old title and is the king's brother-in-law and dearest friend." Katherine was doubtful. "John strives for no position and, God knoweth, I want none. There are few at court whose friendship I miss. Only Mary."

"Well, she's still allowed no visitors, my dear, and believe me, I've prodded Charles about this. But he says to leave well enough alone. However, every once in a while Lady Bryan comes to court. Things go poorly in that household, Katherine! I try to see her and give her messages to take back to Mary. Nothing written, of course, only that we all still love and pray for her. Lady Bryan says Mary lives in little rooms at the back of the house and gets very little exercise. You remember how she loved to ride and hunt and hawk! Now she keeps to herself and suffers badly from her teeth and headaches if she reads too much. Lady Bryan says sometimes she stays in bed all day! She is still allowed to write her mother and receives letters in return. But I wonder how long that will last? Jesu, Katherine, did you know the old queen lives in only one room with Maria who cooks her meals over a fire? She is so afraid of poison or murder she won't go outside at all!"

"Does Mary know all this?"

"I'm certain those who guard her—they're all relatives of the Boleyn—make certain she hears!" Kate's wrath was evident in her flushed cheeks. "Lady Bryan told me that one day Mary was so lonely, she even came to the nursery and saw little Elizabeth for the first time. I hear the child is quite beguiling and you know how Mary loves children. Anyway, after that, Mary went back often. It helped pass the time and gave her a chance to talk to someone other than Susan. Whenever the queen's ladies arrived, Mary always left. She refuses to have anything to do with them and calls them her jailers."

"Mary is her mother's daughter." Katherine shook her head, angrily. "It is heartbreaking the way they struggle so. But you and I know, Kate dear, they can do nothing else."

Kate Brandon warmed to her tale. "One day, Mary was in the nursery, playing with little Elizabeth when, without any notice at all, the queen appeared in the doorway. She was speechless at the sight of Mary cosseting the child. She thought perhaps Mary had now come to her senses and would be eager to submit to her father. Anne Boleyn wants that submission very badly, Katherine! So when Mary prepared to leave, Anne blocked the doorway and wouldn't let her pass. She said she'd like to make her peace with Mary and be friends. If she did so, she promised that all Mary's material comforts would be restored and soon she'd be back at court with her father."

"And what did Mary say?"

"Lady Bryan said Mary just stood there, gazing at the queen as she spoke. Anne was wearing a very rich fur cape and a plumed cap with jewels. Mary has had no new garments in almost three years and she just looked at her with contempt. She drew herself up and said, 'I know of no other queen in

England, my lady, except Her Grace, my mother. I would be obliged to you if you would tell this to my father, the king.'"

Katherine gasped. "Oh, Kate, that sounds so like Mary! But at what cost to her!"

"It didn't help," the duchess replied grimly. "The queen was shocked and lost her temper. She shouted at Mary, telling her what a bad girl she was and said she'd bring down her unbridled Spanish blood if it was the last thing she ever did. Lady Bryan said it spoiled the whole visit with Elizabeth, for Anne was shaking with anger and barely had time for her little girl. She told Lady Bryan she was going to tell Lady Shelton and her companions who live in the house to beat Mary if she misbehaved again."

"Jesu, let us pray it never comes to that," Katherine whispered, near tears.

Kate Brandon then said that several days after meeting with the queen, the household was ordered to Hunsdon. Mary had been sick and thought because she was unwell, she'd be allowed to stay at Hatfield and follow later. But when everyone was ready to leave, she was ordered to go with them, sick or not. She'd appeared in the hallway, expecting the first litter to be hers. When she saw it was for Elizabeth, she'd refused to go, telling everyone the Princess of Wales had precedence.

"And, as she waited there, Elizabeth was brought out and placed in the litter and off it went. When the next one arrived and Mary still refused to go, Lady Shelton's husband picked her up and threw her into the litter, telling her if she made any more trouble, they'd make her walk. Ah, Katherine, I tell you, I cried for an hour after I heard that story. I was so heartsick! But Charles says there is little that can be done—it has gone on so long now that people are liable to forget. All except the new queen, of course. She never forgets."

* * *

When Lord Latimer also urged Katherine to appear at court, Kate Brandon insisted her friend's wardrobe must be replenished. "You're very unstylish, my dear, and the court is—thanks to the queen—more fashionable than ever. Everyone who returns from the Continent brings back a new mode. You must appear in proper dress, Lady Latimer, or you'll shame your brother and sister who, I think, carry their fortunes on their back!"

Several days later, the two visited the stalls and shops of Bishopsgate, selecting kirtles, mantle veils, several new pointed hoods and matching waistcoats embroidered with seed pearls and heavy with Venice gold thread. They spent hours searching and choosing fans of feather, gold enamel or the new parchment-like paper, painted and pleated, into which tiny jewels were embedded. Bits of embroidery, laces and ribbons, yards of silver and gold fringe, with jeweled buttons to adorn the gowns—Katherine forgot prudence entirely.

Fingering the brightly colored silks and sateens, the brocades adorned with heavy, raised mosswork, Katherine felt less extravagant as Kate Brandon bought recklessly. One shining bolt of violet velvet was put aside for Maria. Kate said she was rebuilding part of her mother's Barbican house, refurbishing it inside as well. "The old queen can't last much longer, it saddens me to say," she told Katherine. "I haven't seen my lady mother since she was at The More. She always said if she ever left the queen, she'd not be allowed to return."

"Oh, Kate, that was almost five years ago! You and Maria have had so little time together!"

"She'd have it no other way, Katherine. We'll have to become reacquainted when she returns!" The young duchess smiled. "But I intend to see she comes home to a suitable house. After all she's been through, she deserves that at least. Only then will I tell the duke what all those men crawling over the roof and rebuilding the wall have cost!" Then, reflectively, "I think my lady mother has been happy in her way. She was never the same after my father died. They were devoted to each other."

"As were mine. . . ." Katherine recalled the day Maud Parr had swooned when informed of her husband's death. Of the weeks she'd spent in a semi-darkened room, a slight, forlorn figure, huddled on the bed, consumed by a pain that was almost physical.

Now, after two husbands, Katherine knew her parents had possessed a rare special passion which seemed to have eluded her. The French queen had had it with Charles Brandon and now Kate was obviously reveling in a similarly satisfying relationship with the duke. Anne Boleyn had, for a long time, held Henry Tudor an enthralled prisoner. All of them had been shamelessly and happily lost in an enchantment she'd never experienced. Lately, she'd felt a resentment which, guiltily, she'd tried to stifle. Magic stimuli could wane; the present queen was a good example of that. Her two husbands had cherished her and given her wealth and security; she already had abundant good health and every physical attraction a woman could hope for. What more could she want?

Inevitably, the picture of Thomas Seymour rose in her consciousness. She recalled how those piercing dark eyes had turned her legs to rubber as he held her hands. Was that the emotion of which the balladeers sang, which fortune-tellers prophesied for unwedded maidens and for which maids of honor blushed when courtiers carried their favors in the lists? Why had it eluded her? She remembered the gypsy in the woods outside Richmond Palace. What had he predicted for her? Crowns, scepters, castles and a title. Not one man, but many.

In a way, that prophecy had already come true. She'd had two marriages, lived in a castle and bore a title. But the crown? Could it be the little circlet Katherine of Aragon had given Maud Parr at her birth? Katherine treasured the gift as much as her mother had and at least once a year, alone and feeling a little foolish, she would remove it from the napkin with the queen's insignia, lay it atop her head and regard herself in a hand glass. Then the napkin would be freshly laundered and pressed before the circlet was once more consigned to her jewel chest.

*　*　*

Several days later, her new finery packed in chests stowed at one end of the Latimer barge, Katherine rode with her husband and the Duke and Duchess of Suffolk to Richmond Palace for the queen's thirty-second birthday celebration. Henry and Anne had recently returned from a progress through Hampshire. They'd enjoyed hunting and hawking and, as Ann Parr Herbert told her sister, "they seemed pleased with one another again."

Katherine looked forward to the Richmond gala. There would be jousts on the Green and fireworks from the boats anchored in the Thames to accompany the revelry in the Great Hall and on the river terrace. Earlier that day, John told her that little Princess Elizabeth was being brought from Hunsdon so the court might pay homage to the three-year-old heir.

"If the baby princess is coming, then so will Lady Bryan!" Katherine was exultant. "Oh, John, do you think Mary might be there also?"

"It would be a blessing for Mary, Katherine, but don't pin your hopes upon it." John shook his head. "Enjoy yourself, my dear, you haven't had much time for merriment in the past few years. You've busied yourself so much with me and my family." He took his wife's hand in his. "Keep your memories in the past and don't look back. You'll only spoil the present with remembrance of things that can't happen again."

Soberly, Katherine agreed.

Yet, as the barge rounded a bend in the river, her spirits rose at the sight of the old red-brick palace. Trees growing along the riverbank were larger and thicker than she remembered. The building itself had mellowed since the days she and the palace children had romped with her mother and the French queen in its woods or sung their lusty songs with the old queen from a small boat near the waterstairs.

Kate Brandon seemed to be lost in thought also. "It looks the same but so much is different," she whispered, "I almost dread what might happen during this gala, Katherine. Charles said Edward Seymour told him the king believes Anne Boleyn has practiced witchcraft to entrap him in marriage. Jesu! —he is blaming all his troubles with the church and with people like Fisher and More on her. I see nothing good ahead for her. . . ."

Katherine shivered. "I wish I could feel sorry for her, but I can't. Most of her trouble she's brought upon herself!"

"That's true, but now it is the king who takes the lead. He still shows great favor for that pale-faced Seymour wench and her brothers, the estimable Viscount Beauchamp and Sir Thomas—did you know he was knighted? —encourage her to please the king, no matter what. Anne doesn't help the situation for she flirts outrageously, seeking the attention she used to get from her husband. But she has to look to those of lower degree, for she hasn't a true friend at court except perhaps your sister and that odious Lady

Rochford. There are some who flatter and praise her, who think they might still gain something from her and, in this way, she thinks she makes the king jealous. Her brother is a great consolation, but even the rest of her family almost shun her for they think she may be their downfall. Sometimes I think she is doomed. . . ."

"Sir Thomas Seymour—has he wed?" Katherine wondered if he would be at Richmond for the celebration. How would she react if she met his wife?

"No, Katherine, my dear Lady Latimer, the splendid Tom Seymour has not married. Not that there aren't plenty of wenches eager to share his bed—especially now that his sister enjoys such royal favor! He's always admired you, my dear, I've heard him say so. And I think you're a little intrigued?"

When Katherine, astonished at her friend's frankness, didn't reply, Kate swung a shapely foot, beautifully shod in cream-colored Spanish boots from beneath her long skirt. "I like the shoes I'm in, my dear, and so should you." Glancing at John and Charles Brandon, deep in conversation, she lowered her voice. "Your husband is still besotted with you. You'll always be able to trust John Neville for he is like a rock. Too many others are like pebbles—beware of the shifting sands they lie in! They'll do you no good, my dear!"

Katherine felt herself blushing and, waving an affectionate hand at the duchess, realized she hadn't fooled her friend. There was little doubt that Kate regarded Thomas Seymour as an ordinary "pebble."

Several hours later, as they waited in the Great Hall for the king and queen's arrival, rumor swept the palace that Mary Tudor had also arrived at Richmond in the entourage of the little princess.

"Yes, she is here," a reluctant Charles Brandon told his excited wife, "but it was supposed to be a secret. The Privy Councillors wish to speak with her, but no one else is allowed."

Katherine clutched John's arm. He nodded understandingly. "Remember Woburn?" he shook his head, "I'm afraid, my dear, that no disguise will do it this time. Charles told me in the barge Mary was to be here but it's only because her father wishes to talk to her. It was easier to have her come with Princess Elizabeth than for the king to go to her. He's ordered she should have no visitors."

Before Katherine or Kate could reply, silver trumpets heralded the arrival of the royal pair. The great doors opened and, for the first time in almost three years, Katherine set eyes on her sovereign. As Henry held out his hand, Queen Anne placed hers on his and together they entered the room, walking slowly apace as the spectators bowed or sank to their knees.

"He's in a good mood," Charles Brandon whispered to his companion. "Perhaps we'll have the good fortune for the evening to pass joyously," he winked at Katherine, "sometimes it doesn't. . . ."

Waiting for the right moment to curtsey, Katherine studied the royal pair. Anne wore a crimson satin gown with sleeves of gold tissue cloth. The vibrant colors emphasized her olive complexion and hair, black as a raven's wing, from which a diadem blazed with jewels. A blood-red ruby, the size of a pigeon's egg, hung from the three rows of pearls clasped about her neck. The long tapering fingers of which she was so vain lay along her husband's heavy square hand, the gems from numerous rings flashing and winking in the light of hundreds of candles. The queen smiled, seemingly happy, as she greeted acquaintances or relatives. Yet Katherine sensed a tension or anxiety in the woman she'd never seen before.

Henry, however, was relaxed and buoyant with good humor. Aware he looked his best in the cloth-of-gold doublet with its ermine-trimmed surcoat, his scarlet hose still emphasizing the fine turn to his calf with its Garter insignia, he nodded and smiled as he passed. His figure had thickened since Katherine had last seen him, but his great height and bright auburn hair under its golden velvet cap, the ruddy healthiness of his skin still caught the eye.

As they approached, Katherine felt that almost mystical glow of pride in her sovereign, a fascination bordering on bewitchment, a pleasure almost physical. Wryly, she accepted that part of the excitement was vanity—that she should be so close to the power that was royalty. Yet visions of monks bound to hurdles, heads rotting on poles and bloodied quarters hanging over monastery gates were swept away as the two shining figures stopped to speak to a foreign ambassador just ahead. There were tiny beads of perspiration on the queen's upper lip. *She is nervous,* Katherine thought, wondering why. Looking beyond the bowing foreigner, she saw Edward Seymour, his wife and sister Jane, whom the king was now raising from her curtsey as Anne looked on, her expression wary. Just beyond Jane another tall, imposing figure, his cap tucked respectfully beneath his arm, smiled in appreciation of the compliment paid to his sister.

Eagerly, Katherine gazed at Thomas Seymour, as splendidly dressed as his brother and sister. While bowing to the king, he exchanged a gallantry with the queen which caused much laughter. Even so, Anne's fingers tightened on her husband and she urged him to continue along. Katherine found it difficult to tear her eyes away from Seymour. The man looked more mature, though he still possessed that supreme self-confidence she could almost feel from a distance. Again there was a tiny roil of pleasure in her breast, a little pulse of excitement in her loins. What would she say when they met?

Then, suddenly the king and queen were directly in front and, along with the duchess, Katherine curtsied, reaching for the hand Henry Tudor extended.

"My dear Kate! How fine to see you again! Let us see you at court more often and don't suffer this greedy husband to keep you so to himself. Life in the North must agree with you, Kate! You look wonderfully happy, my dear!"

Katherine felt the warmth of a blush as the king's eyes boldly slipped over her figure in its deep purple velvet gown. All thought of Tom Seymour disappeared. Henry lifted her hand to his lips. "And God knoweth, you are more like your mother every day." She felt the rough touch of his beard on her fingers. "Latimer is a fortunate man, my dear Kate. And you know it, John?" He inclined his head toward her husband, who bowed and smiled in return as the Suffolks joined in the laughter.

"I do, Your Grace, indeed I do." Katherine heard his reply, hoping her blush would not deepen. She felt the queen's eyes upon her. Anne said nothing, but merely smiled at her husband's words. Some of the tension seemed to have left her, but her eyes bore a hooded look as she urged her husband along.

"An honor, my dear, His Majesty was most gracious," John sounded pleased and proud. Again Brandon winked at her, whispered something to his wife, which caused Kate to hide her mirth behind her fan and shake a knowing finger at Katherine.

And then it happened. As the royal pair reached the dais at the room's end, there was Thomas Seymour before her, bowing to her husband and the Suffolks, taking both hands in his as if they were close dear friends who saw each other often instead of once every two or three years.

"My dear Lady Latimer! Such a fortunate occasion to see you again and you, my lord. Only the other day you were the subject of discussion in Hans Holbein's studio!"

Katherine felt the familiar tingling spark at Seymour's touch. The man was blessed—or cursed?—with a magnetism which equaled the king's own; she felt colorless and insignificant beside him. Yet no one must see her uncertainty. She sought the right tone.

"Master Holbein? Now what, Thomas Seymour, could the king's sergeant-painter have said of Lord Latimer's wife?"

"That he has an unfinished portrait he yearns to complete." Seymour's gaze bore into hers. "That he'd had two sittings before you, sir"—he gestured toward John in mock horror—"swept this lady off her feet to the North! Hans has lamented ever since it was never completed. I think"—once more his gaze was for Katherine alone—"he would very much like to see Lady Latimer again."

The words, innocent enough, were clear. Seymour was asking—and was aware she knew—that he would like to see her also.

"His studio is still in Westminster?" Katherine, her poise returned, found she was enjoying the little game. "We left for Snape very hurriedly after our marriage, Sir Thomas. Will you please tell Master Holbein I'll wait upon him soon so he may finish the portrait?"

Outside a thunderous explosion signaled the fireworks had begun. The Great Hall was lit by shards of falling flame, the candlelight paling in the shining aura. Quickly, John urged everyone onto the terrace. Bowing, Thomas pressed Katherine's hand. "Don't disappoint Hans again, my dear Lady Latimer. He dislikes unfinished business. So do I. . . ." And he touched his lips to the fingers the king had so recently kissed and was gone.

As she watched the sky lit bright as day by a huge burst of color and flame, Katherine recognized the implication of Seymour's words. She hadn't fooled him. He knew that he affected her and was saying he felt the same. He wanted to see her again and knew she was similarly intrigued. The admission—that she yearned to see another man—stunned Katherine. She loved and respected her husband—she'd never thought of herself as disloyal. Yet she was little better than the loose ladies of the court about whom Kate Brandon spoke so disparagingly. She hoped the duchess suspected nothing, for she knew she could never discuss it with her. Yet she'd never kept anything from Kate before.

The thought made her resentful and a little sad. As the fiery colors cascaded to a trailing death into the Thames, Katherine moved closer to her husband. Tucking her fingers into the crook of his elbow, as if seeking sanctuary, she felt his hand close over hers. The gesture was comforting and safe, the same as her marriage. Yet her pulse beat no faster. There was no consuming warmth or curiosity that left her literally breathless.

Suddenly, John's protective gesture filled her with shame. Damn Thomas Seymour! What had she been thinking of? An assignation with a man whose reputation was a little unsavory, but whose physical attraction was such that she could lose sight of all the values she cherished? If all she'd heard of Seymour was true, he wasn't worth her husband's little finger. Men of great charm usually made poor husbands, someone had once said. The king certainly possessed his fair share of that mercurial trait, but old Queen Katherine had fared poorly at his hands and Queen Anne was hardly the picture of happiness.

Except—she faced the fact squarely—Thomas Seymour, damn him all she would, could still rouse her as no other man ever had. And he knew it.

CHAPTER XIV

The following morning as John joined the king's party for hawking in the Surrey countryside, Katherine eagerly made her way to the royal nursery. If Mary's chamber was nearby, they might meet by accident. She missed Kate Brandon. The king had, to the duchess' irritation, ordered Charles to London on a mysterious errand, and the duke had intimated it might be diplomatic for Kate to visit her stepdaughter, Lady Frances Grey. They'd left before daylight when Kate had sent a message indicating where the nursery was.

A sentry on duty outside the door insisted on summoning Lady Bryan before Katherine was admitted.

"Kate, you're a sight for these old eyes!" Margaret Bryan's plain features lit up at the sight of her visitor. "Come—we'll have a good visit!"

She led Katherine into a small richly furnished chamber with handsome Flemish tapestries depicting biblical scenes on its walls. Though the room, with only one small window faced away from the river, candles burned brightly and a fire blazed in the massive fireplace. At the window, chattering excitedly to the nurse who held her up so she might better see outside, a small child pointed and laughed, clapping her hands with delight, looking to see if the older woman was similarly pleased.

"Come and see my lady princess." Lady Bryan drew Katherine toward the window. At their approach, the little girl turned and held up her arms. She wore a simple dress of white lawn, trimmed with delicately embroidered lace, over a stiff petticoat of pale yellow taffeta. Bright auburn hair—the exact shade of her father's—was almost hidden under a morning cap of the same yellow taffeta. The baby princess' skin was pale, very unlike her mother's. But Anne Boleyn's black eyes, tilted and piercing in their glance, sparkled with a similar intensity in her small daughter's face. They appeared even larger as the brows above them were not black, but pale auburn. Elizabeth had the same long tapering fingers as her mother. Swiftly, one reached out for Lady Bryan's white cap which would have gone askew had it not been firmly tied beneath her chin.

"Child! Child!" the governess cried, "this cap is mine, not yours!" Holding Elizabeth's hand firmly in her own, she said, "We have a visitor, my little lady, and you must behave and do me credit!"

Katherine held out her hand and the child grasped her fingers tightly.

Suddenly she noticed the thick gold chain with its large single pearl that Katherine wore around her neck. Fascinated by the bauble, the princess gazed at it silently for a moment and then reached for it.

Quickly, Katherine covered the jewel, laughing as she touched the child's smooth cheek. "You're very pretty, my lady, and a very taking one!" Deprived of the treat, Elizabeth similarly patted Lady Bryan's cheek, while everyone laughed. Katherine wondered how often Anne Boleyn saw the entrancing little creature. For most of her short life, Elizabeth—for reasons of health and security—had lived away from London and the queen could not have seen much of the daughter whose rights to the throne she guarded so zealously.

As the sound of a herald's trumpet signaled the return of the king's hunting party, Elizabeth wriggled in Lady Bryan's grasp. Her pale little face was pink with excitement and she struggled until the governess put her on the floor. Quickly, she ran to the window, waving her arms for the nurse to pick her up again so she might see outside.

"She recognizes the sound," Lady Bryan smiled, "and knows it means her mother or father are nearby. And she'll wait all day—not very patiently, I'm afraid—until they come. And God knoweth, I have to have a ready excuse if they don't appear! Then she becomes very upset."

As Lady Bryan and Katherine watched, the child waved her fists, drumming them on the window as if to let everyone know she was there. Below, they could see the king's party breaking up. As the stableboys led the horses away, the king thumped his smiling falconer, Robert Cheseman, on the shoulder before dismissing him. Nearby, Katherine saw her husband bow and make his farewell. Soon he would be looking for her. But before leaving she wanted to find out if she could see Mary.

As the king remained below, little Elizabeth's lips trembled and she appeared about to cry. Firmly, Lady Bryan urged the nurse and child into the adjoining room. "Your father, the king, has much to see to, my dear. When he's finished, I'm sure he'll come and see you," she explained, kissing the top of the child's head. "Be my good Elizabeth, little one, and old Lala may give you a sweetmeat before your nap."

Obediently, the little girl clung to the nurse, her face suddenly expressionless. Katherine's heart ached for the tiny princess. She knew the tears were only held in abeyance. She wanted to run outside and tell the king the most important thing he could do now was to forget his falconer, his horses and his hunting friends and come and see his little daughter.

Lady Bryan sighed as nurse and child left the room. She and Katherine stood near the window, still watching the scene below. Soon, only the king remained. He appeared to be waiting for someone, looking in all directions and rubbing his hands impatiently. Suddenly, he raised his hand in greeting, walking from the courtyard to the open field beyond. "How unusual!" Katherine exclaimed as she saw his step quicken.

"Yes, it is," Lady Bryan whispered, "he's going to meet Mary. See, there she is, out in the field. . . ."

Eagerly, Katherine watched as the king's elder daughter approached. She doubted if they could be seen from the window, shaded as it was by an overhead parapet. Slowly, Mary drew nearer her father. As the two met, the girl sank to her knees in a low curtsey and her father held out a welcoming hand, raising her to her feet. Though he removed his cap, tucking it beneath his arm, there was no embrace.

The two women gazed silently as father and daughter saw each other for the first time in almost three years. Mary was very thin. She wore a simple gray cloak without any of the jewels, ribbons or laces of a princess. She appeared to be doing most of the talking while the king listened. Several times she held out her hands in a pleading gesture.

"She looks so unhappy," Katherine whispered. "Jesu, I cannot believe Mary could be so wretched. . . ." Hot tears welled in her eyes and her voice shook with a sullen anger bordering on rage. "After all these years, I would think everyone would realize Mary is never going to submit. Why can't they just leave her alone?" She clasped her fingers tightly, afraid she might rap on the windowpane and interrupt the heartrending tableau.

Lady Bryan did not reply. She and Katherine watched as the king—waving his cap for emphasis—talked to Mary whose shoulders had visibly slumped from the proud carriage with which she'd greeted him. At one point, she raised shaking fingers to her face to wipe away a tear. The king, apparently softening, put an arm on her shoulder, though he did not embrace her. But Mary only shook her head while Henry gazed off in the palace direction as if wondering what to say next. After a moment, he bowed abruptly and Mary curtsied again. The king then turned quickly and strode back toward the courtyard. Mary, the picture of despair, walked through the field, disappearing around the wall which abutted on the friars' woods where they'd all romped long ago.

As Katherine sighed, Lady Bryan muttered, "Now what could have caused that? He saw something. . . ." Glancing below, her nose almost pressed to the glass, she cried, "Ah, I might have known! Fie!" Her voice shook as she drew Katherine nearer. "See, it is that Shelton woman, the queen's cousin. She is still Mary's guardian. She was spying on them and now she'll tell everyone Mary has seen her father. It will not set well with the queen! She was very upset when the king asked that Mary come here."

"Please, my lady, tell me everything, for my husband awaits me," Katherine implored. Walking toward the door, the governess said that Queen Katherine still lived in fear of her life, remaining in one room where her meals were prepared in the fireplace to avoid poisoning. She knew her own cause was lost, yet still clung to the fervent hope her rebellion would safeguard her daughter's rights. In a letter which Mary had shown Lady Bryan, the queen had urged her daughter to "show her teeth" to her father.

"Show her teeth!" Katherine was scornful. "That's all Mary has done for the last three years and it has worsened her lot! The old queen can't realize how it is at court now. If Queen Anne has a son, Mary's inheritance would still come after the Princess Elizabeth's! Must her whole life be ruined for something that can never be?"

"Mary has many supporters, Kate," Lady Bryan whispered. "You'd be surprised at those who come here to see my little lady princess. They bow and curtsey and are very respectful. Yet in the hall, the guard hears them laugh and make scornful remarks on her birth. Or say that she'll never be queen because the Pope has ruled that Mary is the legal heir and her cousin, the Spanish emperor, might even make war on England to protect her rights! I believe they think the guard has no ears! They still call Katherine the true queen, even though they've submitted to the king, on the surface at least. But they don't like it that the old queen's confessors, Father Abel and Father Forrest, are now in the Tower. They don't like it that Cromwell becomes more powerful every day. My son says that many who once courted Anne Boleyn now shrink from her for she's lost her hold on the king. Now they hate and blame her for what has happened to the church and they rejoice she hasn't given the king a son. . . ."

Francis Bryan, Katherine knew, would certainly know the political undercurrents at court. During a youthful escapade, Prince Henry had dubbed him the "Vicar of Hell" and the two had remained close over the years. Katherine had heard similar rumors—that the king was so angry with his daughter and the old queen for the wide support and affection they still had from the people, that he'd even considered making his illegitimate son, Henry Fitzroy, his heir.

A cry from the next room interrupted the conversation. "I must go to the princess." Lady Bryan pressed her visitor's hand. "I only hope the king comes today. But now that Mary has upset him so he probably won't unless the queen insists. I vow, Katherine, I often wish someone else had this responsibility! But I would miss my little princess. She is a very toward child. . . ."

Katherine embraced the older woman. "Be of good cheer, my lady, you do much good. And you see Mary more often than anyone else—I know it comforts her! I'll come again if I can. Tell Mary I grieve for her, that I long to see her and that we all love her very much."

Retracing her steps through the winding corridors to her chamber, Katherine found a message from her husband that he was with the king in the Privy Chamber where both would welcome her presence.

Smoothing her hair under its fine damask cap, her hands lingering on the pearl which had so fascinated the baby princess, Katherine set out for the Privy Chamber, wondering what would require her presence there so late in the morning. Whatever it was, she, too, had something to say to the king. Making her way toward where His Majesty waited, Katherine thought of numerous ploys by which she might remind Henry Tudor that away in her own room—and probably far from his thoughts—a small, auburn-haired child waited, listening for the footstep that might be his.

* * *

The Privy Chamber was crowded. Several courtiers played at primero or dice, while others stood quietly talking together. The king and queen were seated at a small table near the window overlooking the river. Anne's greyhound, Urien, lay at her feet. Henry was somber as he rolled the dice; the queen appeared drawn and distracted. Katherine sensed their tension and was thankful at John's approach.

"We've not been dismissed, my dear, and cannot leave until the king and queen do," he whispered. "Did you see Lady Bryan?"

In a low voice, Katherine described the scene in the fields.

"That explains it." John appeared relieved. "The king joined us here shortly after the hunting party broke up. He was very angry and told Cromwell to consider a bill of attainder against the old queen and Mary. Everyone was shocked and I think it upset our new Vicar-General very much." He inclined his head toward the fireplace where Thomas Cromwell was in deep conversation with Chancellor Audley. "Cromwell would rather have Mary's compliance. It would improve the king's relationship with Spain for one thing. But, more important, rabble-rousers would have little reason to make trouble then. Lady Bryan is right. There's a great deal of support for Mary and her mother and Cromwell knows it. That's one of the reasons he wanted the king to see his daughter now. But I don't think he thought Henry would be so angry he'd threaten her with imprisonment—or worse!"

Before Katherine could reply, Charles Brandon, accompanied by the Duke of Norfolk, entered the chamber. Without greeting anyone, they strode toward the king, knelt and whispered in his ear. Henry paled visibly and rose to speak with the two dukes. For the first time, Katherine saw her sovereign without his usual self-assurance; now he appeared troubled and unsettled. As Brandon and Norfolk bowed and left, he turned to the gaming table where Anne gazed at him questioningly.

"Yes, it is done." Henry threw the dice angrily on the table, his color returning. "It is done, madame, and I hold you responsible for this good man's death!"

Anne rose, holding out a hand to her husband. The greyhound, his delicate head cocked to one side at the king's unusual tone, drew closer to her.

"You must be satisfied now, dear lady. Your most illustrious opponent is no more." Without a word to anyone, he brushed by his wife and strode from the room.

In the shocked silence, Katherine urged her husband to follow. Everyone was making their way toward the door, noticeably avoiding the queen who remained apart, her back to the group, looking out the window, her hand caressing the dog's ear.

In the hallway, they joined the group surrounding Charles Brandon and

Norfolk. "We went to London at the king's order," Charles was explaining. "It was to witness Tom More's execution."

At the astonished cries of protest, the duke raised his hand for silence. "The king gave him every chance. As did the Vicar-General"—Charles nodded in the direction of Cromwell—"but he would not relent. He said he was the king's faithful subject who thought no harm but wished everybody good. He said if that was not enough to keep a man alive, then in faith, he did not long to live. But he would not swear the Oath. . . .'"

"He died well?" someone asked.

"He died well," Brandon replied grimly, "as one would expect. He asked the guard to help him up to the scaffold, for he found the ladder a bit steep for his strength. But, he said with some mirth, he would need no help in coming down. His last words were that he was 'the king's true subject, but God's first. . . .'"

Tears welled in Katherine's eyes. Thomas More had been her parents' close friend. It was hard to believe he'd had his head cut off that morning. Now that head would undoubtedly adorn a pole on London Bridge along with other traitors. Yet how could anyone think More was a traitor? He was not a man of the cloth refusing the royal supremacy. Nor had he communicated with foreign powers or involved himself with malcontents such as the Nun of Kent.

John agreed. "It is a dire thing, my lords, for More was popular with the people and his death will only anger them further. We should be trying to win their support not their criticism." He stopped as the queen emerged from the Privy Chamber, the greyhound following obediently behind her. Looking straight ahead, she disappeared around the corner. Katherine hoped she was on her way to see her little daughter.

"He did it for her, *une grande putain*." Norfolk almost spit the words out, gesturing toward Anne's retreating figure. Katherine was shocked at the vulgarity, for the queen was the duke's niece, the child of his youngest sister. "The king did it for her," Norfolk continued. "Tom More was imprisoned because the queen insisted no favoritism be shown. Everyone must swear the Oath. It's no secret she became his enemy when he absented himself from her coronation. Once in the Tower, it became a battle of wills between the king and his prisoner. I don't think anyone knew the depth of More's own conscience in this matter. He lost—but so did the king. Yet the queen may be the greatest loser of all."

* * *

While Katherine and John remained at Chartreuse, Katherine of Aragon died at Kimbolton Castle in the arms of Kate Brandon's mother, the beloved Maria. Though it had hardly been unexpected, the old queen's death sent Katherine to her bed in tears. The knowledge that the king had refused to let Mary see her mother at the end only added to her dejection.

Later, as she and John slipped into the Charterhouse church to say a prayer for the old queen's soul, Katherine could only guess at Mary's heartbreak. She must be wondering about her mother's last hours—had God taken her or had her end been hastened with poison? It could increase her hatred of the new queen.

Hoping to lighten the sadness in her home, Katherine showed John the little circlet the queen had given Maud Parr at her birth. Placing it on her head she told him of the gypsy's prophecy. "So much for the gypsy's words!" she cried, snapping her fingers. "I wouldn't exchange places with any queen! God be praised the old man was wrong." She kissed John warmly. "He made a little girl very excited and happy with his prophesying. But there'll be no crowns or scepters in *my* life. I'm just as happy as I am. . . ."

News of the Princess-Dowager's death swept the City and at once the churches filled with those who affectionately remembered the woman who'd been their queen for nearly a quarter of a century. And, in wealthy homes as well as hovels, in churches, inns and taverns, they wondered at the nature of her death. Soon, the finger of suspicion was pointed at Queen Anne, causing Cromwell to obtain a statement from Katherine's Spanish physician that the Princess-Dowager had refused additional medical help offered by the king, saying " 'I will in no wise have any other physician, but wholly commit myself to the pleasure of God."

At court, Anne remained vindictive. "I am grieved," she cried, "not that she is dead, but for the vaunting of the good end she made!" William Parr told Katherine now that there was no one to defy her, Anne Boleyn felt she was truly a queen at last.

Henry was also relieved, exclaiming that now neither the Spanish emperor nor the French king had reason to make war on England. Defiantly, he carried an ecstatic little Princess Elizabeth about the court, boasting of her beauty and intelligence, so cosseting the child that she was all but delirious with the unusual attention. Even the Spanish ambassador's sharp remonstrance that it had been inhuman to keep the Lady Mary from providing some solace for her mother at the end could not detract from Henry's good humor.

"You cannot try my patience today, senor!" the king clapped a hand on the ambassador's shoulder. "We are rid of a great burden—your country as well as mine. There is just one difference. I admit it, but you will not!" He gave the ambassador a gentle shove. "What good would it have done for Mary to visit her mother? They haven't seen one another for years! It would have been a great strain for both, particularly the Princess-Dowager and may even have hastened her end. Mary may not have wanted to leave her and there would have been a scene. She is not a well girl. Nothing would have been served."

The king and queen appeared reconciled once again. In the weeks following Thomas More's execution, placards had been nailed to Paul's Cross and scurrilous leaflets dropped in the streets, accusing the queen of murderous acts, charging her next targets would be the old queen and the Lady Mary.

In the midst of the unrest, Henry had pointedly left Anne at Whitehall and gone to visit Jane Seymour at Wolf Hall in Somerset. William Parr told Katherine the Seymour family—especially Edward and Thomas—had advised their elder sister to stay away from court since the queen was so unpopular.

Often, as Katherine rode from Westminster Abbey toward the handsome gate at Whitehall Palace which Hans Holbein had designed, she saw the artist's little studio near the royal cockpit. There, she'd virtually promised to meet Thomas Seymour. She knew all she had to do was present herself for a sitting and—unless he was away on the king's business—he'd certainly be there the following day. For the hundredth time, she wondered what such a meeting might bring. The court was always alive with gossip of new flirtations or the progress of old affairs. Nothing Tom Seymour did would likely surprise the jaded nobles. What *would* cause talk would be Lady Latimer's involvement! Katherine wondered if she, regarded by everyone as level-headed and steadfast, could bear the whispering and laughter, the loss of admiration and respect as the gossip's finger was pointed toward her? Could she think of the wound even a mild flirtation would bring to her husband should he find out? Or the disillusionment of her stepchildren? Invariably, she hastened past the little studio, intrigued but still undecided, knowing that once she acted, there'd be no backtracking. She'd be in a situation over which she'd have little control.

As plans for the old queen's funeral were made, however, fate ended Katherine's doubts. She and John were awakened one morning by the early arrival of a steward from Snape. He hadn't trusted a written message by courier, he explained to his hastily robed master and mistress, but felt he must come himself.

"There is dire trouble at home, my lord," he told John. "When the old queen died, people said she was poisoned and they are angry. They mislike what the king does—that he makes everyone swear the Oath so my Lady Mary will not be heir. And they wonder what he plans for the church, for he lets my Lord Cromwell send untutored men to investigate our holy houses. They pretend to find sinful living and corrupt practices and threaten to close our churches. But what they really want, my lord, are the church's treasures and land!"

Katherine ordered refreshments for the agitated man and after hungrily munching his bread, meat and ale, he told the Latimers the old queen's death had aroused the Northerners' deep resentment. They were further sickened at the treason laws which sent Chancellor More to his death, shocked at the old queen's treatment which they felt had hastened her death and infuriated at the persecution of her daughter.

"They love my Lady Mary, my lord. They feel the king is surrounded by evil advisers and they want to make their wishes known at court. They want you, my lord, to come home and tell them what they should do. They are talking of sending a delegation to London."

Visibly shaken, John told the man he'd be in Yorkshire within the week. Katherine knew he was concerned with what excuses he could make at court. But she said nothing, her head filled with all that must be done. There would be time for talk later on.

Later, after speaking with the surprised servants and her disappointed stepchildren, her thoughts revolved about what appeared to be open rebellion in the North. She could understand the people's discontent, though she knew few at court would appreciate their dissatisfaction. Secure in their hilly fiefdoms, a world apart from London and the court, the Northerners had always regarded their southern cousins somewhat contemptuously. They were a people apart, with strong pride in local custom and traditions. Through the centuries, they'd wrested a living from the soil with little time for cultural pursuits. Katherine knew many elderly servants, living their days out in tiny cottages on the Snape or Kendal estates, who still believed in demons, fiends, angels, witchcraft and other magic. How easy it would be for them to rebel when their queen or princess, their faith or tradition was concerned! She knew they would rise to defend their holy houses or protect their churches for, whether they worshiped in a parish church or the vastness of York Minster, their response was the same. They were comforted at the sight of saints, safe in their niches, the flowers and foliage of the fields heaped at their feet. Wealthier counties might beautify their statues with jewels or gold, but the Northerner lay the treasure of his sweat and toil at their feet. Did Cromwell really believe he could send strangers—always a source of suspicion in the North—to investigate their holy houses which they considered a source of pride and reaffirmation of their faith? Did he really think he could assess the Northerner's world and deal with it as he might in other areas of the country? The king and Cromwell, Katherine felt, might eventually be surprised.

Yet, for all her disappointment that her London visit was so short and apprehensive of what she might find at Snape, Katherine felt a niggling sense of relief. As she packed the little gold circlet, the darkly handsome image of Thomas Seymour rose before her. Now he and Holbein's portrait seemed of little importance. Even as she worked, however, she recalled his merry banter, the derisive smile, the almost insolent familiarity in his gaze which seemed meant for her alone. So much for her fine words and uplifting thoughts! The man would not be driven from her mind. And, by doing nothing since their last meeting, Katherine knew she was only keeping him alive in her imagination.

When her packing was complete, she wrote a little note to Holbein informing him of their departure. Certainly the news would ultimately reach Thomas Seymour. Now she'd have all the long winter-filled Northern nights ahead to amuse herself of what might have been. She wondered if he'd be disappointed, admitting at the same time her own regret was probably greater. Perhaps fate had saved her from an indiscretion which would have been costly and she should be grateful. But now she'd never know.

*   *   *

The Latimers arrived at Snape to find the country, as the courier had said, in the grip of rebellion. Everywhere people talked of the brutal murder of Chancellor More and wondered if the queen had been poisoned. They were as angry at excessive taxation as they were at the persecution of their princess. And above all they despised Thomas Cromwell whom they considered too baseborn to serve the king.

While they'd grumbled for months at these injustices, it was finally the sight of their monasteries being desecrated—the hand of man defiling the house of God—which shocked them to their simple cores and set them on the path of open rebellion. In her first days at home, Katherine heard it often—the complaint of "something must have happened to the king's Grace that he would condone such acts!" The harvest that year was the worst in living memory. Obviously God was angry that they'd let an ancient loyalty to their sovereign obscure a higher loyalty to His Son's teachings?

At first, John tried to placate his neighbors—those aristocratic landowners and other gentry who'd flocked to Snape to hear news of the court. Katherine could see her husband was torn. A true Northerner, he understood better than most the depth of the people's feelings.

"I'm shocked at the way they speak of the king, but I know why they do it," he told Katherine after obtaining the release from prison of one of his own tenant farmers. The man had complained loudly that all the problems besetting the county from the weather to the price of wool was the king's fault and it would get no better while he reigned. Promising to see to the man's future behavior, John had sent him home. Yet each day brought new insults to the sovereign. Katherine had never felt so uncomfortable in her country home and wondered what her parents might have done.

Her uncle, William Parr, as much a Northerner as John, still remained at court. He wrote that the queen was again pregnant. "Pray for a son, Katherine, it would settle so many issues and problems now if the king had a male heir." Katherine found it easy to pray for such a blessing. It would make life easier for Mary and perhaps calm the turbulent spirit of the North.

Her hopes, however, were dashed by a letter from Kate Brandon which arrived in the middle of winter, a letter delayed for almost a week by the heavy Yorkshire snows. John had gone to York to prepare for a meeting of the Council of the North at which the heavy taxes on wool and property, along with the people's other dissatisfaction would be discussed. Eagerly, Katherine read the duchess' words:

February 6, 1536
Westhorpe

My dearest Katherine,

As Charles is sending letters by courier to John at the Council of the North, I enclose this to you which brings news of the court. Some is fearful and I know you will read between the lines. The courier, who is a trusted servant, may give you by tongue that which I am too craven to write.

The king suffered a massive injury less than a week ago. He was jousting in the tiltyard even though Dr. Butts had told him—as had Charles and the queen—that with his sore leg and his added weight, he should not do so. He was thrown from his horse and, for almost two hours, lay as one dead. Upon removing the armor, the sore on his leg had split and was very bloodied. The king looked as dead as anyone on a field of battle, Charles said, and a priest was summoned while all knelt in prayer. During this time, someone told me, my Charles was so overwrought he wept, lamenting, "It is such a waste, a waste! Who will take his place?"

Miraculously, after two hours he was revived, being very weak with a massive ache in his head and joints. But he was alive, for which Jesu be praised!

But now, alas, I come to the part which makes me as fearful as sad. You know the queen was again pregnant? She had softened during the last few weeks and spoke of the boy she would bring forth. Even the king appeared kinder to her and the court was a pleasant place to be. But during the king's fall, that fool Norfolk, her uncle, ran to her chamber and told her the king was dead or soon would be. Anne shrieked that she'd told him he must not ride —she berated her uncle, beating him with fists about the shoulders for encouraging the king in his tomfoolery—as if anyone could prevent Henry from doing as he wist!

Everyone tried to soothe her, but she would have none and oh, Katherine, it grieves me to say that within an hour she went into labor. It was long and painful and for a while, as the king lay as dead, we thought the queen might join him. At last she brought forth her baby and you will lament to hear it was a boy. But it was dead. It was too soon to be born and could not survive. The queen, on being told her son was gone, fainted away.

The next day there was much dolor in the palace and, as Mary had been brought with Elizabeth to see her father because of his injury, I took a chance and, with Lady Bryan's help, hid in her chamber for the space of an hour. Oh Katherine, it was so good to see her after so long! She grieves still for her mother, but says her heart is at peace as now she is with God and not suffering the insults of her last days on earth. She, too, fears poisoning, but has resigned herself to her fate.

Breathless, Katherine put the letter aside, wondering if John was hearing the same thing at York. She wondered at the almost heavenly retribution which the queen had suffered. It seemed God would deny her the son he'd denied the old queen. She picked up the letter again:

Later, Lady Bryan told me the king had seen Anne who was very ill from her ordeal. He was angry with her and loudly accused her of killing his boy. Lady Bryan said it was truly pitiful the things they said to each other. Anne blamed the shock of her loss on him, saying if he'd spent more time with her to quiet her heart instead of playing the braggart on the tiltyard, they might have had their son. And all this was said while little Elizabeth was in the room before Lady Bryan took her away. The child cried terribly all the way back to the nursery. Lady Bryan said the last thing she heard was the king telling the queen he'd have no more boys by her for he no longer wished to live with her.

What makes this even more frightening, Katherine, is that the king's accident and the queen's miscarriage occurred on the day when the old queen was being buried at Peterborough Abbey and the unlit tapers about her tomb lit of themselves. A *Deo Gratias* was sung by the choir and then the tapers went dark. This was witnessed by too many to be false. People said it was as if her spirit returned to Whitehall and wreaked a justice impossible in her lifetime. Is it likely the shade of a departed one can do this? It is the talk of London and many at court too. . . .

When John returned from York, tired and discouraged, he told Katherine that Brandon had written much the same thing. "He says the king will not tolerate this situation for long, Katherine, and he'll find some way of ridding himself of the queen. Soon, I fear, Elizabeth will be in the same position as Mary! And still the king will not have an heir." He shook his head sadly. "Ah, the situation is rife, my dear. I see no good coming of it, mark my words. I don't know where it is worse—here, or at court. Still, I'm glad we're out of it."

As spring came to the Northern valleys, Katherine honored a promise to take young John and Margaret to visit her Borough stepchildren at Gainsborough. Margaret was now nearly the age she herself had been when she'd arrived as a bride, looking for the handsome russet-haired man in the medallion. At Gainsborough, she walked through the warm mellow rooms where she'd learned to be a wife and mistress of a large estate. Bemused, she told Bessie, "It's like another lifetime. Were we ever that young, Bess?"

"Kate, my dear, you're still only twenty-four!" Her companion smiled, giving Katherine a little shake. "I see no gray hairs yet, Lady Latimer!"

One morning as Katherine prepared for a ride through the spring-freshening Yorkshire hills, a courier arrived from court with a packet for her Borough stepson. Henry Borough's voice shook as he read to his family the news that at a May Day joust at Greenwich, Queen Anne Boleyn had been arrested, charged with adultery with Sir Henry Norreys, Sir William Brereton, Sir Francis Weston and a court musician, Mark Smeaton. "The men are aghast, their families unbelieving," the message read, "and Weston's family have offered Cromwell 100,000 marks for his release. They all strongly deny the charges and Norreys told the king to his face there was nothing between him and the queen. Only Smeaton seems to have provided some evidence and it is common knowledge he was tortured at Cromwell's own house to make such an admission. The queen stays now at the Tower awaiting trial with the others. . . ."

Katherine was incredulous. As the group followed her stepson back into the house, their ride forgotten, she asked Henry Borough, "Why, if the king wants to be rid of the queen, doesn't he simply divorce her as he did the old queen?"

The young man folded the letter carefully. "I'm sure, my dear Katherine, our dear Vicar-General Cromwell has a reason for all this. Probably he thinks the king might not be strong enough to resist Anne's pleas not to forsake her. He might no longer love her, but she could appeal to his senses— or his pride—and he might not be able to go through with it." Henry Borough's voice was wry. "But now, by this letter and many others like it, Cromwell has made certain the charges are so horrible that once the truth is known—and see how little time it took to arrive here, hundreds of miles away?—there will be no looking back for the king." He slapped the letter against his thigh. "A clever move for Cromwell! Now the king is the innocent and offended party. His wife is so certain of being judged guilty of a foul crime, they'll have to kill her to get rid of her."

The words remained in Katherine's mind as she and her stepchildren rode back to Snape. The picture of the unfortunate Boleyn, her sensuous charm, the mercurial, almost quicksilver personality of the dark-haired woman with the sparkling almond-shaped black eyes rose before her. Later, discussing it with her husband, she said, "You must know those men are innocent, John. Norreys attended the king when he married Anne. He's almost as close to Henry as Charles Brandon! Brereton and Weston are good men—they were great friends of my parents. The musician I don't recall. How can the king convince himself of these disgusting charges?" John could only shake his head obviously bewildered by the news.

In the following days, as everyone waited further news from court, Katherine wondered about Anne Boleyn. Was she, perhaps, in the same Tower cell where her old foe Thomas More had languished? Where Lady Salisbury, now free but out of favor at court, had been incarcerated? And what, she wondered, would happen to little Elizabeth? Would the queen have time to see the daughter whose rights to the throne she'd so zealously guarded she'd put the king's eldest daughter through almost six years of hell? What would they tell the little girl when the trumpets sounded and no queen-mother appeared?

And what would Mary Tudor think of the shameful charges? Would she laugh for joy, cry for pity or what? Katherine asked John and then, not waiting for an answer, said, "No, being Mary, she'll dutifully pray for that poor woman. She'd have every right to cheer and bless the event. But if I know Mary, she'll be on her knees, praying for the abandoned soul of Mistress Anne Boleyn. Even now, she'll never call her anything else. . . ."

CHAPTER XV

Throughout the summer and fall of 1536, the Latimers of Snape Hall lived with the uneasy knowledge that their neighbors, friends and families were rapidly becoming more deeply embroiled in a covert rebellion against Cromwell's influence with the king. John and several other nobles had helped quell the defiant resentment of early spring, but the shameful travesty of Queen Anne's trial and brutal execution followed by Henry's indecently quick marriage to Jane Seymour, only added more fuel to a barely quenched flame. When two of Cromwell's investigators, the infamous Richard Layton and Thomas Legh, arrived in Hexham in Northumberland to determine which monasteries would be dissolved, they were met with the first armed resistance. Local citizens with pikes and clubs were joined by monks carrying any garden tool they could lay their hands on. Everyone was prepared to defend the holy houses. The stunned investigators, hinting bribery might save the day, were roughly handled and soon put on the road south. The citizens were now beyond compromise.

Soon afterward, Sir William Parr arrived at Snape on his way to Westmorland where his Kendal tenants were as aroused as their Yorkshire neighbors. Sir William had witnessed Queen Anne's execution and did not spare his niece and her husband in his account of it.

"It was not a pretty sight, but I trow the queen had already put this life behind her. I think Brereton, Weston and Norreys' death and that of the wretch Smeaton had drained her of any emotion," he said. "And that other charge, of incest with her brother, Lord Rochford, had so numbed her, she was like a puppet on the scaffold. She knew her queenship was over, that the king wanted everyone to witness her disgrace and hear the shocking charges for which death was the only punishment. I never liked the woman, but at the end she had all the dignity she never showed as queen."

When Katherine asked how true the charges were, her uncle replied, "Cromwell was very clever. There was just enough innocent flirting and evil tongues eager to accuse that the poor woman never had a chance. When Lady Rochford made that monstrous charge against her husband and the queen, Anne knew there was no hope for the only way the king could get rid of her was by her death."

"That vile woman!" Katherine was incensed. "She used the queen's disgrace as a means to get rid of her husband for she always hated George

Boleyn. Her father, that miserable Lord Morley, made her marry George who wasn't too pleased with the match himself. So of course he had to die! Jesu, what an abomination! And how fares my Lady Rochford at court now, Uncle?"

"She preens and tells everyone that many times she saw her husband visit the queen in her bedchamber and once, when Anne was sick, saw him lean over and kiss her full on the mouth. She's almost convinced herself the shameful charge is true. But you know the real reason George Boleyn had to die?"

Katherine shook her head.

"Otherwise, he'd have spent his life avenging his sister's honor, my dear! You know they were always very close." He glanced out the window at the splendor of Snape's hills vivid in their autumn color. "That was Cromwell's warning to everyone who gets in his way. He prides himself on doing the king's business and when Henry wanted to be free of Anne Boleyn, our Vicar-General cared little about the means employed. One life, more or less, was little price to keep the king's favor."

When William Parr left the next morning, he had a private word with his niece. "Katherine, be careful what you write and send to court. Be careful what you say and to whom you say it. Cromwell has spies everywhere. He is determined to close most of the holy houses—suppression and eventual dissolution he calls it—and the king looks the other way because his coffers are empty and the church has great wealth." He kissed Katherine's cheek. "We're facing a time of trial, my dear. John knows it and he has great faith in our people to do the right thing. I wish I were as certain! People can be pushed just so far. But the mistreatment of the old queen and Mary and his new marriage has made everyone here lose faith in him. I'm afraid of outright rebellion and, if that happens, God help us all. He has no son now, only two bastard daughters, for Elizabeth was illegitimatized when her mother died. It wouldn't surprise me if someone tried to take his crown. There are still some alive who remember King Richard, whose Plantagenet relatives still live in uneasy truce with the king. Cromwell is, I'm certain, determined to deal with them one way or the other."

In the weeks following her uncle's departure, Katherine went uneasily about her tasks, agreeing with John that the inclement weather that had so greatly damaged their crops would necessitate further supplies being purchased for winter. Their people would look to Snape for sustenance in their time of need, John said. Katherine wondered how those freeholders in their tiny cottages with a wife and many children to feed and clothe would manage throughout the long months of a Northern winter.

Within days she had her answer. It arrived in the form of her stepson, Henry, Lord Borough, who told the Latimers that over twenty thousand rebels from other counties were planning a march on Yorkshire and they should be prepared for trouble. Quickly, John summoned several of his tenants and stewards and, within the hour, they'd all fanned out in different directions to inform their neighbors what was happening. Each householder—from castle, manor or cottage—must defend himself; there was no walled courtyard or moat at Snape. At the day's end, a tired husband and stepson returned to join Katherine as she and Bessie ate their evening meal.

"It's too early to say if the people—some are even calling them rebels!—will come this far," John said wearily, "but we've learned much today, Katherine, and it's worse than I thought. Everyone says things are not right in England. The king should not allow the desecration of holy lands and buildings, which many have seen plundered, with the stone carted away for other building and their old statues taken tb London for burning at Holborn. And Cromwell, so old Lord Darcy says, has not lived up to his promise to use the monastery monies for hospitals, schools or orphans' homes. Old Darcy says he wrote the king the men were marching in protest against unjust taxes and the enclosure of their common lands. He said the king may suffer holy houses around London to be closed, but in the North these griev-ances have incurred a good deal of ill will. And he said the king must use caution and tact in dealing with the people. I don't think Henry's going to like that. He doesn't like opposition, as you know."

Katherine put an arm about her husband's slumping shoulders. She could imagine Darcy, white-maned and bluff, every inch the proud Northern lord she'd known since childhood, writing his charges to the king. Really to Cromwell, she thought. How would the king and his new Lord Privy Seal react? She put the question to her husband.

"I think they're going to be disappointed," John said as he eagerly began the hot meal a servant placed in front of him. "They are innocent and be-lieve they can tell the king their grievances and, being their good sovereign, he will act to right their wrongs. But you and I know the Privy Council will advise the king to retaliate more severely. I don't think our people know what they risk! Neither Cromwell nor the king will tolerate this rebellion for any length of time. If these rebels are allowed to continue, they'll gather more support along the way. We must do something to stop them before the king sends soldiers to fire on them, poor devils. They don't, I trow, have a cannon amongst them!"

Though they lacked arms, the rebels had strength as was evident when, at twilight several days later, a frightened, white-faced and bloodied Sir William Askew was brought to Snape's gate. He'd been collecting the local taxes as was his duty, he explained to Katherine and John, when the local people set upon him.

"And I thought my end was near." The man, weakened from his loss of blood, submitted to the ministrations of the Snape apothecary, as Katherine sent Bess for some herbal oils from her stillroom. "The ruffians are now in Pontefract Castle and ask others to join them. They've lit beacons on the tors to summon those from neighboring counties and everywhere marchers are pouring into the castle." The man shook his bandaged head. "What are we coming to, my lord, when farmer and ploughman think they can take such matters into their own hands?"

Hoping to distract him, Katherine asked after his daughter Anne.

"The girl is daft in her mind, it gives me no pleasure to say," Sir William grumbled. "You remember she was such a one for learning? I think it has addled her brain! Thomas Kyme, as good a man as could be found for her, has about put up with all he'll take from Mistress Anne! She neglects her husband, home and children who rarely see their mother! It's been well my wife is willing to see to their care for their own mother might as well be a traveling pedlar-woman!" He touched his head with a bruised hand as if to dispel such unhappy thoughts. "She spends her time riding to meetings and preaching to anyone who will listen. She calls it 'gospeling.' Whatever it is, it's full of every evil the devil ever thought of and every lie one can tell about our Holy Father in Rome. She questions the Mass, the sacraments, the way churches are built and managed, the saints we worship and laughs at heaven and hell alike! She is so full of heresy, I wonder our Lord allows her to live!"

Shaken at the vehemence of Sir William's words, Katherine guiltily recalled an impatient little Anne's eagerness to learn, the bright intelligence she'd brought to her studies. It had all seemed so innocent then.

Anne Askew was not Sir William's only complaint. He too blamed Cromwell, the king and Sir Richard Rich, the Lord Privy Seal's colleague, for mishandling the suppression of the monasteries. "I warned them, but they wouldn't listen. Had they sent someone to explain and appease these rebels, they'd never have gathered such strength. No, my lord, I think it's too late and we'll see more violence unless someone with common sense who has the rebels' respect will take charge." He looked at John. "You would do well, my lord. You family is well known and admired in these parts. And then there's young Aske—Robert Aske, that is. He also has the people's trust and possesses as bold a tongue as I've seen. He can soothe or rouse like no one else. Will you see him, John? This uprising must go no further if we can help it!"

Wearily, John nodded his head.

Two days later, as Sir William Askew lay abed, still nursing his wounds and awaiting word from Cromwell on how to proceed, Robert Aske arrived at Snape. Despite her intuitive feeing that they should not become further involved, Katherine was impressed by the visitor. Robert Aske was in his midthirties, clearly a man of great spirit and intelligence, of middling height with a shock of flaming red hair no brush could tame nor cap could cover. A lawyer with more idealism than most lawyer-clerks she'd known, his strong square face was stamped with the Northerner's high color. He was clear of eye and direct of gaze. Katherine suspected the stubble of beard on his strong, almost pugnacious chin was there so he might appear even older.

Aske was brutally frank in his assessment of the rebellion. "It's not going to stop, my lady," he told Katherine. "We have priests, monks, artisans, farmers, laborers, tradesmen and many others who've joined in this march. They call it a pilgrimage for they are bound to preserve Christ's church and their holy houses. They think the king is in the clutches of evil advisers and is giving away—or selling—holy property. Do you know old John Russell has purchased Woburn Abbey? And the king's great friend, Sir Anthony Brown, has been given Chertsey Abbey and Guildford Priory and much land in Surrey, while Cromwell himself has annexed St. Osyth's monastery and Lewes Priory for himself? This we know for certain, but you may be sure there is much we don't know. Our people see their way of life being threatened and they will no longer suffer to have their taxes raised, their lands enclosed and their holy houses violated. Some of what Cromwell's men have done is nothing but pure vandalism and they are destroying the beauties of our realm! The king and council don't understand our problems or feelings and we can no longer tolerate that we should be so governed without any say in the matter at all!"

Robert Aske was impressive—he was all William Askew had said. He exuded confidence, a sense of justice and moral courage and an independence that reminded Katherine of her father. She could not imagine him practicing any duplicity.

As he and John discussed the rebels, Katherine was amused as Rob Aske's eyes often strayed to where Bessie sat quietly, her slim fingers busy with her needlework. Aware of his glances, the girl only bent her head lower, her cheeks deeply pink, her usually calm demeanor suddenly confused. Katherine tried not to stare. Few things flustered her Bess—plainspoken Mistress Bellingham who'd become such a staunch companion. Katherine had always promised a handsome dowry for Bessie, also in her early thirties, should she find a mate.

But Bessie had not been optimistic. "If my prince comes calling, sweeps me off my feet and leaves me in a swoon, I won't be backward about accepting your offer, Kate," she said, "but I don't want *anyone*—just to be a married maid! You know me better than that! As long as you want me with you, I'm happy as I am. I can't waste time looking and waiting for any lad. . . ."

Touched, Katherine had accepted that spinsterhood would probably be her friend's lot. Bessie lacked nothing in remaining unwed and now, in her advanced maidenhood, it would take a man of unusual and special character even to interest her, let alone win her heart.

But, as Katherine watched and listened to Robert Aske, some small flash of intuition told her that even if Bessie didn't know it, the man had arrived. That was the pleasantest thing that had happened since her arrival at Snape.

* * *

As conditions worsened in the North, the king reacted with tolerant amusement, confident his Northern lords such as old Darcy, Hussey and Latimer would quiet any rebellion.

When Sir William Fitzwilliam, the Lord Admiral, reported there was much sympathy for the rebels' cause in some of the southern counties, the king merely shrugged. He was certain of his Northern lords; they'd quell any rebellion. He considered getting the queen with child more important than negotiating with a group of uncouth, illiterate Northerners who thought they could dictate to a king.

* * *

At Snape, Katherine and John were apprehensive as several of the aristocracy—Lords Lumley, Scrope, Conyers and even the Earl of Westmorland —ignored all pleas for restraint. The movement had swelled to over thirty thousand rebels and, when two tax collectors, Sir Robert Tyrwhitt and Sir Thomas Misselden, were captured and imprisoned at Louth, the insurgents' hatred and resentment boiled over. Throughout the countryside, the dales were soon alive as men from small hamlets and villages, from castle, manor house and yeoman's cottage poured forth in a movement as spontaneous as it was devout. The devastating harvest, the pillaging of their holy houses were reasons enough for God's wrath, the marchers cried. On the highest tors, beacons were again lit to summon those in neighboring counties. Calling themselves pilgrims, they streamed across the craggy hills, their banner— depicting the Five Wounds of Christ—held high. It was a Pilgrimage of Grace, someone shouted to an incredulous ploughman as a crowd of protesters tramped across his land toward a meeting place, a Pilgrimage of Grace to pluck the king from the clutches of those determined to change their ancient way of life.

As Michaelmas approached, Katherine and John remained at Snape, apprehensive that the king had finally sent Thomas Howard, the old Duke of Norfolk, to Doncaster with an armed force. Henry had at last reluctantly recognized the militant nature of the uprising. Each day the Snape courtyard was filled with couriers going from one camp to another, wolfing down food and drink before hoisting their banner of the Five Wounds and marching off again. Katherine knew it was depleting their store of winter provisions, yet she could hardly refuse her hungry countrymen for every neighboring house was sharing what it had with the rebels. If food was all they lost, Bessie said grimly, they would be lucky.

As Katherine had suspected, the attraction between her close companion and Robert Aske had grown and deepened in the past few weeks and Bessie now made little secret that her heart was as involved in the uprising as any pilgrim's. Robert Aske made Snape his headquarters while he attempted to bring order among the villagers and the nobels' retinues that clogged the roads as they assembled in various parts of the county. Bessie and he were often together as Katherine, to John's amusement, made excuses to leave them alone. Still Bessie, ever the taciturn Northerner, said nothing. Finally, unable to bear it any longer, Katherine shook her friend lightly, asking, "Well, my girl, when are you going to tell me?"

"He's the one, Kate, the one I said would have to sweep me off my feet!"

Bessie laughed, ducking her head against Katherine's shoulder. "But of course, there's no time to do that. Robert wants our people to be heard and hopes old Darcy and Hussey will be able to treat with my Lord of Norfolk at Doncaster. They all know each other well. When everything is over, he'll come back here for me. Until then, we can't make any plans."

Katherine hugged her friend, a catch in her throat. "Ah, Bess, I'm happy for you! Robert Aske is a fine match. John has only good words for him—sensible, strong and not looking to profit himself." She embraced Bessie again. "And he's also pleasing to look upon and has a kindly way with him. We'll give you a fine wedding, my Bess, and a well-earned dowry when this trouble is over. And it must be over soon! Winter is coming and people cannot march in the snow!"

Yet two nights later, Katherine wasn't so sure. An icy wind had brought down several trees in the park while the first frost had blackened what was left in the gardens. A great fire blazed in the hall where Sir Francis Bigod from Mogreve Castle in Blakemore had come to talk of a match between his son and Margaret Neville, now fourteen years old. It was the first meal Katherine had shared with her husband in days. Usually Bessie joined them at mealtime, but she had asked to be alone with Robert Aske.

Suddenly, a rumble like distant thunder or a strong wind could be heard. As it grew louder, John went to the window, his face graying as he looked outside. "God's blood . . . they wouldn't dare!" he cried. In a moment, a servant ran into the room crying, "My lord, my lord! Come quickly! In the courtyard at the back . . . !" Without a word, John and Sir Francis ran from the room.

Quickly, Katherine was at the window, Margaret and John beside her. In a moment, Bessie joined them. "Robert has gone with my lord, Kate. Is this a dream we're seeing or is this for real?" Soberly, they all gazed at the scene below.

The courtyard of Snape was filled and, as far as they could see to the fields beyond the gate, there were men—men on horseback, on foot, some in wagons and carts, some carrying pikes, staves, halberds or clubs. Great torches flamed from enough hands to light the scene as if it were day. Katherine saw many familiar faces while Bessie recognized others. "At least they're not ruffians, Kate. I think we're safe!" She sounded relieved.

"No one is safe where there's a mob, Bess! They've come for something, but in God's name, what? Pray we can help them!" Katherine saw the leader, Sir Robert Constable, calling to John, Sir Francis and Robert Aske who stood on a courtyard balcony. "Let's hope it keeps them from coming in," Margaret whispered as her hand sought Katherine's. "What do they want from Father?"

Bessie opened the window and the sharp cool air brought the burning smell of torches and the marchers' body sweat into the room. A great cheer went up as Sir Robert Constable stepped forward, calling to those on the balcony that everyone from the surrounding countryside—some two thousand men—were there. At which the mob cheered again.

"And what is it that we can do for your good men, Sir Robert?" John called out. Incongruously, Katherine saw he still held his dinner napkin, waving it as he spoke, causing several of the rebels to jiggle their banners in response.

"We want leaders, my lord," Constable called, "leaders to take these pilgrims to Doncaster! They want you and young Aske! You know our grievances! Our farms are decaying because outsiders have enclosed the lands to raise sheep for wool. Many people will go hungry this year, my lord, for we cannot eat wool! We'll get no relief from the holy houses because they're gone—desecrated and looted—by those who use abbots' copes for their doublets and decorate their saddles with altar cloths! They will sell off our ancestors' graveyards, for nothing is sacred! We're even forbidden to celebrate any saints' days! We cannot exist this way, my lord—it is unjust! Surely our king has heard of the unruly conditions here, of the unjust taxation and of how our hearts are sore smitten! Now Norfolk has come at the king's orders and we want you and young Aske to talk with him for us!"

John nodded. Calling to Constable, he advised that everyone douse their torches and camp overnight in the fields outside the gates. He and Aske would talk, he said, and at daylight he'd tell them their decision. As he left the balcony, a muttering began among those in the forefront and Katherine's heart sank. She noticed that Aske was obviously dissatisfied. Plainly, he thought John should have listened to them longer and given them more assurance. But relief swept through her and Margaret's taut hand went limp as, one by one, the torches were doused and the sound of campers settling down for the night could be heard.

After Bigod had left and the children reluctantly gone to bed, the two men continued to talk. What should they do? Never before had Katherine seen her husband so uncertain, nor had she herself felt so doubtful. Her heart was with her countrymen lying outside now in the cold and damp. Their grievances were just. Yet Parrs and Latimers were always loyal to the king. Never for one moment could either she or John rebel against Henry Tudor.

"It isn't rebellion in that sense, my lord," Robert Aske explained. "What these people want is a full hearing. Injustices have driven them to this point and they want some redress and an agreement that it won't happen again."

"You make it sound so simple, Robert," Bessie said shyly, her hand seeking his, pride shining from her eyes, "and so good. Their cause *is* just! You should go with them! They all have such confidence in you and Lord Latimer. Certainly you can convince my Lord of Norfolk that none here are traitors! Ah, go with them, Robert, and with my blessing!"

As Katherine watched her husband, still doubtful and unsure, a picture of Henry Tudor flashed into her mind. The king as she knew him: gracious, smiling, witty and pleasant. And then the remembrance of monks bound to hurdles, a queen possibly poisoned and one beheaded. What would happen if Henry should judge those men outside—perhaps even John and Robert Aske—as traitors?

"John, I'm as fearful as you," she whispered anxiously, "but think how my Lord of Norfolk might greet Rob Constable's men! They might even quarrel before they talk. But if *you* go, Norfolk will certainly see you. You can make sure the people's grievances are sympathetically presented. It might prevent the marchers from fighting the king's soldiers. At least they'll know they've had a hearing. Norfolk is an old friend, John. You can give him your own opinion of all that has happened here."

Suddenly, it all seemed quite simple. With Constable, Rob Aske, Lord Hussey and the Nortons, Moncktons and Danbys—neighbors and land-owners all—John would go to Doncaster and help settle the matter once and for all. The king was no monster. Poor communication on both sides had helped bring about the terrible impasse which would only worsen if the mob outside challenged Norfolk.

Finally, it was decided, John and Robert Aske would lead the marchers in their pilgrimage. Before they went to bed that evening, both John and Katherine went to the small Snape chapel to pray for divine guidance on their mission.

* * *

Within days, the first of several couriers John had taken to Doncaster arrived at Snape with news of confrontation. Over thirty thousand pilgrims had assembled at one end of Doncaster Bridge with Norfolk's army of eight thousand soldiers at the other end. The duke, said the courier, had been greatly surprised by the people's strength. There was no violence, although Sir Robert Constable had vehemently told Lord Latimer and Rob Aske that the rebels should "show their teeth" to the king's forces. But both John and Aske felt they might win more by a show of strength rather than bloodshed. Later that same day, John's first letter arrived. Greatly relieved, Katherine read aloud to an anxious Bessie, concerned as much for her lover as for her mistress' husband:

> "Norfolk is much with us in spirit, my dear. He said to me (though I am certain he would not wish this to go further), 'what does it gain the realm already beset with heresy if all the Catholic lords like yourself die on the field of battle? What comfort that would be to those who encourage such hatred of the Pope and the Catholic church!' He means Cromwell and Cranmer, of course. He feels many of our grievances are just and that the people have been poorly handled. He's promised to take our complaints personally to the king."

"Then they should be home soon!" Bessie cried, relief apparent in her plain features. "Oh, Kate, now my lord and Robert will make it right with the king and his ministers!"

When, ten days later, John and Robert Aske returned home, they were similarly optimistic. They said that Norfolk had asked them to return to London to be with him when he met with the king and council.

"One thing we wish to be certain of is that everyone participating in this pilgrimage will be pardoned, and Norfolk thinks Rob and I should make this request," John explained. "There were many who said a pardon was not enough, that they had not spent so many months arraying themselves to march at great cost to their families and land only to ask a pardon of the king and Cromwell. Old Rob Constable was nigh undone when we said we would go. He thinks it is a trick of Norfolk's and once we're in London we'll be clapped into the Tower to suffer for our good intentions!" He shrugged his shoulders. "And who's to say we might not be? I pray we've made the right decision."

More than once in the following days, as they traveled southward to London, Katherine prayed also. If ever the Latimers needed the king's goodwill, it was now, for only God knew what he'd heard since the meeting at Doncaster. There'd been no news from court—only that Norfolk was awaiting the arrival of Lord Latimer and Robert Aske—before reporting to the king, Cromwell and the Privy Council.

Making their way through the little Yorkshire villages, the Latimer entourage was cheered by villagers when they saw the banner of the Five Wounds which some of the travelers carried. All about them, Katherine saw reminders of the uprising—market crosses with blasphemous placards protesting the king's actions, with as many others protesting the Doncaster compromise. She was heartsick as, rounding a wooded valley, a small monastery she'd visited as a child lay skeletal to the sky, its roof gone, the great columns of stone scattered on the hard Yorkshire soil. Sheep now nibbled at grass sprouting within the holy precincts. She noted the small marketplace shops appeared almost destitute of goods. Conditions were worse than she, safe at Snape, had ever realized.

At Peterborough, the cavalcade halted while Katherine and John slipped into the abbey church to view the magnificent tomb of Katherine of Aragon. Everywhere, tapers burned as a constant stream of visitors knelt before the hearse, beads in their hands, praying for the one they'd regarded as their true queen. Katherine's cheeks were wet with tears as she viewed the last resting place of Mary's mother, knowing that Mary—even some eleven months later —had yet to see it. It was evidence that Henry Tudor was not all wit and gracious affability. Many as close to him had felt the king's displeasure.

Emerging from the church to the shady cloister, Katherine said another silent prayer for her husband and his mission. For the first time in her life, she acknowledged, she was afraid of London and the court. And, more important, of the king himself.

CHAPTER XVI

Cromwell, it is thou that art the very special and chief causer of all this rebellion and mischief, and art likewise causer of the apprehension of us that be detained, and dost daily earnestly travail to bring us to our ends, and to strike off our heads. I trust that ere thou die, though thou wouldest procure all the noblemen's heads within the realm to be stricken off, yet shall there one head remain that shall strike off thy head!

—Lord Darcy of Templehurst to Lord Privy Seal Cromwell, April 1537

At Chartreuse, John awaited his summons to court. The king and queen were at her family home in Somerset, William Parr said and, at their return, the Privy Council would meet. Katherine was grateful, for the respite gave John time to assess his position. When she told her uncle that many at Snape had thought their coming to London might be a trick, that once at court they'd be charged with treason or at least mischief-making or disloyalty, Sir William Parr shook his head vigorously.

"The Parrs and Latimers, thanks be to God, have friends at court, Kate!" he patted his niece's shoulder. "I have had access to the king and your sister talks freely to the queen. Your brother has spoken with young Fitzroy and Charles Brandon has stood at the council table and told everyone the truth—that you joined the pilgrimage to control any violence or property destruction and to prevent the rabble from looting and profiting themselves. Even our cousin, Cuthbert Tunstall, sent a strong message to the king from York that Latimer's involvement had helped bring the situation under control."

"And what did the king say?"

"Ah, one day he lauds his leaders for their work and then the next, after someone has fed him rumors of plots involving the Pole family or old Lady Salisbury, his temper flares again. They tell him the Yorkshire rising only encourages similar rebellion in other counties and I must admit there is some truth in that. But remember, both of you, that all the misery you have seen was brought about by Parliamentary decree. All the laws our Northern friends disapprove of will remain and their way of life is going to change forever," Sir William spoke dispassionately, but Katherine could see he was disturbed. "The land will be enclosed for sheep raising and many small farms will disappear. Those who worked them will have to find something else to do. The community life which revolved about the parish church or the nearest religious house will suffer for those meeting places will be closed, perhaps destroyed. And yet, they'll be expected to pay their fair share of taxes." He shook his head wearily. "I'm sorry if I sound harsh, my dear, but I hear these things at court. I know there are many who look at the situation very differently. John should be prepared for that before he meets with them."

Later, Sir William told John the Charterhouse and its land would soon be for sale and he suggested the Latimers purchase it.

"I wouldn't own one plot of consecrated earth, especially that next door!" John shook his head vehemently. "I've accepted all the king and his ministers have done, Will, but it hasn't been easy. If I had my way, I'd happily spend the rest of my days in Yorkshire and say farewell to the court with no backward glance. Reforming the church is one thing. Destroying it and killing those who object to the king's methods is another. Cromwell is not observing the standards set for closing the monasteries—that's one of the things our people complain about the most. I think you've all found it easy to overlook and have become hardened to certain practices our countrymen find evil!"

"There's a whole new group at court now, John, a group who care little about what you or I—or even old Norfolk or Charles Brandon—think. These are the new men Henry has used and rewarded—the Seymours, the Bryans, the Wriotheseleys and the Dudleys. In order to flout Spain and the Pope—and keep France at a distance—they woo the Lutherans and the German princes. Cromwell and his followers are all for reforming the church, but not because they have any really sincere religious beliefs. It's all a matter of politics. They've obtained power through the king, by using religion as a stalking horse. If Cromwell can gain the support of enough of these people and keep his influence with the king, he can fight everyone who opposes him—the old nobility, the bishops, France or the emperor. And all in the guise of cleansing or reforming the church."

William Parr's words lingered in Katherine's mind after John finally left for court. Her uncle had confirmed everything Anne Askew had said many months ago—that the religious changes in England would really be political in nature. If the people in the North were to be hurt—as William Parr seemed to think was their fate—might not many others suffer also?

Taking some books for study out to the garden, Katherine walked beside the old Charterhouse wall, hoping to soothe her restlessness. She felt the ghosts walking with her. Not only the gentle Houghton, but the French queen and Maud Parr. Would they have fed and cared for those rebelling against the king? And what would the old queen, so devout, think of a holy man's dismembered body hanging over the house he'd served so loyally?

Walking through the stiff crispness of fallen leaves, Katherine was glad they were not alive to see an England where influential intelligent men used the church to hide their greed for power, their lust for land and money. She remembered what Charles Brandon had said of the nobles' eagerness to acquire the dissolved monasteries and their land. "If the king feathers enough nests," Charles had laughed dispiritedly, "then the rooks will give him no further trouble. It's a good way of keeping new friends' loyalty, for they'll never forfeit such loot. Besides, the king needs the money badly."

And it would be these same men, Katherine realized, who would be sitting around the council table, ready to judge her husband and Robert Aske.

* * *

At Whitehall, the Privy Council assembled at midmorning. Lord Latimer, Robert Aske and the Duke of Norfolk stood apart at a window overlooking the river. None of the councillors had spoken to them as they'd filed toward the council table. Once seated, Lord Chancellor Audley said Henry had hunted that morning as far as Hackney village. "But his leg is sore bothering him," he explained, "and His Grace may be a bit tardy." Everyone talked with each other, pretending not to see the two visitors. John was relieved when Charles Brandon entered the chamber and hurried to join them.

"John, I think this will go well," the duke grasped his friend's arm. "Henry was in a terrible mood when he returned. He really shouldn't ride at all, his leg is so swollen. Yet he'll listen to no one! But when he saw the queen, he heard good news!"

"And what was that?"

"The queen is definitely with child," Brandon whispered. "Henry couldn't wait to tell me and naturally his mood changed for the better! The queen is very clever in her own way, quiet and passive, not like the other one." The duke shook his head at remembrance of Jane's predecessor. "I think she's known for several days, yet waited to tell him when it suited her. She's no friend of Cromwell's and has told the king he'll cause great trouble by closing the monasteries. She begs continually for Mary's return to court. I think they became close when she was maid of honor to the old queen. With such news as he's just heard, I can't believe Henry will do anything to cause her pain."

The door opened and everyone bowed deeply as the king hobbled into the room. He seated himself at one end of the long table while the councillors, shuffling their papers, coughed discreetly and looked with sidelong glances at Latimer, Aske and the Duke of Norfolk.

"They're wondering which way he's going to go and ready to follow whatever lead he throws out to them," Norfolk whispered to his companions. "I think even Cromwell doesn't know the king's mind today." He gestured toward the portly Lord Privy Seal, dressed in his usual black, in strong contrast to the more handsomely garbed councillors. Cromwell sat silently, drumming his fingers on his sheaf of papers, waiting for the king to speak.

Henry gestured for a gentleman-usher to place a cushion on an adjoining chair and, settling his leg comfortably upon it, he spoke to Cromwell. "Ask the petitioners to step forward, identify themselves and present their cases for our hearing."

At Cromwell's command, the Duke of Norfolk came forth.

"I went to Doncaster as Your Majesty ordered," he said, "to meet the forces which had caused an uprising throughout Lincolnshire and York-shire." Norfolk spoke slowly as everyone leaned forward so as not to miss a word. "I met with the rebels' representatives who are here with me today. They told me their grievances and, in many instances, I think their complaints are just. I pray Your Majesty will agree." There was another rustling of papers at such a strong statement. Norfolk continued. "It was beyond my province to rule on or attempt to settle any grievances, for I did not possess the authority to do so. Armed combat was not considered for I was outnumbered from the start. I feel, sire, I acquitted myself with honor. I trust to God Your Majesty will feel so, too."

"Ah, you always know our wishes. Sometimes too well!" As everyone laughed, Henry gestured to the duke. "Over here, Thomas! Come and take your seat. You followed our command and were our good servant and, even though these rebels seem to have caught your sympathy, you despatched your commission with your usual authority. Now we'll hear from Latimer and his young friend. . . ." Henry looked at the paper in front of him. "Aske, is that right?"

"I am Robert Aske, Your Majesty," Robert bowed deeply.

Henry observed the young man with the bright red hair and beard not unlike his own. Robert's gaze did not flicker. There was respect, even admiration in his eyes, but no awe. The king's eyes lingered on the petitioner's dress, for Robert had chosen to wear a humble doublet of deep green Kendal cloth, unadorned except for a large badge which covered his chest. It was the sign of the Pilgrimage of Grace, a red field covered with the Five Wounds of Christ. John had implored Robert to remove the badge, but the man had been insistent. "I come as a pilgrim and I must look like one. I am here for all those others left behind." Now, John could see, the king was fascinated with the sight.

"An interesting insignia you have there, Aske. Perhaps you would be good enough to tell us why you wear it here?"

"Because I come as one of your loyal subjects from the North, Your Majesty." Robert's tone was pleasant, but firm. "This badge represents all our people who took part in the pilgrimage. They meant no harm to your realm or your person. But they think you are served by evil council who take from the North to profit themselves. Still they believe in Your Majesty's goodness. They hope, through me, to tell you what is in their hearts, so you will know their cause is just."

The room was silent. John wondered what those Robert had called "evil" were thinking. Did they—and the king—admire his courage or consider him foolishly ignorant?

"Thirty thousand people think we need to be saved from evil council?"

Henry appeared incredulous. He waved his arm toward the councillors. "Here's our 'evil council,' Master Aske! Look at them! Do they have horns on their heads and cloven hands and feet? They have served us well and some of them for a long time. They do not insist we do their bidding. We insist they do ours!" His face flushed with anger and his words came faster. "We will tell you, Robert Aske, that you represent a presumptuous people, who live in one of the most ignorant and backward parts of our land. You are bound to obey and serve your king—that is God's law. What foolhardiness gives these people any thought that they can tell the king of England what to do? No one can do that . . . except, of course, sometimes the queen." Henry smiled broadly as the councillors laughed spontaneously and pounded the table in appreciation.

The king moved his leg, the gentleman-usher hurrying to turn the pillow. "Now Aske, let us hear your complaints. You have a handful of papers there. We—my leg and I—would be grateful if you make a short end of all this."

Obediently, Robert began. "These are what my people, your loyal subjects, sire, have found odious. I will make a short end as you suggest. It is the content of our grievances, not the length, which made our people rebellious."

First Robert mentioned the heretical works of such as Luther, Wycliffe and Melanchthon which should be destroyed. Then the king must renounce his churchly supremacy and effect a reunion with Rome, restore the monasteries which Cromwell had confiscated and return their lands and goods. "At this request, sire, I should say that the standard set for closing only the smaller houses with two hundred pounds a year or an insignificant number of inmates has not been followed. The royal commissioners, who call themselves 'visitors,' have at times handled the fathers very roughly, threatening them bodily and seeking to corrupt them by bribery. They have despoiled many noble religious houses mainly for what they could get"—Aske looked directly at Cromwell as he spoke—"and the work is continuing even at this moment."

The king looked at Cromwell, who only shook his head. Robert laid down the last sheet of paper. "And lastly, Your Majesty, our people humbly petition you to restore the Lady Mary to your favor and to her just title. She is much loved and our people lament the dire condition she has lived in for these past long years."

The king shifted his leg again saying, "We would hear now from Lord Latimer."

John stepped forward, wishing he could look into Henry's mind. Robert's words had been strong and in direct contrast to the king and council's policies. He knew he could add very little to what had already been said, but he chose his words carefully.

"Sire, Master Aske has given you the specific grievances of the people of Lincolnshire and Yorkshire, grievances they've suffered for many years. It has taken little of your time. But it took them a very long time to come together in a Pilgrimage of Grace to seek redress from their plight. By its very title, the pilgrimage shows desire for good, not evil, and the badge which Master Aske wears so proudly is representative of a good and simple people, loyal to Your Majesty, who are concerned you pay so little attention to their needs. Contented subjects do not rise in rebellion, sire. And they've caused no destruction or death, though a few of your representatives were rumpled a bit, I believe. But that is all. Our people need your attention and compassion. They've waited a long time, with stout patience, for justice. I think, sire, as loyal subjects, they hope Your Majesty will try to understand what is in their hearts and give them some relief."

It had been a long speech for John and he felt the sweat rising in his palms. The king appeared to be considering all he'd heard. Shifting his leg again, he spoke directly to Robert Aske.

"Master Aske, here is what we wish you to take back to your pilgrim friends. Ignorant people should not attempt to instruct us in matters of theology. We think they have a madness of the brain to think they can tell their king—who has governed this realm for twenty-seven years—what he should or should not do. Some of what you call heresy, others call logic or reform. We do not seek to destroy the church, merely to cleanse it! The church in this country will have but one head and it will be your king, for the Pope is forever damned in England! Tell your people if they are looking for evil, when the last Pope was laid out for burial, the Roman peasants had to be restrained from entering his bedroom so they might mutilate the body of a hated man! Tell that to your fellow rebels, Master Aske!

"When you speak of our closing the abbeys and monasteries," the anger in the king's voice lessened, as if he were explaining to a difficult child, "you talk as if they were all privileged places where only the most highly principled brethren lived. This is not what we found when we looked into their management! There was much corruption, high living, slack control and many of the same venal sins of which you accuse our commissioners! Do you know the wealth the church possesses, Master Aske? Let us tell you! The church is richer than the Crown, the wealthiest landowner, farm owner, mine owner, jewel and cattle owner and has more treasures than your king! What do you think of that, Master Aske? If all this is true—and it is, you have our word for it—then why didn't those monks, friars, abbots, priors and those poor frightened nuns help those destitute farmers, those despairing neighbors and pilgrims of which you so sadly speak? What did they *really* do? They did, we're certain, dole out bread and ale at their gates and probably visited the sick before they buried them and then read their wills prior to collecting a comfortable tithe for the hundreds of masses the dead one bought for admission to heaven. But it was all paid for by *you*, Master Aske, and all your friends who worked the abbey lands and fed the cattle belonging to them."

No one dared speak, yet Robert Aske's glance never wavered. Drawing a long breath, Henry continued. "The closing of the religious houses, Master

Aske, is not an act, will or fantasy of any one councillor or minister, but has been done by an Act of Parliament. But we will, in an act of goodness directed to our Northern subjects, remind those undertaking this task to be on their honor that no worthy house be suppressed. As to the Lady Mary, she is our daughter and we will treat her as a natural loving father when she behaves as a natural loving daughter. She has been obstinate, obdurate and hazards her very existence daily by such continued stubbornness. We will say no more of her."

Standing close to Robert Aske, John felt relief seeping into his bones. He knew that, for the moment, the king was not going to take any direct action. Otherwise, he'd never have listened as patiently and answered as freely and fully as he had. And, by striving for an understanding with the petitioners, he'd taken the responsibility for judgment from Cromwell, for which the Lord Privy Seal was undoubtedly grateful. Now whatever happened would be Henry's fault, not his. He was amused as he noted several councillors' encouraging glances.

"Now you, Lord Latimer, we thank you," the king interrupted his reverie, "for what we know must have been a most disagreeable task. To ride amongst rebels against your king! But we know why you did it and we must say, John, if we hadn't, your family, and that of your good wife, my Lady Katherine—has given us no peace in explaining your position at Snape and your later behavior." For the first time, the king smiled broadly and the councillors at last regarded John as though seeing him for the first time. "We are convinced you prevented the rebels from doing harm to our soldiers or to themselves. We hope it helps convince Master Aske we are hardly surrounded by dullards or devils. Our problem now is what to do with Master Aske?"

Robert stepped forward. "I am willing to receive whatever Your Majesty in the goodness of his heart wishes to give me." His words carried a quiet dignity and Henry's face softened. He turned to whisper to the gentleman-usher who left the room. Then he spoke once more to Robert.

"Master Aske, you will take these words back to your friends in the North. You will tell them to worry no more about their sovereign. There will be no return to popery and we concede nothing where the Lady Mary is concerned. She appears to be mistress of her own fate. So be it. Tell them their insurrection has not impressed us and we think it a folly bordering on treason whereby you have shamed only yourselves. We charge you, therefore, to order your friends to withdraw to their own houses and cause the mischief-makers and provokers to be jailed. Tell your people we will talk with our advisers, good men all, about the taxes. They are lawyers, priests and soldiers, but they are not miracle workers. And tell your people, Aske, there is one thing their king *will* do for them. Tell them next year—after they've had time to work out their differences—we will have a Parliament at York. And when it is time for the queen's coronation, we will have her anointed there also. We will show ourselves to your people so they may

know they have a true king who has their welfare at heart and who"—
Henry relaxed visibly, enjoying the rapt attention of his audience—"when
he comes may also, God willing, bring a prince with him. My friends, the
queen is with child."

Immediately, a great commotion broke out as the councillors applauded or
loudly banged the table. Charles Brandon, with a brother-in-law's privilege,
thumped Henry on the shoulder. The king was all smiles, beaming at the secret no longer his, his ruddy complexion heightened by the excitement. Even
Cromwell had unbent, clapping his hands and shouting as loudly as the
others.

"It will be in the fall of the year, so says Her Grace," the king explained.
"Pray for us, gentlemen. She is a hardy, healthy lady and we want a hardy,
healthy son."

At that moment, the door opened and the gentleman-usher returned carrying a scarlet piece of satin on his arm. Henry motioned Robert Aske to his
side. "You will pardon your king that we do not stand up, young Aske."
Henry smiled, taking the scarlet cloth in his hands. "See here, we have two
gifts for you. One is this coat." He held it up so everyone could see it was actually a handsome doublet of bright red trimmed with gold braid. "Now,
Aske, we want you to take off that badge and, as a gift from your king and a
pledge from your sovereign, wear your red coat home. Show this to your people as a sign of our goodwill. And, as a second gift, tell them we give you a
pardon and it will extend several weeks. This will give you time to gather
your leaders together and tell them they are pardoned for their crude and ignorant action. Tell them if they put as much effort into the peace as they
have into the uprising, there will be no further trouble. Go in good faith,
Master Aske, and wear your coat with pleasure."

Overcome with the gift and pardon, Robert fell to his knees. He grasped
the hand the king offered and solemnly kissed the ring-covered fingers. Observing the scene, John felt his eyes mist over. He knew the king was enjoying himself, relishing Aske's penitent submission as much as he enjoyed
Cromwell's obvious discomfort.

Yet, John wondered, did Aske and Cromwell realize how little the king
had given? He'd promised an heir, a coronation and a Parliament. He'd
given their chief rebel a pardon and a scarlet coat. That was all. It had
affected everyone in the room and was yet another instance of Henry
Tudor's evanescent charm and magnetism which had little to do with his extravagant dress or bejeweled fingers. By virtue of his own will, the man could
still sway, even with a swollen leg, one vein of which John could see still
throbbed painfully.

As the councillors rose and thronged about the king, John hoped young
Aske could describe the scene for Katherine better than he. His own feeling
was one of vast relief. He and his wife had come through the crisis un-
scathed, their property and lives intact. And it might so easily have gone the
other way. Everyone present had recognized the delicacy of their position.

Their fate had all depended upon the decision of the heavy, bearded man, his head thrown back in laughter now, the sound ringing throughout the room. Henry was as pleased and proud of his impending fatherhood as any man many years his junior.

As he went to thank the king, John thought that perhaps, after all, the one he should feel grateful to for his good fortune was Queen Jane Seymour.

No one could have timed a pregnancy better.

*   *   *

Back at Snape, Robert Aske met with the rebels to explain the king's pardon. The Latimers were stunned at the lack of response among the Northern people. And, despite the pardon, the promise of a coronation and a Parliament in the North, a new uprising soon commenced at Scarborough. The leader was Sir Francis Bigod whose son was plighted to wed John's daughter, Margaret, in the spring.

A frightened Bessie, thinner than ever from worry, said Robert rode constantly about the countryside mustering the people at market crosses and churchyards, in taverns, open fields or castle courtyards—anywhere they would listen to him. He urged that they return to their homes and go about their own business. By continuing to assemble and dissent, he told them, they were endangering their lives and property as well as the pardon. He understood their disappointment that no royal seal dangled impressively from the written proclamation which he read to those unable to do so. Yet the king had promised to consider their problems. What more did they want? They were lucky to be alive, he cried. To which the rebels responded with derisive hoots and shouts.

Soon the beacons flared again from Scarborough to Hull to Beverley. As John Hallam, a Latimer neighbor, warned, "Liberal sayings fill the air!" while rebel bands gathered in several other counties. When the city of Newcastle refused to pay its taxes until the king outlined specifically what relief they might expect, Sir Francis Bigod demanded other counties also do the same. Obviously, Aske and his companions had been deceived by the king's promises, he said. What relief had the North actually received?

When John denounced Bigod for encouraging a new insurrection, Sir Francis snapped, "While you met with the king and Cromwell, I've listened to the people's laments. I've seen their misery and the suffering caused by these new laws and I think, my lord, the king has tricked you. So does Rob Constable, Lord Darcy and others. And until we have some relief, we mean to make our wishes known, by force if necessary. We have more support than you think, my lord!"

John then bluntly told his friend he'd have nothing further to do with the cause and, after an angry Sir Francis left, he burnt the marriage contract between the Bigod heir and his daughter.

"He feels he is right and God knoweth this will break Margaret's heart,"

John later told Katherine, "but the man is irresponsible and will endanger us all. There was nothing else I could do."

Katherine felt Bigod's treachery deeply. He was a dedicated Humanist, devoted to the "New Learning" and she knew she'd miss him. In the past they'd often shared books, spending hours discussing the religious upheaval on the Continent and in England. Bigod was a truly educated man with a seeking mind and a great desire to learn, rare among her neighbors, many of whom could still only sign their name. It had been largely due to her efforts that John had even entertained Sir Francis's marriage proposal for Margaret Neville. John had hesitated exposing his young daughter to Bigod's philosophy which he'd surely passed on to his son. However, young Bigod seemed a sensible lad and Margaret had a mind of her own. She would not be easily swayed from her training and heritage. It saddened both Latimers to think of the girl's heartbreak for she was genuinely fond of her young fiancé. But it could not be helped. John wanted no further part in any movement against the king.

For days Margaret moped in her room or appeared, red-eyed and quiet, at mealtimes. Bessie, in constant fear for Robert Aske's life, spent every moment she could with him. Katherine sought to console her old friend, stressing how much Aske was respected, how well he could speak for the king.

"Ah, Kate, that is true," Bessie agreed, "but the more time passes and nothing comes from London confirming Robert's words, the less people believe him. Some even call out at meetings that he sold them out for a red satin coat!" Bessie's voice shook with hurt as Katherine put an arm about her.

She felt many of the same fears. These were frightening days for anyone with a father, husband, son or lover, for every family seemed to have someone in the uprising. And, try as she would, Katherine could not still a stirring of doubt. Why didn't the king send an official pardon and some further word of his promises to Robert and John? What would happen if the people refused to do as he'd commanded? The pardon was to last only two months.

A letter from her uncle, William Parr, did not help. Sir William wrote, "I cannot predict, John, what lamentable fate will await our friends if the king's pardon continues to be so disregarded. He is very disappointed young Aske has accomplished so little and roundly belabors Bigod and his friends who continue to stir up unrest. Cromwell is waiting like a man with a baited trap to release the spring! Henry has sent Norfolk back to Doncaster, and Suffolk will go to Stamford with soldiers. They will take matters into their own hands once the pardon has expired. If you and Aske cannot control your people, I would advise that you and Katherine return to London or go elsewhere so you will not be again implicated in what I see—God forgive them all—as a great tragedy in the making."

Bessie, so happy at having Robert home again, wept softly as John read the letter aloud. For the first time, Katherine felt a burning anger toward both her husband and Robert Aske. She was angrier still at Bigod and Constable and all those foolish others who thought they might dictate to a king and his minister. She wanted to shout aloud they were all a pack of naïve fools, marching about like children, frightening the countryside into thinking they could challenge the Crown. Couldn't they see they were risking civil war and encouraging those very factions that hungered after Henry's throne? She recognized the good intentions with which the pilgrimage had originally started. But somewhere, somehow, something had gone awry and she was sick with indignation at the sight of Bessie being tortured with uncertainty for her lover's welfare. She was almost glad when John and Robert decided to meet with the Duke of Suffolk at Stamford. John intended to question Charles Brandon about Cromwell and the king's state of mind regarding this latest outbreak. If nothing but armed confrontation was contemplated, they would all return to London. Whether Bessie would accompany them or stay with Robert Aske was something Katherine dared not think upon.

Several days after John had left, as the family was dining, the Snape courtyard filled with an angry mob. Margaret saw it first and, white-faced and trembling, returned from the window, crying, "They've knocked down the gatekeeper and are coming into the house!"

With a rapidly beating heart, Katherine ran to the balcony where John had, months ago, spoken to a similar gathering. This time there were no friendly faces. Those gazing up at her were ragged, with angry, sullen expressions and appeared spoiling for trouble. Feeling her mouth go dry and thrusting her hands in her skirt to hide their trembling, she called out to them, "What is it you want?"

"Lord Latimer—he has betrayed us! He and that scoundrel, Aske! They've gone over to my lord of Suffolk!" Loudly, the mob yelled its support of the speaker.

"You are wrong," Katherine shouted, "they have gone to Stamford to try and explain why the peace is being continually broken and the king's pardon ignored!" She felt her courage returning. "It is such as you who have caused him to meet with the duke to explain so no harm will come to you!"

"Ha!" The spokesman, one-eyed and filthy, waved a pitchfork which, for a moment, Katherine thought he meant to throw upward at her. "He goes to save us does he, dear lady? From what? From ourselves? He goes to trick us —for he and Aske have deserted us all! They went to London and the king rewarded them with fine clothes and probably lands and money as well. What did we get in return? Nothing, my fine lady! Nothing! The king has sent no word at all. Now we want an explanation."

"I've told you all I know," Katherine cried again, trying to hold their attention. "Remember when the king brings the queen to York to be crowned, there will be a Parliament. That is when you will be heard. You should return to your homes and not endanger your pardon!"

Only a few heard for, curiosity getting the better of them, more began to enter the house. "Oh, Kate, they'll destroy everything," Bessie cried. "If there was one familiar face in that stinking mob, I'd go below and call out every

Northern curse I know! But these are not from hereabout—these are trouble-makers and looters!"

Katherine thought of the treasures John's family had collected from many lands and the gifts from the old king that graced the massive cupboards and sideboards. Probably much of it would find its way into torn, scruffy pockets. But, miraculously, no one was coming up the stairs and, if they got what they wanted below, perhaps they'd be content to loot and leave three defense-less women alone. Turning to speak to Margaret, she found the girl had disappeared.

"Bess! Where did she go? I didn't see her leave!" Quickly, Katherine ran from the balcony into the adjacent room. It, too, was empty. She heard the rumble of conversation from downstairs, some hooting calls and jeers and then a sharp retort. Suddenly, there was silence, as if everyone were listen-ing.

Opening the door, she and Bessie crept out into the hallway. At one end, a stairway led steeply into the hall below where the mob now gathered. A bright light flickered up the stairwell; it was a moment before Katherine real-ized they'd brought their torches inside. Dear God!—she prayed—help keep them in control so old Snape Hall will not go up in flames this night! As she and Bessie, staying well back against the wall, crept toward the brightness, a slight figure loomed ahead.

"It's Margaret!" Katherine gasped.

Whenever John's daughter had left, or why, she stood now halfway down the stairs talking with the rabble below. Lady Margaret Neville was a strik-ing-looking girl for one only fourteen years old, and she was blessed with the authoritative manner of one of her high birth. She spoke to the same one-eyed ringleader they'd seen from the balcony.

"You are wrong, good sirs, about my father and Master Aske. You do them great harm by coming into our home this way. Has my father ever invaded your house with bad intent, frightening everyone?"

There was a long silence as several shuffled their feet, coughing nervously and muttering amongst themselves. Katherine stifled a desire to laugh or cry or just run down and join Margaret. Yet instinct told her to leave the girl alone.

"Now hear what I have to tell you and then you must leave." Margaret's clear voice carried back to the shadows where Katherine and Bessie waited. "I will ask my father, when he returns, to forgive the fact that you dared enter his house and push his servants to the ground and frighten his wife and me. He would not spare one minute before finding out all your names and coming with the sheriff to rout you from your beds and shame you be-fore your neighbors, your family and your wives! Do your wives know what you do this night, good sirs?"

There was much laughter and waving of pitchforks and torches as some-one shouted his wife was glad to be rid of him. Margaret also laughed to humor them. "Now my good stepmother has told you my father and Master

Aske have gone to Stamford to intercede for you with my lord of Suffolk. They'll be returning here in a day or so. Why don't you wait until then to see them? They have nothing to gain from the king! What good will it do to despoil the house of a man who is trying to help you? Is this the way you repay him? I say, good sirs, it is for shame! My father is a good man. Master Aske has worked himself ill for you. And one day I will wed with young Bigod. His father is your leader, is he not?"

As cheers sounded through the old hall, Katherine felt light-headed with relief. Tears welled in her eyes and Bessie shook her head, a half smile on her pale lips. Margaret had hit upon the key word, "Bigod." The whole county knew of her contract to wed the boy. Apparently, they hadn't heard John had broken the agreement. Margaret was using her own heartbreak to save her home and the lives of everyone in it.

Katherine's eyes smarted with admiration for her stepdaughter. From the silence downstairs, it was apparent the girl had made a great impression. Watching them, Margaret's shoulders straightened and, as Katherine gazed at her with pride and awe, she seemed to grow taller in authority. Now she had mastery over the rebels and she knew it. Yet it might all have been so different. Her beauty alone might have proved an enticement to some who could have turned the ugly situation into destruction for them all.

Still, Margaret remained silent. Then, suddenly, she was waving her hand in farewell. Katherine heard the clumping of feet and smelt the rancid torches as they passed by the banister only a few feet below. The light was lessening. "Jesu be praised," she cried to a jubilant Bess, "they are leaving!" No matter what they'd taken, no matter if they'd broken all the treasures downstairs, the house and their lives had been spared. She'd have to get word to John at once. Any servant would ride with the speed of a demon after what he'd witnessed tonight. They could no longer stay at Snape with such malcontents roaming the countryside.

As the door banged shut, she and Bessie flew to embrace a triumphant Margaret, Katherine still at a loss for words to praise her stepdaughter's courage and poise.

But words were not needed. As the two women sped down the stairway, calling their blessings on Margaret, they came upon the girl just before the hand with which she'd clutched the railing gave way and, moaning with stunned relief, she crumpled like a broken figurine into their waiting arms.

* * *

Katherine's cry for help reached John at Malton near York and, with only one servant for company, he rode frantically for Snape, over frostbitten roads, plunging deeply into thick woods whenever smoky wisps from a rebel campfire could be seen over the treetops. He spent his first night in stables adjoining the burnt-out hulk of a manor house he'd known since his youth; the destruction appalled and sickened him. He thought constantly of his family's welfare and only his first glimpse of Snape, still whole in its park-like setting, lessened his anxiety. Certainly if the house remained, his family was safe! Gaining the hilltop overlooking the park, he saw Katherine and the servants running into the courtyard and, tears in his eyes, he thanked God for their deliverance.

Late that evening after the household was quiet, John said they must leave Snape. Charles Brandon had told him the king was enraged with the way his pardon was being ignored and he'd suggested the Latimers disassociate themselves from the rebel cause that had so endangered them all. Cromwell was only waiting until the pardon expired. Then the soldiers sent to keep the peace would take their reprisal.

"I see all too clearly for my soul's comfort, Kate, there will be bloodshed before this is over. Henry's tolerance is lessening and Cromwell fans the flame. Remember, once this new insurrection is put down—as indeed it will be—there will be great prizes in land and buildings for the victors. But they will not be our people, my dear. . . ." John said Bigod and his companions encouraged further rebellion saying the pardon was a snare, that the king never meant any relief, that there was nothing in writing. He even wrote Cromwell and taunted him by saying, "The king has given us the faucet, but you have kept the spigot!" John suggested they leave within the week for London.

The next day as Katherine and Bessie looked to the safekeeping of the Latimer treasures, as they placed several servants with neighborhood families or sent others to their homes, they saw the beacons burning now even in daylight. Outside Snape, the roads were clogged with malcontents making traveling hazardous and increasing the suffering of those hoping to remain free of any involvement. "All this marching about and rioting have brought us nothing, John!" Katherine cried, impatient and angry, "I can't wait to leave this place. It is too heartbreaking to see them marching to their own destruction. I don't know who is more foolish—we for trying or they for hoping!"

Bessie still worried constantly for Robert Aske. He wanted to go to London again to explain the failure of the peace to the king. "If he goes, Kate, he'll not return," the girl said gloomily. "No one has tried harder than my Rob, but the king and Cromwell will see only the failure, not the effort." Katherine, too disheartened to attempt any comfort, could only put an arm about her old friend, sick at the potential disaster she saw facing her countrymen.

* * *

It came sooner than expected. In London, spies had kept Cromwell advised of rebel activities. Some monks and nuns had returned to several formerly closed monasteries, they reported, "and the abbots wax fat with pride." No taxes had been collected for over a year and similar uprisings were forming in Westmorland and Cumberland. Hull Harbor, the spies said, was guarded so supplies might not reach the king's forces and rebel garrisons had been established at Newcastle and Scarborough by Bigod's followers.

When the rabble of Kendal, Richmond and Hexham attacked Carlisle, Cromwell's anger boiled over and, within days, martial law was proclaimed. The two dukes, Suffolk and Norfolk, were ordered to advance and put down the revolutionaries once and for all. Soon, Sir Francis Bigod was captured at Carlisle and eight rebel leaders were hung in chains. Two hundred pilgrims died in battle on the frosty roads while others filled the county prisons. Some remorse, however, attended Norfolk's efforts, for he wrote the king: "Westmorland has been very badly handled in the past by excessive taxes, enclosures and oppressions which I and others here think is the only cause of this rebellion." He hoped the Lord Privy Seal would see his words.

When Henry read the depositions taken from Bigod and other prisoners, he marveled that his own generosity had been so abused. Daily, Cromwell brought reports to the Privy Council involving Lords Darcy, Dacre, Hussey and others Henry had thought loyal. Fragments of intercepted mail showed Robert Aske had hoped to "accomplish a great enterprise and so playing my part that all England shall perceive it." Putting his own interpretation on the words, Cromwell suggested Aske had betrayed the king. There was hardly a man in the whole North who hadn't assisted the rebels with arms or money, he said, and the crisis was spreading into other counties. All about him Henry perceived treason, disloyalty and a challenge to his throne. At last, he acted. He wrote to Norfolk that because of the great treachery he'd suffered, Norfolk was to "cause such dreadful execution upon a good number of inhabitants of every village, town and hamlet that have offended, as they may be a fearful spectacle to all others hereafter that would practice any like matter. . . ."

Norfolk was dismayed at the order. Yet he had no alternative but to obey, for since the death of his niece, Anne Boleyn, he'd lived under a cloud. Cromwell hated him more than any other noble. If he had not hesitated to strike at a queen, would he ignore the opportunity to destroy England's chief noble and all his house?

Yet many did not deserve to die. Quickly, Norfolk sent unsigned letters to Darcy, Constable and Robert Aske, urging they flee into Scotland or France. In no other way could they be saved, he said. The old duke felt no disloyalty in so doing. He realized the rebels' animosity was really directed against Cromwell and not the king. Once the letters went off, he would carry out the king's orders for he meant his return to court to be with Henry Tudor's full confidence. Catholic though he might be in a country where the Pope was damned, he was the king's man first. And both Henry Tudor and Thomas Cromwell would know it.

*   *   *

Henry's injunction to cause dreadful executions spared no one. Farmer, blacksmith, joiner, mason, squire, lawyer, noble or servant—anyone who'd worn the banner of the Five Wounds, or aided or abetted those that had, was apprehended. Soon, corpses dangled from tavern post, village gibbet, churchyard or cottage doorway or hung in chains over the town gates. Many swung from trees in their own gardens. Weeping crowds of women and young children accompanied the victims to their executions as, over the dales and hills of the North, the beacons were extinguished. Village squares and marketplaces were fouled with blood as countless unfortunates were hanged, drawn and quartered.

As the wagons and carts were packed for the Latimer journey, Bessie awaited each courier with grim hopefulness. Katherine's heart ached for the girl, still anxious for Robert Aske's safety. Never before had anyone won her heart and if anything happened to Rob—Katherine crossed herself and said a silent prayer—she knew Bessie would accept no other mate. No harm would come to the man, she told Bess constantly, for he'd taken no part in the Bigod uprising. But with the country under martial law, it might be difficult for him to reach Snape, for travel was greatly curtailed. Yet Katherine had little real conviction. She had no more confidence that Aske would be safe than she did the queen's child would be a boy.

John made one final hurried trip to see Charles Brandon at Stamford and was again advised to make haste to return to London. Who knew what stories might be told at court if they remained too long in the North where the king's soldiers were reaping a grim justice? The journey had been a brutal one for John. "The executions are proceeding," he reported, drawn and shaken, "but it's sickened my soul and spirit, Katherine. Many have suffered for very little cause. They've left behind little ones and families who are dependent upon them. It sears my heart to wonder what will happen with no father or husband to care for them. I feel I am a coward to leave! But both Norfolk and Charles say I must, upon my life, I must!"

Katherine asked if he feared how the king might receive him.

"Charles says he is certain a kind reception awaits us if we leave soon. But I fear not what awaits me, for after what I've seen here, a swift death might even be more desirable. But you and my children must be safe! Lord Darcy and Rob Constable are prisoners and have been taken to London to answer charges which I doubt they can explain. I've inquired constantly after young Aske but no one has seen him. Norfolk thinks he may have gone to Scotland or France. It puzzles me that he left no word with anyone."

The possibility gave Bessie new spirit. "It will make us wait longer to be together, but if he's safe, that's all that matters!" she said with the first smile Katherine had seen in days. "He'll get word to us as soon as he can, Kate, you'll see!"

A light frosting of snow covered Snape park on the morning of their departure. Katherine's servants busily loaded carts and wagons with clothing and household goods, her beloved books and John's treasures. They left little of value behind and, mounting the hilltop that formed part of the rim of Snape park, Katherine saw tears in her husband's eyes. She knew he was wondering if they'd ever see his beloved home again. Bessie, too, gazed sadly at the place where she'd found her true love. London would be even farther away from Robert Aske, no matter where he was.

While Katherine understood their sadness, for herself she was relieved to go. Soon they'd be safe in their beds at Chartreuse and the peaceful quiet of the venerable old house would do much to mend tired bodies and saddened spirits. A new suitor must be found for Margaret. And it would be a trying time for her stepson, for John was a country lad to his noble fingertips. There would be problems, but nothing like the heartbreaking ones she'd lived with for almost three years. It was bewildering and ironic, Katherine thought, that she now regarded London as a refuge, much as she'd once thought of Snape as a sanctuary from the court.

Once free of the park, they met an old monk hobbling along the road, begging for alms. Shocked, John instructed the steward to give the man a few coins as Katherine asked him why he must beg.

"Ah, my lady," the old man replied, crossing himself, "I have no place to go. So I go from house to house, for that is what the world is now. It was not so in your father's day nor mine! Now it is a perilous world, for we will have no pilgrimages and no saints' days for we are forbidden to venerate them. And all religion is suspect! Oh Lord, have mercy on us"—he wiped a shaking hand across a lined forehead—"I would live as my forefathers have done. I would believe as they believed. . . ."

Moved, Katherine suggested he join their caravan. Undoubtedly the old man had lived a life of worship in one of those ruined monasteries one saw everywhere and was completely unfit for anything else. He was no longer young and it would be impossible to find a place where he might labor for his keep. "Come with us," Katherine touched his shoulder, disturbed at his frailness and ragged clothes. "We go to London and there perhaps we can find you shelter."

Tears in his eyes, the old monk shook his head, his formerly tonsured locks now uncut and dirty. "London, you say, my lady? Ah, I would not wish for London! That is from whence comes all our trouble—from the king and his devil Cromwell! If I die, as I'm certain I will, my lady, I will die in these hills where all my life I've served my people and my God with all my heart. . . ." He turned away and Katherine winced at his torn sandals and scarred feet. Opening the purse attached to her waist, she emptied it of several coins and suggested he accompany them to York. "There my steward will get you a warm cloak and boots and you'll not suffer so from the cold. At least ride with us to York." She was pleased when the monk, making the sign of the cross, thanked her for the coins and sank wearily into the rear of one of the wagons.

The next hour was an ordeal. Once out on the open road, everywhere Katherine looked there were corpses hanging from tree limbs, village gibbets and castle gateways. One even dangled from the heavy cross of a village church spire. At each, the old monk made the sign of the cross. Katherine stared first in disbelief, then with sickness threatening, averted her eyes, feeling hot shame at such cowardice. These were her people and they'd died for a cause they believed in. The least she could do was pray! But as they rode toward York the brutal scenes only increased. No one spoke. John and his son were up in front with the steward. Bessie rode silently beside her, her usually cheery face pale and stolid. Margaret was quiet at the horror through which they passed. Families walked along the road, some carrying bodies that they'd cut down under cover of darkness. Katherine was almost violently ill at the sight of a man carrying a young boy's head wrapped in a bloody cloth. The man's face was swollen with grief; he appeared heedless of the Latimer entourage as it clattered along beside him.

The ugly sickening scenes were repeated endlessly until, numbed, Katherine advised Bessie and Margaret to keep looking straight ahead. "There's nothing we can do. Pray we'll be out of this soon!"

As the ancient gates of York appeared ahead, John signaled the procession to halt. He rode back to say since the city was under martial law, each must wait his turn and possibly be searched before going through the gates. Katherine wondered if all their treasures would be safe. Soldiers or not, John might have to bribe them to get through the gates. As she'd given all her coins to the old monk, she suggested Bessie go back and retrieve the money. "Tell him we may need it at the gate and once inside, we'll repay him." The woman jumped lightly from her horse and ran toward the rear.

As the line moved closer to the gate, Katherine's nervousness increased. Certainly, nothing could harm them now? John was well known in the area and undoubtedly either Norfolk or Charles Brandon had sent deputies to escort them from York. Neither duke would have insisted they leave Snape if danger still existed. That many tragedies had occurred in York also was obvious for, slowing her horse as he inched forward, she noted at least a dozen corpses hanging over the gates. She watched in sickening fascination as the bodies, amply hung in chains, twirled in the cold morning air. Katherine tried to be calm. She'd wanted to think they were probably criminals or looters such as had invaded Snape. Undoubtedly they deserved their fate. Yet, inside, she was outraged. No one deserved such an end. But, if what they'd seen for the last hour was typical, there would probably be many more horrible scenes before they reached Doncaster. She'd better get used to it.

Suddenly, her eyes lit on one chained figure. It was in the center, directly over the gate and from its condition, she could see it had been there for several days. Great carrion birds had picked at the clothing as well as the flesh. Already the eyes were gone as were parts of the chin. The fingers had been plucked to the bare bone. Katherine watched it twirl endlessly in the pale sunlight, not wanting to believe what she saw, her gorge rising as she accepted the reality that the figure rotting in the chains still showed a goodly crown of bright auburn hair and beard. Even as one part of her screamed that bright auburn hair was hardly a rarity in the North, another part—

shocked and revolted—realized that the figure was clothed in a scarlet satin coat.

As a searing anger surged through her, her numbness disappeared as she sought disbelief from what her eyes were plainly telling her. Riding nearer, she knew without a shadow of a doubt the identity of the man in the chains. Her next thought was of Bessie. Whirling around, losing her place in line, she galloped toward the rear. Bess must not see the mutilated thing hanging over the gate. Somehow, she must be protected.

But she was too late. Katherine pulled at her horse for Bessie was now running back with the coins from the old monk. Suddenly, she stopped abruptly, gazing upward. She turned to Katherine, her face white with an agonizing horror as the coins fell from her limp fingers to the ground.

"Kate!" she screamed, "it has a red coat! A red satin coat! Oh, Jesu in heaven, 'tis Rob!" Covering her face with shaking hands as if to wipe out the terrifying image, the girl screamed again and again. Hurriedly, Katherine dismounted as John and the children ran to her side. "What is it? Oh, Bess, what is it?" Margaret was trembling. "Why are you screaming?"

Katherine reached Bessie first. Her screams continued until—the full impact of the loathsome sight seared forever in her brain—she turned away and was sick by the roadside. Grimly, Katherine pointed upward as John, his face as white as chalk, stared unbelievingly. The steward covered his eyes as Margaret gasped and quickly looked away. She, too, had recognized the red satin coat.

Katherine knelt by Bess in the roadway and, after a few moments, helped her to her feet. As they approached the gate, John took his cloak and wrapped the girl tightly in it. Picking her up, he lay her in the wagon with the old monk. "Put the cloak over your head, Bess," he whispered. But Bess had already done so—anything to hide from the ghastly sight under which they were now ready to pass.

CHAPTER XVII

Weeks later, Katherine still suffered the effects of their ghastly journey to London. Her sleep was disturbed as scenes, seared forever in her memory, recurred. After Doncaster, there was further evidence of the royal reprisal in the frozen quartered bodies displayed at town gates or hung in chains from gallows. Many abbots, friars and monks swung in empty church naves or from the steeples of the monasteries to which they'd returned. Nearing London, the Latimers heard that Francis Bigod, Tom Percy, John Hussey and old Lord Lumley had died at Tyburn while, on a Friday market day, Rob Constable had been hung in chains above the Beverley Gate at Hull. The first news that reached them at Chartreuse was that old Lord Darcy had been beheaded on Tower Hill.

Every day, it seemed, brought more tragedy along with the sight of Bessie's deep and unrelenting grief. Once away from York, she'd never again referred to the abominable sight above the gate. John learned from Norfolk that the old duke had tried to save Bessie's lover. "He sent young Aske a letter warning him," he told Katherine, "but perchance it never reached him. Each city has its own sheriff and soldiers and, under martial law, they do as they will. Rob had many enemies who thought he'd betrayed them to the king. Someone probably took him in revenge."

Katherine had another opinion. "It was Cromwell!" she cried, the remembered sickness welling up in her, "for he hated it when the king was so generous to Rob. His spies did as much to stir up trouble as did Bigod's men, you know that, John! Ah, I hope I live to see the day he overreaches himself! He's grown big with his own power!"

Katherine sought an early reunion with her sister, Ann Parr Herbert, now a lady-in-waiting to Queen Jane. She was pleased to see the girl was less critical and self-seeking; the Boleyn tragedy seemed to have softened Ann Parr. Or perhaps, as William Parr intimated, her husband had ambition and guile enough for both of them. "If the king changed his mind five times in as many days, Will Herbert would be the first to applaud Henry's wisdom each time. He's very typical, my dear, of those about the king. All have their hands outstretched for any largesse. Henry likes him and Cromwell finds him useful. I predict he'll do very well for himself."

Within several days, Kate Brandon, the Duchess of Suffolk, arrived at Chartreuse for her first meeting with Katherine in over a year. The day before, as she and Charles had accompanied the king and queen to vespers, she said Henry had received the Lady Mary's written submission.

"I don't believe it!" Katherine was appalled. "Mary hasn't held out this long only to submit when the queen might have a son who would be the heir. What would she gain?"

"In this instance, I think very possibly her life," Kate replied dryly. "Cromwell told her if she continued to resist, she would be forbidden ever to write to him or her father again. Henry hasn't answered a letter of hers in five years. Cromwell said her position—since she had none except as the king's bastard daughter—wouldn't save her from imprisonment or worse."

Katherine recalled the last time she'd seen Mary and her father at Richmond Palace. "These last years have been hell for her," she said sadly, "and so little of it any fault of her own."

"Well, that's all changed now. The king has sent her a thousand crowns—for her little pleasures, he said—and the queen sent her a diamond ring. Mary will be coming to see her father soon, Katherine, and I've told Charles when that happens I want to be there! And so will you, my dear, if you're still in London. We have much to catch up on, you, Mary and I!"

Mary was often on Katherine's mind as she went about London with the duchess seeking materials for refurbishing Chartreuse. Passing the crumbling old palace of Westminster, she gazed up at the little window under the tallest of the eaves, remembering the classroom where her mother, distracted by the French queen's mischievous children, had slapped their hands with birch tally sticks, while Vives intoned the virtues of scholarly learning. Riding along Whitehall, heading for the Strand, she remembered romping with the neighborhood children along the riverbank.

And how that riverbank had changed! Now the great church palaces were owned by Henry's nobles and bore their names. In gardens where monks had toiled, there were only family servants and laborers, with animals running free and small children playing in the orchards.

And in the church itself, the king continued to make changes, denouncing any belief in Purgatory and abolishing many saints' days—an unpopular move with the people whose few holy days were their only respite from hard toil. Katherine had seen little provocative in the act, telling her husband it was merely a cleansing of the clutter, of man's overlay of what was, in essence, a simple worship of one's God.

"I've told you before, Katherine, you may believe as you will"—John was angrier than she'd ever seen him—"but please don't tell me your radical opinions! I suppose we should be thankful the king has left us baptism, penance and the Eucharist! But a mortal, even a king, should never tamper with the church's authority! That comes directly from Christ. Henry has outraged the clergy."

"Only because they didn't make the changes themselves, my lord." Katherine could not resist the challenge. "Had the clergy made those decisions, you'd not be so upset. It is because it comes from the king and *not* the church that you are so grieved!" John was about to respond but, thinking better of it, left the room, slamming the door behind him. They'd not referred to the subject again.

But Katherine recalled it as, riding through Westminster, she passed Hans Holbein's little studio. Impulsively, she went to the door, puzzled to find it dark and locked. A neighboring artist, frankly in awe at one he assumed from her rich clothing and handsome horse to be a great lady of the court, bowed and tugged at his cap. "Master Holbein is on the Continent, my lady," he explained, "and he'll not be back until next spring." Katherine was disappointed. It seemed ordained her portrait would remain unfinished.

* * *

For his service to the king during the Pilgrimage of Grace, Lord Latimer was made a Chamberlain of the Household and, in that capacity, was commanded to appear at Richmond Palace at the reunion of the Lady Mary and her father. Promptly at eleven o'clock on an October morning, Katherine and John arrived at the old palace, traveling from London with the Duke and Duchess of Suffolk in their barge.

Katherine was so excited she'd barely slept the night before and, walking the endless corridors toward the Presence Chamber, could scarcely contain her happiness. After so much misfortune, it was pleasant to be back in the old building where the very hallways were alive with memories. There were the old queen's apartments and, farther down the hall, she passed the rooms the French queen and her consort, now the husband of the youthful duchess at her side, had shared.

Entering the Presence Chamber, they found the king and queen talking with attendants and friends. Katherine remembered the day Anne Boleyn had so furiously torn a chain from Jane's neck. How sure the girl had been of herself to wear the king's portrait in the queen's presence! Katherine had decided then that Jane's demure passiveness undoubtedly hid a strong will and she said as much to Kate Brandon, adding there was much about the woman that was commendable.

"Indeed there is," Kate laughed, "for she has remarkable patience, restraint and docility. And she's always been a great friend of Mary's. But she's also devious, not unlike her brothers who work only for the family's good. Ah, see, there they are!"

Startled, Katherine searched the group about the king and queen. There was Anne Stanhope Seymour, Lady Beauchamp, beautifully dressed in a gown of dark blue velvet with pearls and diamonds set into the neckline. Her hood was extremely pointed with the same gems sparkling against her dark, lustrous hair. Katherine wondered if she'd remember how angry she'd been the night the king hadn't chosen her as a dance partner. Anne stood beside her tall, imposing husband whose dark hair and beard were now flecked with touches of gray. Lord Beauchamp was talking animatedly with his brother Thomas as the Latimers approached.

Immediately, Thomas caught Katherine's eye and once again she felt that intangible force reaching out to enfold her. It was that missing something, almost a bewitchment—that quick, warm, soft and pleasurable something— that always occurred when she saw Tom Seymour. He bowed now, glanced from her to the queen, with a private humor that seemed to say, "Who would have thought this could happen? Once I told you I was the king's glorified messenger. And now, madame, see this! I am his brother-in-law and may enter the Presence Chamber at will!"

Katherine knelt before Jane Seymour. "Your Majesty," she whispered, impressed in spite of herself at the self-confidence of this tiny woman who now carried England's hope of an heir. Outwardly, Jane had changed little from her days as lady-in-waiting to two queens. She was magnificently dressed in a damask gown of old rose and the color, reflected in the gleaming diamonds about her neck and the small circlet on her pale blond hair, bathed her in a rosy glow. There was another subtle difference. Love, marriage and now a pregnancy had softened the sharpness of her features, even deepening the bluish-gray cast of her small eyes.

Katherine had no time to greet the king, for the doors opened almost immediately as a herald announced, "The Lady Mary!"

Everyone knelt as Mary Tudor entered. Looking neither right nor left, the girl passed down the long room, her eyes only for the man and woman at the other end. Katherine noted the taut line of Mary's chin and the way her hands, ringless except for the diamond the queen had sent, were clutched tightly to her breast. Mary looked older and more worn than her twenty-one years. Katherine wanted to rush out and embrace her old friend, to say how much they'd all missed her and how she must now forget the misery of those dreadful years when she'd lost her mother and father, her title and, very nearly, her life.

Now everyone held their breath as Mary knelt, penitent, before Henry and Jane. There were tears in the queen's eyes and Henry's mouth was working. Nervously, he brushed his hands against his doublet before rising to embrace his daughter warmly. His voice was low; his words were for her alone. Even the queen could not hear his greeting. As he put an arm about her shoulders, Mary's eyes filled with tears and she trembled. For a moment, Katherine feared her poise might desert her. But quickly, Mary squared her shoulders and dropped to her knees before the queen. Soon Jane, too, had her arms about Mary. After a silent moment, she turned with the king to present the girl to the kneeling guests.

Then, all at once, everyone was clustering about Mary. She greeted them warmly, as if she'd seen them all only days, not years, before. But her struggle for composure was evident when her dark eyes lit on Katherine and Kate Brandon. As both swept her deep curtsies before they embraced, they all struggled to hold back the tears. Mary was obviously finding it hard to conceal her emotions. Her nerves were raw and she hadn't expected to see her old friends so soon. Quickly, before the tears spilled over, Kate Brandon spoke.

"Mary, do you know I have two children?" Gesturing toward her husband, she smiled. "He's been a father and a grandfather—all in the same year! That takes a fine bit of doing, my lady, and also our Lord's indulgence!"

Everyone laughed and, Katherine was pleased to see, Mary was slowly regaining her composure, accepting a cup of wine from the king's hand. Henry gazed at his daughter with affection and pride. Obviously, the king loved Mary. Yet for years, he'd treated her as a traitor, almost a criminal, forcing her to live beneath her rank, depriving her of love, friends, her own home and his presence. How could he justify such behavior?

Yet Mary, too, had reacted as strongly. She'd been stubborn and inflexible, retaliating in the only way she knew. In her obstinately perverse way, Mary had attempted to save the Crown for a Tudor, since she believed little Elizabeth was not the king's child. It was all so muddling and confusing, Katherine thought, this yearning for a crown with its promise of power and a divinity from heaven itself. Those with any claim to it must always be ready for any sacrifice. She did not envy Queen Jane.

Henry's voice interrupted her reverie. Standing by the fire, a cup of wine in his hands, he took Mary by the hand, saying, "You have seen our pleasure today in the return to our side of our most beloved daughter, the Lady Mary. She will live now at her own will, with our blessing, and be with us as much as she wishes and our duties allow." Henry had had several cups of wine and the firelight, flickering on his ruddy features, only enhanced the wine's flush. He gestured somewhat angrily to no one in particular, saying, in almost a petulant tone, "Some of you were desirous that we should put this jewel to death . . . !"

Queen Jane gasped and stepped forward beside Mary, who had grown very pale. The queen put her hand on her husband's arm. "That would have been a great pity, sire," she whispered, "to have lost your chiefest jewel of England. . . ."

"Nay!" The king laughed. He looked at his petite queen. "Nay!" Boldly, he reached out and patted the small protuberance that could be seen in the queen's rose damask gown. "Edward! Edward! That will be our name for our son. And he will be our chiefest jewel. There will be no other. . . ."

Mary stood apart, watching the king and queen. All she understood was that her father had once contemplated her execution and he could now even make merry of the fact! Remembrance of her lost years of humiliation and deprivation rose before her and she wondered—was this a trap? Had she forsworn her birthright to be caught publicly amongst her oldest and dearest friends like a captive animal? Was she doomed to a more horrible fate? Was all this fine reception merely to make her realize what she'd lost by her obstinacy and rebellion?

As everyone laughed at the sight of the king patting the queen's stomach,

there was a low moan and, before everyone's horrified eyes, Mary's composure crumpled. Her courage deserting her, she fell to the floor unconscious,
while her father and the others looked on, wondering what had happened.

* * *

Until Mary could once more have her old household, the king sent her to
his little manor house at Chelsea. It was near the handsome old home where
Sir Thomas More's family still lived off the produce of their gardens, orchards and the fish they took from the stream that ran through the vast park
above the Knight's Bridge.

In contrast to the More estate with its splendid terraces and carefully
tended land, the king's small house was simple, three stories high, built of
red brick and dressed stone, the Tudor coat of arms over the door. There was
no gateway or waterstairs, merely a simple wooden fence which enclosed a
small garden and fishpond. It turned sharply, running along the riverbank
where small boats or barges left their passengers to leap upon the thick
boards held in place by boulders so the tide would not wash them away.

But Mary Tudor cared little that the house was not as grand as Beaulieu,
Hatfield or Hunsdon. The manor house represented freedom—freedom from
constant supervision, spying and restraint. Here she often went on the river
or astride her horse with a pack of greyhounds running alongside, as she
coursed through the thickly wooded areas until she reached "the king's
road." Dr. Voisey, who took care of the king's daughters, told Mary the air
was more sweet at Chelsea than anywhere else along the Thames.

Within weeks, Mary was eating and sleeping better. Her headaches and
stomach pains lessened as each day brought a semblance of her former well-
ordered life. One by one her old servants arrived—some on foot, others by
horseback or the river. Margaret Baynton, Mary Brown, Anthony Roke and
Randall Dodd—each made a deep curtsey or bow before being embraced by
a tearful Mary. These were the people she'd known since childhood; many
had served her mother. Their years away from her hadn't been easy and
Mary noted sadly how much they'd aged.

They, in turn, regarded their young mistress with affection, looking for
traces of the sunny, sweet-tempered girl they'd remembered. There was less
laughter in Mary, little naïvete and her eyes, strained by poor vision, were
wary and grave. Old Margaret Baynton told Randall Dodd it seemed something was festering within the girl, poisoning her simplest reaction or decision.

"She has to learn to trust again," the old Welshman muttered, "and we
must all be patient with her. Remember what happened to her mother and
how quickly her fine friends left her when she needed them most!"

The servants were, therefore, pleased to see that among the first to call
upon Mary were Lady Latimer and the Duchess of Suffolk. Katherine and
Kate Brandon arrived one morning shortly after Mary had moved to Chelsea. They disembarked from the handsome Suffolk barge onto the large

boards set into the river's mud. Breaking into a run, holding their skirts high, they ran to Mary's side, where they made a deep curtsey to their old friend.

"A duchess does not curtsey to a mere lady, Kate, don't you know that?" Mary's voice was steely. "We'll have no more such nonsense!" Then, happiness returning, she hugged her friends warmly. "Oh, it's so good to see you! Have you seen the king's house before? Come upstairs, we'll be able to talk like we used to! No one will say you have to leave, no one will listen outside my door and write lies about what I've done! Oh, my two dear Kates, it's so fine to be back!"

Mary's chamber was a spacious room with windows overlooking the river on one side and the small garden with the fishpond on the other. Firelight cast dancing patterns of gold on the richly embroidered purple velvet bed hangings. Everyone admired the sleek Turkey carpet as Mary guided them to benches and chairs covered in the same velvet.

"This is where the king stays," she explained proudly. "It's very different from what I've had these last few years!" She shook herself as if casting off a bad memory. "But that is over now and the king says I may have Beaulieu for my own."

"My mother used to stay there when it belonged to your great-grandmother, Lady Margaret," Katherine said quietly, thinking how much Maud Parr would have enjoyed this reunion. "She always said Beaulieu was her favorite." Then, remembering the enchanting little girl she'd met at Richmond, she asked, "And where will the Lady Elizabeth live?"

"Wherever the king sends her." Mary appeared remote. "She's here now with Lady Bryan, but when I go to Beaulieu, Elizabeth will be sent to another house. I shall miss Lady Bryan, for she's getting old and now fancies being in her own house. She says she's raised us all—in one fashion or another! I don't know who will take her place. Elizabeth is too little to know all that has happened, so it will be easier for her than it was for me. But even so, she'll wonder when she doesn't see the king so often."

"But surely he will watch out for his own daughter?" Katherine wondered if the little girl knew what had happened to her mother. Who would tell her such a thing? Or would the king do it himself?

"Elizabeth is not the king's child!" Mary's lips tightened and her voice was raspy as she repeated the words. "There is none of my father's blood in her!"

Aghast, Kate Brandon looked about the room. "Jesu, Mary—be careful what you say! The child has been bastardized and removed from the succession, yes. But you cast doubts on her parentage to your own peril. Why do you say such a thing?"

Mary then told her story. She'd come to Greenwich by the king's order, as custom demanded, to be present at the birth of his son. Several of Anne Boleyn's ladies—her *own* ladies, she stressed—told her they doubted Henry was the father of the queen's child.

"My Lady Anne's conduct was such that they had strong opinions that the father was really Mark Smeaton, the musician. They said the Boleyn had favored him many times, even though he was one of low degree. They said she called him her "marmalade" for his fair skin and reddish hair. Elizabeth even has the same complexion and hair!"

Katherine wanted to say the king had similar coloring, but knew that would only upset her hostess. "It's a matter that can never be resolved, Mary," she answered, "and in trying you'll only kindle a great heat! You must be more careful! You can lose your freedom and your father's love with such words. Anyone who told you such a thing was no friend!"

"I think the Boleyn bore it on her conscience always," Mary said. "I think she feared it would be found out and it ate away at her nerves so she became almost unmanageable. I'm even more certain since she had arranged to have Lady Kingston come to me after her death to make amends for all the calamities she'd caused to fall upon me."

Mary told her astonished friends how, two days after Anne's death, Lady Kingston, wife of the Lieutenant-General of the Tower, had come to Hunsdon to beg a dead woman's forgiveness for Mary's years of humiliation, deprivation and the constant assaults on her integrity, privacy and honor.

"Lady Kingston said the Boleyn had asked her to get down on her knees and kneel in front of me. She was to say that Anne could not tolerate my father's love for me, that I was too much a reminder of my mother, that she did not want me around to take his attention from her new daughter. Lady Kingston said that during her last hours the Lady Anne's conscience was such she could not die until she knew someone would beg my forgiveness."

"And you believe she feared someone would find out Elizabeth was not the king's child?" The distasteful words made Katherine so uncomfortable, she could barely whisper them.

"I don't believe the king thinks she's his daughter either!" Mary cried. "But as long as he and that woman were wed, he put a good face on it. There was always the possibility of a son. It was more important to acknowledge Elizabeth than to disown her for, in doing so, he'd have had to put that woman away at once. Remember, as soon as she died, he took away Elizabeth's title! Had he really believed she was his daughter, he could have left her in the succession until he had a boy. Now he rarely sees the child. . . ."

Before anyone could speak, the door opened and Elizabeth, red curls flying, ran to greet Mary. Lady Bryan followed her into the room, smiling as Mary returned the child's tight embrace. Katherine could see the little girl's pleasure in being fondled and petted. She turned to Katherine, asking, "Did you bring me something?"

"Ah, my little lady, we didn't know you were to be here." Katherine put her hand on the child's shining hair. Elizabeth was only four, but she appeared older. Her dark Boleyn eyes missed nothing. "Next time I promise to bring you a present."

Mollified, the child turned to Mary again, clutching her hand. "My lady governess says I must have a new dress." She fingered the hem of her little green cambric gown. "See, Mary, it is torn here. . . ." The hem, Katherine could see, had been turned and patched so often it was indeed ragged.

Mary took the child's hand and said, "Lady Bryan will see to your clothing, Elizabeth. Now I would talk with my friends. Come, I will take you to Lala so Lady Bryan may have a rest." She took Elizabeth's hand and, reluctantly, the little girl followed her. Katherine was touched as the child's exuberance disappeared and, listlessly, she accompanied Mary from the room.

Lady Bryan sighed, accepting the cup of wine Katherine poured for her. "I will miss them both," she said, "but it is time to go to my own home now. Someone else must take over for me."

"You've been a great comfort, especially to Mary," Kate Brandon smiled, "and, but for you, Elizabeth would have had only Lady Shelton."

"Yes, and it has nigh undone me." Lady Bryan drank her wine gratefully. "Tell me, do you find Lady Mary well?"

Without waiting for an answer, Lady Bryan continued. "She is well on the surface, perchance, but underneath, she is still stricken at having given in to her father. But Jesu, she could do nothing else! Cromwell was threatening her with imprisonment or worse! I told her she had to do as her father ordered. Cromwell had enclosed the submission statements—all she had to do was sign."

"That doesn't seem too fearful, after all she'd been through," Kate Brandon reflected.

"Yes, but it was what Cromwell had written that made it so terrible for Mary. When she signed, she admitted her disobedience in not acknowledging the king as head of the church and disavowing the Pope. But the worst of all—I know because it made Mary physically ill—she agreed that her parents' marriage was incestuous and illegal. But I talked to her—oh, how I talked to her! I told her she'd had years of abuse and argument, persecution and abandonment. How much longer could it go on? I told her she had no choice—that if her mother had been alive, she'd say "sign!" She'd want her daughter to have some sort of decent life. I told her the old queen was elderly when she defied the king. Mary is twenty-one and already her life is half over!"

"You gave her good advice, my dear Lady Bryan," Katherine whispered, knowing the agony of conscience Mary had endured.

"I hope so"—Lady Bryan drank the last of the wine—"but sometimes I wonder if she'll ever put it behind her. Only the other day, she said she thought Christ Himself had deserted her, for she's had no peace in her heart since her submission. Perhaps it will be better when she's in her own house. She's happy to be able to see her father, but she can't forget what she did to her mother. When she signed Cromwell's statements, she feels she signed away her birthright and her mother's honor. For several days, Kate, she was prostrate with grief! She told me then if she died, she'd probably even be forbidden heaven. I thought she'd be relieved, but I know she feels she's done something monstrous."

Lady Bryan rose and embraced her friends. "Now mind you both, see Mary whenever you can. She needs to occupy her mind with today and not dwell upon the past. In some ways, it's a good thing little Elizabeth will go elsewhere for she reminds Mary of all that's happened. But then I worry about the babe, too, for no one at court seems to bother with her anymore! Ah, my ladies, 'tis a good thing I'm going to my own home. I worry more about the king's children than I do my own! But remember—help Mary to forget and be happy again."

*   *   *

As she returned to London, Katherine's thoughts revolved about the meeting. Mary's strained manner, her firm belief that Elizabeth was another man's child and the poignant description of a dead queen's apology was still in her mind as she sought her husband. She must tell John how bleak Tom More's house looked. Perhaps they could help Sir Thomas's old widow. Walking toward her bedchamber, she saw Bessie running down the hall.

"Kate, come quickly! My lord has been taken ill. Oh, I thought you'd never return! I'd have sent a messenger to Chelsea, but was certain you'd already be on the river. . . ."

Katherine pushed past Bess to the bedchamber. John was in bed and appeared to be asleep. His face was pale and strained; his rasping breathing filled the room. Hearing her footsteps, he roused himself to greet her, only to cough into a basin until exhausted. "I've sent for the doctor, Kate," Bessie whispered, "and he should be here soon. This came upon my lord very quickly."

Suddenly, a great burst of light lit the dim room followed by a thunderous explosion. Running to the window, Katherine pulled back the heavy hangings. "What could it be, Bess?" she cried. Below, Dr. Butts was dismounting in the courtyard. Beyond the monastery wall, framed by the Charterhouse spire and chimneys, fireworks were exploding near old Westminster Abbey and the sounds of people shouting and cheering drifted northward from the river. Suddenly another salvo from the direction of the Tower shook the room.

"Bess, 'tis the queen! She's had her child! And it's alive!" Katherine ran to meet Dr. Butts on the landing.

"Is it the queen, Doctor?" she asked breathlessly, relieved the physician, whose girth exceeded even that of the king, was smiling broadly.

"It is indeed, Lady Latimer, and we have an heir! I have just returned from Hampton Court where my colleagues and I helped deliver, by the grace of God, a son!"

Katherine clasped her hands as tears misted her eyes. A boy, a *prince!* At last Henry Tudor had his son and heir. "Oh, Doctor, what joyful news! Jesu be praised!" Katherine crossed herself and then pulled at the man's heavy cloak. "It will make my husband want to get up and give thanks. I think his illness is more of the spirit than that his body's humors fail him. Come quickly, Doctor, and tell him the good news!"

John still lay quietly. Katherine shook him lightly. "My lord, we have a prince!" Again tears filled her eyes. "The queen has had her child and it is a boy. I trow it should make you feel better! Oh, John, think what this means to the king!"

"And the queen . . ." her husband whispered, his voice grating and tight. "She has naught to worry about now, our queen, for Henry will deny her nothing. All the jewels of Cathay—even if they come from our churches and shrines. And all honors for her family! She has only to ask and the king will wave his golden scepter and everything will appear as if by magic." He smiled weakly. "She's done well, has Jane Seymour. And now Edward and Thomas have a nephew who will one day be king. There will be many more changes. . . ." He groped for Katherine's hand. "With a son to follow him and with such as the king now surrounds himself, even our new ways may not be enough to satisfy those who have power." He struggled to rise, clutching her hand tightly, his forehead beaded with sweat. "I don't think *you* are in any danger, my dear. Your family is close to the king and your own feelings are with the 'New Thinking' or the 'New Learning,' whatever it is that has turned our country and its people upside down. But oh, I do fear for my children, Katherine! They know naught but the old ways and it is those who know nothing but the old who will suffer most. Just as many have already suffered. . . ." He stopped, listening quietly to the bells pealing from the Charterhouse next door. "It's the first time in months I've heard bells that aren't tolling for death. . . ."

As Dr. Butts loosened her husband's clothing to examine him, John appeared exhausted by his speech. He turned his face to the wall, ignoring the physician. He'd spoken of his family, Katherine thought, almost as if he feared he'd be unable to protect them. Was he more ill than he appeared?

Outside the joyous sounds continued. Each new salvo from the Tower wafted over the river to reverberate throughout the room. But, Katherine noted, her husband appeared to hear nothing. The happy cheers and singing were growing louder and suddenly all the church bells of London pealed forth, reflecting the joy at Hampton Court where even now a proud king held a son in his arms.

Suddenly, Dr. Butts was shaking the sleeping man. "What is it, Doctor? What is wrong?" Katherine cried, alarmed at the physician's efforts. "John is all right, isn't he?" Then, incredibly, she saw the doctor delicately closing each eyelid.

"Lady Latimer, your husband is dead. There was nothing anyone could do. His consumption had gone too far and he had no strength to fight it."

There was a stifled gasp from Bessie in the corner as a servant, groaning, left the room. Stunned, Katherine reacted. In a moment, she knew, the Chartreuse servants would be lining up in the hall, sobbing and wailing. Quickly, she called out, "Tell them to stay downstairs, Bess! I want no one outside this door! If they must mourn, they must do it by themselves!" Before she confronted those who'd served John for years, Katherine knew she must first find his children.

Yet she could not take her eyes from the man in the bed. Had John known he was going to die? There was so much she'd liked to have said to him. How could he have left her and his children without so much as a fare-well?

Dr. Butts put a consoling hand on her shoulder and Katherine felt her throat constrict painfully. "He tried to do too much," she whispered to the physician. "He was such a good man, he couldn't let others suffer. We forgot he wasn't young." She glanced at the quiet figure again. Every line in John's face, every gray hair in his head and beard, was testimony to a man who'd dedicated himself to his responsibilities. Remembering the miserable events of the past year, she explained, "It was all too much for him in every way. But none of us realized it then. I know I didn't help as much as I might have." She lay her hand on her husband's. He'd striven as hard for his neighbors as either Aske or Constable. Katherine knew she should be thank-ful he'd died in his bed. Yet John Neville, Lord Latimer, was as much a vic-tim of the Pilgrimage of Grace as anyone who'd hung from a gate, tree or church steeple.

As Dr. Butts left, Katherine again remembered the children. They would be devastated by their loss. She must find them before any servant blurted out the news. She must tell them their father's last words had been of them.

Downstairs, she found Bessie waiting with a cloak. "They are in the gar-den, Kate. I think they suspect something for they saw Dr. Butts arrive. But they think their father is only sick. Can I help?"

Katherine shook her head, wondering what she'd say to John's son and daughter. Throwing the cloak about her, she walked slowly to the garden where the cries of celebration were even louder. When someone died, she thought, it should be quiet and solemn, not joyous and festive. She saw two figures seated on the bench against the old monastery wall. John and Mar-garet were waiting.

As she walked toward them, Katherine realized that once more she was a widow and must bear not only her own sorrow, but also the sadness of a hus-band's children. She prayed she'd be more of a comfort to the orphaned pair now waiting for her than she'd been to her older Borough stepchildren.

* * *

Six days later, after her farewell to family members who'd come from the North for Lord Latimer's interment in St. Paul's Cathedral, Kate Brandon told Katherine that on the same day Prince Edward was born, her step-daughter Frances Brandon Grey had given birth to a girl whom they'd named for the queen. The marchioness and her husband were disappointed the child wasn't a boy but, according to its grandfather, Charles Brandon, the baby was most comely and he'd asked his duchess to find a suitable christening gift.

Glad of the distraction, Katherine flew to her coffer for she, too, must find something for the king's grandniece. She took out the little gold circlet that Katherine of Aragon had given to Maud Parr at her birth. It would make a handsome present for the new baby. She was now a widow, nearing the age when her mother had died and unlikely ever to have any children of her own.

But, removing the shining little crown from its wrappings, Katherine knew she could never part with it. It had been a gift of love, a tangible mark of affection and respect for the Parr family. She, as well as Katherine Brandon, would have to find something else for little Lady Jane Grey.

CHAPTER XVIII

The joy of the English people at little Prince Edward's birth turned to a disbelieving sorrow twelve days later when the London bells tolled at Jane Seymour's death. A distraught Ann Parr Herbert soon arrived at Chartreuse and, weeping, told Katherine how greatly Jane had suffered at the little prince's birth.

"She was nigh dead for she travailed nearly thirty hours before they cut her and took the child," Ann sobbed. "We thought it a miracle she survived! Then she wanted to take part in the christening celebrations and it was more than she could stand." Ann said the king was devastated by the loss of his queen.

Katherine recalled the slight pale-skinned woman with the sly eyes and thin lips whose ambition had exceeded her physical strength. Jane Seymour had yearned for a crown belonging to another, caring little for the bitter remarks on the virtue of one who'd encouraged a king while his imprisoned queen awaited the headsman's axe. Jane had won her crown and bore the son which certainly would have ensured her queenship and, quite possibly, her husband's continuing love. Yet, after seventeen months, the attainment of both had killed her.

After the funeral at Windsor, Katherine told her stepchildren she was going to the manor of Wyke which their father had left her in his will. There, amongst the Worcestershire hills, she hoped to mend a body and spirit emotionally depleted by the horrors of the Pilgrimage of Grace, the death of her husband and now, the queen. Margaret, determined still to wed young Francis Bigod, tearfully said goodbye before returning to Snape with her brother John. Katherine promised to visit them well before the wedding.

Old Wyke manor house near Pershore lay in a valley enclosed by surrounding hills covered with dense woods in which tenant farmhouses, modest dwellings for workers and other more imposing homes of the nobility had graced the cleared land for several hundred years. Wyke was a handsome two-story building of brick and timber, crenellated and gabled, with a wondrous number of new chimneys of twisted brickwork, a rare aspect of country living that still caused the elders of Pershore—more used to a hole in the ceiling to rid themselves of smoke—to shake their heads in disbelief. The chimneys' new bricks were in sharp contrast to the mellowed walls of the ancient moat with its decaying drawbridge minus the portcullis that had been removed years ago. Wyke had always been a favored Latimer dwelling because of its halfway position between London and the North. Graduated terraces on the southern side, a recent innovation when the Latimer children were little, led to a small lake where colorful skiffs were kept in a great grove of oak trees. In good weather, it was possible to row across the lake and picnic in a modest octagonal banqueting pavilion built for the first Lady Latimer. Wyke, John had once told Katherine, was a house of pleasure and relaxation away from the demanding responsibilities of court life and she'd been pleased he'd left it to her.

Sir William Parr, recently retired as head chamberlain in the household of young Henry Fitzroy, accompanied Katherine to Wyke. Before the king could appoint him elsewhere, Sir William had begged to return permanently to Kendal and Henry had affably granted his request. Yet there was little doubt he still expected Parr to be of service, for he'd been appointed Chief Commissioner of the Peace for Westmorland, a county still recovering from the destructive effects of the Pilgrimage of Grace. Though anxious to be in the dales about his beloved Kendal home, Sir William remained at Wyke long enough to explain to Katherine the importance of her husband's bequests.

In addition to Chartreuse in London and Wyke manor, John had also left his wife the manors of Nunmonckton and Hamerton, several tin mines in the West Country as well as many profitable leaseholds around London and the southern counties. Young John had been left a small fortune and Snape, while a generous sum was set aside for Margaret's dowry.

"You'll never have to worry, my dear, these are very sizable holdings!" William Parr elatedly told his niece. "Together with what Edward Borough left you and your own Parr inheritance, you have quite a fortune!" The rents from whole villages, profits from the tin mines and fees from parks and other leaseholds would produce more annually than she could ever spend, he said.

The extent of John's generosity had stunned Katherine. Observing friends like Kate Brandon bemoaning the cost of the new roof at Westhorpe or the additional servants needed at Suffolk House for her babies, she often felt a twinge of guilt. When an exasperated Mary Tudor said she'd had to write Thomas Cromwell several times to remind him her annual stipend of forty pounds had not been paid, Katherine could only marvel that a princess and a duchess should be so pressed for funds, while she had only to ask her uncle for any reasonable sum and it was soon in her hands.

Both her brother and sister also appeared in constant need of money. Young Will Parr's wife, Anne, daughter of the Earl of Essex, incessantly carped that the boy's modest inheritance was so much less impressive than her dowry. Ann Parr Herbert and her husband were notorious spendthrifts, always in the clutches of the moneylenders. When, guiltily, Katherine told her uncle she'd like to assist her brother and sister, William Parr shook his head vigorously.

"Once you commence helping, Kate, they'll give you no peace and become

like leeches! Will is twenty-one and has a good future if he can just use common sense where that flighty wife of his is concerned. Don't worry about
Will! The king often says how much he reminds him of your father. Will is
extravagant, I know, but he must learn to be more prudent in his spending.
Ann's husband will take good care of her and let no moral nicety blind him
if he has a chance to gain in his purse.

"Remember, my dear," he concluded as Katherine smiled at his astute
assessment of her brother and sister, "by right you should leave your estates
to your Borough and Latimer families, since you have no children of your
own. They'd be shocked if you disposed of anything without consulting
them. The holdings are yours for life, but we must be good stewards of what
God has given you."

Katherine wanted to reply that God had had little to do with it. She'd
married two old men, submitted to their desires, led the life they preferred,
taken care of their children, homes, servants and tenants, remained constantly at their beck and call, all the while lending the considerable Parr
prestige to their names. She'd respected her first husband and had a genuine
affection for her second. If, out of these unions, had come great wealth and
more honor, she wanted now to live as *she* wished—with proper time for
friends, family, books and study. Perhaps even a bit of travel abroad on the
Continent.

Katherine was, she decided in those first quiet months at Wyke, tired of
being *used*—in house or in bed—especially when it was not accompanied by
that elusive, intangible something that still brought a blush to the cheek of
the twenty-one-year-old Duchess of Suffolk when Charles Brandon watched
her with a certain light in his eye or caressed her bare arm when he thought
no one was looking. All around her, Katherine had seen marriages of convenience where there was little if any love.

But there were others such as Joan Champernowne recently wed to one of
the king's oldest friends, Sir Anthony Denny. And Joan Guildford, a friend
of palace schoolroom days. Joan had wed Sir John Dudley and was now the
mother of six-year-old Robert who shared the same birthday as Princess
Elizabeth. Each time Katherine saw the Brandons, Dudleys or Dennys, she
was impressed and envious of that intimate evanescent something they all
shared that had somehow eluded her.

Even Bess had experienced a rare closeness with Rob Aske during their
brief courtship. Why had she herself failed to find it? Was she destined
never to feel that rapturous excitement, that passionate bewitchment with
someone she could adore and cherish—one who would return her love a
hundred times over? Was she never to have children or wait impatiently for
a lover's return at night to experience something other than mere physical
coupling?

Once, during the end of her first year at Wyke, Kate Brandon, the Duchess of Suffolk, arrived for a visit. The king had recently made Charles Brandon the Lord Great Master, responsible for the royal household. Conse-

quently, the duke was spending more time at court leaving his wife free to visit her closest friend. Shortly after their reunion, Katherine tried to express her thoughts to Kate Brandon, stammering and blushing, and finally waving her hands in despair at describing how she felt at the lack of honest love in her two marriages.

"Ah, Katherine, you're too modest, my girl! Do stop blushing for I know what you mean!" The duchess laughed. "Marriage is a lot more than four legs in a bed and that's about what you've had, although you must know that both your husbands *adored* you! The French queen used to tell me during her own sickness what an unusual young girl you were. Now that you're no longer so young and she's no longer here, I'll tell you what she said, for it can do no harm. She said, 'Kate is like my darling Maud who was made for a man to love and was lucky enough to get Tom Parr. But Kate isn't that lucky and she's using all that hidden disappointment, that sense of frustration, to make herself the perfect wife and stepmother. All her stepchildren idolize her to the point of idiocy. And that only makes their father love her even more. But it's not fair to her! She deserves better than a graybeard! I hope someday she finds the right man!' "

"Well, he might even try looking for me," Katherine laughed to hide how deeply the French queen's words had touched her. "Think of all the scrutiny he'll face—not only from my uncle, but both my Borough and Latimer families, too! I may end up a dowager-spinster yet, Kate!"

When Katherine asked for gossip of the court, Kate Brandon replied that her husband, the duke, had welcomed the king's appointment because, in addition to being responsible for the royal household, Charles also served as President of the Privy Council. By spending more time at court, Kate said, her husband hoped to help guide or control Thomas Cromwell.

"There are those who think the man is a genius," Kate explained, "for he manages the king's affairs very well. But he's made so many enemies— usually those close to the king from the old nobility who are rich but now have little power. The councillors are afraid of those Cromwell has placed in all parts of the government. People like that abominable Richard Rich who lied so at Sir Thomas More's trial. He receives all the monies and treasure from the sale of the holy houses. I think Henry appointed Charles because he's really the only one he can trust!"

Kate said the king was being urged to marry again. "He's sent for a portrait of Mary of Guise, the Duke of Lorraine's daughter. There are those who say she's the rarest beauty of the French court, but the king only fancied her after he'd heard the French king had pledged her to Henry's nephew, James Stuart! Now Henry is angry for Mary is not only beautiful, but well educated and said to be quite charming. She's also tall and Henry told Charles he's a big man and needs a big wife! But King Francis will do nothing—he only insists she marry the Scottish king. You know how Francis has always favored and encouraged the Scots so they'll make trouble along our border and otherwise meddle in our affairs! Charles says Cromwell will do anything to prevent the wedding, for he doesn't want a queen with strong Catholic leanings. He's already casting about for someone the king might marry."

"Can't Henry choose for himself?" Katherine laughed. "If a king cannot choose, pray, who can? Isn't there a lady willing to wed her sovereign? Isn't there one big enough? Or, perchance, with one wife exiled and persecuted, another beheaded, another dead in childbirth, there is no one anxious to share the royal bed and person, no matter how big?" At which both ladies dissolved in mirth, wiping their eyes at the thought of Henry Tudor, frustrated at winning the one woman whose portrait and reputation had so beguiled him. To waste such a woman on his sister Margaret's son whose youthful whoring at the Scottish court was already legendary!

"You see, my girl," Kate Brandon laughed merrily, "you're not the only one with problems of the heart! But now that you're approaching middle age, you'll be allowed to choose, for you have more money and land than any suitor. Yet even a king cannot do that! Yes, Henry will wed again. But this time, I trow, Cromwell will pull the strings. Unless, of course, Charles and others like Norfolk and Sussex can stop him. . . ."

* * *

Within a year of Kate Brandon's visit, Katherine knew the duchess' words had been prophetic. France and Spain signed a ten-year truce and with it rose the likely threat of an invasion by two Catholic countries determined to deal with the heretical English king. At the same time, Pope Paul III issued a bull denouncing Henry and absolving all English Catholics from any allegiance to their sovereign. From Rome, Reginald Pole wrote his family and other Catholic friends, encouraging them to crusade against the king whom he called "cruel and abominable."

Stung by the French-Spanish alliance, Henry ordered that defenses along the Thames estuary, the Kentish coast and Cornwall be improved. Dikes were repaired, many by women and children digging and shoring, as the royal engineers dealt with the more complicated task of reinforcing decaying coastal castles built by the Normans. Around the country—even at Wyke—musters were held and, once again, the beacons flared, reviving painful memories for both Katherine and Bessie.

Katherine had just returned from a visit with her stepchildren when she heard that Henry had finally selected a bride. Margaret Neville had become a mother for the second time and all Katherine's Borough grandchildren were now having babies of their own. A packet of mail from friends at court informed her that Henry had sent Hans Holbein to paint the portrait of Anne, daughter of the Duke of Cleves, baron of several small duchies along the lower Rhine. The result had been acceptable to His Grace and even now the princess was en route to England.

Katherine wondered what had happened to her own still-unfinished portrait. Was it stacked along with others in the artist's Westminster studio?

The portrait also brought Sir Thomas Seymour to mind. Where was the handsome courtier whose sister had been briefly queen and given England its heir? Remembering the man's strong impact and the assignation she'd almost kept at a time when she was Latimer's wife, Katherine could only shake her head at her own foolishness. Certainly, fate had intervened when her own good sense had seemingly deserted her.

The Seymours had come a long way, higher than any of them could ever have dreamed. One had been queen, two were now uncles of the heir, Prince Edward. She wondered what the court of King Henry and another Queen Anne would be like. It would be different from the quiet, closely knit court of the old queen and be very unlike the gay, sophisticated court of Anne Boleyn, bent upon entertainment and diversion. The court of Jane Seymour had been marred by the Northern rebellion and her early death. Certainly it would be a challenge to the Flemish Anne to imprint her personality on a court full of memories, loving or otherwise, of three dead queens.

Her uncle, Sir William Parr, was dubious about the marriage. He wrote Katherine, "Henry is marrying this woman only to show the French king, the Spanish emperor and the Pope that England does not need their friendship, that he is a strong sovereign in his country. Cromwell has no true religious feelings, my dear. He is either very astute politically—or foolhardy beyond belief. It all depends upon how the king regards Princess Anne. Because the court, you may be sure, will act upon that. Only Mary has been truly honest. She told your brother Will she doesn't know how to address a stepmother of her own age, one who understands no English and who believes in a church ritual which she, herself, despises. Ah, it's going to be a time of testing at court, Katherine. The lines have been drawn and this woman may, all unknowing, determine the victor."

*   *   *

Three weeks later, in answer to a royal command to attend the wedding of Henry of England and Anne of Cleves, Katherine returned to Parr House. It had been almost three years since she'd been in her old home and she wandered, misty-eyed, through the spacious rooms, her throat constricting as she entered her parents' bedchamber with its familiar hangings and the great wardrobe where Maud Parr had kept her precious satins, damasks and velvets. Her own room was smaller than she remembered and, over the years, had been refurbished. The view of the river—so exciting to a small child— would now mean only an icy dampness and she directed her steward to place her belongings in her parents' chamber. At last she'd sleep in the bed where undoubtedly she'd been conceived. The thought, while poignant, did not distress her. It still surprised Katherine how much she missed her mother. Maud Parr's vital presence, even after almost a dozen years, still lingered in the rooms and garden where familiar trees and bushes had grown to great height.

On the day of Anne of Cleves's arrival, the Parr family joined the Duke and Duchess of Suffolk as they rode to Shooters Hill where the princess would be formally welcomed to London. Before leaving, everyone toasted young Will Parr whom the king had recently made Baron Parr of Kendal. Katherine thought her brother had matured into a handsome, firm-fleshed young man with high color, his father's straight nose and his mother's preference for expensive finery and jewels. Beside him, his plain-faced wife appeared almost insipid and graceless. The marriage was obviously not a happy one. How terrible, Katherine thought, to be bound so young in a loveless union! It had happened to her but, each time, there'd been an early release. Unless there was some accident of nature, she knew there'd be no such release here. As if reading her thoughts, Charles Brandon cleared his throat and, selecting his words carefully, remarked that the day might be difficult for the king apparently did not care for his new bride-to-be.

"I see only trouble ahead," he told the stunned group, standing in the sunlight of Parr House's river room, wine cup in hand. Outside, the stablemen could be heard readying the horses that would take them to Shooters Hill. "I cannot say that I blame His Grace for when I first saw the woman, I could scarce contain my bewilderment." Brandon's voice was puzzled. "You all know that Master Holbein always captures an excellent likeness, but he sees something in this lady I do not. She looks much older than her years—not unlike the Lady Mary at the time of her troubles. Her skin is dark and without any luster and is pitted from the pox." He glanced away in exasperation, waving his hand angrily. "How could the man have been so wrong? He knows how delicate the king is in his preference for fairness! Ah, I despair at what he will do!"

Katherine was aghast. How could Holbein have made such a mistake? Henry Tudor had never liked the inferior. Even Anne Boleyn, for all her reputation and irrational behavior, had been a Howard. All his other queens had had their own distinctive beauty or talent. She recalled Holbein once telling her he could paint only what he saw. Yet the king had thought the painting excellent and the sitter most comely. How could Anne be so different from her portrait? What had Holbein seen that Charles Brandon and Henry Tudor could not?

Within three hours, at the foot of Shooters Hill on the plain of Blackheath, Katherine had her answer. There Londoners had their first glimpse of Anne of Cleves as she rode in procession to meet her new subjects. The Flemish woman was escorted by her duchy's ambassador, the Earl of Overstein, and several of the English nobles. They rode together, their banners whipped by the slicing January winds toward the palace of Greenwich where, after Twelfth Night festivities, the wedding would take place.

Katherine's impression as she waited to take her place in the entourage, was of a woman—taller than most—who appeared much older than her twenty-three years. Her high forehead was framed by two strands of dull brown hair covered by a dark green coif which made her skin appear even more sallow. Anne wore a flat cap with elongated flaps which covered her ears and emphasized the long thin face and prominent nose. Her large dark eyes peered intently; Katherine suspected the pox might have affected her eyesight as much as it had scarred her skin. Anne appeared full-busted and was garbed in a riding costume which, while probably the height of fashion in the German countries, made her appear overdressed and old-fashioned in comparison with the English ladies.

Once in the palace, Katherine hurried to shed her cloak and find her place in the procession to the princess' chamber. She saw Anne was plainly bewildered and uncomfortable at the tone of the English ladies' chatter which, while she could not understand what was being said, told her all was not well. Their stares and whispers were blatantly scornful. They were plainly aghast at the foreign visitors who did not even appear eager to change their rumpled traveling clothes to something more suitable.

Katherine felt sorry for the woman now so much at her new country-women's mercy. Kneeling at her presentation, she smiled at Anne, hoping to convey that not everyone was unfriendly and was rewarded by a large smile which softened the Flemish princess' heavy features as she bobbed her head in response and changed her expression enormously. It lent a sparkle to her plain brown eyes and a lightness to her stolid Dutch features. Katherine felt if they could converse she would find Anne's plain looks forgotten, that the woman would be bright and charming. She remembered how beguiled the king had been with her portrait. Though the picture was solemn, had Anne chattered with the artist in a language they both understood? Had Holbein made the experience of posing so pleasant he'd caught a pleasant-featured, relaxed woman on canvas? Had Anne been happy and secure then, even as she was now tense and uncertain?

As her attendants and the English ladies commenced to wrangle over who would serve her, Anne's spontaneous smile vanished. Each time a suggestion was made, she stoutly answered, "Ja!" though Katherine felt she might just as frequently wished to say "Nein!" Katherine almost said it for her when the sharp-featured Lady Rochford, the widow of George Boleyn, who'd given such damaging testimony at her sister-in-law's trial, was appointed chief lady-in-waiting. But there were others she was certain the new queen would like. Joan Dudley and the stately Countess of Rutland would be kind. Little Catherine Howard, the old Duke of Norfolk's niece, would chatter endlessly, flirt without discretion and laugh and giggle constantly. They would be a contrast to Anne's own more serious, apparently humorless companions who appeared as bewildered as she at their luxurious chambers, the extravagance of fire and candles and the colorful, expensive English ladies' clothing.

During the following day, as the king argued that his council must find a way out of a distasteful marriage, Anne of Cleves remained in her chamber, the center of attention and dispute between her countrywomen and the English ladies. She knew Henry was disappointed in her and, alone with her own women, they'd talked in low whispers of what she must do to endure this man who made so little effort to hide his discontent. Soberly, they reminded her that other wives hadn't fared so well under the yoke of his displeasure. Close to tears, Anne had vowed nothing unpleasant would happen to her if she could help it. One day at a time, her ladies advised and, ears and eyes open, she listened carefully when the Englishwomen advised a more stylish coiffure. Since she would be the tallest of Henry's wives, they said, she should dress her hair in a fashion which did not accent her height. Anne had almost laughed aloud at the suggestion until she realized they were serious. Could she help it if she was tall? Was it true her dresses were too cumbersome, in an outmoded fashion and in unflattering colors? Was it so terrible that while she spoke French and Spanish fluently, she'd never learned English?

Katherine offered to help Anne with her new language and teach her the card games and dances which would help pass the time. "I've taught before, Your Grace," she told Anne through the interpreter. "I'd like to help."

But Anne had little hope that anything would change Henry's attitude. "The king does not like me, Lady Latimer," she told Katherine with blunt frankness. "He's scarcely seen me since my arrival. Will it help if I wear my hair another way, if I change the dresses my mother and sisters thought suitable for me with those more English, if I learn your games and dances and speech?" Anne's face flushed with embarrassment as she struggled to let the interpreter know her exact feelings. "What will it matter if the king does not like *me*? Everyone says I must be more witty and clever, almost a flirt! At home we do not compete to be witty or clever and we take our duties seriously. There the man is dominant and we are content to be patient and understanding and let him lead the way. We are always ourselves," she said, her strong jaw jutting out. "We do not play games with each other."

Katherine understood. How often had she herself played games with two husbands, pretending love and affection, spending her days in dull household tasks she could easily have given to a servant, hiding her reading and learning? How often had she, docile and passive, spent days at her husband's side caring for his family, home and servants, riding his lands, visiting his relatives or lay in his arms, unfeeling and passive, at night? Each day, as she watched Anne struggling to adapt to new ways, her admiration and sympathy for the foreign woman grew.

Yet it was obvious Henry's dislike of his intended bride had not waned. Her uncle told Katherine the king had strongly chastised Thomas Cromwell for arranging the marriage with the Lutheran princess, elating those Privy Councillors with strong Catholic feelings. William Parr said it was providential Hans Holbein had remained on the Continent for he thought Henry would have sent him to the Tower.

But at last the king realized he had no valid reason for not marrying Anne of Cleves. Repeatedly, Charles Brandon explained that to evade the union would bring dishonor to the house of Cleves and push Anne's brother and all his duchies straight into the Spanish emperor's arms. Thomas Cranmer, the Archbishop of Canterbury, and Katherine's cousin, Cuthbert Tunstall, the Bishop of Durham, both pronounced there was no real reason why the wedding should not take place.

"God's blood!" the king lamented, "is there no way for us but to put our head into the yoke?" When no one spoke, he cried, "My lords, if it were not that she has come so far into our realm and the great preparations that have been made for her and for the fear of making a ruffle in the world and of driving her brother into the hands of the emperor and the French king, we would not marry her!"

Katherine was in Anne's chambers when Lady Rochford, preening, arrived to say the king had agreed to the marriage. Since he'd stressed there was no hurry, she said there might be time for a new, more proper wedding gown to be made. Katherine could cheerfully have shaken the woman as she prattled on, telling Anne that since the marriage was now definite, Lady Mary and Lady Elizabeth, the king's daughters, would soon pay their respects to their future stepmother.

Anne had kept her eyes fixed on her needlework as Lady Rochford talked and her interpreter explained how much had to be done. At last she laid the cloth aside and, her jaw settling more firmly, spoke through the interpreter whose face was as flushed with anger as her own.

"My lady, you will do me the honor to ask His Grace what is the reason for the delay? It is not in my power, nor his, to set our wedding aside! Like it or not, we must be married. That has been agreed upon by my brother, your king and all their ambassadors! This cannot be undone and you may tell your king if I am willing to put up with him, he can at least do the same. I think you should tell him it was not *my* idea to come to England to wed your Henry." Anne's eyes sparkled with anger and Katherine wanted to cheer. "That was a decision made *for* me. If I can accept him—and there were several others like Christina, the Duchess of Milan, who refused his offer, my ladies, you must recall that?—then he might behave in the goodly manner I would expect from someone who has been so graciously praised as intelligent and pleasant. I've seen very little of these things in your king since my arrival, Lady Rochford, and you would do me a favor to tell him so. I will listen to no more excuses and I urge His Grace to set a date for our wedding soon. I will rely on you to inform him, my lady, since my own ambassador is too angry over my reception and I fear would only enrage your king even more if I asked him to take these words to him."

Everyone was silent as Lady Rochford, mouth open in shock, appeared as if she'd been struck. Several of the English ladies smiled encouragingly as others bustled about or busied themselves with their duties. Anne again picked up her needlework, her large square fingers holding the cloth delicately. On her right hand she wore a heavy gold band, a gift from her parents. On the inside, she'd told Katherine, was the inscription "God Send Me Well To Keep."

Anne fingered the ring, as if remembering the words. Stifling her laughter,

Katherine wanted to tell Anne she had little doubt that He certainly would. Anne of Cleves was obviously as little impressed with Henry of England as he was with her. But perhaps he'd met his match in this stolid Flemish woman. Katherine suspected if the king didn't make up his mind soon, the royal fireworks—planned for the Greenwich wedding reception—might not be needed.

Later, stung by the princess' remarks which a hesitant Lady Rochford repeated to Charles Brandon, Henry allowed that if Anne was so eager to be married, the ceremony could take place the following morning. Anne insisted on wearing her own gown of cloth of gold embroidered with flowers of large oriental pearls, which the expression on the English ladies' faces plainly told her they thought unfitting. But Anne knew she had the advantage, however fleeting it might be. She was finally going to do that for which she'd been sent to England: marry its king. In somewhat garbled English, she thanked Katherine for her kindness. "You've been a great help, Lady Latimer, and I'll not forget. I'm puzzled by many things I've found here, but I know goodness when I see it. Pray for me today. And pray for the king also," she added, somewhat as an afterthought.

After the ceremony, as the royal couple left the festivities, Katherine did as Anne of Cleves had asked. But, she told Kate Brandon with a smile, she prayed a little harder for the king.

* * *

Three days later, when Anne went to Richmond to meet her infant stepson, Katherine returned home and, in the weeks that followed, Parr House became a meeting place for friends whose ties to each other went back many years. The handsome rooms rang with the laughter of ladies, fashionable, well educated and wealthy, many the wives of those with powerful positions at court. Lady Denny and Lady Dudley—her "two Joans," Champernowne and Guildford—were often there. Mary Tudor came from Richmond where she'd left Elizabeth with Queen Anne. "The child is beside herself with excitement at meeting her stepmother," Mary smiled, "but the king is very angry that Elizabeth wanted to meet her. Sometimes he forgets how young she is!" Katherine saw Mary was upset. "He told her she had a mother so different from the queen it was better not to go. I had to remind Elizabeth not to repeat what he'd said. My father is not improving with age, Katherine, and his leg only makes it worse!"

Once again Mary was at odds with the king for considering a marriage for her with Anne of Cleves's brother. The thought of such a union with a man so closely allied to the Lutheran cause and countries had appalled Mary and she'd been almost ill with anxiety ever since. "I told my father I preferred the single life," she told Katherine, "but he just waved me away and said my Lord Cromwell would continue negotiations." Mary was close to tears and, with an arm about the slight girl, Katherine drew her into the large chamber where her friends bantered with each other, as their children and dogs scampered about in front of the open fire. All rose to curtsey to Mary before sitting down again to their needlework and gossip.

One day, the Marchioness of Dorset, Frances Brandon Grey, brought her children, Jane, Katherine and Mary to Parr House. The girls, named for two dead queens and a former princess, were almost too quiet and well behaved for their ages, Katherine thought. She hadn't seen her former schoolmate—so troublesome to her mother—since the birth of three-year-old Lady Jane. The little girl greatly resembled her beautiful grandmother, the French queen, while Lady Frances looked more like her uncle, the king. Her voice was similar, but marred by a whining tinge of petulance. She is still a crosspatch, Katherine thought, always complaining, never pleased, probably the scourge of her household. Kate Brandon said she constantly irritated her husband and behaved like a devil with her children. It bewildered and angered Katherine that one should so tyrannize her little girls who, young as they were, obviously feared the large-framed, domineering woman. Jane, particularly, appeared agitated and frightened of her mother. On one occasion, as the woman gave the little girl a vicious pinch, Kate Brandon protested.

"Jesu, Frances, she is but a mere babe! Tell her what you want and don't change your mind so often. If you can't do that, give the child to her nurse. She can't be expected to remain like a mouse when she doesn't know what you want!"

Frances Grey was about to reply but, noting the disdain in other eyes, summoned a servant and a tearful little Lady Jane was led from the room, rubbing the red wound on her arm. Katherine wondered how often the child was slapped or pinched when no one was around to defend her. Even more, she wondered why the marchioness so obviously hated the little girl whose beauty, so reminiscent of Frances's own mother, made her all the more endearing.

After years in the North where conversation centered about county activities, the weather and crops, family feuds and the latest marital alliances, Katherine found the Parr House conversation stimulating and refreshing. All her friends' husbands were intimately involved in the king's affairs, and they spoke as knowledgeably of court politics and continental alliances as they did of their families and households.

Everyone agreed the religious changes plaguing the country were coming too fast. "It's hard to keep up with what we're supposed to believe," sniffed Joan Dudley. "When people like Hugh Latimer and Nicholas Shaxton resign their bishoprics and Cromwell hangs old Abbot Whiting on a Glastonbury tor, one wonders if the reformers are not causing more trouble than even they want. Such changes must take time and should be explained to the people."

Katherine turned aside at the words, saying she wished to hear no more of violence. The brutal scenes on the York Road still burned in her mind after nearly four years.

"You remember what we were all taught," Katherine said. "You remember we were taught that if we are to have faith, we must have knowledge! That's what my mother, my grandmother and many of *your* grandmothers all said years ago in these very rooms!"

Katherine felt exhilarated by speaking out at last. "I know there are many people—perhaps the greater number—who follow my Lord of Norfolk and my Lady Mary, who do not believe as we do. If Mary were here today, she'd be the first to argue with us! Both my husbands followed where the priest led. Today my sister and brother do also. They say we must accept everything on faith. Yet priests argue among themselves as to what we should believe! If the 'New Learning' has done nothing else, it has made people think. I remember years ago, a little girl, Anne Askew, saw more concerning religion than I or anyone else did."

Kate Brandon nodded in agreement. "Everyone agrees that religious beliefs must be the same. We can't have one group believing one thing and others believing something else. But let it come without violence—with study and education—with the church and king leading the way peacefully."

Joan Dudley said she believed that religion should be kept separate from politics. The king's marriage to Anne of Cleves was a good case in point. "Cromwell arranged the marriage to please the reformers and to spite the French and Spanish. Now, to plague Cromwell for the marriage he so dislikes, the king courts old Norfolk, showing more of an eye for his niece, Catherine Howard, than bodes good for the queen. My husband says and aye, I agree, 'twould be better if religion and politics were not mixed!"

"And if the king continues to favor the Catholics on the council, such as Norfolk," Katherine replied bitterly, "they will only urge him to more changes in the church. All of which will lead to more bloodshed." She gestured impatiently, her face flushed, "It is such a waste . . . !"

Kate Brandon leaned over to pat Katherine's hand. "You've seen more tragedy, my dear, more waste and sorrow caused by religion than all of us put together." Kate's voice was grave. "We all know there is only one Jesus Christ and He told us what to believe in the Bible. So I agree—why not let the people read for themselves and make up their own minds? Yet Charles tells me it isn't that simple. To give the king credit, he tries. I think he believes much as we do. Remember the Lady Margaret, his grandmother, had his ear for many years when he was a child!" Kate explained that at council meetings the king had been firm, saying that leaving a choice of belief in the hands of the uninformed or the troublemakers only resulted in rioting and violence. "People argue, families disagree, bishops resign and other churchmen and the common people find themselves at each other's throats. The reformers cry, 'If it isn't in the Bible, it isn't so!' To which those of the old faith cry 'heretic!' When the Northerners tried to protect their religion and their holy houses, the king finally saw the issue might tear England apart. Had he not seen it, believe me, Cromwell would have been the first to inform him."

As Katherine gestured to a servant to pour wine, someone said the king appeared to enjoy confusing his queen and Cromwell about his religious preferences and, as if to spite his unhappy marriage, was lessening his support of the reformers who'd anticipated more cooperation with the advent of Queen Anne of Cleves. Now several protesters had gone to the stake for refusing to recant their belief that the body of Christ was not actually present in the communion wafer, but merely symbolic. Another had been hanged for eating meat on Friday. Even priestly celibacy was once more mandatory.

"A black day for old Cranmer," Kate Brandon giggled over the wine, "he's had to send his wife back to Germany!"

Soon the room was filled with laughter again.

CHAPTER XIX

Level, level with the ground
  The towers do lie,
Which with their golden glittering tops
  Pierced once to the sky!
Where were gates, no gates are now;
  The ways unknown
Where the press of peers did pass
  While her fame far was blown
Owls do shriek where the sweetest hymns
  Lately were sung;
Toads and serpents hold their dens
  Where the palmers did throng.
—Ballad describing the destruction of Our Lady of Walsingham shrine,
  1540

The spring of 1540 brought a welcome relief to Londoners from one
of the most severe winters in memory. Again the Thames had frozen over;
each morning stiff bodies of beggars, the weak and sick or the dispossessed
were found on its icy banks. Now sporadic uprisings commenced once more
in the North and in London the warmer weather brought the frightening
threat of the plague.

Yet the one constant irritation was the king's unhappy marriage. Only his
younger daughter seemed oblivious of her father's discontent. Elizabeth sent
a constant stream of notes to the king, their childish script tidily neat and eloquent of her desire to see him. With a rueful smile, Mary Tudor told
Katherine the king wondered if his Flemish queen encouraged the child to
continue writing him. Anne of Cleves was devoted to little Elizabeth and
constantly urged Henry to pay more attention to her.

"And what does the king say?" Katherine asked Mary. "The queen only
wants to be a good stepmother."

"My father listens to her, Kate, and then with a flip of the hand, a shrug
of the shoulder, a goodly bow and, cap in hand, he is gone! He leaves it all
to Cromwell who tells the queen she waxes willful and stubborn in suggesting how a father should behave with his children. Then she is quiet for a

while at least. She fears if she troubles him too much he might not let her see Elizabeth and Edward at all. God knows they would miss her! She's the only one—along with me and sometimes Lady Bryan—who visits them. Cromwell knows the king doesn't like the queen so he feels he, too, can treat her as he chooses." There was genuine concern in Mary's voice. Despite their religious differences, Anne had won Mary's trust and affection.

Once, visiting the queen at Richmond, Anne told Katherine that Mary had been so poorly treated by her father, she still felt abandoned, a feeling Anne said she now understood and appreciated.

"I don't want it to happen to the other children." Anne's tone was firm as she glanced toward Elizabeth and her cousin, little three-year-old Jane Grey, playing in the reeds along the riverbank. "I do what I can, Lady Latimer, but the king will not let my Elizabeth or Edward live with me. It would be so much better if they did."

They had just emerged, along with several ladies-in-waiting, from the deserted cloister of the Franciscan Friars, walking to join the children being watched over by two elderly nurses seated on the waterstairs wall nearby. Spring had brought an early green life to the river and a soft, moist air, alive with freshening fragrances, blew from the south. The children's voices were joyous as Elizabeth, growing taller each day, waded in the water, pulling at the reeds. All the while she kept an eye on the nurses and Jane, safe on dry ground.

"See, she likes an audience, that one!" Anne whispered with a smile. "Elizabeth knows everyone is watching her. She didn't want the nurses about and told me she'd watch out for Jane herself. I had to tell her the king would be very angry if I didn't let the nurses stay, too."

Handing a fistful of reeds to Jane, Elizabeth showed her how to plait a basket. Jane, eyes solemn, watched as the older girl deftly wove the reeds as Lady Bryan had taught her. The king's daughter and grandniece—two little auburn-haired girls engrossed in a simple pastime—made a pleasant picture, Katherine thought.

She knew their happiness—for the moment at least—was largely due to the kindly interest of the plain, strong-featured woman at her side. With her guttural speech, her large, square hands waving vigorously to Elizabeth and Jane as they held up their reeds for her to see, with the river's mud on her hemline, Anne of Cleves was hardly the picture of royalty the French queen and Katherine of Aragon had presented on this very riverbank so many years ago. In spite of the fact that everyone at court knew the king had refused to consummate the marriage, Anne had kept her dignity. She had also kept her trousseau clothing and still wore her hair in the old fashion. While Henry blamed Thomas Cromwell for the unfortunate union, he'd raised him to the earldom of Essex, as if to show everyone the marriage was not important. Anne had been determined, however, no matter if the king had rejected her, that no one would ever be able to accuse her of not being as good a step-mother as her husband would allow.

To help in the task, Katherine often invited the queen and her stepchildren to Parr House. Anne found Richmond lonely without Elizabeth and Edward and relished any chance to absent herself from the court. It was on just such an April day as Katherine waited on the terrace for the queen's barge that her brother, William Parr, appeared and in a hushed voice said that a bill of attainder would soon be issued against Margaret Pole, the Countess of Salisbury. Will emphasized Katherine should tell no one; he should not even be telling her! But he'd heard she'd visited the countess recently and he warned her that in the future, she must disassociate herself from all the Poles.

"If our uncle were here, he'd tell you the same thing, Kate," Will explained as his sister appeared speechless with shock, "because we cannot afford to be close to traitors."

"Traitors? Lady Salisbury is a traitor?" Katherine was ill at the thought of the countess' plight and enraged at her brother's callousness. "Lady Salisbury is no traitor! She was the old queen's dearest friend—next to Maria—and she's almost crippled with an illness in her bones. What in the name of our Lady has she done? What does the king want with such a sick person? Ah, but it is not the king, I know! It is Cromwell who's responsible for this!"

"That poor sick crippled person has written her son, Reginald Pole, who is now a cardinal in Rome and urged that further treasonous writings against the king be sent to England. Exeter calls everyone about the king a knave and says once those who think as he does have power, they will raise the West Country where loyalty to the Plantagenet is still strong. They remember the old queen and Lady Salisbury always wished a marriage between Lady Mary and Reginald Pole. They say it's the only way to save the true religion in England. Cromwell has convinced the king that many listen to Pole and his ravings and they plot with his relatives urging the Romish Catholics to rise. Ah, Kate, there is truth in what he says! The Poles have been a canker in the king's side as bad as the one in his leg. I think he's shown great patience for those who brag about their Plantagenet blood! Now Cromwell must show the king he can handle such a dangerous challenge. He hopes it will make up for the part he played in the king's unhappiness with the queen."

"I haven't noted His Majesty's unhappiness!" Katherine retorted hotly, still shaken at her brother's words. "The last time I saw him he was so taken with Catherine Howard that one would have thought he was a sprig of a boy rather than a man nearing fifty winters! And her uncle—I thought Norfolk had more sense! Yet he urges Mistress Howard on, mindful we now have a new queen who is making the best of a poor bargain. Why? Because he despises Cromwell and yearns to make trouble for him with the king. So they make religion their tilting ground. Cromwell for the new and Norfolk for the old! And may the best man win with little regard for whoever falls in battle before the contest is over!" There were tears in Katherine's eyes as she gestured impatiently. "I am tired of the lot of you—you care not one whit for the queen's feelings, for Lady Salisbury's sickness or those foolish Poles whose talk is mostly bragging for ears only too willing to listen! Cromwell is no fool—he must be desperate to go this far. But mark you, this will give him larger sins to answer for than being born of low degree and choosing a bride the king doesn't like!"

Her brother's face, lean and handsome, flushed at Katherine's disdainful glance. "You need not twit me, Kate! I tell only what I see and hear and I know the attainder will be issued soon. But Lady Salisbury is only the beginning. Things have to change, for they are not to the king's liking. The union with the Cleves will bring forth no children, for he does not bed with the queen and he's determined to rid himself of her. Cromwell remembers, if you and I don't, how the Boleyn brought about his Master Wolsey's downfall. He won't allow the lady of Cleves to do that to him!" Will Parr sighed. "Kate, the king is a man! And Mistress Howard is winsome and merry and pleases him very much."

"Mistress Howard has pleased several men." Katherine ignored her brother's raised eyebrows. "Last winter when the chamberers and launderers from Howard House came from Lambeth when their own chimney and roof gave way under the snow, Bessie heard them out in the laundry talking about Mistress Howard. They were laughing about how she fools the old Dowager-Duchess of Norfolk, the duke's stepmother, who is supposed to be her guardian. They said she was more strict with her maids than she was with her own niece! She's had several love affairs, Will, even though she looks like a child. How old is she—seventeen, eighteen?" When Will shrugged his shoulders, Katherine snapped her fingers contemptuously. "She isn't what the king is looking for unless it's a quick tumble on the heath at Hampstead or the park at Richmond. She's pretty, I trow, with her wide eyes and dimples and the way she laughs and glances sideways at the king. I know she's much to his liking. But so was her cousin, Anne Boleyn. They seem to fascinate him, these Howards! Which gives old Norfolk one up on Tom Cromwell because she'll act in religious matters as the duke says. She may sing and dance and be merry as a lark, Will Parr, but I doubt she can sign her name and I'm certain the changes in the church mean little to her! She'll be nothing but trouble for the king and he deserves better. She's been petty to my Lady Mary and rude to Kate Brandon. She seems not to know her place. . . ."

Katherine stopped, short of breath and still irritated with her brother. She saw the barge from Richmond had landed and already her visitors were climbing the waterstairs, calling and waving. Little Elizabeth, clutching Jane Grey's hand, was running toward the terrace ahead of the others. Out of the corner of her eye, Katherine saw her brother bound toward the courtyard and his waiting horse. She wanted to shout after him how wrong it all was, how he should not be part of Cromwell's desperate scheme to regain the king's favor.

Instead, she smoothed the hair about her cap and, taking a deep breath to rid herself of anger, forced a smile as she opened her arms to the two little girls. Mary Tudor and Queen Anne, accompanied by several ladies-in-waiting, walked more leisurely as Katherine, a child by each hand, waited, wondering how she could face Mary and not tell her the appalling news of her beloved old governess.

* * *

The Countess of Salisbury's detention typified the unsettled conditions at court caused by the king's marital unhappiness and the shamelessly political maneuverings of such newly influential people as Cromwell, Richard Rich, the Seymours and Carews.

And, Katherine had to admit, the king did nothing to stabilize his court by good example. His attention to Mistress Catherine Howard was as open as it was deliberate. The Countess of Rutland, in charge of Queen Anne's ladies-in-waiting, swore the girl would be the death of her. "She seems not to know her place!" she cried, using the same words Katherine had cried to her brother. "She is devious, leaves the queen's chambers when she pleases and with no excuse. Today she sent word she was staying at Howard House to care for the old duchess who has been ill. But later I found out from a servant who brought quince from their orchards for Her Grace that she really wished to stay because her old piano tutor has returned to Lambeth and she wanted to see him. So she's stayed to play a piece of her own choosing with a musician! You see how upsetting she can be? When the queen asked after her, I told her the truth!"

"And what did Her Grace say?" Jane Dudley's eyes were wide. Even Katherine held her breath. Had Anne of Cleves noticed her lady-in-waiting's interest in the king?

"She said, 'Let her stay for I don't want her about me. She will return and by that time I will have gone to Richmond. Then she will find the king, my husband, and he will not be lonely.' Ah, she is like a little wild thing. She doesn't know where she belongs or what is expected of her. She has no manners and laughs when you try to help. 'Oh, I have no need of that, my lady,' she'll say and run off. Only Jesu knows where! I wish the duchess would take her back. I'm sure the queen would consent."

Soon after the Countess of Salisbury's incarceration, Katherine was stunned when her uncle, Sir George Throckmorton, told her spies had been set to watch him. Throckmorton had been a great supporter of the old queen and Cromwell now accused him of denying Henry's supremacy in the church during the time of her exile. His brother, Michael Throckmorton, was a well-known Papist and worked with Cardinal Pole in Rome. Though it could not be proved, Cromwell intimated that young Throckmorton had aided the uprisings in the North. His association with the Poles was enough to insure suspicion, the minister said. He was certain more evidence would be uncovered. Soon Sir George Throckmorton entered the Tower of London where, along with Lady Salisbury, he stoutly maintained his innocence.

"It will cost us dearly," a grim Sir William told an appalled Katherine and her younger brother. Will Parr looked uncomfortable. Notoriously spend-thrift, he knew he could contribute little toward his uncle's release unless it came from his wife's estates.

Katherine shook her head angrily. "He's had no trial, no chance to prove his innocence and neither has my Lady Salisbury nor her family. And the king does nothing, but leaves it all to Cromwell. I think his new title and the wealth it brings him makes my new Lord Essex ever more greedy. But no matter the amount, Uncle, we will pay. You've said I need never worry about money. Take what is needed from what John left me and get my uncle out of the Tower. Try to hold onto Wyke, if you can."

The next day, Sir William and Will Parr approached Cromwell. Clearly understanding their mission, he wasted little time in bargaining, agreeing to purchase part of Lord Latimer's Buckinghamshire lands for a good deal less than their true value, as all three were aware. Through Richard Rich, his colleague in collecting the wealth of the holy houses, he also bought the old abbey of Nunmonckton and all its lands in Yorkshire, again at an in-significant price. But he refused to release George Throckmorton without an admission of guilt or some confiscation of his property.

"He agreed your uncle would be made more comfortable," Sir William said. "I trust him there for he keeps easy promises. But look for no early release, Katherine, the man is still trying to end the marriage with the queen. It's the best we could do, my dear."

When the transfer documents were placed before her, Katherine noted her uncle had toted up her losses. She'd sold lands which, at her death, should rightfully have gone to John and Margaret, for a fraction of their real worth. According to her uncle's figure, the visit to Cromwell had cost her over two thousand pounds.

Angered by her uncle's seeming acceptance of the situation, she protested. "There must be some way to stop him if only to protect our honor! He uses a highwayman's methods to take what he wants and silences everyone by fear. If he wants some admission of guilt by our kin, he will wait forever. What he really wants is Coughton Court!"

Sir William put an arm about Katherine's shoulders. "Kate, fifteen years ago if anyone had told me I'd live to see the day when a king's minister, and one as base as Cromwell, would covet my cousin's birthright—and have a good chance of getting it—I'd have thought them mad. But he's not alone! Richard Rich, who has the foulest mouth at court and seems to bear the sin of Tom More's execution on his soul very lightly, has just taken old St. Bartholomew's Church and leased it out for trade. Edward Seymour has been given so many parcels of land, he'll yet make the fortune that wife of his yearns for. Even our saintly Archbishop of Canterbury, Thomas Cranmer, has begged Shelford Priory for his brother and the Greyfriars near his cathedral for another relative. Everyone, your dear brother included,

Kate, is scrambling for the church's spoils and the king lets Cromwell lead the way."

* * *

On May Day, 1540, a great tournament held at the tiltyard at Westminster brought together representatives from the Continent to challenge the English nobles in jousting, tourneying and foot combat. Queen Anne, in a rare appearance, sat with the king, Mary and little Elizabeth in an especially constructed pavilion covered with cloth of gold. Charles Brandon, too old at forty-nine to participate, sorely missed his wife who'd taken her mother, the aging Maria, to Westhorpe for a visit. "It will be like the old days," he told Katherine and her uncle gleefully, "with enough rough and tumble to please everyone, including Henry, who regrets—as do I—that he can no longer join in the sport."

The Suffolk entourage was one of the first, lined up by rank, to enter the tiltyard. The day was perfect with soft warm air creating just enough breeze from the Thames to keep the banners rippling above the royal pavilion. The king greeted Katherine warmly. She embraced Mary and Elizabeth, noting how impressed the little girl was by the noise and the presence of so many splendidly garbed people. Elizabeth jumped as a brace of silver trumpets heralded the contestants' arrival. She clasped Katherine's fingers in excitement as each one—in full armor and carrying his colors—rode the length of the field. Spectators cheered each appearance and soon the entire four sides of the tiltyard were lined with courtiers waiting to begin. The last time Katherine had seen anything comparable for grandeur and color had been Anne Boleyn's coronation festivities.

The last one to ride into the yard sat proudly astride his stallion, causing her breath to quicken and her pulse to plummet. She'd forgotten how magnificently Thomas Seymour bore himself and never before had she seen him well horsed and ready for combat. With his visor down and armor shining, carrying the Seymour colors of black, gold and scarlet, the man held his lance as if it were a toy, while he and his black Spanish jennet moved as one. From the shouts of acclaim that greeted his appearance, there was little doubt of his popularity.

At Katherine's questioning look, Charles Brandon whispered, "I cannot abide the man's arrogance, but he has no equal on the field." She longed to ask more, but could scarcely take her eyes off Seymour as he rode about the tiltyard, inclining his head toward friends, holding his lance high and beaming at the accolade. In front of the royal pavilion at last, he bowed low to Henry and Anne as the king called affectionately to his brother-in-law. For a moment, before he rode off, his gaze met hers and there was a flicker of surprise and then appreciation in his eyes. Katherine felt herself blush as she caught Mary's amused smile.

Fascinated, she watched as the English met the French, Scotch and

Spanish challengers. She was unfamiliar with most of the rules for neither her uncle nor her husbands had ever been tournament contestants. As events proceeded, Charles explained the finer points of the exercises while Mary, who loved all sports, told her the skills she must watch for, especially in the Spanish. Both she and Mary were pleased when the Flemish contestant bested his English counterpart, noting the flush of pleasure on Queen Anne's face as she nodded graciously to the breathless man when at last he stood in front of the pavilion, headgear in hand, sweat pouring down his face.

But the day belonged to Thomas Seymour. Two hours later, he still remained undefeated in any event. When he bested Henry Howard, Lord Surrey, the Duke of Norfolk's son in foot combat, the crowd exploded. Though he might be no favorite at court, Seymour appeared immensely popular with others, while Surrey seemed heartily disliked. Katherine saw the young nobleman's manner was insufferably pompous and his petulance and anger were evident in the rough manner directed at his attendants as he left the field.

Then Thomas Seymour was standing bareheaded before the royal box. Henry called out his congratulations as the queen, taking a scarf from her neck, threw it down to the man who expertly caught it on the point of his lance. He bowed again at this sign of royal favor from the woman who'd replaced his dead sister, smiling and waving to the crowd as they pelted him with the May Day flowers picked in the fields on their way to the tiltyard.

Later, at Durham House in the Strand, she saw Seymour in the courtyard and wondered if he'd recall the last time they'd met when she'd practically agreed to an assignation at Holbein's studio. As the procession to the Banqueting Hall began to form, he was suddenly beside her, bowing. "My dear Lady Latimer! I was surprised and pleased to see you with the king's Grace today. It has been a long time! How many years since we made something of an appointment?" Not waiting for a reply, for which Katherine, suddenly tongue-tied, was grateful, he asked, "Will you honor me, my lady, as my partner for the banquet which awaits us? I long to hear of all that has happened since last we met. I heard of Lord Latimer's passing, but only many months afterward, for I was in Brussels for almost a year. . . ."

A long trumpet blast sent the last of the guests scurrying for places in the procession and, as Katherine took her seat near the royal table, her poise returned. She tried to reason with herself, admitting that Seymour was disarming, but he was just another man. More attractive than most with a pleasant vibrant voice, as magnificently dressed and full of grace and charm as ever. Was this why so many like Charles Brandon and her uncle disliked him? Yet Thomas appeared a favorite of the king who, his queen beaming at his side, now rose in a toast to all challengers. Then, with the special flourish so like him, he filled his wine cup again, asking all to stand and honor "our dear brother, Tom Seymour, who rides as well as he speaks and tilts as well as he looks!"

It was a rare honor and, for a moment, Seymour appeared nonplussed. But only for a moment. Then, in a gracious speech, he thanked the king and others, especially the brave challengers who'd so stoutly defended their countries' honor. At the end, when he included "that noble contestant, my Lord of Surrey," the spectators cheered at Seymour's gracious inclusion of his opponent. But the young nobleman, sitting near the king with his mother and cousin Catherine Howard, merely nodded to Seymour, then glanced away and pretended not to hear the acclamation. The rebuff was observed by everyone including the king who flushed with anger.

But Seymour turned to Katherine as if nothing had happened. He asked after her Borough and Latimer families and inquired if she expected to remain in London. When she nodded, he said, "Then you will be here when my brother is made a Knight of the Garter and entertains the king at Wolf Hall. Perchance you will even come with others of the court?" Thomas threw back his head and laughed lightly. "Ah, Lady Latimer! I wish my good father had lived to see the day when a son wore the Garter!"

Katherine could not resist. "He lived to see a daughter wear the crown," she smiled, "and a son become an earl."

Thomas sipped his wine, his lips tightening. There was a moment's silence, awkward and heavy.

"Yes, my older brother is a great comfort to the king. While I travel on my sovereign's business to Spain, Vienna or Calais, avoiding trouble with the Hapsburgs who are having difficulty with the Turks, who are spoiling for a fight with the emperor, who is pondering a war with the French—well aware that both of them are at odds with the Italians—well, it is a solace to know that Edward Seymour, Earl of Hertford, is here advising the king on domestic matters while his lady rears a son and looks to the king for signs of further favor."

"I am certain the king regards you as highly, Sir Thomas. He would never entrust you with such weighty matters if it were otherwise."

"Weighty or not, my lady, to be a member of the Privy Chamber, as I am, is not the same as being a member of the Privy Council, which my brother is! And there he can look to his own good while paying little heed to any that might come my way."

The last, said with bitterness, startled Katherine. The quick rise of the Seymours—who had given England a queen and an heir—was unusual. Often, she'd heard her cousin Tunstall comment on the intelligence, sobriety and resourcefulness of Edward Seymour. Ever since he'd gone to France as a twelve-year-old page in the entourage of the French queen, he'd served the Crown in one way or another, being knighted for courage and leadership during the French campaign. He understood, so said her cousin, the economic, social and religious problems confronting the king and Henry had listened to his advice and acted upon it within the council. And he'd rewarded the elder Seymour with lands in Somerset and Wiltshire allowing him to purchase several influential government offices profitable enough to build a fine home, Chester Place, in the Strand.

There was probably some justification for Thomas's envy of his older brother, Katherine thought, but she wondered why the king hadn't similarly rewarded the younger Seymour for services which, in their way, were as valuable. As if aware of her thought, her companion raised his wine cup and said, "Enough of this, my lady. But I will not keep calling you 'my lady' for you are not *my* lady! Lady Katherine, if I may, let us drink to my brother-in-law who has honored the Seymours more than we ever dreamt! I jest not—I am content. I like my king as a man and we have much joy in each other for Henry likes a man who can laugh. Edward, on the other hand, is content with a smile. . . ."

"As long as there is goodwill, it matters little." Suddenly, Katherine felt at ease with Tom Seymour. "And I agree, since I am not your lady, perchance 'Lady Katherine' would be best!" She raised her cup in response.

As the festivities ended and the queen left for Richmond, everyone rose to leave. "I hope it will not be as long until we meet again." Thomas bowed. "If I may call at Parr House, perhaps we can shorten the time?" Hoping to hide her nervousness—and pleasure—Katherine nodded.

The spell cast by Seymour's charm lingered as she made her way to bid her cousin Tunstall farewell. Standing at his side, she was surprised as another guest, Sir Thomas Wriothesley, his consumption of wine evident in a ruddy face and slurred speech, gazed at her boldly. "My Lady Latimer! I recognize the name, for you are celebrated, you know." At Katherine's puzzled look, he laughed loudly. "For the *salon* you keep, my lady. Mistress Howard has said that you and your friends speak of the 'New Thinking' or the 'New Learning' as if it is your religion! That you question what we on the council —all privy to the king's wishes—do to bring those in the church and country to think as one. I hear that you would have it differently—with study and education—and then everyone would love each other and believe the same. Can that be, my lady? Why are we mere men kept from such discussions? Perchance we might contribute to your knowledge! Would Lord Latimer have approved such talk? Would the king approve? It has done little good for old Throckmorton, my lady, has it?"

Katherine felt a frightening chill as Wriothesley stood, a foolish smile on his face, enjoying her discomfort. The man had caught her completely off guard. Bishop Tunstall, hearing his words, quickly greeted the next guest, forcing Wriothesley to move on. "Say nothing, Katherine, be quiet," he whispered as her mind revolved about the man's disturbing words and insolent manner.

Later, at Parr House, Tunstall explained. "Tom Wriothesley is secretary to Cromwell and a very valuable man about the court. He has little honor, no conscience and lacks any common sense, as you've just seen. He does Cromwell's dirty work and with Richard Rich they make quite a pair! Keep away from him, Katherine, and don't antagonize him. He can be a formidable enemy for he has all of Cromwell's power to back him."

Bishop Tunstall told her of the heartbreaking plight in the North. "Between Cromwell, Rich and their colleagues, they've made certain the monastic life is over in England, Katherine. Even Thomas à Becket's shrine at Canterbury has been looted. I think the example of a bishop who bested a king could no longer be tolerated! The dissolution is almost complete—but old Durham Abbey still stands! I can only pray the king's Grace realizes the extent of what Cromwell tells him. If, indeed, Cromwell tells him everything—which I doubt. Unfortunately, I think all Henry sees is the treasure."

* * *

Several days later, when she was denied permission to visit Sir George Throckmorton in the Tower, Katherine's anger boiled over. She remembered her lost lands, her uncle's calm acceptance that there was nothing that could be done about Throckmorton's continued detention. "And my cousin Tunstall tells me I mustn't protest too much," she raged to Bessie, "for Cromwell has a long memory and either he or that snake Wriothesley might bring up old charges against the Latimer family for John's activities during the uprisings." Katherine hated referring to that dreadful time that had cost Bessie a lover. Her dearest companion was no longer a girl, but a woman in her midthirties with gray in her hair. She still cherished the shining image of Rob Aske as a martyred saviour of his people.

"He is right, Kate, it is useless to protest." Bessie soberly folded linen for her corner cupboard. "My father writes that everywhere in the North there is decay. Farms rot because there is no one to work them and those who now own them—Londoners mostly, important at court—enclose the land for sheep so they grow rich on wool. The people are starving since they've been forced from their cottages and there are no holy houses to dole out clothing, food or medicine. People die of sickness, especially in the winter, or else they freeze to death."

The devastating effects of the dissolution were also evident in London. Beggars were everywhere, reminding Katherine of the old monk she'd befriended on the York Road. He was one of the lucky ones, she thought. Other monks or nuns, young or old, had not fared as well and had been forced into vagrancy. They joined the tradespeople who'd supplied the monasteries and were also now penniless and evicted from their homes. Forming bands for protection and traveling from village to village, seeking food, shelter and work, they were often met by the local sheriff's men who whipped or beat them, threatening slavery or death if they did not keep on traveling. Almost overnight, a small army of vagrants covered the roads of rural England, especially in the North.

Everywhere, Katherine saw the results of Henry's supremacy in the church. Anyone denying the king's authority or the doctrine preached since the separation from Rome placed himself in great danger. Those who, like herself, believed in a purified religion, regarded the bread and wine served at the altar as symbolic of Christ's body and not a real presence as the Romish Catholics believed. Though such a belief had been tolerated and even encouraged during the reign of Anne Boleyn and Jane Seymour, now many were persecuted for the same opinion.

Katherine often thought of her mother's simple belief that silent prayer, a direct communion with God and the asking of forgiveness for her sins, was as powerful as confessing to a priest. The simpler the better had been Maud Parr's teaching—teachings that had come from the king's grandmother and her own grandmother. People should go to the Bible in their search for salvation. Henry, who considered himself a good Catholic and not as much of a "reformer" or "protestant" as many others, had agreed and an English Bible was now in every church. He'd insisted that priest and layperson alike be given instruction in its contents and learn the Lord's Prayer, the Creed and the Ten Commandments in English. Katherine believed—as did many of those ladies who shared her afternoons—that with such gradual instruction, the superstitious entrapment that had grown and permeated the Catholic doctrine during the centuries might eventually be discarded and a cleaner, purer religion would find peaceful root in England.

But the divorce from the old queen and the persecution of Princess Mary, who remained as staunchly Catholic as ever, had divided the country into two religious groups—Catholic and those beginning to be called Protestants. Cromwell repeatedly warned that those who differed in their belief from the prescribed state doctrine would suffer, though the king—probably to spite the queen's Lutheran relatives who wished for more reform—appeared to be swinging back to the old Catholic doctrine, minus any allegiance to the Pope.

"The king is having his cake and eating it, too," William Parr told Katherine with a wry smile. "Mainly it's due to old Norfolk's influence and that of Stephen Gardiner, the Bishop of Winchester. He appeases those of the old belief by approving the sacrament of communion and insisting on priestly celibacy and confession. Yet he placates the believers in the new faith by placing Bibles in all the churches—though half the congregation can't read!—and by giving everyone who disagrees with him a chance to recant. It's not the way Cromwell—who appears to be losing influence to Norfolk and those other Catholics on the Council—had expected things to go!"

That many refused to recant, however, was evident whenever Katherine and Bessie went abroad. They learned to avoid Smithfield where those staunch advocates of the new faith were burnt. Each burning was a blow to Cromwell as his Catholic opponents, Norfolk and Gardiner, became more influential. Katherine wondered how she'd react if taken into custody and forced to state her own beliefs, point by point. Church doctrine, it appeared, changed as power among those near the monarch also shifted. She feared what would happen to the Poles and Lady Salisbury, as well as her uncle whose freedom still seemed elusive. She wondered what the king had been told about old George Throckmorton. Did he believe everything Cromwell told him? Was it so easy to put aside the years of devoted service an aged

countess had given to his first wife and daughter? Did he truly understand
what had happened in the North?

Katherine found it difficult to believe a monarch as loving of his subjects
as Henry professed would approve laws which caused such heartbreak and
physical suffering. She wished she might talk with the king and realized, almost immediately, how foolish she would appear. How could she, a mere
woman, influence his thinking? And she wanted to talk to someone about
her imprisoned uncle. She wanted to find out if there was to be any relief
for the North. But there was no one she trusted to understand. Her brother
and sister were the king's people and would go where he led. Lady Mary refused to speak of politics and had vowed she'd never again allow herself to
be exiled and persecuted. When informed of the attainder against her old
governess, Lady Salisbury, she'd turned white with shock, as if someone had
dealt her a physical blow. Still, she'd remained silent, excusing herself to return to her chamber where she'd stayed alone until the following day. Kate
Brandon was still with her ailing mother at Westhorpe and, though
Katherine might have talked to her "two Joans," Lady Denny and Lady
Dudley, caution made her keep her own counsel. She still remembered
Wriothesley's menacing words.

Yet in the days following the tournament, as her uncle's incarceration continued, the thought that she see the king kept recurring. Each night,
Katherine prayed for guidance, seeking that strong certainty which would
encourage any action that did not humiliate or endanger her family.
Recently, Lady Throckmorton had written a tear-stained letter telling of her
fears that her husband would never return. If he did, undoubtedly they'd be
forced off their land which had belonged to the family for generations. "I
know not what to do, Kate. We will have to start over. George is not a court
favorite as you know and I fear it may be the end of him for his heart is not
strong."

The injustice of it all gnawed at Katherine's conscience and she wondered
if it would be possible to see the king without Cromwell's knowledge. When
she heard the minister had gone to Essex to visit St. Osyth's Priory, a holding of the Essex earldom, she realized the time was opportune. That night,
almost asleep, Bessie's sad face floated before her and with it the mangled
remains of a bright-haired man in a red satin coat. Her last thought before
falling asleep was that she must act. To do nothing would be cowardly.
Henry might laugh and consider her behavior a whim. But if she asked his
confidence, she was certain he'd grant it. He'd always shown great affection
for the Parr family. What had she to be afraid of?

In the morning, refreshed and heartened, she said nothing of her plan to
Bessie, writing a hasty note to Charles Brandon asking if he would arrange a
meeting with the king. She cited Lady Throckmorton's letter; that would explain the reason for the visit. Within hours, her servant brought a return
note that the king would be happy to receive her at four o'clock that afternoon.

Whitehall was almost deserted when Katherine arrived. Following a gentleman-usher to the Presence Chamber, she again prayed for guidance. Entering, she saw the king at a table, signing his name to a pile of documents. Henry looked tired; the tournament and the following days of festivities had taken their toll. As the usher announced her name, he glanced up with a pleased smile and, putting away his pen, rose to greet her.

Raising her from her curtsey, he indicated a chair and smiled. "Ah, Kate, it is good to see you. We didn't have a chance to talk at tournament time, but it was a splendid affair, was it not? We trust you enjoyed our brother-in-law's performance?" There was a bantering tone in the king's voice and an amused smile on his lips. Katherine wondered if he'd noticed Tom Seymour's close attention to her at the banquet. If he hadn't, someone had surely mentioned it. Gossip was as important in the palace as it was in the streets.

They spoke briefly of the tournament and Katherine inquired after the health of the prince. The king visibly relaxed, his face shining with pleasure as he talked of his three-year-old son. "But you didn't come to see us about the prince, Kate. There must be other reasons. What can we do for you? Everyone who seeks the king wants something, my dear."

Katherine flushed, angry at herself for not taking the initiative and annoyed with Henry for putting it so bluntly. But he was right. Swallowing hard and clutching her hands together to hide her nervousness, she replied, "You are right, sire. I do want something. Not for myself, but for my uncle."

"Old George is still in the Tower? Cromwell tells us the man has strong Papist sympathies and works with those who want a return to the old religion. Come now, Kate, you know we can't have that! He deserves his imprisonment and will come out a stronger man and we hope a more wise and sensible one. We doubt he is suffering much. Some of the Tower lodgings are as comfortable as here."

"That's not the whole story, sire." Katherine's composure returned and with it that strong certainty that what she was doing was right. "I'd like to tell you what I know if you'll be good enough to hear it all."

Henry nodded and, pulling a chair nearby, put his bad leg upon it, grimacing as he did so. "Let me help, sire," Katherine rose and placed the chair more comfortably. The king patted her hand as she did so and smiled. Katherine noticed the gray in his reddish beard, the lines around his eyes and mouth. He's not well, she thought, and he's getting old. But the look was kind and his gesture comforting. It gave her courage and she plunged on.

For the next half hour, the king remained silent as Katherine detailed the whole controversy over the Coughton Court boundary. His dismay was plainly evident when she called the two thousand pounds paid to Cromwell and Rich "a corrupt bribe." Pointedly, she emphasized the minister was feared more than anyone else in the kingdom and that many Northern families had suffered similar extortion. Warming to her task, she recalled her years at Snape and, in several poignant incidents, told how her family and others less fortunate had survived the losses of loved ones, the confiscation of property, all usually without a trial or hearing of any kind. She mentioned the wealth of the despoiled holy houses which went to Richard Rich, implying that perhaps not all of the treasure reached the king's coffers. Much of what she was saying, she'd seen herself, she told the king, recounting some of the scenes observed on the York Road. She did not spare Henry, even mentioning the man in a red coat hung in chains over York gate. The king gazed out the window as she spoke and she knew remembrance of Robert Aske must be vivid in his mind.

"What all this means, sire," Katherine said in a strong voice, "is that Cromwell is so despised in the North, there will never be peace while he is in office. They fear and hate him so, they will never stop fighting. He does not listen to them or even think of compromise. He is very certain of himself, sire."

"Yes, we know," Henry's mouth curled in a quizzical smile. "Humility is not one of my Lord Essex's deeper qualities."

"He takes you much for granted, sire, and appears to feel you'll always accept his advice." Katherine was rewarded by the first small show of anger as the king's eyes widened. "He does! He realizes you depend upon him. But often, I believe he forgets to tell you things that might cause you to act differently than he wishes." Suddenly, she was fearful she might have gone too far, telling her sovereign quite plainly that he'd been manipulated. It was possible the king's Tudor pride might quickly turn against her. But except for the irritation in his eyes and a deeper flush on his cheeks, Henry continued to listen.

"All I ask, sire, is a trial for my uncle for such a hearing will show Your Grace and everyone else he is no Papist. He loved the Lady Mary's mother and also your daughter. He loves *you*, sire. It is hard for an old man to give up his first loyalties." Katherine knew she was treading on delicate ground, but she had to be honest.

Henry was reflective. "We will see to Throckmorton at once, Kate." He smiled as if to reassure her. "If he's as loyal as you say, he shouldn't be in the Tower. We promise you our help."

Relief flooded Katherine and with it, more confidence and certainty than ever. "And the North, sire? I assure you there will only be continued risings as long as Cromwell is in charge. The people don't trust him. And I must say, they have little reason to do so. He knows all this, but the wealth he takes from them and the appearance he gives that he's fighting for a just religious settlement makes it profitable for him not to resolve the matter."

The king was silent for a moment. Then gingerly removing his leg from the chair, he stood up, indicating the meeting was at an end. Quickly, Katherine rose, sinking in a low curtsey. "Sire, I thank you for seeing me and for any help you can give my uncle Throckmorton."

Henry held out his hand and, as he'd done so often in the past, briefly kissed her cheek. "Kate, we thank you for coming to us. You remind us so much of your mother, but it was not Lady Maud talking to us today, but our good friend, Tom Parr. Remember, we Tudors have always trusted the Parrs! You'll be hearing from us soon, my dear." Katherine bowed, kissing the bejeweled hand which still held hers and, tears in her eyes, spoke again of her appreciation.

After the door had closed behind her, Henry limped to the desk and began making notes of the conversation. Katherine Parr's words had given him a different view of his minister. Or—the king was truthful—if he'd suspected some of the things he'd just heard, he hadn't dwelt on them long. Tom Cromwell was the most able man who'd held office in his long reign. Better even than his old master, Tom Wolsey. For a moment, Henry almost hoped Katherine might be wrong. For, if she was right, he had little recourse other than to confront the new Earl of Essex with her charges.

*   *   *

It was Charles Brandon who rode to Parr House to tell Katherine of her uncle Throckmorton's release from the Tower. "He came to see the king at once," Charles said jubilantly. "He is thin and somewhat frail, Kate, but otherwise all right. He told Henry he was no Papist and he reminded him of the days when he and Lady Throckmorton had been close to Henry's father, how his wife had served the old queen and how overjoyed they'd been when Mary was born. He told Henry it was not easy to change the belief of a lifetime, but he said he loved the king and would always be a loyal subject. He said though it pleased my Lord Cromwell to say he was a Papist, it was not so and that a man his age and with such a noble record of service to the king should not be so harassed."

Relieved, Katherine wished she could tell Charles of her conversation with the king. But that would only place her and the Latimer family in peril. She was certain now that her uncle had been released from an unjust and dishonorable detention, Thomas Cromwell would leave the Throckmortons alone.

Charles had other news also. "Richard Rich visited the king after your uncle left and had a long talk with His Grace. I trow I cannot understand what the king would want with the man unless it had something to do with Cromwell's business that must be done while he's away in Essex. 'Tis odd and queer, Katherine, for the man was very nervous and quite unlike himself. It is more his manner to play the bully! He swaggered into the Presence Chamber but looked like a man undone to the death when he came out. The king then left to see old Norfolk or I'd have stayed to find out what had happened."

Katherine said nothing, her mind was revolving fast on Charles's message. Was the king acting on her charges? She knew he'd believed her, but supposing Richard Rich—and Cromwell when he returned—could convince Henry they'd been unduly attacked and blamed for things they couldn't help, their good names tarnished by a woman's careless words? If the king believed them, she knew Cromwell's revenge would make her uncle's imprisonment look like a child's game of hide-and-seek. Her joy at her uncle's release diminished and, remembering the menacing Wriothesley's words, she thought how terrible it would be to be at the mercy of Cromwell or Rich. If that ever happened, there'd be no place in England safe for her or her family.

After Charles left, she went out into the garden to sit on the old bench near the monastery wall. It was a day of soft air, the overhead sun sending a warmth into the grounds and along the terrace. But Katherine did not feel the warmth. She was uncertain and afraid, aghast that she'd confronted the king with such strong charges against his powerful minister. How had she dared? What would happen now after the king, apparently, had acted upon her words? As she sat leaning against the warm bricks, the thought came that she might have paid with more than two thousand pounds for her uncle's release.

CHAPTER XX

Katherine heard of Cromwell's arrest from Thomas Seymour. The king's brother-in-law had soon appeared at Parr House and jubilantly recounted the fallen minister's disgrace. Richard Rich had told the king many instances of bribery and extortion, of information grossly exaggerated or withheld altogether, of an abuse of power in dealing with the Northern people that led Henry to wonder if similar examples of injustice or rapacity might not be found within his government. The man whom Cromwell, more than anyone else, had helped to power and riches beyond his wildest dreams, had little conscience in accusing his patron. Neither he nor his colleagues, when questioned, showed any pity or concern or attempted to explain those occasions when Cromwell's intent might be judged two ways. Many appeared eager to speak against him; few wished to defend him. And no mention was made of his long efficient service to the Crown. Instead, his preference for the Lutheran alliance was stressed and regarded with the same disdain the king exhibited toward his queen whom Cromwell had chosen. Several of the councillors even muttered "heresy" when discussing the earl's religious beliefs, forgetting that months before they'd been as eager to seek the Cleves union as Cromwell or the king.

"What convinced Henry, I trow, was Tom Cromwell's untimely remark that the Lutheran doctrine was best for England," Seymour told Katherine. "He said if any Catholic lord opposed him, he'd make such an example of them, the country would never forget. But *he* forgot that was not his decision to make! The king was very angry, though Tom Cranmer tried to save the man, saying he'd served with great loyalty. But all the other lords could hardly wait to accuse him and when he returned from Essex, he was arrested for heresy and treason. Norfolk tore the Garter from his neck and the king took away his privileges and title and the town criers have proclaimed he'll be known only as 'Cromwell, cloth carder.' Now he's in the Tower, and the Privy Council, so says my good brother Edward, is meeting to deal with this new move. I think finally my lord is beginning to realize his danger."

Riding with Thomas in the woods outside Whitehall, Katherine wondered at her lack of feeling for the fallen minister. There was no pity, but neither was there any elation such as her companion showed. It was as if an unpleasant force had been removed from her life and other lives as well. One of the strongest reasons for any continued Northern dissension was now gone and she felt that the man in the bright satin coat and the abbot hanged from high Glastonbury tor, as well as those countless victims of brutality on the York Road, had been avenged.

And, thankfully, no one but the king would ever know of her part in the tragedy for Henry had kept her confidence. Even now, smiling at Thomas, she marveled at her own action. Where had that inspiration and courage come from? She'd been impetuous and foolhardy, but luckily the king's affection and respect for her family had made him listen. Then, later, he'd found what he wanted. She could hardly wait to get home, run upstairs, embrace Bessie and say that Rob Aske's martyrdom had been avenged. But even then, she must be careful.

The great expanse of Whitehall forest, barred to commoners and used for the royal hunt and chase, was filled with other courtiers riding for exercise or to and from St. James's Palace, a small gem of a building set in its own little park at the forest's northern edge. Both Katherine and Thomas nodded and waved to friends who cantered leisurely toward "the king's road."

The June morning was fresh, the air washed clean by an overnight thunderstorm. Carefully, Thomas guided their mounts over twigs and small branches that had fallen to the ground.

Riding through the sunlit-patterned woods, Katherine observed her companion fondly, for his actions during the last few weeks left little doubt that he was attracted to her and liked being in her company. Almost daily, he'd appeared at Parr House, either by prearrangement or otherwise, delighting her with his robust humor and an infectious charm other male acquaintances lacked. His presence filled the quietly sedate rooms with a spontaneous and easy amiability. Gladly, Katherine would put aside her needlework or book and follow where he led—to the park, the river, to her own garden or those at Whitehall. There the sight of the widow Latimer and Tom Seymour walking quietly along a graveled path or talking animatedly in one of the green arbors, caused many an amazed look and raised eyebrow among other courtiers.

At times, Thomas chided her for spending so much time reading and studying. "I am not bookish, Katherine," he smiled, "for my father thought it sufficient for me to hunt, hawk, blow a decent horn, learn to tilt and wrestle. The scholar in the family is Edward." Again, there was a tinge of bitterness at the mention of his older brother. Edward, the Earl of Hertford, was a learned man though she suspected it was not his knowledge that Thomas envied.

"One must use one's own skills, my lord, we have all too few as it is," she said quietly. "I was taught to read and write—and do both well—when I was very little. My mother was a woman who sought knowledge and I do the same. I could not change for any reason." She was gratified that Seymour did not argue. For months, she'd relished the freedom of widowhood—the first freedom she'd had in years. Never again was anyone going to forbid her to study and speak as she chose.

"I promise not to tax you with my opinions, my lord," she finished, "but mayhap if you listened, you would be challenged or interested to learn more?"

But Thomas shook his head. "Katherine, I've listened to you and your friends when you talk about religion. But my own faith does not run deep. I know there is a God and I'll worship Him in any manner the king or council says I must. Beyond that, why seek anything else?"

Katherine remained silent. How could she convince Thomas it was more fulfilling to commune with God without priestly intercession? How could she explain how difficult she found it to believe the church was the only way to salvation? She knew he had little real interest. She must try to find those things that did interest him—especially if they continued to see each other.

She still enjoyed the weekly meetings at Parr House with those court ladies who held beliefs similar to her own. The liberty to explore and discuss, to speak and listen to such as Miles Coverdale and the noted John Parkhurst was exciting and satisfying. But she knew Thomas's interest would be only polite and perfunctory. So whenever he appeared, she hurriedly put away her books and notepaper, knowing such evidence of learning would not interest him. There would be plenty of time when he was gone.

And when that happened, Katherine was startled at how much she missed him, what a void his leaving caused. Is this what falling in love is like? she wondered. Is this what Kate and Charles Brandon have, what makes the Dennys and Dudleys so special and so happy with each other?

Yet she kept her feelings to herself. Kate Brandon, the only one to whom she might have confided, was overseeing the building of a new Suffolk home in Lincolnshire. But she knew instinctively the duchess would not approve, as Bessie so obviously did not. There was just enough of the raffish about Thomas Seymour that always provoked a strong reaction. No matter that his sister had been queen, that his brother was now an earl and a stalwart and valued councillor, Thomas's outrageous lack of deference or respect toward those who felt they merited both had angered many in and out of court.

When Katherine—who considered his attitude harmless if somewhat careless—told him so, Thomas only laughed at her reproach. "Don't worry about it, Kate," he said easily. "I take pleasure in deflating large bags of wind —the bigger the better! You must admit pride of place is not limited to those nearest the king. What harm if I help lower a few heads who aim too high?"

Two weeks after Thomas's first visit to Parr House, Katherine knew her feelings toward him had become stronger. Each day they were together, a surge of joyous expectation almost overwhelmed her. Each time he left, she felt lost and bereft. Their time alone was the best part of the day and she knew Thomas felt the same. Every smile, gesture, the intimate tone of his voice, the strong hands that lingered on her shoulders as he helped her dismount revealed his feelings. How much longer would it be before he spoke? I'm almost twenty-eight, Katherine thought, and now, for the first time recognize what love can be like.

Recalling her two marriages, she felt herself blushing imagining what being Tom Seymour's wife might be like. Of being with him every day and every night, sharing a home and a bed. Making love with Thomas would not, she was certain, be the huffing performance of Lord Borough or the precise and careful coupling of Lord Latimer. What would it be like—being Lady Seymour?

At the thought, Katherine felt her body grow warm with an unusual and pleasant desire. She remembered what her childhood tutor, Vives, had said, "They that marry for love shall spend their lives in sorrow!" Vives had called love an "affliction," declaring any good woman resisted it, not listening to her lover any more than she'd listen to a sorcerer. She recalled her cousin Tunstall's sermons when he'd thundered on about lust and carnal copulation. It revived the image of the sensual Boleyn stroking the king's thigh.

Obviously, Katherine thought, there were pleasures she'd never experienced. And, just as obviously, there was no doubt that if she ever hoped to share them, she wanted Tom Seymour as her partner.

* * *

Nine days after his arrest, an act of attainder—ironically the same instrument by which he'd seized the Countess of Salisbury and executed her son and nephew—was issued against Thomas Cromwell. Everywhere, especially in the North, the people exulted. The man who'd encouraged the destruction of the holy houses, hounded a queen to the scaffold and proved a scourge to the aristocracy was now vulnerable and his enemies showed no mercy. The Duke of Norfolk and Stephen Gardiner, the Bishop of Winchester, told Henry that Cromwell had often acted without royal permission in cases of treason and heresy; they emphasized the numerous licenses issued for profit in his own name. "The man has made a mockery of the rights and liberties which Your Grace has promised to the meanest subjects!" they cried. "Cromwell is a most false and corrupt traitor and deceiver!" There was more than enough evidence to support their charges in the fortune taken from his Austin Friars home—trenchers of gold with matching cups and ewers, silver and gold-worked dishes and handsome jeweled crosses were sent, along with the rich silks and velvets imported from the Continent for the new earl's wardrobe, to the royal treasury.

The disgraced minister languished in the Tower for only seven weeks. Vigorously, he denied being a traitor or heretic, telling his inquisitors, "I have acted so often for the king and meddled in so many matters, it is not possible to answer to all the charges." Ever the realist, he knew disgrace and the loss of his fortune and power were inevitable. He might even expect to serve some time in prison. At first, he busily mustered his defenses, readying himself to answer his accusers. But as week after week passed and still no sentence was given, it at last occurred to Cromwell that he was in even greater danger—that the king might, in fact, desire his death.

Henry had been shocked and angered at the revelations of Cromwell's transgressions. Uncomfortable at how easily he'd been manipulated, the king vowed that never again would he give anyone such power. Yet the remaining thought, uppermost in his mind, was how to free himself from the unwanted, undesirable wife Cromwell had foisted on him. Several years previously, Anne of Cleves had been contracted to wed the Duke of Lorraine's son and that, coupled with the fact that he'd never consummated the marriage—thereby depriving himself of any issue—now appeared ample reason for an annulment. When the final papers were drawn, the accommodating Thomas Cranmer, Archbishop of Canterbury—already responsible for dissolving two royal marriages in seven years—pronounced the marriage null and void.

And with it Cromwell's doom was sealed; the king no longer needed him. Waiting in his Tower cell, the man who for years had served as the king's ablest administrator at last realized what awaited him. Frightened, he wrote the king, "I am ready to take the death when it shall please God and Your Majesty. Yet the frail flesh incites me to call to Your Grace for mercy and pardon for my offenses!" When there was no answer, Cromwell knew his royal patron had deserted him. Now it was merely a matter of time and how quickly his enemies could persuade the king to execute him.

*   *   *

Concerned with the speedy annulment of his marriage, Henry sent a copy of Cranmer's decree to the queen at Richmond. Remembering the fate of her predecessors, Anne had suffered nightmares as her husband's quest for a divorce went on. What would happen to her? Exile, false charges leading to execution, poison? When Charles Brandon, the Duke of Suffolk, accompanied by Thomas Wriothesley, now discharging many of Cromwell's duties, appeared to obtain her signature to the decree, Anne was faint with relief.

"I am eager to abide by the king's wishes," she told the kneeling visitors through her interpreter. "Whatever my dear husband desires, I am certain will be for the best."

Brandon, taken aback by Anne's quick consent, patiently explained that she must also relinquish the title of "queen." He hoped the woman understood. Memories of Katherine of Aragon's staunch refusal to give up her title —the harassment and persecution she'd suffered because of it—still remained with the duke after eight years.

"You will be known as 'the king's sister,' Your Grace," he told Anne, who continued to nod happily, "and you will enjoy precedence over every other court lady except the king's two daughters and, of course, any future wife the king may take." Before she could object, Brandon hurried on. "His Grace has great affection for you and wishes to be generous. My colleague, Wriothesley, has brought documents which he will give to your ambassador. They attest to His Grace's great desire for your comfort." Wriothesley, scanning the documents, mentioned that Anne would have four thousand pounds a year for her pleasure, with no accounting of how she spent it. And the manor of Bletchingly, known to have substantial income in rents, tithes and leases, as well as the palace of Richmond which the king knew she loved, would be hers for life.

Dazed by her interpreter's account of her sudden riches, Anne could only shake her head to show she understood and repeat a hearty "Ja!" Even the last condition—that she remain in England for the rest of her life—failed to trouble her. Of course—she bobbed her head to show she understood—it *would* be inconceivable that she return home to marry again. No former queen of England could possibly become another man's wife! Scrawling her signature on the heavy documents, Anne could still scarcely believe her good fortune. Why should she desire to return to a dull homeland where her brother might want to marry her off again when she could remain in this country, with stepchildren she'd grown to love, and a fortune of her own to spend as she wished?

After Brandon left—still amazed at the ease with which the emotionally explosive situation had been settled—Anne quickly wrote a letter to her "good brother" and thanked him for his generous settlement. She affirmed she wished only to please Henry in all things and, as a token of her cooperation, returned her wedding ring. Prudently, she signed the letter, "Anna, Duchess of Cleves and your loving sister."

The next letter was to her real brother advising him to raise no objections. If he felt his country and family's honor had been impugned, Anne told the Duke of Cleves bluntly, such feeling must be put aside. She was happy, she said, and she was safe.

With the two letters out of the way, Anne called Mother Lowe, her chief attendant, and all her ladies-in-waiting and there was a great celebration in the queen's quarters. Anne felt a great load had been lifted from her shoulders and she wanted to share her joy with her countrywomen who for the past five months had shared her disgrace. Wine cups in hand, they embraced each other, laughed and wept all at the same time. For the first time since their arrival in England, everyone felt free.

Once the festivities were over, Anne summoned her Dutch chamberlain and instructed the man to obtain a strict accounting of how much her new properties yielded annually. Then, she told a surprised steward, there were changes she intended to make in her living quarters, changes more to her taste. Later, with her mistress of the wardrobe, she took a long careful look at her clothing which, after months of being criticized by her English friends, suddenly appeared heavy, stiff and in all the wrong colors.

Three days later, an English dressmaker arrived at Richmond and soon afterward Anne's maids were startled to receive gifts of the former queen's clothing. "I am no longer a queen and have no use for these garments," she told her surprised companions. Soon they would see her new wardrobe and by the time they did, she'd have a more fashionable coiffure. Anne meant to commence her new life with a new look. If she was to be an Englishwoman, she must appear as one and, in so doing, she'd show her gratitude to those kind English ladies by dressing and living as they'd advised. She hoped to keep their friendship as well as that of Lady Mary, little Elizabeth and her young stepson.

Once her wedding ring was gone, Anne put the heavy gold band her parents had given her on her finger, smiling at the inscription inside. God had, indeed, sent her "well to keep." She'd survived her disastrous marriage and never, in all her life, had she been so content. And she intended to remain that way.

* * *

Astonished that his queen had given him up so easily, Henry Tudor prepared to wed again. But before that there was other business to attend to. Once the annulment decree was issued, the king signed the death warrant for Thomas Cromwell and, on a hot July day, pounds thinner—but with the firm stance of the soldier he'd once been—the disgraced minister mounted a scaffold at Tyburn where an executioner, new to the trade, sweatily hacked away at his neck, strokes that mercifully rendered the man unconscious, though the head did not sever easily.

"The foul churl is dead at last!" exulted Norfolk as he left the scene to inform the king the deed was done. Norfolk had more than one reason to celebrate. The king's intended bride was his niece, Catherine Howard. Though the girl was a ninny and too flighty, she'd do as told, and the duke meant to exercise his avuncular privileges. There'd be no more nonsense about popery. Even though Cromwell with his Lutheran tastes was now gone, Norfolk still did not desire any return to Rome. When the holy houses had been dissolved, the Howard coffers had been greatly enriched with several church properties. But at least the constant appraisal of what sacraments were official and the needless debating of whether one should read Scripture for one's own instruction might now be a thing of the past. Norfolk knew Henry wanted peace in the church and through the new queen and with the help of Stephen Gardiner, the Bishop of Winchester, the duke meant to have not only peace, but a return to the conservative religion of his youth.

"I've never read Scripture nor never will read it!" he later told the king and Charles Brandon. "It was merry in England before the 'New Learning' came up. And I wish all things as they were in times past!"

With his chief enemy now dead and another niece likely to become queen, he had little doubt but what that happy time would soon come to pass.

* * *

At Parr House, Katherine was again startled at her lack of remorse at Cromwell's fate. Obviously the king had found matters even worse than she'd thought. Never once had Henry referred to her visit to Whitehall, nor had she mentioned it to Bessie. Her part in Cromwell's disgrace and death would apparently remain a secret for which she was thankful and relieved. She knew she'd risked a great deal but, she acknowledged with a wry smile, it meant as much to Henry's pride that they both remain silent. What sovereign would want his court and subjects to know that charges substantial enough to bring about a powerful minister's downfall had come from a mere woman?

But she was completely unprepared for Henry's generosity in disposing of Cromwell's property in which he greatly favored the Parrs. Oursley, the disputed land adjoining Coughton Court, was awarded to her delighted uncle, George Throckmorton, and spendthrift brother Will happily received several of Cromwell's Essex properties. Then, to her great discomfort, the king presented Katherine with Cromwell's home at Wimbledon. She knew it to be Henry's way of showing his appreciation, but still could not bring herself to visit the house which Tom Seymour said was a fair lodging set in its own impressive park. Instead, she asked her uncle to let it out on a long lease.

Within days after Cromwell's execution, Henry married Catherine Howard in a candlelight ceremony at the small manor of Oatlands and, a week later, Katherine waited with the entire court to welcome the king and his bride to Eltham Palace. She was curious to see the new queen—thirty years younger than her forty-nine-year-old husband—and wondered what Henry could see in the girl who still looked like a child. That he was infatuated with her was obvious for, reminiscent of her Boleyn cousin, Catherine had the same vivacity, the sparkling black eyes and dark hair which, unlike Anne, curled in an aureole about her face. It emphasized the rosy cast to her fresh complexion and the retroussé nose above a laughing, sensual mouth. Everything about Catherine—her melodic laugh, voluptuous body and bubbling good spirits—reflected a joyous temperament.

"And that's what seduced His Grace!" a scornful Kate Brandon told Katherine during the welcoming festivities. "You remember she's an orphan and she's so played on the king's sympathy he denies her nothing. You'd think she was a vendor's daughter instead of a Howard if you could hear her talk! And oh, how she loves to dance and gamble. There was a torchlight celebration on the river at Windsor which kept us up 'til daylight! I trow she even makes the king forget his bad leg!"

The Suffolks, Katherine and Tom Seymour were among those who rode with the honeymooning royal couple for early morning hunting and hawking, later attending the midmorning meal at the palace. They joined Henry and Catherine in the royal barge for a musical evening on the Thames and rode in procession to Windsor and Greenwich for Garter and May Day festivities. The king delighted in Tom Seymour's company and Katherine was keenly aware of the envious glances of the other ladies impressed with the

handsome courtier's virile good looks. Irrepressible as always, Thomas made
light of them with outlandish remarks interspersed with the flamboyant oaths
of which he was the undisputed court champion, even surpassing old
"Swearing Russell," now the Earl of Bedford and proud possessor of venerable old Woburn Abbey.

Their relationship still puzzled Katherine. At times, watching Thomas
ride hell-bent with the king to plant a standard on a far hilltop, she knew
how much she loved him, how necessary he was to the peace of her days.
Ruefully, she admitted Seymour had captured her heart as easily and as
quickly as he now plunged his standard into the soft hilltop turf. It amused
her as she wondered what others would think if they knew she, the poised
and beautiful Lady Latimer, so envied at court for her closeness to the sovereigns, noted for her learning, impeccable background and gracious manners,
was as intrigued with Seymour as the king was with his youthful wife.
Often she felt awkward and uncertain and, as if aware, Thomas would take
her hand, clasp her shoulder and whisper in her ear until her poise and
humor returned.

And then, one memorable day, on the Westminster waterstairs, as they
watched a spectacular sunset on the blood-red roofs of Lambeth Palace across
the Thames, in full view of whoever might be watching, he enfolded her in
his arms and kissed her long and deeply. Afterward, her head on his shoulder, he stroked her long, unbound hair, as she waited for him to say he loved
her and wanted to be with her always. Yet he said nothing, only whispering,
"I marvel at your sweetness, Kate. You are so untouched. . . ."

It was not what she'd expected and she hadn't known what to say.
Shouldn't she be angry with him for not declaring himself? Instead, she was
only angry with herself for wanting to hear it so desperately.

Back at Parr House, the scene remained in her mind and heart for days
while she told herself repeatedly that a kiss and an embrace was hardly a
thing to become so exercised about. Especially with someone like Thomas.
He was a man, obviously as attracted to her as she was to him. But he'd also
been attracted to many others, whereas she'd never known anyone who
aroused her so strongly. Katherine knew herself well enough to know she
could never become involved in a casual affair, the like of which was so
rampant at court. Was that what Thomas wanted? Did he hope to persuade
her a love affair would be enough? Shaking herself, she tried to erase the
possibility from her mind. But it persisted—only to upset her for admitting
that Seymour's attraction was so intense she might be unable to refuse him,
so great was her desire to taste the passion and love she'd never before experienced.

As the weeks passed, Thomas remained faithfully attentive. They enjoyed
each other's company and the now more passionate kisses and embraces that
always left Katherine dissatisfied and hungering for more. Yet he never mentioned love or marriage, nor gave any indication their affair might be more

serious. It was mystifying and frustrating, but Katherine knew she'd never forsake him for another.

* * *

At summer's end, the king announced that at last he would fulfill his promise to visit his Northern counties. Immediately, courtiers vied with each other for the privilege of attending the royal couple on the progress. Henry meant to be triumphant as well as conciliatory. Once, he reminded the court, he'd promised to present a queen to his Northern subjects and now he'd bring one such as they'd never before seen, his own "rose without a thorn." Once they saw her he had little doubt his formerly rebellious subjects would love her as much as he did.

Although Katherine was delighted with the king's plans—for he was at last honoring his promise to the Northern people—she prayed she'd not be summoned to attend the queen. She had no desire to mingle with a festive court amidst remembered scenes of horror and heartbreak. Cromwell's death, the Pole executions and the continued incarceration of an ill Countess of Salisbury had kept her on edge. Even though Thomas, as a Gentleman of the Privy Chamber, would accompany the court, she knew there'd be little time for them to be together.

And Thomas so obviously wanted to go. "For once, Kate, I'm not to be sent abroad at a time when the court will be together for days on end. Who knows what will happen? It will be a time of celebration, for the king is so besotted with the queen they appear to have a continual honeymoon. Why, Henry hasn't mentioned taxes, conspiracies, heretics, France, Spain or Scotland in weeks! Catherine has the same sorcery as the Boleyn, but she uses it differently. Anne used to make Henry beg, but Catherine anticipates his every wish. She likes wedded life, the new clothes and the jewels," he smiled knowingly, "and Henry likes to indulge her. It makes him forget how old he is."

Yet when the last wagon had rumbled out of Westminster and the great cavalcade of five thousand courtiers, nobles, bishops, retainers and servants had set upon the Great North Road, Katherine found she was desolate without Thomas. Again for the hundredth time, she wondered if he'd ever declare himself. And then was angry with herself for feeling an uncertainty he never would. Was he so used to years of living alone, of irresponsible relationships with no home or the duties of a husband that he regarded them with apprehension? Katherine felt his reluctance to speak out was a little of all of these. Yet inwardly she knew that Thomas was more concerned with his brother's advancement, an almost blind obsession to match or surpass Edward Seymour in authority and wealth. As far as money was concerned, she had enough for both, though she sensibly recognized her wealth was one reason why her uncle and brother regarded Seymour with so little enthusiasm.

But no matter. Hadn't she spent too many years married to older men who, though kind, had given her little bodily pleasure or mental stimulation? She'd had little joy in shared activities or the happiness of a child. Katherine knew if she was to bear and rear a child it must be soon. She was nearing thirty and Thomas was several years older. Perhaps this time apart would make him think more of their future together.

*　*　*

To shake off the depression caused by Thomas's absence, Katherine threw herself into her neglected studies avidly reading the new books that had lain unopened all summer. She invited her Borough and Latimer stepchildren to London; Margaret was again pregnant and John had wed that spring. Though her brother and sister had gone north with the king, there were enough friends left at court to have musicales and evenings of cards, dancing and feasting. The Parr House servants grumbled at the unusual activity, but Katherine was glad to be kept preoccupied. When Mary Tudor asked her to Richmond for a visit with Anne of Cleves, she accepted at once. The former queen, Mary wrote, was anxious to see them. She thought Anne was quite lonely now that several of her countrywomen had returned home and she was no longer at court.

The next day Katherine and Bessie rode to Westminster waterstairs for the barge Anne was sending for them. She was happy at the thought of seeing Richmond again; the palace always gave her a great sense of well-being and contentment and seeing Mary and Anne would take her mind off Thomas. And she and Bessie, usually so busy with their tasks at Parr House, would have time for a long chat while on the river.

It promised to be a fine day. Already, at eight o'clock the Strand was alive with apprentices removing shutters from their masters' stalls and shops. Vendors carried great trays of pies, hot oatcakes and fresh herrings to stands outside St. Paul's. Small boys running errands were pushed aside by more officious servants who themselves hurried out of the path of a group of knights in full armor as they raced toward the Tower. Outside St. Paul's, a lengthy procession of grave-faced churchmen, splendid in copes and miters, walked toward the cathedral. In Paul's Churchyard, Katherine sought to control her horse made skittish by merchants setting up the trestle stalls outside bookshops and stationers' shops. She remembered years ago when Bessie had gone almost daily to these very shops to find materials for little Anne Askew. Nothing had changed. Overhead, the brightly painted signs of the Bishop's Head, the Angel, the Holy Ghost and her favorite, the Holy Lamb, reminded Katherine of the satisfying hours she herself had spent browsing through the stalls for reading material for herself and her young guest.

Pushing on out of the Churchyard, through the throng that grew as barges from Baynards Castle and the Temple dislodged their occupants, Katherine saw a gathering ahead, one large enough to impede their progress. Her steward pointed toward a dry path along the muddy Strand roadway and Katherine, her mind still on the girl, followed his lead. Bessie chattered beside her, hoping aloud the weather would not turn and spoil their river journey. Suddenly, a great shout went up from the crowd ahead. Katherine hurried her horse along, wondering if a thief had been caught. She had no desire to witness some poor wretch being carried off in chains, the objects of blows, with mud and stones thrown at him along the way. She averted her glance, intent upon following the steward's lead when Bessie cried loudly, "Jesu in Heaven, I don't believe it! Kate, look! 'Tis Anne!"

Had Bessie not mentioned her name, Katherine thought she might have merely conjured up a vision of the girl she'd taught in a Lincolnshire manor house so many years ago. For there, mounted on a makeshift pulpit, was the slim figure of Anne Askew, garbed in a colorless gray, her pointed hood slightly tilted from shouting and waving her hands. Her face was alight with enthusiasm and intense with fervor as she spoke.

"And I say to you that if you would know the truth, you must read Scripture for yourself and aye, if you cannot read, find someone who thinks as you do to read it for you!" Anne held aloft a Bible. "The truth is there, my good people, and not in the minds and hearts of those yonder who parade in costly garments and mumble a ritual they do not themselves understand!" She gestured disdainfully toward the priests as they entered the cathedral. Suddenly, as her eyes scanned the crowd, she saw Katherine and Bessie. Waving the Bible, she cried, "My lady! My lady!" and, pushing her way through the throng was suddenly there on the dry path beside them.

Katherine dismounted and hugged the girl, now as tall as she, noting her clothing was shabby and none too clean. "Anne dear, what brings you to London? And what are you doing there?" She pointed toward the rickety pulpit now occupied by another speaker. "Where is your husband? And who is caring for your children?"

Bessie had urged them into a doorway of a small shop while the steward, plainly annoyed at the interruption, resignedly took the horses out of the busy traffic. Anne, breathless, her face wreathed in smiles, turned to hug Bessie as she explained. "My mother cares for my little ones, my lady, for I wish to minister to many, not just a few. And my husband? Well, my husband has forbade me my home which pleases me well for I never wished to wed with him nor become a mother either. "This"—she clutched the Bible to her breast—"this is what I was born for! To make people study and think. To make them learn—that's what I've always wished to do. You remember, my lady, years ago I told you that?"

Katherine nodded, still stunned by the unexpected encounter. She listened with dismay as Anne said she'd translated the Scriptures, a work which had taken years and kept her sane in her unhappy marriage. "Oh, my lady," she kissed Katherine's hand, "how often I blessed you for your teaching! You opened my eyes to the world and through what you gave me, I have found my life's work." Anne said her husband, Squire Thomas Kyme, had objected to her constant studying, her work in translating the holy words, and forbade her to continue. "But I did not let it bother me," she said cheerfully, tossing her head, her freckles gleaming even more strongly in the early morning sunlight. "I went on gospeling whenever I chose and found many ready to listen to my words. That was more than I found at home, my lady! It finally became so bad I decided to leave. So one evening I crept out and left the children with my lady mother and came to London. Along the way I preached wherever I could—I even spoke in Lincoln Cathedral, my lady! At least I did until the dean found out about it and had me carried out!"

Disturbed, Katherine wondered how anyone could leave their husband and children. Especially for a belief she might have kept as long as she remained silent and did not provoke her family and neighbors. Why endanger one's reputation—perhaps even one's safety—in as conspicuous a place as Lincoln Cathedral and Paul's Churchyard, with views that might be viewed as treasonous or heretical, depending upon whatever the king and his council believed at the moment?

As if understanding her old friend's quandary, Anne responded, "Oh, my lady, this is what I was born to do! I must spread this gospel of truth. I must correct the wrong thinking that harbors saints and superstition, penance and popery! This is what I wish to do with my life. My mission is divinely inspired, my lady, and I have you to thank for showing me the way!"

Katherine felt an unusual resentment at Anne Askew's words. She wanted to say she thought Anne arrogant and careless, lacking in the more normal feelings a mother and wife should possess, and using religious study as a means of escaping responsibilities that bored her. But she knew that would only provoke argument and Bessie's silence confirmed her thoughts. Hoping to turn the conversation in another direction, she asked where Anne was living.

"I lodge with the Wadloe family in the Temple, over yon," Anne pointed, "and oh, my lady, I am so happy there! They do not think as I do. They think more like the bishop, my lord of Winchester, while I think more like the archbishop, my lord of Canterbury. We have many lively discussions before it is dark, my lady!"

Katherine hugged Anne again, explaining they would miss their barge if they stayed any longer. She did not ask Anne to call at Parr House nor did the girl suggest another meeting. Mounting her horse, she saw Anne had rejoined the throng surrounding the speaker and, with rapt expression, was lost in absorbing his words. "She's forgotten us already, Bess," she whispered, pointing to the girl. Bessie shook her head, shrugging her shoulders, as she urged her horse on. Yet all the way to Westminster, the vision of the fervent Anne remained. Dismayed, Katherine found she could not shake the uneasy conviction that with the girl living so nearby, she'd really seen the last of her.

* * *

Anne was still on her mind when the barge left them at the Richmond waterstairs. Katherine felt her spirits lift at the sight of the handsome palace, its pennons taut against a cerulean sky and the King's Beasts gracing each turret and tower, looking ready to lunge in combat in the bright sunlight. Following the cries coming from the garden, they found little Elizabeth holding a stick over the fishpond hoping to bait one of the carp that swam in its deep greenish depths. Susan Clarencieux, Mary's favorite maid of honor, sat on the grass, fashioning fish hooks, while Mary waved to them from the pond's opposite side.

"Come here, ladies, while this wench catches her fish and then we'll all see the Lady Anne!" Mary cried, while Elizabeth waved exuberantly. Katherine was pleased to see her old friend looking so well and in such apparent good humor. The Privy Council was again considering her marriage and each time that happened, Mary had bouts of depression and melancholy, spending part of each day in bed.

When, amidst exultant cheers, Elizabeth at last pulled a squirming carp from the pond, they all made ready to leave. "I will take it to my Lady Anne," the child cried, running to gather leaves to put around the slippery fish. A short time later, as they walked through the woods adjoining the now deserted Franciscan Friars monastery, Mary recalled the old gypsy's prophecy. "Crowns and scepters, he promised you, Kate, and I remember I did not know what he meant!" Mary laughed. "Thankfully, my father now has a prince. The crown and scepter will be Edward's. It's just as well I'd never set my heart on them."

Before Katherine could reply, Elizabeth cried out, lamenting that everyone was going too fast for her. Wasn't there a shorter way to the palace and Lady Anne? she wailed. Her fish was not quite dead and it was hard to carry. Mary ignored the little girl's complaints and, if anything, increased her pace, still disregarding Elizabeth's cries that she could not keep up with them. After a few moments, as her belligerent remarks continued, Mary turned, crying, "Then walk alone with Susan and Bess and don't be such a scold! You don't have to walk here with my Lady Latimer and me!" Elizabeth's face flushed at the reprimand and tears welled in her eyes. The hands cradling the fish trembled and, as if not wanting anyone to see her cry, she hung her head.

"She always wants to be with me. . . ." Mary explained, aware of the surprised look in Katherine's eyes. "I know, Kate, I am probably harsh. But I am not her mother and she treats me as though I am." When Katherine still did not reply, Mary whispered, "I don't wish to be cruel to the child. But I have to show her she must not depend upon me as much as she does. When I wish to act the mother, I want it to be with my own child!"

Katherine mentioned the council negotiations. "That may come sooner than you think, my girl, if the foreign ambassador and your father's advisers have their way and agree upon terms."

Mary laughed bitterly. "Ah, Kate, don't be taken in by all the playacting. That's all it is. Now that I'm illegitimate again—and so is poor Elizabeth back there—we have less value than we did years ago. And my father's pride is such that he would still demand the best for me, no matter what he says.

He fancies now and then to listen to offers or make one himself, but it will amount to nothing, you'll see." She sighed. "No, Kate. I would marry with Spain, my mother's country, but nowhere else. And Spain is not interested."

Katherine put her arms about Mary's thin shoulders. At twenty-five, the girl had never had a suitor who'd roused her interest much less touched her heart. And always about her, the speaking, demanding, living reminder of the woman who'd caused all "the troubles." She could understand Mary's resentment.

But she was still aware of Elizabeth's misery and her heart went out to the little girl, the laggard way in which she walked, the joy in the fish she'd caught for her stepmother lost in Mary's sharp criticism. Turning to Susan and Bessie who walked on beside the little girl, she called out, "Now then, you three—Mary and I will race you to the gate. Hoist your skirts and off we go!"

Handing her fish to Susan, Elizabeth screamed in delight as Mary, rising to the challenge, started off across the grass and they all sped toward the startled guards who watched from each side of the old gate. On they ran, Elizabeth's shrieks filling the air, her little legs flying over the grass in an effort to keep up with the others. Then, in unspoken consent, all four adults slowed down just enough so that as they arrived, breathless, at the old stone archway, the little girl was the first to reach the guards who snapped to attention at the sight of the king's two daughters, racing like country maids, across the greensward.

"I won! I won!" Elizabeth cried happily, snatching the fish back from Susan, her black eyes, so like her mother's, dancing with joy.

"You did and well done"—Mary took Elizabeth's proffered hand—"and when we see my Lady of Cleves, remember to tell her how fast you ran." As the three entered the vast hall, their footsteps echoing behind the chamberlain, Katherine's eyes sought Mary's. She smiled and patted her friend's shoulder fondly.

"And you, too, Mary. Well done."

* * *

Returning to Parr House, the events of the day occupied Katherine's thoughts. Beginning with the unexpected meeting with Anne Askew and the poignant episode with little Elizabeth in the Richmond woods, the meeting with Anne of Cleves had been anything but what she'd expected. Instead of a lonely and hurt ex-queen, whose pride might justifiably have been touched by the suddenness of the king's remarriage, they'd found a handsome woman whose lighthearted gaiety and satisfaction in her new rich clothes and more attractive appearance were heartening to see.

"And you are all to blame!" she'd told Mary and Katherine. "You and all your friends. I can't wait for the Duchess of Suffolk and the Countess of Rutland to return so they, too, can see how much they have done for me." Anne smoothed the heavy plum-colored velvet with her large, square hand

and thrust a shapely sandal of the same material out from beneath the skirt for all to see. Together they'd admired the newly refurbished rooms with costly hangings of arras, the new furniture and the rich table at which they'd all been served a meal, eating the English dishes which, Anne said, was all she now served. As she chattered and laughed, ruffling little Elizabeth's hair affectionately, Katherine saw traces of the woman Holbein had painted. She wondered what Henry would say when he next saw his ex-wife. Anne was not in exile and could go to court whenever she chose. In her fine new clothes and jewels, her easier manner, her new language and, particularly, her gaiety and graciousness, Anne of Cleves bore little resemblance to the bewildered, almost miserable woman who'd arrived in England a scarce six months ago.

But she was obviously happy and content. Katherine had been pleased. Her only remark concerning her successor was when Mary spoke of how much she missed her father and hoped for his early return. And then, she'd dutifully mentioned she missed the queen also. "Ah, Madame Catherine," Anne waved a hand disdainfully, "she has taken quite a burden upon herself. . . ."

Now, settling herself in front of her fire, wine cup in hand, Katherine took the bundle of letters delivered to Parr House by courier that day. She did not expect one from Thomas. Before leaving, he'd explained writing was such an effort, he'd given it up long ago. But, he promised, he'd remember everything to tell her upon his return.

One letter was from her sister. Painfully scrawled, for Ann Parr Herbert was no scholar, she wrote of triumphal entries into cities Katherine knew well, of festivities in Northern castles she'd often visited with John or Lord Borough. From Pontefract Castle, east to Hull and then to York, Ann noted, progress had been slow, no more than fifteen miles a day. She wrote of rain, floods and Henry's concern that his nephew, King James V, might not cross the Scottish border to meet him. Ann described the king's gracious manner toward the masses that lined the roads everywhere to see the royal cavalcade pass, as well as the fêtes given by nobles who, Katherine knew, would undoubtedly be impoverished for a year after such costly celebrations. Ann did not mention Thomas Seymour or, more strangely, the queen.

Katherine had saved a letter from Kate Brandon for last. She opened it eagerly, thinking there might be word of Thomas in it.

Grimsthorpe
August 5, 1541

My dearest Katherine,

Though I am as near death from exhaustion as ever I expect to be, I must still write to you of the king's visit while it is all fresh in my mind. It was glorious and I thought so often how you would have loved it—you and Mary. She would have delighted in seeing her father so at peace with himself. Even Charles says Henry hasn't looked so well in years. They both mounted horses and tilted on our green one fine afternoon while everyone cheered and I held my breath.

Everything has gone well but the weather has been foul and made it wearisome to move so many people from one place to another. The king has promised more attention to our problems with more new people on our Northern Council. But there is still much bitterness with the spoliation of the holy houses and the changes in the church. Those who complain the loudest, Charles says, are those who first conveyed away the stone blocks and carved wood for their own homes! The king has not hurt his cause by this visit, but it hasn't done as much good as we wished.

For the most part, this has been holiday time and everyone—the Seymours, the Lisles, the Carews, Dennys and Dudleys—all seemed to enjoy themselves. The pressure for the king's favor still goes on— all, I have to say, except for my dearest mother. I had dreaded this visit for one reason only and that was the reaction of my mother to seeing the king again, for they hadn't met since the old queen's death. But habit is strong and when, at our first evening's banquet, mother made her entry alone—which is as she wished it—ah, Kate, you could have heard a pin drop! She walked to the king, made a low bow and then turned as if to walk away, not expecting anything.

But Henry would not have it so. He rose, put out both hands to her and said, "Maria, it has been too long since we have seen you. And you have hardly changed at all. Oh, Maria, how we still miss our friend Willoughby. . . ." The queen was, thankfully, not yet in her place at table. She is not very punctual and the king had waited long enough. But I was happy my dear mother was excused from paying homage to another queen named Catherine. She was very moved by the king's gracious words for I saw tears in her eyes as well as his. She bowed again and he kissed her hand and let her go. I vow, Kate, it made we weep, too!

Katherine felt her own eyes mist over. Maria de Salinas, one of Maud Parr's closest friends, must be nearly fifty-five years old. It was well she'd made peace with her sovereign and in her daughter's presence. She continued reading:

Now, Katherine, I will write of something else, but this is not to be mentioned to anyone. I would not put this to paper if it were not being delivered by Christian, my most trusted courier. The truth is that Charles is almost out of his mind with worry and I know that several of the council are also deeply troubled by what they see in the queen's behavior.

I cannot understand the girl. She is quite beautiful and it's hardly a secret that Henry loves her. His eyes follow her everywhere and he fondles her openly. While I thought her very light-headed last year, I did not think her stupid. Now, I trow, I know not what to believe! It is easy to see she is a flirt and has a very light way with her. But many who like merrymaking also have a more sober side which this young lady does not appear to possess. She needs constant entertainment, cannot bear to be alone and talks too much to her ladies.

But my real concern, Katherine, is that I think she plays the king for a fool! During those times when he is in council or with the men, she seeks her own companions and some are very odd indeed. Her favorite is Tom Culpepper, her cousin, and they are together a great deal. Another favorite is her former music master! It troubles me that she is so careless and depends on the wrong people. The one who encourages her the most is that silly Lady Rochford who I think would have learned her lesson during the time of the Boleyn. The two are very close and conspire. I am troubled at what might follow. . . .

Katherine lay the letter aside, as puzzled as she was troubled. Everyone knew the queen was a silly girl, but she was a Howard and, now married to a king, one could hope she'd change her irresponsible ways. The enormity of Kate Brandon's implication gnawed at Katherine for the remainder of the evening. Henry deserved better. Couldn't someone say something to the spoiled young girl?

But who would speak up? Not Lady Rochford and she knew her "two Joans," so secure with their husbands and their own reputations undoubtedly had not even heard the gossip that Charles Brandon had given his wife. She wondered if Thomas had observed Catherine Howard's foolish conduct. If the queen's indiscretions were so obvious, he could hardly have avoided doing so, for she knew he was an intimate friend of Tom Culpepper's.

Another hateful thought came to mind. Could Thomas in any way be involved with the queen? Or was he intrigued with another court lady who was chancing an affair, as the queen seemed to be doing? The possibility caused Katherine such anguish that she hurriedly thrust Kate's letter into a cabinet, not wanting to read it again. It depressed her that a slip of a girl might be cuckolding a husband who'd raised her, an orphan child, to the highest position in the land. It depressed her even more that Tom Seymour, who'd taken first her fancy and then her heart, might be a part of it all.

CHAPTER XXI

The elegance and pomp of the royal progress ended on November 1, 1541 when the king and queen arrived at Hampton Court to celebrate All Saints' Day. As courtiers returned to the homes and families they'd left four months earlier, Katherine waited at Parr House for Thomas Seymour. All night long, she'd listened to the shouts and clatter of horses' hoofs on the Strand crowded with the nobles' carts and wagons, as weary servants plodded toward house and country estate. She wondered if Thomas was already at court. When would they meet? How would he greet her? Should she tell him how much she'd missed him? Four months was a long time and he might have changed. And what if he were involved with the queen? That suspicion, she admitted to herself as the first lightening rays of daylight crept between her shuttered windows, was what had eaten away at her peace of mind for weeks. Today she'd have her answer.

By midmorning the barking of dogs in the courtyard announced an arrival and, in a few moments, she was being held tightly, her face covered with kisses. "Kate, Kate, I've missed you so!" Thomas whispered, shaking her lightly. "Ah, love, it is so good to hold you again. It has been so long. . . ." Another deep kiss and all Katherine's worried suspicions vanished. Thomas was back, holding her in strong arms, his eyes as loving as she remembered. It was as if she was discovering him all over again—his clean brisk manner, the invigorating scent tinged with the slightest smell of horseflesh and good leather, his plumed cap set as rakishly as ever. Above all, she welcomed the tenderness in his smile, the love in his eyes that told her she'd been genuinely missed.

Over wine, Thomas told her of the progress. Henry was very angry with his nephew, the young Scottish king James, who'd pointedly snubbed his uncle, refusing to venture onto English soil for a meeting. Wed to the beautiful French Mary of Guise, whom Henry had coveted for himself, James was now being wooed by France.

Henry had not taken the snub kindly. "It means the Border raids will continue," Thomas said. He told Katherine that several on the English council in Ireland had mutinied, resulting in charges of treason. On the Continent, England was in disfavor with the Lutherans for Henry's abandonment of Anne of Cleves while the Low Countries were threatening to break off trade agreements in retaliation.

"You speak knowledgeably, Thomas," Katherine regarded her companion fondly. "This time away with the court has been worthwhile to you?"

"I was not privy to council meetings, Kate, if that's what you mean," he laughed, "but people talk outside the council chamber, especially when the wine flows during the evening galas. Henry knows that since he now has no Cromwell to rely upon, he himself must handle those factions within the council who vie with each other. He does this by favoring first one and then another—it keeps them confused, but on their toes! Norfolk, on one side, urges the king to restraint and fewer changes in the church. Cranmer and to some extent my noble brother on the opposite side feel differently. But Norfolk's niece is queen and for the moment he seems to have the upper hand."

"And the queen?" She must find out what Thomas knew. "Catherine is so young! Does she meddle in court business like the Boleyn? Does she play favorites?"

Thomas threw back his head in laughter. "Kate, the queen tells the king nothing except how wonderful he is, how much his subjects love him and how much *she* loves him. She meddles naught in court affairs, for, I trow, she wouldn't know how. But playing favorites—ah, there I am puzzled. And also fearful."

"In what way?"

Thomas's face was sober. "I believe the queen is in great trouble, Katherine," he said quietly, "and the sad thing is, I don't think she even knows it. For if she did, she would not have acted as she has these past months."

"And how was that?" Katherine felt the tightness seep from her body. Thomas spoke so easily of Catherine Howard, he could hardly be involved with her.

Drawing two chairs close to the fire, Thomas impressed upon Katherine that his words must remain a secret. The queen was deeply in love with Tom Culpepper, he whispered. Katherine remembered the handsome youth with the chestnut-brown hair and trim beard, full of pranks and good humor, one genuinely liked at court. Of course it would be someone like that—so much the opposite of the king—who would catch a young girl's fancy! She listened as Thomas recalled the occasions Catherine, with the help of Jane Rochford, George Boleyn's widow, had contrived to meet Culpepper at night.

"Lady Rochford helps the queen keep her trysts?" Katherine cried disdainfully. "Sometimes I think that woman is addled in her mind and stirs up trouble only to be in the center of things. And the king knows nothing of it?"

Thomas shook his head. "Henry sees nothing but his rosy little bride, who usually manages to be there when he wants her. And she ruffles his thinning hair, claps her hands and all the while urges him to be merry. He acts like a schoolboy with his first real love. Let us just hope that now everyone is home, it may all be over. But Culpepper seems smitten, too."

"Perhaps someone should warn her—or him." Katherine found it difficult to comprehend the risks the queen had taken. Flirting was one thing. Even the king liked a coquette. But serious dalliance with a trusted courtier—was the height of folly. Exasperated, she threw up her hands, repeating, "Why doesn't someone warn her?"

"It would do little good, my love, and I, for one, wish no part of her madness." Thomas went on to tell Katherine of the gossip rampant at court concerning the queen's girlhood at Howard House. When only thirteen or fourteen years old, Catherine had shared the sleeping quarters of the older girls in the household. Each evening after the old Dowager-Duchess of Norfolk had retired, many of the young gallants who also lived in the house went to the large dormitory room where Catherine's blooming young beauty stood out among her more ordinary companions. There, Thomas said, Henry Manox, a young music teacher in the Norfolk employ, had determinedly announced he'd be the first to seduce the duke's niece. Everyone had encouraged the affair and it was certain Catherine had allowed him great liberties. That is, until she began to pay more attention to the well-bred Francis Dereham, a gentleman-pensioner at Howard House.

"Why wasn't the girl more straitly kept?" Katherine was appalled, remembering her two husbands' protective attitude toward their own daughters.

"I don't know. But remember she was very young and had no chamber of her own." Thomas's tone was compassionate. "No one seems to have ever paid much attention to her. One should pity her, perhaps, for such foolishness. I suppose with so many others doing as they wished, she wanted to be like everyone else. Only she forgot she was a Howard and a duke's niece."

The affair had apparently lasted for almost a year. While others changed partners as their fancy dictated, Catherine liked Dereham who nightly disappeared into her bed. In no time at all, he was calling her his "wife," and Catherine appeared happy to have him do so. "They both overlooked the fact that such an agreement, coupled with intimacy, constitutes a legal marriage in the eyes of the church," Thomas explained, "and now she has taken Dereham into service as her private secretary and has obtained important court posts for many who have knowledge of those old dormitory days. This has caused much gossip and there are many who might use it for their own ends. My esteemed brother, for one, considers himself responsible for the morals of the court and regards the matter quite seriously. In his ponderous way, though hardly of the old faith, he is more like Norfolk than anyone else. For myself, I can only think what this will do to the king. He is obsessed with the girl. . . ."

Thomas said that when the old Dowager-Duchess finally realized what was happening, she'd had Catherine appointed maid of honor to Anne of Cleves. By that time, Henry had noticed the nubile young girl who'd been happy to discard Dereham, especially when she knew the king would never stay married to his Lutheran bride.

"Catherine Howard is either generous, foolish—or frightened—for otherwise she'd never allow those old companions about her now. For they talk, poor ignorant souls! They boast of their friendship with the queen and hint of what they know." Thomas put his wine cup down and strode nervously about the room. "They don't know that Tom Wriothesley has worked night and day to find out everything he can about the queen's youthful escapades. He's never forgiven Norfolk for the part he played in Cromwell's downfall and execution. And for my dear brother, who is now an earl, it is a heaven-sent opportunity to further the new religion and perhaps even pluck a ripe Norfolk holding should the old duke incur Henry's disfavor!"

Katherine remembered the sly, slightly drunken councillor who'd taunted her at Durham House for those afternoons of study with her lady companions. Had Thomas Wriothesley anything to gain, she doubted he'd have much pity for his victim, even if she were a queen. But what of the king? Had anyone considered his pride in and love for his young wife? Perhaps her actions since her marriage, foolish and imprudent as they might be, had ceased short of adultery. Wriothesley and his colleagues were certainly looking for a way to involve Norfolk, to bring about his downfall and thus vindicate all Cromwell's religious efforts. But did they care if a foolish, thoughtless girl was sacrificed?

"The matter is now in Thomas Cranmer's hands." Thomas's voice, edged in sarcasm, interrupted her thoughts. "But my Lord of Canterbury quails at the thought of telling his king for he knows how marvelously set Henry is upon the queen. Perhaps he'll be able to convince the others to leave well enough alone, although he had little influence—or else dared not use it—when the old queen and the Boleyn were in similar circumstances!" Thomas prepared to leave. "Now that everyone is home and about their own affairs, it may all soon be forgotten. I pray so! I don't know what the king would do if he ever found out."

* * *

Within days, Katherine learned from a letter brought by Kate Brandon's courier that Henry would soon issue an order for the execution of Margaret Pole, the Countess of Salisbury. The Privy Council and the king, Kate wrote, wished to remove such a prominent figure of the old faith, one who still regarded Henry's marriage to Katherine of Aragon as his only legal union and Mary his only heir. Now that he had his son, her belief was treasonous in the king's eyes. Along with her son and nephew, she'd plotted for a Plantagenet restoration to the Crown; Cromwell had gathered the evidence before his own execution.

"But it's really that fool son of hers, Cardinal Pole, who's as much to blame as anyone!" Kate wrote, her strong handwriting uneven, evidence of her distress. "He still harangues the king and prattles on to all who will listen what heresy is practiced in England. When no one listens, he obligingly writes everything out and smuggles it here where it circulates among those of the old faith. Charles says the king's patience is at an end—and so, too, may be Lady Salisbury."

But the end came sooner than anyone expected. Several days later, without trial or notice, without any opportunity to send word to those who loved or feared for her, Margaret Pole was dragged from her fetid cell and brought to Tower Green. Quickly, word of the execution swept the city for one of the last Plantagenets did not go quietly. Seeing the scaffold, she'd refused to ascend and when someone called her a traitor and ordered her to climb up, she'd rounded on her accuser saying, "I am no traitor!"

Quickly, she was pushed up the steps and ordered to lay her head on the block.

"If you wish my head, you must get it the best you can!" the frail woman shouted.

Taking her at her word, the executioner swung his ax, but the countess was too quick for him. Eluding his grasp, she made for the scaffold stairs. There two soldiers caught her, bringing her back to face the hooded axman. With deadly aim, he swung once more at the thin neck. The woman, tightly clutched, could not move. All she could do was twist her head from side to side, as if encouraging the butchery. It was not until seven blows had caught her that the seventy-year-old countess' head was severed and the sundered body thrown in the straw.

Shocked that the king had allowed such a barbarous end for her mother's old friend, Katherine knelt in tearful prayer in Parr House chapel. Later Thomas tried to comfort her. "Now that the king has a son, he'll have small pity for anyone of the old faith for he considers their belief a threat to the boy's legitimacy. And Cardinal Pole's influence with those of the old faith is strong. I think this was the king's way of showing Pole he'll stop at nothing to eliminate those who oppose him."

Her uncle said the same thing. "It's the Crown, Katherine. Security for the Crown—that's what Henry wants for his son. The Tudors took the Crown from the Plantagenets and any who remain must walk a very narrow path. Pole works constantly to restore the Pope here. Lady Salisbury was as loyal to Rome as the old queen was and as Mary Tudor still is. Politically, the king was right. Morally, he was wrong. But when has morality been the foundation of a Crown's strength?"

Distraught, Katherine and Kate Brandon set out for Richmond to comfort Mary Tudor. Soon they were walking through rooms reminiscent of the dead countess' presence—rooms in which Margaret Pole had often sat with the old queen and her young daughter as they worked with their needles, the flickering candlelight haloing her silver hair. Katherine still found it difficult to accept the woman's shameful death. Even more she feared its impact on Mary.

They found the king's elder daughter dressed all in black returning from her devotions at the small prie-dieu at the chamber's end. The strong morning light emphasized her swollen eyes and pale pinched features. Wordlessly, they embraced Mary who, in a choking voice, told them of the message the countess had given to be sent in case of her death.

"It was the last request she made," Mary's voice trembled. "She said, 'Tell my Lady Mary she has never been far from my thoughts, as I know I have never been far from hers. She has acted as her mother would have wished and I have had much love and joy in her good sense. Tell her I am content, even though I am sure the end is near.'" Mary clasped Katherine's shoulder. "Oh, don't you see? She was telling me she understood why I never went to see her! She knew I never dared even write a letter or send things for her comfort though I yearned to do so. There were too many on the council waiting to pounce on me for any misadventure. And I have hated myself for not having the courage to do so anyway! But now, I know she understood."

"She knew the danger," Kate Brandon whispered, "and she knew how much you'd suffered already. Above all, she wanted you to be safe."

"Her words give me some peace of mind, for I cannot believe my father would permit such an end for her." Mary walked to the window and gazed out at the arbored gardens near the river. "All those years at Ludlow—you remember, my Kates?—she wrote my mother every day and, by return courier, the queen sent word of how I was to be dressed, what I should eat and study—even how much exercise I should have." Mary's eyes mirrored the tears that shone in her companions'. "Later, my good mother told me it was the only way she could stand the separation. She always hoped I might marry with Lady Salisbury's son before he entered the church. . . ." The girl's eyes flashed angrily. "Now I think the cardinal must be mad! He should never have put his mother's life in such peril!" She strode nervously about the room.

"I know you two don't believe in churchly matters as I do. But are things any better since my father replaced the Pope? I still believe everything my Lady Salisbury—and my good Duke of Norfolk—believe. How can the church's teachings of centuries be changed in a few years? What was won by cutting off the heads of the godly Fisher and Tom More? What did all the Northern fighting gain? This would never have happened had my mother still been queen. It's all that wretched Boleyn's fault!" Mary waved her hand impatiently. "Ah, my good friends, I long for the old ways. When things were ordered and dependable and beautiful. How can one forget a lifetime of learning? Now all the abbeys are gone or so destroyed they are mockeries and those who lived in them try to fend in a world they don't understand. I cry at the dishonored shrines and am sick for the poor tormented souls who roast at Smithfield for a belief so new they often don't even understand it, except it's supposed to be better than when the Pope was their heavenly father on earth." Mary wiped her eyes.

"Forgive me, my ladies, I thought all my tears were gone. I haven't thought upon this for a long time. I think losing my dear Lady Salisbury has brought back memories of all the lovely old peaceful ways. Our visits to Ditton or Hanworth and then on to Greenwich for Christmas with everyone making ready to gild the Boar's head and the mummers fighting over who would play the Shipman and the Fool. And all those gifts on New Year's Day at Windsor! It was all so lovely then, when I was little"—Mary turned away, her voice choking—"and now they've cut off her head!"

The sound of the door opening grated in the silence. Susan Clarencieux and little Elizabeth stood in the doorway. "She saw the visitors, my lady, and wanted to come," the older girl explained.

Katherine waited for Mary to reply, but the girl was still struggling for composure. She noticed Elizabeth, pale and very unlike her usual boisterous self, was hanging back, waiting permission to join them. Had the child heard the words "and now they've cut off her head"? She wondered if anyone had ever told Elizabeth what had happened to her mother. Now, as the little girl waited tensely, she realized someone had. She yearned to open her arms to the frightened child and comfort her, but dared not. This was Mary's chamber, not hers or Elizabeth's.

She was relieved when Mary gestured for them to enter. "Come and see our visitors," she called. "Come and show them how much you've grown, Bess." After curtseying to the little girl, Katherine put an arm about Elizabeth. The child's color had returned and she was tugging at Mary's sleeve, wanting to whisper in her older sister's ear. "Of course," Mary straightened up, a little smile about her lips, "of course you can tell them what you're making for the king for New Year's giving. And you must tell them what he brought you from the North. It will cheer us all, for we have been sad. . . ."

A servant entered and thrust a piece of paper at Mary. As she scanned the note, her face paled and she cried, "Get my heavy cloak, Susan, and some for my lady guests." Waving the paper, she cried, "It's from Lady Bryan. She said she was summoned because Edward is ill! She sounds as if she's at her wit's end. She's summoned the king and asks that I come too!" As Elizabeth tugged again at her sleeve, she pushed the hand away. "No, Bess, you cannot go. The king's Grace will be worried enough about Edward without having to worry about you too!" At Elizabeth's disappointed look, her tone softened and she put an arm about the little girl. "We don't want you to get sick too, Bess. Stay here with Susan, that's a good child. I promise to send word as soon as I know how Edward is. . . ."

As the three women bundled into their cloaks and hurried through the halls, Mary whispered, "Ah, Kate, if anything happens to Edward. . . ." She stopped, appalled at her own words. "If anything happens to him, I think it would be the end of my father, too!"

* * *

At Whitehall, the Privy Council debated the fate of the queen. No one wanted to tell the king of his wife's indiscretions, yet all the councillors wanted him to know. Edward Seymour, the Earl of Hertford, and old Chancellor Audley, avowed enemies of the queen's uncle, the Duke of Norfolk, also hated Stephen Gardiner, the Bishop of Winchester, whom they suspected would welcome a return to popery. Any action against the queen was an action against both Norfolk and Gardiner.

At last they'd persuaded Thomas Cranmer to act. The archbishop had sent a note by messenger telling Henry of his wife's corrupt living as a girl and her suspected infidelities while she was queen. The king, disbelieving, at once summoned his council and affirmed his belief in his wife's innocence. "I command you to find the perpetrators of such gross calumnies and see to their punishment!" he cried to Lord Privy Seal Fitzwilliam. The king, who'd bragged he'd spared no man in his anger and no woman in his lust, felt it imperative his young bride be protected. Contemptuously, he threw the letter on the council table and went hunting.

The next day the councillors and king met again. Silently, they laid before Henry indubitable proof of Catherine Howard's indiscretions, naming names, places and a signed confession by one of her lovers of intimacies over a long period of time. It was because of such a sinful background, they explained to the stunned monarch, that they'd paid even closer attention to rumors of the young queen's involvement with Thomas Culpepper whom she'd greatly favored all during the Northern progress. Just how favored they did not explain but left it for the king to draw his own conclusion.

Henry appeared stunned. Struggling for composure, his corpulent face flushed hotly and his mouth worked, evidence of the anger and shame consuming him. Everyone remained silent and several, such as Charles Brandon who genuinely loved the man, turned from the sight as the reality of the accusations struck at the sovereign's self-esteem, vanity and faith in his queen. Henry had often boasted of his wife's beauty and virtue and now, feeling the humiliation of the cuckold, he called for a sword to slay the woman who'd tricked him. Then suddenly, before anyone could reply, his feelings overwhelmed him and, shoulders hunched, he covered his face to hide the tears as great wrenching sobs filled the room.

The councillors rustled their papers and avoided glancing at each other, embarrassed at the sight of their invincible monarch displaying the sorrow of an ordinary man. Charles Brandon rose from his chair as if to go to Henry, but at a glance from Cranmer, who shook his head, quickly sat down again.

In a moment, the king recovered his poise. In a voice ragged with emotion, he thanked the council for their endeavors which, he was certain, had not been easy for them. He said he recognized their desire to protect him and the integrity of the Crown and, for that reason, they must confront the queen who was at Hampton Court with their accusations and inform him of her reaction. He would accompany them, he said, but under no circumstances did he wish to see the woman again.

* * *

At Hampton Court, a concerned Mary Tudor, Katherine and Kate Brandon hurried through the Base Court of Wolsey's riverside palace. Everywhere, as the queen was in residence, an unusual number of servants went about their duties. Katherine wondered if Edward had seen his stepmother. Mary had been scornful of Catherine Howard's lack of interest in her younger stepchildren. "I'm seven years older," she told Katherine, "and we have so little in common, I think she feels uncomfortable about me. But she could pay more attention to Bess and Edward! What they'd do without my Lady of Cleves, I don't know!"

A chamberlain told them Edward was suffering from quartan fever and had not responded to treatment. He left them with a tearful Lady Bryan at the nursery door and, after curtseying to Mary, she led them into a stale-smelling room lit only by several small candles. Katherine saw the old governess was nearly ill with worry and fatigue.

"I've done all the doctor said," she explained wearily. "We've kept the child in bed, away from noxious airs and given him only broths and milk puddings to eat. But he is very contrary and seems to lose strength." Katherine realized Lady Bryan was also very frightened, knowing things would not go well for her if anything happened to Henry's heir.

Mary tiptoed to Edward's bed. The little boy appeared half-asleep, his fair hair matted and damp against the pale skin so like his mother's. "He's very unlike himself and quite irritable," Lady Bryan whispered. "He refuses to eat until he's hungry and then he devours everything we bring and it's more than his little stomach can hold."

Katherine glanced about the room. There were no toys, no one to play with or talk to, no sunlight or good air. The child had been deprived of playthings, his pet dogs and harassed by good intent. No wonder he lay so still, with all his attendants speaking in such whispers he must think he might be dying. She said as much to Mary.

It was all Mary, obviously thinking the same thing, needed. "Give us some light, for the love of God and open the windows!" she cried to a nurse. "It is not winter! You say he does not like the broths and puddings and keeps asking for meat? Then bring him some meat!" Distraught, she strode about the room, flinging windows open and asking Lady Bryan to find some toys and have the prince's dogs brought for a visit.

The child, his interest aroused by the unusual activity and hearing a promise of something decent to eat, began to cry. He held up his arms to Mary who soothed him with a tight embrace, stroking his little forehead. "See, Katherine?"—she hugged the child—"He's sad because he doesn't feel well. But now he's going to get better, aren't you, Edward? A good dish of meat will soon be here and you must eat every bite. Then your dogs will come to visit and tomorrow, if you sleep well, I'll take you outside for some good air and perhaps a ride on your pony!"

At that moment, the door opened and as the king entered everyone fell to their knees. Worried, tired and still devastated by the council's news, Henry had met Dr. Butts on arrival at Hampton Court and was told of his son's illness. The doctor now hovered anxiously while the king greeted Mary with a kiss on both cheeks. He nodded to Katherine and Kate Brandon, but his concern was clearly for his son. Katherine had never seen him look so miserable, so *vulnerable*. Henry Tudor looked every bit of his fifty years and was obviously fearful a cruel caprice might now rob him of his only boy. Again Katherine wondered at this fearful, anxious and very human man who ordered beheadings and burnings, exiled queens and bastardized daughters with no apparent looking back.

But Mary saw only that her father was there. Her tired face was wreathed in smiles as they sat and spoke to the little prince who, still weak but relieved someone was at last going to make him well, climbed upon his father's knee to be petted.

Almost at once, a hot meal arrived and Edward began to eat quickly as Mary, finger to lips, caught her father's questioning look and shook her head. They stood together, Henry's arm about Mary's shoulders, until the child finished the dish. Without thinking, Dr. Butts put his hand on Edward's forehead and asked gently if the child wished to vomit.

It was almost more than the little boy could bear. His food had been tasty, the fresh air reviving, his father was there and he felt fine. He'd had enough of darkened rooms and worried governesses and nurses. He gazed at the solicitous physician and, patience gone, waved a clenched fist in the air. "Go away, fool!" he struck at Butts's hand. "I would see my father and sister!"

Everyone laughed at the child's impudence and the relieved king motioned the doctor away. Silently, Katherine tugged at his arm, signaling she'd go with him. "Ah, my lady," the doctor said happily, "I would tarry until he called me a knave to see him so well!"

Kate Brandon was waiting at the door. As they all left the room, Henry and Mary remained at the prince's bedside. It was not often Mary had a chance to be alone with her father and brother, and Katherine knew she meant to make the most of those precious moments. Passing a window bordering on the Base Court below, she was startled to see Charles Brandon, the Duke of Norfolk and several councillors striding into the courtyard.

"Odd," Kate Brandon whispered when Katherine drew her to the window. "Charles said nothing of coming to Hampton today. But 'tis just as well. We can all return home in his barge."

"Perhaps they've heard of the prince's illness also," Katherine suggested, watching the men disappear into an adjoining wing, "and wished to be here if anything happened."

In a moment, Henry emerged from Edward's chamber, relief at his son's improved health still evident on his haggard face. Mary was smiling happily. For the moment at least, the shocking death of her beloved old governess—and the fact that the man at her side was responsible for it—was forgotten in her joy at seeing him. She was reluctant to say goodbye. The king, however, seemed anxious to be off. As everyone bowed, he indicated he'd go to the chapel to give thanks for his son's restored health. The three women watched silently as he walked down the long rounding staircase to the heavy chapel doors.

As they closed behind him, a long anguished wail reverberated about them. Katherine looked at her companions who appeared as frozen and fearful as she herself felt.

"What . . . ?" Mary looked back at Edward's room, thinking Lady Bryan had cried out. But the door opened at once and the old governess came running to join them at the balustrade, for the sound appeared now to be coming from below. The screams continued, becoming more loud and shrill. Katherine clutched Mary's arm. Someone must be in great pain! Couldn't the king hear the crying also? Outside the chapel doors, the two armed guards standing duty listened to the strident noise and, as it became louder, hoisted their halberds in readiness.

At last the sound was upon them. All four women watched in horrified disbelief as Catherine Howard appeared in headlong flight round the corner and ran down the opposite flight of stairs toward the chapel. Breathless now from screaming and the long journey from her chamber, she reached the entrance. There the guards respectfully but firmly crossed their halberds, stating they could admit no one.

Scornfully, Catherine pushed them aside and pounded on the door. "My lord! My lord!" she cried, her small hands hammering on the heavy door desperately. Suddenly, as if in pursuit, Charles Brandon and Thomas Wriothesley were on the stairs and shouted to the guards to remove the queen. The king no longer wished to see her, they said.

At the incredible words, the distraught Catherine gazed at the guards' impassive faces. Pale, frightened, and struggling to understand, she cried aloud again, tears streaming down her cheeks.

"Come, madame, you are not to enter," one guard spoke firmly. "Return with my Lord of Suffolk to your chamber."

When the girl shook her head obstinately and made as if to pound on the door again, Charles Brandon motioned quickly to the guards. As Katherine and her companions watched in astonishment, they both took firm hold of the queen. Struggling to be free, Catherine Howard appeared suddenly consumed by an all-consuming terror and she fought the guards with the strength of youth imperiled by shock and fright. The two guards clutched tightly at her arms and quickly dragged the now hysterical woman outside, her tiny velvet-shod feet making a scratching sound in the Base Court gravel.

On the stairs, still unobserved by Brandon or the guards, the four women remained in stunned silence listening to Catherine Howard's receding sobs. As, with one accord they turned toward Edward's chamber, the king emerged from the chapel, his shoulders slumped as he walked slowly, his limp more noticeable than ever, in the opposite direction.

It was then Katherine realized the queen's secrets were no longer her own.

*   *   *

Katherine had planned a festive Christmas season at Parr House with her Borough and Latimer stepchildren and their families, but in the weeks after

Catherine Howard's arrest, the Duke of Suffolk suggested she arrange to stay at court during the holiday where those close to the king and his three children would be in residence.

"You are more needed there, Katherine," Charles Brandon explained. "The king is almost ill with worry—I've never seen him so pensive. The queen has struck at his pride and he thinks of little else but how she has deceived him. He needs those he trusts to be about him now and you know how he has always esteemed the Parrs! Lady Dudley is to bring Edward from Eltham and Lady Denny will come with my Lady Mary and Elizabeth from Richmond. Let us hope a quiet time with the family and loving friends will help His Grace in this time of sadness."

Obediently, Katherine ordered her servants to prepare for her departure. Her stepchildren would understand though she suspected their own younger family members would regret being deprived of Christmas in London. The City had been unusually quiet since the queen's arrest although the gossip continued in the brothels, taverns, inns and citizens' homes. The arrest of Lady Rochford as an accomplice and witness to the queen's indiscretions was cheered; no one had ever liked George Boleyn's tart-tongued widow. But Thomas Culpepper's apprehension had been viewed with dismay for the likable young man was a great favorite, even outside the court.

Thomas Seymour escorted Katherine to Greenwich. Soon, he said, he would travel to the North to treat with James V, the Scottish king. James, said Thomas, was listening more to the blandishments of François, the French king, than he was to his own uncle, Henry Tudor.

"He swaggers with his own importance," Thomas laughed. "His wife is pregnant and prays daily for a son. That would please her uncles who are as powerful in France as its king. François has broken his truce with Spain and sends money to James so he'll keep harassing our Northern Border. He hopes Henry will send his troops to fight in the North so there'll be none left here to fight on the Continent should it come to war. Now that our king is once more friends with Spain—whose emperor chooses to forget the way the old queen and her daughter were treated—it is possible England might send an army to help Spain fight France! Ah, Kate, it will take the talent of a sorcerer to sort out this mess and I wonder if even my brother and the old Earl of Rutland who are already at Berwick can do anything at all."

Katherine put her arms about Seymour's waist. "I will miss you, Thomas," she whispered, laying her head on his shoulder. "We never seem to have much time together. I hate it when we're apart."

In response, Thomas kissed her lightly on the cheek with teasing little caresses. Softly, as he traced her chin with his lips, she felt her eagerness mount and wondered, for the hundredth time, if he'd ever declare himself. Finally, after one long deep kiss, his arm about her waist, he drew her toward the window to watch other barges arriving at the waterstairs. Katherine wanted to shake him for, in the past few weeks, her passion for the handsome Seymour had increased. She was certain his desire was as real and as urgent as her own. Was he waiting for her to make the first move toward submission? Often, she thought he might be testing her, wondering if she would yield. It was almost like playing a game—a game where she was unfamiliar with the rules. But, though she longed to submit, something held her back.

Later, alone and more in control of her senses, she admitted ruefully that remembrance of her mother and the French queen—even of the old queen—was still strong. In a court where many members engaged in sexual liaisons very easily—some even with the knowledge of their spouses—Maud Parr and her close friends never had.

Katherine knew she could not give herself that easily. When Kate Brandon teased her for tolerating Seymour's silence, Katherine had defended him. Her lover valued her sufficiently, she said, and in time, when his own future was settled, she was certain he would propose marriage. "He is no beggar, Kate," she told the duchess, "but he hasn't had the same good fortune as his brother. It seems to gnaw at him and everything else takes second place." She laughed, making a wry face. "Even me. . . ."

The duchess had shaken her head doubtfully, but said nothing. Katherine knew Kate was not alone in her dislike of the younger Seymour. Even her uncle, William Parr, made no attempt to hide his disdain of the man. "His brother may be an earl," he remarked when he'd arrived at court, "but young Tom is not of the same caliber and never was. Oh, I admit he is very courtly in his fashion and personable enough to turn any woman's head. I think he's turned quite a few in his time." At a rare and unusually angry glance from his niece, he shook his head. "I would be remiss in my duty, Katherine, if I didn't say what I thought. The man is magnificent to look at and a delight to be with, I know. He is very witty and Henry values him only slightly less than Edward Seymour. But there's not much up here." He tapped his head significantly. "He's not for you, my dear. And now I promise not to mention it again, for I have done what your dear father would want me to do. And your own brother also."

Katherine had remained silent, deferring to the elder man's opinion although inside she was hurt and resentful. Did everyone think she could be so easily deceived? Granted Thomas had not won the same honors as Edward Seymour, but how many other courtiers had a wife like Anne Stanhope with her steely determination that her husband was going to succeed no matter what the cost? Katherine felt Thomas was being unfairly condemned. But when her brother Will, also present at court for Christmas, spoke disparagingly of the man, Katherine exploded.

"You tend to your affairs, Will Parr, and I'll tend to mine!" she snapped angrily. "And in so doing I hope to make a better success of my life than you've done with yours so far!" Will's young wife had just left him, calling him such a spendthrift she was certain he'd impoverish her if he didn't bore her to death first. Angrily, her brother had stormed out of Parr House and they'd not referred to the matter again.

In the following weeks, after Thomas had gone to Berwick, Katherine concerned herself with the needs of the king's family and the king himself. She found Henry a bewildering contrast in moods. For hours, he'd remain in the Privy Chamber, alone, dejected and quiet, while she played cards or dice with her "two Joans" or Mary and Kate Brandon. Then he'd emerge unexpectedly and, as everyone bowed, call for the minstrels and there'd be dancing and laughter with the two younger children, Edward and Elizabeth, brought hurriedly to sit with Mary at the king's table when the meal was served. Their happiness in being with their father whom they all clearly adored was poignant to see. In several days, soon after the New Year's gift-giving, they'd all leave for their separate homes. Katherine wondered why the king just didn't keep them with him since he appeared so lonely.

Yet even as she watched, it was obvious the king's thoughts were elsewhere. One evening, with no apparent cause, he became angry and, leaving the table, struck his Fool, Will Somers, a stinging blow. As everyone bowed while Henry stalked away, limping, his shoulders hunched angrily, Katherine went to the Fool. She knew how fond Henry was of Will Somers. The old Fool was rubbing his chin and, at Katherine's look of astonishment, said quietly, "Don't blame him, my lady. He's really striking at everyone who's put him in this position. Our Hal is a very unhappy man, my lady."

* * *

The happiest moment of Katherine's stay at Greenwich was the time she spent with Henry's younger children. Elizabeth with her quick mind, boundless energy and ready wit had always been a delight and she'd loved Mary for years as a companion and friend. But she soon lost her heart completely to the handsome precocious little prince. Edward was startlingly beautiful.

Holbein had recently painted the boy, but even his awesome skill had not captured the almost quicksilver personality of the pale-skinned boy with hair the color of winter wheat, whose deep gray eyes gleamed with an intelligence his mother, whom he so greatly resembled, had lacked. Edward's infectious laugh filled the nursery, making everyone smile; his governess, nurses, rockers and all the servants obviously loved him dearly. Even his tutor, Richard Cox, a Provost of Eton and a Canon of Westminster, was charmed by the boy. Along with his alphabet, Edward was learning Greek and Latin. Yet, Cox told Katherine, he found it difficult to handle his pen, to make the simple letters that would ultimately form handwriting. Edward later told Katherine he didn't like to write. He'd much rather be outside riding, playing at quoits or stickball with other court children—even just walking with Mary or Bess! Lady Bryan said that all the child's activities were even more rigidly supervised since his illness for Edward was not as robust as Elizabeth. When he was deprived, the lady sighed, there were often difficult scenes in the royal nursery.

Even for one so young, Edward Tudor was very aware of his position. At times, Katherine hid a smile as he stood, imitating his father, his small feet wide apart, as she and other court ladies bowed to him. Once that was accomplished, he was as likely to fling himself upon an adoring Mary or grab Elizabeth's hand and cry, "Bess, come and see the sword our father has brought!" Or, "My Lady Latimer, I am tired of being indoors! I would ride and see my dogs!"

In the late afternoon, Katherine often sat in the nursery with Kate Brandon or Mary when Lady Bryan went for a visit with friends or simply for a much-needed walk. Anytime the weather was inclement or if Edward coughed or sneezed, he was made to stay inside. Once, feeling bored and deprived, when he knew even a display of childish temper wouldn't work, he climbed on Katherine's knee and asked to be told a story. Katherine recounted several tales Maud Parr had made a nightly ritual and several others she'd learned from her stepchildren in the North. Edward appeared willing to listen endlessly and, when even tears would not gain him outside freedom, he frequently sought Katherine out to hear more. Katherine sent Bessie to Parr House for those books she herself had favored as a child. Some might be beyond the boy's understanding, but she knew that just the solace of being held, her chin on his shining hair, was comforting to the child and as much an attraction as the tales she told.

It was on just such a day as Katherine was reading of dragons, sorcerers and spirits that the king unexpectedly entered the nursery. Edward flew to his father who swept him up but, as Katherine prepared to leave, Henry urged her to stay. Together, they helped Edward arrange a New Year's gift —tiny wagons and carts, with servants and household officials—in a procession such as he'd often seen from his nursery window. At the head was a lordly figure on horseback and behind him the courtiers and horses to draw the vehicles wherever the majestic figure commanded. After much thought, the buildings—little cottages, inns, a church and a noble mansion—were placed about a small green some distance from the procession. Willingly, the king deferred to his son when Edward suggested the mansion be put nearer the church.

"Then no one will get wet when they walk to worship." Henry smiled as he dropped the tiny church near the larger building.

"But don't you see it is better to watch what goes on in the church?" Edward was impatient to be understood. "The church causes you such trouble I wonder you wouldn't want to see what they do!" The boy reached out and moved the building even closer. "Now no one will honor the Pope here"— he pointed to the church—"or those who live here"—pointing to the mansion—"will see and tell the king." Proudly, he picked up the little carved figure at the procession's head and placed it as if to enter the mansion.

Henry smiled and shook his head, ruffling his son's hair fondly, while Katherine wondered how and what Edward had heard of his father's trouble with the church. She kissed the child affectionately as, reluctantly, he went off with Lady Bryan for his afternoon nap. Making ready to leave, Henry indicated he'd accompany her. In the outside hall, he lifted her hand to his lips. "You've been very good to us these many weeks, Kate," he said, "and we are grateful. Mary told us only yesterday what a help you've been with the children. They've all missed having a mother—all except Mary, and God knoweth that was as much sadness as if there'd been a death." He stopped, still holding her hand. "There are times, Kate, when we remember what it was like with Tom and Maud Parr. Childhood seemed much easier then! We know it has been difficult for the children. . . ."

A sudden noise from the courtyard caught the king's attention. At the window Katherine saw several councillors—Chancellor Audley, Charles Brandon, Anthony Denny and Lord Privy Seal Fitzwilliam—dismounting from their horses, as Thomas Wriothesley brought up the rear.

Quickly, with only a sudden handclasp, the king was gone, walking as fast as his bad leg permitted. Katherine made her way toward her chamber, thinking the Suffolks could escort her back to Parr House. Now that Charles was there, he must get permission from the king for her to leave. She'd have mentioned it herself if Henry hadn't left so hurriedly. She was telling Bessie as much when the door opened and a white-faced Kate Brandon gasped and said, "It's been decided today. The queen, that Rochford woman and young Culpepper are all guilty. They are to die."

CHAPTER XXII

Oh, what a godly act should it be to Your Excellent Highness to bring such a sort of people to a knowledge of God's laws, the country so necessary to your dominions, by reason whereof so many souls should live in quietness. . . .

—Lord Lisle to Henry VIII during the English campaign to subdue Scotland

Two months later, the queen remained at Sion House where she'd been sent after her arrest. Katherine's sister, Ann Parr Herbert and a Borough stepdaughter, now Lady Tyrwhit, her ladies-in-waiting, were ordered not to leave her side. Katherine, genuinely concerned for the queen, learned from her sister Ann's almost undecipherable handwriting that Catherine Howard was fretful, often sad and, at times, hysterical. Then, quickly, the mood would pass and she'd urge them to sing and dance, vowing the king was so much in love with her he'd forgive her and see she came to no harm.

But at court Katherine heard differently. There the Privy Council made little secret it was eager to carry out the death sentence before the king changed his mind. Thomas Wriothesley had interrogated all the queen's friends from Lambeth House days. "They've even put the old Dowager-Duchess in the Tower, telling her she ran a bawdy house instead of a home!" Kate Brandon said angrily. "The man is a snake and he'll make the most of this chance to fight Norfolk's influence with the council. After all, the duke is the one who promoted Catherine's chances with the king." Kate said the duke was frightened half out of his wits and had fled to his country home, Kenninghall, in Norfolk. "And I think this time he has good cause for worry for he also promoted the Boleyn's cause and the king is not likely to forget that both women were his nieces. Now he only wants to be as far away from Henry as possible. He wrote the king he thought the queen's actions abominable and said he was very perplexed. Charles says he's never seen him so disturbed."

"He paid scant attention to Catherine until she was queen. Then he was eager for the Howards to receive great favors from the king's hand. And now that she needs them, they fly like gulls to a safe haven!" Katherine was scornful. "This girl is not like the others. The old queen gave as good as she got and the Boleyn was dragged down proclaiming her innocence and fighting to the last. This one does not have the wits! The king has always found an excuse when he wanted his freedom. He could have this marriage annulled and put her in a nunnery. I think, left alone, that is what he would choose." But deep in her heart Katherine wondered if even the king would stand against the council on a matter that touched him so deeply.

Within days she had her answer and the council had its way. Descriptions of Catherine Howard's intimacies with Francis Dereham were bruited about openly in the City and, though both the queen and Thomas Culpepper denied their backstair meetings throughout the Northern progress had been adulterous, the situation emphasized a sexual need on the queen's part that the king apparently was not satisfying. The implication that he was impotent or inept in bed—also implied in the Boleyn trial—struck deeply at Henry's self-esteem, just as Wriothesley and his colleagues intended. Quickly, he ordered the sentence on Dereham and Culpepper carried out. On a cold December day, the two men were drawn on hurdles from the Tower to Tyburn. There Culpepper was beheaded—a last minute indulgence from the king for his former Gentleman of the Privy Chamber. But there was no such clemency for Dereham. He was hanged, taken down, his innards ripped out and then quartered. Both heads were later set on London Bridge.

In the following days, as the City held its breath waiting for action against the queen, Katherine went to Whitehall to visit Mary Tudor. One result of the queen's misfortune was that the king had asked his elder daughter, now living at Hanworth, to stay at court. Mary was overjoyed to have her father so near. They often rode together, coursing through the great forest outside Whitehall or along "the king's road" to Chelsea, once even spending the night at Henry's little manor house with only a few attendants. Mary told Katherine her father was devastated by the queen's infidelities. On one hand he wanted her to suffer as much as he was suffering. On the other, he blamed her orphaned youth and lax relatives.

Katherine found the Duchess Anne of Cleves in Mary's chambers. She had brought Elizabeth from Richmond for a visit with her father. Mary, looking happier and healthier than Katherine had seen her in months, was at the virginals playing while Anne and the little girl capered about the room. The king's elder daughter was a superb musician, a talent Katherine did not possess but could appreciate and, at the duchess' urging, she joined them in a circle as Mary played even faster and they spun swiftly about the room.

Suddenly the door opened and, with no announcement, the king entered. Quickly, everyone fell to their knees as Henry gestured impatiently.

"Enough, my ladies! Get to your feet again and let us see your merriment! It is more cheerful here than in there," he gestured toward the Privy Council door.

As Elizabeth ran to embrace him, Katherine thought the king was going to brush her away but, sighing, he leaned down and kissed her on the cheek as she clung to his arm. Katherine was surprised at how greatly Henry had aged. He'd always been—with his unusual height—an ageless giant she'd known since childhood, bluff and good-humored, his ringing laugh and high color impressively distinctive. Now his eyes were red-rimmed with fatigue and the pouches beneath them more prominent than before. Overnight, he'd become an old man. There was more white than auburn in his hair and his girth had widened tremendously. Charles Brandon said that Henry often took out his frustration at the table with too frequent glasses of wine and hippocras in between.

He stood now, his younger daughter gazing up at him adoringly, obviously at a loss what to do. Katherine wondered what she might suggest. Suddenly Mary, smiling broadly, began playing again. The king responding took Elizabeth to the center of the room and bowed deeply. The little girl was enchanted. With precise formality, she made a deep curtsey, then took the king's extended hand. Together they danced in a circular fashion about the room as Katherine and Anne watched. Mary deliberately kept the music's beat slow for it was obvious the king's leg did not allow him to leap and prance about as he had years ago. Katherine saw him wince several times, but he gamely led the little girl to the dance's end, then sat down, breathing hard, next to the Duchess Anne.

"Ah, Your Grace still dances well . . . and you have pleased both your daughters and Lady Katherine and me, sire!" Anne beamed, her pleasure at seeing her former husband and his children together very evident. Katherine could see Henry was still puzzled by the transformation his Flemish queen had undergone as soon as she was divorced. Previously, he'd disapproved of and ridiculed her outmoded dress and coiffure, her guttural speech and the belligerent manner she'd adopted to hide her early disappointment and confusion. Now, Katherine had to avert her face to hide her smile as he gazed appreciatively at the smartly dressed, beautifully coiffed woman with her regal bearing and exquisite jewels. Even Anne's accent made her English speech all the more charming. The Cleves woman had endeared herself to everyone; Katherine had grown especially fond of her and was impressed by the way she'd solved her formidable problem. She'd given Henry everything he wanted, accepting her freedom and a fortune in return. And then she'd proceeded to make herself as physically attractive as possible, eagerly studying her new language and her adopted country's customs, wearing what she pleased and doing as she chose. One result of the transformation had been that both Mary and Elizabeth now had easy access to visit their stepmother who was treated at court as the king's "beloved sister."

Katherine wondered if Henry would ever realize what Anne had accomplished—and why. Without uttering a reproachful word, she'd shown the king how wrong he'd been. Now there appeared to be genuine understanding and even affection between them. If for no other reason than such a relationship was good for Henry's three children, Katherine was happy that one queen at least had escaped heartbreak or worse.

* * *

Thomas Cranmer made one final effort to save Catherine Howard's life. If she'd admit to a precontract with Francis Dereham, of engaging in carnal relations with him, he told the girl, then in the eyes of God and the church she was a married woman. As such, she'd never been legally wed to Henry Tudor or been a Queen of England.

But Catherine would not agree. She was a Howard, she cried, and never would she have taken Dereham as a husband! She'd been foolish and misguided, yes. She'd accepted his gifts and admitted him to her bed. But there'd been no precontract and under no circumstances would she ever have married him.

Her forceful rejection could have only one result and on a lowering February day, while darkness mercifully hid the rotting heads of her former lovers still impaled on London Bridge, Charles Brandon escorted the queen to the Tower. There, still waited upon by Ann Parr Herbert and Lady Tyrwhit, she prepared to die.

"It's almost as if she's glad her agony will soon be over," Ann told Katherine on a quick visit to Parr House to borrow some clothing, her own being too far away to obtain in the little time she could leave her royal charge. "She's even begged the council not to inflict their displeasure with her on her family. Family, ha! They've all fled and left her to her fate." Ann wiped her eyes. "Jesu, Kate, she's but a child! Wise beyond her years in many ways, but a child in others. But she says there's nothing left for her. Should she be pardoned, what could she—a former queen—do? She would hate a nunnery and could never marry again. She says death will wash away her sins, though she never thought her actions sinful at the time. She has sworn to me, crossing herself and crying, that she never knew Culpepper carnally. Dereham, yes, but not Tom Culpepper and she feels by flirting with him, she sent him to his death. She says she wanted to lie with him and had there been a safe opportunity, she'd have done so. I think the king knows this—and now he'll never rest until she's gone."

On the night before she was to die, Catherine Howard requested the block be brought to her Tower cell so she might practice fitting her head onto it, for she was determined to make a dignified end. The next morning, composed, accompanied by her tearful ladies-in-waiting and a subdued and chastened Lady Rochford who was accused of aiding the queen in her frivolous and romantic pursuits, Catherine left her cell for the last time. Uttering her belief in Christ and asking the people's prayers, the queen meekly lay her head on the block. The executioner was swift and her end was merciful. She was followed by Lady Rochford who said her sentence was just, for she'd made shameful evidence against her husband, George Boleyn, years ago. Within moments of her speech, two bloodied, headless bodies were wrapped in sheets and quickly removed from the scaffold.

A few miles away, at Whitehall's gate, Catherine Howard's brother William and cousin Henry Howard, the Earl of Surrey, paraded through the streets, finely dressed and in a festive mood. It was their way of showing they did not share the family disgrace and approved of the queen's brutal end.

*　*　*

England's worsening relationship with Scotland soon erupted into outright war. Margaret Tudor, Henry's older sister, the mother of young King James V, had recently died and it was soon evident that France's ploy to keep the English army busy with their Northern neighbor, thus eliminating any aid to Spain, had succeeded.

But suppressing the Scots was not as easy as Henry and his advisers had anticipated. At Haddon Rig, ten thousand Scots confronted the English who, vastly outnumbered, had little recourse but to fall back or be slaughtered. Shocked, Henry ordered the aging Duke of Norfolk—eager now to be back in the Crown's good graces—with forty thousand English to cross the Scottish border. During the five-day rout, his troops burnt villages, destroyed an abundant harvest, put the torch to homesteads and churches and laid waste to the countryside along the Tweed which Norfolk wrote, was "barren, wild, cold and utterly ungarnished with wood." Henry hoped the lesson would be obvious to James, writing the young monarch he regretted having to use arms.

But, unexpectedly, James retaliated. Courageously raising a larger army, he advanced on the Border's western end where he knew Sir Thomas Wharton had only two thousand men. Although outnumbered, Wharton, a brilliant strategist, kept his head, cleverly maneuvering the Scots into a swamp, Solway Moss, where they were trapped by the River Esk swollen with heavy rains. Panic, insubordination and terror engulfed the weary Scotsmen and there followed a debacle during which many were drowned or taken prisoner. The thirty-year-old Scottish king, watching from a nearby hilltop, could scarcely believe what his uncle's army was inflicting upon the pride of Scotland. Ill with fever and heartbroken, James returned to Falkland Palace. There he learned that his wife, Mary of Guise, had given birth to a daughter, Mary Stuart, at Linlithgow Castle, three days earlier. The king's fever did not abate and, within a day, with no display of the fiery temper and reckless disposition for which he was known, James V quietly died. With no male heirs, the little girl would one day be Queen of Scots.

In London, there was a joyous celebration, dampened for Katherine by the news that Thomas Seymour had gone directly from the North on an embassy to Vienna. She wept with disappointment for word of the victory had meant one thing—that Thomas would soon be back at her side. He'd scrawled a few lines which Charles Brandon gave her when he returned with the victorious Norfolk. "I hate to go, my Kate, but I have no choice. I miss you more each day, my love, and long for us to be together. But I am not sorry to leave this carnage. . . ."

Tearful, Katherine put the letter away, glad Thomas had left the desolate Border. She knew the scenes he must have witnessed. Just the same as during the Pilgrimage of Grace—bloody, brutal, unjust and often needless. She wished he could have come directly home where she could have offered some comfort. Why was it that fate seemed determined to keep them apart?

* * *

To temper her disappointment, Katherine went to Snape Hall, her former Yorkshire home, to see her Latimer stepchildren, John and Margaret, both parents of broods of handsome children. She wandered through Snape's comfortable old rooms and galleries, still reminiscent of John's presence. All his beloved treasures were in place reminding her of the night she'd feared for them, the night Margaret had confronted the pilgrimage marchers on the stairs. She missed Bessie, who'd been so much a part of her life at Snape. But Bess had decided to use the opportunity to visit her parents at Burneside. Katherine knew her companion did not want to see the rooms and terraces, the familiar walkways where she'd fallen in love with Robert Aske or the courtyard where she'd said her last goodbye.

Katherine was shocked at the ruins she saw on her way north. The holy houses were now gone. All that remained were roofless walls bearing delicate traceried stonework almost black against the gray sky. Inside, the tombs, shrines, the glorious sculptures, carvings and paintings had been ruthlessly ripped, torn, hammered and mutilated. The destruction of the monasteries was now complete, her stepson said, and the more profitable nunneries, chantries, hospitals and other religious buildings—even coalfields which had been their property—all had been sold or given away and their wealth distributed to those who were the king's friends.

"There's a whole new gentry up here now, Katherine, wealthier and with more holdings than even the Parrs. And most of them weren't even known at the old king's court! It's a good way for Henry to insure their loyalty. I'm glad my father didn't live to see it, although he often said my world would not be like his." John's smile held a trace of bitterness. "Those families aren't likely to forget the source of their new wealth and they'll do as the king orders whether it concerns the church or the government. Henry learned much from Cromwell. . . ."

Katherine used her time at Snape for the studies she'd neglected for Thomas Seymour's company. Parliament had recently enacted several acts that gave Henry Tudor—already a king—the powers of an emperor and a Pope as well. In the church, articles now declared how one should regard and accept the sacraments. They demanded priestly celibacy, the necessity of the Mass and confession. Henry had made it known he expected his nobles and those newly wealthy families to set a good example by steadfast compliance to his new religious doctrine. Properties once given could just as easily be taken back.

Katherine read the reformers' tracts, the books and pamphlets now smuggled into England. She did not discuss them with her stepchildren, still as true to the old faith as their father had been. But when John questioned her about what was happening to religion in London, she was truthful.

"I think the king is returning more to the Romish belief, John, although he'll never acknowledge the Pope again. He calls him 'the Bishop of Rome.' He listened to Norfolk before the queen's disgrace, although I know many on the council prefer the reforming beliefs of such as old Cranmer, the Archbishop of Canterbury. But the man is a scholar, not a zealot like Stephen Gardiner or the Bishop of London. It is difficult to know what the king really believes for he follows the advice of many who have only their own interests at heart. He does not always consider what the people really want." Katherine was surprised at so easily putting into words what she'd felt for many months, for it appeared Henry Tudor could vacillate like the common man where his faith was concerned. And the more he wavered or changed his mind, the more people took matters into their own hands, seeking for themselves and for their children. A whole new generation had grown up knowing only that the Pope must be reviled. Most did not even know why, Katherine told John.

"That's not so here in the North, Kate, and never will be," John replied, looking more like his father than ever. "It will never happen here. People have died for the belief once and they'd do it again."

"Pray it never comes to that, John," Katherine whispered, "but as for London—I don't know. I don't know. . . ."

* * *

On her return to Parr House, Katherine again commenced the weekly study sessions with Kate Brandon, Joan Dudley, Joan Denny and others who were enthusiastic for church reform.

It was at such a study session that Bessie brought Anne Askew to Parr House. While at her parents' Northern home, Bessie learned that Anne had visited her husband. Squire Kyme ordered her to be an honest mother to those children who scarcely remembered Anne; she'd been away for over two years. He wanted a wife at home, not a religious zealot some called a heretic, flaunting her misguided knowledge in front of decent people and endangering them all!

Bessie said Anne had refused all his demands. She cared little whether he thought her a heretic or not. It was her mission in life to spread the Word of God and if Squire Kyme wanted a divorce, that was fine with her for she never intended to live with him again.

Anne's father had consoled his son-in-law, Bessie said, and privately she felt the Askews were relieved to see Anne go. For years, she'd been nothing but trouble and it had all come from learning to read and write. Katherine felt that roiling of guilt, that feeling that she alone was responsible for the way Anne had chosen to live her life.

Yet when Anne arrived with Bessie, her delight in being at Parr House again very evident, Katherine felt only a genuine affection for the tall, handsome, well-formed woman with her high color and piercingly alive eyes. She greeted Anne warmly, touched by her pleasure at seeing her teacher again. There was really little difference, Katherine realized, in what she or Anne Askew thought on religious matters. But the way they pursued that interest was very different indeed. Katherine was content to study, to read, think and discuss. Anne wanted to instruct, argue, harangue if necessary and insist—always—that her opinion was the true one, the only one that mattered.

Katherine had greeted Anne warmly, touched by her evident pleasure at seeing her old confidante and teacher again. Later, after the others had left, she accompanied Anne while the girl pored over the books in Katherine's chamber. Stroking them lovingly, she cried, "I remember when we read that one, my lady. Oh, that meant so much to me! I owe you so much, Lady Latimer, so much! I want you to be proud of me."

Katherine wanted to reply she'd be prouder if Anne used more conservative and less strident methods to pursue her calling, but she knew the girl would go her own way. She suspected that no matter who said what about any subject that interested Anne, if the opinion wasn't what the girl herself believed, neither king, council nor church would change her mind. And again she knew, with disturbing awareness, that she was more than partly to blame.

* * *

Then all thoughts of Anne Askew were cast aside. Thomas was back. With no notice whatsoever, he appeared one late afternoon in the Parr House courtyard, thinner and less jovial, with a maturity only the battlefield could give stamped on his features. There were no words as he enfolded Katherine in his arms and kissed her. She clung to him, reveling in the tight embrace, the feel of his lips on her cheeks and neck. "Kate, my Kate!" he whispered, "God knoweth it has been too long, sweetheart. How I've waited for this moment. . . ." And he kissed her again, long and deeply, uncaring as was Katherine that behind them the Parr House servants were watching from kitchen, stable and house.

Once inside, over refreshments, it was as if the months apart had not happened at all. Thomas said he could not describe the conflict on the Border. Though it had sickened him, he was exuberant that the English had won. "I find there is more of the soldier in me than I thought," he laughed, his arm about her as they sat near the fire and Katherine poured more wine for him.

"I know the sights only too well, my lord," she said quietly. "Though the cause was different during the pilgrimage, I am sure the results were the same: death, torture, bloody quarters of what had been men hung high. And desperate hardship afterward for their families. Don't tell me any more, Thomas. I've seen it all before. Have you seen the king?"

Thomas shook his head. "Not yet. But tomorrow I will see him and report to the council. Edward is at Hampton Court also and I want to see the boy. It's been almost a year! I hear he looks more like my good sister every day." Katherine recounted the scene with the little prince and Dr. Butts during which Thomas laughed delightedly, his white teeth gleaming below the black mustache, his handsome features relaxed and appealing. A new leanness emphasized an almost saturnine look that neither Jane nor Edward Seymour possessed. Clearly, Thomas was a throwback to a non-Seymour ancestor. Hoping to sound casual, she asked about his plans.

"I will see the king and report on my activities these many months, Kate. I'll also tell His Grace that your brother is very well liked in his new position and has won much support from the people. He administers justice carefully and honestly, although I don't know how long he'll be content to live in the North! I want to ask the king for a residence away from court. I'm not as young as I was and the embassies he's sent me on have been trying, Kate. Older men, used to their firesides, withstood the Scottish discomforts better than I! Now I'd like a home and an assurance that I may serve my king at court in some position nearby, although Jesu forbid he send me to Wales or even to Ireland. And I do not long for the Continent again. Now I think I might ask for some grace and favor and then . . ." he leaned over to embrace her, "and then, my Kate, we must talk."

Katherine felt tears behind her eyes. It was just as she'd thought and as she so often told her sister and Kate Brandon. Thomas did love her and they'd wed as soon as he knew his future was assured. The king was getting no younger either and if he was to give Thomas a just reward, it must be soon. She said as much to her companion.

"Don't be surprised when you see Henry, my lord. He looks older than you remember—the queen's death was nigh his undoing. He's worried for more than a year about the war. Be patient if he doesn't succour you at once."

Later, as Katherine kissed him goodbye in the courtyard, Thomas told her the first news he'd heard that morning on arrival in London was of Hans Holbein's death. "I was surprised and sad," he said as they walked toward the servant holding his horse. "He never finished that portrait of you, did he, my dear? A pity, for he was the best. And he wasn't even that old."

As she went in search of Bessie to tell her of Thomas's return, she thought that—in an odd way—Holbein had died at a time when there was to be a great change in her own life. Her first association with the king's sergeant-painter had occurred during the time when she'd first met Tom Seymour. When he'd been nothing but a teasing, witty gallant, intent upon flirting and impressing her, wondering if she was likely material for a casual affair.

And now, with Holbein's death, so apparently had ended all resemblance to that eager courtier, hoping for an extramarital romp with any willing court lady. Thomas had returned from the war and his diplomatic embassy visibly matured and anxious for a settled future with a wife of his own. And once he'd seen the king, Katherine thought, Henry could hardly help but reward him. Then he'd come back to her and they could make their plans.

*   *   *

The following day, accompanied by Lady Denny and Lady Dudley, whose husbands had left earlier for the court, Katherine went to Whitehall where she entered the procession bound for the Presence Chamber.

There Katherine saw her brother for the first time in months. Anne Stanhope Seymour, now the Countess of Hertford, was talking with Ann Herbert who appeared recovered from her ordeal of attending the dead queen. The countess—easily the most distinguished woman in the room—was splendidly dressed in deep crimson velvet with broad bands of cloth of gold, dotted with tiny jewels, at the neckline and sleeves. The gown must have cost a fortune and Katherine wondered how Edward Seymour, even with the bounty the king had given him, could afford such extravagance. As her eyes met those of the countess, Anne Seymour appeared to read her thoughts and pointedly looked in the other direction. It had not been a snub; she simply appeared not to have seen Katherine.

As she crossed the room to join Mary and Kate, a fanfare of trumpets announced Henry's appearance and, with the others, she went on her knees as the king appeared with the former queen at his side. Following Henry at a discreet distance was Thomas Seymour. Katherine's heart beat more strongly. If his sister-in-law was the most distinguished woman in the room, Thomas was the most striking man. His dark hair, newly trimmed, gleamed in the light of hundreds of candles. He carried his cap beneath one arm; the other was clasped tightly on the hilt of the sword at his waist. If Thomas had been with the king—before Henry had seen anyone else—then perhaps his fortune had been accomplished. What a celebration they would have! She hoped he'd come to find her, but instead he went to his brother Edward and whispered something in his ear. Quickly, they both slipped out a nearby door—an unusual and impolitic gesture—since the king was already in the room and no one was supposed to leave until he did, unless given express permission. Katherine wondered where Thomas had gone and why he appeared so somber on such a happy occasion.

For the next hour, absorbed as she was in seeing her friends, Katherine watched for Thomas's return. Suddenly, the trumpets blew again and Henry prepared to leave. Aghast she hadn't paid her respects, she moved quickly forward toward the dais where Henry waited. Suddenly, Lord Sussex came forward and, bowing, said, "My Lady Latimer, the king would like you to remain after the others have gone. He will see you in his chamber." He nodded toward the room from which the king had entered. Puzzled, Katherine followed Sussex, wondering what the others would think. Again she wished Thomas would return. Perhaps they might even see the king together.

It was Henry's private sitting room beyond which, undoubtedly, was the royal bedroom. This was the room in which the Duchess Anne and Thomas had seen the king. What could have concerned such an odd trio?

From the window, as she waited for the king, Katherine watched the horses, wagons and litters waiting to take the nobles back to the country homes they'd left months ago. Everywhere, people joyously called to one another, waving and shouting as they left the palace courtyard. She looked for Thomas in the crowd, but neither he nor his brother nor sister-in-law was in sight.

At last Henry entered and, after making a deep curtsey, she sat in the chair he indicated opposite him. Candlelight touched the grayed auburn hair and beard, emphasizing the lined and seamed face, the heavy pouches under his eyes—eyes that suddenly appeared nervous and uncertain. Katherine had never seen the king when he was not in command of every situation and she waited, wondering what she should say and why she'd been summoned. She was surprised as he fidgeted restlessly with the gold braid on his cap before clapping it back on his head. She was about to inquire after the health of the little prince—always a safe subject—when Henry, sighing, turned to her, his face serious.

"Kate, my dear, we know you're wondering why you were summoned here, especially after such a large gathering. We should have had you here alone. But this has been a taxing time for everyone and we thank God for the victory He has given us." As he crossed himself, Katherine did the same. "We go to Hampton tomorrow for everyone has gone to see the families they left behind and we would see our son Edward for soon it will be his birthday."

Katherine, apprehensive, wondered if Henry's diffidence concerned Thomas and the Duchess Anne of Cleves. Should she ask? If it concerned something unpleasant, something she must explain or defend, she might fail and incur Henry's displeasure. She felt the palms of her hands grow moist as a fearful anticipation filled her. Angry with herself for not having put the king at ease more quickly, she replied, "He will be six, sire, isn't that right?"

"Six, Kate, six years since his mother left us." Henry sighed, glancing out the window, still preoccupied. "They have not been happy years, my dear, as you know. But we accept our share of any mistakes. . . ." Sighing again, he turned and then, surprisingly, pulled his chair closer and took both her hands in his.

"My dear Kate, you know how often we've told you of our love for your parents. You know how well your family has served our father and us. We've always known, but only recently realized, how much you've given to our children and to those families and friends close to us, like my Lord and Lady of Suffolk. And our good servants Dudley and Denny. We've noted for the past year, Kate, a very unpleasant year, how quietly and . . ."—Henry sought the right word—"how *elegantly* you fit into every aspect of our life— family, court and wherever we may be. Your mother and our sister were dear friends. Now you and our daughter are as close as Maud Parr and Mary were. My children, every one of them, love you dearly. You're more a sister to our Mary than poor Bess will ever be—and it isn't just the difference in their ages. Ah, Kate, we have few secrets from you or your family. You know us well! We remember you growing up in the schoolroom at Westminster. There's not been a year or an event you haven't shared with us since then."

Why, Katherine wondered, was the king rambling on in such a fashion? It was almost as if he were reminiscing to himself. Little beads of perspiration mingled amongst the reddish-gray hairs of his beard. He was looking directly at her and the eyes she remembered as so intensely blue were now faded and tired. Then, suddenly, he was no longer apprehensive; he seemed to know what he wanted to say.

"Kate, my dear, we would like you to be our wife . . . and queen."

For a moment, Katherine felt as if she'd been struck. Fear, hot and thrusting, invaded her very innards, engulfing her as her legs grew weak. She seemed to have lost completely the power to speak and knew her voice would be a mere squeak if she used it. But her brain was alive—alive with the implication of the king's words. A wife, a *queen*. Now she understood why the Duchess Anne had looked so stunned. Henry had paid his only living ex-queen the courtesy of telling her his plans. Then, shocked and sickened, Katherine realized he must have told Thomas also. But why Thomas? Of all the courtiers and nobles, the soldiers and prelates gathered in the chamber outside, Thomas Seymour was one of the least important. Why had the king told him?

Then she realized that somehow the king knew Thomas had planned to marry her. If Thomas had told his brother, Edward had probably told the king. If his countess knew it, she might have told Anne of Cleves. Somehow the king had known.

Yet she and Thomas had made no commitment—not yet. Both were still free. That was probably what the king had asked Thomas. If he were to marry again, there should be no precontract, no agreement with the woman he wished to be his wife. And, she was certain, the confirmation that there'd been no sexual relationship between his former queen's brother and the woman who'd now be his sixth queen.

All this ran swiftly through Katherine's mind as the king waited for her answer. But her brain was so involved with all she'd heard, she found it difficult to speak. How to word what she wanted to say? Then, suddenly, she heard herself blurting out the truth. Words she hadn't meant to say, but which came straight from her heart.

"Ah, sire, a queen? No, 'twould be more meet if I were to be your mistress!" Appalled at her words she could only clap a shaking hand to her lips, wishing she could recall what she'd said. How had she dared?

Henry rose to stand directly in front of her and, holding out his hands, drew her to her feet. His expression was half-humorous, but there was a glint of anger in his eyes. It was enough to make her regret her careless words. She should have been more circumspect and even humble. Henry had every right to be angry.

But instead, as he put his arms about her, she saw the anger disappearing and he laughed with delight.

"Now we know, my dear Lady Latimer, that we can trust you to speak honestly with us always. We knew that it would be so! But 'tis not a mistress we want, Kate, we want a wife! And someone to minister to our children! We don't have a lot of years left and we would try to make them happy ones for you. Would you do that for your king, Kate? You are young enough to live on after us and still have another life. Although, God knoweth, I've always wondered why your uncle didn't place you after John died. Only recently, we found the answer. We heard of Tom Seymour's attachment to you. We asked him about it today."

"And what did he say, sire?" Katherine held her breath. It was as she'd thought. Someone had informed the king and he'd questioned Thomas—and told Anne of Cleves—before he'd approached her. He was very sure, she thought. Henry Tudor was very sure of himself indeed.

"Tom said in all honesty he was greatly surprised by what we had in mind for you. We think in fact he was astonished as was our good sister of Cleves! Neither one said much after we told them what we were planning. Tom said he had only the greatest regard for you, but that he'd not spoken his mind and you'd promised him nothing. Is that right, my dear?"

Katherine nodded, seeing the scene in her mind's eye, even as she felt tears at the back of her throat. "Yes, sire, that is right. And what else did he say?"

"After that, we discussed his future. We've made plans which will be beneficial to him, Kate, and he will leave tomorrow on an embassy to Brussels, where he will go as our ambassador to the Queen-Regent with Dr. Wotten, Dean of Canterbury. If what I think will happen does happen, then he will go to Calais as Marshall of the Army. It is an important post and I think, after what I heard of his conduct in the North, one that he's equal to. He will receive other rewards in the purse and still continue to be our good brother-in-law and our son's uncle." Henry tipped Katherine's chin up so he looked her straight in the eye. "We don't think, Kate, his heart is very broken. His pride is even somewhat enlarged that someone he coveted—and might have won—is also coveted by a king. We love Tom as a man, Kate, but he's not the one for you. He is shallow and vain, very unlike his brother who is neither and he has an ambition that is not matched by his talents. You can do better, Kate. We're asking you to do better!"

Katherine knew if she didn't get away from the king soon the tears forcing themselves painfully in her throat were going to overflow. Certainly, Henry was not lying. Thomas had accepted his good fortune in exchange for no contest in the matter of a wife. It was as simple as that. She felt sadness, hurt and anger. Yet, she had to be fair—no one else in Henry Tudor's realm would challenge him in his choice of a wife, either! Thomas might be all the things the king said he was, but he was not a witless fool. Undoubtedly, he'd put as good a face as possible on a situation foisted on him without any foreknowledge at all.

Jesu! She felt her palms grow moist. Henry was twenty-one years older than she—old enough to be her father. Once again, an older man would be her husband and there would be another brood of stepchildren, this time royal. What, she wondered, would Kate Brandon say? And Mary? She'd be Mary's *stepmother!* She'd live in a palace with this heavyset bearded man at her side, share the intimacies of the royal bed and tolerate the royal mood. She wondered, a little bitterly, why fate had determined to choose her husbands when her heart lay with that younger courtier who'd just left for God knew where without any word to her at all?

The thought of Thomas brought tears to her eyes, tears she hoped Henry would think the emotional result of surprise and indecision. For how could anyone refuse a king? What would happen if she did? The fate of Catherine Howard was as fresh in her mind as what had happened to Anne Boleyn. The old queen had died alone and rejected. How could anyone regard Henry Tudor—no matter how appealing for the moment—and not be fearful?

Suddenly, Katherine remembered the old gypsy's prophecy. "Castles and a title. Not one man, but many," he'd said. And hands that were meant to touch crowns and scepters. Well, she'd wed twice, borne two illustrious titles and now a king was offering her a crown and scepter. If the gypsy had been right, how could she—a mere woman—fight what appeared to be her destiny? Wouldn't it be wiser to place her faith in God and hope for the best?

Never before had Katherine longed for someone, most of all her mother, to talk to. How proud both parents would be to see her in the queen's chair of estate, the wife of the man to whom they'd given love, friendship and service all their lives.

Gazing at Henry, Katherine's tears at last brimmed over and she shook her head in assent. There was no other way; she must make the best of it.

"Sire, you pay me great honor," she whispered, "and I beg you to forget my careless remark. I will indeed try to be a loving wife and a good mother to your children. I will try to undo the unhappy years, sire. . . ." She put a hand to Henry's beard, feeling the bristles sharp against her skin. As he smiled broadly and embraced her, she had a momentary glimpse of the young, splendidly handsome and confident giant she remembered before all "the troubles" began. Moved in spite of herself, she returned the embrace and kiss. The tears had disappeared.

As Henry released her, Katherine curtsied and said she must see her family. She would send a courier off that evening to the North, but the king must tell everyone else. Henry said he would inform the Privy Council immediately for he was going to Hampton Court to see his son.

Hampton Court. Katherine remembered that Thomas, too, planned to be at Hampton to see his nephew. She wondered what would happen when the man she'd hoped to marry met the brother-in-law she *would* marry. Would Thomas be surprised to hear she'd accepted the king's proposal? Probably not. Having stepped out of the picture at his sovereign's request, he'd left her little alternative. He hadn't even fibbed a bit and admitted he and Katherine Parr had planned to wed, that they had a precontract.

As she left the room, the king kissing her cheek gently at the door before summoning a chamberlain to escort her to the courtyard, Katherine wondered at her seemingly easy acceptance of this overwhelming situation that was going to change her life forever. She'd entered Whitehall relatively carefree and deeply in love with a man she hoped to marry. She was leaving the court destined to marry a king and hoping to forget the man who'd abandoned her. Why wasn't she shattered by this rebuff to her pride from one man and the exalting gift of sovereignty from another?

As she hurried to her servant holding her horse in readiness, she thought that old Senor Vives had been right. Vives had said that romantic love was dangerous and any woman marrying for such a reason would be duped and spend her life in sorrow. How much better then to be courageous and optimistic and proud!

Pride. That was it. Katherine had never spared herself in assessing her feelings or motives and now, she acknowledged, she was *proud*. Henry Tudor had chosen her for his queen knowing Parr blood was every bit as good—perhaps even better—than Tudor blood. The Parrs had been great lords of the North when young Owen Tudor, Henry's great-grandfather, had come out of Wales, a penniless and obscure nobody who would one day marry a king's widow and found a dynasty.

Riding quietly behind her steward, Katherine's confidence grew. Yes, she was proud—guilty of that glaring, exorbitant pride that priests and bishops all said was such a deadly sin. It was a welcoming feeling after all those months when her self-esteem had been battered by Tom Seymour's reluctance to speak out, to assure her he loved and wanted her only. Well, Tom Seymour had lost and she'd won a king, a crown, a family and all the honor England could give.

Arriving at Parr House, Katherine went in search of Bessie who'd be the first to know. She wondered what the man back at the palace was feeling. Was he thinking: I've won Kate Parr, twice widowed, thirty-one years old, daughter of dear friends, well educated and wealthy, one who will be kind to my children who love her, who will grace my bed and palace with beauty, charm and distinction? Was he thinking he, too, had done well?

Then she remembered all those other queens. What had they thought when the king proposed? Had they been proud, afraid, happy or despairing? Each had been different. And she, too, intended to be different. She would do her best to be a loving wife and a good stepmother, no matter that one daughter was only three years younger. She would strive to make a good life for all the family but, most of all, she meant to survive.

Katherine, the Queen K.P.
1543

CHAPTER XXIII

The long windows of St. George's Chapel at Windsor were dully gray, lacking the sunlight that normally caused the brightly hued figures of saints, angels, kings and princes to come alive. No slanting ray of gold, rose or blue curved about the massive pillars that soared to the vaulted ceiling the old king had commenced and his son finished some twenty-five years ago. Instead, the dimly shadowed light emphasized the carved bosses that ornamented the ceiling. Newly gilded and painted, they and the delicate stonework provided a fitting canopy for the tombs, statues and recumbent figures of knights and their ladies lying on alabaster pillows, hands clasped in eternal prayer.

Late-arriving courtiers stood at the chapel's rear with the common folk of the little village of Windsor. Though it was damply cold for an August day, everyone wanted to be there—to see the king, queen and the court and to pay their last respects to the great Duke of Suffolk whose body lay in the casket at the altar, covered by a purple and rose tapestry bearing the Suffolk coat of arms.

Seated in the first row, Queen Katherine sat between the king and a grieving Kate Brandon clothed in her widow's black. They listened as the priest extolled Charles Brandon's virtues—his service to king and country, his love of family and outstanding regard for duty and honor. Recently, said the prelate, the duke had distinguished himself during the war with France though he'd not been well. But he'd gone anyway, as his conscience dictated and God, in His infinite wisdom had brought him home safely to see his beloved wife and children before he died.

As the eulogy continued, Katherine held the duchess' hand. She knew Kate was still in shock for Charles had gone so quickly. Theirs had been a real love match and happy beyond what each had expected; the deep pain of Kate's loss was yet to come. The king had told her she should praise God her husband had died so suddenly for no one had despised weakness and illness more.

Katherine knew that Henry, too, felt the duke's death keenly. They were of the same age—fifty-four—and had been together since boyhood. The king had often said Charles was as dear to him as any brother, for Brandon had seen him through the loss of all his children by the old queen, each subsequent marriage and the unfaithfulness of two wives. There was nothing they hadn't shared.

It was just a little over two years since that July day Katherine had taken her place beside Henry in a small chamber at Hampton Court and, in a simple ceremony with their two families and closest friends watching, exchanged the vows by which she'd become Queen of England and wife to Henry Tudor. Charles had been absent in Scotland with her brother, but everyone else was there. A beaming Lady Mary and an exuberant Lady Elizabeth, each holding a hand of little Prince Edward, sober and obviously awed at the occasion by which, he'd been told, that nice Lady Latimer would become his stepmother. Edward Seymour, the Earl of Hertford and his countess, Anne Stanhope, had been properly deferential. Thomas had left on his embassy to Brussels several days before. A smiling Anthony Denny brought the best wishes of his wife, Joan, at home for the birth of their third child, while Joan Dudley lamented that her husband, now the Lord Admiral, was on duty with the navy in the Channel.

After the ceremony, Henry, beaming and proud, had taken Katherine by the hand and turning to the others said, "We give you your queen. . . ." As everyone went on their knees, she'd felt a startling awareness that, no matter how much she'd vowed not to change, everything and everyone about her was now different. There was now only one to whom *she* must bow and he was the portly, jovial man at her side, his seamed face wreathed in smiles, the blue eyes laughing and happy, much as she remembered him when he'd ruffled her hair in her father's presence and called her a "comely wench." Now he was her lord, master and king, as well as her husband and Katherine realized—no matter that those kneeling reverently were her own flesh and blood as well as friends who'd been dear for years—that she was isolated with Henry in that mystical aura that surrounded royalty. Now she was a queen and if she ever forgot it—which wasn't likely—someone kneeling or waiting to be spoken to or given a welcoming hand would certainly remind her.

As she held Kate Brandon's taut hand and listened to the priest's comforting words, her mind wandered. She had no need to hear anyone laud Charles Brandon for she'd known and loved the duke all her life, ever since her mother had told her that romantic tale of the time he'd gone to France to escort the French queen home—and then stayed to marry her himself. She knew his was a devastating loss and how the stricken woman beside her must feel. But the duke's two sturdy boys, Henry and Charles, sitting on their mother's other side, their eyes fixed firmly on the tapestry-covered casket, would be a comfort. Kate would not be alone.

Katherine thought of all that had happened since that simple wedding ceremony. She recalled the tears in her sister Ann's eyes and the pride in Will Herbert's that his sister-in-law was now the queen. Kate Brandon's joy had been infectious as she'd hugged Mary and Katherine together as Mary whispered, "my dearest *stepmother*, Kate!" which had caused all three to much laughter which they'd refused to explain.

Shortly after the ceremony, Katherine had given Mary two magnificent gold and ruby bracelets which, with Henry's permission, she'd taken from the royal collection in the Jewel Tower. Without his knowing, she'd added twenty-five pounds, for Mary's household was continually short of money. She'd also found a small necklace with a tiny diamond pendant for Elizabeth who was enchanted with her first piece of jewelry. Little Edward had bowed his blond head in submission and then quickly climbed onto her lap to look with interest on the supple Spanish riding gloves with small jeweled cuffs that she'd had made especially for him.

As his grateful children showed off their gifts, returning to embrace Katherine again, Henry had looked on nonplussed. "It's unusual for him to have all three about in the same room at the same time!" Ann Parr Herbert had whispered. "He doesn't know what to make of it! I can't remember that I've ever seen the prince with both his sisters at the same time. . . ."

Katherine had noticed their happiness too and on that long lazy summer progress that was her honeymoon, as the royal cavalcade wound through Surrey, danced and feasted through Buckinghamshire and Bedford, held musicales and pageants in Hertfordshire before returning to Nonsuch Palace in Surrey for a reunion with the children, Katherine had wondered how to approach her husband about having Mary, Elizabeth and Edward live at court.

Already, Henry had given her so much. Shortly before their first Christmas together, Sir William Parr had been summoned out of retirement and made Lord Parr of Horton and Henry's Lord Chamberlain. His namesake, Will Parr, raised to the rank of earl had been given Cromwell's old holding of Essex. Will Herbert was made the Earl of Pembroke with the gift of Wilton Abbey. Katherine had appointed her sister Ann, her "two Joans" and stepdaughters Margaret Neville and Lady Tyrwhit as ladies of her bedchamber. As her jointure, the king had signed over more manors, castles, boroughs, lands and leaseholds than she could remember; the one that pleased her the most was the little manor house in Chelsea. Her uncle had said, with great satisfaction, she was without doubt the wealthiest woman in England. When she jokingly repeated this to the king, Henry had laughed and said, "You probably have more money than we, Kate. But we have the Crown jewels and lands! However, you'll find you can spend only so much. The rest is only a responsibility." And he'd been wise enough to appoint her uncle, Sir Thomas Arundel, and her stepson-in-law, Rob Tyrwhit, to administer her estates and fortune.

She might, as her uncle and husband said, be extremely wealthy, but she'd been unprepared for the luxury that now surrounded her every waking and sleeping moment. Henry Tudor was a connoisseur of the rare and beautiful and at Whitehall, Richmond, Greenwich, Eltham, Oking and Oatlands, the palaces, manors and castles were filled with exquisite furniture of carved ebony, cedarwood, walnut or oak, inlaid with mother-of-pearl, ivory or rich gold or silver artwork. Heavy silks, satins, brocades, trimmed and lined with cloth of gold, seed pearls or other jewels, covered the chairs, bedsteads, couches or stools. Persian "Turkey" carpets lay on the floors and corridors, complementing the costly tapestries and arras hanging on the walls. The plunder of the churches and the loot of the monasteries and abbeys were evident in the great golden candlesticks, the illuminated manuscripts that adorned the royal library. With Kate Brandon at her side, Katherine had wandered through the Hampton Court rooms admiring the Venetian brocades, curtains of French lace and Chinese silks, the walls adorned with Flemish tapestries. She'd always considered her parents' treasures impressive, but they paled when compared to the hundreds of gold, silver, bronze and crystal ornaments, chandeliers, sconces and golden candle wheels in all the royal residences. There were porcelains, ewers and basins, plates, goblets, glasses and coffers, richly embossed, carved, gilded and jeweled in the staterooms and chambers used by the courtiers and those foreign dignitaries who seemed in constant residence.

All these riches were cared for by innumerable household servants from the lowly scullions to those keepers appointed by the king who kept the royal wardrobe, horses, dogs, birds, woodyards, pantries, chapels and stillrooms in order. There were more apothecaries, ushers, cupbearers, carvers, choirs, musicians, cooks, gardeners and secretaries than Katherine knew she'd ever get to know, although the king seemed at ease with most, many of whom had served him for years.

She was particularly fond of Will Somers, the king's Fool, with his slightly hunched back and craggy face. Will had a privileged position with Henry, for he'd lived at court for twenty years. Will was not treated—as some noblemen treated their household Fools—as a stupid pet, often forcing them to behave as such. He performed no outrageous antics or pranks, nor was he ever dismissed by a wave of the royal hand. Henry delighted in his mocking talk, his frank opinions, his unquestioned loyalty and his complete disregard of the royal temper. "My, my, Our Majesty is in a nasty state today," he'd say when Henry bellowed at someone. If the king glared at him, Will Somers glared back, a staring match that often caused Henry to whoop with delight as he watched his Fool attempting to restrain a smile. Many had tried to use Will's influence with the king for their own good, but he'd have none of it and, with the same fearlessness he showed his sovereign, he scathingly denounced any attempt at bribery or coercion.

At Whitehall, Katherine and Kate crept into the Privy Council Room—where neither had ever been before—to gaze at the great wall fresco of King Henry VIII which Hans Holbein had completed just before his death. The artist had caught the king in a typical and familiar pose—feet apart, hand on hip, his eyes below his plumed cap gazing with cool indifference at the onlooker. His furred coat was richly adorned with rubies and diamonds, the great chain, heavy with gold, rubies and garnets and the small "H's" wrought throughout had been rendered with meticulous care. It was her husband to the life and Katherine marveled again at Holbein's incredible artistry. She wondered what he'd have made of her own portrait had she ever had it completed.

During those first months of her marriage, as she struggled to adapt to her new position, Katherine thought again about having her stepchildren live at court. Henry loved them all, but in different ways. He thoroughly enjoyed his elder daughter's company for Mary always made an unusual effort to please him. She'd play the virginals and they'd sing together, father and daughter, for both had excellent voices. Edward was his father's pride and delight and he always found it difficult to leave the boy. It was almost as if he still could not believe he had a son. Katherine worried about Edward. She wished he were sturdier, more demonstrative and outgiving, such as Elizabeth. His exercise, diet and studies were strictly ordered and observed, yet he remained pale and thin and more sober than she thought any six-year-old should be. Edward was so used to being surrounded by deferential servants, his nurse Sybil Penn, and other maids that once, when he was left alone with Katherine for a day, she found him ill at ease without more attendants about. It had taken some time for the boy to be comfortable with the attention of only one and some time before he truly believed he could call her "mother" which he now delighted in doing.

With Elizabeth it had always been different. If Henry ever allowed himself any unusual feeling of guilt for Mary's years of persecution and exile, for the fact that she was approaching a spinster's age because he'd made no marriage for her, his attitude toward his younger daughter was puzzling. Elizabeth's natural high spirits and intelligence often made him testy and impatient. She would sulk and then, feeling she wasn't receiving her fair share of attention, continue sullen until, exasperated, the king either sent her off with her governess or, sighing, would be more attentive until she was again smiling. Katherine soon realized Elizabeth's temperament was very similar to her mother's. Obviously Henry, too, saw a great deal of Anne Boleyn in her daughter. Yet, Katherine reasoned, Elizabeth was his daughter and should not suffer for the sins of the mother. Often she looked for traces of Henry in the little girl's features, remembering Mary's insistence that Elizabeth was not the king's child. The only resemblance was their almost identical coloring. Otherwise the child's oval face, dark eyes and long fingers were all Anne's.

Katherine wondered if Henry had any doubts regarding Elizabeth's parentage. Before he'd gone to the French War, she'd suggested he settle the Succession and a subsequent Act of Parliament had restored both Mary and Elizabeth to succeed to the Crown after Edward and his heirs. Henry had said at the time he did so with ease because Edward would marry young and certainly there would be heirs. There was precious chance the throne would ever go to Mary who, unwed, would be at the mercy of her council or her husband if she married later. Or, God forbid that it should pass to Elizabeth who was too bright and assertive for her own good, much less England's!

Once the honeymoon was over, Katherine spoke with Henry about having his children live at court. She stressed they'd never had a real home and that, with his myriad duties and obligations, he'd missed many of the joys of fatherhood. Henry didn't like to think he'd missed anything and, anxious to please his new queen, Katherine had had her way. Within weeks, whenever the court was at London, Greenwich or Richmond, the king's children were there also. It had brought Mary and Katherine closer than ever, had made both Mary and Henry more tolerant of Elizabeth and given sober-faced little Edward many moments of pure pleasure, especially when his father took him shooting at the butts in Smithfield or watched his riding lessons in the tiltyard or the back stableyard at Whitehall. When Henry's leg was so painful it was difficult to walk, he'd watch from his horse.

Katherine often took the younger children on the river in the royal barge and was rewarded by a show of color in the prince's fair skin and a tired Elizabeth who, unused to so much attention and activity, was sleepy-eyed and fatigued by the time they returned to Whitehall Stairs. On one memorable day, she and Mary rode with the children to the old schoolroom in Westminster Palace. The building had burned several years earlier, but the schoolroom wing was still standing. Picking their way through the debris left by Londoners looting the grounds for building materials, they'd arrived at the little chamber which the children gazed at with wide-eyed interest.

"It's so small," Elizabeth said, a bit disdainfully. And Katherine had to agree. Dust and dirt had settled on the shelves she remembered as bursting with books, tablets, writing materials and maps. Several little chairs with missing legs lay in one corner; no desks were left at all. The room where her mother, Princess Mary, the Brandon girls and other court children had studied was indeed smaller and grimier than she remembered and fetid now with the musty damp smells of river and decaying vermin. It was a dead place, with none of Vives's magical presence or Maud Parr's bright stimulation to lift the gloom. Seeing Mary felt the same, Katherine almost wished they hadn't come or that the wing had burned too.

*   *   *

Now, as the priest commenced a long chanting prayer, Katherine heard Elizabeth in the pew behind them whispering to little eight-year-old Lady Jane Grey. Henry said the child had behaved outrageously upon hearing of her grandfather's death. She'd locked herself in her room and cried throughout the night which had earned her her mother's loud condemnation and a heavy clout when she'd emerged for the funeral. Katherine sighed. She'd never understand Frances Brandon Grey and why the woman so disliked her little daughter for Jane Grey was a beautiful child, the image of the French queen with her long red-gold hair and large blue eyes. The rosy complexion that had earned her grandmother the title of "the Tudor Rose" was, in Jane, covered with freckles. Katherine wondered if Frances treated Jane so badly because she looked like her own mother. Frances had never been a beautiful child, always gaining attention through mischievous deviltry and arrogance. Perhaps that had made more of a difference than anyone thought. Jane often spent time at court as a playmate for the prince, for they were of the same age. Katherine never failed to wonder at the difference in the child when she was away from her mother's ominous presence. Jane was as smart as Elizabeth, as loving as the prince and as deeply religious as Mary. She enjoyed their companionship and it wrenched Katherine's heart to see how she always hated to go home.

As the chanting continued, Katherine listened to Elizabeth's whispers. Elizabeth knew all about sorrow and angry parents for, soon after she'd joined the royal household, she'd felt the full force of her father's anger. Katherine had been so delighted to have her stepchildren under one roof, she'd overlooked the challenge or danger of such proximity. An easy familiarity with his children was difficult for the king. Always before, their rare visits had been arranged, formal and predictable.

One evening, they'd all gathered in the little room off the Presence Chamber for prayers before bedtime. The king had been at his desk, ruffling through papers of monastic grants made by his Privy Council and, as Katherine knew, wondering who to name as Lord Chancellor for old Audley had died the week before. Katherine sat with Mary and Elizabeth by the fire, the prince engrossed with a toy at her feet. She'd taught Elizabeth a new embroidery stitch for a scarf the child was making for her governess' birthday. Elizabeth was quick to learn. Soon she was skillfully executing the stitch. After one row was done, she ran to show it to the king. As the child left her side without any warning, Katherine bit her lip. Henry never liked being interrupted—just as Elizabeth never liked being told what she couldn't do.

The king had looked at the embroidery, smiled absentmindedly and nodded, returning to his papers. But Elizabeth wanted more. She shook his arm, thrusting the embroidered cloth so the papers were obscured and forcing him to look at it more closely. Sighing, he did so, saying, "Yes, Bess. It is very pretty and we're sure the queen has been a help. You are very clever. Now leave off and go back to your chair for we have work to do and then we will have prayers."

Elizabeth had either resented her father's quick dismissal or the inference that her stepmother deserved more credit than she. Instead of leaving, she stood her ground, her childish anger visible by two red spots on each cheek. Katherine was about to bring her back to the fire when incredibly, in a clear voice, Elizabeth asked, "Did you treat my mother that way?"

For a moment, Katherine could not believe what she'd heard. Surely Elizabeth would never ask such a question! But then, the insistent little voice continued, "Why did you cut off her head?"

Henry's face paled as Katherine rose, frightened, hoping to get Elizabeth

out of the room before the king struck her. She saw that already the girl regretted her words and knew there was no escape from her father's anger.
Henry had stood up looking even taller than his six feet, his face now
flushed, the blue eyes narrowed with anger and even dislike. His fists were
clenched and Katherine knew if they'd been alone, he'd have slapped
Elizabeth—a blow the child appeared to expect. There were tears in her eyes
and her shoulders slumped as they always did when she was disappointed or
hurt. Katherine's heart went out to Elizabeth. What she'd said was deplorable and uncalled for, but she was still only eleven years old. Somewhere,
she'd heard about her mother. Heard, God knew what?

But Henry was beyond excusing his daughter. She'd committed an unbelievable blunder in mentioning someone he was determined at all costs to forget. Which was difficult at best when Anne Boleyn's daughter was now present every day, as demanding in life as her mother had been. As Katherine
held her breath, he'd looked at the girl and said, "Go to your chamber, Bess.
We don't wish to talk to you again. No, don't bother the queen. Just go
right now." Elizabeth, tears now brimming over, had dropped her needlework to the floor and quickly run from the room. Mary had sat with her
head bent over the embroidery she held in shaking hands. The little prince
was so engrossed in his own playing, he appeared not to have heard a thing,
although Katherine suspected he knew something was wrong, yet chose to
remain apart.

It had taken time to calm Henry, Katherine remembered. She'd tried to
mollify him and, at the same time, explain Elizabeth's behavior, regrettable
though it had been. In the end, she'd found—as she'd often found since—
that it was the wisest course when the king was in such a mood, simply to do
nothing. Not that she felt Henry's action wasn't justified. Elizabeth had
acted without thinking, bringing up a subject she intuitively knew was forbidden. Yet she'd gone ahead anyway. The king had a right to be angry with
such childish impudence.

Katherine had thought that in a day or two, the whole episode would be
forgotten. But the king would not be calmed. The following day he ordered
that Elizabeth be taken by Sir Thomas Heneage, her governess and several
servants to St. James's Palace and remain there at his pleasure.

"We built it for her mother and we'll see to it she finds that out too, if she
wants to be so inquisitive! She can stay there until we can bear to look upon
her again!" he'd shouted when Katherine asked to say goodbye to the child.
Henry had forbidden it and so she'd watched alone from a window as the
forlorn little girl and her companions walked toward the litter which would
take her to the palace at the edge of the Westminster fields. Neither
Katherine, the king nor Elizabeth knew then how long she'd have to stay.

It had been longer than anyone expected. Within weeks, England and
Spain had declared war on France and the king had gone abroad in person
to participate in the taking of Boulogne. Before his departure, he'd insisted
his wife act as Queen-Regent in his absence. It was a great honor and had

taken Katherine completely by surprise, for she'd expected he'd name Edward Seymour or Thomas Cranmer to rule with the aid of the Privy Council. When she said as much to the king, he bluntly told her she was the only one he trusted.

"The rest have their ambitions, Kate, and though they'd never betray us, they'll look too much for their own good along the way. With our absence, it would be easy to foster cliques and make decisions more for their benefit than ours. Seymour would be too generous with our properties and titles and would bedevil those councillors too old or too weak to stop him. Cranmer would work for more changes in the church's ritual than Gardiner or old Bonner want. No, we learned our lesson with Wolsey and Cromwell! We will make you our Regent and your good brain and kind heart will not forget whose place you take!" So Henry had gone, designating Seymour and Cranmer, along with the new Lord Chancellor, Thomas Wriothesley, to advise and support the queen. But her decisions were to be final.

Katherine went to Dover where the great fleet awaited its sovereign. Along the way, Henry reminisced about that other time he'd gone to France to attend the Field of Cloth of Gold. It was almost a quarter of a century ago, he said. "And your dear mother was with us, Kate, although we'd lost your father. Ah, but you were but a child then."

"Yes, sire, a little girl, but I can remember her leaving." Katherine wondered what Maud Parr would say now if she could see her daughter retracing her steps and left to rule during the king's absence. It would have been beyond Maud's belief that her seven-year-old Katherine, left so complacently at home, would one day occupy the place of her dear Katherine of Aragon.

During her regency, Katherine had acted as seriously as Henry had intended. She went to Hampton Court with Mary and Edward and couriers daily went to France with letters giving the king news of country, the court and his family. The Privy Council kept her informed, presenting the documents requiring her signature. Any that she judged important were written about to the king before signing. She became familiar with trade licenses, import fees, university and church personnel and more completely informed on the political situation in Scotland whose own Queen-Regent, Mary of Guise, had just refused an offer of marriage for her baby daughter, Mary Stuart, with little Prince Edward. Katherine knew how disappointed Henry would be for he'd considered the betrothal a good way of uniting Scotland and England. She became more aware of the jockeying within the Privy Council for position and influence as well as in the church whose bishops were bent on preserving their own authority and keeping the ritual from the sullying hands of the "re-formers" or "protest-ants."

One of the first letters Katherine wrote as Queen-Regent went to Elizabeth still in disgrace at St. James's Palace. If Henry had left all decisions to her, she reasoned, then her first decision would be to write to his younger daughter telling her of her father's absence. She couldn't bring Bess home but she could at least send the child a packet of new books and let her know she wasn't completely forgotten. At the letter's end she wrote her signature, "Katherine, the Queen-Regent." The letter was hardly of momentous importance—except to the child who would receive it. But the signature bothered her. Katherine remembered two others who'd borne the same name—the old queen and the Howard girl who'd treated her title and crown with less care than Edward took of his beloved toys. She wanted something in that signature to make it her own. Quickly, she took the pen and initialed "K.P." after the title, gazing at it with satisfaction. Now she'd not be confused with any other queen with the same name.

Ever since then, Katherine had written "K.P." in tiny neat capitals after her signature. No matter that Edward Seymour had lifted an eyebrow and Cranmer had smiled when they'd first seen it. Later, upon his return, the king had laughed outright when he reread part of her correspondence. Yet he'd never forbidden the initials.

She'd had an immediate answer from Elizabeth—a long letter in which the child poured out her loneliness and shame at being so humiliated and disgraced. She begged Katherine to ask for the king's forgiveness. Between the lines, it was easy to see Elizabeth Tudor had learned a valuable lesson. Direct and forthright confrontation might not be the best way to attain one's heart's desire—or the answer to one's problems. She didn't think Elizabeth would ever make the same mistake again.

But she did as the child asked and in each letter that went from Hampton Court to France, the king was told of his children's health and how much they loved and missed him. When he returned his greetings and affection to all *three* of his offspring, Katherine sent a letter flying to Elizabeth, receiving a quick reply from the girl, exultant that her father had apparently forgiven her.

By the time the king had returned, aglow with his triumphs, he was willing that his penitent daughter return to court. Elizabeth, now almost as tall as Katherine, had arrived just before her twelfth birthday. Approaching the king, she'd dropped a deep curtsey, waiting for his reaction. Henry had raised her gently and then embraced her; there was no reference to her year-long exile or the reason for it. Instead, he said he'd have her portrait painted by a talented artist—one almost as good as Holbein—who'd begged passage aboard the royal ship when it returned to England.

In the following days, as they selected a gown of bright crimson velvet with cloth of gold sleeves heavy with raised mosswork and a matching cap embroidered in pearls for the sitting, Katherine noted Elizabeth's sedate behavior, her hesitant responses and quiet preoccupation.

Only when they were first alone had Elizabeth shed her new seriousness and, throwing her arms about Katherine, had cried, "Oh, madame, it is so good to be back! I know how much I owe you, madame, and I can never thank you enough!" There were tears in both their eyes as Katherine embraced Elizabeth, musing somewhat sadly that she'd miss the impulsive, warmhearted little girl with her easy chatter and beguiling ways. Elizabeth had gone away a wounded child; she'd returned a wary and cautious adult.

The priest had finished the service at last and, amidst the scraping of chairs and the rustle of those kneeling in final prayer, Katherine and Henry prepared to leave. As the king rose, she placed her hand on his, for they must leave the chapel first. As Kate Brandon and her sons followed behind, Katherine glanced at Elizabeth. She had her arm about little Jane Grey who was still staring at the casket with swollen red-rimmed eyes. Katherine could almost read their thoughts. Jane had lost a grandfather, a defender, a belovedly secure giant. Elizabeth had almost lost someone too and she knew how devastated the little girl must feel. But now she was reunited with him and, luckier than Jane, she'd never again risk losing his love or approval.

* * *

In the months following the duke's death, Katherine found her husband's moods difficult and exasperating. She was no stranger to the obvious differences in marriage to an older man; Lord Borough had been four times her age and Lord Latimer over twice as old. Henry Tudor was no different. His opinions, standards and behavior were those of a fifty-five-year-old man who was also a king. And his health, primarily the leg condition he'd had for years, only made it worse. Dr. Butts had recently died and Henry fretted about his successor, Dr. Wendy, who seemed unable to please.

"We felt fine in France, rode comfortably and better than most and we return to find this!" The king pointed to the open leg wound which, unbandaged, was bloody with infected flesh that would not heal. The physician wanted to say that the constant riding and walking Henry had done during the French campaign had undoubtedly resulted in extra stress on the leg. He could only guess at the pain.

Katherine went through her mother's stillroom recipes, tried to recall what concoctions her stepdaughters had made at Gainsborough and, with the help of the royal apothecaries, brought preservatives, lozenges, cinnamon comfits and licorice pastilles for the king's enjoyment as he sat for hours with his leg propped upon a chair. When these failed to satisfy, Henry consulted astrologers and alchemists, dosing himself with stomach and liver plasters and applying one made from powdered pearls to his leg. Katherine found ointments and salves for dressing the ulcerated leg and even took that task upon herself when the doctor was absent. It was a messy task and not one she relished but a clean dressing was comforting to Henry. When he was restless she read to him, played dice or primero and, as tactfully as possible, urged less consumption of the strong mead and spicy dishes he favored. At times Henry complied; on other occasions he would snap at her sharply, saying he was not a child and she could keep her opinions to herself. Then she knew his leg was paining him more than usual.

"I know it hurts, but he should take better care of himself," Mary told

Katherine in an unusual criticism of her father. "The more anyone tries to help, the more he pretends he doesn't need it. But the time is coming when he won't be able to walk on that leg. And then what will he do?"

The same thought had occurred to Katherine. If her days could now be marred by the king's temper, what would they be like when he was completely incapacitated? Finally she and Mary—for Mary insisted on sharing the responsibility in case her father made a fuss—devised a large chair, strongly secured to a platform which had four poles, not unlike a litter. Six men—one at each pole and one on either side of the platform—could lift the king comfortably and carry him from room to room, to courtyard, terrace and horse. "It will save you steps, sire, and save your strength," Katherine explained when at first Henry had stubbornly refused to use the conveyance. "Your leg will have a chance to heal and then you won't need it." At last he'd agreed and, with no comment, had used the chair whenever he could not walk. Within weeks the leg was somewhat improved and he resumed his morning hawking or merely went with some courtiers into the park and shot at the popinjays.

Henry's illness and the fact that she was now living at court had brought Princess Mary even closer to Katherine. They shared time sitting with the king, rode with him when he was well and sighed with relief when he went off to the council room or to the countryside to hunt. Both took a close interest in Prince Edward's education. At her marriage, Edward's teacher was Dr. Richard Cox, Provost of Eton, a gentle scholar and staunch supporter of the "new religion."

After two years, when Edward was almost nine, Katherine suggested a change to the king. She felt a younger man might challenge Edward's mind and be more of a companion than the older Cox. Ultimately, John Cheke, a fellow of St. John's, Cambridge, replaced Dr. Cox, whom Katherine tactfully made her Almoner. Cheke was also sympathetic to the Humanistic principles, and young William Cecil, who'd married Cheke's sister Mary, said the man was also sensitive and knowledgeable. "He has a winning way teaching young boys. I think he will do very well," he told Katherine.

Cheke had only been in residence for about six months when Katherine heard from her ladies-in-waiting, that source of all court gossip, that Bishop Gardiner was particularly disappointed by the choice of John Cheke and further offended when William Grindal was appointed to teach Princess Elizabeth. When Katherine protested that thirteen-year-old Elizabeth could now speak French, Italian, Spanish, Flemish and Latin with ease, that she was proficient in mathematics and wrote passable poetry in a beautiful handwriting, Ann Parr Herbert replied that the bishop didn't think Cheke and Grindal were godly men. "He thinks they'll have a bad influence on Bess and Edward, Kate. He'd rather have a priest!"

"He's been angry with me ever since the king failed to appoint him an adviser along with Seymour and Cranmer during my regency," Katherine laughed. "Henry thinks Gardiner is spoiled and willful and looks to his own good too much. The children fare well. They are learning and appear content to do so. I think Gardiner is just being spiteful. The king is satisfied and so am I."

Busy as she was Katherine missed Kate Brandon. Kate had taken her two sons to Westhorpe to sort out Charles Brandon's possessions for the new duke, fifteen-year-old Henry. "My dearest stepdaughter, Frances, is not too pleased with this," Kate wrote that first week. "If her father hadn't married again and had a son, the title would have gone to her husband. It's one more thing for her to complain about, so I'm not unhappy to be away for a while. But I miss our times together, my dearest friend and queen, and I hope you're not too lonely."

Katherine realized then how much she and the duchess depended upon each other. In her younger years, married to older men, she'd had a great deal to learn and stepchildren to care for. Now there were hundreds of servants for her households and her present stepchildren, governed by rigid royal protocol and tradition, needed her companionship and supervision, but not her everyday care. As queen she could not go to the royal stables and select from the numerous royal mounts and, on impulse, go cantering through the woods to Chelsea or Islington as Lady Latimer often had.

And those months when she'd been widowed had spoiled her. Then she'd had freedom and leisure to do as she pleased, see whom she wanted or do nothing if she chose. Now if she found her lack of freedom restricting and her husband demanding, if the wardrobes full of costly gowns, the castles and palaces teeming with treasures and servants were taken for granted, if she often felt stifled, she must learn to accept it with good grace. She'd vowed at God's altar to be what Henry wanted and to take care of him, much as she'd taken care of her other husbands. Sometimes, she thought, that's what God intended for her—to take care of older husbands and their children.

Katherine allowed herself moments of private rebellion. When Henry was with the council or away hunting overnight, she'd dismiss her ladies and, safely off in a small chamber surrounded by books and a fire, she'd read until the candle gave out. Working with her stepchildren's tutors, she found their enthusiasm for scholarship rubbing off on her and she began to write out, for the first time, her thoughts regarding the diverse religious beliefs that had caused so much tumult in England. It had been easier than she'd thought and soon pride and satisfaction mingled together as the stiff pages, covered with her neat handwriting, piled up. Only Bessie knew what she was doing and where she kept the manuscript. It was her secret and she'd show Henry and Mary—and Kate Brandon when she returned—if she chose to. In the end, she might destroy it. But now she was grateful since the activity occupied her mind, kept her from thinking of the king's health and moods and the fact that the next day—and the day after—might all be very much the same.

Safely in her bed, knowing the king would not arrive, she often wondered

about Thomas Seymour. Then guilt made her determined to sleep and she'd
snuff out the candle and try not to think of her former lover. Yet it was
difficult for Thomas was often at court. When Charles Brandon died, Henry
had given Edward Seymour his post of Lord Great Chamberlain, causing his
wife, Anne Stanhope, to remark it was because her husband was the only
man the king truly trusted.

But Henry had seen that Thomas shared also in honors and wealth, grant-
ing him several profitable export licenses and naming him Keeper of the
King's Forest at Farleigh Hungerford. Later, in an impressive court ceremony, Thomas Seymour was created Master of the Ordnance, a Vice-Admiral of the Navy and Warden of the Cinque Ports with his headquarters at
Dover. With all his responsibilities, he was in and out of the council room
frequently and it was impossible not to meet at court galas. Several times
Katherine had had to restrain herself from asking the man, impressive now
with his new honors, yet still as irreverent, blithe and witty as ever, if he was
at last content. While Thomas did not equal his brother in influence or
wealth, he had come a long way since that fateful day at Whitehall when
he'd talked with the king and allowed their lives to be forever separate. To
do anything that reminded him of that time now would be pointless. Henry
seemed to have forgotten about her attachment to Seymour and now, in
those rare private moments she found for herself, Katherine thought of
Thomas and those months they'd had together as a fantasy, a dream she'd
once had and from which she'd awakened too soon.

* * *

Katherine's marriage to Henry Tudor had held some surprises. On the first
night of her marriage, she'd gone to the queen's chamber, disrobed and with
the help of several ladies including her sister Ann, put on her nightrail of
fine linen with rows of tiny pleated satin ribbons at neck and wrists and
climbed into the large bed wondering how long it would be before the king
arrived. She remembered that first painful night with Lord Borough and
those years with Lord Latimer; John had always appeared embarrassed that
he enjoyed her body—so much so she'd often wondered if the pleasure was
worth the assault on his conscience. She doubted that Henry Tudor would
be embarrassed.

She grew more anxious as the moments passed and still the king did not
come. Jesu! She was waiting now for a *king*! What if she displeased him?
Henry had had far more experience than both her husbands combined. How
could she satisfy the lust he'd felt for the Boleyn or inspire the honest love
he'd had for Jane Seymour? How was she supposed to feel as she waited for
her lord, master, husband and king—she who two weeks ago was dreaming
of another man, one who'd aroused her as no one had before?

She'd waited long, absorbed in her thoughts and was almost asleep when,
suddenly, the darkened room was ablaze as two servants, torches held high,
opened the great chamber door and escorted the king inside. Henry was in

his nightrail with a large furred cloak about his shoulders, a woolen nightcap on his bald head. Within moments, he was in the large bed, thrusting his bad leg first under the heavy coverlet. The servants bowed, closed the doors and the room was once more dark.

Henry had reached for her, pulling her head to his shoulder, his arm heavy and clumsily uncomfortable along her back. "Kate, my Kate," he said laughing, "we've had quite a day! Did you enjoy it, my dear?" As Katherine nodded, he pressed his lips to her forehead, hugging her even more closely. "Ah, Kate, it made everyone happy and you make us happy, too. We will be good to you, my dear, you must not be frightened."

And Katherine had found that she wasn't frightened or anxious and that if his leg didn't bother him or his fluctuating moods hinder him, Henry Tudor was a considerate and expert lover. If she paid no attention to the huge weight upon her, the bad leg that at times lost its dressing leaving blood on the bedsheets and a disagreeable odor on her body, but responded only to her husband's urgency, the experience was not unpleasant. It was natural of Katherine to want to please and her husband's obvious pleasure made it easy to answer his need. Henry could be rough and he could be tender. If nothing else, his lovemaking was unpredictable and that alone allowed little of the complacency she'd had with her other husbands.

Within days she was waiting for the king at night without any anxiety and he rarely failed to arrive. Often, he spent the whole night in her bed rather than return to his own. Henry had pleasured himself with her so much those first months, Katherine thought she'd surely be pregnant. But it hadn't happened. I must be barren, she thought, there's no other reason. Three husbands and no child? It had to be her fault.

Then, after his return from France, Henry had come less and less to her chamber. When he did, to her great surprise, he would often merely enfold her in his arms, kiss her quietly and comfortingly, rest his head on her shoulder—and fall asleep. By morning, she'd find he had gone. She never mentioned his unusual behavior but wondered if she'd displeased him. Then memories of other remarks, of implied instances of impotency, or a lack on the king's part in satisfying the voracious Boleyn and the wanton Howard rose in her mind and she wondered: had there been truth in both queens' complaints? How could anyone as virile-looking and as hugely male as the king not be a true husband? She knew that for herself, at least, she'd not experienced that elusive excitement, pleasure and satisfaction such as Kate and Charles Brandon had shared or that her sister Ann had with Will Herbert. She knew she was not an adequate judge, but should a husband's attentions cease after a year or so of marriage? She longed to talk to someone about it.

And then, just about the time she'd accepted the situation and settled herself comfortably in her bed, Henry would appear in the doorway either to talk or tumble her about in the great bed and she'd be left wondering again at the strange habits of husband and wife, even if they were the king and queen.

Ultimately, Kate Brandon had ferreted enough information out of Katherine to explain at least part of the story.

"Several years ago, Henry told Charles there'd never been any problem with the old queen and God knows there were enough babies so it appears to be true. Also, they were both very young." Kate chose her words carefully. "But after he and the Boleyn were married, he told Charles that at times she made fun of him or simply refused him, making him take her by force as if it were all a splendid game! Then often she'd insist when he was tired or worried—or even after they'd just been together and, when he could not pleasure her as she wished, she'd jest and make fun of him or accuse him of trifling with another woman. Henry said he was worried enough to have a girl brought over from a Southwark brothel to find out if he was incapable. He'd had no trouble with the girl at all. Yet when he went to his wife—or she came to him—often nothing happened at all. And it went from bad to worse, for Anne would harp on it all the time, making the king more worried, angry and humiliated."

Katherine was greatly relieved. The king hadn't found her undesirable or lacking. Pondering Kate's words, she understood how one confrontation could lead to another, causing Anne to flirt and encourage courtiers—even a court musician—hoping to make her husband jealous. What Anne hadn't foreseen was that such behavior might kill any genuine emotion the king had for her, making their rare couplings more out of anger than love. In the end, she'd brought about her own downfall.

What a relief Jane Seymour must have been to a king whose faith in his own manhood had been so badly shaken! Now Katherine knew why the birth of Prince Edward had meant more to Henry Tudor than an heir for the throne. He'd fathered a son and, had Jane lived, would presumably have had more. For the first time, Katherine understood his attitude toward Anne of Cleves. The woman had repelled him for some reason and he'd gone no further, not wanting to experience the disastrous effects he'd suffered before.

"So," Kate Brandon finished, "you can see what a disaster it was for Henry when the Howard woman played him false! For months she was everything he wanted and he'd had no difficulty at all. She was a beautiful child—always glad to see him—and he doted on her. Then he found out that she, too, seemingly found it necessary to look elsewhere for pleasure and satisfaction. I know she vowed she'd never been untrue to the king and I don't think she had. But she'd *thought* about it and certainly spent enough time with young Culpepper so it looked as though she had. I think the king would have pardoned her and sent her away if the council hadn't seen to it that everything she'd done was quickly made public. Henry was so shaken and humiliated, with everyone laughing at him for being a cuckold, what could he do?"

Katherine was vastly relieved after her talk with Kate Brandon. From that time on, she did not worry about the king's attentions—or lack of them. When he came to her chamber, she welcomed him gladly and, as she sat with her needlework beside the fire, Henry would sip his wine and talk, sharing his thoughts with her, knowing she would understand and be discreet in repeating them.

"You have the gift of common sense, my Kate," he said, "and we can talk with you like no one else and know we'll get an honest answer." The king appeared proud of her learning, saying it was also a relief to talk to someone who could and would answer without thinking first of their reputation or purse.

As he beamed and sipped his wine contentedly, Katherine bent her head over her embroidery to hide a smile. What, she wondered, would Henry say if reminded it was Senor Vives with his advanced study programs who had contributed so much to her education? And she'd shared in it because her mother was a dear friend of Katherine of Aragon who'd insisted that Maud Parr's daughter share the education of a princess? Katherine always recalled the old queen with love and gratitude.

But she doubted Henry would be equally grateful. One thing she'd learned very early in her marriage. As far as all his queens were concerned— even including his "beloved sister," the Duchess Anne of Cleves—there was no looking back. Aragon, Boleyn, Seymour or Howard—they were all gone and Henry did not wish to be reminded of any of them.

CHAPTER XXIV

I am very sorry to know and to hear how unreverently that most precious jewel, the Word of God, is disputed, rhymed, sung and jangled in every alehouse and tavern. . . .

I am sure that charity was never so faint among you, and virtuous and godly living was never less used, nor God Himself among Christians was never less reverenced, honored or served.

—Henry VIII addressing his last Parliament, November 23, 1545

During the years following the French War, Henry Tudor needed every ounce of his failing strength to face the political and religious problems facing England. When he wasn't meeting with the emissaries of those Catholic nations determined to deal with the heretic king of England, he visited coastal fortifications, seeing to their improvement in case war should come. With Lord Admiral John Dudley, now the Viscount Lisle, he checked sites for new ports, observed the decaying castle fortresses and increased the number of warning beacons. He congratulated Vice-Admiral Thomas Seymour, his brother-in-law, who, after several days of pursuing French galleons in the English Channel, confiscated their stores of wine, cheese, salt herring and dried cod, later sending them to be stored in the empty monasteries in London. Should invasion come, everyone agreed the supplies would be useful for the harvest that year had been disappointing. When time and weather permitted, the king and his companions enjoyed a pleasant morning hawking or hunting, but Henry's deteriorating leg condition soon made it necessary to return to Whitehall.

There he found several of his council solemn-faced, insisting that the troublemakers in the church also be dealt with. The English people, cried the old Duke of Norfolk, were frustrated with so many religious changes. Thomas Cranmer, the Archbishop of Canterbury agreed, explaining what they really wanted was a simple creed and ritual in their own language which they might understand and revere. Religion was meaningless unless the worshiper could understand its ceremonies. Not so, shouted Stephen Gardiner, the Bishop of Winchester. What people really desired was the familiar ceremony with its mystical Latin and their rosaries—to be allowed to venerate saints and celebrate the Mass as their forefathers had! All were aware what confusion and disorder had resulted when the English Bibles were placed in the churches so all might read Scripture for themselves. Everyone had had a different interpretation and the experiment had ended miserably in increased religious dissension.

With the help of Thomas Cranmer, Henry had set forth his own opinions in *A Necessary Doctrine and Erudition for Any Christian Man.* The reformers considered it too Catholic; the Catholics considered it too Lutheran. But "the King's Book" was popular and accepted by the more malleable young who had no recollection of a time when England had revered the Pope. It was scorned by those Catholics who viewed Cranmer's new Prayer Book with loathing and worked constantly for a religious settlement that would preserve the more familiar and beloved tenets of their faith.

When Henry discussed his problems with the church, Katherine did not hold back. She knew that much of her thinking was contrary to what her husband felt his subjects or churchmen would accept. But, she pointed out to the king, she could not give up her lifelong belief—a belief that had come from his own grandmother, old Lady Margaret Beaufort. She did not mention that other queen, Anne Boleyn, who'd also been a staunch supporter of the "new faith"—although she suspected it was primarily Anne's way of getting back at the Pope who'd hindered her marriage for so many years.

When Katherine told Henry she dreamt of a day when everyone's religious belief would be a matter for their own conscience, the king slapped his thigh and laughed loudly. "Ah, Kate sweetheart, if it were only that simple! Priests don't want education—they want power! They want the saints' days for the opportunity it gives them for intercession! They wanted the holy houses to remain for the comfort, the wealth and the chance to instruct others who would think exactly the same. By preaching eternal hell for those who don't believe as they do, they control minds by ignorance and fear. If you instruct people to read the Word of God for themselves, what is left for the churchmen? No, Kate, we must please both sides as much as we can. . . ."

* * *

"If the king can fight the bishops, so can the queen," Katherine later told Bessie and, within several days, study sessions similar to those she'd held at Parr House commenced again within Whitehall Palace. For the first time since her marriage, Katherine felt a sense of purposefulness. Now she could use her strong personal convictions, her own Parr determination, all buttressed by the Crown's authority and resources, to further a cause as dear to her heart as it had been to her mother's.

In the following weeks, the noted reformers, Nicholas Shaxton, Hugh Latimer, Nicholas Ridley and Myles Coverdale, who'd worked with Tyndale on his English translation of the Gospels, came to Whitehall to speak with the queen and her ladies. There they expounded faith in Jesus as the redeemer, spoke of life everlasting after death and ridiculed the idea of purgatory as being shameful to Christ's Infinite Mercy. Listening with rapt attention were the queen's sister, Ann, Lady Herbert, Kate Brandon, the Duchess of Suffolk, Lady Tyrwhit, the queen's "two Joans" and, on occasion, Anne Stanhope Seymour, the Countess of Hertford.

At one study session, Frances Brandon Grey arrived with her daughter, nine-year-old Lady Jane, who was promptly sent off to play in Prince Edward's quarters. Explaining she had a guest, Frances left the room to return with a tall red-haired woman who bowed graciously to the queen and murmured her pleasure at being received.

At first, Katherine did not recognize Anne Askew. Anne was taller, more mature and subdued than she remembered. But the high color in her bright, inquisitive face was still there, her eyes alive with intelligence and good humor. As the girl kissed her hand, Katherine greeted her warmly. She was shocked when Frances Grey said Anne had just been released after serving an eleven-day sentence in Compter jail.

"They had me first at Sadler's Hall, madame," Anne explained as everyone hung wide-eyed on each word. "They tried to trap me by asking if I disagreed with His Majesty's churchly decrees. I told them I'd rather read five lines of the Bible than listen to five Masses for one instructs me and the other gives me nothing!"

"And you were imprisoned for that?" Katherine was relieved to see that her guest bore no evidence of ill-treatment. Indeed, she suspected that Anne, firebrand that she was, had rather enjoyed tilting verbal lances with old Will Laxton, the Lord Mayor of London, who'd been her chief inquisitor.

"No, madame, I was imprisoned for telling Bonner, the Bishop of London, that I believe as Scripture teaches me. But when he asked me what that teaching was, I refused to answer, for I knew it was but a trick to make me tell him what he could have heard at Paul's Cross any morning! But I would not satisfy him! He became very angry, madame, and said I was but a woman and should not question a bishop. But because I was wellborn and he knew I had good friends, he would show me mercy. The mercy was eleven days in prison." Anne smiled broadly, but her voice held a trace of bitterness. "I suppose I was lucky for others have been burnt for less. Some friends did come to help me. . . ." She indicated the ample figure of Frances Grey. "And since I can't preach in public for some time—I am certain old Bonner will put his spies onto me!—my Lady Frances was kind enough to say I might come and listen to your disputations here, madame."

Katherine was annoyed that Lady Frances assumed she might bring anyone to the queen's chambers. But she said nothing. It was very like Frances Grey whose little intellectual capacity often made it difficult for her to comprehend what Katherine and her ladies were talking about. Frances cared little about religious problems and less about what might be done to solve them. Her main interest in the group, Katherine suspected, was purely social. She wanted to be in the center of things as far as the queen and her ladies were concerned and if that meant she must listen to dull educational and religious talk from freethinking professors or visiting dignitaries, she could bear it as long as it was only once a week and didn't interfere with her real pleasures of riding and hunting. She'd brought Anne Askew simply because she didn't want to be bothered with the girl herself and now Anne was Katherine's responsibility.

Yet within weeks, Anne had ceased attending the palace study groups. "I'm sure she found us all rather tiresome, merely talking and reading," Katherine told Bessie when she'd inquired after the woman. "She's more one for doing. Although God knows what she'll do now! I'm sure old Bonner or Bishop Gardiner are having her watched. But it will matter little to her. If she finds out who the spies are, she'll only try to convert them!"

* * *

In the spring of 1546, the plague again threatened London. Henry ordered Elizabeth and Edward to Ashridge and Mary to Beaulieu, her Essex home. All three were upset at leaving the warm, comforting life they'd had for the past three years with their father and stepmother—the only real home Elizabeth and Edward had ever known.

Elizabeth, particularly, made no attempt to hide her feelings. "Oh, madame, I don't want to go!" she cried tearfully. "Can't I remain here if I don't go out of the palace? I won't even go into the courtyard! It might be for all summer, madame!" The tears came freely then and she hung her head as if to hide them.

"Bess, you know the king is only looking to your safety." Katherine put an arm about the trembling girl for she knew Elizabeth was remembering that year of exile with only her governess and servants for company. "Your father and I are to go to Oking and it simply is not large enough for all you children and your servants. The king is doing this for your own good, Bess. We'll write often and visit if we can. But London is not safe and you must leave soon." She was relieved at last to see acceptance in Elizabeth's mutinous face.

Returning to her quarters, she found Mary directing the packing of the clothing and household items that would go to Beaulieu later that day. "I need some exercise," she wearily told her stepmother. Soon she and Katherine, arms linked, were outside, setting off down the graveled path at the fast pace Mary loved. Rounding a corner, they saw Eustace Chapuys, the Spanish ambassador, so severely crippled with gout he was seated in a chair similar to the king's, being carried in their direction. Seeing the two women, he attempted to leave the chair to pay his respects.

Quickly, Katherine urged him to remain seated. Bowing his head, the old man explained he had just taken leave of the king. After sixteen years in England, he said, he was at last going home.

"Oh, senor," Mary's eyes filled with tears as she held out her hand which the old ambassador grasped affectionately. "You have done my father—and my mother when she was alive—great service. I am sad that we'll not see you again. . . ." Her voice quivered and she seemed at a loss for words.

Tactfully, Katherine bade Chapuys farewell, asking that she be remembered to the emperor. "I shall walk on ahead and wait for the princess," she said. "You both have much to say to each other. . . ."

Before Mary could respond, she walked rapidly down the path to a seat under a trellised arbor. Relishing the rare moment of privacy and solitude, Katherine leaned her head against the trellis, watching the gouty old man in the chair as he and Mary talked together. As they both began gesturing excitedly, she realized they were speaking in Spanish, an opportunity Mary did not often have.

She will miss him, Katherine thought, watching as Mary wiped her eyes and Chapuys patted her on the shoulder in a fatherly fashion. She could guess at the conversation. Mary was telling the old Spaniard how much his support and companionship had meant to her mother—and to her—during all those years of "the troubles." Chapuys had been with her mother only hours before she died; he was almost Mary's last living link with Katherine of Aragon now that Maria de Salinas was dead. It must sadden her to know that now he, too, would soon be gone.

She doubted if Mary knew that age was not the only reason for the ambassador's return. France was spoiling for a fight to regain Boulogne and urging Spain to invade England before too much harm was done to the true religion in such a heretical country. Everyone knew Henry Tudor was in failing health, that his daughter was strongly Catholic as opposed to a king who had his own version of the old religion and a queen who was helping instruct his two younger children in the "new faith." Everything she and her ladies believed in would certainly be considered heretical by the gouty old man now bowing his head for the last time to the girl he'd never considered anything but a princess and the king's only legitimate daughter, no matter that Parliament had ruled otherwise. He could at least return to Spain with the consolation that Mary had regained her title and was now named in the Succession.

As Mary walked slowly to rejoin her, Katherine felt a strong surge of sympathy for her old childhood friend. Mary had really regained nothing that hadn't been hers by right all along. She'd suffered years of persecution and exile and those scars still remained, no matter how much she tried to hide them. She was husbandless and likely to remain so as long as the religious and political situation remained as it was. No Catholic prince would seek a bride from a country that had separated itself from Rome. Katherine thought it ironical that she, herself, might believe differently and be queen. But Mary, staunchly Catholic and a princess as well, was denied a husband.

Katherine hoped that some religious settlement would be made soon, if for no other reason than Mary's future might be secured. Then those like Anne Askew could preach as they chose or realize what their danger was if they disagreed. Then Mary might have children before she became too old.

Katherine knew, with chilling intuition, it must be soon. The king was not well and hardly likely to get better. When he went, what would happen to them all?

* * *

Returning to London after another threatening plague, the king and queen made a leisurely progress through Portsmouth, Farnham, Guildford, Nonsuch Palace and Greenwich. At Portsmouth, word arrived that the French fleet of three hundred ships was anchored off the Isle of Wight and soon the beacons flared with the threat of invasion. A small French force landed and burnt a dozen houses before the inhabitants, armed with clubs, pitchforks, bows and arrows drove them back. The fleet then sailed to Dover, but again the English ousted them into the Channel where Admiral Lisle pursued them until they were in French waters. There he ordered his seamen ashore to wreak a similar vengeance on French coastal towns.

The invasion threat and rigors of the progress—the constant riding, hunting and entertaining that the nobles in their great houses provided along the way—had taken its toll on Henry. At Nonsuch he'd fainted and been unconscious for almost an hour, sending his courtiers into a panic. Once revived, the king made light of the incident but later, mentioning old Chancellor Audley, Dr. Butts, Sir Thomas Wyatt and several others who'd recently died, Katherine saw her husband was facing the reality of his own mortality.

Settled back into Whitehall, she soon resumed her weekly study sessions. Though her ladies said nothing, it was obvious the king's poor health was as much on their minds as her own. What would happen to England when Henry Tudor was gone? Lately, the king had favored the more Protestant element—Edward Seymour, John Dudley, old Will Paget and Tom Wriothesley, now the Lord Chancellor—who had scarcely bothered to hide their delight at the discomfiture of the aging Duke of Norfolk. Along with Stephen Gardiner, the Bishop of Winchester, Norfolk was the council's most prominent Catholic. Together, they wooed Van der Delft, the new Spanish ambassador, who told the council the emperor would retaliate if England pursued a closer alliance with the Lutheran states.

No seer with the gift of prophecy was needed to see that a mighty power struggle would result when the king died. Not that the possibility was ever publicly mentioned. Even Henry never spoke of the future nor had he made a will. But Katherine knew he was worried. Rumors of plots and counterplots surfaced regularly, undermining confidence in his courtiers and bluntly demonstrating a failing ability to control his unruly councillors. In order to attend more meetings, he used his chair frequently, for it was now almost impossible to walk any great distance. Yet he continued to indulge at the table, increasing his weight and making his leg more painful than before. The result was an irritable husband, a monarch sensitive to any reference to his condition and a deteriorating effectiveness in council and court.

Although Katherine often thought the only one who could really handle the king was his Fool, Will Somers, Henry appeared comfortable with Thomas Cranmer and Edward Seymour, the Earl of Hertford. The bishops, particularly Stephen Gardiner, invariably upset him, ponderously predicting the wrath of France and Spain if the king tampered further with religious rituals or failed to take stronger measures against the heretics who were undermining the foundation of the church he'd created. They lamented, if not directly, his younger children's exposure to such heretical instructions as Queen Katherine had recommended and pointed with pride to Princess Mary, still true to the old faith.

Katherine was greatly relieved and heartened by the Duchess of Suffolk's return from Westhorpe. Kate Brandon said living at her country home was a grim experience without Charles and she now planned to reside at Suffolk House across the river in Southwark. Katherine dismissed her ladies-in-waiting so she and her old friend might spend a quiet afternoon alone, talking of Charles and those long-ago days.

When it appeared Kate might speak of Thomas Seymour, Katherine quickly interrupted saying how worried she was about the king's health, of his lack of future planning, and how much stronger those younger councillors had become mainly because of his illness.

"Don't expect you can change anything," the duchess advised, laughing. "I know you're worried, my dear, and not without cause. Charles was the same as Henry. He wouldn't change his habits either, even when he knew they were bad for him. When he could exercise, he did so, often to the point of injuring himself tilting or the like. Then when he was ill and needed to exercise, he was unable to do so! So save your strength, Katherine. In the end, Henry will have his own way!"

So while the king nursed his leg and struggled with an embattled council, Katherine spent her days with her ladies. She missed her stepchildren. Because of the invasion threat, Henry had ordered all three to remain in their own homes. Sight unseen, she persuaded the king to hire Catherine Champernowne, a West Country relative of Joan Denny's, to act as Elizabeth's governess and soon her stepdaughter's letters bore out her pleasure in having Catherine's companionship.

Between the lines of Mary's letters, however, it was evident poor health and depression still plagued the princess. To brighten Mary's days, Katherine sent books and bolts of cloth from the Wardrobe, angered as always that the council would not provide sufficient funds for the princess' household, for she was certain anxiety contributed to Mary's condition. While the girl's residences were self-sustaining with ample gardens and orchards, there was little ready cash and Katherine knew that small gifts of money were also welcome.

When she told the king how much she missed his children, he said, "Visit them if you must, Kate, but leave them where they are for now." When she complained to Kate Brandon, the duchess was not surprised. "I know you're disappointed, my dear, but remember, Henry's only had them around since you married him. I suspect constant fatherhood was more of a charge than a pleasure. . . ."

One day after Katherine returned from Suffolk House where she'd spent the afternoon with the duchess, a lady-in-waiting announced a visitor in the queen's Privy Chamber. Entering the room, she found Anne Askew reading one of her books. In a moment the young woman—looking more drawn than she had eight months before—was kneeling before her. She said she'd come to warn of a plot against the queen.

"A plot, Anne?" Katherine was puzzled. "Why in the name of our Lord would anyone plot against the queen? What have I done to warrant such action?"

"Oh, my lady, I must tell you everything," Anne reverted to the address she'd used as a child. "You are in great danger! You've been away and could hardly know all this, but I have heard the story from my sources and you must be very careful."

Anne explained that while the king and queen had been away on progress, the rift between the Catholics and Protestants in the council had deepened and become more serious than even the king recognized. This rift had widened to the point, said Anne, where there would never be any healing. It had been further aggravated by an incident involving Henry Howard, the handsome young Earl of Surrey, the Duke of Norfolk's son. Katherine remembered the ill-tempered young man whom Thomas Seymour had bested in the May Day tournament—the one who'd behaved so arrogantly he'd displeased the king.

"He is very proud, this Surrey, and sneers at my Lord Hertford, saying the Seymours are arrivistes, that if their sister had not become queen, they'd have been nothing. He drinks too much and leads a rackety life brawling in the streets at midnight, pelting stones at peaceful persons' windows. Finally, he was arrested and brought before the council when my Lord Hertford was presiding."

Katherine understood. Edward Seymour would hardly miss an opportunity to chastise the vain Surrey. "And my Lord Hertford settled a few scores?"

Anne nodded. "Surrey had been arrested before, for eating flesh on an abstinence day." Her lips curled in disdain. "As if it mattered anyway—would Christ have cared?"

When Katherine remained silent, Anne said Surrey had been sent to the Fleet prison to ponder his sins. After his release, he and Hertford had met at Hampton Court and Surrey, still vengeful, had picked a quarrel with Hertford and the two had come to blows. Fighting within the bounds of the royal palace was a crime punishable by the loss of a hand. But old Norfolk had pleaded so deeply for his son, the case had been dismissed. Hoping to make amends, Norfolk suggested one of Surrey's sons marry Hertford's eldest daughter but Surrey had indignantly rejected the offer which Hertford had taken as an insult. Immediately all those partial to Hertford ranged themselves against Norfolk and Surrey and the situation had become explosive.

"Hertford has vowed he'll ruin Surrey," Anne whispered. "The old duke has taken his son home to Norfolk, but the council still works against them."

As Anne told her story, breathless, Katherine sat stunned. Previously, she'd heard rumors of young Surrey's brawling, his tendency to drink too much and fight, a trait hardly unusual among the younger courtiers and one the king viewed leniently as long as no serious crime was committed. She was certain Henry was not aware of what had happened and wondered why Edward Seymour had kept the story from him. She asked Anne as much.

"Because, my lady, it means that—for the moment at least—my Lord Hertford and his colleagues like Wriothesley, Richard Rich and even old Cranmer, have bested that other Catholic, Bishop Gardiner. And they know how the king dislikes such petty behavior especially regarding religion. But Bishop Gardiner is wroth, my lady, that so few came to Surrey's defense, that it was kept from the king on the pretext that he, a sick man, should not be bothered with a young man's pranks. Gardiner disputes this and says they are hounding Surrey because of his religion and through him they will bring down the father, too. When they do that, they will have eliminated the strongest Catholic on the council."

"Do you believe this, Anne?"

"I do, my lady, I do. And I think they will succeed in destroying Surrey. They are looking for evidence right now. The man has a reputation for being overproud, remember, and not too clever when it comes to using his head instead of his fists. But it is really the father they want."

"But what does this have to do with me, Anne? *I* have no fault with my Lord Surrey except, as you say, he can be troublesome and for little cause. He can be exasperating, but what. . . ."

Anne interrupted, placing her hand on Katherine's. "Don't you see, my lady? Who do you think Gardiner blames for the predominance of the reformers on the council? Who has written about and encouraged the 'new faith'? Who has placed two reform-thinking and preaching tutors to teach the Princess Elizabeth and my lord prince? Who has ladies here each week to talk about the 'new religion' and laugh at the old? Who owns all those books written by heretics and sent from the Continent as soon as they are published so she might read and then discuss them with her younger stepchildren and their father? Who has a friend who calls her little dog 'Gardiner'?"

At that, Katherine laughed aloud. "Oh, Anne . . ." she shook her head wryly. Kate Brandon did, indeed, call her little dog, "Gardiner." Because of his barrel-shaped chest and thrust-out jaw, the animal's undisputed manner of stalking into a room and waiting to be complimented or noticed, Kate had one day convulsed the ladies by pointing out his resemblance to Stephen Gardiner. Thereafter, everyone called the dog by the prelate's name. It was a harmless if tasteless jest, Katherine admitted. But how could he know of it?

"There is little that goes on *anywhere* that the council doesn't know."

Anne looked at Katherine almost with pity, as if she, the queen, should be aware of such things. "Everything I've said is true. Gardiner has put it this way. He said he will 'bend his bow to bring down the head deer.' For a time he looked to see if you continued with affection for Thomas Seymour, but you have been so prudent, they found nothing." Katherine was almost speechless at the girl's presumption, but Anne appeared not to notice. "You must believe me, my lady," she emphasized, pressing Katherine's hand. "You must be aware of the danger! I have heard people say Gardiner is so maddened he's vowed vengeance on all the Seymour faction. You may be the queen, my lady, but you believe in religion as they do. And you have a more prominent position. What better way to attack my Lord Hertford than through the queen? They think you have too much influence on the king but they can hardly attack *him*. They don't think he's as honest in his beliefs as you are, my lady, for he's wavered too much and changed so often. But *you* must be careful."

After Anne had gone, Katherine sat, stunned and frightened, in the darkening room, waving away the servants who came to light the candles. She wished she had someone to talk to for she could think of little else but Anne's story. But there was no one. Her sister Ann, even now in another part of the palace, was a chatterer and would certainly tell her husband. Her uncle, William Parr, sighing for the peacefulness of Kendal and stating he was too old and unsuited for the intrigues of court life, had returned to the North. How would he advise her? What would Kate Brandon say if, tomorrow, she rode at once to Suffolk House and recounted Anne's story?

Yet instinct told her otherwise. Instinct warned her not to say anything—even to her husband. Perhaps, most of all, to her husband. Suddenly her hands were clammy and she felt a roiling surge of chilling fear. She'd only wanted to seek what she truly thought was best for the English people—a purer and more honest religion—with the opportunity to obtain their own solace from Scripture than from a priest. She'd felt so secure as Henry Tudor's wife; her queenship was her greatest protection. But now, after listening to Anne, she wondered if it might not be her greatest danger.

* * *

Three weeks later in the sunny river room at Parr House, Katherine sat for her portrait. The artist, William Scrotts, was a friend of the Flemish painter whose portrait of the Princess Elizabeth was so striking that Henry had ordered it—to the intense delight of his younger daughter—to be hung in his Privy Chamber. Remembering how her tardiness in meeting with Hans Holbein had resulted in his loss, Katherine made the appointment with Scrotts at once.

Then, for reasons she didn't understand anymore than she could explain why she always put "K.P." after her royal signature, she requested the sittings take place at Parr House. Perhaps some memory of Maud Parr, paper in hand, fretting over the dowry she must pay some greedy Northern lord for marrying her daughter, made that child, now a queen, want her portrait painted in her old home. When she asked permission of her husband, Henry had shrugged and said to do whatever she wished.

With Kate Brandon, she'd spent a considerable amount of thought on the proper gown and jewels for her sitting. Ultimately, they'd selected a deep crimson velvet, cut in the latest fashion, with huge billowing sleeves, the whole trimmed with broad bands of heavily embroidered goldwork. Beneath the gown's bodice, Katherine wore a blouse of stiff Spanish lace, delicately patterned in gold threads. Kate suggested the blouse's collar stand up rather than lie flat on her shoulders, thus framing Katherine's slim neck with its necklace of rubies, garnets and pearls from which hung a golden pendant with a pearl the size of a robin's egg. Lacy cuffs emerged from the crimson and gold sleeves and half covered her hands resplendent with several rings. Katherine particularly liked her headdress. The old pointed hood favored by Katherine of Aragon and the Boleyn had given way to a flat, more appealing cap-like covering that was trimmed with similar bands of gold and pearls from which a luxuriantly creamy plume curled about the cap lending its luster to her fair skin and red-gold hair.

It was on the fourth day of sitting when, as she held the pose—hands clasped lightly in front, looking just to the right where she might watch the river's traffic—and listened to Kate Brandon's chatter as the duchess worked on her embroidery—that Will Parr arrived. Will was now about the age of Tom Parr when he'd died so suddenly; he strongly resembled his father. Will was accompanied by an obviously distraught Bessie Bellingham, her eyes dark with a fear Katherine hadn't seen since the Pilgrimage of Grace days. Her first thought was that something had happened to Henry or one of the children and she rose, clutching the crimson gown as Bessie reached her side crying, "They have her, Katherine, they've taken her. Oh, you must see to it at once. . . ."

"See to what?" Fearful, Katherine put an arm about Bessie as her brother motioned the artist to leave the room.

"Mistress Askew has been taken into custody, Katherine, and she's made such a fuss I warrant the council will never be the same," he explained.

"The council? The Privy Council?" Katherine asked, stunned. "What has the Privy Council to do with Anne Askew?"

"They have her husband, too. . . ." Bessie whispered. "Oh, Katherine, she is in great trouble this time!"

Weakly, Katherine sat down on her chair as Will Parr strode about the room, describing the scene that morning at the Guildhall. It was only several weeks ago that Anne had warned her that she, the queen, was in great danger. Had she known then the council might question her and she might not have time later to see her old friend? Or had the council learned of her visit and arrested her *because* she'd warned the queen? She sat quietly, listening to her brother, a cold sinking feeling in her stomach and legs.

Thomas Kyme, Anne's husband, had been summoned from Lincolnshire to explain his wife's behavior. Standing at the council table, he told his listeners he'd always disapproved of Anne's gospeling, for she was a strident, contentious woman who'd disgraced her family and hastened her father's death a year before. Even her brother, Francis Askew, knighted for bravery in fighting the king's war at Boulogne, had washed his hands of her.

Gravely, the councillors had shaken their heads and dismissed Squire Kyme. "By now, he's probably halfway back to Lincoln," Will Parr said, "but Anne has gone to Newgate."

"What are the charges?" Katherine's voice quivered. Newgate Prison was foul and dangerous. Anne was a strong woman who, given a chance, could take care of herself. But Newgate might prove too much for her. She wondered what she could do to help.

"Charges?" Will Parr said. "She made a fool of herself by distributing a pamphlet about the City ridiculing the priests for arresting her last year. She's asked for this, Katherine, just as if she'd gone to the councillors and handed them her complaints. You must not interfere, for it would only make the case more important, and you'd do yourself no good."

"I'm not looking to do good for myself, Will. I'm looking to help Anne."

"She's well able to take care of herself! When Tom Wriothesley told her this morning that the king wished to know her religious opinions, she said she'd gladly tell the king anytime he asked. When Bishop Gardiner said it was not meet that the king be troubled with the likes of her, a mere woman, she told him that was unfortunate, that even King Solomon who was known as the wisest man of his time had not objected to listening to two common women. And, said she, she did not consider herself a common woman, but an instrument of God. After that old Paget sought to match her quotations from the Bible, but she corrected him several times and said there was no one, not even Bishop Gardiner, who knew Scripture as well as she did. She said she'd tell them naught of her religious convictions. She said she spoke publicly because she wanted to give people the true Word as the Bible taught it. They had a choice and didn't have to listen or accept it if they didn't believe what she said. She said she didn't think that was a crime, that the council was guiltier since they hounded people because of the way they worshiped God."

Katherine felt her eyes mist over. Anne Askew—child, girl and woman— had always meant well, asking only to be left in peace to speak her own deep convictions. Yet her manner and behavior was, as her husband had said, so contentious that whatever gift she had of true belief was lost in her contempt for any kind of authority.

"So she's at Newgate," Will Parr continued, "and there she'll remain at the council's pleasure. I came to you, Katherine, and I'm glad my Lady Suffolk is here also, because I know you both are fond of the woman. The council knows she's been to Whitehall many times to listen to your speakers, so you must be careful. I've already told Bessie she must stay away also, for this time, I trow, the Askew woman has gone too far. There is much going on at court, Katherine, which I'm not privy to talk about now. But you must be careful. Everyone knows of your association with Anne Askew, although so far, they've asked her nothing concerning it. But for now, for the sake of us all, leave her alone."

CHAPTER XXV

Aware of her brother's warning not to meddle and realizing that to do so might do Anne more harm than good, Katherine sent Joan Denny to Newgate Prison with clothing, writing materials, a warm cloak and some money to buy whatever else she needed. But after the guards questioned her closely and Lady Denny had to say the gifts were from her, Katherine did not ask her to go again. Joan was frightened that her husband, a trusted councillor, would find out what she'd done.

Katherine longed to speak to Henry about Anne; a word from him would free her immediately. Then she could probably convince Anne to return to the North if only for a few months. Anything to get her out of London, away from those who would be looking for any lapse on her part.

But instinct told her the time was not right. Henry's leg, complicated by dropsy, was extremely painful and though he put on a confident manner for the foreign ambassadors, she knew the political situation abroad—rife with rumors of an alliance between Spain and France—had never been worse. The combination of pain and nagging worry made him irascible and unpredictable.

Anne had been in Newgate about a week when Katherine sat, as she often did, with the king in the Presence Chamber. He was discussing with Bishop Gardiner the difficulty of keeping supplies in Boulogne, of how defenseless England would be if France joined with Spain for invasion, and whether or not the German states might now feel friendlier toward a king who'd cast aside a Lutheran queen and forbidden her to return home. An alliance with those German princes might now be feasible, Henry said, glaring at the bishop, though he was certain the prelate would hardly agree. The king had always enjoyed baiting his councillors and churchmen. Now his painful leg and concern over the political situation at home and abroad only spurred him on. When he asked Gardiner to go to Spain and treat with the Emperor Charles directly, since they were both such good Catholics, the sarcasm was not lost on the bishop and he looked momentarily uncomfortable and baffled.

Katherine watched Stephen Gardiner closely. The man was clearly not enthusiastic. It was well known he still hoped to reconcile Henry and the Pope; his absence from the council might lead to Cranmer, Hertford and other reformers making undesirable progress against him. Neither did he want to lose control of the situation created by Anne Askew's arrest or be unable to protect Henry Howard, the Earl of Surrey, if any charges were brought against him.

Hoping to distract Henry and ease the awkward moment for the bishop, Katherine mentioned what an admiral replacement Van der Delft, the new Spanish ambassador, was for old Chapuys. Henry turned to her and in a tight voice asked, "And you, too, Kate? The man may have charm but he means no good to us! He is clever and bargains well, but he'd have us change all that we've worked so hard for. He wants the Pope welcomed again in England and says Holy Writ should only be taught through the priests. Unlike Cranmer, he thinks the saints' days should be restored and the Mass be said in Latin. Even *you* don't believe that, Kate!"

Katherine warmed to the discussion. Anything that would ease Henry's pain and give him some respite from the irritating Gardiner would be satisfying. "Then, sire," she said lightly, "if you want people to know Holy Writ, you must let them read it for themselves! Once you thought so too and made Scripture available to everyone. And then you took away all the Bibles and issued a proclamation forbidding people to read them in English. How can Holy Writ be served by such action?" She looked up, smiling expectantly. Henry often enjoyed a good theological joust; any intellectual exercise stimulated him and made him forget his inflamed leg. They'd discussed more serious religious issues than this and she only hoped the bishop would not spoil it by argument.

But the king was not smiling. His eyes narrowed as he looked at her. In the strained atmosphere, Gardiner remained silent as a statue. Surprised and suddenly apprehensive, Katherine wondered what to say. She knew her husband's attitude was caused as much by his discomfort as her remark. But to say anything further might only make it worse. She was angry with herself also for feeling suddenly frightened. Why would Henry be so impatient over such an innocent remark?

"You may go now, Kate"—the king turned away—"we will talk with the bishop for a while." Resentfully, Katherine gathered her needlework together and curtsied. She did not, as she often did, kiss her husband on the cheek or pat his hand before leaving. As a servant opened the door, she heard Henry mutter. "A good thing it is when women become such clerks! It's little comfort to us in our old age to be taught by a wife!" As the door closed behind her, Gardiner was murmuring solicitously.

In the following days, Katherine resumed her portrait sittings and forgot the incident. Henry had gone almost immediately to Greenwich to examine the evidence the Privy Council had gathered on the Earl of Surrey. She was ashamed at her feeling of relief when word came he might be away for a week or longer. If he was to be absent that long, she told Bessie, then she'd ask his permission to visit Edward and Elizabeth. He could hardly be angry with her for that.

One evening as she lay reading in bed by candlelight, she heard footsteps and whispering outside her door. Hurriedly, she donned a robe for the flaring of torchlight beneath her door might mean the king had unexpectedly returned. Instead, a lady-in-waiting, who usually slept in the adjoining room, entered saying her brother was waiting outside. In a moment, Will Parr was at her side.

"Will! What is it?" Something must have happened to Henry. "What brings you here at this hour? Is it the king?"

"No, Katherine, nothing has happened to the king." Will looked overwrought. "But sit down, my dear, for I have grievous news. And we must find a way to deal with it, for only God knows what they may have found out from that woman."

"What woman? What are you talking about, Will?"

"The Askew woman. You know how Gardiner has been determined to find out who she's been involved with. He wants to make enough of a case to keep her in prison, perhaps even execute her! If he can implicate Hertford, that would be even better. And this time he may have succeeded."

Weakly, Katherine sat down. In Henry's present mood, it would not take much provocation to convince him of disloyalty or disagreement. But she was not prepared for her brother's next words.

"Anne has been sent to the Tower and questioned every day. So far she's refused to associate herself with anyone, saying she's her own woman and never needed anyone. She says she wished only to speak the Word of God and to teach anyone who listened. Though the council knows she's been to Whitehall with your ladies, she's disclaimed any friendship with any of them, saying she went only to hear the speakers. She says the articles she received in prison were brought by servants she didn't recognize. She says no one has helped her or encouraged her."

"Well, she's right. She's always been one to do for herself. She wants to be beholden to no one."

"I don't think the interrogators believed her. She treats their questions with amusement or is so proud she remains silent which only makes them angrier. Yesterday, she maddened them so they sent her to the Tower. And this afternoon, Anthony Knyvet, the Lieutenant-General of the Tower, arrived during a council meeting. He was very upset, saying he must speak with the king. He was told to speak up then and there and he did so saying that Anne Askew had been racked—and rather badly, I gather. He said he'd objected since he'd had no order for such a thing and he wanted the whole council to know he wasn't responsible."

Katherine fought back a nausea that stifled the cry welling up within her. The thought of Anne's long slim body stretched upon the vile Tower rack was almost more than she could bear.

"Why didn't he stop it?" she cried tearfully. "He's the Lieutenant-General! What manner of man is he that he'd allow this without an order? Can't he control his own men?"

"Anne wasn't racked by anyone in the Tower, Katherine. She was racked by Bishop Gardiner and Tom Wriothesley." Will's voice sank to a whisper. "I think the council was as stunned as the king. Henry waved the man away, saying if the deed was already done, at least the woman was not dead and he'd deal with them both. But he wasn't as angry as Cranmer or Hertford or as many of us were."

"The Bishop of Winchester and the Lord Chancellor of England took it upon themselves to rack a helpless woman?" Nausea was replaced by an anger so violent Katherine found it difficult not to scream and pound the wall in frustration. "They dared? God forgive them! Why? Why? Why?" Her voice was rasping, choking on tears of disgust and hatred. "Anne may be a nuisance on the London streets with her gospeling, but she's done nothing else! She hasn't robbed, maimed or killed. She has no family anymore and very few friends. . . ."

"She has the queen. . . ." Will's voice was curt. Suddenly, he grasped her shoulders and shook her not too gently.

"Kate, when are you going to wake up? You've known the woman since she was a child! Some people say you taught her all she knows, although—to her credit—*she's* never said that! She goes in and out of your chambers as if she were an old friend. Bessie Bellingham takes a great interest in her because their families are old friends in the North. She's been seen in the company of Frances Grey and Hertford's wife, Anne. Don't you see how all of you are involved and this is what Gardiner wants? If he can bring down the lot of you, every Catholic in the country—and there are more of them than there are reformers!—will rally to his cause. Cranmer would have to go and Hertford would be ruined." He shook her again. "Don't you see how dangerous this is for you?"

But Katherine was beyond reasoning. She sat down, one part of her mind listening to Will, accepting what he said, but seeing only Anne, stretched on a rack as two strong men—a bishop and a Lord Chancellor—worked the rack to pull her joints apart. The specter was so dreadful, she was sobbing uncontrollably as Bessie, paper in hand, entered the room, her face contorted with fright. Obviously, Katherine thought, wiping away her tears, she's heard the same news. How can I comfort her? As she took the paper from Bessie, her hand shook so badly it was difficult to read the words. Perhaps Anne had confessed . . . what? Anything would satisfy such animals as Gardiner and Wriothesley.

Hoping to comfort Bessie, she put an arm about her as she read the long official-looking document, but it had nothing to do with Anne. For there, at the top was her own name.

Clutching the document, Katherine scanned it quickly. At the bottom, "Henry R" was scrawled in her husband's now-wavering handwriting. Unable to believe the words, she went back to read it from the beginning. There must be a mistake. What she held was an order for the arrest and detention of Queen Katherine who was to remain in her apartments until further notice of the king. There was no mention of the crime with which she was charged.

*   *   *

Shocked, Katherine spent a restless night. Each time she briefly slept, her dreams were little nightmares of creaking racks manipulated by black-gowned bishops and a riotously laughing Tom Wriothesley. Once *she* was on the rack, hearing her own cries, awakening in such sickening terror, she was sobbing noiselessly. Over and over, she heard Catherine Howard's screams as she was dragged from the chapel door at Hampton Court. Had the Boleyn, waiting in the Tower to hear her fate, experienced such fright that she'd cried out into the blackness of the courtyard where she would soon be executed?

Deliberately Katherine willed herself to calmness, telling herself how lucky she was to have this time since the indictment had been served. Bessie had found the paper on the chapel floor when she'd gone for evening prayers. Who had dropped it there—a friend or an enemy? Finding it gave her time to wonder what made the king take drastic action. She was inno-cent of any crime; the council could prove nothing. The king had *wanted* to rid himself of Anne Boleyn and with Catherine Howard the council had given him no choice. But what had *she* done? How should she respond?

Her brother had been no help, hurrying back to Greenwich immediately. She was grateful Will was on the council in addition to her many other friends. Certainly Cranmer, Denny, Dudley, Will Herbert, and Rob Tyr-whit would stand by her? Or would they? Hadn't old Norfolk forsaken two nieces? Hadn't Tom More, with similar friends in high places, still lost his head nearly eleven years ago? Who would stand up to the king?

Inevitably, as she watched the first rays of daylight about her long cham-ber windows, fright turned to anger. She'd done nothing . . . *nothing* to be placed in such a position! She was Katherine Parr, daughter of two of her husband's dearest friends, whose uncle, brother and sister had served the king, as Parrs had served the Tudors for years. She was as learned as her husband, with wealth that almost equaled his, the beloved of his family and friends. She was no opportunist like one queen or wanton like another. How dare he order her arrest, as if she was a Newgate vendor accused of common thievery or a strumpet from the Southwark stews who'd disturbed the peace on a drunken night!

Calmly, she tried to assess her position. Whatever reasons Henry had for ordering her detention, they were false and certainly the work of those ene-mies Anne Askew had described. The thought of Anne, injured and still in the Tower, made her ill again—a sickness compounded by rage. She would fight the king, she decided, and not go as bitterly as the Boleyn or as hysteri-cally as the Howard woman. Parrs had knelt to the king in reverence; she'd not kneel in terror.

By the time Bessie arrived, her face gray with despair, Katherine had control of herself. She'd thought of everything that had happened during the past two weeks and there could be no reason for any restraining order except the incident when she'd tried to amuse and divert Henry from pain and politics by the sort of discussion they'd enjoyed dozens of times before. But Stephen Gardiner had been there and he'd stayed with the king. And it was Gardiner, so Anne Askew had said, who hated the queen's influence on her husband and his younger children.

"It has to be the bishop," she told Bessie, repeating Anne's story. "He had a hand in this. But I must find out what the charges are! Gardiner must have told His Grace many lies. He's an abomination and a disgrace to his office, but he *is* the Bishop of Winchester. In his present mood the king might believe anything he was told. If only I could see him!" She paced about the room, the image of the terrified Howard pounding on the chapel door, recurring in her mind.

In the afternoon Bessie brought word the king had returned and was in his apartments. Katherine, weak with relief, dressed herself with care. Surely he'd come to see her? He must know how mystified and frightened she was.

But Henry did not come and, by late afternoon, her apprehension increased. Was the king testing her? Had he been told such lies and falsehoods it would be impossible for him to show any justice as it had been made impossible for him to extend Catherine Howard any mercy? The thought cleared her mind. She would not accept this situation, she would not spend another night only to arise in the morning, more ill than ever from fear and loss of sleep. Tomorrow might be the most important day of her life and she had to be ready for it.

But Bessie had other thoughts. She, too, had caught some of Katherine's fear and indignation and, after a thoughtful time at the window looking out at the river, she knelt and put her arms about Katherine's waist.

"We've got to do something, Kate. I have an idea. It may not work but at least we'll not be sitting here like two geese waiting to be taken to market!" For the next half hour, Bessie explained what they must do. Several times Katherine, near tears, lapsed into laughter, edgy with nervousness, but a welcome relief from tension nevertheless. At last they were ready to put their plan into action.

Bessie placed Katherine near the door. Then, walking to the opposite side of the room, she held her hand high and cried in a quivering voice, "Yell, my queen! Yell good and loud! Oh, Kate, scream like you've never screamed before!"

Katherine opened her mouth and almost jumped from fright as a long, terrified wail filled the room. As her companion flung herself about the room, jumping up and down, urging her to even louder tones, much as if she were conducting a band of minstrels in the gallery down the hall, Katherine kept on screaming. At one point she thought of Anne Askew and moaned loudly, relieved to be giving visible vent to her anger and revulsion. When, at last, she gestured that she was becoming tired, her throat raw, Bessie nodded and began to keen softly. After several moments, her voice rose and she sobbed as realistically as if she were the accused. The noise was deafening. Once, as Bessie's wails reverberated loudly, Katherine put her hands over her ears, even as she smiled encouragement to her friend who was enjoying her own release from the fearful predicament.

After about an hour, both women pressed their heads to the door. They sensed the guards' presence outside and heard footsteps going in the direction of the king's quarters. Katherine looked at Bessie uncertainly. "Oh, Bess, what if he's not there? We don't know that he is! He may have returned to Greenwich or gone to Richmond and all this little make-believe will be for nothing!"

"Someone is out there, Kate, and no matter where His Grace is, he'll be told of this, you may be sure of it." Bessie sounded so cheerfully certain, Katherine reached out to hug her. Bessie's calm good sense was just what she needed. She knew her fear was only quiescent because of the ridiculous behavior of the past few hours.

As if sensing her thought, Bessie whispered, "Now once more, Kate! Whoever's out there, let him hear how you feel!" She raised her hand and again Katherine screamed, a long piercing wail, ending in a terrified moan as she threw herself exhausted on the bed while Bessie silently applauded.

Katherine lay there, waiting, while Bessie stood near the door, listening for sounds from the hall. Suddenly there was a loud exchange of words and the familiar tread of those porters who carried the king's chair could be heard. Exultant, Bessie signaled Katherine, running across the room to lead her to a nearby chair. "He's coming, Kate! The king is coming—I know it!" she whispered tightly. "Oh, Kate, pretend you are faint. Pretend your heart is broken that he would do this. And find out why!" She flew to the door as it opened and Henry, in robe and nightcap, was carried into the room. The porters put the chair on the floor, bowed and hurried out the door with Bessie behind them.

Katherine and Henry gazed at one another. The king looked old, ill and sullen. But he did not look like the ogre who would sentence her to a fate similar to two other queens. As she held out the incriminating paper, Katherine felt her anger return but knew she must hide it. Though she'd never grovel, she must be humble and as contrite as she'd ever been in her life. Softly, in a quivering voice, she asked, "Sire, I have this paper. I am horrified that you should regard or trust me so little. What have I done? Can't we talk about this? I am very upset, sire. . . ."

"Yes, Kate, we've heard how upset you are," Henry's voice was cool but she discerned a touch of humor in it. "We think the whole palace is very aware of your distress. We've been severely discommoded by such noise. We could not sleep."

"I am sorry, sire. I am very grieved and beg your forgiveness." Katherine let the paper fall to the floor. After the long sleepless hours, the anxiety of the day, her voice was faint and tears rose in her eyes.

Henry looked at Katherine as she stood in her rumpled robe, her face pale and distraught, swaying slightly from fatigue. It was almost as if he were seeing her for the first time. But it was Maud Parr standing there. Maud with her remarkable green eyes, her red-gold hair in disarray as she now waited for some explanation of the horror on the paper. Then Maud's image changed to that of her daughter. Kate, who'd mothered his children, dressed his infected leg, lain in his arms at night when he was too preoccupied or ill to do anything to comfort or pleasure her. And nagging at the back of his mind was what he'd say to Cuthbert Tunstall, to young Will Parr and old William Parr, to Ann and Will Herbert. His council was divided enough as it was and it took all his strength to control those factions who fought each other and themselves. Should he alienate some of those old and valued people who'd always been so loyal? Now, confronted by his wife and queen, he wondered what had so angered him that he'd issued the order that Gardiner had insisted upon. He remembered at the time he'd thought only to frighten his wife and teach her a lesson, so she'd keep her knowledge to herself and not parade it in front of unfriendly bishops.

Katherine saw the fleeting glimpse of uncertainty on her husband's face and knew, knew as if he'd said so, she would not go to the Tower. Not that she was out of danger. If someone had persuaded Henry to take such measures against her, he must be a bitter enemy indeed and he could strike again. The danger was not over; it was merely put aside. Now it was up to her to win her husband's trust again. Hadn't she determined before her marriage she would be a survivor?

"Kate," the king said wearily, "this has been a bad time for you. We will send Dr. Wendy to you in the morning. But now you must be content and rest. Don't belabor yourself—or us—anymore. Go to bed and don't worry. We will see you tomorrow." It was the nearest to an apology Katherine had ever heard Henry make.

Gratefully, she took his hand and kissed it. "I thank you for coming, sire. You have greatly renewed my spirit."

Henry patted her shouder. "Go to bed, Kate . . ." he half-smiled, "go to bed and be quiet." Then he called for his porters.

As the door closed behind him, Katherine tore the accusing paper in half and then lay down on the bed. She was drained of any emotion, even of guilt and fear for Anne Askew or concern for young Surrey. She must rest so that tomorrow she would be at her best when she saw Dr. Wendy and the king.

But even as she prayed for rest, it was a long time before she slept.

* * *

In the morning, Dr. Wendy told Katherine the king was in a conciliatory mood, but she should be careful not to irk him again. Lowering his voice, he said it was the incident with Bishop Gardiner that had infuriated Henry. After she'd left, the bishop had sympathized with Henry in tolerating a queen who—along with her ladies—flouted his desire for religious conformity. Katherine knew that had they been alone, Henry might only have shouted or sulked. But Gardiner had taken advantage of her husband's anger, disclosing that a friend of the queen's had recently been arrested, and intimated additional heresy within the palace might be discovered if he had the authority. He was certain the woman would give evidence proving the queen was a political burden and a religious nuisance. And so Henry had ordered his wife's detention hoping to frighten those other passionate reformers while awaiting whatever evidence Anne Askew would give.

It was then Katherine realized how desperate Gardiner had become. For the moment, he was dominant in the council and in a position to protect the Catholic Earl of Surrey against whom, Dr. Wendy implied, dangerous evidence had been found. He said Katherine must remain silent until the king decided what he would do. She now knew why Gardiner had become so maddened that he could forget his high office and personally rack a woman so he could obtain enough incriminating evidence to justify what he'd told the king.

But instead—with a courage he'd never envisioned—Anne had remained silent, refusing to involve the queen and her ladies. While Katherine was relieved Henry was no longer angry with her, she was heartsick knowing she was the cause of Anne's imprisonment and suffering.

Whispering her thanks to Dr. Wendy, she tried to compose herself so as to be at her best before the king. When her sister Ann appeared at midmorning, there was a tearful reunion and they walked together to the king's chambers. It was the first time in almost three days Katherine had left her own quarters and she was almost light-headed with relief as she entered the Privy Chamber. The king was not alone. Several councillors, among them the Earl of Hertford, Archbishop Cranmer and her brother Will, were present. None of Gardiner's colleagues were there. For the moment at least, the bishop was still in disfavor and those who thought as she did—and as the king once had—were present to witness her vindication.

Quickly, Katherine knelt before Henry. After inquiring if she'd slept well, he said she was there because he held her in such affection and respect he wanted his good councillors to hear her views on the charges made against her. No one mentioned, of course, that the indictment contained no charges whatsoever.

Sinking back in his chair, obviously enjoying the moment, his corpulent figure relaxed and confident, Henry pondered what question he might ask. Katherine took a deep breath and laughed lightly. "Ah, sire, you make merry at my expense! How could a poor silly woman with all the imperfections of her sex understand such diffuse questions of religion? What would my judgment be worth? There is only one head, one supreme head, sire, and that is Your Majesty. Next to God in Heaven, you are the one we must all lean unto!" She was rewarded by a gleam of humorous appreciation in Henry's eyes.

"Not so, by St. Mary!" Henry pounded the chair arm enthusiastically. "You have become almost a doctor yourself, Kate, one to instruct us, not to be directed by us."

"If Your Majesty take it so," Katherine laughed again, waving her hand aimlessly as if it held an invisible fan, "then you have mistaken me." She went on to explain she thought it unseemly for any woman to instruct her husband. "Rather I think she should be taught by him," she finished, as the image of John Neville, Lord Latimer, slamming doors against her arguments rose in her mind. If this was what the king and his councillors wanted, so be it. They all knew better, but if this little farce must be played out, she'd give them what was expected.

"Sire," she leaned over to take the hand Henry extended, "very often your pain has been such that I have sought to distract you with discussions that might entertain you so you might forget your discomfort. And, many times, you have instructed me to my profit! What is lost by such discussion? You have explained and I have learned."

Clearly pleased with his queen's performance, Henry arose and embraced her, kissing her loudly as his relieved councillors smiled broadly. "Is it so, sweetheart?" he asked tenderly. "Your arguments were to no worse end? Then we are perfect friends again as much as we have ever been. Your words are more welcome to me than one hundred thousand pounds!"

While everyone beamed, a loud stomping of feet could be heard outside the Privy Chamber and suddenly, Lord Chancellor Wriothesley entered with a band of the king's guard behind him. Startled, Katherine looked at Henry. Was this a trick—a shameful trick by which she'd humbly acted the submissive wife, only now to be carted off to the Tower? Then she realized it was a trick, but not a trick against her. Weak with relief, she sat down in her chair next to her husband's to watch Henry play out the rest of his comedy.

Expectantly, the Lord Chancellor stood silently, the order for the queen's arrest in his hand. As he noted the councillors and the apparent goodwill of king and queen, his self-satisfied look faded. Shifting from one foot to the other, he was clearly at a loss what to say. Then Henry exploded.

"Knave—you are a very knave, Wriothesley! A beast and a fool! Take your false order and leave us alone. We cannot stand the sight of you in our presence!"

Remembering this was the man who'd sadistically racked Anne Askew, Katherine tried to hide her disgust and revulsion. Wriothesley was really Gardiner's tool; any mercy shown him might extend to their helpless prisoner, now that their plot had backfired. Touching Henry on the arm, she said, "Perhaps there is a mistake, sire? Perhaps my Lord Chancellor is only carrying out his orders and is not himself to blame?" If nothing else, her words would inform the stunned and crestfallen Wriothesley that she, the queen, was well aware of how the whole plot had begun.

But for the moment, she could see anger—an honest anger—possessed the king. "No, it is not so, my Kate, and you little know how evil he deserves any grace at your hands. On my honor, sweetheart, he has behaved like a very knave!" Turning to Wriothesley, he shouted bitterly, "Get out of our presence, knave, you and your cohorts! We do not wish to see you again! Nor the face of anyone else who has committed this folly!"

Wriothesley now understood. Pale and silent, he bowed and, hoping to salvage any remaining remnants of poise, he backed out of the room. But he could hardly help hearing, as he walked quickly down the hall to the court-yard, the explosion of laughter in the Privy Chamber behind.

*   *   *

The following morning, Archbishop Cranmer visited Katherine. He said both Wriothesley and Bishop Gardiner had been forbidden to come into Henry's presence. When she inquired after Anne Askew, Cranmer promised to do everything in his power to obtain her release. But Katherine must remember she had two bitter enemies in the Lord Chancellor and the prelate and they would not make it easy. Since yesterday news of their disgrace had been celebrated all over the City as well as the court.

Katherine determined to put the whole dreadful episode behind her and she asked Henry's permission to stay at the little Chelsea manor house which he'd given her at their marriage. If Princess Mary and Princess Elizabeth could join her, perhaps Frances Grey would let daughter Jane visit, too. Katherine knew Prince Edward was too busy with his studies to be at Chelsea and the house was not large enough for his servants and tutors. She told Henry when the council's business wearied him that he, too, might enjoy the good Chelsea air and the absence of state business.

Affably, Henry agreed and that day couriers were dispatched to Mary and Elizabeth and to the Duchess Anne of Cleves so she might visit from Richmond. Katherine wrote the little prince explaining that he must especially practice his riding since the French ambassador would soon arrive at the English court and Edward would be expected to play the heir's part in the festivities. She knew it would satisfy the sensitive child who might otherwise be hurt by not joining his sisters.

Within three days Mary—looking better than she had in months—arrived with Susan Clarencieux. Much as she loved being with her father, it was apparent Mary was more comfortable in her own home with those close servants and ladies with whom she'd grown up. There she was free of any lingering memories of her mother and father when they'd been together. At Beaulieu, there were no familiar rooms with unpleasant associations, no enemies or treasonous friends, no father whose mood could change—with a bewildering swiftness and for reasons she never understood—from warm affection one moment to icy impatience or bitter sarcasm the next. At Chelsea, which she loved as much as Katherine, Mary was the girl who'd listened years ago to the gypsy's prophecy in the Richmond woods. She was the child watching Maud Parr and the French queen surreptitiously talk of the

Boleyn woman on the Parr House terrace and the little girl who'd hid behind a Cheapside pillar to watch the glowing triumph of her parents' return from progress.

The next morning, Katherine rode with Mary for an hour or more in the woods above the manor house. Later they wandered, silent and thoughtful, about Tom More's old home with its now overgrown gardens, its upswept terrace and littered path to the river. The property had reverted to the Crown and old Dame Alice More and her family, the young Ropers, now lived elsewhere. The thought of the gracious and witty Lord Chancellor More—how different from the present one!—depressed Katherine and she shivered recalling her own dire predicament only a week ago. Mary had not heard of the incident and Katherine had cautioned Bessie not to mention it. She intended to forget it had ever happened; she knew she would never forget *how* it had happened.

In the late afternoon, the two women sat on the river wall eating cherries that Mary had brought from Beaulieu. They watched a barge approaching in the distance and, as it neared, saw Elizabeth standing impatiently in the prow. No sooner had it beached than the girl agilely leapt onto the boards so as not to muddy her gown and, after a quick curtsey, flung herself on Katherine, crying, "Oh, madame, it is so good to see you!" She turned and embraced a smiling Mary.

"Bess, you've grown so! You are taller than either of us!" Mary spun the ecstatic Elizabeth about. It was true; Elizabeth was almost a head taller than both of them. Katherine felt a catch in her throat, remembering the frantic little girl beating her fists against the window to catch her father's attention. And the silent young daughter, tearless and despairing, who'd abjectly gone off to a year's exile because she'd dared ask about her mother. Elizabeth was now fourteen, but clearly she was no longer a child. It was not only her height, but a maturity of face and manner that gave her the appearance of being older. She has poise, Katherine thought; at least now she's not letting her emotions rule. She's using her head instead of her heart.

Behind Elizabeth, her companion waited to kneel before Katherine. "This is Catherine Ashley, but we call her Cat. She was Mistress Champernowne and kin to my Lady Denny. She has just wed and now has to leave her husband so soon!" Elizabeth's laugh pealed out causing Cat Ashley's young cheeks to redden. Katherine smiled at the handsome girl, hoping to put her at ease. Cat Ashley looked sensible and equal to the task of handling the volatile Elizabeth. She indicated Cat might walk with them to the manor house but, predictably, Elizabeth soon clutched the girl by the arm and pulled her toward arbor and fishpond to show all the secret little places she'd enjoyed as a child in the king's little riverside home.

As Mary indulgently shook her head, Katherine linked arms with her and they walked toward the house. Jane Grey would arrive the next day and then, for several weeks, they would cast aside court protocol and forget the troublesome issues facing king and country. They would picnic in the surrounding woods, wade in the Thames or take a boat as the old queen and Maud Parr had done years ago, singing their songs and throwing food to the fishes and herons that waded in the shore waters. It would take Jane a few days to relax and realize she would not be chastened or pinched for some imagined offense, that she might scamper with cousin Elizabeth and talk with her stepgrand-aunt, the queen, without any reproach. Katherine knew the joy and relief of these next few weeks would replenish her own depleted emotional reserves and give her the strength to return to London and a king whose health was dangerously poor, where those in the council and court jockeyed for the power and influence that would follow upon his death.

And what, she thought, watching Mary and Elizabeth, would happen to them? As princesses of the realm, they would owe obedience and loyalty to young Prince Edward. But, because of his youth, the strong leadership his father had always provided must be administered by someone else. Who would that someone be? The religious issues that had torn the country apart since the 1530s were all personified in Princess Mary, a Catholic, and the two younger children, who'd been taught by reformers and could never remember a time when the Pope was revered in England. No matter who gained power within the council, the king's children would be vitally affected.

Katherine did not worry for herself. Once Henry had gone—and the thought in itself was so treasonous she always crossed herself when it entered her mind—she would live out her days at Wyke and in her little riverside dower house here in Chelsea. She could visit John at Chartreuse or Snape and pay long visits to Margaret and her Borough stepchildren in the North. She would spend the remainder of her days as a beloved and respected Dowager-Queen.

Or would she? Inevitably, such thoughts brought Thomas Seymour to mind. Thomas had done well in the past few years, yet he'd never married. Katherine was always shaken by the intensity of her yearning to be back in that time—now over three years ago—when they'd been in love. What would happen when she no longer had a husband?

The forbidden thoughts would not go away. They only made her feel foolishly guilty and all the more determined to enjoy this brief respite at Chelsea. Each day the king grew older and the future more uncertain. Such peace might never come again.

* * *

At dusk the following day, Katherine, Mary and Elizabeth emerged from the woods above the manor house and, walking toward the little building silhouetted against the river in the waning sunlight, saw the Suffolk barge at the landing.

"My Lady Suffolk is here!" Elizabeth clapped her hands delightedly. Long ago, Kate Brandon had endeared herself to the princess with her caustic wit and forthright tongue—indulgences Elizabeth now realized she was not allowed. They were much alike, Katherine thought, the princess and the duchess.

She wondered what had brought the duchess to Chelsea. She'd waited until late morning for the Grey's barge to bring Lady Jane, but it had not arrived. It would be just like Frances Grey, she told Bessie, to make Jane wait and spoil the day for her. Bessie promised to look after the child if she arrived so Katherine and her stepdaughters might go on their picnic.

Once inside the house, the three looked expectantly about the candle-lit rooms. Ascending the stairs they met Bessie on the landing. Bess had been crying; her eyes were swollen and red and she would not meet Katherine's alarmed look. Behind her in the shadows was Catherine Ashley. Instinctively, Elizabeth moved toward her companion, who put an arm about her.

"Bess, what is it? Has something happened to my Lady Suffolk?" Katherine looked about the landing as Kate Brandon, holding little Jane Grey by the hand, appeared in the doorway. Bessie seemed unable to speak and gestured toward the duchess who came forward to embrace Katherine.

"My dear, I bring tragic news and I'm loathe to be the one to tell you. But better I perhaps than anyone else." She looked about at the others, still staring helplessly, although Jane had run to Mary to hide her face in the folds of her skirt.

"Well, Kate, speak up!" Mary's deep voice was impatient. "What is it? Is it the king?"

"No, it is not the king," Kate's voice was tight. "He is well, for which God be praised. He and his council have worked hard. I trust they all have their rest untroubled this night. If they do, they will be one of the few in London who do so." As Katherine stared, bewildered and sickened with a foreboding she thought she'd put behind her, Kate Brandon explained in a voice strong with emotion.

"Anne Askew was executed today, Katherine. She went to Smithfield and was burnt alive. She had to be carried because of her damaged legs. She died with two others, with that spineless priest Shaxton, who used to speak with us and who later recanted, offering a pardon if she named those who believed as she did. Your cousin Throckmorton went to offer solace but was told to leave and not endanger himself or his family. Before she went to Smithfield, Anne somehow bribed someone to come to me and say she'd not told the council or anyone else anything that would endanger you. She said she died happy, that she was keeping her word with the Lord."

A numbness crept over Katherine as she gazed at her dearest friend, willing her to say it was a vile mistake, that Anne was still in prison—in distress even—but alive. But Kate said nothing and the numbness grew as the image of Anne, bound tightly because her legs were useless, waited until the faggots were lit and the flames consumed her. As the image assaulted her brain and senses, there was a moan that Katherine did not recognize as her own and her legs seemingly disappeared beneath her. She heard Elizabeth crying, "Oh, madame, madame . . . !" The doorway spun about in a circle and then someone was holding her by the shoulders. The abominable picture of Anne Askew amidst flames then darkened, finally disappearing into darkness. It was more than her mind could bear.

CHAPTER XXVI

In the throne room at Hampton Court Palace, Queen Katherine and King Henry were seated on the dais awaiting Claude d'Annebault, the Governor of Normandy and Admiral of France, who had come to England to ratify the French peace. The August day was warm and Katherine was grateful she was not riding, clad in heavy velvets, to meet the ambassador at Hounslow Heath. Instead, the king had ordered that Prince Edward, with several councillors, greet the ambassador and escort him to the palace. Edward had been proudly pleased until, at the last moment, as his entourage of nobles, knights and gentlemen waited on their mounts in the Base Court, he became a nine-year-old boy instead of the king's son. Tugging Katherine's sleeve, he'd whispered, "Do you think the ambassador will know what I say if I speak to him in Latin?"

Katherine understood the child's anxiety. Edward was not as skillful in languages as his sisters and was worried that even his Latin might not be good enough. She'd soothed the nervous prince, telling him that—when the occasion arose—certainly his uncle, the Earl of Hertford, or his godfather, Archbishop Cranmer, would suggest something appropriate. It seemed to mollify the anxious child and Katherine had then led him to a mirror to show him how magnificent he looked.

She'd helped select his crimson and white satin doublet scattered with tiny diamonds and jewels about the collar and cuffs. Though only nine, the prince was taller than his two good friends, little Barnaby Fitzpatrick and Robert Dudley, Joan Dudley's son, who lounged about him now, respectful and more than a little awed. But one of Edward's shoulders was higher than the other and this tended to make him self-conscious and shy. Edward had needed all the cosseting and love Katherine had been able to give—needed it more than the aggressive Elizabeth or the embittered Mary. As he left the room, his pale skin flushed, his wheat-blond hair covered with a white satin cap, hiding his apprehension as best he could, her heart ached and she prayed the ambassador would be kindly tolerant toward the child.

Now while the court milled about, as Henry slapped his Fool, Will Somers, affectionately on the back as he changed the pillow on which the king's leg rested, Katherine thought how much she'd prayed for solace and strength in the weeks following Anne Askew's death. The appalling news had spoiled the Chelsea holiday and, within days, Mary and Elizabeth had returned home. Katherine wanted to get back to Whitehall, to her brother, sister and husband—to anyone who could explain the tragedy. Why was Anne burnt? Wasn't Gardiner now in disrepute? Hadn't Cranmer said he'd do his best to protect her?

She'd had her answer from Will Parr, waiting at Whitehall. Katherine had sent word she wanted to see her brother even before she saw the king. Will described what had happened.

"Kate, there was no way the Askew woman could be saved. She didn't *want* to be saved! She'd convinced herself that to be a martyr for her belief would be her strongest statement against superstition and the Roman corruption of what Christ taught. She said if she couldn't die for what she knew to be true, how could she make people believe her faith was honest?" As Katherine wept, pacing about the room, Will did not spare her. "Anne was brought to the stake and tied securely because her legs were so disjointed she couldn't stand. When she saw the Throckmortons, she told them they did no good to themselves and advised them to leave. She cried out to the other prisoners to be cheerful as they were going to meet God face-to-face, that there would be no pain. For her it could not come too quickly. After old Shaxton had preached his sermon, a messenger came from the king offering a pardon if she would recant. She told him she hadn't traveled such a long road to deny her Lord and Master now. She pleaded with the others not to weaken and they didn't. There was no choice but to light the fire."

Katherine could imagine the scene. Anne transcendent with a glorious courage, eager to show the depth of her faith. Had she cried out against Bishop Shaxton, calling him a liar and a hypocrite—he who months before had preached those same beliefs for which she was dying—only to lose his nerve and recant when the Privy Council took him to task? Had she laughed at the king's messenger?

Whatever it was, said Will, Anne's death had angered Londoners more than anything since the execution of Prior Houghton and the Carthusian monks. And they'd made their displeasure known to all who'd signed the death warrant—Gardiner, Wriothesley and Cranmer—by demonstrations at Smithfield, Lambeth Palace and Winchester House in Southwark where Gardiner lived.

"Cranmer signed the death warrant?" Katherine asked, disbelievingly. "He said he'd try to save Anne if he could!"

"Well, he couldn't and my lord archbishop is not one to take a stand," Will explained gently, "and the Privy Council, the bishop and the chancellor wanted this woman out of the way. She was not just an ordinary nuisance."

"And she was a friend of the queen. . . ." Katherine turned away, her throat closing against her sobs. "This is something I will bear to my death, Will. Anne was a sacrifice, don't you see? A sacrifice to the enmity of the bishop and the hatred of the chancellor who've both been disgraced because the king chose to protect his queen at their expense. Oh, Jesu, that no one could stop it . . . !"

"No one could, Kate." Will put an arm about his sister's shoulders. "Anne had determined to die and to die in the way she did. In the end, she got what she wanted! She got the best of everyone—she won! Her death made more of an impact on those who believe as she did than a dozen sermons by Cranmer or his colleagues. At the end, I think she was half in that other world she spoke of so strongly. Really, she made fools of those who sent her to the stake, for none have gained anything by it. Mark you, they lost too."

* * *

The sound of trumpets interrupted Katherine's thoughts and suddenly, at the room's end, there stood a visibly triumphant Edward accompanied by a tall, distinguished, gray-bearded Admiral d'Annebault. Behind them a cordon of English and French knights waited to enter. D'Annebault's left hand was covered by Edward's small palm and, at a signal from the head usher, the trumpets blew again and together the prince and ambassador walked the length of the room. Quickly, an aide removed Henry's stool and Katherine deftly put out a hand to steady her husband as he struggled to his feet to greet the man who'd led the French invasion on the Isle of Wight two years ago. She smiled at Edward as he stepped aside so the king and ambassador might exchange pleasantries. Off to one side, Edward Seymour, the Earl of Hertford, caught her eye, nodding and smiling toward Edward. It was his way of telling her the prince, his nephew, had behaved admirably and all was well.

Just to Hertford's right she saw another familiar figure. Thomas Seymour was gazing at her, his glance as outwardly casual as his brother's, but with a familiarity and awareness he knew only she would recognize. She was glad of the chatter and activity for otherwise she might have shown her surprise. Of course, Thomas would be present for so important an occasion. How could it be otherwise? He was the prince's uncle, the king's brother-in-law and Vice-Admiral of the Navy as well. And her former lover. Her eyes locked with his and the strain of the past few weeks melted away in pleasure at the sight of him. Thomas looked splendid, his plumed cap tucked beneath his arm; his rust-brown velvet doublet, slashed with small puffs of cream-colored satin, fitted the lean, hard figure with distinction. Katherine was startled at the intensity of her longing to run from the dais, to fling herself into his arms, to forget for a while the strain and sorrow of the past few weeks, the king's poor health and the constant necessity of being smilingly gracious —even to one's enemies. Thomas represented love and wit, an awareness and teasing familiarity she'd relished because it made her feel genuinely desirable. Why be a hypocrite and not admit it?

She was still shaken when, later that evening, as the welcoming festivities for the visiting Frenchmen commenced in old Wolsey's vast Banqueting

Hall, Thomas claimed her for the first masque. While the queen traditionally never covered her face, Katherine recognized him at once. He stood before her in white satin with a cloth of gold trim, his masque a satyr's face sprinkled with jewels, and held out his hand. It was the first time he'd held her since their parting and that deliciously warm limpness swept over her. *I am being stupidly foolish,* she thought, as she followed his expert lead. *By the time this dance is over, I must be in control.* Thomas remained silent, yet never took his eyes from her face.

At the end, she was the first to speak. Gazing at him, she took the masque admiring its delicacy. "A lovely disguise, my lord"—she held it to his face again—"but I recognized you at once. Welcome home, Thomas! Did not my lord prince do well today?" Common sense had returned and she felt very proud of herself.

But Thomas was not in the mood for banter. "I want to see you, Katherine. I must see you." He put out his hand and, not wishing to cause a scene, she took it indicating she'd return to Henry's side. Instead, Thomas led her to a corner where elderly court members were gathered. They bowed to the queen and her companion who was loudly and humorously recounting events of d'Annebault's reception at Hounslow. Katherine turned her back to them. "Thomas, this is unwise. I must return to my place. Please take me back."

"Kate, it's all right. I'm no fool. Everyone is busy with the Frenchmen now. We're the prince's uncle and stepmother speaking of him here together, right in plain view of everyone!" He lowered his voice. "But I must see you. . . ."

"Thomas, I will not see you alone. I must make that plain." Katherine was firm. How could this man who'd walked away from her three years ago because the king had indicated his own interest, now think their relationship could be resumed? How dare Thomas think she'd be that easily persuaded? If he didn't return her immediately, she would leave him alone and that would cause those busy elders to more gossip than the occasion demanded.

Scowling, Thomas replied, "Then you leave me no alternative but to speak now." He looked about again and then, laughing heartily as if she'd just said something very amusing, drew her to the long window as if to show her something outside on the river.

"Now, Kate, listen quietly. I know the king is failing—failing more than perhaps even you realize. And he has yet to make a will! I know that evidence will soon come out that my Lord Surrey and his father, Norfolk, have plotted—because of their rotten Plantagenet blood—to try and take the throne when Henry dies." At Katherine's incredulous look, his face hardened and he went on. "They have! Don't look so surprised! If anything happens to the king, you must remember there are more Catholics than there are reformers. They'd rise up to support Norfolk and there'd be as bloody a rebellion as you told me of in the North! And he might succeed! My brother is sick with worry over the whole thing. Kate, Kate, I could shake you! Don't you see? Doesn't Henry understand?

"He's settled the Succession, everyone knows that. The crown goes to Edward. But who is to protect the boy's rights? Henry must name someone! He must make a will designating a Protector or a Regent. Who will deal with the problem of religion? Someone has to make it plain what people should believe so the issue can be put aside and the real problems dealt with. Our currency is so debased it is the laughingstock of the Antwerp moneylenders. Look about London, Kate! We have a small army of soldiers and sailors who fought in France who haven't been paid. They're starving outside Whitehall's gates and any church they can get into to say a final prayer. If they have any strength left when Henry goes, they'll side with anyone who'll feed them and dress their wounds. I was shocked, Kate, when I returned from France to see how Henry has failed—he's bloated with dropsy and my lord brother says that leg is going to have to be cauterized, it's become so infected. Otherwise the doctors are afraid it might rot away. Kate, do you understand what I'm saying?"

"I understand what you're saying, Thomas, and you know there are people in this room—the king, for instance—who would consider your words treasonous." She felt a little stab of pleasure at the dismay on her companion's face. It wasn't often she'd had the better of Tom Seymour! "But don't be afraid, Thomas, I will not repeat what you say. I know you mean well and much of what you say is true. I know you want Edward's inheritance protected. So do I! I want Mary and Elizabeth's future assured also, as well as my own! As uncle of the heir, however, I can understand your concern for Edward's well-being."

As Thomas's face flushed a deep red, Katherine looked about the room to see if they'd been noticed. The king, seated on the throne and in deep conversation with d'Annebault and his companions, appeared not to miss her. Edward Seymour and his beautiful countess, Anne Stanhope, were in the center of a large cluster apart from the throne, waiting for the minstrels to commence their next piece.

Katherine put her hand out for Thomas. "I must return, my lord, but I'll remember what you say. The king may listen and he may not. Sometimes my advice is not welcome." She shivered slightly, remembering the events preceding Anne Askew's death. She saw Edward had joined his father. As the boy bowed low, saying his good-night to the French ambassador, the king ruffled his hair fondly. Katherine wanted to see her stepson before he left and she hurried Thomas along. "We must say good-night to Edward also, my lord. Remember to tell him how well he conducted himself today. The ambassador said he has beautiful manners and was very gallant for one so young. But the prince is not an overly proud boy, you know, and he lacks confidence. Now he looks quite pleased—I'm certain his uncle's praise will be welcome."

Thomas squeezed her hand, nodding. "And you'll remember what I said, Kate?"

"I'll remember what you said, Thomas."

*   *   *

As if justifying Thomas Seymour's concern, within weeks of d'Annebault's departure and the arrival of the new French ambassador, Odet de Selve, the king became ill. Henry considered the peace terms—that England would hold Boulogne for eight years after which France would redeem it for two million crowns—his own personal victory. But the splendor of the French visit —the mumming and banqueting, the early hunting at dawn, the jousts and tournaments at which he'd stood for long periods to reward the contestants had taken its toll.

Katherine was relieved when Henry at last went uncomplainingly to bed. She heard his groan of distress as the doctors cauterized the open running leg sores; he was pale for hours after the treatment. He slept for short periods, his corpulent, bloated body restless in the vast canopied bed. A few old and trusted courtiers visited and he attended to the official paperwork, but shortly before Christmas, even those activities became too much and Edward Seymour was designated to represent the king at the council table and court functions. The action was not lost on those councillors whose trust of each other was fleeting at best. If he had to stay in bed and pamper his leg, Henry grudgingly told Katherine, there was at least some reward, for it was an amusing game to wonder which councillor would overstep his authority first.

Henry's idle comment, made as she sat at his bedside with her needle-work, while Will Somers played a flute nearby, gave Katherine the opportunity she'd been looking for.

"If they plague you, sire, then you should meet them on their own ground and put them in their place. They take advantage of your sickness. . . ." Katherine knew better than to imply that her husband's illness was more than a badly infected leg. "You've always been there to keep one group from getting the best of the other. If you must be away because you're not well, what will stop my Lord Hertford and Cranmer from fighting with Wriothesley and old Paget? What will prevent Gardiner's friends to work to get him back on the council?"

Katherine knew she wasn't telling the king anything he didn't already know. He'd dismissed Stephen Gardiner from the council after the attempt to discredit and arrest her and, in so doing, the council's balance of power had swung back to the Hertford faction again. But *she* felt better that Henry knew her concern. Whatever he decided for the future vitally affected her as well as his children and the English people. Each day she was more visibly convinced of the king's physical deterioration and, realist that she was, wondered what would happen when this capricious giant was gone.

His next words startled her. "We know your thoughts, Kate." He held out his hand. "We look in the mirror and see our gray hairs and beard just like old Will's!" He smiled at the Fool who bowed his head with a sadness Katherine had never seen before. She took her husband's hand, startled to find it trembling. Compassionately she held it to her cheek, shaken at Henry Tudor's bitter realization that he was mortal, that his vitality and exuberance were slowly draining away. Not only was that huge majestic frame, once so gloriously lean and healthy, now almost unrecognizable, but even that clever brain, usually so quick to respond to challenge, to recognize deceit and intrigue, was as tired as his body. The old excitement of baiting councillors and rival ambassadors, keeping the balance of power by standing between them—the ultimate decision always his, of course—had diminished also. As Katherine felt his anger and resentment, heartache mingled with concern, for she recognized something else in Henry's attitude. Acceptance. Was nature this kind, she wondered, that it could make so powerful a sovereign, so self-assured a man, agree that he must give way and turn his power and authority to others? That he, heretofore supremely invincible, was no longer capable of determining his own fate?

Henry saw her foreboding. "Kate, no tears. We will have no tears! Those eyes of yours, filled with tears, remind us of emeralds, Kate, and we have some which should be yours." Quickly, he motioned to a gentleman-usher at the door and whispered a few words to the man who quickly left the room. "Now we will have some wine, Kate, and then we must get up, whether our leg thinks so or not. We must meet with the council. But we will sup tonight, sweetheart, and soon you will have your jewels." As she handed him the wine cup he reached out from the bed to embrace her, the old gray head level with her shoulder. She held him close for a moment as he whispered "But *I*, Kate, *I*, not we—*I* have the best jewel of all. . . ."

The next morning, after Henry left for the council room, the gentleman-usher arrived and placed a small rosewood coffer before Katherine. She'd been writing Princess Mary and, laying down her pen, cried, "Come, Bess, and see the king's gift. Emeralds, he said. Come and see!" As the messenger discreetly left the room, she took the key from the soft animal skin pouch tied to the coffer and unlocked it.

She could scarcely believe her eyes. Henry had said emeralds and she'd expected a necklace, perhaps several rings and brooches. But Bessie's gasp of amazement echoed her own. For there in the coffer was a king's treasure of diamonds, pearls, garnets, rubies, turquoise and heavy gold pieces carved and twisted into "friars' knotts," small jeweled fans, feathers, beasts and chains. There were several crosses of gold or wood studded with jewels, obviously stripped from church ornaments. A small pouch held loose stones from other religious relics. And there at the bottom, lay the emeralds—a long necklace of perfect, deeply green-glowing emeralds, as green as her mother's eyes. Taking them from the velvet-lined case, Katherine thought how Maud Parr would have loved this rich display. While Bessie held a mirror so Katherine could see the emeralds against her neck, the messenger spoke. "The king chose them all, madame. I brought back much more, but these were the ones he wanted you to have. He said they were the most perfect."

Dazed, Katherine nodded. Bessie had put several stones together, suggesting what a pretty brooch they'd make. "No, Bess," she said. "Let's wait. It will be Christmas soon and some of this can be shared with Mary and Elizabeth. Not the emeralds, of course. His Grace meant those for me. But these others." She indicated an ivory cross, delicate with tiny bands of diamonds and turquoise. "Mary would like that. And how Bess would love these pearls—you know they're her favorite!" Henry would not care if some of his treasure went to his children. And she must find a pale amethyst for Edward; lavender was his favorite color. How proud he'd be to wear one on his small thumb, the same as his father did.

They were still admiring the jewels when the king returned to his chamber and Katherine crossed the corridor to see him. Henry was sitting at his desk, his face flushed a deep angry red. A messenger waited, as he signed a long document similar to the one she'd recently held in her own hands. As he gave it to the messenger, waving him away, Katherine cried, "What is wrong, sire? Are you all right? You look distressed. . . ."

Henry sighed, putting away his pen. Though some of the flush was leaving his cheeks, Katherine saw he was still disturbed. The main business of the Privy Council that morning, the king explained, had been Henry Howard, the Earl of Surrey and his father, the Duke of Norfolk. And it had been worse than even he had thought. For months, evidence had been gathered from a variety of witnesses—many former friends of the earl and the duke—and it now appeared that Surrey and Norfolk had practiced treasonous activities. The document was an order for their arrest.

At Katherine's stunned look, Henry described the escutcheon found at Kenninghall, the Howard home in Norfolk, which had the royal arms of England in one quarter. The motto, *Honi soit qui mal y pense* had been replaced with "Till then thus." More than once the earl had said that, when the king was gone, there was none so capable of guiding Prince Edward than the Duke of Norfolk. Otherwise, he predicted, such creatures as Hertford and Cranmer would rule, ridding themselves of others of noble blood and surrounding the prince with low persons such as themselves.

"His explanation was that his father's first wife was our aunt, Princess Anne Plantagenet, and if she had the right to quarter arms on her shield, why not he?" Henry's voice was rasping, the thick purplish veins about his neck distended. "He forgets our father defeated the Plantagenet at Bosworth Field! He forgets he's been dear to us, as dear as a son! But he has made idle boasts and is overly proud and is insolently contemptuous of those who serve us well, like Hertford. He told Cranmer he'd rather see his son in his coffin than wed to Hertford's daughter. He sneers at the Seymours and forgets a Seymour was our son's mother! When he went before the council last night at Wriothesley's house in Holborn, he was so scornful of their charges, he suggested he and the chancellor remove their doublets and wrestle with each other. If he won he would be innocent! He was surprised no one took him seriously. . . ."

"He is his own worst enemy, sire, but perhaps one can forgive him his youth. . . ."

"There will be no forgiveness, Kate, for he and his father have plotted against us. And you may be certain Gardiner had a hand in this. You know he and Norfolk have always been close—both of them hoping we'd make a friend again of the Pope! They fight constantly with Hertford and do all they can to undermine Cranmer. We will not tolerate it any longer! They were even plotting, once we were no longer here, to get my lord prince's person and rule in his place!" Henry paced slowly about the chamber, his wrath returning as he comprehended the enormity of the Howards' treachery. "We have little choice, Kate. Surrey is too brash for his own good. He never thinks of the consequences. As for Norfolk," Henry's voice wavered a bit, "we can only think it was a father looking out for his son which led old Tom to forsake us. Now he knows *we* will look out for our son, too!" Despite his bravado, Henry appeared troubled as well as angry. Thomas Howard, the aging Duke of Norfolk, was the premier peer of the realm, the only other duke being Kate and Charles Brandon's son, the seventeen-year-old Duke of Suffolk. Norfolk had been a friend since childhood. Yet both Howards had dared to touch his scepter, as two Howard queens had made a fool of him. Was he remembering them now, Katherine wondered, still too shaken to reply.

She was comforted when later that evening, Henry said that he would meet with Hertford and several other councillors. At that time he meant to speak with Cranmer and Hertford about his will.

* * *

The splendid Christmas revels at Greenwich, while outwardly merry, were marred for Katherine by a visibly ill husband. But she did her best to cheer Henry and his children during the day while keeping the mummers and minstrels busy each evening. On several occasions, the king was absent, meeting with his councillors across the courtyard to discuss the imprisonment of Surrey and Norfolk. Katherine danced with young Edward, who proudly wore his amethyst ring and twirled his stepmother and sisters in the festivities that followed the mumming. Each morning, the prince, happy to be relieved of his studies, escorted Katherine, Mary and Elizabeth to the top of Greenwich hill and then, shouting as loudly as a tinker's lad, held his lance high, pointing straight ahead, as he led all three racing across the fields, Elizabeth's long red hair, unbound and streaming behind, her dark eyes fixed on that distance where she meant to arrive first. Sometimes she did, but often, Edward was there ahead, laughing and jubilantly waving his lance. Moments later, Katherine and Mary joined them at a more sedate pace.

"Don't you want to be first, Mary? Don't you want to win?" Elizabeth cried, puzzled, as she wound her hair away from her flushed and sweating face. "You could win if you tried!"

"It depends upon the prize, Bess. When I was your age, I rode like you. Now I, and the queen, too, are just as happy to give way. In the end, you see, we're here with you both. It just took a little longer. And along the way, we were not uncomfortable, we could relish the wind in our face and appreciate the skill of our horse. It doesn't matter that we weren't first." Mary winked at Katherine. It was incomprehensible to Elizabeth that one should not try to win.

It was after such an outing, with Kate Brandon and her fifteen-year-old son Charles accompanying them, that Katherine again met Thomas Seymour. As everyone dismounted in the palace courtyard, she saw several councillors gathered near the stables, obviously waiting for their mounts. Edward flew to greet his uncle. As everyone bowed respectfully, Thomas put an arm about the prince, explaining to Katherine, "We await His Grace, madame, for we leave for London at once."

Katherine was surprised. Henry had not indicated the court would be leaving Greenwich. As Edward ran off to the stables, she started to leave saying there was much to do. But Thomas stopped her.

"That won't be necessary, madame. The court will remain here. Only those you see here are leaving." At her puzzled look, he lowered his voice. "Surrey will die soon. He made a fool of himself at the trial and did his father, who is still in the Tower, little good with his proud boasting. He reviled practically everyone here—one of his friends said that after the king died, Surrey had even bragged how we'd all smart for it! Had he admitted his foolishness, had he repented and thrown himself on the king's mercy, I think he might have been saved. But he's angered Henry too much, and everyone agrees there is nothing more to be done. I think his punishment will show everyone that the king will not tolerate any challenge to Edward's inheritance."

"I remember the May Day you bested him, Thomas. It was all so silly and wasteful the way he acted. That overweening pride has been his death! Did he and Norfolk really think they could stir up such trouble? If so, they deserve to die. . . ." Katherine said remembering the scenes along the York Road.

"Ah, it is all such a waste!" Recalling their last conversation, she said, "But Henry has made his will, Thomas. I'm sure you know that. It should settle the matter once and for all."

"I wish I were that certain, Kate." Suddenly, his look was that of the Thomas of old. "But we'll talk of it no more. I'll miss you at court. I miss you much of the time, Kate. I. . . ." He was interrupted as the grooms brought the horses forward and the king, with Cranmer and Lord Hertford, appeared in the doorway. The children ran to him and Katherine joined Mary to say goodbye. She was amazed at her composure. She'd just heard that a young and proud scion of England's noblest family was to die and it had left her unmoved. She pitied old Norfolk more. Her husband was leaving without her and she should be disappointed; instead she was relieved. Now she, Kate Brandon and Mary, too, if she chose to stay, might enjoy the luxury and solitude of Greenwich without the formal court etiquette that always surrounded the king. Edward and Elizabeth would return to their studies. She would miss them for she'd counted on their company for a few more weeks.

But, she admitted ruefully as she knelt before her husband to say farewell, what she missed most of all was what Thomas Seymour had been about to say.

* * *

Ten days later, Bessie Bellingham awakened her shortly after midnight. The king was ill and wished to see her, Bessie explained dolefully. The barge was being readied and an escort was waiting, so they must leave at once. Mary had been sent for from Beaulieu, but no one was to tell the two younger children. It was the king's express wish.

In a moment, Kate Brandon was there in her robe, her long hair braided about her shoulders, helping the other ladies-in-waiting pack some of the queen's belongings. "Take only what you need, my dear, and I'll see to the rest. Take Bessie with you." She hugged Katherine. Both were near tears, guessing the summons meant the king's condition had worsened.

Katherine's apprehension increased during the ride back to London. It had been years since she'd been on the river so late and the mist, rising from the sluicing water alongside the barge, twirled about her into eerily thickening shapes and forms. Sitting with Bessie in the prow, she drew her cloak close about her against the cutting damp, watching the cloak's hemline disappear in the curling fingers of mist seeping into the barge itself. There were faint cries from those on the shore who—from the dozens of lanterns placed about it—recognized the royal barge. In a few hours it would be light and the City would begin to stir. What would happen when its citizens heard their king might be dying? Or was already dead? What would she find at Whitehall? The thought made her so miserable, she clasped Bessie's hands and the two sat, wordless, until Whitehall stairs loomed in the mist before them and the bargemen cried out for the waiting attendants.

In the doorway of the king's chamber, the sentries respectfully stepped aside and there in the great gilded bed, with its canopy of crimson velvet and cloth of gold embroidery, lay her husband. Dr. Wendy was on one side, Archbishop Cranmer on the other. Edward Seymour, the Earl of Hertford, came forward to greet her, his footsteps muffled on the heavy Turkey carpet. In the shadows against the crimson velvet draperies that covered the windows facing the Thames, a stricken Will Somers nodded. As she neared the bed, their eyes met. The Fool shook his head ever so slightly, tears welling up in his eyes. The glance told Katherine all she wanted to know and his misery affected her more than anything else.

Then she was there, holding out her hand to the gray-faced man. Henry wore his nightcap and, although the room was noticeably warm, a heavy fur robe covered the bed. Weakly he clasped her hand with hot swollen fingers. "My Kate." He attempted a smile through fever-cracked lips. "We didn't send for you, my dear, for we are no prize to see now! But our brother Cranmer insisted you'd want to see us!" Katherine glanced gratefully at the mild-faced archbishop. Cranmer nodded. "Princess Mary will be here very soon, Your Grace," he whispered, "she was sent for the same time as you, but has further to come." He rose from his chair. "I'll leave you now. . . ."

"No!" Henry waved a hand. "We want all of you to listen to what we have to say. You, our brother in the church and you, Edward, our brother in fact. We want you to know that if it is God's will that we should part, we now order you to honor and treat our beloved wife, Katherine Parr, as if we were living still. If it is her pleasure to marry again, so be it, and she should have a jointure for it. She is to keep all her jewelry and ornaments. . . ." The effort to speak was almost too much and Henry's breathing became more difficult. His words had moved everyone, Katherine most of all, and, tearfully, she leaned over the bed. "Rest now, sire. Will is here and he'll stay with you. Rest for a while. . . ." The king nodded and closed his eyes.

Back in her chamber, Katherine tried to compose herself. She must accept the reality of a life without Henry Tudor. The king was dying, there was little doubt of that. Always before, after periods of illness, that great body had risen again, his lust for life as great as his lust for power, as deep as his lust for women had once been. But no more. Anyone would be a fool to think the king would ever arise from his sickbed, that he could again be an effective monarch.

It would be such a shock to Edward and Elizabeth. Both were so young they still saw him with the eyes of youth. Their father was king and invincible; they'd never seen him when he wasn't in command. Neither could remember their mothers; this would be the first great sadness of their lives. And Edward would be king. A boy not ten until October! At the moment that was almost more than Katherine could bear thinking of. She'd hoped to convince Henry to name her Regent so she might guide and help Edward with his awesome responsibility. When the king had worked on his will, she'd mentioned the possibility, reminding him of her regency when he'd been in France.

But the king had only laughed, saying, "You must not be hurt, Kate, but it would not do. You are clever, intelligent and have great political skill. We have listened much to you and been the better for it. But the Privy Council would not accept it, my dear. They'd fight and snap behind your back, while fawning to your face, and little by little, control would be taken from you. No, we must think of a way so that no one person is predominant—so that all will be safe for Edward."

She remembered Thomas's whispered words, his seeming doubt, about Henry's will. What could the king have done that made his brother-in-law so uncertain?

She was just finishing letters to Edward and Elizabeth when Princess Mary entered her chamber. As they embraced, Katherine felt her tears start again, for Mary appeared devastated. "Oh, Kate, he's going to die! I can't believe it!" Her voice was choked and her hands shook uncontrollably. "He told me he regretted the sorrow he'd caused me and that he'd not given me in marriage. He said it was because of the unhappy state of his affairs, that he could do nothing else." Mary's eyes were stark with remembrance of those long bitter years of exile. "And he asked me," she sobbed, "to be a kind and loving mother to Edward, as you would be also, for he was leaving such a helpless child too soon. . . ." She wrenched herself from Katherine's embrace. "Kate, can you believe this? Can you believe he's going to die?"

Seeing the quiet acceptance in her stepmother's face, Mary began to cry again. Katherine put an arm about her shoulders. "Calm yourself, Mary, as best you can. Your father is making his peace with everyone and we must help him by being here when he wants to see us. Now I think we should go to the chapel and pray—pray that God will take him painlessly and easily." No one, she thought, as she and Mary walked the long corridor to the chapel, could be that ill and linger long.

* * *

But Katherine was mistaken. Henry lingered for another ten days. Each time she and Mary asked to see him, word came back that it was Henry's own wish that he have no visitors. Angrily, Katherine demanded she be admitted to the king's chamber. But Will Somers sought her in the hall and explained, "Your Grace, it is the king's request and he does it for your own good. At times he is not himself. It is not pleasant to see him play more of a fool than I! He is being nursed, but it is not the same as if he could bathe and do for himself. Our Henry still has his pride, my queen, and he wishes to see no one. He has said his goodbye. . . ." The Fool touched her softly on the shoulder. "Your Grace will pay greater honor to him to remember him as he was. . . ." Fighting the lump in her throat, Katherine nodded, saying she would see Princess Mary and explain they could do little else but wait.

While Henry lay wasting and feverish in his bed, as the palace became hushed and small crowds formed outside the gates, the Earl of Surrey was executed at Tower Hill. His father's execution would follow the next day. "If nothing else," said Will Parr, shaking the rain from his fine cloak, as he visited Katherine in her chamber, "it has taken people's minds off the king's condition. God, what a day!" He looked out at the gray river with its surprisingly light traffic. "Everyone is either at the gates here or at the Tower to see Surrey's blood spilled."

"I don't want to hear of it, Will." Katherine turned away, sickened. "At least death was kind to young Howard. He went fast. It is taking longer here." The gloom enveloping the whole palace was becoming almost more than she could bear.

The next day she was pleased to see sunlight. *It will dry the blood on Tower Green,* she thought, *and fill the river with busy traffic again.* But it did little to lighten the tension in the dark and silent rooms. She thought of going to Chelsea and even spent one morning making plans to wait out the death vigil there with Mary. When the worst happened, they could return within the hour and there'd be no moping about these shadowy chambers, with nothing to do, forbidden to see her dying husband, with only silent, saddened ladies-in-waiting for company.

She thought of Edward at Hertford Castle and Elizabeth at Enfield. They hadn't heard from their father since Christmas, almost a month ago. Did they wonder what was going on? How heartless not to think of their anxiety! If she went to Chelsea, perhaps she could bring them to stay with her. But, she finally realized, that was impossible. The king had to give his permission and he was beyond that.

By morning, however, Henry Tudor's trials were over. Sometime after midnight, a pale and tired Edward Seymour came to Katherine's chamber and told her the king had died, his hand held by Thomas Cranmer. Though speechless at the end, he'd been aware of what was happening. When the archbishop asked if he died in the belief of Jesus Christ and His Infinite Mercy, Henry had nodded his head and wrung Cranmer's hand strongly. There had been no pain, said Hertford.

"And my Lady Mary has been told?" Katherine asked. "And my lord prince and the princess?"

"Even now, Your Grace, a messenger is on his way to my Lady Elizabeth and I, personally, will go with my brother Thomas to give our nephew this sad news. But we have not told anyone outside these chambers, Your Grace. The court doesn't know and neither do the people at the gates." At Katherine's questioning look, he replied smoothly, "These are troublesome times, madame, and before such dire news is given out, we must have the king here in person. No one must know of his father's death until he is safe in the Tower."

Katherine nodded, stunned by Hertford's frankness, even as she appreciated the truth of his words. *The king is dead, long live the king,* she thought. How would they tell Edward? she wondered. Would they shake him from sleep and, kneeling, call him "Majesty" and "Your Grace" without thinking of a young boy's sadness or grief? And Elizabeth? The girl adored her father; she'd be as devastated as Mary at his loss. Perhaps Cat Ashley would be equal to the task of comforting.

Never had Katherine wished so much to be with her younger stepchildren. Together, she and Mary could have told them more easily, cried with them and shared their loss. But she knew, gazing at Hertford, who was obviously eager to be off, the decision was no longer hers to make. She was the

Queen-Dowager now and as such had little influence. Her power and authority had expired when that last breath had departed from the diseased and wasted body down the hall. Once more, for the third time, she was a widow with stepchildren to console. But this time it would not be easy. One was a king, the other two in direct line for their father's crown. Now others would direct and influence, eager to mold and control the minds and behavior of the younger children, particularly Edward. The only supremacy she'd ever had with them had been that of mutual love and respect. She hoped it would be enough for them all in the days ahead.

CHAPTER XXVII

Henry's body, sealed in a leaden coffin covered with a silken cloth of woven Tudor roses, lay in Whitehall's Royal Chapel, newly hung with black cloth and the banners of St. George, their strong colors reflecting the light of eighty wax tapers in huge silver candlesticks arranged about the catafalque. At the entrance, a herald cried, "Of your charity, pray for the soul of the most high and mighty Prince Henry VIII, our Sovereign Lord and King." And, for ten days, the citizens of London and the surrounding countryside came to kneel and weep for their monarch.

At last, on the morning of February 16, the funeral cortege, four miles long, wound its way from Whitehall, through Charing Cross, over the Knight's Bridge en route to Chiswick and Sion. Along the way, immense crowds formed. Many mourners held lighted torches, the better to see the great hearse drawn by eight black horses whose caparisons bore the arms of England and the house of Tudor. Noblemen, knights, gentlemen, family and household attendants followed on horseback or in litters, while others walked miles before taking to the wagons and carts that brought up the rear. At Sion, someone remembered that it was the fifth anniversary of Catherine Howard's execution; she had gone to the Tower from Sion.

At noon, the next day, the procession arrived at Windsor Castle where Henry would be buried next to Jane Seymour. Prince Edward was not present among the male members of the court attending the service in the great room where Charles Brandon had been eulogized only two years ago. Because of his youth and the demands of the forthcoming coronation festivities, he was to remain in the Tower. The Privy Council had also decided that because there were two queens and numerous other female members of Henry's family, they would stay in London. Relieved, Katherine took Elizabeth and Mary, Kate Brandon, Frances Grey and her daughters for prayers in the Royal Chapel at the same time Stephen Gardiner was conducting the funeral services at Windsor.

The selection of Gardiner startled many for it was well known the Bishop of Winchester had been removed from the Privy Council by the dead king's command. Kate Brandon explained, "It's Hertford's way of mending fences. Just as the council raced to save Norfolk from execution the morning after Henry died. He may not have wanted Gardiner as an adviser, but he never took away his office. Now Hertford wants the bishop's goodwill. Remember what Charles used to say? If you want to feather a nest, you must be prepared to share it with many rooks! But I wonder what Tom Cranmer had to say about it?"

Katherine reflected on the truth of Kate's words. Each day had brought a startling awareness of how much her own life had changed with Henry's death. While outwardly all respect was still paid to the Queen-Dowager, her influence and authority of the past three and a half years was gone. It was very evident when she'd requested an audience with her stepson shortly after he'd arrived at the Tower. A tearful Elizabeth had told her, with quivering lips, of how Edward had cried when he'd heard his father had died. Katherine had wanted to tell him how proud his father was of him, to give the boy some solace and support for the demanding days ahead. But the Privy Council had sent word the young king could not be brought to court, nor could anyone other than the councillors see him. Edward was mourning his father, even as he was being instructed in the affairs of state and trying to continue with his studies. The queen should be satisfied with the companionship of her two stepdaughters and other family members, for the young king now had more important matters to attend to.

"Like watching them divide up Norfolk and Surrey's estates!" Kate Brandon cried when Katherine complained. "And spying on each other to see that no one gets Edward's ear to benefit themselves. Poor Norfolk! Perhaps he thought life imprisonment would save his estates from confiscation. He told Cranmer he's like a wounded bird that can no longer fly and he might as well be dead."

Katherine remembered those councillors who'd fawned over her whenever they sought to use her influence in a private matter between them and the king. And the churchmen who'd praised her learning and patronage of the reformed religion. Now they were all silent, waiting to see which way the council and the new king would take. She'd been grateful Norfolk's execution—scheduled for the morning after Henry's death—had been canceled. The seventy-three-year-old duke had been kind to her during the trying days of the Pilgrimage of Grace and she'd always thought his sins were more his son's than his own. Life imprisonment would give the councillors the old nobleman's riches. There was little need to execute him and sparing him might win them credit from the Catholics. The family's destruction would be more diplomatically sound than his death. A lesson had been learned: fear was often more useful than an army. Even the selection of a chastened Gardiner to serve at the funeral services was a sop to religious and political unity.

That had been Henry Tudor's aim and in his will, he'd tried his best to preserve a united governing body to guide his young heir until Edward reached his majority at sixteen. Will Parr had given Katherine a copy of the will, one given to him by Archbishop Cranmer. It explained much of what had happened since Henry's death.

According to the will, the Crown passed to Edward and his heirs. Failing any issue by the young king—which Henry had never doubted—the heirs would be Princess Mary, Princess Elizabeth and the daughters of Frances Grey, whose grandmother had been the French queen, Henry's sister. Henry had ignored five-year-old Mary Stuart, the little Queen of Scots, grand-daughter of his other sister, Margaret. Katherine knew that had he lived, Henry intended to continue to pursue a marriage between Mary and Edward, thus peacefully uniting Scotland and England.

To preserve the Succession, Henry had appointed his Privy Council, six-teen strong, as his executors. Among them, there was a sprinkling of those who favored the old religion, yet had given the king no trouble with his reforms. There were others, such as Hertford, Cranmer, Dudley, Denny and Herbert, who were strong reformers. The king's intent was clear. He meant the entire council to be responsible for protecting Edward's inheritance, with no one person or faction predominant.

Reading the clear sentences, skillfully written by the royal secretary, with the wavering "Henry R" scrawled at the bottom, Katherine wondered about Thomas Seymour's doubt when she'd told him the will would settle all prob-lems. "I wish I were that certain, Kate," he'd said. If he'd been unsure, presumably his brother, Hertford, had felt the same way. Why then, hadn't they discussed it with Henry before he died?

For his queen, there'd been no doubt of Henry's intentions. Praising her love, obedience, chastity and wisdom, Henry had left Queen Katherine one thousand pounds in cash, three thousand pounds in plate, household furnish-ings and all her jewels. Along with her dower property and a jointure for any future marriage already confirmed by Parliament, he'd also willed her the manors of Hanworth and Chelsea.

But, most of all, what Katherine remembered was his deathbed insistence that after he was gone, she was to be treated the same as if he were still liv-ing. So far she'd seen little evidence of that order. With no political favors to bestow, no opportunity to influence councillor or courtier, no chance even to see a beloved stepson, she knew she'd have to be content with being the richest widow in the realm, one who must seek to visit her stepchildren whenever the council allowed, fulfill whatever role they might give her at royal functions and, most of all, stay out of their way. A chapter in her life had closed forever. Heretofore, she'd been very much a part of her stepchil-dren's lives, but now the council stood between her and Mary, Elizabeth and Edward. They were the heirs. She was merely the king's relict, a Queen-Dowager. Their future was ahead; hers was in the past.

* * *

Two days after the funeral, the public jousts and tournaments, the daylong celebration following the coronation of Edward VI was over. The splendid procession from the Tower was headed by the young king, garbed in silver, with a white velvet waistcoat and a cloak slashed with Venetian sil-ver brocade, embroidered with pearls. On either side, his two uncles, Edward

and Thomas Seymour, rode to Westminster Abbey where, robed in a surcoat, train and gown of crimson velvet trimmed in miniver, he sat in St. Edward's Chair, pale but exhilarated, while Thomas Cranmer performed the
ceremony by which he became "His Sacred and Royal Majesty, Edward VI,
Defender of the Faith, King of England, Scotland, Ireland and France." It
was nine hours later before the exhausted boy went to sleep in the bed in
which his father had died.

The next day Katherine went to Chelsea. On the afternoon preceding the
coronation, she'd seen Edward briefly. She'd hoped for privacy, for an opportunity to quiet any fears, to say how proud of him she and his sisters were, to
tell him that once that great day in the old abbey when the Crown of England was placed upon his head was over, she hoped he'd come to Chelsea.
In her own way, she wanted him to know that behind all the formality, the
pageants and speeches, his family waited.

But the visit had been a great disappointment. She'd knelt before Edward
who looked small and frail, his feet dangling from his father's chair of estate
with its red velvet canopy. His eyes were guarded and apprehensive, as if
he were trying to remember everything he must do and say—and do and say
it perfectly—rather than enjoy this brief reunion with a beloved stepmother.
He appeared very aware of his uncles nearby, of his godfather Cranmer, as
well as John Dudley who watched with wife Joan from behind him.

With no privacy, there was little Katherine could say. She wanted to embrace the boy and comfort him as she had before d'Annebault's arrival, but
knew it was hopeless. Instead, she'd bowed gracefully and said her goodbye,
so blinded with tears as she left the Tower room, she was grateful for Bessie
Bellingham's guidance down the long twisting flight of stone stairs. The
heartache had remained for days.

But Chelsea had always been a delight and never more so than now. The
little manor house built by the king as a royal nursery was now hers. And, in
a week, the clean fresh river air, the raw pungent smell of the spring earth
being turned in the adjoining garden, the long walks on the beach or around
Tom More's old home and the early morning canters with her ladies up the
path of "the king's road" had worked their magic.

"I trow I'm beginning to feel like Kate Parr again," she told Bessie as they
sat one evening on the terrace gazing westward at the fading sun. Soon it
would be March—always one of her favorite months at Chelsea—and now
she could remain as long as she wished. There was no husband or court duty
to call her back to London and she suspected the longer she stayed away, the
more pleased the council would be. With luck, she might even get their permission to have Mary and Elizabeth visit during April and May. Later, she'd
travel to Kendal Castle and see her uncle William Parr and her cousin,
Cuthbert Tunstall, at Durham. Both were now old and she could give them
the attention they'd never had while she was queen. There was a whole passel of Borough and Latimer grandchildren she didn't know well; some she'd
never even seen. And Wyke would be splendid for the summer. She'd have

Bessie and certainly Kate Brandon and her boys would come. Perhaps even her "two Joans" and her sister Ann might visit. Their husbands would be busier than ever with state business.

By mid-March, Chelsea had worked its magic. "Bess, I'm sleeping like I haven't since I was at Snape!" Katherine delightedly told her companion. "Perhaps I've worried about Edward too much. Everything seems to have worked as Henry wished it and we must give thanks there has been no trouble." From those brief messages from her brother and sister, Katherine heard the City of London appeared quiet, content with its handsome boy-king and relieved there were no quartered corpses hanging over its gates. The fires of Smithfield where Anne Askew had suffered had been dampened and swept away.

"It will be a new beginning for everyone," Katherine said, "and tomorrow we'll send a messenger to dear old Duchess Anne and ask her to come from Richmond for a visit. She, too, will be concerned about the children. . . ."

* * *

Before the courier left with the message for Anne of Cleves, Katherine had her first visitor. She was just settling down to the task of selecting music books for both Mary and Elizabeth and wondering what she might send Edward so he'd know he was in her thoughts, when Thomas Seymour walked in unannounced, a scowling Bessie behind him.

"Thomas!" Katherine put the books aside, her face warm with pleasure at the sight of her former lover. She held out her hands. "Thomas! What brings you to Chelsea? Is everything all right with the king?"

"Edward is fine, Katherine, as fine as he's allowed to be. He's safe and follows his studies and does as he's told. I must say he reminds me more of his mother every day. Jane was not one to complain or fuss, remember. Edward is her son. At times I wish he had more of Henry in him!"

As a servant arrived with wine and sweetmeats, Thomas flung himself into a chair, his long lean body in its deep brown riding suit, leaning forward to take the wine. Katherine had to restrain a smile. Every day she was more potently aware of her changed position. Only a short while ago, Thomas would not have dared such a discourtesy unless the queen sat first. But she said nothing, waiting for him to speak, aware of the warm pleasure the sight of the handsome Seymour always gave her.

"Kate, no one knows I'm here and that's the way it must be. Remember to tell Bessie to be quiet. I don't think anyone saw me come in."

Puzzled, Katherine nodded. Thomas appeared disturbed. Had anything happened to Edward? Or perhaps to Mary or Elizabeth?

"Kate, I had to talk to someone and I'm coming to you because . . ." Seemingly at a loss for words, Thomas was silent for a moment. ". . . because we're old friends. I know I can count on your discretion." Sipping his wine, he explained. "My good brother, the esteemed Hertford, has just shaken up the council and I trow I don't know what to do about it. I never thought Henry's will was the answer, but this is not what he intended! I think some of the others feel the same, but they go along with my brother anyway. They're all in it together!"

Katherine could not resist. "And you, Thomas? Where are you? What have they done?"

Other than a slight touch of color in each cheek, there was no evidence her guest had heard her first two questions. "What have they done?" He took a long sip of wine. "My dear brother Hertford has named himself Lord Protector of the Realm! Henry meant the whole council to protect Edward's rights and if he'd wanted a Protector, he'd have named one!" Setting the wine cup aside, Thomas strode nervously about the room. "My brother worked it all out with Will Paget. Now I know why they were walking up and down the corridor for hours after Henry died! Now I know what kind of bird they were hatching!"

"But Thomas, how could they do this if it was Henry's written wish that the council govern as one body?"

"With money, my dear, or lands or power. And titles! Everyone has been elevated, my brother first of all. Edward is now the Duke of Somerset and John Dudley the new Earl of Warwick. Between the two of them they've picked Norfolk and Surrey's estates clean. Your brother Will is the Marquess of Northampton. That sniffling Wriothesley is the Earl of Southampton and even Richard Rich was made a baron! Everyone has more manors, money, hundreds of servants and a power, my dear, that your husband would have run them through with his sword for the taking! You know how chary Henry was of giving honors or elevating his advisers. Frankly, I often thought he was less than generous, but now my brother says the nobility must be freshened by new blood since the old nobility has diminished through death and attainder. Suddenly, everyone has a wealth and authority they'd never dared have dreamt of less than three months ago! And they've convinced young Edward he has no choice but to agree. He's signed their letters of patent already."

"I doubt he could do otherwise, with the entire council recommending it to him." Katherine defended Edward even as she sadly remembered those Somerset lands, which Edward Seymour now owned, had once been the property of Margaret Pole, the Countess of Salisbury. They'd reverted to the Crown at her execution and now the new Duke of Somerset had picked himself a ripe plum.

Katherine felt an anger matching that of her guest. She remembered Henry's assessment of Thomas Seymour. What had he called him? Shallow? Vain? With ambitions not matching his talents? Obviously if Thomas was now dissatisfied with the council's actions, they'd not been as generous as with the older Seymour. "And you, Thomas? You must have been remembered, too!"

"Ah, yes, Kate, I was remembered. With my brother handing out such honors so that your brother, for instance, is second in command after him—a fine ploy to keep John Dudley from becoming too ambitious!—with all the grants and titles he gave, it was only fitting to remember his own brother. I am now, madame"—Thomas turned and swept her a deep bow—"none other than the new Lord High Admiral of the Royal Navy, replacing Dudley and then, for something new, Lord Seymour of Sudeley, a godforsaken manor in Gloucestershire where, I'm certain, my brother hopes I shall bury myself and not bother him anymore. That's when I'm not at sea with the navy, committed to being out of the country for long periods of time."

"I understand." Katherine poured herself a glass of wine with a shaking hand, sickened by what she'd just heard. "How could this happen? I am shocked! It goes against Henry's express wish! Why only a few days ago, I was telling Bessie how well things must be at court. I'd never believe the king's wishes could so easily be put aside. Won't Parliament protest?"

"Why would Parliament do so?" Wine cup in hand, Thomas paced about the room. "Our new Protector and his colleagues will distribute some of their largesse to its members. And they have other friends there who will stumble all over themselves to do whatever the new leader wants. They've left nothing to chance. The Protector even says if the religious settlement Henry wanted is to be preserved, someone must be named to protect it before the Catholics get more power and sweep away all the king did during his reign."

Now Katherine understood. Of course Edward Seymour would use religion as his political stalking horse. And if anyone challenged him, the Smithfield fires would again be lit and the executioners be busy with knives, swords and ropes to place mangled human remains about London and the countryside again. How naïve she'd been to think such horror might be over!

"Then it's all been decided? There's nothing anyone can do?"

"Nothing." Thomas took a deep breath. "My brother has no strong rivals. Who will challenge the king's elder uncle, the one who's just made himself Protector? Edward has seven more years until he's sixteen. My brother can go no further, but he'll find enough sops for everyone else during that time to keep them in line. If he forgets, that wife of his—that hateful, conniving, domineering woman!—will be sure to remind him. Already, she's taken on airs that would rival an empress and is grander than any of our queens. And I've known them all since the old queen. . . ." Thomas sipped his wine. "Anne Stanhope is quite pleased with all that's happened. She's always been ambitious, God knows. So now she's a duchess. The first duchess in the realm, really, since old Norfolk's wife hasn't anything. Not even her husband, who'll stay in prison until he dies."

Katherine shivered. The thought of Anne Stanhope taking precedence over everyone at court—except the queen and the princesses—was so unpleasant it almost made her ill. The woman would have no time for Edward, but look more to the advancement of her own three sons.

Pondering Thomas's words, Katherine felt the peace of Chelsea dissolving. With Henry dead a little over six weeks, already those left with the power he'd given them had made a mockery of his will, his intent and trust. Young

Edward Tudor would be a figurehead whom they'd train, keep from outside influence—most of all his stepmother's—and use as they manipulated his government and plundered the wealth of those who opposed them. By the time he was sixteen, they'd still be there, most of them, swollen with their riches, their ambitions still endless, bent upon controlling the guileless boy they'd made so dependent upon them. As Thomas said, Edward was Jane Seymour's son. Of all his children, Katherine thought ironically, it was Elizabeth who had her father's aggressive conviction and strength. And of all his children, it was poor Bess who had the least chance of ever using those gifts for herself or her country.

Suddenly, Thomas was there, pulling her toward him and she felt his body hard against hers. "Kate, my Kate," he whispered, his lips warm against her neck, "I remember how it used to be. I've never forgotten, my dearest, though you may think otherwise. You've never been far from my thoughts. It was hard to watch you from so far. Hard to think you were happy. . . ." The rest of his words were blotted out as he kissed her long and deeply.

Again Katherine felt the sheer physical sensuality of this man who had the power to turn her bones to water, to make her forget his weaknesses. Hungrily she returned his kiss. It was so long since she'd been held tightly, so long since passion and pleasure mingled so pleasantly she didn't care if Bessie or one of her ladies saw them. The devil take the council and the whole pack of beasts back at Whitehall! She was at Chelsea and Thomas was there. For now that was all that mattered.

*   *   *

Shortly after Edward Seymour became Protector, the French king, Francis I, died and his son Henri II ascended the throne. Frequent meetings of the English Privy Council reflected their concern that the new king, deeply influenced by the noble Guise family—whose most prominent member, Mary of Guise, was Queen-Regent of Scotland—would meddle in that country's affairs. It was not long before their worst fears were realized.

English possession of Boulogne, which Henry VIII had won in his last war effort, still rankled the French. When the English council offered its return in exchange for a large amount of money and the marriage of their boy-king to Mary Stuart, the little Queen of Scots, the French were indignant. Never would the Catholic Mary be joined in marriage to a king who governed a country where shrines, images, holy relics and all mystical celebrations of the Mass were forbidden and the Pope an object of derision and scorn!

The French king's reaction emboldened the Scots who had little heart for the English marriage. Secretly, they sent support to Henri when he tried and failed to retake Boulogne by force. When the jubilant English retaliated by fortifying the harbor, the French sent their ambassadors to Scotland further muddying the diplomatic waters. As the future of the half-Guise Mary Stuart was pondered in all three courts, bloody skirmishes on the Border alarmed the English council who pleaded with the Protector to resolve the issue for England could not afford another war.

The Protector, dictatorial and domineering, was little help. In letters, speeches and proclamations normally issued by the king, Edward Seymour used the royal "we," yet signed his own name. In an opening prayer to the council, he intoned, "Thou, Lord, has caused us to rule . . ." which angered many councillors. And one day, referring to the young French king as his "brother"—such as Henry VIII and Francis I had when they were on good terms—he was severely rebuked by the French ambassador, de Vieilleville, who reminded Seymour he was no "brother" but merely the king's uncle.

Katherine returned to court to attend the ambassador's reception held prior to the bargaining sessions. While her old suite of rooms remained at Whitehall, she chose instead to go to the little red-brick palace of St. James's in the fields bordering on the park where she'd ridden and hunted since she was a child. Mary was still at Beaulieu and Elizabeth at Enfield; both had been given permission to visit her at Chelsea in May. Her main concern now was to see Edward and she'd made it plain to Thomas Cranmer she wanted to visit him without ceremony or with councillors listening to their every word. Her request had been granted and, soon after her arrival at the palace, Thomas Seymour escorted her to Whitehall.

It was two months to the day since Henry had died and she wondered if Edward would remember. Walking the long corridor toward his chamber, Katherine tried to think of everything she wanted to say for she must make the most of this meeting. Suddenly they were there and, as she curtsied and Thomas bowed, Edward rose from his canopied chair on the little dais and then, quickly, she had her arms about him, stroking the small wheat-blond head as the boy burrowed his face against her breast. He'd grown a bit, she noticed, yet seemed thinner and more wan with a paleness that came from being indoors too much. At the corner of the room, the tall black-robed figure of John Cheke, his tutor, kept a discreet distance, allowing privacy but not solitude.

For the next half hour, they sat together and Katherine asked Edward how he spent his days. Ticking his fingers off meticulously, he mentioned early morning prayers and then his studies. He was beginning Plutarch, geometry and Italian and had begun to write his geography and history lessons in the Latin that had previously given him so much trouble. He studied the Bible in English and was making a special study of Proverbs, Ecclesiastes and the four Gospels. Barnaby Fitzpatrick, Robert Dudley, the Earl of Warwick's son, and two of the Protector's boys were his classroom companions. There were no girls, but whenever Jane Grey and her sisters came to Whitehall to stay, Jane was allowed to attend. "And she's smarter than all of us!" Edward cried delightedly with a sidelong glance at his tutor.

The lessons were formidable for one not yet ten, Katherine thought. But since his curriculum had been determined by John Cheke, Thomas Cranmer and approved by the council, it would only irk everyone to suggest music, dancing, some poetry or drawing to lighten the long study hours. Seeing her reaction, Thomas said Edward and his schoolmates also had the run of palace corridors and galleries for racing on inclement days and were often taken to the park to shoot at the mark, play stickball or run in the ring. "And I think, Edward, you should tell your stepmother what happened last week, when you lost your tongue. . . ."

Edward colored a bit. "I swore, Your Grace, I swore a lot! And all the boys cheered!" He laughed and clapped his hands again as more color came into his cheeks. "I said every bad thing I'd ever heard, mostly from you, my good uncle!" He pointed at Thomas who covered his eyes in mock shame. Katherine joined in their laughter. Thomas's oaths—at which he excelled— were as much a part of his temperament as Henry's had been and she was used to them. But she could imagine how a young boy would be impressed.

"And what happened, Edward?"

"Well, Barnaby is my whipping boy and he had to take the punishment. But it wasn't a bad whipping, Your Grace, even he said so. But Master Cheke says if it happens again, *I'll* have to take the whipping myself!"

As they rose to leave, Edward hugged Katherine, imploring her to come more often. "I shall tell my uncle I wish it," he said soberly. "This uncle," wringing Thomas's hand, "already knows how much I miss you and want to see you." He kissed Katherine once on each cheek and then, stepping back, held out his hand as she and Thomas bowed. Already, Edward had taken on that aura of majesty that had surrounded his father. As they left the room, Katherine saw him run to the window so he might watch them leave the courtyard below. In the background, Master Cheke, surrounded by books, pens and paper, waited respectfully for the boy to return.

* * *

"It was all so different when we were young," Katherine said, remembering the gentle Senor Vives as she and Thomas returned to St. James. "Our studies didn't take so long. We went outside to play each day there was sunlight. We raced about the gardens and played on the beach watching the horse ferry take passengers over to Lambeth Palace. Our mothers often came with us for they thought it was as good for them as for us to be away from the court. When they couldn't come, they sent Lady Bryan or Bessie out on the river with us and no one knew who we were! Who will see that Edward has a little fun? Who'll take him hawking or shooting at the butts in Smithfield like Henry used to do? He loves to race—at Greenwich we raced every morning! He could race through the park here!" She flung her arm about, angry at the thought of the cloistered youth back at Whitehall.

"Kate, of course you and Mary had an easier time," Thomas replied. "The old queen was there to see to it and so was your mother. But remember, the king still hoped then to have a son. Mary wasn't seriously considered his heir! Edward is *the king!* God's blood, he can't just go out and tumble about in the mud or fish from the riverbank. Everyone knows who he is! It would be dangerous and unhealthy and he's frail enough as it is. When he goes abroad, he has a proper escort and at Whitehall he has his tutor and servants to care for him. He's all right. I think you worry too much."

Once back at Chelsea, Katherine put the matter aside for there was little she could do. If Thomas sided with the Protector on their nephew's care and education, it was one of the few instances where they agreed. Thomas resented and envied his brother's power and he thought war with Scotland and France unnecessary. "It would be difficult to protect one flank with the ships we have—much less two!" he'd remarked dispiritedly, "and I don't want to be away from you, my darling, no matter what." Pulling her toward him, he held her so tightly she felt every clasp, fold and button of his doublet.

When Thomas made love to her, everything else faded from Katherine's mind. She was a widow of eight weeks and should be in mourning for her husband, spending more time in prayer and good works. Instead, she was deeply in love with another man and it was only a matter of time before the fact became common gossip. How would she react when it was known the Queen-Dowager was in love with the Lord High Admiral? Never before had her name—or her mother's before her—been tinged with gossip, nor had any of her friends' reputations been soiled with rumor or speculation. It worried Katherine, torn between duty and desire.

When Edward Seymour began to build a magnificent home, Somerset House in the Strand, Thomas made such a fuss the Protector gave him the adjoining old episcopal mansion, Bath House. With some lands confiscated from the executed Earl of Surrey's estates that bordered on one side, it made a handsome gift. Thomas renamed the whole area Seymour Place and promptly began to remodel the mansion into a sumptuous dwelling, setting out fine orchards and gardens, one with an aviary. The work kept him in London more than Katherine liked, but she wrote him daily, her courier speeding off early each morning. Thomas still did not like to write, but after she suggested he add a secretary to his rapidly growing household staff, communication became easier. But the letters were less than she wished. Nothing could take the place of Thomas being with her.

Just when she thought she could bear his absence no longer, Thomas would arrive unannounced, riding over the fields or leaping from his barge and come upon her in the terrace or garden. Sweeping her up in his arms, he'd sit on a stone bench with her on his lap and kiss her passionately, no matter that a gardener was in full view, that her ladies or Bessie might be watching from a window. Other times when he sent word of his coming, Katherine would dismiss her ladies and, walking the mile or so to the gate that bordered on the fields, wait happily for the man who suddenly filled her whole world to the exclusion of everything else.

One morning, about two weeks after they'd seen Edward, Thomas arrived meeting Katherine at the gate. Instead of walking back to the manor house, the horse following behind, he suddenly pulled her down into the grass, covering her body with his as he traced an arc of warm kisses from her neck to her eyes and then hungrily kissed her on the lips. Katherine strained toward him, her pulse beating, her body fluid as the hot blood raced through her. As he whispered his love, she felt his hands on the laces at her bodice. The sound of his voice brought her to her senses and she pushed him away, sitting up, still dazed with longing but aware of what had been about to happen. Fornication was not a pretty word; it was not a minor sin.

"Thomas, we must stop! I'm not going to meet you like this again, it's too difficult for both of us." She gazed at the lean face, each vibrant feature etched in her mind with the sharpness only love could give. Thomas pulled her to her feet, an amused look in his dark eyes and a wry turn to the lips that had just devoured hers so eagerly.

"God's blood, Kate!" he laughed outright, making a great show of lacing up her bodice again, "we're not children! You've had three husbands, my dear. What did you think they were made of? If you don't want me to act as any lover or husband should, then don't meet me here alone, dressed as a country wench, with your hair all loose and your eyes looking anxious and hungry. . . ." He reached out and touched the long reddish-gold hair hanging about her shoulders.

Katherine felt longing rise again. "My lord, if my being here as I am has given the wrong impression, I'm sorry." She turned away stiffly. It was always easier to talk to Thomas when she couldn't see him. When he made no move toward her, she felt more comfortable and it was easier to tell him, as she wound a vine of honeysuckle about her fingers, that she could not submit to him, much as she wished to, for her honor would not allow it. She'd been a widow for such a short time!

Behind her, Thomas roared so heartily, a covey of birds rose, startled, from their sanctuary and flew off with an angry flapping of wings. He spun Katherine around. "So you're worried what people will think? My dear, your great, late husband was betrothed to Edward's mother the same day his former wife had her head cut off! He married Elizabeth's mother before he'd even divorced the old queen and anyone who can count on their fingers knows why! Ha, a fine thing it is to be taunted about one's morals when our own king did not set such a good example! And look at his great friend Brandon—how often was he wed? Three times and the last time to one young enough to be his grandchild and a mere two months after the French queen died. And he'd married *her*, you recall, against the king and old Wolsey's express wishes! Kate, Kate." He pulled her to him laughing, all desire gone, anxious now only to chide and humor her. "Who cares? Will all of England fall in a heap if their queen loves the king's uncle? I think Edward might even approve—Edward the king, that is, not Edward the Protector.

No matter *what* I do, that Edward will criticize and complain and if he doesn't, his wife will find other faults to cry about. How she loves to make a great ruffle! But Kate, look you here"—he held her so she was forced to gaze into his eyes—"I'm not seeking a quick tumble in the grass, my dear. I love you and I want to marry you. I thought you knew that." He picked up the horse's rein and, an arm about Katherine's waist, glanced at her quizzically. "Would you have me, Kate? The wife of the Lord Admiral is not the same as being the wife of a king. But I think I could make you happy, my dearest. But it must be soon. I may get sent to Scotland, to France or God knows where. We can't go on like this, snatching little pieces of time to be together."

Tears of frustration welled in Katherine's eyes. "Thomas, we must wait at least a year. To do otherwise would not be honorable. What would people say? What would the children think?" Wiping away the tears, she felt the warm redness on her cheek that just the thought of being Thomas's wife brought.

Suddenly, he clutched her waist and, pinning her against a tree, then spread both his arms over her shoulders, each palm against the tree trunk. Laughing, his teeth gleaming against his tanned skin, he whispered, "Now I'm not going to let you go until you answer me. What do you think people will say if we wed? Who cares? What will the king's children think? They love you, don't they? I'll tell you what will happen, Kate. Our marriage will be a nine-day circus at court and on the tenth, people will forget. Something else will come along to catch their fancy. And the children? How about Mary?" He pressed his body close against hers and caressed her hair again. "Mary? Who knows what Mary will think? Has anyone ever made love to Mary? Like this?" There was a long moment of silence as he greedily kissed her. "Mary is a premature old maid, my dear, her only love is the love of Jesus Christ and she spends hours every day on her knees in worship before an outmoded altar in a ceremony that will soon be called heretical. And Elizabeth?" He released Katherine and, an arm about her waist, they walked on. "Now there's a wench with all the hot blood of her father and her mother's determination. I think Elizabeth will be very pleased. She'll think it all very romantic and it will mean another proper household for her to visit away from that guardian, Cat Ashley."

"And Edward? How will he feel? He has to be told of our marriage, he and the council both. It would be better to have their permission and good wishes than not. Edward is a child and could be persuaded, I'm sure, but the council? And your brother? Suppose they forbid it?" Katherine's voice trailed off. "It's too soon, my darling, and I still think we must wait at least a year. We don't want to ask and be refused—think of the gossip! Oh, can't you see that Anne Stanhope preening? To be the wife of a man who could forbid his younger brother to marry a woman she's intensely disliked for years!"

The thought was so discouraging, she lapsed into silence as they walked slowly back to the manor house.

And, how could she wait a whole year?

* * *

During the following days, after Thomas returned to Seymour Place, Katherine thought about their marriage. What might happen in a year, presuming she could put him off for that long? War with Scotland? With France? If so, Thomas, as Lord Admiral, might be away for months. She longed to have someone to talk to besides Bessie and, one afternoon, wrote her "two Joans" inviting them for a long week at Chelsea. She was shocked and hurt at their quick refusal, citing the pressure of court duties and family responsibilities. It was the Duchess of Suffolk who explained why Joan Dudley, now the Countess of Warwick, and Joan, Lady Denny, would not come to Chelsea.

Kate Brandon had arrived unannounced the next day. Seeing the approaching barge, Bessie cried, "It's my Lady Suffolk!" Quickly, Katherine ran to the beach and was waiting with a welcoming embrace when the duchess leapt onto the boards. Kate explained she'd left her sons at Grimsthorpe, her Lincolnshire home, and now she had time—the first since Henry had died— to be with Katherine. "Especially when I heard you'd asked Lady Dudley and Denny to come and neither would," she explained. "A fine pair, those two, although at times I think they'd like it otherwise. They are fond of you, my dear. Why shouldn't they be? But John Dudley says if Joan leaves their boys—they have four, you know!—he'll send her to Warwick Castle. He wants Rob Dudley to be with the king as much as possible and the other boys, especially Guildford, are to keep their noses in their books and do their father proud. No matter that he himself can hardly read! I trow, Katherine, he plays the Protector false behind his back. He's always been angry he was placed in a position where he had to agree to Edward Seymour becoming the Protector. Even the earldom he got in exchange wasn't enough, I think."

"So the court hasn't changed much," Katherine laughed, hugging the duchess. The intrigue and petty conspiracies, the cunning, gallant manners, which often hid overbearing pride and ambition, were still prevalent. "It all seems far away at Chelsea," she said, "even time seems shorter here. Instead of two months, it seems only yesterday I was a wife and queen. I don't like being a widow, Kate."

"Well, it's not for want of any suitors, I hear." The duchess smiled at Katherine's look of surprise. "Joan Denny told me the Lord Admiral comes to see you often. I think that's one reason Anthony Denny wouldn't let her visit you—there's little love lost between those two! And Lady Paget said when you were last at court to see the king, every time Thomas came into a room, you colored up so prettily, she wondered what was going on. Everyone remembers what passed between you both before you married Henry, my dear. Are you going to tell me or do I have to spend the next few days prying it out of you?"

It was such a relief to unburden herself that, once started, Katherine left nothing out. She told Kate of her deep love for Seymour and how she could think of nothing else. If she wrote her stepchildren, she found her mind wandering. In talking with her ladies, she thought only of Thomas and her longing to be with him. She had no desire for further study, no wish to plan for her future. How could she think of visiting Wyke or Snape? They were too far away! And always, in the forefront of her mind, was his insistence that they wed at once. So much could happen if they waited a year! "I don't want to lose out again," she whispered.

Kate Brandon lit a candle against the encroaching dusk and sitting beside Katherine clasped her hand. "My dear, when I came here today, I came for a reason. I'd heard all about you and Seymour in London. No, the gossip isn't vicious nor widespread. But it's only a matter of time before it will be twisted out of all proportion and the council will make a fuss. I remember how everyone was askance when Charles and I were married. Sometimes you simply have to decide these things for yourself. On the other hand, *I* was not the Queen-Dowager, but my husband *was* the king's brother-in-law and best friend. We survived it."

"Then you think it would be all right for me to marry Thomas now?"

"When I came here today, I was going to advise you to think carefully and wait at least a year," the duchess paused, "but now, after what you've just told me, I'm not so certain. Oh, my dear, you've had so little happiness—real happiness—in your life! I remember my lady mother telling me once of a conversation with your mother when Lady Parr had just sent you north to marry Lord Borough. Your mother wasn't at all certain she'd done the right thing. But her pride was such that she felt it would be dishonorable to accept anything less than a peer for you and Lord Borough was the only peer available. I think she sensed that my mother disapproved. Remember, my mother waited a long time for my father, Lord Willoughby. She once told me she'd resigned herself to being a spinster. So she'd waited for happiness and won. I think she wanted your mother to do that for you, for you were very young."

Katherine felt a mist over her eyes. It was so long since she'd thought of Maria de Salinas, Katherine of Aragon's closest friend. Yet it was only twenty years since that conversation with Lady Parr. How many lifetimes had she lived since then?

"And, of course, I remember John Neville," Kate said. "I think you were happier as Latimer's wife—you were older and he was younger for one thing —but it still wasn't the same as if you'd been truly in love. You were wonderful to him, my darling Katherine, all during that dangerous time in the North. And his children adored you—*all* your stepchildren adore you! And then, you'd just found Seymour again when Henry interfered. Ha, wouldn't our dear king shout if he could hear me calling him 'interfering'? But he did!"

"He said Thomas wasn't good enough for me. He said he thought I could do better," Katherine whispered. "I often remember his words now."

"Well, he was right and you probably could do better. I have no illusions about Tom Seymour, Kate, or Edward, our sainted Protector, either. They are both vain, ambitious and greedy. But Edward is also quite competent in his way and without that wife of his urging him on might even become tactful and obliging and I do think he has the country's good at heart. But Thomas, my dear, you must know doesn't have Edward's level head, his efficiency or determination. Thomas is Lord Admiral and he has yet to set foot on a ship since his elevation. John Dudley is livid about it and says that when *he* was admiral morale was high and the navy was well looked after. Now morale as well as the ships are deteriorating since Thomas leaves everything to his subordinates. But, I suppose this should not concern you. *You* are the one Thomas Seymour loves and, if you were married, perhaps you could temper that fine ambition of his and set some common sense into that handsome and roguish head. When I see how much you love him and especially when I remember how you've served three husbands with so little in return, I must ask myself why you shouldn't marry him? You're thirty-four years old and if you want children it must be soon. It may be too late already, but at least you'd have some happiness just being his wife."

Katherine thought of her future if she remained single. Thomas would be off with the navy fighting England's wars. Her stepchildren, especially the two younger ones, would grow further and further apart—from her and from each other—for it would not be easy for Edward to see his family informally or often. Her closest friends were no longer willing or even permitted to visit her casually and everything she herself wanted to do would be subject to the council's permission. With Thomas as her husband, she'd not be lonely and he'd be there to fight her battles for her—perhaps even fight them too well!

As she was leaving the darkening room, her arm about the duchess' waist, her mind was suddenly made up. She was going to be as selfishly practical as her "two Joans" and change her mind as easily as Kate Brandon had changed hers. She was tired of putting Thomas off. It would serve her right if one day he'd ride off, with one of his great oaths, over the Chelsea fields and not come back. The thought was so heartbreaking that even thinking of it chilled her. But it renewed her conviction. She was going to marry Thomas and before she went to bed tonight, she'd write and tell him so.

Lady Seymour of Sudeley

1547

CHAPTER XXVIII

The Lord Seymour of Sudeley married the queen, whose name was Katherine, with which marriage the Lord Protector was much offended.

—King Edward VI, written in his own hand in his journal, *A Chronicle,* Summer 1547

In comparison with her other three marriages, surrounded by family and celebrated with music, dancing and feasting, the marriage of Katherine, Queen-Dowager, and Thomas, Baron Sudeley and the Lord High Admiral, took place in a small chamber at Lambeth Palace with the Archbishop of Canterbury officiating. No one else was present.

"The less anyone knows, the less dangerous it will be for them," Katherine told the Duchess of Suffolk on the day they'd said goodbye at Chelsea. "Oh, Kate, I wish it weren't so! I wish on the day it happens, you could be there. But even my sister Ann is suspicious of Thomas's coming here to see me and she questions him constantly. She says we must wait since Henry has been gone such a short time. But Thomas says he'll tell his brother and the king only when he thinks it's proper."

Once she'd made up her mind, however, Katherine had refused to think of family, of the Protector or her stepson, Edward. Worry hadn't lessened her lover's ardor; if anything, it made him more insistent on their marriage than ever. And Katherine was content it remain a secret for she could no more deny Thomas anything than she could stop breathing. It would hurt no one and she'd already waited too many years for happiness. How did anyone know when the proper moment would be? If she waited much longer, Thomas might be sent to Scotland or France or ordered abroad for months with the navy. The very thought of his absence made her eager to marry him as soon as possible.

However now, as she rode to St. James's Palace, accompanied only by Bessie, her confidence wavered. She'd left her other ladies-in-waiting—much to their disappointment—at Chelsea. As far as the court was concerned, she was still at the little riverside manor house with them.

In the unfamiliar rooms, gazing out at the great wooded park, greening now in the soft spring weather, she wondered if she was doing the right thing. Whenever Thomas was with her, there was no doubt. How much easier it would be if the council, the Protector and the king approved! Katherine had never liked the surreptitious; she was not by nature secretive or devious. But perhaps this was the price one must pay for true happiness? Kate Brandon's reasoning, as well as Thomas's obvious joy reflected, she was certain, what others would think and feel when the marriage was at last announced.

In accordance with their plan, Thomas appeared the next morning, less boisterous, with a new calm she found endearing and her doubts disappeared. He was splendid in a rust-colored doublet trimmed with gold braid over tawny breeches, a plumed cap embroidered with gold and laced with small jewels set jauntily on his shining black hair. He pulled Katherine into his arms, crushing the sea-green velvet gown she'd so carefully chosen for the ceremony. As he held her off, his eyes caressed and admired the smooth hair that Bessie had swept into a sleek coil intricately woven with tiny bejeweled ribbons. Katherine blushed at the intensity of his gaze, murmuring, "I wish I had my emeralds . . ." as he kissed her roughly with mounting eagerness.

"You're enough of a jewel, my Kate." His lips brushed her cheek and she remembered Henry saying almost the same thing. She'd left the coffer containing the emeralds in her suite at Whitehall for, whenever she went to Chelsea, she took only what was needed. Now everything would be brought to Thomas's elegant new home off the Strand and she'd be mistress of Seymour Place, the manor house at Chelsea and those other homes the king had left her. Perhaps once their marriage was known, she and Thomas might make their own small progress and visit her new possessions.

The thought of a future with the man she loved so deeply kept Katherine smiling as they rode through the park to the horse ferry where the Lord Admiral's barge waited. In a few moments, they were at the Lambeth Palace landing and, as the sun rose toward its highest point, were ushered into the small crypt near the waterstairs entrance where Thomas Cranmer waited. The archbishop had put on his finest vestments and a richly decorated altar replete with candles and plate stood at the crypt's end. Katherine heard the gentle sound of the river outside as small wavelets lapped the old building's foundations. Pale sunlight beamed down from a small window high up in the wall, lending a serenity to the crypt and bathing its venerable, oyster-colored stone in golden light.

Her heart lifted at the sight and at the kindly Cranmer's apparent pleasure. She had been greatly surprised when he consented to marry them and knew, even as he smiled indicating their places, that it was because of his regard for her. She and the archishop had always had a special affinity founded mainly in their religious beliefs and she knew he was her friend. Thomas said Cranmer had insisted that if they must marry without the council's permission or the young king's knowledge, then he must be the one to perform the ceremony for no one else could be trusted to keep the marriage a secret. Then, when the news was made public in the future, should anyone accuse him of disloyalty, he could always say he was a bishop sent to do God's work first and the council's second. Who could accuse him of anything treasonous if he'd performed a wedding ceremony for a couple determined to marry?

Standing at the altar with Thomas, Katherine listened to the words that now took on new significance. "To love, honor and obey" had never been as meaningful as now, not even when she'd promised her loyalty to a king. To love and honor Thomas, to obey him certainly was her dearest wish and she felt her eyes misting when he solemnly repeated the words. Her hand shook as he slipped a plain gold circlet on her finger. It reminded her of the small circlet Katherine of Aragon had given Maud Parr for her firstborn daughter. I've had a crown, she thought, which the old queen could hardly have foreseen. But this little ring means much more. It was the first one ever placed on her finger in true love.

As the archbishop bowed at the ceremony's end, Thomas embraced her and they quickly said their farewells. As Cranmer pressed her hand with silent good wishes, Katherine made a mental note that, when she received her coffer of jewels, she'd send him a rich gem as a token of her appreciation.

At Seymour Place, a courier was just leaving as the bride and groom returned. Thomas took the letter a servant handed him and after reading it swore loudly, handing it to Katherine, who recognize Princess Mary's handwriting.

> My Lord,
> My most hearty commendations to you and to say also I have received your letter in which I perceive strange news concerning a suit you have in hand to the queen for marriage whereof you seem to think that my letters might do you good.
> My lord, in this case, I trust you do remember that if it were for my nearest kinsman and dearest friend alive, of all other creatures in the world, it stands least with my poor honor to be a meddler in this matter, considering whose wife Her Grace was of late, and besides that if she be minded to grant your suit, my letters will be hardly necessary. On the other side, if the remembrance of the king's Majesty, my father, will not suffer her to grant your suit, I am nothing able to persuade her to forget the loss of him, *who is as yet very ripe in mine own remembrance.* . . .

Thomas swore again as Katherine handed him the letter. "I wrote her asking for her good wishes *if* we were to marry," he said, his voice rasping with anger. "It wouldn't have hurt her to say she would be pleased! Must one mourn forever?" He threw the letter distastefully aside. "By God's precious soul, must she sound so disillusioned?"

"She is hurt. I know Mary well, Thomas. She is hurt and, I think, disappointed in me. I'm sorry you wrote that letter! I could have told you what her reaction would be. Mary loved her father very much and she loved me, too. As a friend, as well as a stepmother." Katherine felt her throat constrict. She was dismayed—and resentful—that Mary's gentle rebuke should hurt so much. Why couldn't she feel, as Thomas apparently did, that Mary should think less of her father who was dead and more of her stepmother who was alive and deserved, as Kate Brandon had said, some genuine happiness? Mary liked Thomas and, in a year, might have been very enthusiastic about their union. But she was shocked at Katherine's apparent desire for an early marriage and resented being used as an intermediary. Mary was an especial friend of the Protector's wife, Anne Stanhope, and would know that was one reason why Thomas wanted her approval.

Katherine reached for the letter again to read the remainder, but Thomas's hand closed strongly about her wrist and he pulled her to her feet. "Enough of our sainted princess," he muttered, pressing her close. "They are all a pack of hypocrites with their pious do's and don'ts. Thank God Cranmer was a realist! I think he knew he'd better marry us or I'd have swept you on my horse, ridden for Dover and taken you to France to live happily ever after!" He kissed Katherine deeply, forcing her head back to fondle her neck and breast. He reached up and, with one gesture, pulled the coiled hair apart, the ribbons falling like bright feathers onto the floor. "The devil take all the king's children. We don't need them, although I think Bess will cheer when she hears what we've done. 'Tis you and I, Kate, my darling, wonderful, beautiful Kate, you're mine now, *mine*. . . ." He picked her up and lay her on the bed, his fingers busy with the laces at her bodice.

Katherine demurred. This was not as she'd planned. As on any bridal night, a bride waited to receive her husband in bed in her wedding nightrail. She'd expect him to be gentle—even the king had been gentle—and certainly it would be dark. This was midafternoon!

But Thomas would not be deterred. Covering her mouth with his, she felt her whole bodice pulled free from her shoulders as her husband hungrily fondled her breasts. "Kate, you're so beautiful, so warm, my darling, so untouched. . . ."

Katherine felt her passion rise as Thomas removed her gown. Jesu, she'd never made love in the daylight before! She should be covered with embarrassment at her nakedness, especially as Thomas fondled her intimately, his eyes loving her beauty as much as his lips and hands roused feelings in her she'd never experienced before. Then he, now as naked as she, stood above her, raking her body with a hot lustful glance that, had she been younger—or more modest—might have frightened her.

But she was not frightened. She was glad and proud her beauty excited Thomas. The thought of the long wasted years when husbands had pleasured themselves with her at will rose in her mind and she lay back, turning on her side so each curve was visible and, with one arm, reached up to bring Thomas down beside her. Daylight be damned, she didn't care. Not even of what the servants might think.

Any further thought was suddenly drowned in a glow of passion and hot blinding need as Thomas pressed his lean body against hers whispering words into her ear—words she'd never heard before—as he kissed her so harshly it was painful. But she was drowning in lust for him as much as he was for her. If this was the sinful carnal feelings the bishops deplored, she cared little. This was what she'd missed all those years when others had used her, leaving her a passionless creature who now was as wantonly and sinfully enraptured as her husband.

But, she thought, Thomas, now truly in love for the first time, may have missed something too. Although from the deft, experienced and knowing way in which he touched, stroked and caressed her, the eagerness and obvious delight with which he deliberately aroused her—only to hold off while his mouth traced a warm loving path about her body—there was little doubt but that he knew what he was doing.

And now it was all hers, this gasping, hot, sharp, sliding and cresting feeling that filled her so entirely she thought she must cry out. Who could believe the proper Lady Latimer and the dignified Queen-Dowager could lie in bed in broad daylight with a man who was using her as she'd never been used before—more like the ladies of the Southwark stews—and she was reveling in it? It was worth everything to feel the hot and thrusting joy of her husband and her own glorious response and release. Then her body lay, captive with his, their warm sweat mingled together.

Winding her arms across Thomas's bare back, feeling the pounding of his heart and the pressure of his dark head against her breasts, Katherine felt that—no matter what happened, even if she lost friends and family—it was a small price to pay for this deep and exultantly vibrant emotion, hers now for the rest of her life.

* * *

In the next few weeks, she was happier than ever before. Though Thomas was often away at court, he spoke little of his activities with the council or the navy. But she knew he saw young Edward at every opportunity, waiting for the right moment to tell him of the marriage. She'd wanted to stay in London with him but Thomas insisted that until their news was made public, it would be better to remain at Chelsea. Katherine agreed, knowing it would be difficult to hide her happiness from the prying eyes of family and the court.

She counted the hours until Thomas joined her in the little riverside house, for his absence lent a sharp expectancy to every day. He rarely missed returning each night and every time they were together, they so much exceeded their earlier pleasure, Katherine wondered how long such delight could last.

But the secrecy still bothered her and she hoped the marriage would soon be known, if only to eliminate the look of reproach on her ladies' faces when the intimacy of their royal mistress and the Lord Admiral was there for all to see. Bessie said the ladies were scandalized and it made her miserable not to be able to defend Katherine.

When Mary Tudor sent word asking to be excused from her May visit, Katherine realized the princess' shock and disapproval still lingered. What would she say now if she knew the friend she'd loved and the stepmother and queen she'd venerated had already followed her heart and slept in Thomas's arms each night? Katherine felt it wise to pretend she saw nothing wrong with Mary's letter and replied that she hoped the princess would visit at a later date. Elizabeth was still coming in May and would be bitterly disappointed if Mary wasn't there also.

If, as she suspected, Mary had written Elizabeth, it was not obvious when she arrived at Chelsea. Thomas was there the day the barge brought the princess and Cat Ashley. As she leapt onto the boards, he swept Elizabeth up in his arms and with much laughter carried her up to the seawall where Katherine waited. Elizabeth's pale skin was rosily pink as he set her down and, after a curtsey, she flung her arms about Katherine. "Oh, madame, how wonderful to be here with you!" Her dark eyes were laughing and sparkling. "And to see my Lord Admiral too!" She hugged Katherine again as they all walked back to the manor house.

Elizabeth's enthusiasm was balm to Katherine's spirit and she realized again how much she'd missed her stepchildren, how much Mary's rebuff had hurt. She was thankful the princess hadn't written Elizabeth for then she might have remained away from Chelsea too. But later as the two talked excitedly in her chamber, it appeared Mary had written.

"Yes, she did." Elizabeth hung her head as she always did when caught off guard, a spot of color in each cheek. "She wrote of the Lord Admiral's letter and said I should not dishonor my father by coming. I told her you had always had my great affection and I was not ungrateful." Katherine realized how much an affront this would be to Mary and hoped it would not rebound in her treatment of Elizabeth. The girl appeared glad to be able to speak of the episode. "But oh, madame, I don't think it wrong if you wish to wed again! Didn't my father leave a jointure for you to do so? I told Mary I didn't think you'd dishonored our father for he didn't expect you to remain unwed forever. . . ." She twisted the pearl ring Katherine had given her about a long, slim finger. "I think you and my Lord Admiral will be very happy."

Katherine reached out and hugged Elizabeth wishing she could tell her she was already married. Thomas was right. Anne Boleyn's daughter saw the romance and love so missing in her own life and understood Katherine's love for Thomas Seymour. Mary had seen only a rejection of her father. She prayed that in the future she'd be able to make Mary understand.

* * *

Then, suddenly, it was no longer a secret and Katherine was grateful her clandestine marriage was now out in the open. One afternoon, Thomas, riding hard from London, arrived at Chelsea, clattering unexpectedly into the courtyard with Will Parr, the Marquis of Northampton, and brother-in-law Will Herbert. There was a sullen look on Thomas's face and his companions' expressions were sober. Watching them from a balcony window, Katherine knew at once what had happened.

She waited for them on the terrace facing the river and, in a moment, Thomas was there explaining as his companions listened. He'd visited Edward several times, he said, hoping to get the child to agree to the marriage. But Edward had demurred and, toward the end, John Cheke had deliberately given Thomas little opportunity to see the boy. Finally, that morning, Thomas had obtained a letter which, he insisted, was Edward's permission for the Queen-Dowager to wed.

"He says," Thomas read, " 'You should not fear any grief to come or suspect any lack of aid . . . and if you require my help, I am ready. I pray you may live without grief and I will provide for you both, that if any grief or trouble befalls you, I shall be a sufficient succor to you both.' "

Katherine saw the letter was in Edward's childish handwriting. She wondered if Thomas had told the child everything and if he understood the true meaning of those words by which he challenged his other uncle, the Protector, as well as the Privy Council, to take any extreme action against the Lord Admiral and his new wife.

She asked her brother and brother-in-law. "And how say you both?"

Will Parr cleared his throat and, avoiding Thomas's angry gaze, replied, "I wish it had been otherwise, Katherine. As Queen-Dowager, you owed more respect to the king's memory. You could have waited a little longer. As your brother, I feel you might have consulted me or our cousin, Cuthbert Tunstall. We might have advised you otherwise. Certainly the council should have been notified first, not Edward."

"Of course you'd advise her otherwise!" Thomas's face flushed an ugly red. "You'd have wished someone other than the Protector's brother for her, too! Isn't that right?"

"I'd have wished for someone with more thought for her welfare than you have shown, my lord," Will replied stiffly, "and my brother Herbert feels the same way. I say your actions are devious and you have shown poor judgment, doing ill service to our house, to the king's memory and our sister's reputation. I think you seek your own good, my lord, for you are ill-equipped to provide for her future. You have no jointure to give, yet she brings a handsome dowry!"

"Ah, that's what's bothering you, is it, Will?" Thomas's voice was tight. "I shall provide for my wife, sir, and you needn't trouble me with petty talk of a wife's welfare. You didn't do too well with your own marriage, my fine Northampton!" he sneered, striding angrily about the room, slapping Edward's letter against his thigh. "I've told my brother that the deed is done and shown him this letter. I've told him it is a happy thing for my wife and myself, that we mean to take our place at court—she is still the Queen-

Dowager, remember!—and we'll live at Seymour Place. And, by God's precious blood, I'll run my sword through the first man who disparages our union, who talks of my finances or tries to discredit me with the king or the council. I think the Protector understands." He put an arm about Katherine who was startled to feel it shaking. Will Parr hadn't been very diplomatic and she didn't blame her husband for being upset.

"Why shouldn't we find happiness?" she cried, giving Thomas time to calm down. "I've married before, remember, as I was told or thought best. I've brought honor to this family and now, if I wish to marry as my heart chooses, I think it is my affair! Thomas and I will deal with it." Both men bowed as she prepared to leave the room. "I'm going now to tell Bess before someone else tells her. You might want to know," she smiled, her green eyes sparkling wickedly, "that the king's daughter will probably dance for joy and shout with happiness when she hears the news. If Bess can feel that way, perhaps you should take a lesson from her!"

                                        *   *   *

But public reaction was not as understanding as Katherine had hoped. The Protector was angered at his brother's presumption and the Privy Council outraged at Thomas Seymour's audacity in touching the Crown so closely. The gossip prevalent in the inns, taverns and hovels of the poor echoed the condemnation and criticism of the nobles and the London gentry. The nine-day wonder that Thomas had predicted did not abate on the tenth day. Instead Katherine found her daily life challenged by happenings over which she had no control but that affected her deeply. To a woman used to making her own decisions and for a queen with the power to bestow favor, give counsel, effect political and religious affairs, it took time to understand what was happening and more time to think how she should deal with it.

Within two weeks of the marriage announcement, one of her ladies tearfully told Katherine her family insisted she return home. "I have no choice, madame," she wept, "I must do as they say."

"And what do they say?"

"That it is dangerous for me to be here, madame, because my Lord Admiral has angered his brother, that the councillors give the Protector little peace, saying he must deal with the matter before my Lord Admiral becomes more presumptuous. Begging pardon, madame, but they do not want me to share in what they see as a future disgrace which might be frightening for me. Oh, madame, I am so sorry!"

Katherine, frustrated and more upset than she cared to admit, comforted the woman. Her departure the following day cast gloom upon the remaining attendants and, when she met with them later in the afternoon for their usual companionship, the silence was so heavy she excused them soon afterward. She wished there was someone other than Elizabeth or Bessie with whom she could talk. Kate Brandon was still in the North with her sons and would be hearing the news any day now. Katherine hoped she'd soon return to court.

Two weeks later, Thomas said they must return to Seymour Place. The Scottish situation was worsening and his brother was preparing the country for war. "I don't think we need this war and most of the council doesn't either, but if nothing else it will take the attention away from us, my darling Kate. I think our nine-day wonder is over!" He nuzzled Katherine's ear. "And you see, everything turned out all right."

Katherine returned the caress, but did not reply. It would only anger her husband and cause him to storm out of the room in a temper if she told him about losing a lady-in-waiting and the silent recrimination she felt from the others. She had yet to hear from her own sister or from Mary Tudor. Thomas had been right in predicting that Elizabeth would be enchanted with their marriage, but how would she feel back at court when she heard indignation and censure from others? It was difficult to admit even to herself that the loss of self-esteem and pride in the Parr name hurt. She'd refused even to think of what her mother might have said, pushing the thought to the back of her mind. It was a relief to give herself up to Thomas's embrace; the warm, sensuous feeling was balm to her troubled spirit and body. As she held him tightly, she thought—if this is what I have, it is a wondrous thing I've never had before. If others chose to consider her happiness a deadly sin or a moral affront, she'd show them how wrong they were. Anything lost could be regained. She was still Katherine, the Queen-Dowager, K.P. as well as Lady Seymour and now, when she could be as loving and as loved as she'd never been before, her first duty would be to regain her tarnished honor, to show everyone how wrong they'd been.

* * *

All the Protector's efforts to conciliate the French had failed for they still wanted the return of Boulogne. In Scotland, the ruling party refused to consider any marriage between young King Edward and the five-year-old Scottish queen, Mary Stuart. When in late July, the French bombarded St. Andrew's Castle and many Scots freely left for France, English hostility boiled over. In this atmosphere of war preparation—of mobilization, ordnance building, of confiscated supplies piling up in country warehouses and coastal docks for victuals for the soldiers and sailors who would fight the war no one wanted—Katherine and Thomas returned to court. And on their first evening in London, they went to Whitehall.

It had been six months since Henry Tudor had died and, walking the long corridor to the Presence Chamber, the aura of the restless, imperious giant who'd been her husband for five years still lingered. There was the door of her own chamber, still held for her use, where she and Bessie had wailed and screamed that wretched afternoon and evening after finding the paper ordering her detention. In one bend of the corridor, the chair she and Mary had ordered made to carry the king looked shabby and smaller than she remembered. Through another door, she saw someone was sitting at the virginals Mary had often played while Elizabeth and Edward danced, sometimes with her, sometimes with their father.

Entering the room where Henry had held court, Katherine felt an unfamiliar anxiety. How would everyone react to seeing Lord and Lady Seymour of Sudeley? Edward was not there. Possibly he did not attend these functions because of his youth. Standing beside the empty chair of estate, the Duchess of Rutland and Lady Paget were talking to Anne Stanhope, the Protector's wife. Now the Countess of Somerset and the mother of five children, Anne's beauty was at its peak. Only a few telltale gray hairs escaped her lavishly jeweled cap and the heavy white damask gown furred with ermine at the hem emphasized her handsome figure and complexion. Her straight posture was almost regal. Nearby, her husband, the Protector, was speaking vigorously with William Paget, Lord Dacre and the Earl of Sussex.

The Master of the Horse, old Anthony Browne, saw her first and, skillfully hiding his surprise, came forward at once and bowed gracefully. Conversation lessened as Katherine, Thomas following discreetly behind, began to walk the length of the room. Acknowledging the bows and curtsies with a nod or smile, she stopped at one point to take the hand of Lady Wriothesley whose son had just died.

At last she was there facing the Protector of England and now her brother-in-law. Edward Seymour's face was flushed, more from surprise than animosity, Katherine felt. He was not as handsome or as exuberant as Thomas, but there was an attractive maturity and sobriety, a calmness Thomas lacked, which gave him an impressive authority. Now he bowed low and reached for the hand that Katherine extended.

"Madame, welcome," he smiled, "and may a brother-in-law kiss his good sister?"

It was the right touch and behind her, Katherine heard the slight laughter and shuffling of feet, a lessening of tension and felt her own composure return. Edward Seymour obviously meant to make the best of a situation that could not be changed. Katherine suspected neither he nor anyone else had ever controlled Thomas Seymour, that he had had a good deal of experience in living with his brother's deeds.

The thought was still amusing her as she turned to Edward's wife. The duchess' face was expressionless and she met Katherine's smile with a stony stare. Quickly, Katherine passed by, remembering the night Henry had chosen not to dance with young Anne Stanhope and the look of hatred on the girl's face. Anne had never forgiven her for that as well as for other numerous inconsequential reasons that had often puzzled Katherine. Anne had chosen to remain on the fringes of the court ladies, considering herself a touch above most of them. She'd been bound to honor a queen but now, apparently, felt no longer obliged. Katherine, relieved to pass as if not seeing her, resolved not to let it spoil the evening.

Nor did it. At the close of the festivities, after numerous conversations with old friends who appeared impressed by her happiness and her delight in seeing them, Katherine looked for Thomas. She found him talking to Henry Grey, the Marquis of Dorset, who explained how regrettable it was that his wife, Frances Brandon, had to miss such a happy event. Frances was at Bradgate, their Leicestershire home, but she wished Katherine and Thomas well. Katherine doubted Henry's words. Along with Anne Stanhope, Frances Brandon's first concern was for herself; she rarely wished anyone well. Before she could reply, Thomas said Jane Grey was coming to live with them.

"Coming to us?" Katherine was startled and then delighted. Ten-year-old Jane was a sweet child and one desperately unhappy in a home where her bright mind and scholarly manner did not fit in with two doltish sisters and parents who were never happy unless they were ahorse, enjoying the pursuit and killing of some hapless animal. "That will be a happy day, my lord." She held out her hand to Henry Grey. "Tell Jane we'll await her arrival with pleasure."

As they walked the long corridor toward the courtyard, Katherine impulsively drew Thomas into her own chamber. While she meant to keep these apartments, she'd had no desire to live in them, to share Henry's bed with Thomas. But now, she thought, she might take the jewels the king had given her. They were there in the great cupboard at the room's end, in a small secret enclosure that only she and Bessie knew how to find. Thomas could hide the coffer under his cloak until they were safely in the courtyard where darkness would hide the fact that the Queen-Dowager was carrying home a king's ransom of jewels.

Thomas stood in the doorway waving to departing couples as she went to the cupboard. She was anxious to have the jewels again, particularly the emeralds that so became her and that Henry had intended as a special gift. She remembered the affection in the king's voice when he'd called her "my jewel."

She opened the cupboard door. Several gowns still hung there, each with little matching velvet sandals. One special drawer had been built for papers, small trinkets and fans or jeweled bibelots. Seeking the small knob, which could only be found by touch, Katherine turned it eagerly, pulling the drawer forward to the light. It was several seconds before she realized the drawer was empty. All that lay in the bottom were several whorls of dust.

Stunned, she turned to Thomas, holding out the empty drawer. Had someone removed the jewels for safekeeping? Or had they been stolen? Whom could she ask? The thought of anyone handling Henry's gems sickened her. For a moment she wished the king were back so he might bellow his anger that the queen did not have her baubles and where were they? She realized even as she tried to explain to Thomas, she didn't have any evidence—other than Bessie—that Henry had given her the jewels. Or the slightest knowledge of how to get them back.

* * *

At Seymour Place the following morning, Katherine anxiously awaited Thomas's return from court. First he intended to question the royal chamberlain at Whitehall for if he knew nothing of her jewels, the loss must then be reported to the Privy Council. Thomas was confident that someone had removed them for safekeeping during Katherine's long absence at Chelsea. But she wasn't so certain.

One look at her husband's face when he returned told her he did not have the coffer. Recently, Thomas had begun to grow a full beard, the same as the Protector, and the darkening stubble emphasized the flush of anger on each cheek. Throwing his cap on a chair, he shook his head at Katherine's questioning look, saying, "My brother has the jewels."

"Edward?" Katherine was stunned. "He dared take my property and won't give it back? Well, he must return it to me at once!"

"He says he can't do that, Kate, because the jewels are heirlooms to the Crown and must remain in its possession."

"He dares!" Katherine cried out. "Who does he think I am? I am the Queen-Dowager! Who has a better right? The king *gave* me those jewels and on his deathbed told your brother and everyone else they were mine. . . ."

"I reminded Edward of what Henry said, but he says the king meant those jewels he gave you when you were married. Oh, yes, I told him that wasn't so, that Henry had given the coffer to you before he died. Edward finds it more profitable to disagree and his lady, I understand, often wears the baubles."

Katherine was speechless, consumed by such anger she felt almost violent, sickened at the thought of the glorious emeralds about Anne Stanhope's throat. The maliciously haughty countess would take great pleasure in wearing them, not only for their beauty, but because she could keep them from their rightful owner whom she'd always hated. "If she were here, I might choke her, that spiteful, hateful woman!" Katherine's anger gave way to tears and she flung herself in Thomas's arms. "My lord, those are *my* jewels and I want them back! I will not have that woman wearing them! You must go to the council and explain or else I will see my stepson and tell him your brother has robbed me of my rightful property."

"I think that your stepson has already been told, Kate." Thomas sank wearily in a chair, his eyes puzzled. "What they told him, I don't know, but Anne says as the Protector's wife she takes precedence over everyone else since he is the guardian of the realm. She says that by marrying me, you have forfeited your place as well as your jewels and that she has more right to them than you. I doubt, my darling, that with the Protector, the king and the council agreeing, there is little else we can do. But we will try. . . ."

Katherine was about to reply, to urge Thomas to return to London—she'd even go with him—and they'd explain to the king. Then she saw Elizabeth passing in the corridor and turned away, seeking to quiet herself in case the girl joined them. She did not intend to let the king's daughter know what had happened to her jewels—not yet. But get them back she would, if it was the last thing she ever did.

*   *   *

Two weeks later, Jane Grey arrived at Chelsea. With her came several ladies-in-waiting but her tutor remained at Bradgate since her mother was agreeable that she share Master Grindal with Elizabeth. "That is, if you think it proper," she told Katherine, the soft, velvety blue eyes of the French queen gazing at her shyly. Every time she saw the girl, she looked more like her grandmother. Jane was a lovable child, soft-spoken with beautiful manners and a capacity to amuse herself that, Katherine thought, must be the result of hours of being left alone by her parents. Not for Jane the complaints of Elizabeth whenever she felt slighted or put upon. Nor would it occur to the young girl to ask for anything—attention, a new gown or book, or insist upon a certain horse, such as Elizabeth did. To Katherine's surprise, she seemed oblivious of rank or precedence and Elizabeth was forever pulling her forward into her proper place when the procession formed for the midday meal that everyone ate together. If Katherine wished to take the girls on the river or for an early morning canter before studies, she often had to send someone to look for Jane. They'd find her in an out-of-the-way spot curled up with a book or her needlework, at devotions in her room, or just gazing serenely out at the river as she watched the herons marching in their spindle-legged parade about the muddy shore.

Curious, Katherine sought her out one day and asked if she'd rather be left alone. "I want you to have a good time here, Jane dear, and if you want to be by yourself you must say so. Remember, the king built this little house for his children and you can have many adventures in the woods or on the river. We like your company but if you'd rather be by yourself, you must say so."

To her surprise, Jane came forward and clasped her arms about Katherine's waist. "Oh no, madame, you mustn't think that," she whispered into the folds of Katherine's skirt. "I just don't want to be a burden, madame. My lady mother says I must never be a burden. At home, I think they look upon me as such."

"Why in God's name would they think you a burden?" Katherine asked, puzzled.

"I don't know, but they do." Jane turned away, tears in her eyes. "Whenever I am with either my mother or father, whether I speak, keep silent, sit, stand or go, eat, drink, be merry or sad, be sewing, playing, dancing or doing anything else, I must do it so perfectly—as perfectly as God made the earth, madame!—or else I am so taunted and threatened and pinched with nips and bobs and other things, that sometimes I think I am in hell. . . ." Then, as if she couldn't bear the reality of her words, the tears flowed over. "It is so different here, madame. . . ."

Appalled, Katherine put her arms about the little girl, who made no effort to hide her tears. "My darling Jane . . ." she whispered into the soft hair. As the child sobbed softly, she pulled her onto her lap, rocking her back and forth, wanting to thrash the weak Henry Grey and scratch Frances Brandon's malicious face for making their daughter's life so miserable. "And so you stay away from them and go off by yourself?"

"As much as I can, madame." Jane began to hiccup. "But I'm happiest when I go to Master Aylmer. He's my schoolmaster and he teaches me gently and pleasantly and encourages me so that the time passes quickly and happily and I forget what I will go back to. Sometimes, it makes me cry. So it's easier to take a book and hide where no one will see me."

"Well, you don't have to do that here, Jane." Katherine kissed the child's wet cheek. "You must remember we *want* you to join us for we *like* having you around. And no one will give you nips and bobs, except perhaps a horse or a dog! My Lord Admiral and I want this to be a happy summer for you, Jane. For you and Bess and, mayhap, for Princess Mary too. You do understand? No more nips and bobs!"

She was pleased to see Jane's tears disappearing and, when Bessie passed by the chamber door, Katherine called out. "Bessie! Come and take our Lady Jane to find Elizabeth. She's probably in the stables. This wench is now going to ride and sail with the rest of us."

As Jane, her demure face now wreathed in smiles, went off with Bessie, Katherine realized that, for the first time in weeks, she'd forgotten about her jewels, Mary's silence and the Privy Council's reluctance to cooperate in the matter of her confiscated gems. Thomas had hired two lawyers from Chancery telling them, "My brother is wondrous hot in helping every man to his right, save me! But I'll find a way—our sainted Protector and that witch who sleeps in his bed haven't heard the last of this matter!" Now, watching Jane chattering contentedly with Bessie, the jewels didn't seem as important as the release from the past hostility and resentment.

*   *   *

The summer months at Chelsea passed quickly, marred for Katherine only by Mary's continued silence and Edward's absence. In late July, the Protector took the English army to Scotland and on a "Black Saturday" in September, shattered the Scottish forces in the battle of Pinkie Cleuch, leaving mutilated corpses, burnt villages and a ruined harvest in his fiery wake. After hurriedly burying a decimated Scottish nobility beneath the peat hags of their despoiled land, an exuberant Edward Seymour triumphantly returned to London, ignorant of the fact that any possibility of a marriage between Mary Stuart and young Edward Tudor was ended forever.

The war with the Scots had been a land war and while the navy patrolled the English Channel and the coastal Scottish towns, its Lord Admiral thought it more prudent to be at court or the council table, to protect his absent brother's authority. If the council sat late, Thomas remained at Seymour Place overnight. But early the next day, he'd arrive whooping and clattering with several attendants into the courtyard and shout, "What's this? No wenches to see me? A fine thing it is for a man who's risen with the sun and foregone a whole day's hunting . . . !" Katherine, Elizabeth and Jane would race to the courtyard for embraces and kisses and later, in simple dress, they'd all go on the river to picnic in some secluded cove between Chelsea, Richmond or Hampton Court. Once, in sight of the palace, they all fished from the barge and never even went ashore. Both Elizabeth and Jane, fair-skinned and easily burnt, had to wear large netted caps to hide their faces from the sun. Even so, Jane's arms were freckled and brown.

Each time Katherine saw the child's happy face and relaxed manner, her enjoyment of their rollicking good times, she felt immense satisfaction. If only she could have had Edward whisked from Whitehall to join his cousin and half sister, her happiness would be complete. She couldn't bear to think of Jane having to return to the Greys at summer's end.

And then, incredibly, Thomas said Jane would never go back. "I've bought her wardship," he told Katherine, almost reluctantly, one evening as they lay in bed, her head on his shoulder, enjoying the cool breezes from the river through an open window. "She'll live with us—wherever we are."

Katherine sat up, looking at her husband with disbelief. "Henry and Frances agreed to this, Thomas?" And then, teasingly, "What did it cost?" No matter what he'd paid, she meant him to know what Jane had told her, that it would be worth every penny for the girl to live away from such brutal parents.

"Henry Grey said last week it was time his daughter came home and he'd come and escort her. It was then I realized how happy she seems here, so I offered him two thousand pounds for her wardship. The papers are being drawn up and when I pay the first five hundred pounds we'll be her legal guardians."

"Oh, Thomas!" Katherine hugged him, "she'll be so happy! And Bess will be pleased for they get on well together. You are kind to do this, Thomas! It will make such a difference to Jane! Henry Grey might have sold her wardship to someone else." Katherine knew of many instances where families placed their sons and daughters—much as Bessie Bellingham had come to Maud Parr years ago—where the wardship money, not the safety, comfort or even the happiness of the child was important. Bessie had been happy with her lot; many children were not.

She told Thomas of Jane's life with her family. "I can believe it," he mused, "for that fool of a father spends more time at the gaming tables than he does with his family. I'm sure that's what this money will go for—to pay what he owes—or try to recoup his losses. And Frances has always treated her dogs and horses better than her family. She's never gotten over the fact that she hasn't a son!"

As Thomas spoke, Katherine thought of Jane's future in her home. She would study with Elizabeth or perhaps that kindly tutor could come from Bradgate. If Henry Grey had placed his child with her so she might enjoy the "advantages" of living with the Queen-Dowager and the Lord High Admiral, Katherine meant to see that Jane received that boon—even if it had been bought with money.

But it stunned and sickened her to think the Marchioness of Dorset, the French queen's daughter, would give up the winsome child, Henry's grandniece, so easily. And it amused her to wonder if Frances knew the real reason that Henry Grey was parting with his oldest daughter—not for any "advantages," but in reality for enough money to pay his gambling debts.

*   *   *

When Elizabeth, her face mutinous, heard Jane was to remain in Katherine's household, she said she would not go back to Enfield, Hatfield or Ashridge; she wanted to stay with her stepmother, too! And, if Thomas didn't ask for her, then she'd write the Protector himself! "There's room here for me, madame. I can let some of my ladies go and keep just Cat Ashley and Tom Parry, my cofferer. I don't want to live by myself. I want to be with you and my lord!"

She stood silently, waiting for Katherine to speak, no hanging of head now, her black eyes sharp and determined. While Elizabeth twisted the rings on her long delicate fingers, as she often did when nervous, Katherine was reminded of Anne Boleyn's intensity and perseverance. Elizabeth was now almost fifteen, as tall as she'd ever be, with small round fully formed breasts, the long oval Boleyn face, the rich auburn coloring in hair and eyebrows the only evidence of her Tudor blood.

Gazing at the determined girl, Katherine remembered Mary Tudor's insistence that Elizabeth was the bastard child of Mark Smeaton, the minstrel youth accused of adultery with Anne Boleyn. Now, after years of living closely with Elizabeth, Katherine had abandoned the thought. Her father's coloring might be all she had of him physically, but Elizabeth had more of Henry Tudor's nature and personality than either Mary or Edward. She was aggressive—resolute enough to say she'd write the Protector himself!—and with all the king's charm and vigor, his sharp mind, even his love of music. And while Henry had never been as fond of Elizabeth as he was of Mary and Edward, she was more truly his child in every way than the other two. The thought of having Elizabeth in her household, of watching her blossom into womanhood, intrigued and delighted Katherine and she asked Thomas if the Privy Council might consent.

Within a week, Thomas brought the answer to Chelsea. The council had agreed that Princess Elizabeth might continue to live with her stepmother while she pursued her studies. Later, other arrangements would have to be made for a proper household such as Mary had. For by then, of course, her marriage would be of the utmost importance.

Elizabeth was ecstatic. Cat Ashley and Thomas Parry were dispatched, along with the princess' head steward, to Enfield to bring all her books, clothing and her favorite horse to Chelsea. Awaiting the Protector's return, Thomas spent more time at the little manor house to the girl's obvious delight. They were much alike, the admiral and the princess—strong in their opinions, yet sensitive, witty, with an intense personal pride which did not belie their enviable rank and comfortable security. Both enjoyed each other's sense of humor. When Thomas twitted Elizabeth about always reading and studying, calling her "My Lady Bookworm," she saucily replied, "If I am, my lord, I shall be happy and die with a full stomach as I eat my way through the pages." From then on, it was a game as to who would best the other in riddle, puzzle or quick-witted retort.

Both were extremely musical. Thomas had a full, deep baritone and, with an arm about the slim princess, they often sat on the terrace facing the river, Elizabeth's sweet soprano mingling with his, until suddenly, Thomas would parody the familiar verse, using naughty phrases that made Elizabeth blush. If she smiled at a serving man or was overly gracious to a stablehand, he'd loudly lament that she cease such folderol and remember her position! Bewildered, Elizabeth would defend herself hotly, explaining she'd been taught good manners that my Lord Admiral sometimes overlooked. And then, one look at Thomas's smiling face told her that again he'd mocked her innocent behavior and won.

In the early morning, as the sun rose over the river, a sleepy Katherine often heard Thomas walk down the hall to Elizabeth's chambers. In a moment, she'd hear loud oaths and laughter and doors banging as Elizabeth's attendants and Cat Ashley greeted the admiral still in his nightrail and robe. Burrowing deeper into her bed, Katherine listened to Jane Grey's piping voice joining the others. Inside and out, her household was stirring as stablehands brought horses for Thomas's early morning ride. Since he disliked riding alone, Katherine often rose and went with him; other times Elizabeth or even Jane accompanied him. It was all comfortable, happy, secure, the sort of life she'd dreamt of during those empty years at Gainsborough, Snape or Chartreuse. Often she'd make herself rise from her bed so as not to miss a precious moment, for soon they must all return to court. The only thing she wanted in London was to see Edward and somehow force the Protector to return her jewels. Katherine had put that issue out of her mind, determined nothing would cloud this precious summer.

On one visit, her sister told her that the Protector's wife had made many enemies at court. "She has a monstrous pride and is intolerable!" Ann Herbert sighed. "And since her husband's victory, she's lorded it over everyone, even the Countess of Rutland and old Lady Paget!" Ann said the elder members of the court, who could remember the old king and who'd attended young Henry's first marriage, kept their distance from Anne Stanhope. But the wives of the newly enriched young men continued to fawn all over her with the lavish compliments and extravagant promises of loyalty that she relished.

One of her best friends, Ann said, was Princess Mary. She often came to court to see young Edward and invariably visited Anne Stanhope. Each time Anne inquired if the Protector could do anything for Mary's comfort or pleasure, whether it be a new household, a better-equipped stable or merely finding residences or pensions for those servants who'd served the princess for years and were now retiring from royal service. Katherine said nothing, thinking it ironic that a woman who ten years ago was largely known as the wife of Jane Seymour's brother, should now be in a position to dispense favors to the king's daughter. It still troubled and hurt Katherine that Mary had never replied to her letter suggesting a later visit to Chelsea. Now, it seemed, the woman who wore her confiscated jewels had also stolen her best friend and a stepdaughter's affection.

And then, suddenly, Elizabeth solved everything with shrewdness and audacity. She appeared in Katherine's chambers one morning with a letter, from which Princess Mary's seal dangled, clutched tightly in her hand. "She's coming, madame," she said, pink cheeks betraying her pleasure. "At first I thought it should be a surprise, but mayhap it is best you know before she arrives." She handed the letter to Katherine who read aloud:

> "Beaulieu
> October 5, 1547
>
> My dearest sister,
>   I have received your letter by the hand of my courier Bastion in reply to one of mine and wish to say that I will be at Chelsea by the middle of this month if it pleases the Queen-Dowager. I have not been in good health for this is the time of the year—as the leaves begin to fall—which is always a troublesome time for me, as you may remember. Perhaps the river's coolness will be more comforting.
>   I have read your complaint that Master Grindal, being sickly, does not pursue *The Aeneid* as fully as you wish and you think you might benefit by my tutelage if I were there. I think I could help in that respect as well as any other that your teacher does not have time or health for, especially as he also instructs our cousin, Lady Jane. I am certain the Queen-Dowager has done all she could. With her great responsibilities—duties at court and my Lord Admiral, now so busy with the navy after our victory over the Scots—I fully marvel if she has any time left for such schoolroom adventures.
>   So, my Bess, I would be happy to come to Chelsea for mayhap I can relieve the Queen-Dowager which will be to me a great happiness. . . ."

"Bess, you sly wench!" Katherine laughed so heartily she fell back among the pillows. The sight of Mary's handwriting brought a lump to her throat and tears mingled with laughter as Elizabeth joined her on the bed, grinning from ear to ear that she hadn't been reprimanded. "What a clever one you are," Katherine hugged her as they read the letter again.

"Mary wasn't happy either, Your Grace," Elizabeth whispered, "but she is so proud! And she didn't know how to see you again after being quiet for so long! But now she's coming to our aid because you and Master Grindal don't have time for my studies. . . ."

Their loud laughter erupted again as they recalled the hours Katherine had spent consulting with the old tutor, deciding what studies were appropriate for Elizabeth and Jane who assimilated everything set before them with an ease at which Katherine never ceased to wonder.

Katherine rose from the bed, her eyes shining. "We must make plans, Bess. We'll have a reunion here at Chelsea and I'll ask Mary's friends from court." The arrival of the king's elder daughter, she thought, would also serve another purpose. Not even her "two Joans," whose husbands hadn't wanted them visiting the newlywed Queen-Dowager, could hardly refuse to see Princess Mary. It would be like old times for by then Kate Brandon would be home. They could all go to Richmond and see Anne of Cleves who was still devoted to her stepchildren. And by then, it would be time to return to court, with the family reunited once more and all because Bess had been such a clever girl.

As Katherine smoothed her rumpled skirts, the large pearl pendant she often wore slipped to the floor, its chain broken in half. As Elizabeth retrieved it, Katherine was reminded of the little redheaded girl in Lady Bryan's arms who'd once reached out for this very pearl.

"No, Bess, it's yours," she said as the princess handed it back. "When you were little, you wanted this very badly. I don't know why I've waited so long, but I think now you should have it. 'Tis not of great value, but it belonged to my mother—and her mother before her, I think—so it means a great deal to me. But you've done me a good service, my darling Bess, and as soon as the chain is repaired, it is yours."

Elizabeth's black eyes glowed as she held the gem in her palm. Pearls were her favorite and she didn't have many. "I'll treasure it, madame, always because it was yours. . . ." Then, suddenly a child again, she ran off to show her prize to Lady Jane.

CHAPTER XXIX

Seven months after their marriage, Thomas announced they must return to Whitehall Palace, a move Katherine viewed with some misgiving. She much preferred the privacy of Seymour Place, but Thomas was insistent that Whitehall was where they should be.

"You're still the Queen-Dowager, Kate, even though some appear to have forgotten that since our marriage. The palace is your official residence and I don't intend anyone to overlook that again!"

It was over two weeks since that day Katherine and Princess Mary had ended their six-month estrangement. Mary had leapt from her barge and quietly reached out for the embrace that had shaken them both. "Kate, it's been too long . . ." she whispered. Katherine was shocked at how thin Mary had become. She was thirty-one, only three years younger, but her sallow coloring and shadowed eyes made her look much older. Even the short climb up to the seawall and the manor house terrace made her breathless and she walked noticeably slower than the others. Later Susan Clarencieux told Katherine that Mary suffered from poor eyesight that gave her blinding headaches. She had to exercise each day and be especially careful of her diet. "She leads a very lonely and restricted life at Beaulieu," Susan explained, "and still misses her father very much. She worries about the king, too, thinking he's so young to be alone. She needs her family, Your Grace."

Katherine was determined that Mary would not be lonely again and asked that her rooms at Whitehall be near her own. Elizabeth and Jane and their households were on the floor above and in that first week there was much visiting back and forth.

One day Katherine took Elizabeth and an intrigued Jane Grey and, with the palace chamberlain, sought a proper schoolroom. Later, when Jane excitedly told Thomas of her difficulty in finding her way through the maze of corridors, of her awe at the great Royal Chapel and delight in the panorama of a silvery river running by her window, Katherine thought how ironic it was that the palace she'd frequently visited as a young woman and lived in as a queen should be so new and enthralling to members of the king's family. While Elizabeth had lived there too, she now saw many things for the first time since that miserable year of exile.

Edward had been sent to Woburn Abbey, Katherine learned, to meet the Protector on his return from Scotland. She assumed he would be there until the City's streets and lanes could be decorated with bunting and banners to welcome the victorious Seymour and his soldiers home. She was surprised when a few days after her arrival, the chamber door opened and Edward stood in the doorway, taller than she remembered, his blond hair in disarray, cheeks pink with excitement. Katherine held out her arms as Edward ran to her, laughing with delight at her surprise.

"I came by myself, madame," he said proudly. "Last week I went to see my Lord Protector at Woburn to thank him for his great victory. He'll be back in a day or so. When I came home today I heard you and my sisters and cousin were here. So I just decided to come to see you and I didn't ask anyone—and no one stopped me!"

Katherine was touched by the child's innocent happiness, his pride in simply walking a few corridors alone and vowed again to find some amusements normal for a ten-year-old. Edward was as lonely as Mary.

She hadn't counted on Elizabeth and Jane. They urged the boy to join them whenever his studies were complete and soon he was spending more time in Katherine's chambers, playing cards, dice or Blind Man's Buff. Later, when Mary played the virginals, all three children danced, showing their stepmother the new steps their dancing master had taught them. Katherine was pleased that the bonds forged in those years when they'd lived with her and their father under one roof—bonds which had been strained many times —still held.

But each of Henry's children was different from the other and the passage of time, as well as the political events of the last year, had affected them in surprising ways. One day, riding through Clerkenwell, they passed a monastery that had been sacked and destroyed. It had not been a large religious house and the rubbled heap was not impressive. But Edward, his interest aroused, rode apart from them to peer into the building's desolate shadowed interior. Grass sprouted everywhere among the fallen stones and along the chancel floors where the tiling had been ripped out. Tendrils of ivy curled about the traceried windows and crept across the damp stone. Puzzled, he turned and asked what the building had been.

"A religious house, Your Grace, dissolved and demolished by order of your father, King Henry, for abuses," an attendant replied hesitantly, glancing at Katherine who'd reined in her horse nearby.

"Abuses?" Edward was bewildered. "I don't understand why my father the king didn't just punish the offenders and yet let such a good building stand. And put better men in them—men who might have lived here and governed right!" Shaking his head again, the boy reached out and plucked a long ivy tendril from a fragment of wall. Mary, gazing at Katherine, shrugged. Usually, she avoided seeing any despoiled religious house if she could help it, often going considerably out of her way to do so. This one, unpretentious and unknown, had come upon them by accident. Katherine wondered what Edward would think if he could see the great holy houses of the North standing roofless to the elements, their riches plundered, the land standing wasteful and overgrown.

The boy was busy with the long ivy vine, his fingers plaiting and smoothing as he pulled a leaf from one place and tucked the long tendril into a weaving pattern. Triumphantly, he held it up for everyone to see and then, laughing, handed it to his stepmother. "For you, madame," he said, "an ivy crown for my queen mother. . . ."

Touched, Katherine bent her head as Edward placed the little circlet on her hair, wondering again at the folly of fate that caused Jane Seymour's son to place a crown of green upon her head while Katherine of Aragon's daughter, Anne Boleyn's child and the French queen's granddaughter watched with pleased smiles. Even Lady Bryan, who'd taught all the king's children to plait, would have been startled at Edward's gift. Remembering the little circlet of gold that the old queen had given Maud Parr, she thought suddenly of the gypsy's prophecy. It had all come true. Four husbands, one of them a king. And she'd had a crown—one from a queen and one from a king. And now this one, woven in love, which was as precious as the others.

* * *

The tranquillity of Whitehall vanished a week later when the Protector returned to London. Katherine and Thomas had relished these few weeks together, with more privacy in their comfortable chambers than the small Chelsea manor house provided. They'd seen family and old friends and Katherine had gone to Parr House and to Chartreuse where her stepson, John Neville, now Lord Latimer, was raising a brood of handsome children.

"But now duty calls," Thomas said as he dressed for an early morning session of the Privy Council. "We must welcome the victorious Protector properly so all the people can see him. And there's certain to be a great gala, Kate, so be sure you have a rich gown. Remember, you'll be the most important lady there"—he caught her to him—"and certainly the most beautiful." Katherine responded to his kiss eagerly; the passion of their first weeks of marriage had not worn off. If anything, it was even more intense, a delight she'd never anticipated and still regarded as almost a miracle.

Mindful of Thomas's suggestion, she called for bolts of fabric from the Wardrobe and several pattern books and spent the morning discussing her gown with Mary Tudor. There hadn't been many ceremonial festivities during Henry's last year. Only the French ambassador's reception where she'd met Thomas again after such a long absence. She wanted to look as beautiful now as she had then for, as Queen-Dowager, she'd have an important role to play.

Mary, too, was excited at the prospect of music and dancing with minstrels and mumming gracing the huge Banqueting Hall that had been silent for so long. "It won't be like the old days, Kate, but there'll be fireworks on the river again, the people will have their bonfires and all the conduits will flow with wine! Do you realize the children have never seen all this? And you, my Kate, will be the prettiest lady there. I've never seen you look so well. . . ."

It was, Katherine realized, Mary's way of conferring a belated blessing upon her disputed marriage. Thomas had held no grudge since their reunion, welcoming Mary to the manor house with great courtesy, as if nothing had happened. He treated her with much the same joking amiability as Elizabeth and Jane, which made Mary, more quiet and more sober, laugh as much as the others.

As they sat poring over the court pattern books and comparing bright samples of costly damasks, satins and brocades, with piles of trim and jeweled sleeves about them, Thomas returned from the Privy Council meeting. He strode in, no sight of amiability now on his handsome flushed face, his lips tight between the darkly luxuriant mustache and beard. Calling for wine, he flung himself into a chair muttering, "My brother and I have had a disagreement. . . ."

Katherine sighed. Life had been pleasant the past few months because the Seymour brothers had been separated by the war. Thomas's envy and jealousy of Edward Seymour had given way to pride in the Protector's Scottish victory, in the prestige he now enjoyed as husband of the Queen-Dowager. Yet the moment the two were reunited, all the old animosities were revived.

Sensing Thomas's mood, Mary quietly left the room, murmuring she'd watch out for Kate Brandon who was to join them. After a moment, Thomas explained, "My brother is wondrous angry with me for bringing Princess Elizabeth to live here. And he wonders why I bought Jane's wardship? Ha, Henry Grey was sitting right there listening but he said nothing! What was I to say? So that my Lord Grey could pay his gambling debts? Or that they were miserable parents and abused their daughter? And then our Protector also is disturbed that Edward comes to see you so freely. I told him the boy had decided on his own—that it will only make him, my brother, look foolish if he protests and orders Edward to stay away. He said the boy would never have taken so much upon himself if he hadn't been encouraged."

Katherine looked at her husband thoughtfully. "And he was encouraged, my lord?"

Thomas set down his wine cup, laughed heartily and reached out for her. "And what would you do if I say he was? Ah, Kate, the boy is kept too straitly! One of his attendants told me that first day we arrived here that he's never alone for more than fifteen minutes. But it's always a tutor, a guard, a steward or some servant who's with him. He never has any time for himself and you know why? Because my saintly brother is too worried he'll be influenced by others not to his liking. Why, the Protector won't even give the child an allowance!"

"And you do?"

Thomas's cheeks colored. Katherine hadn't meant to sound so critical, but it angered her that her husband would use her stepson to provoke his brother. She loved having Edward visit—the freedom had done the boy a great deal of good. But if such visits were only going to increase bad feelings between the Seymour brothers, it would all rebound eventually upon Edward who would feel he was to blame and probably be more restrained than ever. She also suspected neither brother really sought the boy's well-being, but thought only of themselves. "My lord, you take it too lightly," she said, pulling away. "I've said it before, if you'd try to work things out with my Lord Protector. . . ."

"God's blood, there's no working things out, Kate! My brother will do as he pleases, but I don't intend to stand by and fawn all over him as the others do! Nor will I allow him to tell my nephew what he may or may not do. I'm the boy's uncle, too. You seem to forget that!"

Katherine turned away. She rarely got the better of Thomas in an argument. Should she do so, he'd storm from the room, shouting one of his great oaths and stay away for a day or so. She never knew where he went, but had learned not to worry. She'd never expected life with Thomas Seymour to be as well ordered or as predictable as her other marriages. Wasn't that one of his great attractions, one of the reasons she still loved him so much and treasured the moments spent with him?

"It's the other side of his nature," she told her sister, Ann, after a shouting match between Thomas and Ann's husband, Will Herbert, "and one we have to accept. But sometimes, Ann, I fear for him! I wonder how this relationship with his brother will end? Can it go on this way for six more years until the king can rule for himself? Six years of the Seymour brothers at each other's throats, suspicious and antagonistic all the time?"

Thomas's bitterness and envy was the one cloud under which Katherine lived, for she knew she could never control or influence her husband. Not in the important ways that mattered. It worried her for she wanted nothing to spoil her happiness nor the well-being of those in her care. It never ceased to bother her that something as simple as the relationship between two brothers —men she hadn't even known fifteen years ago—could now determine the tenor of her days and the possibility of a secure future.

* * *

The vast Banqueting Hall, hung with banners, their colors shimmering in the light of hundreds of fat candles set into the great overhead wheels, lit up the scene of the Protector's victory celebration. Everywhere people milled about and, as the trumpets blew announcing their arrival, Katherine and Thomas walked in procession to the end of the room where King Edward waited, bowing and nodding to acquaintances as they went.

Edward smiled as they went on their knees, more at ease than Katherine had ever seen him. Indicating the guest of honor, he said, "My Lord Protector and his lady, madame. . . ."

Greeting Edward Seymour, Katherine was conscious of his wife standing by his side. She was handsomely dressed in vivid golden velvet and about her neck Katherine saw several of her own gems; others were on the

woman's gown and in her hair. Undoubtedly, Anne Stanhope had worn
them deliberately, hoping to provoke, and Katherine steeled herself, vowing
not to let her anger show. Instead, she let her glance slide away from Anne
and turned her full attention to the Protector. "A great victory, my lord, and
all England is very proud," she murmured. "You must accept my great joy in
your safe return which so affects us all."

It was the right speech with the right tone and, relieved, Katherine moved
on, aware of the consternation in the countess' eyes that her presence had
not been acknowledged. Katherine was glad the awkward moment was over
and cared little what the woman thought, wondering why she—the Queen-
Dowager—should feel on the defensive? The Lord Protector had earned his
moment of glory; she felt no reluctance in complimenting him. Nor did she
feel he bore her any ill will. After all, by virtue of her marriage to Thomas,
they were relatives. Yet he must be aware of his wife's animosity.

Mingling with the crowd bent upon celebrating Edward Seymour's success, Katherine met Joan Dudley and Joan Denny. In a moment, months of
separation were forgotten as they eagerly talked about life at Chelsea, Joan
Denny's new baby and the Protector's competence and goodwill. Both
women complimented Katherine on her obvious happiness and she forgave
their neglect of the past months for they were as pleased to see her as she
was to see them.

Taking her place in a circle forming for the dance, she found handsome
young William Cecil, the Protector's secretary, as her partner. Across the
room her brother, Will Parr, flirted with young Lady Fitzwilliam as her
older husband tolerantly looked on. Will would never change she thought,
sighing. As Thomas danced by she caught the amused look in his eye and
knew he'd also seen Will bent on another feminine conquest. Near Edward's
small throne, Kate Brandon and her elder son Henry, now the Duke of
Suffolk, were talking with the Greys. Frances Brandon Grey had put on
weight which her heavily bejeweled gown only emphasized. Katherine wondered if she and her husband had visited their daughter, asleep now in another wing of the palace.

In a moment, she saw Mary Tudor embracing a slight, gray-haired lady
and, once the dance was over, Will Cecil escorted her to the princess. "Lady
Bryan," Katherine smiled, embracing the older woman. She wondered where
the years had gone since this lady—smaller now than she remembered—had
taken Mary, Kate Brandon and herself on childhood excursions on the river,
in the woods and along the City's streets, had babied and cosseted young
Elizabeth and worried about a little prince's well-being. Kate Brandon joined
them as they all listened to Lady Bryan's account of a quiet life in her Essex
home.

"Ah, yes, my ladies, I miss you all," she smiled, "but my son brings me
gossip of the court and I have my own fireside and garden." She smoothed
the twisted gold cord along the sleeve of her simple gown. "I would be too
old for all this now," she gestured about the room. "But my son thought I

should see this great celebration, for there might naught be another for me. . . ." Across the room, Sir Francis Bryan, Henry's old gambling and hunting companion, raised a wine cup in his mother's direction.

Then suddenly it was all over and everyone prepared to leave. Quickly, Katherine embraced Lady Bryan, promising to meet her the next morning so she might visit Elizabeth and Edward, who would be delighted to see her. Then there'd be enough time to sit and talk, share a meal and have a real reunion.

With Thomas at her side they went toward the door. As Queen-Dowager, she must leave before the others could follow. The entrance was crowded and the Protector, bowing, made way for Katherine. But his countess would not budge. Glancing coldly at Katherine, she spoke to her husband. "Come, my lord, no one can leave until we do. . . ."

It was a deliberate affront, meant to antagonize and insult. Thomas stiffened and, about them, those who'd heard Anne's words, gasped. But Katherine was too outraged to care. Even fear of a scene, of hot words and possible physical violence between the brothers did not lessen her fury. Never had she hated anyone as much as the insolent woman who stood there wearing her jewels, a malicious smile on her handsome face, taking unto herself a precedence and authority that, by ancient decree and custom, belonged to royalty. Without thinking further, Katherine stepped forward.

"Your place, madame, I think you don't know your place." Quickly, she put one foot on the train of the countess' long velvet gown so she could not move without tearing it badly. There was momentary panic in the woman's eyes for all about her others were watching. Even the Protector looked nonplussed while Thomas's expression changed to one of guarded satisfaction.

But Katherine was beyond caring. "Your place, madame, I think is here," she said in a low voice. Removing her foot, she stepped forward one more pace causing Anne to move backward several paces. But not before it appeared the two women were jostling each other for position.

The advantage of surprise was Katherine's, however, and at the doorway, she held out her hand to Thomas. "Come, my lord," she said loudly, repeating Anne's exact words, "no one can leave until we do. . . ." Nodding toward the stunned Protector and with Thomas barely concealing his laughter, she went out the door as satisfied titters could be heard among the guests.

Behind her, an affronted countess, near tears, turned to her husband. "And you stand there, my lord," she cried, "and let Latimer's widow, who is now merely the wife of the young brother of England's Protector, take precedence over she who is the wife of that guardian! Shame on you, my lord! If Master Admiral teaches his wife no better manners, I am she that will!"

* * *

A truce between the Queen-Dowager and the Countess of Somerset was declared when Will Parr patiently explained to Anne Stanhope that by an

Act of Henry VIII, his wife, Katherine Parr, his "beloved sister," Anne of Cleves, as well as his two daughters all enjoyed precedence over her. The mortified countess accepted the decision but continued to beleaguer her husband who hoped to keep the sisters-in-law apart as much as possible.

Knowing how embittered Anne was, Katherine vowed to avoid her whenever she could. It was not difficult for the relationship between Edward and Thomas Seymour was rapidly deteriorating. Thomas felt neither the Protector nor the Privy Council gave him the regard that was his due. His wife was a queen; a princess of the realm as well as a royal grandniece lodged in his home and he was Lord High Admiral of the Navy. Why wasn't he more trusted, given further honors and estates? Why didn't the councillors rely on his advice and leadership as they did his brother's?

Katherine tried to explain to her husband that perhaps his aggressive attitude was to blame. "You weaken your position, my lord, when you harass the councillors. You irk your brother by demands he cannot possibly satisfy. Be patient—do the work you've been given and do it well. Ah, Thomas love, we have so much! Don't let what you think are slights to your pride or honor poison what could be a good life! Your brother *is* the Protector! Accept it and help him, offer your services for whatever he may want you to do."

"I do that and I'll find myself in Spain, Brussels or Calais," Thomas grumbled. "Edward would be very agreeable to having me out of the country. Or else he'd like me dead. No, I must stay right at hand and guard my interests —and those of my Lady Jane and Bess, too."

Katherine wanted to reply that the girls' future was hardly Thomas's concern. But she remained silent, aware once more of the turbulent spirit she'd married. The two sides of this complex man who still held her in thrall were something she must accept and tolerate if they were to be together. She could only hope that about the court and at the council table, Thomas would eventually behave with more propriety and soberness, that he would try to make peace with his brother.

She was surprised when, two days later, sitting with her "two Joans," the brothers' animosity was openly discussed. It was of particular interest to the council, Joan Dudley explained, because Thomas Seymour had married a queen, taken a princess of the realm into his home and obtained the guardianship of Henry's grandniece.

Katherine scoffed. "My ladies, you pay too much attention to gossip and not enough to fact. My Lady Elizabeth is my stepdaughter and Thomas honorably bought Lady Jane's wardship! That is not unusual! We're both very concerned for their future. . . ." Puzzled, she asked why the councillors shouldn't be pleased Thomas had taken on such a responsibility? Why should his actions anger them?

Joan Dudley looked at her old friend with disbelief. "Because of their status, Kate. These are marriageable young ladies, remember. The Privy Council will decide on the matter, of course. But your husband can make it difficult because he has great influence on both girls. More, perhaps, than even you, my dear! But what really concerns them the most is that he works to poison the mind of the king against the Protector."

As Katherine started to protest, Joan Dudley held up her hand. "Now hear me out, Kate. I'm glad to be able to talk like this for mayhap you can warn Thomas he goes too far. My husband sits at the council table daily and he tells me what goes on! He says Thomas spends endless time with young Edward, so much so that John Cheke has complained about it. He says my Lord Admiral urges the king to speak out against the Protector, saying he wants to rule more than he does. He hurts the boy's feelings by saying he's not a real king, that all the Protector does is let him sign papers that someone else writes. He taunts the boy that he never has enough pocket money so that he's a penniless king who hasn't a farthing to spend." Two bright spots of color on each cheek emphasized Joan's anger. "It's all very troublesome, Kate. And the Protector's wife constantly urges that her husband get rid of Thomas. She says if he doesn't, he is cursed, for the brother works for his death."

Katherine was appalled that Thomas was the target of so much talk. Determined not to show it, she lightly reminded her two old friends that more damage was done by gossip than anything else. "If the Privy Council and my Lord Protector are angry or resentful, let them talk to Thomas. Make him explain why he's done as he has and settle the arguments once and for all," she advised. But even as she spoke, she wondered if such a confrontation might not enrage her husband even more. Or would it clear the air and bring peace to their days?

She remembered the conversation later in the day as she unexpectedly came upon Thomas and Jane Grey's father in the Whitehall gardens. Walking toward them, she heard Henry Grey's last words, ". . . and you will match her with the king?" Catching sight of his wife, Thomas smiled broadly, shook his head at his companion and all three continued back to the palace courtyard.

After Henry Grey had bowed his farewell, Katherine asked, "And what did he mean, my lord? Who will be matched with the king?"

Thomas looked about the empty courtyard. Putting a finger to his lips, they continued on in silence. When at last inside, he replied, "Well, if you must know, Kate, I would match Jane with young Edward. They are both old enough to be betrothed and it would settle many questions. With the Stuart lass whisked away to France—thanks to my dear brother's murderous victory in Scotland—there'll be no marriage there! Who else is Edward to wed? No Catholic princess on the Continent will have him. Both he and Jane believe in the 'new religion.' They would do well together."

"And what does the Protector think?" Katherine was uneasily reminded of Joan Dudley's conversation. She wished Thomas would not make decisions that were not his responsibility.

"Aye, what does my brother think? Well, my brother thinks Jane Grey should marry his son, Lord Hertford. And he'd be just as pleased if the king married daughter Jane, named after our sainted sister who was queen. Or, if that can't be arranged, he'd be pleased to have it the other way around, with Jane Grey marrying the king! And he has the effrontery to accuse me of being too ambitious and, as he says, having too many strings to my bow. What you heard me tell Jane's father was that I would work to match her with the king."

Katherine's patience disappeared. "I think you both take too much upon yourselves!" she cried angrily. "It sickens me to know that either of you think you can decide what is right for Henry's son and grandniece. When the time is right, the Privy Council and the bishops will settle the matter!" She wanted to say that the Protector's ambition appeared to exceed her husband's.

But, she realized with a pang, Thomas had spoken a vital truth. With their love for the reformed religion, Elizabeth, Edward and Jane Grey —recipients of hours of study and discussion with her on the tenets of the "new faith" that Mary Tudor so despised—had grown up far removed from Catholicism as it was practiced abroad. It would be difficult if not impossible to find Catholic spouses for them. So they must look for matches at home and as such, the Seymour brothers—unknown to her mother and father's generation except as minor country gentry—might look with hope to allying their blood with royalty.

It disturbed Katherine more than she dared admit. Who were these two men—come to power because their sister married a king—who felt they might so easily decide the fate of a ten-year-old boy and girl and possibly a nubile fourteen-year-old princess? They hadn't mentioned Elizabeth. But the girl was older now than she herself had been when she'd gone north to wed Lord Borough.

If he had any thoughts regarding Elizabeth, Thomas did not say. Seeing his wife's anger, he only laughed, called for wine and suggested they might soon return to Chelsea. "There, my darling Kate, you won't be hearing all this gossip that makes you angry with your husband and his brother. I want a wife who's a comfort, not a nag! My brother and I have the king's children's interests at heart, believe me. How much better can their interests be protected than if they are wed with the family who has the authority and power to maintain that safety? Do you want Jane marrying a Dudley, or Edward one of the Howard wenches or Bess paired off with my young Lord of Suffolk, old Charles Brandon's sprig? Get you off to Chelsea with the girls, my darling wife, and don't worry your lovely head about something you can do nothing about."

After Thomas had gone, Katherine ruefully reflected there was, indeed, little she could do about her stepchildren's future. The power lay at the council table and with the bishops. But with the Seymour brothers now firmly entrenched at court—and jockeying each other for power and influence—she wondered if either group would be a match for them.

* * *

After the holiday festivities—restrained in view of the fact that the court was still in official mourning—Katherine moved her household back to Chelsea. Mary returned to Beaulieu, refreshed after being with her family and relieved her tie with Katherine had been renewed. Elizabeth and Jane were glad to be free of the endless court protocol and processions, of being constantly surrounded by ceremony. Everyone was saddened at leaving Edward who maintained, as they said goodbye, that no matter what anyone said, he'd visit his stepmother at Whitsun. If Mary came from Beaulieu at the same time, they'd all be a family again.

Katherine put the court squabbles, the disappointment over her failure to recover her jewels and her heartache at Edward's absence behind her and looked forward to enjoying another Chelsea spring. Thomas still came to the riverside house almost every night; it was nearly a year to the day since he'd come riding down "the king's road" back into her life to change it forever.

She'd been there less than two weeks when, rising from her bed one morning, listening to the loud shouts and laughter from Elizabeth's quarters where Thomas was again awakening the girl and her ladies-in-waiting, she felt a sickly dizziness overwhelm her. Lying back in bed, the sounds from down the corridors receding and then almost overpowering her, she fought back a nausea that confirmed something she'd suspected for days. Uncomfortable as she was, she wanted to rise and run down the hallway and shout the news to everyone. How their laughter would turn to pure joy! Always, she'd felt she must be barren, but this weakness, this churning inside her must mean only one thing—she was pregnant. Gloriously, uncomfortably and undeniably pregnant.

Lying in bed, with her stomach settling and the weakness subsiding, she wondered if she should tell Thomas. She might be mistaken, though every instinct told her she was not. Kate Brandon was arriving with her two boys at the end of the week. Perhaps it would be better to wait and see what a few more mornings brought. If Kate agreed she was indeed going to have a child, she'd get young Dr. Huyck down from Whitehall and then tell Thomas.

She was just drifting back to sleep when suddenly her door opened and, with no permission to enter, someone banged the door shut. Suddenly, Cat Ashley was looming over her, red-faced and angry. Curtseying briefly, she explained.

"Your Grace, this is unseemly of me, but I protest before you as I have before my Lord Admiral, he must cease from coming into my lady princess' room so early! Some mornings, my lady is not even awake, madame! He pulls the curtains aside and tickles her and frightens her so that upon awakening, she must burrow under the covers because it is all so sudden and she knows not where she is . . . !" Cat's tone was indignant. "I think it unseemly, madame, that a man garbed only in nightclothes should come into a maiden's room so early in the morning and before she is awake!"

Stunned at Cat's outburst Katherine was about to rise when Thomas, returning, heard her last words.

"By God's precious blood! I will tell everyone including the Protector how I am slandered! I will not leave off for I mean no evil!" He glared at Mistress Ashley who glared back. "If you want to be so careful, my good woman, watch your little lady who's not above kissing a strange lad out in the garden. I saw her myself at the gallery window yesterday. . . ."

As Cat gasped in surprise, Katherine struggled to her feet, taking the robe Thomas handed her. Again he rounded on Elizabeth's companion. "Tell my Lady Elizabeth to lock her doors if she doesn't want any interruptions! I trow she enjoys our romps as much as I do and so do all the other ladies! Has no one ever tickled you in your bed, Mistress Ashley?" His voice had an unpleasant tone and Cat, shaken by the question, looked at Katherine imploringly.

"Thank you, mistress. . . ." Katherine motioned the upset girl out of the room. It had taken courage for Cat Ashley to confront her and Thomas. "We'll talk about it later."

As the door closed, she lay back on the bed, her robe covering her, hoping Thomas wouldn't notice how ill she felt. She was about to ask him to call Bessie Bellingham when he was suddenly there beside her, holding her in his arms, stroking her hair. "She's a spiteful woman, that Ashley," he whispered, "now she's disturbed your rest and I think made you unwell, Kate. Lie quiet now and don't get up. Try to go back to sleep, my darling. I'll stay here with you until you do."

Gratefully, Katherine stretched out in his arms, his warmth and reassuring words comforting, her nausea disappearing. Sooner or later, she'd have to deal with Cat Ashley's outburst and Thomas's report that Elizabeth had dallied in the garden with . . . who? It was so unlike Bess to involve herself that way. She was proud, prouder than Mary of being a king's daughter and not likely to take up with someone below her station. Katherine's last thought before sleep overtook her was that if Elizabeth indeed had reached the stage where she could flirt with a stablehand or other servant, then perhaps she, more than the other two royal children, should be married soon.

* * *

Cat Ashley was waiting the following morning when Katherine asked if the girls were with their new tutor, Roger Ascham, who'd come to Chelsea after old Will Grindal's death. Cat nodded and waited, for both knew what must be discussed—the charge that Thomas had made the previous day of seeing Elizabeth embracing someone in the manor house garden.

"I asked her, Your Grace, and told her what my Lord Admiral said. I repeated his exact words. She was very upset and said my lord was making a joke, that she'd embraced no one. I was quite insistent, madame. She wept woefully and said again and again there was nothing to the charge, that she sees no men except my Lord Admiral and her tutor."

"And you believe her?"

"I believe her, madame. I know my lady princess well and she does not lie. She was indignant that someone should accuse her of such a thing. I'm indignant too, madame, for I believe my lord is having fun at my Lady Elizabeth's expense."

Katherine was torn. Thomas was capable of such a tasteless joke and capable of leaving her to deal with it. She wanted to believe Cat Ashley for she did not think Elizabeth would be so foolish. It would be difficult for her to misbehave for she was rarely unattended. But she might knowingly or unknowingly have encouraged one of the attractive boys about the household or stables to look beyond his station. And might she not, like Anne Boleyn when aroused, act and then think about it later? Katherine remembered the time the child had asked Henry about cutting off her mother's head. She'd acted instinctively and paid for it. But it had been an honest question.

And if Elizabeth, denied the company of proper young boys her own age, was seeking companionship from unsuitable ones, wasn't it her responsibility to deal with it? Bess would give her little trouble once the danger was pointed out, for she had a practical mind and sound temperament. More than censure, she needed guidance and a warning that there would always be those ready to take advantage of her innocence.

With her mind made up, Katherine dismissed Cat Ashley, whose tone and expression softened when she saw her charge wasn't going to be condemned unheard. "Speak to her, Your Grace," she said as she left, "and you'll see she is innocent."

Katherine made her way down the narrow corridor past the window where Thomas said he'd seen Elizabeth kissing a stranger. Hearing low murmurs in an adjoining chamber, she opened the door. Thomas was standing in front of the fireplace, his arms about a slight figure who gazed up at him, eyes lit with wonder, her flushed face and hurried breathing telling Katherine that only now had Elizabeth experienced her first kiss.

Both turned as the door opened, presenting a tableau of stunned amazement. Elizabeth gasped, covering the lips Thomas Seymour had just kissed with a shaking hand. Her face crumpled. "Oh, madame . . . !" Thomas looked pale, his usual proud, high-spirited swagger fading before his wife's shocked and disbelieving gaze.

Katherine's heart beat so wildly she thought she might faint. I will not cry, she thought, I will not let Thomas see this hurt. . . .

"Bess, go to your room." Her voice sounded distant and rasping. Elizabeth, pale and now visibly shaking, curtsied and ran quickly from the room.

"What am I to think, Thomas?" She turned to the man who, poise returning, walked toward her, a slight smile on his lips, with a calm she found infuriating. "I was on my way to chide Bess about your story. Were *you* the man who enjoyed her embrace yesterday? Or was this the first time? Was this some game between the two of you to see who might dishonor your wife?"

As he tried to take her shaking hands, she flung herself from him. "Stay away from me, Thomas! You've gone too far, my lord, and I will not be quieted. She is fifteen, Thomas, *fifteen,* old enough for you to caress and old enough for you to want. But she is an innocent and you know it and still you were willing to take advantage of her." As he started to speak, Katherine raised a hand, stifling a desire to slap her husband's handsome face, to scratch and claw so he might physically feel the pain he'd inflicted upon her. "But she is a king's daughter and I am a king's widow. How dare you attempt such a ruse! I will not have it in my house—and this is *my* house, Thomas—for never have I tolerated indecency. You may go or stay, my lord, but you go or stay by yourself. Now I will leave you to think of what you've done. And for what, Thomas? For what?"

Not trusting herself any further, she ran from the room. She would never let Thomas Seymour see her cry.

Hours later, after much thought and tears, Katherine went to Elizabeth's chamber. She found the girl sitting on a window seat, looking pensively out at the twilight-lit river. Her eyes were swollen from crying and she looked at her visitor with such fright and dismay that Katherine felt her determination wavering. She held out a hand and, greatly relieved, the girl took it as Katherine sat beside her. Elizabeth hung her head, her lips trembling, but still clutched her stepmother's hand.

"Bess, you know we'll have to do something about what happened here today. I don't know how long this has been going on and I don't want to know. I blame myself for much of this. I should have listened to Ashley about the way Thomas behaved in your chambers, but I trusted you both. Especially Thomas. He knows better, yet chose to pleasure himself, thinking little of your welfare or our honor. But he and I will work that out. Now, the main thing is, what to do about you?"

"Whatever you think best, madame," Elizabeth whispered. "But I want you to know that nothing has been going on. Yes, he came to my chamber often in the morning and enjoyed the pranks he played on my ladies and me. Sometimes when I wouldn't get out of bed, he'd chide me and say I was too modest! Sometimes, madame, I didn't know what to do and I'd call for Ashley. Today, he came up behind me and scared me almost witless because I didn't hear him. He said, 'Now I have you!' and the first thing I knew he was kissing me. . . ." With her confession complete, Elizabeth put her head on Katherine's shoulder and sobbed.

Touched, Katherine put her arms about the shaking girl. She understood all too well the attraction Elizabeth Tudor's chaste young beauty had for Thomas Seymour. "Bess, stop weeping, or better still, have a good cry. Then we'll put this behind us and make plans. But don't make yourself ill, my dear. I know you're not to blame. But you know we can't go on as we were.

Please, Bess, if you want to be forgiven, I forgive you. But we'll have to make some changes."

At the terrified look in the girl's eyes, Katherine wavered, but she went on. "Yes, Bess," she repeated firmly, "we'll have to make some changes. I don't think it's good for you to live here anymore. Talk to Ashley about it—talk to Tom Parry. I think they suspect more than you know. See how quickly they'll agree. I'll work it out, Bess, but I'll need your help. We'll have to talk to the council about where you are to live. But we have to send you away, Bess, as much for your own good as anything else. And I'm sorry —sorrier than you'll ever know."

A footstep was heard in the hall and Cat Ashley appeared in the doorway. Over Elizabeth's bent head and the hot tears now staining her gown, Katherine shook her head slightly, urging the woman away. After Cat left, she held Elizabeth closely and let her own tears mingle with those of the heartbroken princess.

The following morning a devastated Elizabeth left for the home of Joan Denny at Cheshunt. Sir Anthony Denny was a member of the Privy Council that would decide whether the princess would go to Ashridge, Hatfield or her old residence at Enfield. A subdued Thomas Seymour, begging Katherine's understanding of his foolish and unpardonable behavior, would also have to explain to the council why he, once so eager to have a princess live in his household, would now voluntarily send her to Henry and Katherine's old friends.

"Tell them anything you like, my lord, but under no circumstances is Bess to be blamed," Katherine told him coolly. "This has grieved her more than you'll ever know and she's paying dearly for it. No councillor must think she has offended or is at fault."

After a grim Thomas had left, Katherine went to Elizabeth's chamber where servants were packing the bulk of her possessions—books, drawing materials, needlework and her rich court garments—that they'd take to Cheshunt later in the day. On the table she found Maud Parr's pearl pendant and gold chain that she'd given to Elizabeth. The sight of it, neatly laid out so that she'd be sure to see it, started the tears flowing again. Not only for Elizabeth's hurt—for obviously she thought herself unworthy of the gift —but also for her own heartache over Thomas's coarse conduct and the fact that she'd never even told him of the baby.

But she did tell Kate Brandon when she arrived that weekend in Chelsea. The duchess whooped and held her old friend tightly. When, looking at her closely, she said, "But you look peaked, my dear. Are you all right?" Katherine broke into tears and poured out the whole sordid story.

The duchess sat stunned. Recovering her poise, she cried, "Well, he's not the first husband to allow his senses to rule his mind. Nor will he be the last. But that's small consolation to you, my dear, and I know you're hurt. But I'm sorry it was Bess. I could see him whipped for that! But," she looked thoughtful, "it explains much. When I was in London Joan Dudley told me that Elizabeth was at Cheshunt and I wondered why. And I wondered why Thomas behaved as he did with the council."

"And how was that?"

Kate explained that Anthony Denny and John Dudley had tried to warn Thomas that his conduct with the young king was becoming an open scandal. It was no secret he continually urged the boy to ask the next Parliament to revoke the Protector's appointment. He'd even told Edward that Katherine felt the same. But Edward, on the advice of his tutor, John Cheke, would do nothing, not wishing to favor one uncle over the other.

"But I think he frightens the boy," the duchess explained, "because then Edward wonders if those uncles are fighting amongst themselves to take his crown away. And he remembers the story about the boy who would have been Edward V if his uncle hadn't killed him and his little brother in the Tower! Recently Thomas said if Edward wouldn't have the Protector deposed, he could ask to have the appointment shortened. And you know there are always those in the council who feel that in any change, they will gain something. So Thomas has a few supporters. Ah, he's going to need them if any of them ever finds out he tried to seduce a princess! I trow I'd like to be a fly on the wall when he explains that!"

At Katherine's look of distress she rose and put her arms about her old friend. "My dear, I know Thomas loves you very much. As much as he can love anyone. We've never had any secrets, Katherine, and we shouldn't start now. I encouraged you to marry him for I thought you'd had very little real happiness. But you know I never thought much of either Edward or Thomas Seymour! They're only where they are today because their sister married a king and now their nephew is the sovereign, if only in name. It's made them light-headed with power and, unfortunately, whatever else is in their heads, it is not the stuff of wisdom!"

Katherine had to smile at Kate Brandon's ascerbic assessment of her husband and brother-in-law. Maturity had not dulled the duchess' wit or tongue.

"But what do I do now? I've not even told Thomas of the baby."

"I don't think fatherhood will make much of a difference, my dear, for your husband is not the kind that will be tethered. But mayhap now he's learned a lesson."

Thomas's artifice depressed Katherine so much she ended the conversation, praying that his conduct might not doom them all. Already, Bess had suffered for something not basically her fault. And now she herself—and her baby—might be endangered for, should Thomas succeed in getting a bill through Parliament deposing or limiting the Protector's office, everyone would know the source. Apparently everyone already did. And supposing he lost? Katherine could imagine Edward Seymour's justified wrath—and Anne Stanhope's jubilation.

Within two days her fears were somewhat put to rest. Her brother, Will Parr, wrote that Thomas had told the council that his wife's household and that of Lady Jane Grey would be moving to Hanworth, a manor given her by the old king. Will wished her a pleasant journey, saying it was too bad there was no room for Elizabeth, but the council would soon have her removed to Hatfield. The news had caused them little concern and Katherine breathed a sigh of relief. The secret reason of Bess's removal to Cheshunt had been kept.

But, according to Will, what concerned the council more was the Lord High Admiral's motives in working against the Protector, actions they knew as fact and not rumor. In addition to severely reprimanding Thomas, the council denied him any higher wage for his navy duties since he'd paid so little attention to them. Thomas had sworn loudly, Will wrote, and accused them all of impugning his honor and said all they'd heard was a pack of lies. When several councillors threatened a period in the Tower to help restore his memory, Thomas had backtracked somewhat. "At that point, he apologized to the Protector saying his actions had been misunderstood. Everyone was more tolerant than he deserves, Katherine, for he's playing with fire. I've told him you are his greatest protection, that if he was not wed to Henry's queen, he would have been imprisoned. But he just laughs. One who understands better is the Protector's wife who's frankly told her husband again that he should get rid of Thomas for if he doesn't, he will be the death of him. . . ."

* * *

Before leaving for Hanworth, which Thomas said they must do since that's what he'd told the council, Katherine's spirits were revived by a letter from Elizabeth. It was in answer to one in which she told the princess of her pregnancy. In her affectionate reply, Elizabeth rejoiced at the news, said she was happy at the Dennys, busy with her studies and had very little time for leisure. Between the lines, Katherine sensed the girl's loneliness and knew how much she missed the love, security and good times of Chelsea.

From Beaulieu, Mary Tudor wrote that she, too, was overjoyed at Katherine's pregnancy and begged to be kept informed of her whereabouts and condition. "I shall be going to Kenninghall, Kate, for lack of good health has stayed with me all the while and, being so unstable, I find the Norfolk air better for my condition. I pray God Almighty watch out for you and the babe. . . ."

Sighing, Katherine put the letter away. How much better it would have been if the whole family could have been with her now when she felt the child growing each day. There'd been no word from Edward at Whitehall and she wondered if the boy believed what Thomas had told him—that she, too, believed the Protector should be deposed.

Upon returning from London, a repentant Thomas had scoffed at her fears. "He's naught but ten, Katherine, and is kept busy, for every moment of the day must be accounted for. Of course he listens to me. But he listens to the Protector too as well as his household officers, his nurse and playmates. God's blood, why must I be blamed for everything?"

Thomas, in good spirits, again made light of the council's threats Will Parr had described. He would be eight hundred pounds richer each year, he boasted, for at the end of the council session, the Protector had increased his annual income by that amount. "He knows I feel he takes too much upon himself and that I resent it. But now I'm satisfied, Kate, and the sooner we're at Hanworth, I want us to start all over again. I was a fool, stupid and thinking only of myself and I regret that poor Bess had to go. But you have the babe to think about now and Jane still needs your cosseting. Life, my sweetheart, can be good again! Come now, we mustn't live in the past!"

And, Katherine decided, Thomas was right. One couldn't live in the past, continually condemning for an unfortunate momentary mishap. It wasn't her nature to sulk or harbor a grievance. And what convinced her most was her husband's joy in being told he was to be a father. Thomas had held her close and, tears in his eyes, had whispered his love for and pride in her. Together, he said, they'd be the best parents in the world to their son. "You'll see, Kate. All your worries will be for naught. Give me a son and we'll have everything worth living for."

"And if it's a daughter?" she laughed.

"No, it must be a son." Thomas was serious. "A man needs a son and you and I aren't young sprigs with several chances ahead. In his older years a man needs to point with pride to one who will bear his name and carry his blood. . . ."

Katherine laughed again but, several days later at Hanworth, when the news arrived that the Protector's wife had just had her fifth child and third son, Thomas's face darkened. She knew what he was thinking and prayed the child she carried—beginning now to make her unwieldy—was a boy. She really felt it was God's will whatever He sent, and she'd be as content with a fair daughter as a son. But even God's decision apparently would not allay the enmity she knew still existed between the Seymour brothers.

CHAPTER XXX

By mid-June, en route to Sudeley Castle, their reconciliation was complete. Before leaving Hanworth, Katherine wrote Kate Brandon. "I've put it from me, Kate, for Thomas is now as loving and faithful as ever. His mind, he says, was unhinged for a while with all the responsibilities of his work, with the demands of Seymour Place and his jealousy of the Protector. What started in fun with Bess was suddenly something less than a game. Now he laughs at it. I do, too, to make him feel easier but now I think I know my husband better. He's not as clever as he thinks, nor as superior as he feels. But he is kindness itself for *my* welfare and I think being at our new home at Sudeley will complete this miracle of our well-being. I am content and, once our babe is born, perhaps Mary and Elizabeth can join us there. Jesu knows Sudeley is big enough! After Chelsea and Hanworth, it will seem like a palace! I am so happy and content now I care little whether I ever return to London or the court. Thomas says he feels the same. . . ."

It took six long weary days for the journey from Hanworth to Sudeley Castle near Winchcombe in Gloucestershire. Katherine traveled in an especially fitted wagon instead of a litter. It was comfortably lined in the softest of leather, deeply cushioned with crimson velvet and bore the royal arms on its side. But the roads were deeply rutted, mired in mud.

Everyone was eagerly anticipating seeing the castle upon which Thomas had lavished a small fortune since the Protector had given it to him over a year ago. When cresting a hill, he called to his wife, the wagon pulled out of procession and Katherine, thankful for the respite, walked to the hilltop to look down on her new home.

"There's been a house of some sort there since the time of the Romans and the Saxons. . . ." Thomas pointed with his whip to the long range of buildings standing about a rectangular courtyard. Only one tip—bright and green —of what Katherine assumed were the gardens could be seen from where they stood. A banner with the Seymour crest flew atop one huge old tower, its stone mellower than the remaining building, much of it covered with ivy. Similar banners and welcoming flags flew from arched gateways and the battlemented roof. Two towers had mere slits for windows, slits from which archers would have defended the castle hundreds of years ago. Large oriel windows and others with diamond panes or colorful with stained glass were in the newer section. Tiny figures scurried about the courtyard, for one of the chamberlains had galloped on ahead to announce the lord of the manor's arrival. Jane Grey danced about them in excitement, pulling at Lady Tyrwhit's hand, grinning from ear to ear, her freckled face flushed with happiness.

"Oh, madame, it is so lovely!" she cried, "I didn't know it was so old. . . ." Jane loved ancient history—much of which she read in the original Greek—and when Thomas told her there was a large mound on the property thought to be a Roman burial place, she looked awed.

In the weeks that followed, Katherine was more content than she'd ever been, daily discovering something more beautiful or inspiring about her new home. Sudeley had once belonged to a Crusader, Ralph de Sudeleye, whose son, John, had served with King Edward II and the Black Prince, she told a delighted Jane Grey. And when they visited the great tithe barn built in A.D. 811 that had formerly belonged to the Abbey of Winchcombe, it was Jane who told Katherine that Winchcombe had once been the capital of the ancient Saxon kingdom of Mercia. There was so much excitement in each day, Katherine often wished Mary, Elizabeth and Edward could be there to share it with her.

Sudeley was grander than her Gainsborough home and larger than Snape and everywhere showed the results of all of Thomas's lavish spending. From almost any window, the view was of gardens of flowering shrubs, ornamental yew hedges or the green parkland that teemed with deer and wildfowl. There was even a lake hidden from view by a magnificent old forest of black oak. Often Katherine and Thomas walked in the twilight admiring the elegance of their home, the beauty of its land and the softness of its air. Watching the restoration work still being carried on in the great Banqueting Hall, Thomas urged the workmen on, saying when his heir was born, all London would come to celebrate!

The Lord High Admiral, it seemed, was at last content. The households of Seymour Place and Chelsea and pages, chamberlains, grooms and porters from Whitehall were now at Sudeley where Katherine knew she could happily live forever. Each morning Thomas rode his property, seeing to the restocking of streams, overseeing the construction of a dovecote and deciding which range in back of the church would be used for sheep-rearing.

"Impending fatherhood has made him more sober and industrious," Katherine happily wrote Kate Brandon. "I think Thomas needed this responsibility—this maturing time—which perhaps is only natural. We must remember, you and I, that we married older men who'd spent their foolishness during their youth. I think Thomas now realizes he can be happy with what he has and how wasteful it is to spend his days working for what he doesn't need! Now he is all I could ask for and our life together is very satisfying. I am truly content." Away from the aggravation of his brother's success and the competition and challenge of court life, Thomas was, indeed, a new man.

Each day Katherine worked with Lady Tyrwhit and Bessie Bellingham to fit up the room where she'd give birth and the small adjoining chamber that would be the nursery. Six Belgian tapestries, illustrating the story of the nymph Daphne from her mother's old chamber at Parr House, were hung on the walls. There was much excitement the day the new bed hangings and curtains of crimson taffeta she'd ordered from London arrived. There were days when letters from her sister Ann and from Mary and Elizabeth made her miss them more and she wept the day an embroidered hanging of baby animals for the nursery room arrived from Kate Brandon. Kate, who hated embroidering almost as much as Elizabeth, proudly announced she'd made it herself.

The serene weeks passed quickly. Sudeley ran smoothly and the couriers riding constantly to and from London kept Katherine in touch with family and friends. Now she could and did listen to divine service in her own church with no Cromwell or Wriothesley to pry into whether she was observing whatever ritual the king and council had momentarily deemed proper. Now the work of devotees of the "new learning" had resulted in a cleaner, less superstitious religion further honed by those reformers and protestants formerly called "heretics." It was the divine worship as practiced at Sudeley and one from which Katherine and Jane Grey derived great comfort and inspiration. Jane's devotion to her faith was as staunch and deep as Anne Askew's had been and would have worried Katherine except most of what Anne had believed was now more or less accepted. Jane would never be in the danger Anne had been. Katherine knew she'd never lose her heartache over Anne Askew. The girl had died too soon. Had she lived a little longer, she'd have seen many of her most cherished beliefs encouraged. But then, Anne had been more of a political victim than a religious martyr.

Thomas often excused himself from the religious services at Sudeley. "Pray for me and my sins," he told a vexed Katherine, kissing her warmly as she left for the little church behind the castle. "I believe what you believe, my dear, and God will understand He gave me little patience to kneel endlessly and little mind to remember the prayers and responses you and Jane speak so beautifully. Do whatever you wish if it gives you peace. I'll attend to my duties and be as fulfilled and satisfied."

Several times returning from services, Katherine saw visitors arriving from London. One she recognized as Sir Thomas Sherington, Master of the Royal Mint; the other was a stranger. When she questioned Thomas, he brushed aside her question saying only that the stranger was Thomas Fowler who served in young Edward's apartments at Whitehall. "They are unimportant and here merely to help carry out my duties since I'm so far away, Kate. They're well taken care of in rooms in the old tower and will be gone in a day or so. You're not to concern yourself with them." Since someone was constantly arriving from London or elsewhere to keep Thomas in touch with the court, Katherine soon forgot about them.

As she grew more unwieldy she often sat with her companions, reminiscing with Bessie Bellingham about the Gainsborough years, laughing at how ignorant they'd both been. She never spoke of the Yorkshire years during the Pilgrimage of Grace for Bessie still revered the memory of Robert Aske. One day she told her companions there wasn't a time when she could not remember Bessie being with her. Impulsively, she asked if Bess had been satisfied.

"Satisfied? Why Kate, I came—an ignorant country lass from the North— to be with the prettiest and kindest lady I'd ever seen! God was with me the day He sent me to Lady Maud and your father. You were about nine then, but older than your years—just as you've always been. I've lived with you in castles, palaces, manors and country places little better than fortresses and I've never regretted one moment. I always knew you were a queen, my darling Kate, even before a king made you one. Yes, I've been happy. . . ."

"And now the babe will make us all happier." Katherine, near tears at Bessie's words, rose awkwardly to embrace her companion. "And if God wills it, there'll be brothers and sisters, too. We'll take them all to Kendal and have the same happy times we had there when we were with my mother. . . ."

At the end of July, Thomas left for London. "I'll be back in a week," he told a dismayed Katherine. "I must report to the Privy Council and see to my affairs. Then I'll be interrupted no further and can stay here with you until the babe comes, even for the rest of the summer."

Though she was reluctant to have him leave since her time was so near, Katherine let herself be persuaded it was for the best. Thomas said he'd be seeing Sherington and Fowler in London so they'd not have to come to Sudeley again. And he'd see young Edward who'd be eager to hear of Katherine's condition. In the end she decided it was perhaps best her husband be away these last few weeks of waiting. It was comforting to be with her ladies and not have an impatient Thomas, chafing and frustrated at being restrained and at the mercy of an unborn son's arrival. Always, he referred to the baby as a boy and Bessie said his groom told her he'd even consulted a fortune-teller, a palmist, who prophesied he'd have a strong healthy son. Thomas promised to bring the king's own physician, Dr. Huyck, back to Sudeley for only the best could usher the Seymour heir into the world.

After he'd gone, Katherine eagerly waited for his letters. But Thomas still hated to write, so there were few. But one came from young Edward, apparently written at Thomas's urging. It was so unlike the boy—almost guarded in its contents—that it disturbed rather than comforted Katherine. Each day couriers brought letters from Mary or Elizabeth, or from her sister Ann or from Kate Brandon who said she'd soon arrive for Katherine's confinement. There was even a note from the Protector telling her Thomas had again petitioned for the return of her jewels and he'd turned the whole matter over to the Chancery courts to see to its legality.

Perhaps I'll yet wear my emeralds once more, Katherine thought, somewhat disappointed that here in the beauty of her Gloucestershire home, the matter of the royal baubles wasn't as important as her husband and expected child. Perhaps later, when the baby had come and Thomas had settled down to being the husband and father they'd both need, her eagerness to have the king's jewels would return. Now all she wanted was her baby.

* * *

The pains began at midnight on August 29 and before Katherine knew it, Bessie had summoned the midwife, Goody Turner, and Dr. Huyck. Thomas stood at her bedside in his night-robe, concerned and loving. At the doctor's urging, he kissed Katherine's cheek, embraced her lightly and left for his chambers.

Katherine lay in her bed, aware of the mounting intensity of the roiling, grinding sensation in her stomach. She gazed about the beautiful room she and her ladies had worked on with such care, hoping to distract her senses from the white-hot agony that was spreading to other parts of her body. Groaning, she turned her face into the pillow, arching her back as the pressure grew, knowing she was hurting the hand of whoever was holding hers, but caring little. Nothing could hurt as she was being hurt now.

It went on, it seemed, for endless hours. The room became fetid with the warm August air and her own body sweat. Dr. Huyck came again, examined her, patted her arm and said, "You're doing well, Your Grace, but it will be a while yet. Goody will call me when you're ready." As the pain increased, even to her fingertips, toes and the top of her head, Katherine wondered if she'd ever be ready and how long it would be before her terror showed. She was angry too that the doctor appeared so unconcerned. Here she was, spread-eagled on her bed, piercing pincers clutching her innards so that each moment was torture. Impatiently, she cried out, "Goody, this has got to stop, it's getting worse. . . ."

Immediately Goody appeared with Bessie at her side. "Kate, you're doing beautifully—Goody says so," Bessie whispered. "The babe is lower now and Goody says it will not be long. Oh, my darling Kate, I know it's painful but you can do it!" She swabbed a cool damp cloth across Katherine's forehead. "You're strong and healthy, my dear, and there's no need to be fearful. If my Lady Maud, who was tinier than you, could have three, you can have one!"

Bessie's sensible tone comforted Katherine and she tried to forget her torment by sitting upright. Then, finding the position even more painful, she sank back on her bed. "Oh, Jesu," she whispered, "Jesu . . . help me. . . ." Out of the corner of her eye, she saw the midwife cross herself.

"Jesu will help, Your Grace, but you must help too." Goody's tone was compassionate, but professional. Again the doctor came to examine her with probing fingers where she hurt most. "Not yet," she heard him say and again the slashing, surging torment consumed her. Mercifully, then, a haze settled between her and the others. She was aware of time passing, aware of her writhing, sweating body, her smothered moans and the ministrations of her ladies. Once Kate Brandon whispered in her ear that the baby would be born soon, that now, more than ever, Katherine must not give up. She wondered if she were going to die for she couldn't imagine ever recovering from such anguish.

Away, as if in the distance, she heard a scream, animal-like in its intensity and realized it was her own. "It's coming!" someone cried and again she saw the doctor's face, hope lightening his tired features. And then, quickly, Goody was there and they were doing things to her that she hoped would help. If it didn't, she thought, as she heard the scream again, just let me die. Then, clutching Kate Brandon's hands, she felt an almost hysterical relief. Whatever it was that had caused such pain was gone. Through tear-filled eyes, she looked down between her legs. There, bloody and battered, lay something like a lump of raw meat on the bed.

"Oh, Jesu be praised!" Kate Brandon's tears flowed freely as the midwife scooped up the child. "You'll be all right now, Kate. It was a difficult time, but it's over now. You'll be surprised at how soon you're going to feel better!"

"The baby—my baby—where is it?" Katherine asked weakly, grateful for Bessie's cleansing ministrations. "Where is my baby? What is it?"

"It's a girl, Your Grace, a lovely little girl." Goody sounded triumphant. "She's being cleaned and you'll see her in a moment. We must make you presentable first. Jesu, we made a mess between us, we did!" Suddenly, the room, which only a few moments before had held such fright and pain, was filled with laughter. Someone flung open a window and the clean fresh night air was reviving. Someone else applied wet cloths to her damp, sweaty body and the soiled sheets were clumsily replaced. Katherine raised her arms gratefully for a clean nightrail and then, Goody was holding out a bundle for her.

Katherine took the child into her arms and, looking down at the little oval face, almost laughed aloud. Her daughter was almost a miniature of herself and Maud Parr. There was a down of the softest pale gold hair and, as she opened her eyes, she looked at her mother with such solemnity, that Katherine's tears mingled with her laughter. This tiny, soft bundle, a physical representation of her and Thomas's love, was suddenly the most important and dearest thing in her life.

And then, Thomas was at her side, a half smile on his face, looking at the baby with her. "And so it's a wench," he said, one forefinger brushing the child's delicate cheek. "And as pretty as its mother. . . ." He leaned over and kissed Katherine. "The doctor said it was a bad time, Kate, but that you're going to be fine, that the child is healthy. So all is well and God be praised. . . ."

"And you're not disappointed it's a girl?" Looking at her daughter's face, knowing what it had cost her to have this baby, Katherine couldn't imagine anyone being disappointed.

"I wanted a son, Kate, but this is as beautiful a daughter as one could have! And I'm proud of her—just as I'm proud of her mother!" Thomas rose from kneeling and kissed his wife. "You're to rest now, my dear, for soon it will be daylight. And rest as long as you wish. I'll send a courier to the Protector and tell him of our daughter's arrival. My daughter!" He straightened his shoulders and, flinging back his head, laughed loudly. "And what shall we name this beautiful child? Edward is certain to want to know."

Katherine was reluctant to say that since Thomas had refused to discuss the possibility of a daughter, she'd only thought of naming a son for him. But inspiration struck and, impulsively, she cried, "Let's name it for Mary, Thomas. Mary is my oldest friend and she'll be so pleased. Yes, I'd like it named for Mary." Over Thomas's shoulder she saw Kate Brandon's smile of approval.

Saluting his wife with a wave of his hand, Thomas left as Katherine lay in bed, still enchanted with little Mary Seymour. What a life she'd give her daughter! The best of Thomas and herself of course. And books, study, summers in the North and at Sudeley. The best of London and Chelsea. And, someday, a man of her own choice, one she'd marry only for love. Never, Katherine vowed, would she give her daughter for status. What status would the daughter of a Queen-Dowager ever need?

As if aware of Katherine's thoughts, Bessie Bellingham disappeared and returned a moment later bringing the coffer containing the little gold circlet Katherine of Aragon had given Maud Parr at her own daughter's birth. Katherine had discussed it with Bessie before, and now, as Maud Parr had done before her, she opened the coffer and laid the circlet across the bundle, holding the napkin out for Kate Brandon to see.

"See, Kate, here it is. *K.I.P.*" She traced the initials. "That's for *Katerina, Infanta Princess*. It came all the way from Granada with the old queen as part of her dowry. My mother said the Spanish nuns made it for her trousseau. The old queen gave this to my mother the day I was born. And now I give it to my daughter." Her voice choked with happiness as she saw tears in both Bessie and Kate's eyes. "It is hers now to give to her own daughter someday."

The child, unimpressed by the solemnity of the moment, yawned loudly, put fist to mouth and closed her eyes, turning her tiny face away from the three women as their laughter filled the room. Katherine returned the little circlet to Bessie and, reluctantly, the baby to the nurse. She felt weak, but joyous, and above all, relieved. And even the fact that Mary Seymour was not a boy could not dim her happiness.

*   *   *

Within hours swift couriers left for London to announce Mary Seymour's birth. On the following evening, one returned with a letter from the Protector, which Thomas read to Katherine. "We are right glad to understand that the queen has had a happy hour and made you the father of so pretty a daughter. And though we would have been—as we are sure you feel also it would have been—more joy and comfort to have had the firstborn a son, yet the escape from danger and the prophecy of sons to come is no small joy and comfort to us, as we're sure it is to you and Her Grace. . . ." Thomas crumpled the letter into a small ball and threw it to the floor.

The next morning, Katherine asked Thomas why she'd heard such loud activity in the courtyard all night. "Messengers from the council and from Seymour Place," he replied. "My affairs are in disorder, Kate sweetheart, for I've stayed so long at Sudeley. There are many decisions to be made and I must return to London within a day or so."

Katherine said nothing, disappointed that he'd want to leave so soon, but too weak to protest. Now that there was no reason for her husband to remain at her side, it might even be better for him to be away while she convalesced. Nothing would be more trying to a man of Thomas's spirit than a temporarily invalid wife. And Dr. Huyck had said it might be a long time before she recovered from her ordeal.

The doctor came often to her bedside as everyone crowded around to admire the infant, and an enchanted Jane Grey was allowed to hold Mary Seymour. "She looks like one of the little dolls I left at Bradgate," Jane laughed. The baby still regarded everyone solemnly. She rarely cried and was no trouble, the nurse told the beaming doctor. Katherine was relieved the child continued well and wished she, herself, felt better. She was greatly distressed when the doctor said he must return immediately to London.

"But Dr. Huyck, I need you here! I am not yet well and I fear for myself if you go. . . ."

The doctor's pleasant features clouded and he looked perplexed, even fearful. "Your Grace, I must go. There are other patients expecting my services. I hear some are very sickly and have asked for my recall. I've talked with my Lord Admiral and he is content I go." He bowed, kissed Katherine's hand and hurriedly left the room.

Later in the day, as she shakily left her bed so the linens might be changed, Katherine watched from a window as Huyck and Thomas walked in the courtyard. They were talking animatedly and, at one point, Thomas shook his fist in Huyck's face before angrily stalking off. Quickly, the dispirited doctor mounted his horse and rode out Sudeley's tower gate.

Back in her bed, Katherine pondered the sudden departure. Something was going on that she knew nothing about and was in no condition to find out. The moment she saw Thomas, she thought, she'd question him. She was just falling off to sleep when voices in the adjoining room roused her. She recognized one as her brother's, Will Parr, the other was Thomas. She couldn't hear what was being said and at last, frustrated, rose and put on her robe, intent upon surprising them both. Undoubtedly they'd thought her soundly asleep, for she'd dismissed all her ladies, even Bessie who'd spent a good part of the last two days nodding in the corner while her mistress slept.

She was about to open the door when Will Parr shouted angrily as Thomas ordered him to be quiet. "Don't wake Kate, Will. She needs her rest and can do nothing about this. God's blood, you make such a trial of everything! I've done no harm, as you will see. . . ."

"No harm, my lord, except to harass your nephew, calling him a beggar king. That creature Fowler of the Privy Chamber keeps at Edward so constantly that the poor lad knows not what to think of his two uncles and borders between fright and melancholy! Our sainted Protector gives him nothing to do to show he's a king. He's not even allowed to sign a paper and is never told why certain things are done. He's shown little consideration, no one throws him a morsel to sustain his pride. While you, his other uncle, dirty the Protector's name, taunting Edward that others govern in his name. You send him monies by Fowler so he can save face and have coins for servants or a passing beggar. Then Fowler constantly harasses him to write letters to the Parliament that you and my sister are so badly treated the Protector should be deposed or have his term shortened. The council warned you about this, Thomas, months ago! How long can this go on? Everyone, both in the court and out, knows what you've been doing. But now, my lord, you've gone too far and you'll be dealt with. What would my sister say if she knew about this?"

"And how will she know? Will you tell her?" Katherine leaned weakly against the door, clutching the handle for support, grateful for the cooling touch of the gilded wood. She could almost see Thomas, with one eyebrow arrogantly lifted, as he challenged her brother.

"Thomas, you're a fool!" Will Parr's voice was strong. "You don't realize how much of your deceptive scheming is known. You can't deal with an officer of the Royal Mint and keep it secret, my lord. Too many people are involved! You can't buy favor with the king with your shameful coins and not have him ask for advice from others as to what he should do. Do you know what he said to me, Thomas?"

When there was no reply, Will Parr answered. "The last time I saw the boy he said he felt deceived, that he trusted neither you nor the Protector. He said to me, 'You are mine only *honest* uncle. . . .' That's what he said to *me*, Will Parr! He says he'll write nothing more for you and he'll not replace the Protector. Jesu, who would take your brother's place? You? You couldn't replace one of the Protector's chamberlains! You've made a shambles of the navy. Everyone knows it is engaged more in piracy—piracy for *your* profit—than for the country's protection! But Thomas, the thing that will endanger you the most is your duplicity with Sherington."

Appalled, Katherine caught her breath, wondering if she could bear to hear more. Sherington, the Master of the Royal Mint, had made many visits to Sudeley. Why had he come?

"Anything that rascal says is a lie!" Thomas shouted. Katherine recognized the bluster in his voice.

"Four thousand pounds is a lie, my lord?" Will Parr's voice was tinged with irony. "That's what he's admitted clipping from the coinage for your own use. What were you going to do with it, Thomas? Raise an army, depose the Protector, install yourself as saviour of England? Use your disorganized and demoralized sailors to support whomever you could buy or threaten? Jesu, my lord, do you think we are all a passel of fools?"

"I think I've been misunderstood. . . ."

"That's a weak man's defense, Thomas, and no one will believe you. You've been discovered and the least you can do is admit your sins like a man. I don't do this for you, Thomas, I do it for my family's good name and my sister's honor. Understand this, my lord. My sister, the Queen-Dowager, has been your best protection. Without her, you'd have been apprehended a long time ago. But you were given a chance to fail because your wife is one of the best-loved women at court—even in the country! No one wants to hurt her, Thomas. But now you wade in waters too deep and you're not a good swimmer. And, mayhap, now even she can no longer protect you. You saw how quickly Rob Huyck left here when he heard the council and soon the Parliament will deal with your treasonous activities!"

Sickened, Katherine wondered what she should do. Creep back to her bed like the wounded animal she felt and weep? So much was coming clear to her now and at a time when she had no strength to deal with anything other than regaining her health. Stunned by what she'd heard, as that insidious weakness crept over her, she was about to open the door and confront her husband with his treachery when, suddenly, Will and Thomas stood before her. From the tears in her eyes and the distraught look on her face, it was evident that Katherine had heard everything.

Prudently, Will absented himself, muttering, "Thomas will tell you why I'm here, Katherine. Then I want to talk to you and see the babe."

Shattered, Katherine crept back into bed, waiting for some explanation. Thomas strode about the room, calling upon Heaven and all its saints to witness he'd meant no wrong to anyone. When Bessie arrived with a silver basin, cloths, combs and brushes to help with Katherine's toilette, Thomas waved her away. With tight lips, she put the basin aside and, not even acknowledging his presence, whispered in Katherine's ear and left.

"Ah, the good Bess is on her high horse this morning. God's blood, how I hate self-righteousness! I hate it worse than the plague!" Having regained his poise, Thomas grinned down at Katherine.

"Then you must hate yourself, my lord, for I know of no one so self-righteous! I'll hear nothing bad said of Bess! She's an honest woman, Thomas. And honesty is something you know little of, I fear. I don't think you even want to know about it. So don't taunt me anymore. I don't want to hear it."

Surprised by his wife's strong condemnation, Thomas attempted to embrace her, saying he'd send a courier to London to escort Dr. Huyck back for he knew she was still worried about herself.

But Katherine pushed him away. "Leave me alone, Thomas. I believe all that my brother said. You've been carelessly foolish, thinking only of yourself. How could you put the king in such jeopardy? To turn him against the Protector with such excuses that he has no coins in his pocket and doesn't sign enough papers. To tell him he's no true king! He's Henry's son, God be praised, the son Henry waited for for so long. He *is* the king! He may be only eleven, Thomas, but he'll rule one day. But only God knows what this country will be like by the time you and your brother have pitted one faction against the other and, between you, stripped him of all his possessions. How about Sudeley? Is it really yours? Or is it Crown property? If so, Edward may want it back someday!"

"Not as long as it's his stepmother's residence," Thomas was white-faced at her outburst.

"My brother was right." Katherine felt a perverse satisfaction at her husband's discomfort. "You wade in very deep water and I know that you don't swim well. Not any better than you can read or write. Even Dr. Huyck wanted to be out of your presence as soon as even a whiff of a treasonous rumor reached Sudeley. How does it feel, Thomas, to know that even the king's physician doesn't feel comfortable to be in your household? How do you know he'll even come back? He may think it's too dangerous!"

"It's easy for you to talk, Kate," Thomas shouted. "You've always had everything you wanted. First from your mother, then from your husbands, then from a king. Who are you to tell me what is wrong? What I work for, I do for all of us. You and me and our child! I want what is mine by right. I am an uncle of the king!"

"Yes, a king you've terrified and disillusioned with your cajoling and your lies and threats. Have you no conscience, Thomas? You'll never learn—I know that now. You'll keep to your own disastrous course until you've ruined us. Mayhap Anne Stanhope was right when she said you'd be the death of her husband or he of you." She lay weakly back on the bed. The effort of speaking—and under such strain—was too much. How dare Thomas accuse her of always having everything she wanted! He knew of the lack of real love in her marriages, of the long time she'd thought herself barren and what an ordeal little Mary's birth had been. What did he know of those years when she'd melded her life with her husbands', making their needs and interests her duty, but stealing little moments for the study so dear to her, hoping to keep some part of herself for herself? He'd never know how hard she'd worked to win her stepchildren's trust—a trust he'd endangered with Elizabeth—and undoubtedly ruined with Edward. The thought of what Edward Tudor might now think of her made Katherine want to weep.

"Call Bess, Thomas. I'm weary and don't wish to talk any longer. Just call Bess to come back in and when Dr. Huyck returns, I'd like to see him right away."

"He'll be here soon, Kate, don't be uneasy about that. He'll be glad to return in a day or so."

"Don't be too certain, Thomas. Rob Huyck left because he didn't wish to be in the home of a traitor. Once he's explained everything to the council, he may return and then he may not." Thomas, looking as though she'd slapped him, turned quickly, banging the door loudly behind him.

In a moment Bess was there and, putting her hand to Katherine's head, shouted for Lady Tyrwhit and Kate Brandon. Gratefully Katherine relaxed while they sponged her with the stinging fragrance she recognized as one of her stillroom recipes for fever. She drank a glass of water, waiting for the warmth, which seemed now to be in her very bones, to go. But her throat still remained parched and she lay weakly as yet another fresh nightrail was put on her perspiring body. At the worried look on Kate Brandon's face, she smiled, patting the duchess' hand. "It's nothing, just a touch of fever, that's all. And having to deal with Thomas hasn't helped." The tears were so near, her voice quivered and she clutched Kate's hand while the others left the room.

"Sleep now, my dear, I'll stay here with you until you do." Kate lay down on the bed beside her. "Just think of getting well, for your own sake and for little Mary's. Forget everything else. . . ."

* * *

When she wakened, her brother was sitting by her bedside. "I've seen the baby, Katherine, and she's a little beauty. She's very like you." Will Parr leaned over to kiss her. "I'm sorry my being here has marred such a happy occasion. But I had to speak to Thomas."

"Tell me about it, Will." Though it was warm in the room and she was feverishly unsettled, Katherine pulled the covers tightly about her. Never had she felt so vulnerable.

For the next half hour, Will told her everything. Thomas's behavior during the past months was now well known and the council was demanding his arrest. Not only had he tried to turn the young king against Edward Seymour, but he'd bribed several councillors to undermine the Protector's authority. With the help of Sir Thomas Sherington, enough silver had been clipped from the nation's coinage to amass a small fortune, nearly four thousand pounds, to mount a rebellion against the Protector. Several naval officers, openly using English ships, had practiced piracy in the Scilly Isles, later bringing their illegal booty to London for resale—all with Thomas's knowledge and a share in the profits. Thomas Fowler had been removed from the king's quarters and Sherington would probably be imprisoned. But what happened to Thomas was up to the Protector and the council. Will Parr didn't see how they could fail to act.

"They didn't want to do it because of you, Katherine. You were Thomas's greatest protection. He knew that and depended on it. But now he's gone too far."

Katherine nodded, wondering why she hadn't realized Thomas would never forsake his scheming. She'd been so certain he was happy at Sudeley! What more could any normal man want? But that obsession still consumed him and she knew now he'd never be truly content until he had as much as his brother. Fate, however, did not seem eager to place Thomas in that fortunate position. Even his firstborn, his longed-for son, had been a daughter.

And what about that daughter? If Thomas could cause such heartache—and anger—what would happen to her daughter if she didn't get well? It had been nearly a week since little Mary's birth and Katherine felt worse than ever. Aware of her brother's concerned look, she explained, "I fear things are not right with me yet, Will." And then the tears started. "I fear I may not live. . . ."

The door opened and Thomas, Dr. Huyck following, came to her bedside. "Here, Kate, is Rob Huyck back again." Thomas's voice was soothing and he was clearly concerned for his welcome. "I'll wait outside with the ladies. They are all anxious to see you as soon as the doctor is through."

Alone with her, the doctor examined Katherine, asking how she felt. When she explained about the symptoms that hadn't disappeared, his pleasant features were brooding. It told Katherine everything she wanted to know. Now all she wanted was to turn her face into the pillow and weep. Or else strike out angrily at everything or anyone at hand.

Thomas returned, accompanied by a worried Bessie and Kate Brandon. He looked sheepish, with an unusual penitency that made her angry. They'd had so much and he'd treated it so lightly. Why shouldn't he suffer too? Suddenly, she wanted him to know how she felt.

"I'm sorry you feel so badly, my lord." She looked at the others gathered about her bed. "See, look here! Here is Thomas who has cared less about me than he should have and has stood laughing at my grief and weakness. The more I tried to do for him, the less he did for me. I have not been well handled. . . ."

Frowning at his wife's unusual petulance, Thomas whispered, "Why, sweetheart, I wouldn't have you hurt."

"No, my lord, but you've given me many taunts. And you let the doctor go. I'd have given a thousand marks, Thomas, to have had Rob Huyck here the last few days. Now I fear it is too late."

There was a muffled sob from Bessie and Katherine knew, now, there were many things to be done. She must think of her daughter. She must accept the fact that she'd not be around to look after Thomas at a time when he needed her most. That was what she must remember. She must think of the future, not the unhappy present when her husband was in such trouble. For now, at last, he'd be forced to face reality, and common sense told her there was little she could do. But somehow, she felt, they'd all survive. And she didn't want Thomas or any of those dear friends gathered by her bedside, now weeping openly, to remember her as frightened or bitter.

In a forgiving gesture, she held out her hand to Thomas. He took it, kissing her fingers, making no attempt to hide his tears.

"I want you all to know that I am sick unto the death," Katherine whispered. "I am of good mind and perfect memory now, but it may not long be so. If the extremity of death is approaching me, I am persuaded I must make my wishes known. They are that I give all I own to my husband, wishing everything to be a thousand times more than it is. . . ."

Thomas's hand tightened on hers. "Kate, darling, oh my darling, don't leave me. . . ." There was a note in his voice she'd never heard before. She looked at him, green eyes shining. "Thomas, you *did* love me. . . ."

"You're the only one, Kate, you know that." He knelt by her bedside, laying his head on her breast. "Oh, Kate, forgive me. . . ."

Katherine looked at the boyishly handsome dark head. Thomas was no longer young, but he'd hardly changed in those long years since she'd met him with the artist Holbein. She felt his tears staining her nightrail. It was, probably, the first time he'd ever faced a loved one's death.

But suddenly, she wasn't afraid of dying; she was just very tired. Sighing, she closed her eyes and heard Thomas urge everyone from the room. "I'll stretch out beside you, my darling, and quiet you." He lay down with her, winding the long reddish-gold hair away from her face so he might kiss her cheek. "Try to sleep now. I'll stay with you until you do."

* * *

Later she tried to waken. She heard the door open and the doctor speaking with Miles Coverdale, her chaplain. She recognized other voices and heard the scratching of pens. What were they writing? Odd that she couldn't ask them. Then someone muttered "a will" and she supposed Rob Huyck and the others must be attesting to her previously spoken wishes. For some reason it didn't matter as much as she thought it should. All she longed for was a return to that soothing deep sleep.

It was becoming easier now, accepting that she wasn't going to live. The pull toward release was very satisfying, almost tantalizing. The world went on about her, but she wasn't part of it. And she found she didn't really want to be. Doors opened and closed, someone opened a window, voices were muted and far away. Someone bathed her forehead again. She wanted to thank them but couldn't. Once she heard Bessie and Kate Brandon weeping and she wished she could soothe them. But the enveloping warmth had deepened. Thankfully, there was no real pain, only an increasing discomfort and frailty. It seemed better to relax and enjoy the images that had begun to float in her mind.

One moment she was with little Mary Tudor running along a riverbank to a palace with someone who looked like Lady Bryan when she was very young. And then, somewhere in a forest, Mary was looking up at her and asking, "What's a scepter?" An old queen had given her a little lacquered box, which she'd taken to someplace in the North. And there, away in the distance, was her mother—how young she looked!—her tiny sandaled feet flying over the Kendal lawn while baby Will struggled to keep up with two older sisters. The French queen was there, too, in a place called Cantley

Hall at Gainsborough, opening her arms wide to console the bereaved daughter of her best friend.

And children were everywhere—Borough and Latimer stepchildren—and a little redheaded girl shrieking with glee as she raced on fat legs across Richmond Green for a visit with Anne of Cleves. Anne of Cleves. Had anyone told Henry's "beloved sister" that Mary Seymour had been born? She wondered if anyone had told the king and then remembered the king was dead. Long live the king! But which one? Henry or Edward? And which queen had had the baby? Only two queens—no, three—had had babies. The old queen had had many, but only one little girl had lived. Another queen had had a baby and then her head was cut off. And one other queen had a little boy and then she died.

Katherine knew that she, too, was dying and should be frightened. She didn't really want to die. She was only thirty-six, not young anymore, but still with good years ahead. And she wanted to be with her daughter, as well as all those other children. Tomorrow was Elizabeth's fifteenth birthday. How could she be ill or die on such an important day for poor Bess? Yet she still felt dreadful. Why, she wondered, would the images of long-gone days and long-dead people be so vivid if she wasn't dying? Wasn't this what always happened or was she already dead?

Thomas's hand was still in hers but now she longed to be elsewhere. From somewhere, she didn't know where, the pull toward release from discomfort, worry and anger was so strong she could no longer ignore it. Nor did she want to. Somewhere, wherever she was going, there would be those who loved her as much as the ones on earth had loved her. And love was so important; she could never live without love. The love of a man, or children, family and friends. So many had loved her—she'd been very lucky! Maud Parr, the mother she'd lost almost twenty years ago, had loved her very much. Would she see her mother again? And those husbands who'd loved her and left her so soon? Now she was leaving a beloved husband and child as well as those children of other queens she'd loved as her own. Especially Edward with his shining wheat-blond hair. The one who with all the majesty of his rank had placed an ivy crown on her head. She, the only woman he'd ever called "mother."

It was all over now, but strangely, she was not unhappy. With a sigh she withdrew her hand from Thomas's, put it to her cheek and drifted off toward that release which held so much promise.

Afterward

THOMAS SEYMOUR, *the Lord High Admiral*: After Katherine Parr's death from puerperal fever on September 6, 1548, Thomas tried to kidnap Edward Tudor, to force him to depose the Protector. He was arrested, imprisoned in the Tower where he refused to answer any questions. After a month, the Privy Council appealed to the king who said he considered his uncle's action treasonous.

Thomas Seymour was beheaded on Tower Hill on March 19, 1549. When informed of his execution, Princess Elizabeth said, "This day died a man of much wit—and very little judgment."

EDWARD TUDOR, *King Edward VI*: Edward lived a lonely life, torn between duty and the demands of the religious upheaval as England became more Protestant, a condition that inevitably blighted his relationship with his sister, the Catholic Princess Mary. In the summer of 1553, a few months before his sixteenth birthday, he became very ill. After the doctors failed to cure a tubercular condition, his final weeks were tortured by the ministrations of a quack female nurse who fed him arsenic in the hope of restoring his health. He died July 6, 1553, on the eighteenth anniversary of the death of Sir Thomas More and is buried near the tomb of his grandfather, Henry VII, in Westminster Abbey.

MARY TUDOR, *Queen Mary I*: Mary labored from the beginning of her reign to restore the "old religion" to England. She married her cousin, Prince Philip of Spain, in the hope that a strong Catholic alliance would aid her country's return to the papal fold. She was passionately in love with Philip, but he cared nothing for her and spent as little time in England as possible.

By 1558, a brokenhearted Mary was in such poor health, she relinquished control of the government to the church, particularly the Catholic bishops—Stephen Gardiner and Edmund Bonner. Both had suffered imprisonment under the Protector for their beliefs and authority was more than they could wisely handle. To combat the growing Protestant or "heretical" influence, they used the gallows, the stake and the sword to wreak a vengeance that earned the queen the undeserving title, "Bloody Mary," for all time.

Mary Tudor died in 1558 at the age of forty-two and is buried in Westminster Abbey.

JANE GREY, The "Nine-Days Queen": Heartbroken at Katherine Parr's death, Jane Grey returned to her parents' home spending most of her time studying the "new religion" with an intensity heightened by loneliness and the tyranny of her family. When King Edward lay dying, John Dudley, the Duke of Northumberland, connived with Henry Grey to marry Jane to his son Guildford. The dying king was then persuaded to designate Jane Grey and her consort to rule in place of Princess Mary who, once queen, would restore papal rule in England.

Sixteen-year-old Jane was appalled and objected strongly to both the marriage and the queenship, but was forced to accept both. When later the country rallied for Mary Tudor, Jane and her father were sent to the Tower. Mary Tudor, understanding what happened, was persuaded by Frances Brandon Grey to release her husband, though Jane remained in the Tower for safekeeping.

When Mary wed Philip of Spain, Henry Grey foolishly participated in Wyatt's Rebellion, a rebellion doomed from the start for its anti-Catholic cause. In the end, a sad and disillusioned Mary had no choice but to execute Henry and Jane Grey as well as young Guildford Dudley as a lesson to anyone who would challenge her faith and the Crown.

EDWARD SEYMOUR, Earl of Somerset, the Protector: After Thomas Seymour's death, the ambitious Protector incurred the envy and enmity of many on the Privy Council, particularly John Dudley. Even a dukedom did not satisfy Dudley who also worked constantly for the Protector's downfall. He lied to young King Edward that the Protector wished a return to Catholicism, that he meddled in foreign affairs against the country's interests and had little real support from his fellow councillors. Eventually, upon the testimony of unscrupulous witnesses bribed or terrified into coercion, Somerset was sentenced and died on the scaffold on January 22, 1552. On the day of his execution, the young king sadly told the Spanish ambassador, "I would not have believed him to have been a traitor."

ANNE STANHOPE, the Duchess of Somerset: After her husband's execution, Anne was sent to the Tower where she lived in great comfort and style for two years until Mary Tudor became queen. Upon Anne's release, Mary gave her Katherine Parr's old manor of Hanworth. There she married an ordinary house chamberlain, Francis Newdigate. Anne died in 1587, the year before the Armada, at the age of ninety. She is buried (as the Duchess of Somerset) in one of Westminster Abbey's most lavish tombs.

JOHN DUDLEY, the Duke of Northumberland: For his part in the attempted plot to seat Jane Grey on the throne, John Dudley was beheaded on Tower Hill on August 22, 1553, less than two months after King Edward's death. The man who once said, "I think best of the old religion, but seeing a new one begun, run dog, run devil, I will go forward," recanted before his execution and died in the Catholic faith.

JOAN DUDLEY, the Duchess of Northumberland: Widowed by her husband's execution and crushed by the loss of her son, Guildford, Joan Dudley retired to a quiet life. Her son Robert rose greatly in favor of Queen Elizabeth, later becoming the Earl of Leicester, reputedly the only man Elizabeth ever loved. His last letter to her was at her bedside when Elizabeth died.

BESSIE BELLINGHAM: Returned to her family in the North. She never married.

FRANCES BRANDON GREY, the Marquess of Dorset: After her daughter and husband's execution Frances Grey married twenty-one-year-old Adrian Stokes, a groom of her household, fifteen years her junior. She bore Mr. Stokes one daughter who died at birth. Five years later in 1559, at the age of forty-three, Frances Grey died in considerably reduced circumstances. But Queen Elizabeth saw to it that her cousin, the French queen's daughter, had an impressive funeral and her tomb in St. Edmund's Chapel in Westminster Abbey rivals that of Anne Stanhope's for sumptuousness.

ELIZABETH TUDOR, Queen Elizabeth I: After Mary's death, Elizabeth was crowned queen and spent the remainder of her long, impressive, forty-five-year reign juggling her bishops, statesmen, knights and gentry, as well as her lovers—especially Robert Dudley—with extraordinary agility and competence. Elizabeth said she was wedded to the Crown and ignored the pleas of council and country to marry and provide an heir. Instead, she worked ceaselessly for her country's good, built up its navy, fought as few wars as possible and, in general, proved the most effective of all the Tudor monarchs.

Her greatest challenge came from Mary Stuart, the Queen of Scots, who fled into England after the murder of her husband, Lord Darnley. Mary was kept prisoner for nineteen years, until Catholic plots to rescue her and crown her Queen of England could no longer be ignored. She was beheaded on February 8, 1587, at Fotheringhay Castle without ever having met her cousin, the English queen.

A year later, the Spanish Armada posed a life-and-death moment for England that the navy—and the advent of favorable winds at a propitious moment—settled in England's favor.

Elizabeth died at Richmond Palace on March 24, 1603. She was seventy years old, the longest-lived of all the Tudors. The crown then passed to Mary Stuart's son, James VI of Scotland.

KATHERINE WILLOUGHBY BRANDON, the Duchess of Suffolk:
After Thomas Seymour's execution, Katherine Brandon took little Mary
Seymour into her custody at Grimsthorpe, her Lincolnshire home. Two years
later, she was devastated by the loss of her two sons, Henry and Charles,
when they died within hours of each other of the "sweating sickness" at
Buckden Palace. With their death, the Suffolk dukedom passed to Henry
Grey, the husband of Charles Brandon's daughter, Frances Grey.

Still only thirty-five years old, Katherine went into seclusion, finding emotional release and inspiration in the "new religion" that she and Katherine
Parr had studied and worked for for so many years.

In 1553, Katherine Brandon married Richard Bertie, a gentleman-usher of
her household, three years older, an Oxford graduate who shared her
religious views.

When Mary Tudor came to the throne in 1553, Katherine's old enemy,
Stephen Gardiner, the Bishop of Winchester, was released from the Tower,
vowing to help Mary restore the Catholic faith in England. Summoned before the bishop to explain his religious beliefs, Richard Bertie sought asylum
for his family in the Netherlands. On New Year's Day 1555, Katherine and
her baby daughter Susan fled their Barbican home to join Bertie in exile.
Nearly four years of poverty and misery followed until the harassed Berties
reached what is today Lithuania where they lived in peace for nearly a year.
A son, Peregrine, was born in Germany.

When Elizabeth was crowned, the Berties returned to England and received some restitution for their confiscated estates. Safe now from religious
persecution—for after the martyrs of Mary's reign England was more firmly
Protestant than ever—Katherine and Richard Bertie were still greatly disappointed that Queen Elizabeth never made the firm religious commitment
most reformers hoped for. The Berties lived for the most part at Grimsthorpe
and worked continuously to bring the "new religion" to firmer ground.
Katherine Bertie had a copy of the Bible in English placed in every church
near her estate, and area families heard the Gospel, the Ten Commandments
and the Lord's Prayer in their own tongue.

Katherine died September 19, 1580 at the age of sixty; Richard Bertie followed two years later. They are buried at Spilsby Church not far from
Grimsthorpe.

MARY SEYMOUR: The orphaned daughter of Queen Katherine Parr and
Thomas Seymour lived with Katherine Brandon and, according to several accounts, her maintenance was at the duchess' expense which was a great
hardship. When Katherine Parr bequeathed her fortune to Thomas Seymour
—a fortune lost by his execution—Mary Seymour was left virtually penniless.

At the time Katherine and Richard Bertie went into exile on the Continent, Mary disappears from documented history. Some believe she died in
her thirteenth year. But one account, by Agnes Strickland in her *Lives of*

the English Queens, states Mary lived to become the wife of Sir Edward Bushel who, some forty years later, was a gentleman in the household of Anne of Denmark, the queen of James I who succeeded Queen Elizabeth.

When Mary Seymour Bushel's daughter wed, her husband, Silas Johnson, reputedly "obtained a great fortune" for by that time Parliament had restored some of her mother's properties to Mary. Among the possessions was a "fine damask napkin which evidently was made for and brought from Spain by Katherine of Aragon, the first queen of Henry VIII. It was embroidered with the initials *K.I.P.*, which along with four little trumpeters, appeared in each of the four corners."

KATHERINE PARR, Lady Seymour, the Queen-Dowager: Katherine Parr died on Wednesday, the sixth of September 1548, between two and three o'clock in the morning. Lady Jane Grey was the Chief Mourner at the funeral on September 8 held in the Sudeley chapel, which was hung with black cloth. The coffin of lead was borne by six gentlemen of the Seymour household with torches flaring. Miles Coverdale, Katherine's chaplain, officiated at the simple ceremony said in English and the *Te Deum*, sung as the coffin was buried, was also offered in English.

Katherine was buried near the altar of the Sudeley chapel and an alabaster sculpture placed at her tomb. As Sudeley fell into disrepair so did its chapel and inevitably curiosity seekers violated Katherine's tomb, the most irreverent one being in the year 1784, when her body was taken from its coffin and exposed to view overnight until the local vicar had it reinterred.